The Society of Guenevere

The Society of Guenevere

A Dark Academia Novel

Deborah K. Vleck

FTL Publications
Minneapolis, Minnesota

FTL Publications
P O Box 22693
Minneapolis, MN 55433
www.ftlpublications.com
mail@ftlpublications.com

Cover by Getcovers

Printed in the United States of America

ISBN 978-1-936881-83-3

This work is entirely original. No generative AI has been used in the conceptualization, development, or drafting of this work.

About the Author

Deborah K. Vleck (Debby Jones) was a writer, designer, and fiber artist. Creator of many award-winning costumes, she was twice a Best in Show winner of the World Science Fiction Convention Masquerade. She worked as a high school teacher, curriculum researcher, newsletter publisher, database manager, graphic designer, city planner, and full-time mother of two. She was married to a professional astronomer and lived in Canberra, NSW, Australia, as well as Honolulu, HI and St. Paul, MN, USA, among other places. She was one of the co-authors of the science fiction novel, *Autumn World.*

She passed away on July 8, 2023 and is survived by husband Terry and two adult children, Rhiannon and Bryan.

Chapter 1

Monday

From the portico of Paterson Hall, Kerri scanned the Quad for Danger and recited the usual defense in her mind:

> *Veil.*
> *Hide from Them! Hide!*
> *Be invisible. Be quiet and small. Blend in.*
> *Leave no footprint They might see. Make no noise They might hear.*
> *Hide from Them.*
> *Veil....*

She unfolded the note and looked at it again. *How stupid do They think I am,* she asked herself angrily. *Do They suppose I have not learned to be careful?*

It paid to be careful, always. It paid to remember. Kerri was proficient at both taking care and remembering. She could, for instance, recollect every word of her conversation with Professor Greystone's secretary moments ago.

"May I help you? Oh, good afternoon, Miss Dale-Townsend. Have you come to see the Professor?"

"Good afternoon. No, I have no appointment today. I received a message that my regular recitation time has been changed."

"Yes?"

"I should like to confirm the time, please. It is for Thursday."

"I see. One moment. Yes, Miss Dale-Townsend. The Professor has found it necessary to reschedule his Thursday afternoon appointments for this week. He put you down for eleven o'clock, and he'll only be able to meet with you the half hour. Here it is in the book. Will that be all right?"

"Perfectly, thank you. I only wanted confirmation of the message."

"Of course. That is always wise."

Not only wise: necessary. Kerri refolded the note and put it back into her pocket, smiling a small, bitter smile, remembering, as she scanned the Quad for Danger again.

She stood at the top of a sweep of stone steps in the shadow of a fat white column, looking out over her place, her birthright, the ancient University of Yendys. Before her the Great Quadrangle drowsed in smoky afternoon sunshine. Long autumn shadows striped the shaven grass and swept walks, and leaves dropped gently from venerable oaks and eucalyptus over crumbling monuments—the statues and benches, the obelisks, markers, and fountains dedicated in verdigrised bronze to long forgotten graduating classes and unremembered events. It might have been the Age of Dreams, so still and eternal was the afternoon.

The term had barely reached midpoint. Finals were still comfortably far off. Anxiety had not yet begun to hold sway over the temptations of the River, the playing fields, and the Pavilion—plenty of time to doze and dream. Half a dozen students, solitary or in pairs, sprawled on the lawns, bent over books. A pack of soccer players jogged by on their way to the fields, while two Senior Fellows in black gowns strolled sedately down the central walk, long sleeves billowing behind them. An elderly man in overalls and heavy gloves hummed an Escher fugue as he raked fallen leaves into a pile. The black-gowned Senior Fellows passed him without a second glance.

But Kerri, lurking on the porch of Paterson Hall, knew him. Six years out of seven he was a distinguished Professor of Natural History at another university. In this, the seventh year, he was content to let his mind lie fallow to all but music, growing things and the more interesting secrets of a long, productive career. She, newly returned from exile, still dispossessed, could only imagine what those secrets might be.

Briefly the scene erupted into life as men and women spilled out of the venerable stone buildings. The professor leaned pensively upon the handle of his rake, watching them with the air of a farmer surveying a well-grown field. They looked a good lot, the current crop of undergraduates, Kerri reflected, and well they ought to. A good third of them came from fine Academic families. Any number of their parents could be former pupils of the man with the rake. The more uncertain majority would be hopeful Peasants and Cits on their way forward in the world, while the few with brighter plumage and following retinue would be the odd Stockholder son or daughter up for a little polishing before taking on a hereditary round of duties and pleasures.

Suddenly the professor smiled and raised his cap to a young woman approaching him down the center promenade. She was dressed as a student, but her long jacket was daringly cut to suggest the lines of a Fellow's robe, and she moved with the easy assurance that could only belong to an elite Sponsored graduate. Her lips were painted the same red as the scarf that fluttered at her throat. Smooth bobbed hair swung along her jawline like a fringe of black silk.

She raised her eyebrows and smiled at the old man, sketching a bow that startled a pair of passing sophomores. She knew him. One day she would be his equal. This was implicit in the smiles, the bow, the crimson silk scarf.

The enemy. Kerri shrank back into the shadow of the column and hoped Zarah had not noticed her. Surely she was safe. Not only had she taken the usual Precautions, but she was dressed for blending in today, as most days. Her cardigan possessed the requisite Academic redness, her pleated skirt the shortness, her long, honey-colored hair the smooth order of a female student with every promise of the University yet before her. And yet, there was no air of the embryonic Faculty Member about her, nor could there properly be, by right. She could have passed for an undergraduate—and did when it suited her, as it did now.

Holding a notebook against her chest like a shield, she stood motionless a moment longer as the hurrying tide of scholars surged around her on the brick-paved porch. Her anxious brown eyes scanned the grassy space restlessly, returning more than once to the man with the rake and his black-haired companion. He had recognized and greeted Zarah. Might he not remember the scandal? Remember it and recognize Kerri?

As the two separated, she took a deep breath, clutched her notebook a little more firmly, and clumped gracelessly down the wide steps, trailing a painted canvas book bag some seven years out of fashion. Taking cover in the herd of undergraduates, she pulled in close every tendril of her individuality and cloaked it once more with the Veil. The departing graduate, black satin hair swinging behind her, did not turn around or slow her confident march toward the Memorial Library.

Even the distinguished professor, fooled, glanced only briefly at the young woman in the red cardigan. Freshman, he must think, noting the unfinished look, the lolloping gait. Or so Kerri hoped, aware of his eyes on her. The Veil left her unable to detect any beam of recognition, but she had in mind his reputation: He had no eye for the effervescent whims of fashion in, for example, book bags, but he could still pick out a comely pair of legs. These she could not help providing for his appreciation, but she intended to do so for no longer than necessary. She drifted unobtrusively deeper into the nearest knot of noisy pedestrians and then turned off at the path toward the River Gate. When she risked a look back, the old man had returned to his fugue and his raking. There were, after all, many pairs of well-made legs passing daily through his ken. He would forget her before she left the Quad.

At the gate the Kerri paused for a moment in the shade of the arch and crammed the notebook into the canvas bag. Again she scanned the quadrangle, her eyes once more coming to rest on the man with the rake. He had resumed his work, his back to her, and no one else took any notice of her. No eyes followed her now from the open or from any of the hundreds of windows that looked down on walks and lawns.

The Veil had kept her safe. It was fading now just enough to let her feel for Power, for Danger, but the useful, hidden sense was quiescent, cool. She felt no attention focused on her from window, lawn, or doorway, from Them. Their terrifying special awareness was directed elsewhere just now. And Zarah was gone, all unaware.

For several minutes more, color, noise and movement whirled through the quadrangle and then ebbed away, leaving the same landscape of light and shadow and a new arrangement of motionless figures on the grass. Up and down the ancient shaded walks footsteps began to beat in quick time.

In the Old Quad, half a kilometer away, the tower clock announced the hour. It was a safe two minutes fast and had been so for at least three generations. Every quarter hour, Old Paul spoke first to give warning, sending scholars and Fellows alike scurrying toward their destinations. *You have two minutes,* said the voice of Old Paul's great bell. *Hurry!*

As the oaken doors of Tempest Hall closed behind the last black-gowned figure, the bells of the University began to pronounce. High and low, from one end of the campus to the other, they gave Old Paul his affirmation. Four o'clock it was and is and ever shall be, amen. Forever Monday. Eternally April.

Nothing changes here, Kerri reflected. *We come, we depart, we return. The University is the same as it was the day our parents left it, the day our grandparents arrived as freshmen. Intact from the Age of Dreams, it is the heart of our world. Nothing ever alters its steady beat.*

This was an interesting conceit. Hardly original, but interesting. She played with it a few minutes more as she lingered within the arch of the gate, calling up appropriate quotations out of her well-stocked memory.

Assignment in freshman composition: Write an essay comparing the University to a part of the human body. Support your thesis with examples from the classic literature. Four to five pages. To be handed in at noon on Friday.

Kerri smiled. She would tell Nicholas. He would be amused, and the jest would soften her telling of the other thing. Or maybe she would not mention that. Her fingers touched the note from Professor Greystone's secretary, making sure it was safe in her pocket. The Veil melted softly into nothing. She was Real again.

No menace existed, of course, nothing more than some trifling mistake, or someone in the Department playing a juvenile trick, someone who could not tell a worthy target from a straw image. Nothing more, perhaps, than the nervous imaginings of a precariously balanced mind. Kerri shook her head and grimaced to herself. There was nothing like the sight of Zarah to make her feel like a child again, playing stupid prep school games. *Spying and disguises! The enemy!* Absurd to think of Zarah, even Zarah, in such a way. Enemies and warfare were, like so many other miseries of the Age of Dreams, long extinct, and good riddance!

She turned and passed under the arch toward the River, cutting obliquely across the grass between the slender trunks of towering gum trees. Her rough-edged gawkiness disappeared; there was now no trace of freshman awkwardness in her body. She moved with the balanced grace of a Graduate of the University, which indeed she had been for over four years.

She reassured herself that the professor had not recognized her. It would be embarrassing to attract his notice, even as merely her father's daughter. She would rather not bring to his attention the humiliating fact that she had finally given in and returned to her studies—as a Commoner. She remembered that he had sent a note of condolences to her mother at the time of their bereavement, but he had shown no further interest in the widow or daughter of his deceased colleague. Nor was there any reason why he should.

Kerri's only other contact with him had been a formal correspondence seeking Sponsorship for graduate study. In reply to her carefully composed and painstakingly calligraphed letter of application she had received a brief, typewritten notice of refusal from the professor's secretary. It had, with meticulous politeness, conveyed the impression that she was wasting her time (not to mention the far more valuable time of any Faculty member she approached in the matter) seeking a Sponsor.

She had almost given up then. If it had not been for Grandmother she *would* have given up, but Grandmother wouldn't hear of it. "It is no different," she had said to Kerri, "from the reply he gives to all the scholars he turns down. Some of the Faculty are like that. It has nothing to do with that old fuss over that dreadful girl. To be sure, he never paid it any mind if he even heard of it. You keep asking! There is no shame in taking every year the rules allow you to find a Sponsor. This family has been Faculty too long to let go without fighting to the last minute."

Kerri had gone on trying. The sole descendant of six elite generations would persevere to the last. In five bitter years there was scarcely any Fellow at any University she had not asked at least once. This year would be the end, one way or another, whether she went on and finished her degree or not. She would have done her duty to the last minute, and she would have let the family down anyway, if it were not for Nicholas. Their child, if they ever had one, would not be shut out of the Faculty, but it would be from his side they would inherit, not hers.

At least she knew her father's old rival was here in Yendys disguised as a gardener, and naturally he knew Zarah, who had inexplicably changed her name to Arzelle and somehow become the darling of the whole University of Yendys. He was one of Them, by association at least, and now she could be on the lookout to avoid him. The Veil was reliable, but it was safer not to put it too much to the test. That would attract Their attention, sooner or later.

This is frightful! Kerri said to herself. *When will I grow up? I've not been this bad in years. It must be coming back here to be a student again—so strange after so long. And those dementings last month. Everyone's nervous; it isn't just me. But I am a Graduate Student now. I have no time for the old nonsense. The Game is over. From now on I must try to be Real all the time.*

She arrived at the River Path and turned to the right, downstream. She liked the River Path. One could walk it all the way to the lower streetcar stop and catch the trolley after it passed the University Asylum. Indeed, it was the only way to get home without seeing the Asylum at all. And there was a place a little farther along, a flat rock among trees, where she could put in a good half hour of reading before she went to catch her train.

As she rounded the last bend, she saw that her spot was already occupied. A woman of her own age sat upon the rock surrounded by small piles of papers, each weighed down with a stone. She was in the act of sorting several more dusty pages. If these had not been covered with mathematical symbols, Kerri would have taken her for a Cit in her yellow overalls and sandals.

The woman looked up and grinned as Kerri approached. "All over the bloomin' bank!" she exclaimed in the broadest Cit accent. "Any more breeze and they would've 'alf gone in the River. Me notes," she added, to the baffled look on Kerri's face. "I dropped 'em."

"Oh," Kerri replied unencouragingly. The woman was obviously a Cit. The notes, however, looked like graduate mathematics. What the two were doing together on University property was none of Kerri's business. She smiled coolly and prepared to pass on by. She could do her reading at the Station.

"Hold on a minute. I say! I mean, I beg your pardon." The other rose to her feet and pushed a handful of brown curls out of her eyes. "You recite to Professor Greystone, do you not?"

Kerri looked back, startled. The question was bold, almost rude, coming from a Cit, but the woman's accent had vanished. She spoke now in the purest Academic, and her amber eyes looked straight into Kerri's without the shy wariness one so often saw in women of other castes who sought to improve their fortunes in the fastnesses of Academy or University. "I beg your pardon?" Kerri said coldly.

"Forgive me, but I thought I remembered you from the reception at the beginning of term. For Professor Greystone's students? Do you not recite to him?"

"Yes. Yes, I do," Kerri replied cautiously, trying to remember that day, trying to decide if she had ever seen this woman before.

"So do I. That is, he is my Auditor for Classics, this year. I also recite Mathematics to Madame Professor Abbot-Remarque. We met at the reception, but you probably do not remember me."

"I was there. Forgive me, I do not."

"Weberly is my name. Loren Barr Weberly." She dusted off a rather grimy hand and held it out.

Kerri accepted it and shook hands solemnly. "Kerrith Nash Dale-Townsend," she announced herself formally. "I am pleased to make your acquaintance, Miss Weberly."

She had been mistaken. With a name like that, the woman was no Cit; she was Academic, whatever she looked like, and she was a Graduate Student. Professor Greystone did not take undergraduates for coaching and auditing, and he rarely took Cits or Peasants of any degree, although any person who had Graduate status was legally an Academic, whatever caste had given them birth. Furthermore, any graduate student capable of taking on a double program of recitations possessed an intellect to be reckoned with and, probably, a Sponsor. Kerri hoped she had not given offense.

"I am happy to see you again, Miss Dale-Townsend," said Miss Weberly with sincere pleasure. She grinned again. "I do not know many people here yet."

"You did not earn your B.A. here then?"

"No. I graduated from Dalton."

"I see. Well, you will find your way around in no time."

She managed to extricate herself politely with a few more words and continued on along the path. *My reading time,* she thought with annoyance. *Now it's half gone, and the station will be* too *noisy and distracting. Bother chatty people who scatter their miserable papers all over my rock! What an odd person, though. Anyone would think she* wanted *to be taken for a Cit, with that impossible yellow garment and her hair all over the place. And sandals in April! But her accent—she wasn't faking the Academic—and the name was all right. It must have been some kind of joke. Maybe they look upon these things differently in Dalton.*

The streetcar to the Grand Central Station was full of homebound students chattering like currawongs, and the Station itself was noisy, with every bench crowded. There was not a seat to be had anywhere, which was no surprise. Kerri gave up her plan of doing some reading before her train came. She occupied herself with reviewing the lines of the previous week's recitation, giving careful attention to the diction, stress and mood. It was difficult, though, even for a scholar of her experience, when there was so much distraction. After no more than thirty lines she found her mind's voice trailing off, her eyes choosing people to watch.

The cavernous depot was packed with Citizens in bright, untidy clothing, scarfed Peasant women on their way home from the day's market in the city, and little gangs of shrill, uniformed schoolchildren. Most of the University students cleared out immediately, their lodgings being nearby or reached by one of the local cars. Now would be a good time to chat with someone, if studying proved impossible, but Kerri saw nobody she knew.

Suddenly a murmur approached through the babble of the crowd, a sibilant word echoed back and forth with awe. Stockholder! Kerri craned her neck to see the cause of their sensation and caught a glimpse of a tall, elegant figure striding through a path that cleared automatically. There was a flash of jewels, a faint wave of exotic scent. Behind a delicate eye-veil sprinkled with tiny diamonds, grey eyes stared without interest over the heads of the fascinated crowd.

The Stockholder was a woman. Kerri had seen her before and read of her in the newspapers. Her name was Margarethe Girrawang Fairchild, and she had been very much a favorite of the society columns three or four years before, when her eccentricities had still possessed the attraction of novelty. The Cits—and the papers—had grown bored with her, but she was still renowned for the excellence of her taste in all aesthetic matters. Her name never failed to appear among the winners of those esoteric competitions so beloved of the Stockholder caste.

The crowd drew in behind Margarethe Girrawang Fairchild and her retinue, and Kerri lost sight of them. She turned and pushed her way through the people behind her. It was time to board the train for home.

Chapter 2

Evesham

The train was an express, luckily, as far as Rainville, where two-thirds of the passengers got off. After that, Kerri got a seat by the window until Fernly, her own stop, where she changed to her local streetcar and rode to the end of the line. For the last two kilometers she was the only passenger, the only rider to the hamlet of Evesham. When she alighted at the roundabout, she walked over to the switch box and shoved the stiff levers into inbound position.

The trolley man stuck his head out the window and waved. "Ta! Thanks! See ya tomorrow."

Kerri waved back, but she did not linger as she sometimes did to watch the trolley round the circle and set off back down the high road. She turned and made her way up the dirt track toward home. Behind her the click of metal wheels on rails receded northward toward town, leaving a silence gently laced with individual bird voices. Her left eye was dazzled by the low sun, which gilded the fields in the distance and illuminated tall, faded grass along the roadside.

The stillness and golden light pleased Kerri. Living in the country gave her great pleasure, now that she was used to it. Here the gossip and politics of the University District seemed unimportant. People minded their own business. No one had ever gone demented in the middle of the night.

Here she could forget the Game entirely. There was no need to be on guard all the time, to have the Veil ready to her touch. Several of the neighbors carried Power, she had decided, but theirs was quiet and colorless, like Nick's. There was no consciousness in it, no Purpose, no Danger. They themselves did not suspect, of course, and anyway, the houses were nicely far apart. She felt safe here. She felt free.

She passed a ruin surrounded by overgrown thickets of wild rose and blackberry. In clumps of pyracantha beside the track a gang of rosellas, blue, red and green, noisily munched the last of the orange fruit. Kerri whistled at them. The birds took no notice.

It was no small part of her satisfaction to know that she and Nick and their neighbors had made a rather desirable little Academic enclave out at the end of the Fernly trolley line. They had begun with a small spirit of rebellion and desperation, fully expecting to become outcasts, pretending to be resigned to it. Instead they were looked upon as having set something of a fashion. There was no harm in that. It could so easily have been a liability, given the traditional Academic prejudice about living anywhere but the University District.

The trouble was, the District had been crowded to capacity for a generation. Houses, flats, even small rooms were impossible to come by without waiting for months or years, and in spite of tradition, the Evesham Experiment, as it was called, had aroused considerable interest. Any number of graduate students, even junior faculty—packed into tiny rooms in the District or making do with lodgings in less desirable neighborhoods—looked with envy upon the comfortable houses and colorful gardens of the hamlet. And the tragic rash of dementings since the beginning of term had laid a fog of uneasiness over the University and the District. Even people with perfectly good apartments—large ones with two baths and a spare bedroom—talked nervously about moving away, if they could find a good place, a real Academic place.

Nearly every weekend some Academic was seen wandering about sizing up the remaining abandoned dwellings. The most livable ones had already been claimed, naturally. The rest were in varying stages of decay and might not be worth saving unless the stylishness of the location rose still further. There had even been talk of new building, but so far no one had undertaken anything so extreme.

At her own gate Kerri paused to inspect the mailbox. There was a bill, an advertising circular, a letter from Mother—thin for one of hers!—and one from Grandmother addressed with faultless calligraphy. There was a letter to Nick with no return address on the flap.

That was a little odd: impolite, or at least careless.

Finally, she turned over a small envelope bearing the device of the Regents of the University. Her heart lurched painfully. It might be an invitation, it was the right shape and size, but there was no point in being foolishly optimistic, even for Nick's sake. It was addressed to both of them, but he was the one with the Sponsor and gathering glory. He could open it. She tucked it in among the other things and tried to ignore its existence.

She ducked under the arch and carefully latched the wooden gate behind her.

Strolling up the path toward the house, she admired her late roses and Michaelmas daisies and chrysanthemums glowing against the dull brick. This was another advantage of country life: there were abundant cut flowers for the house and her office at the University, just as good as anything for sale in the River Market. Keeping the garden was hard work, especially after so many years of neglect, but to their surprise both she and Nicholas enjoyed the task. In a year they had brought their half hectare of what had been wild tangle almost under control.

Kerri found her latchkey and let herself in through the heavy round-topped front door. Silence greeted her. No book bag reposed on the hall table; Nicholas was not yet home. She halloo-ed anyway for good measure and set down her own bag. Thomas Aquinas trilled from his cage in the kitchen.

"Hallo, Thomas!" Kerri called out. "Mummy's home! Poor bird, is he lonesome?"

She walked down the hall and into the kitchen, cooing and clucking, while the budgie climbed around his cage in a rattle of greeting. The air in the room was gold. Sunlight poured in through the bank of windows. Kerri realized she was still holding Nicholas's letters with her own. She set them at his place on the table.

She lit the fire, put the kettle on, and started getting tea together. After checking the stove to make sure the fire was catching and the boiler was full, she got the rest of Saturday's casserole out of the cooler and put it on to heat. She fixed a salad, cut the bread, set the table, and sat down to read her letters.

Mother's was first. Hers were usually long, chatty and full of local news, but this envelope was unusually slim. There were only four pages, and the writing had an agitated look. Kerri sat up and prepared to skim for the bad news. Fortunately, Mother came to the point at the end of the first page. It wasn't really bad news at all, although it was uncomfortable.

It seemed Mother had been doing some autumn cleaning and had come upon several letters written by her late husband. They were to have been opened in the event of his death. As the event had occurred nearly five years before, Mother was most understandably upset. She felt at fault, although she had not known of the existence of these writings. He had never mentioned them and had hidden them quite out of the way; she did not say where.

Along with some personal messages there were instructions which Father had left to be carried out, tasks left undone. Mother was not specific about what these tasks and instructions were, but she wrote that she could not proceed without Kerri's presence. Kerri must come home as soon as she could get away—of course, she was welcome at any time, always, and dear Nicholas, too—so this unhappy oversight could be mended.

The kettle on the stove uttered a few subdued groans, working up to the white rumble of water coming to the boil. Kerri gazed out the window over the garden and field beyond without seeing the sunset riot of birds. The last of the golden light faded to rose, then lavender.

It can't be, she thought. *It cannot be. She would have told me straight out in her letter. She knows better, but she would never be able to resist. It must be something else.*

Poor Mother! How glad she must have been to find lost letters in his handwriting and how distressed to discover that there was any posthumous trust, no matter how trivial, which had been inadvertently neglected. Not that it could make much difference now.

Poor Father! Kerri could suddenly see him, slightly stooped, with his hands in his pockets and his eyes unfocused and preoccupied, worrying at some knotty mathematical problem—there in the garden where he used to go to think. Five years had gone by since his death, and she suddenly missed him as if it had happened a week ago. There was an empty place in her, beginning to be cobwebbed around the edges, but still capable of echoing with pain.

It was a long time since she had been to the Islands. She would like to have a look at those letters herself, the ones that weren't private for Mother. She would enjoy a few good talks with Grandmother. It would do her good to walk the hillsides of Honowell again and see some old friends.

A year ago, when she had been merely employed at a job, it would have been simple to request a few days' leave for family business. People took time off for far less important reasons, and the money, then, would not have been a problem. Now that she was a scholar again, however, things were much more complicated. Leaving aside the limits imposed by an ungenerous stipend, it was essential to behave correctly always. There were many unwritten laws of University life, and it was perilous to break them.

One of the most stringent customs was that a student must not be absent during term time. Special leave might be granted by one's department in case of severe illness or a true emergency—Kerri had had such leave five years before—but otherwise each student must put in an appearance every working day and leave some written record, usually his or her signature in the department daybook. Cheating could happen, and did, but only the most cunning succeeded. Rivalry was too intense; people were too watchful of each other's mistakes. Being unSponsored and seventeen months away from her Orals, Kerri was an outsider to the keenest competition, but even she would not dare to take such a chance.

Mother offered no evidence of an emergency that would satisfy Kerri's Auditor or the Department Chairman. Kerri had no choice but to wait until the end of term in June and hope that weather would be favorable for a crossing and that Nick might be willing to come along. Mother could not mean come *now*. She knew about Academic life; she must understand.

The kitchen was growing dark. Kerri got up and lit the lamp with a long splinter, kindled from the stove. The kettle gave a piercing whistle at the same moment Nicholas walked in. Kerri felt a turning-over sensation in her middle. After two years of acquaintance and more than one of marriage, his beauty still had the power to rob her of breath. The lamplight seemed to gild him around the edges: his rough tweed jacket, and his hair roughened by the sunset breeze. His smile, though weary, illuminated the room.

He dropped a kiss on Kerri's forehead. "Wasn't there any mail?" he asked.

"Yes. Two letters for you, there by your plate. I was reading one from Mother and never took them back to the hall." Kerri watched his face.

"Ah!" His eyes brightened as he seized the smaller envelope. "Your name is on this, too."

"I wanted to let you open it."

"Coward! Not even a peek?" He turned it over delicately and peered at the edges. "Why not?"

"It's really for you. You know it is."

"Nonsense!" he said. It was a politeness, not a real protest, but he had the grace not to carry it further. Kerri appreciated this.

Nick separated the flap carefully and drew out a gilt-edged card. His grin deepened. "Yes," he said. "It is. We've done it."

"I knew it! Oh, Nick!"

"Listen. ' The Regents of the University request the pleasure of the company of Nicholas Andrade Townsend-Dale, M.A., and Kerrith Nash Dale-Townsend, B.A., at a gala banquet and ball in celebration of the Festival of May. At the Palace of the Arts'—I wondered where they were going to hold it this year. ' Saturday the First of May. Eight O'Clock in the Evening.' Here, look."

Kerri took the card into her own hands and gloated over it. "It really does say what it says. We're going, Nick!"

"Finally." He laughed and hugged her. "Name of the Dreamer! What are we going to wear?"

"I don't know," Kerri said, her smile fading. Costume had always been one of Kerri's strengths in the old days, but since leaving University, she had had little need for ceremonial garb. There being no point in maintaining or adding to her formal wardrobe, she had quite lost interest until she took up with Nick. She was thankful that he, too, had an instinct for costume, especially the showy and elaborate garments required for University rituals and celebrations—it was one of the things that had recommended him to her in the first place.

But the two of them had too little time or money to do anything but dream of the costumes they would create someday. "I suppose our outfits from last year won't do."

"No. Oh, no! Not near good enough, and anyway they've been seen. This calls for something new, something very special. I've thought of it once or twice, but I never said anything. It seemed like tempting fate."

"How much time have we got?" Kerri tried to calculate, but Nick was ahead of her. "One month. Less. Not even four weeks. We'll have to start today. Tonight. Now!"

He flung open a drawer and rummaged for pencil and paper.

She turned to the stove, still laughing. "We can have tea first." She served the casserole onto their plates and sat down.

Visibly forcing himself to come down to earth, Nick propped the invitation on the windowsill and returned to the table. He reached for his other letter, still grinning. He looked at the anonymous envelope, and his face changed abruptly, went blank for two heartbeats, then carefully reassumed a smile. Kerri looked away quickly.

"What did your mother have to say?" Out of the corner of her eye she saw him set aside the letter, half under the tray. He wasn't going to open it in front of her, and he wasn't going to say anything about it.

"Well, it's a little complicated. I shall have to go over to the Islands as soon as I can."

"What has happened? Is anything wrong?"

"Not really wrong, I think, although she was rather vague. It's about Father. She found some letters he left, final instructions—that sort of thing."

"A Legacy?" Nick leaned forward hopefully.

"No. She would have said. Something else. She never even knew these papers existed, and she seems quite distressed. She wants me to come. That is, both of us, if you can."

"What? Now? During term time? You can't be serious, Kerri. It would be worth my career! You have Sponsor applications pending. You can't mean to put yourself at such risk."

"I don't need to be told that," she replied with a touch of irritation. "Of course it's out of the question until the vacation.

"I do admit I'm worried, though. This letter isn't like Mother. She's holding something back, and I'd like to know what. On the other hand, whatever the problem is, it has waited five years. I can't imagine a few more weeks could possibly make much difference. I'd better write to her tonight. Shall you come with me when I go? In June?"

"If I can. Yes, do write to her. She will probably be reassured just to hear from you." He was quite ready to dismiss the whole thing from his mind. After all, they had been invited to the Regents' May Revel, and Kerri's father, whom he had never met, had been dead for a long time. He picked up his spoon and glanced over the oil bill.

Chapter 3

The Society of Guenevere

After tea Kerri began to clear the table, while Nick carried all the correspondence out of the room. He returned in less than a minute and began to organize the washing up. Either it was a very short letter or he hadn't read it. Yes. He knew she was suspicious, and he was saving it to read when he had more time alone.

Or, Kerri told herself, *it is something completely innocent, and I am a fool. Some childhood acquaintance without much education, a Peasant maybe, and he's embarrassed at the lack of form.* "I think I'll get to work," she said aloud.

"Certainly." He glanced over his shoulder. "I won't be long."

As she straightened the chairs around the table she recalled the unread letter from Grandmother. So many things had happened she had almost forgotten it. Now she must set it aside and look forward to reading it during her first study break.

She walked down the hall and into the study, picking up her book bag on the way.

Outside it was full dark. The window was a black mirror reflecting a ghostly image of herself lit by the candle she carried. She touched the flame to the wick of her study lamp, blew out the candle and went to the window to draw the curtains against the night.

Her desk was gratifyingly tidy under the thin layer of a day's dust, unlike Nick's desk, which was awash with papers and books. Kerri had learned years ago to find comfort and reassurance in orderliness. It wasn't always enough, but it helped, especially when things became hard to find. If she could begin by being sure where *she* had put them, it made the fear manageable. It saved time.

Half idly, she glanced about at the trays and cubbyholes while she emptied her canvas bag. The torn-open packet from Mother was in the middle of the blotter, but Grandmother's letter was nowhere in sight.

With a sigh she contemplated again the disorder on the other desk. Nick must have forgotten that she had got two letters and mixed up the second with his own in the dark. He had emptied his book bag on top, too. She swiveled her lamp as far in that direction as it would go and walked around to his side to search the heap.

Luckily, she did not have far to look. The mail was just under his copy of MacNeal's *Commentaries,* and the neat cream square from Grandmother was there with the rest. As she picked it up, she glimpsed out of the corner of her left eye a bit of calligraphy. Her mind read it without conscious intention. It said, "the Society of Guenevere."

She had already turned away to return to her own desk when her attention awoke to the half-seen phrase. The Society of Guenevere. Guenevere. Wife and queen of Arthur, the most enigmatic and interesting of the rulers in the Age of Dreams. All her life she had studied the fragmented writings about this mysterious pair, and all her life she had been fascinated by them. But never in her studies had she heard of such a thing as a Society of Guenevere. The lettering had been remarkably beautiful, too, the kind of work her grandmother would do, or some other master calligrapher, certainly not Nick's hand.

She bent down and looked more carefully where she thought she had seen the words. The light from her desk did not provide much illumination at this distance, but it was bright enough to reveal a piece of writing of such distinction. Under the unidentified letter Nick had received that afternoon (Oh, yes. That. And still unopened.) there appeared to be nothing more than some lists of references, jotted down in Nick's worst private scrawl.

Nothing remotely resembled "the Society of Guenevere" in fine script. She must have imagined it.

Kerri shivered. The words were written as clearly upon her memory as if she were still looking at them: the elegant proportions of the capitals, the controlled grace of the flourishes. Was it a symptom of approaching dementia to see writing that didn't exist? Of course not. Don't think about it. It was some trick of the eye. Her imagination had filled in the rest.

"What the devil are you doing?" The fury in Nick's voice surprised Kerri much more than his sudden appearance in the doorway. "How dare you pry through my papers?" His face was white and distorted. "What are you looking for?"

Kerri froze, too much appalled to do anything but stare at him. She had never seen him so angry. She almost didn't recognize him. His face was pinched and ugly. He advanced two steps into the room, fists clenched before him, but he was not looking at her now, only at the papers she had disturbed. Abruptly she realized that he was as much afraid as he was angry. And it made no sense. They were always rummaging in each other's drawers for paperclips and typing paper....

"I was looking for my letter from Grandmother," she got out at last. "You didn't put it on my desk with Mother's, so I reckoned it was here, and I was right. What on earth has got into you?"

He stared at her for a moment and blinked several times, a flush rising on his face. His expression changed little, but the heat of rage and fear was suddenly gone. He looked at the desk again, and back at her.

"If you must know," Kerri hurried on to fill the silence, "I was admiring your handwriting. What is it you're worried about me seeing? There's nothing there but your usual stuff. You never minded me looking at it before."

"Nothing there," he repeated blankly. He leaned against the doorframe and passed one hand across his face, folding his other arm across his chest. "What am I saying?" He covered his face with his hand again. "Kerri, forgive me. That was monstrous of me. It wasn't even you. Some things happened today. I was going over them in my mind while I was doing the washing up, and then I came in here and...I honestly forgot who I was talking to. I forgot where I was. I think my mind was still on campus." He shrugged wearily.

"I didn't touch your papers," she informed him coldly, unready to forgive. Holding her letter before her like a weapon, she stepped sideways through the two meter space between Nick and his desk and withdrew to her own corner, safe.

"I know. It doesn't matter anyway. I'm very sorry."

He looked like her own Nick again, but pale and tired. Kerri softened. "If you'll allow my asking," she said, "what was it that happened?"

"I don't think you know Charles Mason," Nick said. "He was found in his room this afternoon. Demented. Nothing left."

"Oh, Nick, I am so sorry!" Kerri gasped. "How awful. That's the fifth one this autumn. Did you know him well?"

"Not very. We didn't get on particularly. He was a wart, in fact. But that doesn't make any difference."

"No. One feels dreadful no matter who it was."

"On top of that, someone's been playing tricks around college again—thoroughly petty and aggravating. The place is jittery enough, with Fowler going demented a month ago—at least now we know it can't be him. Someone has been sneaking about, doing the usual vile things, caught two or three of the new graduate students. Not me, thank God, but it was close. I think I'm at least as angry at myself for being careless."

Kerri smiled tentatively. "'A miss is as good as a mile,'" she quoted. "You're safe here." She walked to the doorway and put a hand on his arm, a peace gesture. "Next time put my things on my desk and I won't have to go near yours at all."

"Done," he said, covering her hand with one of his. He squinted at her through his thick lashes. "And I honestly don't care if you go near my desk or not. It was absurd. Will you forgive me?"

"I shall think about it." She moved away to return to her work. "It happened to me today, too," she offered.

"What? A trick?" Nick raised the chimney of his lamp and struck a match. He did not say "You?" disbelievingly, although Kerri could almost hear him thinking it.

It was the third time already since the beginning of term; he ought to be taking it seriously by now. If he believed her. She wasn't completely sure he didn't privately pass these things off as her own absentmindedness.

"I received a note, under the door, telling me Professor Greystone had changed my appointment from two to four o'clock. Before I came home I went to his secretary to confirm it. She showed me the book. The appointment was written down for eleven, not four."

"Did you keep the note?" He adjusted the glowing lampwick, blew out the match and replaced the chimney.

Kerri took it out of her cardigan pocket and handed it to him. "It's her writing," she said.

Nick opened the folded paper and held it near the light. He looked at her and handed the note back without a word.

Kerri looked at it. It said clearly that her regular recitation had been changed to eleven o'clock on Thursday. "But it said four! Nick, it did." She looked at the note again, remembering sharply how she had studied it that afternoon. How she had looked at it again after visiting Professor Greystone's rooms. It had said four—every, every time.

"There was another mark across between the two ones in the eleven, making them look like a four," she insisted. "It's gone now."

Nick came to her and looked over her shoulder at the piece of paper lying in the puddle of lamplight. "Disappearing ink?" he suggested. "Very neat, if that's what it was. Only why have it disappear so soon? What's the use? If you looked again before Thursday it would spoil the whole game."

"Maybe they didn't mean it to. Vanishing ink is hard to control." Kerri studied his face anxiously. "You believe me, don't you, Nick? It did say four when I got it."

He hesitated a second too long. "Oh, I believe you. It seems a clumsy job, that's all. Just as well you went to confirm it. Do you think Professor Greystone's secretary did it?"

Kerri shook her head. "I doubt it. She has been there forever, and she never gets mixed up in the things that go on. I've never known her to take sides. She was willing to show me the appointment book. There is no motive. No, I think someone else intercepted the note and added the pen stroke, gambling that I wouldn't go to check up on it."

"It happens," Nick agreed.

"But who? And why me?"

"The usual reason?" he said. "Maybe you should take it as a compliment."

Kerri made no reply. She refolded the note and tucked it into her appointment book.

She did not blame him for being skeptical about the first two incidents. The book *had* turned up again, and the lost essay had come to light in time—*not* where she had put them, whatever he said about it. But by this time he must admit that there was more at work than forgetfulness.

It was diplomatic of him to suggest that someone was taking her seriously as an academic rival. In his case, of course, a certain amount of sabotage was taken for granted. He was brilliant, handsome, Sponsored, favored by his college. It was not to be wondered if jealous competitors set snares for him in traditional (though publicly deplored) Academic fashion. She, however, was no serious threat to anybody: unSponsored, uncharismatic, her gifts, if any, overlooked by Faculty and students alike—at least since graduation, when she had failed to receive the expected Graduate Sponsorship, in spite of her academic honors and distinguished ancestry.

She had fallen, it seemed, out of the race, and now the only thing she had worth competing for was Nicholas. This was a worrying possibility. She could think of any number of women who envied her, but after all it was a little too late to frighten her off Nick, not to mention a stupid way of going about it. The alternative was that someone thought she was simply too contemptible to be a graduate student at all and was taking a little amusement in harassing her. She had not, up to now, been able to decide which was worse.

Except that now Nick was getting letters with no return identification. And he was suddenly overprotective of his personal papers.

Secrets. The very thought opened a tiny core of terror in her: memories of Val and Zarah, betrayal, the death of love. *Not with Nicholas, not again. I couldn't bear it to happen with Nicholas.*

I'm mad, she thought. *I'm wishing disaster on myself.*

Nicholas was talking about their costumes for the Revel. He was opening his books and preparing to work, musing aloud about sequins and lace and the hazards of velvet. They would have to visit the shops in town, he was saying. "And you know, by this time the pickings will be thin."

Kerri admired his ideas and agreed with everything. She suggested they meet the next afternoon for shopping, and now, if he didn't mind, she must work.

He smiled across at her from his own little island of lamplight. "Am I forgiven, then?"

"What? Of course," she said. "Let us not give it another thought."

Chapter 4

Nicholas

She studied her lines for an hour and then labored over an essay. From time to time she looked at Nick, at the shadows under his brows and cheekbones, at his fine hands as he copied references out of five or six books he had brought home from the library. He wrote very quickly and never seemed to have to hunt for what he wanted or to debate with himself over what to write down. Once he looked up in time to catch her watching him and smiled.

Kerri was aware that some of her acquaintances did not think him at all good-looking. They considered his chief attractions to be his intellectual prowess, which was superior, and his potential for a Faculty career, which was practically guaranteed by his lineage. His mother held the rank of Provost at the University in Urlosa, and one of his great-grandfathers had been a Vice-Chancellor.

He had not the least diffidence about his abilities, which had put Kerri off for all of the first two hours she had spent in his company. But his almost overweening self-confidence was tempered with a great deal of charm. She had fallen for him by the end of the third hour and still felt that her good fortune in having married him was not quite believable.

He did not take anybody completely seriously, least of all himself, except when it came to his work and his position. Scholarship and Academic status counted to Nick, but he was not grimly ambitious like many of his peers. Rather, he seemed to have a supreme confidence that he would achieve. The highest things would come to him because he was the best. He believed it. And so did a great many other people.

Kerri remembered what it was like to feel that, to believe in one's future. Once, she had owned nearly as much confidence as Nicholas—still kept the rags and shreds of it, enough to get by on in public. Before her senior year, before her father's death when the first rips and snags had appeared in the fabric of her destiny, she, too, had been on a straight course for a career among the elite of her caste. She, too, had possessed a future.

But her father had failed, before his early and unexpected death, to will her to one of his colleagues as his Legacy, and it seemed that without this traditional blessing her own achievements, by themselves, were not quite enough. In spite of her excellent record, no Faculty member had been willing to Sponsor her graduate study, and without a Sponsor there was almost no chance of ever being offered a Fellowship. And without a Fellowship, there would never be a place on the Faculty. It appeared that the best chance she had of entering the Faculty world was to marry into it, and Nick was indisputably a prime candidate. If there was a thorn in her feelings about him, this was it.

They had met at a party nearly two years before, a Winter Solstice gathering put on by friends of one of Kerri's friends. The host and hostess, a graduate couple in the College of Philosophy, were unknown to Kerri. She had felt uncomfortably like a gate-crasher, but her friend had assured her that everyone was welcome, there was no formal guest list. It would all be completely informal—not even holiday costumes—and there would be so many people there that no one would take any notice of her. She could hide herself away in a corner, if she liked; no one would bother her.

This was all said in rather a long-suffering way, for Kerri had taken to the habit of hiding in corners when she went to parties, which she did rarely in those days. Then, emerging from the worst period after her divorce, she had felt old, ragged and damaged— quite unequal to frivolity and facing people. Her friends, who had been strong and protective for the first terrible year, were in the second beginning to chafe and turn and tire of the maternal role they had taken on. Gently, and then not so gently, they urged her to face the world again and meet some new men.

Fortunately, there were quite a few unattached Academic males, as well as females, in Kerri's age group. It was the time of life when early student marriages tended to crumble, some amiably, some painfully, and there were many young graduates trying to find their feet again in the social life of their caste. The braver ones, the ones lucky enough to have established stable relationships, gave a great many parties during the holiday season from May Day to late June, for the express purpose of allowing all the recently detached to find each other. It was to one such party that Kerri was dragged reluctantly that particular Solstice Eve.

She had been promised there was absolutely no chance that Val or Zarah would be there, either one alone or in combination, or any of her former classmates from the Classics College. And they weren't, and once she was relieved of that worry and had drunk a glass of very innocent-tasting punch, she ceased to care about much of anything. The party was very large—an unused hall in one of the buildings on the Promenade had been commandeered for it—and it seemed to be composed of dozens of people she had never seen before who all seemed to know each other. She wandered through the crowd, punch cup in hand, feeling relaxed and aimless, almost invisible as she passed little chattering knots of people.

Her perambulations took her back to the refreshment table for a second cup of that not-so-innocent punch, when her opinion was enlisted in an argument going on among the people gathered around the punch bowl. A large and rather obnoxious young man wearing the gown of a Junior Fellow was trying to make a point by appealing to the ladies. The ladies in the group were having none of it, apparently knowing him all too well, so he enlisted the nearest outsider, who happened to be Kerri.

The debate, which she had not heard, had then to be repeated all over again for her benefit, and by chance it happened to pertain to a relatively obscure subject upon which she had written a research paper, one of the ones submitted for judgement for her baccalaureate degree. In fact, it was her own essay—it had won a prize and been printed up in the college proceedings for that year—that stood at the center of the argument.

The Junior Fellow, who had no idea that the blond he had snagged was the paper's author, was citing it to prove his point, but it was obvious to Kerri that he either misunderstood it completely or, more likely, had not read it at all. She was able to set him straight, with remarkable tact considering her detached condition (the punch), thereby handing the argument to his opponent, which she only then really noticed. This, of course, was Nicholas.

Nick was delighted to have got the better of his antagonist so easily, and seemed disposed to regard his new ally in the light of an old friend. He later admitted unselfconsciously that he hadn't read her paper either, just the abstract. In fact he had been bluffing all the time, simply to tease the pompous Junior Fellow. He thought the whole thing was a very good joke. Kerri was not much amused, but she was vastly intrigued by his eyes.

Kerri could never remember just how they lost the rest of the group and drifted to a bench against the wall. They talked together for the next three and a half hours. He saw her home at the end of the party and invited her to lunch the next week. She went to bed that night quite drunk, but she was unable to decide whether it was on the punch or on love. By Solstice morning she knew it was love.

Later her friend complained to the others in their circle: "Nicholas Andrade Townsend, my dears! Like falling off a log! Sixteen other women climbing over each other trying to get him to look at them even once, and she, miserable creature, not even trying to meet anybody and not giving a damn who he is, waltzes off with him to a corner for the rest of the evening, and he hasn't noticed another woman since!"

It was not easy to tell whether Nick had "noticed" other women or not. He had made himself a reputation for being hard to catch. And the fact was that he had married Kerri and seemed to be very satisfied—even relieved to be no longer available. Kerri had been used to Val's flirtations, his jealousies and excesses of mood. Nick was more playful than passionate, although he certainly could be the latter. There was always laughter mixed in, and somehow it was the laughter that got through her defenses and allowed her to trust him.

At ten o'clock Nick got up and went to the kitchen to make their late tea. Kerri noticed he carried the letter with him, no doubt to read it in the privacy of the kitchen. He had not touched it in all the time he had been sitting at his desk. She decided she was heartily tired of the thing and felt a tiny annoyance at him—as if she had any interest in his personal correspondence! This reminded her of her own, and she reached at last for the cream envelope at the corner of her desk.

Although the address and return address on the outside were lettered with flawless elegance, the single page inside was nearly a scribble by comparison. The composition showed the skill of a master calligrapher, but the text had obviously been dashed off in great haste.

My dearest Kerri,

No one is more conscious than I of the duties of a graduate student in her or his first term. Nevertheless, I am writing to beg you to come home to Honowell at the earliest opportunity, as your mother has written to ask. Yes, even before the end of term if you can manage it. Let me remind you that the Long Weekend is approaching. Come then.

The papers your mother has found are even more important than she realizes, especially to you. There is something which could make a great difference to your Academic career. You must act on it without delay.

I have much more to say to you, words that can't be put into a letter.

Do not fail to visit me when you come.

Your loving grandmother,

Aryel Range Stewart-Dale

"As if I would fail!" Kerri muttered to herself. "Strong words, Grandmother!"

She could not imagine why her family were insisting so strongly without giving a reason. Neither of them would tell her why the trip could not be put off until the winter vacation, when a couple of days' delay at either end would not matter. She would be free to come and go as she pleased without risking her career. Grandmother especially ought to know better.

Holding the letter up nearer the light, Kerri read it again, salutation to signature.

The signature. She knew her grandmother's informal signature very well. This one was different. There was an extra flourish at the end of "Range," a peculiar backward coiled line. Kerri's heart began to beat heavily.

It was the Emergency Sign, one of the secret signals her father had taught her when she was a little girl, subtle signs that could be concealed in the ornamentation of ordinary writing. She and he had only used them in fun. She thought he had made them up himself; she never dreamed Grandmother knew about them. And here was the one they had never used, because, he told her, it was serious and Real. It was only to be used if one of them ever truly needed help, or if there was Danger.

Something must be terribly wrong at home, something neither Mother nor Grandmother could bear to put in writing: a scandal, an incurable illness. But repeated readings of both letters failed to reveal any hint of what the disaster might be. There was no sorrow, except the same old grief over a son and husband untimely lost. There *was* anxiety, plain in both letters, and an expressed desire for haste. But now Kerri saw foreboding there, too, where she had not seen it before.

"Something that could make a great difference to your career." Kerri threw her mind back frantically over her whole academic history. Could it be another aftershock of the hideous mess during Prelim. Exams. thirteen years ago? Other than that piece of ancient history, had she done anything, or left undone anything, that could come back to blight her prospects now? How could the damage be alleviated by her absence from Yendys without official leave, leave she would never get on the strength of these vague pleas and warnings? And what had it to do with Father? Or was he simply an excuse?

Grandmother wanted her to act on it, whatever it was, and at once. Grandmother was not in the habit of exaggerating; she was not given to hysteria. She had made herself as plain as she could and added a private signal to emphasize her seriousness.

I must go, Kerri said to herself.

She had not thought about the Long Weekend, but it was a possibility. The University would be officially closed for the coming Friday and the Monday following. If she sailed late Thursday afternoon, she could reach Honowell Friday evening, have Friday night, Saturday, and most of Sunday at her mother's, leave Sunday afternoon, and be home late Monday, well before she needed to put in an appearance at the University Tuesday morning. No damage done. Grandmother implied that such a short visit would be enough time for whatever they needed her for.

No one would need to know she had been gone except Nicholas. The two of them lived so isolated that often they did not even lay eyes on one of their neighbors for an entire weekend. Anyway lots of people went away over the April Long Weekend, even new graduate students. She and Nicholas had even discussed taking some kind of little holiday while the good autumn weather lasted.

The real problem was getting back in time. In autumn the weather could be undependable, and the Sea People were cautious sailors when they carried passengers. They would lay over for storms without regard to anybody's deadline or schedule, including their own. It was a sickening risk. Kerri wished someone would tell her what to do.

Nicholas came in just then with the tea tray. He had been gone an unusually long time, Kerri realized. It hadn't looked like that long a letter.

"I checked the tank," he told her, as if to explain his absence. "The water will still be good and hot in the morning." They had a solar water heater as well as a boiler and used the latter as little as possible for bathing.

"Good," Kerri commented. "Morning showers. Listen, Nick. I think I'd better go to Honowell over the Long Weekend. Grandmother wants me to especially, and she wouldn't ask lightly. Those papers of Father's must be more important than Mother let on."

He set down the tray and poured out the tea. "Did she say what is wrong? Is it something you can get leave for? Did she even hint that it might be a Legacy?"

"No. No details at all. They're being very mysterious. No use even trying to get leave. Neither of them said there was any trouble, exactly, but Grandmother wouldn't ask in such terms if she didn't absolutely mean it. She knows the rules as well as anyone. She knows the risk I'd be taking, and she still begs me to come."

He looked at her alertly but said nothing. She outlined her plan to him. "I'd never consider it if I weren't convinced it is an emergency."

He considered for a moment. "It might work if the weather cooperates. You'd hardly have more than a day, though, and if there's a storm, you might be held up for a week or even more."

"My recitation isn't until Thursday. You could cover for me Tuesday or Wednesday, tell them I'm ill. I would leave notes for you to deliver to my professors and the Common Room. I might even call in at the Infirmary Thursday, put on a good show and get me a waiver. Nobody will think of dropping in here to check. It's too far to come."

"What about the dinner party at Lucia's Thursday? She particularly told me how much she's looking forward to seeing more of you now that you're one of us again."

"Did she?" Kerri was impressed, although she didn't wholly believe this news. Her delayed return to her studies had not yet made her comfortable with Nick's associates in the History College. She strongly suspected they looked down upon her behind her back. They had Sponsors; she did not. On the other hand, they were people useful to know and dangerous to alienate, and Nick needed her to be on good terms with them.

She did not hesitate more than a moment. She was willing to make the effort to enter this social circle more fully, since the opportunity was available, but she was not disappointed to have a good reason not to face them this once. "We could use the same excuse," she said. "I could be coming down with whatever it is. You'll be convinced I've been working far too hard and tell them you've persuaded me to go home early and go to bed. You'll convey my regrets."

He nodded slowly, without approving. "I will do that, if you insist. But, Kerri, you can't be serious about doing this. It would be demented."

"Don't say that!" she snapped.

He raised his eyebrows. "I beg your pardon. You know I didn't mean that literally. Say, ill-advised. I don't like it."

"I know." She sighed. "If I return later than Wednesday I shall simply have to live with the consequences. In fact, I *will* definitely go to the Infirmary. I'm certain I can summon up some convincing symptoms. People do it all the time. I don't like it either, Nick, but I have to go."

"Well." He widened his eyes at her. "I suppose you'd better go, then. I'll cover for you as far as I can. Unless you change your mind. Which would be wise."

"Thank you," said Kerri. She frowned and fidgeted with a pen. She had expected Nick to talk her out of it, as he had every reason to do. Indeed, she had *hoped* he would talk her out of it. The last thing she expected was that he would give way almost at once, with that bland-faced, raised-eyebrow look, as if she were contemplating no more than an excursion to the North Side of the Harbor.

Nick stirred some sugar into his tea. "Anyway," he said, looking down, "it looks as if I shall have to work over the Long Weekend, not to mention at least one of us has to start on the costumes for the Revel. We couldn't have gone away down the coast or anything." It was the first time he had mentioned having to work during the short holiday.

They had made no plans beyond the vague intention to go to Kerri's ancestral cabin in Twilight Country, or down the coast to a favorite beach. He had never suggested he might not be available, until tonight.

They drank their herb tea in silence. Kerri's mind was very far from peaceful.

Chapter 5

The Star Dream

Kerri had the star dream again that night. As always, it began as another quite ordinary dream. She was looking for something in her office at the University. This was not unusual. It was every student's common nightmare to be searching fruitlessly for a mislaid or stolen essay, due in minutes.

But Kerri could not remember what she was looking for. She knew she would recognize it when she saw it—or had she already seen it and not recognized it? She knew it wasn't an essay. No, she remembered. It was the letter from Grandmother, but that was at home. Or had she brought it into town with her? She thought she remembered doing that. Could she have lost it on the way? Why was it so difficult to keep track of things?

Suddenly the search took on great urgency. She must find the letter, or terrible consequences would follow. If anyone else should find it first, she would be ruined, although she couldn't seem to remember why. It had something to do with Nicholas. Papers and books seemed to multiply under her frantic hands, to spill and pour out of drawers and cabinets, as her careful filing systems dissolved into chaos.

She ran out of her office, but the corridor was wrong. The building seemed to change and twist and grow new, unknown rooms—unlit and full of disintegrating furniture and bursting cartons of discarded papers. There was not a sign of another person. She was not in Paterson Hall at all but in a different building, one of the many old, abandoned places used for storage, where great stacks of forgotten things, books, tindery papers lay piled high to cobwebby ceilings. How could she find one letter among so many pieces of yellowed and crumbling paper?

The letter wasn't really from Grandmother, she remembered now. That was only a disguise to fool Them. The letter was from her father, and it contained a message of the greatest importance. They didn't want her to receive the message. They had stolen it. She was not in the dusty building now but outdoors in a small courtyard in a part of the campus she had never seen before. Dry leaves were piled everywhere, great quantities of them, up to the sills of the ground floor windows. The leaves turned to dust as she trod on them. No one was there, but she could hear whispering people just out of sight, watching her, judging her.

She ran out of the courtyard after the thief, only to find herself in another deserted quadrangle where the windows yawned empty and the leaves drifted whispering over lichen covered monuments. She saw that the leaves were not leaves but the crumbling remains of the stacks of papers that cascaded out through the ruined windows. The rustle of malicious voices came from everywhere. The sky was the luminous, sunless blue-purple of Twilight Country.

In growing terror she fled from this dying place. She waded through weedy quadrangles where no one had set foot for generations, climbing over eroding monuments and through tangles of overgrown, neglected shrubbery. All the buildings were locked and dark, the windows opaque and stone-like to her frantic pounding.

Suddenly her way was blocked by a fence of tall iron bars set in a knee-high concrete wall. She grabbed the bars and pulled herself up to stand on the wall, trying to see if the thief had got through somehow. She could see nothing but dreary shrubbery, spilling dead leaves onto moldy ground. She recognized the fence. It was the one that enclosed the grounds of the Asylum. Horrified, she jumped away, turned and ran into the gathering fog. *I'm on the outside,* she gasped to herself, hoping it was true.

She came to a more open avenue, a long walk lined on either side with winter-bare trees. The walk vanished into thickening mist in either direction. She could barely see the fleeing figure of the thief, disappearing into greyness down the path to her left. She followed, knowing that it was not really a letter but Father himself that They had stolen from her.

The fog was so heavy she could not see at all, even the ground beneath her feet. She had not noticed the light dimming, but now it was gone, leaving her in total darkness. This was not the open, windy darkness of a country night far from lights of human habitation but a close, moving blackness, in which she could still almost hear the murmuring of the voices. She had the sensation of being inside an enclosed but unimaginably vast space.

Almost immediately she became aware of tiny points of light scattered through the blackness, dim at first like stars just emerging at dusk. She began to feel an uneasy nudging of memory: this had happened before. Quickly the lights grew brighter and more definite, until she was surrounded by constellations of them. Some were near and bright; others were dim and farther away. She knew that they were not stars but people, and that these were the ones who had pronounced her inadequate, rejected her, condemned her forever to the silent void between stars.

It came to her then that she was dreaming and that she had dreamed this dream before. It was a dream of helplessness, of humiliation and loss. A deep, burning anger began to rise in her heart, anger at Them, at the voices just beyond hearing in the darkness. It was Father they were hiding from her this time. The stars were whispering among themselves, keeping secrets from her, stealing the message from Father. She strained all her will to pick out even one coherent word from that vague whisper as the dream began to shred and dissolve around her. Suddenly a collection of meaningless sounds resolved itself into a phrase, "...for the Society of Guenevere..."

She was awake, staring into the familiar darkness of the bedroom. Nick breathed softly beside her, and a faint paleness crept around the edges of the curtains. She lay still, wide-eyed. She could almost hear the words, still. Again: The Society of Guenevere. And the voice, there was only one voice in the end, a woman's, familiar, but whose?

Anger still crackled around the edges of her mind like summer heat lightning. *They have no right, no right,* something in her kept repeating. *The Star Dream. I have had the Star Dream again.*

It had been years, since before Nicholas. The last time she had dreamed about the Star People was a year or so after her divorce from Val. She couldn't even remember the first time, before she was eleven years old, certainly, before she had entered the Academy Middle School in Honowell. It always started out as an ordinary frustration dream, like this time, and it always left her nearly sick with anxiety, humiliation, and fear—and in later years, grief and anger. It would hang over her like a cloud, poisoning her day with the feelings of being powerless, stupid and inadequate—the way she had felt when she left Val.

Abruptly she sat up and reached for her dressing gown. A glance at Nick reassured her that he was deeply asleep, having dreams of his own, to judge by the movement of his eyes under the closed lids. Moving smoothly and quietly she slid out of bed and wrapped the robe around her. Nick did not move. She watched him for half a minute more to be sure and then slipped out of the room and soundlessly closed the door behind her.

In the study it was less dark. She drew the curtains aside carefully. The western sky was growing light, silhouetting the gum trees and radiata pines at the end of the gardens.

She was glad it was unnecessary to light a lamp. Both she and Nick were conditioned to wake from a sound sleep at the slightest scent of new smoke, and she did not want to take any risk of his surprising her now.

She tiptoed to Nick's desk and scanned the disordered surface. The letter was not in sight, of course. He had moved things around during his evening's work. It was possible that he had simply set other papers and books down on top of the letter, but she knew that if she searched through the pile she would not find it.

And he would know. She began to reach for the handle of one of the drawers. Just before she touched it, she pulled her fingers away.

No. It was wrong. She had no right to pry into his correspondence, his papers, his workplace. She had not even the right to be suspicious. No amount of sad experience, of past betrayal, gave her cause to suspect and worry and pry. If she was not careful, she would create betrayal out of her own imagination, just as she had created the Game, the Power, and the Veil. She had endowed those things with a reality that would not go away, proof of her secret madness. To do the same thing with ideas of Nick being unfaithful would be a disaster.

She hurried out of the study and went to the kitchen where the air was grey and the clock ticked loudly. Thomas was silent in his shrouded cage. She opened the curtains and lit the little oil burner under the kettle. She was getting out bread and yogurt when Nicholas appeared in the doorway suddenly, his eyes wide with alarm. He stared at her for a moment as if he had never seen her before. Then he turned on his heel and vanished into the hall.

Kerri pushed her clenched fists into the pockets of her dressing gown and sat down heavily in the nearest chair. He had gone to the study. She knew it. He knew she had been there, and he thought she had been snooping into his things, although how he could wake up out of a sound sleep aware of her quiet movements she could not guess. And the look he had given her! That could not be allowed to pass. Grimly, Kerri stood and stalked out of the kitchen.

Nick was not in the study. He was in the bathroom, and the water was running. He answered cheerfully to her knock, sounding quite normal and inviting her to come in. As she put her head around the door, he smiled around the edge of the oil-cloth shower curtain and blew her a kiss. Then he noticed her face.

"What is the matter, lady?"

"That's what I wanted to ask you. You came into the kitchen just now with the most ghastly look on your face. Then you barged right out again without so much as a word."

"Did I? I reckon I was still mostly asleep. I just wanted to find out where you had gone. You know, most mornings I have to make a great noise to get you out of bed, and today you weren't there. I wondered if you were all right, and you looked like you were, so I took myself off to have a shower and wake myself up."

"Oh," said Kerri.

He disappeared back behind the curtain. The air was getting very full of steam. "And are you all right?" he called out.

"Yes, of course. I just woke early for some reason. Leave me some hot water, if you please!"

She heard him laughing as she left the bathroom, closing the door behind her. She went and stood in the doorway of the study. There was no change at all that she could see, no sign that he had been in the room. But he had. She did not know how she could be so certain.

And why shouldn't he? she thought. *It is his room, too. It doesn't mean anything. He isn't Val. He isn't even like Val. It's no good if I'm starting to see that kind of thing everywhere. I shall know I really am going mad.*

She willed herself to focus again on the Star Dream as she returned to the kitchen. There had been nothing at all about Nick in the dream. In fact the only connection was the phrase she had hallucinated last night on his desk. *What in the name of the Dreamer is the Society of Guenevere?* she wondered. *If I were studying Arthurian material this term I would suspect a simple echo from work, but all my recitations so far have been in the Sixteens and Seventeens, a lot of dry stuff on the Nature of Man, nothing Arthurian at all. Not even in lectures or reading.*

Had she run across this Society thing before and simply forgotten it? That was possible. Even the most talented memory couldn't retain everything, or pull out every tiny item of information when wanted. That was it. She must have run across a Society of Guenevere sometime in her undergraduate Arthurian studies, and it had popped up in her mind again now for some reason. At least it was a clue. If she could review that old material she might be able to find the reference again and figure out the connection to the present.

Yes, she would do that.

When? Kerri sighed to herself. *With all the work I have to do this term, and sewing for the Revel, and sailing to Honowell, there is no time.*

Then she would make time. Not this week, not until she got back from the Islands.

Afterward. She would make time, because if there were any connection, anything that might help her understand her own troubles, she could gain strength from knowing it. She gave a last vicious slice to the loaf and set the knife down on the counter with a clatter.

She was not going demented; she was not losing Nick. She was simply at a disadvantage through lack of knowledge. Very well, she would acquire the necessary knowledge. She would use this anger. She would learn, she would remember, she would be in control.

Chapter 6

Voyage

On Thursday afternoon Nick went with her to the ship. The west wind was brisk and cold, but there were no clouds. Kerri changed out of her too-Academic clothes in the ladies' room of the ships' terminal. In the nondescript waterproofs of a seagoing Islander, her hair wrapped in a scarf, no one would look at her twice. She regarded herself in the cracked and mottled mirror and added a pair of dark glasses to her disguise. When she emerged, Nick spotted her instantly from across the lobby and laughed.

"You're not going to change your mind?" Nick said when she rejoined him.

"No." She buckled her pack and slung it over her shoulder. "They said the crossing should be fast. The wind is just right, and no storms are expected in the next three days. It will be all right, Nick. I'm going."

"I hope they're right about the weather." He grimaced at the sky. "I wish you were staying."

"You have the letters I wrote, in case?" She glanced around at the milling people but saw nobody she knew or anybody who even looked Academic except Nick. And in his tweed and denim and plaid wool scarf he could be nothing else.

"I have them safe at home. But if you're more than two days overdue..."

"I won't be." She was trying to reassure herself as much as him. "I will be back in time. Let's go out. I want to board."

"Do you want me to wait until you sail?" He took her arm as they strolled toward the double doors leading to the dock.

"No. No use standing about for half an hour or so. You have shopping to do before you show yourself at Lucia's, remember? The shops will be closed Sunday and Monday, and we've got three weeks as of tomorrow."

"You trust my taste?"

"It looks as if I have to!" They smiled at each other. "This time!" she added. "Let's try for the blue and gold brocade and the rest as we planned last night. If it comes to too much money, well, you'll simply have to figure it out without me."

They stopped several meters short of the gate to make their farewells. Nick frowned at the ship. "Don't expect me to get more than the cutting out done before you get back," he said. "Remember, I must work."

"That much? Well, do what you can. And try to spend some time outside at least, while the weather is so fine." *Why are we talking like polite acquaintances?* she wondered. *This is the first time we've parted. We don't know how to take leave of each other.* "Give Lucia and the others my best regards."

Boarding passengers hurried around them. Nicholas said, "I will. Have a safe journey," and gave her a last kiss. They held each other for a moment, and then he backed away through the crowd, waving, until Kerri lost sight of him.

She put her free arm through the other strap of her pack and fumbled in the pocket of her waterproof jacket for her ticket. The line moved quickly. In a few minutes she had put her signature into the passenger book and made her way through the gate and across the gangway. There was a barely perceptible rocking. The deck was crowded. There were many families. It was going to be a noisy passage.

She found her way to her assigned third-class compartment and claimed the last remaining seat near a porthole. She checked the accessibility of her life jacket, located the nearest life boat, and adjusted the ventilation to her liking. Although there were already several seats marked "occupied," there was no one inside. She would probably not see her voyage companions until after the ship sailed. She hoped they would be a quiet lot, not prone to seasickness.

After stowing her pack and securing her locker she returned to the deck and threaded her way through the crowd. The crew were battening down the cargo crane and getting ready to take in the gangway. Passengers crowded the dock-side rails. Kerri elbowed her way through and scanned the people still standing on the dock, but she did not see Nicholas. He had taken her at her word and gone away. For some reason this made her feel completely desolate.

She pushed back out of the press of people and went through the forward lounge to the other side of the ship, which was almost deserted. Leaning on the rail, she stared across at the high nested gables of the Hall of Wings.

Nick was rather silly and endearing, the way he had vacillated between worry over her journey and an almost concealed eagerness to have her gone. As if to prove, she thought, that he could get along very well without her for a few days. No doubt he relished the idea of a little temporary bachelor solitude. That must be what it was. She would not allow herself to think of any other explanation. Sometimes she, too, missed solitude, which was an odd thing to recognize in oneself so soon after being married. She didn't feel in need of being alone now. In fact, she missed Nick rather dreadfully and wished she had never undertaken this ridiculous trip. It was a mistake. Perhaps there was still time to get off.

There was not. The ship was moving away from the dock. The horn sounded, and the bells. Kerri hurried back through the lounge and observed a great flurry of waving and shouting from the people along the rail. She stopped in the lounge doorway. There was no point in looking. He would not be there. He had gone. She was on her way, for good or ill.

The ship began to move out slowly, shepherded by small pilot boats. Her vertical sails remained snugly wrapped in their closed position. They would not be unfurled until the ship passed onto the open ocean. Kerri felt the mysterious vibrations of engines beneath her feet. Sea People, young men and women, scurried around on the top deck. The passengers began to spread out, although most seemed to drift over to the starboard rail to watch as the ship glided past the legendary structure across the water.

Kerri drifted with them. She had seen those soaring roofs many times, but the ancient building still fascinated her. It was said that the Hall of Wings had been built before the Age of Dreams. Which was absurd, according to the Road People, who maintained there was no "before," only various interruptions. They insisted that the Hall of Wings dated back to the founding of the Earth itself, that they, the Road People, had named it and possibly built it, but nobody took this claim very seriously.

Kerri stayed out on deck until just after sunset. She watched the pilot boats stand away and head back to the docks just before the ship left the great harbor. She admired the view of the city and its reflection in the water. She stood in the crowd and looked up with awe as they passed under the magnificent span of the Bridge of Dreams at the harbor entrance. She watched the sails unwind and turn at the bidding of the young sailors. She felt the sudden cessation of vibrations as the engines shut down, giving up their task to the wind.

The wind picked up once the ship left the shelter of the harbor. It grew colder, but she remained on deck, her collar turned up against the breeze. It was another part of her sailing-home ritual to watch the Bridge of Dreams out of sight. This was the best time of day for it. The setting sun gilded the linked fairy towers and web of cable, making the bridge true to its name, for it was also called the Golden Gate, a name which, like the bridge, dated from the Age of Dreams. On the cliffs the seaward windows of the city glittered, Oxinarif of the Haunted Hills to the right of the legendary bridge and Yendys proper on the left. She watched as the lights deepened to red and went out.

The cold forced her at last indoors and sent her to her compartment. She had a vague idea of putting in some time on the next week's recitation and hoped it would be possible to read. Nearly all the seats were occupied by then, by bodies or by notices saying "Occupied." Several mothers were attempting to bed down their small children on the floor or across the rows of seats. There was a lot of noise and not enough light. Kerri got out her text and forced herself to read the first canto of the assignment over six times before she gave up and went to the main lounge.

There the din was even worse, but as she was no longer trying to study she did not care. A group of young passengers were tuning up musical instruments and giving every indication of settling in for an all-night amateur concert. Once upon a time she would have joined them, but it was out of the question this trip.

She went back out on deck. The sky was full dark, wild with stars. The lights of Yendys and the coastal towns were out of sight over the western horizon. There was no moon. It was all very melancholy. Kerri paced the deck restlessly, unable to stand her thoughts, unable to find anything to distract herself from them.

"Eh, Kerri!"

She froze with alarm, clutching the rail.

"Kerri, is that you?" A tall figure in waterproofs stepped into the light from a nearby window. A wide, white grin beamed down at her from the brown face of one of the ship's people.

"Timo!" She laughed with relief. "Eh, Timo! How wonderful! What are you doing here?"

"My job. I work on the ship. Eh, I'm an officer now, didn't you know?"

"I had no idea. Congratulations!" She kissed cheeks with him, delighted. "I've been so out of touch. I'm still living in Yendys, you know."

"Yes, I know. Your grandma comes out to see us every now and then. She brings me up to date. I hear you got married again. Congratulations!"

"Thank you, Timo. I wish you could meet him. He didn't come with me this time. In fact," she lowered her voice, "I shouldn't be here myself. I'm back at University now, first year of graduate study, and if I don't reappear by Tuesday morning, I'll be in for it. So don't mention my presence to anybody, please."

"Oho!" He tapped the side of his nose, and his eyes sparkled. "No worries. As far as the rest of the world is concerned, I never saw you. What is going on?"

She glanced both ways along the deck. "Family business. Will you be free some time on the trip over so we can talk? I want to hear all about your folks at home and what you've been doing. It's been so long!"

"I go off duty at midnight if the weather holds. Will you be up?"

"If I'm not, wake me! I'm in Compartment Six."

He chuckled. "Still sailing third class? Eh, why didn't you marry a rich man while you had the chance?" He ducked her friendly punch and danced away. "I have to get to work. See you!" He winked and hurried off, towering over the few hardy passengers who, like Kerri, felt a need for the open air.

She felt very much better. Just seeing such an old friend, hearing the lilt of the Sea People in his voice, made her feel she was in safe hands. Perhaps she was on a mad expedition, but it was good to be going home.

It was too bad there would be no time on this brief journey to travel to the marai and visit Timo's family. She missed them. They were distant kin to her—Grandmother's mother had been born to the Sea People and had (even more unusual in that generation than now) a sister, Timo's great-grandmother. Kinship was precious in a society where the threads of blood relationship were so attenuated, and the Sea People would be refreshing company after the often stifling atmosphere of life in the Academic world.

Kerri was dozing in her seat in Compartment Six when Timo tapped her on the shoulder. The other passengers were asleep except for one woman knitting near the only light.

"Come on up top," he whispered. When they were in the passage, he asked, "Are you hungry? I haven't eaten yet, and I'm starving."

She shook her head. She felt sleepy and disoriented. "I had a sandwich a few hours ago." she said. "I'll come and sit with you."

They went to the cramped crew's mess and found seats across from each other at one end of the single long table. A few crew members looked at her curiously. She waited while Timo went to the serving hatch. The crew members lost interest and looked away. She felt groggy still, rather sorry she had told Timo to wake her up. He returned with a loaded tray and set a mug in front of her as he sat down. A wisp of steam rose enticingly from the cup.

"Tea," she sighed gratefully. "Ah, thanks, Timo. I can sure use a cuppa."

"My pleasure," he answered.

"How's the wind?"

"She's holding. We're ahead of schedule."

Kerri nodded. Her distant connection to Timo's caste entitled her to a certain amount of the Sea People's arcane knowledge, but she had never been very interested. She preferred to talk about family things, and Timo was glad to tell of his parents and wife and two small children and how well the latter were taking to sailing. Kerri described Nick to Timo and gave him a quick history of her courtship. She told him a minimum of facts about her voyage to Honowell, that there were duties to be carried out in connection with her father's death.

There was no need to explain her desire to travel incognito and to return in time. He had been educated with children of the Academic caste, had been given the opportunity to go on to the University if he had chosen. But his ambition had been to follow the ways of his own people, to become an officer and to have a ship of his own some day. He thought all Academics were slightly crazy and had often said so to Kerri. He said so now.

"You know," he said in a low voice, "it amazes me the things you people do." He meant "you Academics", but out of respect to Kerri's plea for secrecy he didn't say it. "This is the second time within a month that I've seen one of you crossing over and not wanting anybody to know. The last one, I knew him, but he didn't know me."

"Who?" Kerri asked. She made a face. "I shouldn't ask. You don't have to tell me. It wasn't anybody I know, and it isn't any of my business."

"Well," said Timo, narrowing his eyes. "Maybe it is, and maybe it isn't." He leaned forward and lowered his voice. "It happens it was your former spouse." With a flourish he lifted his fork and addressed his pudding.

Chapter 7

Val

"Val?" Kerri had never been more wide awake. "Val sailed over to the Islands? During term? It must have been, if it was within a month. When? I wonder if it was that weekend they closed the University on Friday, the day after the Chancellor died."

"I wouldn't know. It was about three weeks ago, maybe four. It was just luck I saw him to recognize. He took a turn around the deck early in the morning and took off his hat for a minute. Nobody else was around except the crew. I was on the top deck, looking right at him, and I knew who it was. I couldn't miss him. He looked just the same. I went and checked the passenger list later, and his name was on it."

"And he didn't recognize you?"

"Eh, not likely! We only met the once at your wedding, and he didn't take any notice of me at the time. I don't think he even saw me this time. Anyway, I was away from the passengers almost the whole trip. So was he. He went first class and stayed in his cabin the whole time, except for a couple of walks in the fresh air."

"How do you know?"

"I talked to the first class cabin stewards."

"How very odd!" Kerri said. "Of course, he's not first year, so it isn't nearly as critical for him as it is for me. Still, it wasn't good form, and especially not that particular weekend. We were all supposed to attend the memorial. Of course, he could have had a special leave. I wonder what for?" She considered for a moment. "Was he alone? Was he traveling with anyone?"

"No. There was nobody in the cabin with him at any time. He spoke to nobody."

"Did anybody meet him in Honowell?"

"I don't know. I didn't see him leave the ship. And I didn't think to look."

"No reason why you should."

"Eh! Why are you so interested? You still sweet on the guy?"

"Oh, Timo, please! I'm well rid of him. I don't want anything to do with him. In any case," she told him, "Val is also remarried."

"I didn't know," Timo replied. "A Yendys girl?"

"An Island girl. She went to prep school with us. Her name was Zarah Pendrake James."

"Do I know her?"

"You met her several times." Obviously, Timo had never heard about the business with Val and Zarah. Perhaps it had not been as big an item of gossip as she had supposed. Even after so much time, this was a reassuring thought. "You said some very unpleasant things about her then."

"Eh! You don't mean that snotty one, the black-haired girl who got you in trouble that time. The one that was so bad to you? Not that one!"

"That one. That's her. She's changed her name. She is called Arzelle now, that is, by those who know her well enough. I don't move in those circles."

"I hope not. That girl was poison. And she hated you, you know. She was jealous of you."

"Come on, Timo. It was just one of those silly childhood hostilities."

"Sure, she was jealous. You were smarter than her. You got better marks. You had more style. People liked you better. You were prettier..."

"Nonsense!"

"It's true! She decided you were the person in her way, and she hated you. You didn't see it, but everyone else did."

"In her way! No more than she was in mine. We were neck and neck, and now she's left me well and truly in her dust, if it matters. As for what she did to me at Prelims, that was all a long time ago, Timo. Very immature stuff. It doesn't matter now. I was vindicated. I survived. We even became friendly later on for a while. Except I suppose we weren't really, as it turned out."

"I'll bet!" he snorted. "And now that bastard Val is married to her." He chuckled. "I'd say she did it to you again, although it looks like he's got what he deserves."

She met his eyes with a smile. "Yes. I never looked at it that way."

"Had you already separated?" Timo asked. "Or did she...?"

"No, we weren't," Kerri said hastily. She lifted her mug to drink, but it was empty. Timo regarded her sympathetically. "I'm sorry," he said. "Was it bad?"

She shrugged. "At the time. Someday I must tell you all about it," she said.

"There's time now."

"But Timo, you've been working. Don't you need to get some sleep?"

"I don't need much sleep at sea," he informed her stoutly. "Unless you'd rather get some rest yourself."

She thought about what to tell Timo. Was it the kind of tale one could tell a man, even a kinsman? Perhaps in condensed form, with a quick ending if his patience ran out. He was her cousin, he was one of her oldest friends, and he cared about her. He was on her side.

She looked around the room. While they had been talking there had been a steady coming and going of crewmembers, taking their meal without much talk and leaving. She and Timo were alone now except for a couple playing cards at the other end of the table and someone with a beautiful baritone voice singing ancient songs in the galley.

"No," she decided. "I'm awake. I feel like talking. If you're sure you want to listen to such a sordid little story."

"Friends always want to listen!" he said gently. "I'll get us more tea."

He got up and went to the hatch. The singing stopped in mid-phrase. A huge covered teapot muffled in a knit cozy appeared in the hatch. Timo hefted the teapot to the table and slid it down to Kerri. The singing resumed. Timo sat down and poured them each a fresh cup of tea. Kerri doubted if she could have lifted the pot.

"It happened early in the summer after my father died," she began, "just after we'd all graduated. Val was going on, of course. He had a Sponsor—his mother is Faculty, you know. I hadn't got one because Father had made no Legacy..."

"I know," said Timo, sympathy in his eyes. "We were all so very sorry."

"Thank you." Kerri sipped her tea and willed the lump in her throat to disappear. "So I decided not to continue my studies right away. I thought I'd re-apply, that someone would certainly take me on because of Father. I was sure the only problem was the timing of when he died, so close to the deadline.

"I don't know if that had anything to do with any problems Val and I were having. Looking back, I think those had been coming on for a long time. I wasn't happy. I don't think he was either, but it was hard to tell. He wasn't always pleasant to live with. He didn't hurt me or anything, don't think that, but he was thoughtless. He'd say things about me in front of other people; he meant them to be funny."

"You don't call that hurt?" muttered Timo.

"And he took advantage. He expected things to be made easy for him. He didn't pull his weight. Does that make sense?"

Timo nodded.

"Over the winter," Kerri continued, "we had become a little friendly with Zarah— Arzelle, I mean—and her husband Warren. He and Val were in the same department.

"Warren was a kind person. I *did* like him. I guess that was the reason I ever let her get near us. She seemed to have changed. That was after she changed her name but before she got to be so well known. I supposed she had reformed, that she was sorry for having caused me so much trouble ten years before. She even apologized for it once when we were alone. Ooh, that was embarrassing. And such a lie.

"Warren had to go up north that summer. Zarah was supposed to go with him, but she couldn't, she told us, because she had to do some work for some professor. Not her Sponsor, somebody else. They had to give up their flat; they were only subletting it, and the owners wouldn't renew the lease. I don't know how we came to agree to it, but she ended up moving in with us. It was only supposed to be for a couple of weeks until she left for the north.

"She had always flirted a little with Val. He used to make fun of her to me about it. I didn't think he even liked her, although I suspected he was a little attracted to her in a physical way. I didn't think the better of him for it.

"One night, after she'd been sleeping on our couch for about a week, Zarah cooked us all a festive dinner. It was good. We had some wine she said was made by a friend of hers. I didn't have much, I thought, but it really went to my head.

"We all got very silly. Then she stood up and announced that she had a big surprise for us. She was not going up north after all. She and Warren were getting a divorce. In fact, it was final that day. It doesn't take long, you know, when you have a student marriage.

"She had a wonderful idea, she said. She would stay on with us and share Val with me."

"What?" Timo choked on his tea.

"That's right. She seemed to think it was a brilliant notion. Val laughed at her. I think I laughed, too—the wine, you know—but I made it clear I didn't approve. I *thought* I made it clear. I thought Val did, too. In the next breath she passed it off as a joke."

Timo recovered from his coughing spell. "Is that sort of thing acceptable in Yendys?" he croaked. He plainly found the idea offensive.

"Not that I know of," Kerri told him. And Zarah hadn't really intended it seriously, she knew. She had had other intentions, and the outrageous suggestion was merely her next move.

"After that I don't remember what happened. I went to bed, or I was put to bed. Maybe I passed out."

She stopped and glanced at Timo. "I don't do that sort of thing," she said. "I don't drink like that, to unconsciousness. I never did. I can't swear I only had one glass of wine, but that's all I remember having. And it wasn't like ordinary tipsiness. I've felt that in my time. It was like being completely wrapped in invisible wool."

"The wine was drugged!" Timo interjected.

Kerri nodded. "I have no proof, but afterward, the more I thought about it the more certain I became. The others were affected, but not as badly as I was."

"I wouldn't put it past her, the snake!" said Timo darkly. "What happened then? I have a feeling I can guess."

48 Deborah K. Vleck

"You probably have," said Kerri ruefully. "This is the difficult part. I woke up sometime in the night. I felt as if I were still dreaming, but I knew I was awake. It was dark, but I could see somehow. It was like there was a glow coming from just out of sight, like night in Twilight Country.

"Val wasn't there in bed. I went to the door of the bedroom and opened it. I heard them. I saw them even in the dark..." Her voice failed, and her hands clenched on the table.

Timo placed his own broad hand over hers. It was very warm. "You don't have to say," he said.

"It's all right," said Kerri. She took a deep breath. It *was* all right, she realized.

There were no tears, only burning anger. She waited a moment, willing herself to relax, to let the fury drain away.

"It was very strange," she continued in an even voice. "I did not care at that moment. I knew what they were doing, but it was meaningless. I must have still been under the influence of that wine. I felt like I was floating. I closed the door and went back to bed. They didn't see me or hear me, I'm quite sure.

"The next morning I didn't remember a thing about it. Val was with me as usual. At breakfast Zarah joked about how drunk we'd all been, but none of us seemed to have a hangover. I felt marvelous, in fact.

"It was a Thursday. Val and I had intended to go down to Twilight Country for the weekend, to stay in that little house I have down there by the lake. Just the two of us.

"Zarah wasn't coming. I think we had invited her—to be polite; we really didn't want her— but she declined. So very considerate, I thought at the time. I wanted to buy some supplies for the trip. We all went to the River Market to do some shopping.

"It was very crowded. Val and Zarah were on a stairway a little ahead of me, talking and laughing together, and just then I suddenly remembered the whole thing. And I knew it wasn't a dream. It was awful. I thought I would die right there on the spot. I stopped. They went on, in the crowd. They never even noticed they had lost me."

"What did you do?" Timo asked softly, his warm hands over her icy ones.

"I went straight home. I hired a wagoner at the nearest place and had him come around in half an hour. I packed my clothes, personal things, all my papers. Fortunately, I was keeping most of my things in storage because the flat was so small. The man brought boxes, and he helped me with my furniture. I had to be out before they returned. I didn't want to leave anything for Zarah to touch, to pry into."

"I don't blame you."

"Of course, I knew at the time I was surrendering too much, letting him have the flat, but I didn't want to fight him for it. I didn't even want to see either of them again. And I suppose I would have ended up letting him have it in the end. He was still at the University, and I wasn't.

"I wrote a note for Val, telling him I had gone to the cottage. If he didn't join me there by noon the next day, I said, I would take it that our marriage was over. I left it on his desk and had the wagoner take all my things to my family storehouse, except for what I needed for the weekend. Then—I don't know what made me do this, except I suppose I didn't trust Zarah an inch..."

"And rightly!" grumbled Timo.

"...I wrote another letter for Val. I told him about the original note, repeated what I'd said in it, told him if he never found it that it must have been destroyed by Zarah. I was going to mail it to his University post box, but I decided to be extra safe and hire a messenger, deliver to addressee only, return receipt requested."

"Ouweh!"

"Yes, expensive. Then I got on the train for Twilight Country. He didn't arrive by noon the next day. He didn't come until evening just before dark, very much alarmed, he said, at my state of mind." Kerri felt her mouth twist bitterly.

"He told me they'd spent hours looking for me in the Market. He insisted there had been no letter waiting for him when they'd got back to the flat. He refused to believe Zarah could have taken it, or even that I had left it. He thought I must be ill. I know who put that notion into his head!"

Timo pounded a fist once on the table and said grimly, "It is a good thing for him I didn't know about this when I saw him last month."

"I was furious," Kerri assured him. "Even now, after all these years, I am. Later I found out that the messenger had made three attempts to deliver my second letter before Val answered the door Friday morning. The other times Zarah sent him away because he refused to deliver the letter to her.

"But I didn't know that then. I told Val I had seen them that night, dared him to deny it. He didn't deny it, but he didn't admit anything either. He tried to make excuses, to convince me that if he *had* done anything it wasn't wrong. He kept implying there was something wrong with *me!* I made him leave. I returned to Yendys Sunday night, got a room in a boarding house, and filed for a marriage dissolution Monday morning as soon as the Bureau opened."

"Did he ever try to get you back?" Timo asked.

"He did once a few days later, before the divorce became final. He asked me to meet him on campus. I changed it to the steps of the Civil Courthouse." She gave a short laugh. "It wasn't quite the setting he'd had in mind for a reconciliation. He did ask me to forgive him, although he still wouldn't admit to doing anything wrong. Which was ridiculous, because he and Zarah had been together in the flat for nearly a week, and she'd moved her things in. I said I would discuss it with him if he sent her away. He suggested we go and face her together."

"Maybe he was afraid of her and wanted you to rescue him."

"I wonder," said Kerri. "Anyway, I refused. I said he must choose and do what needed to be done. He started again on how irrationally I was behaving. I walked off and left him."

"It was over," Timo observed.

"It was over," Kerri repeated with a sigh. *Except the pain,* she thought. *Except the humiliation. Except the suspicion that Zarah—Arzelle—did it only to hurt me, that she never cared for Val, that she spoiled him, diminished him, made him contemptible.*

"That is a very sad story," Timo said. "I would like to throw both of them overboard."

"Please don't repeat this to anyone, Timo. I can't stand the thought of people talking about it."

He smiled. "Of course not. Your confidence is safe with me. Would you have taken him back, if he had sent her away?"

"No," answered Kerri without hesitation. "No. I think—I think we were finished before Zarah ever came into it. It just had a bad ending, that's all. My life is much happier now than it ever was with him."

"I am glad for you," Timo said.

"Thank you." Kerri smiled. "But I confess I am intrigued by this voyage of his last month. It is very irregular. I would like to know what he was doing, even if it isn't any business of mine. And it isn't."

Timo grinned and hunched closer. "Listen, Kerri, we've known each other a long time. We are family. You can trust me. You know that, or you wouldn't have told me what you just told me. I believe about your father and all, but there's something else. I could see in your face it the minute I first mentioned Val. Secret voyages! People sneaking off to the Islands when they have no business leaving Yendys! What's going on? What's the game?"

The Game. Kerri's breath stopped. She made it start again. Timo did not know. Nobody knew. There was a drop of spilled tea on the table. She ran her finger through it and drew it out into a design.

She was visited by a wild temptation to tell him everything. It would be heavenly to trust someone after so long. Timo was safe, if anybody was safe. He wouldn't laugh. He wouldn't draw back in disgust, or tell her she needed medical care. He wouldn't spread gossip or report her to anybody. He had no power (or desire) to endanger her career. Most important, in all the years she had known him, he had never given her any reason to suppose that he was one of Them. In him there was not the tiniest vestige of the dread Power—or whatever it was in some people that aroused her fear. He might even be able to help somehow.

Yet, it was impossible to begin. Here, now, with so many ears close by, she could not. She only shook her head at him, smiling. She had given him enough of her secrets for one night.

"Well," he said, "what if I find out for you why he went to Honowell when he shouldn't? What if I find out what he's up to, and her, too, if she's in it. Maybe then you'll tell me what is going on?"

The design of spilled tea reached the limit of its complexity and began to evaporate. *Timo,* she said to herself, *if by some strange chance it turns out I am actually persecuted instead of merely pre-demented, you will be the first to know!* "Do that," she suggested. "If there is anything in it, and if I discover what it is, I shall tell you. I promise."

She realized she meant it. Even if he only found her some weapon against Val and Zarah, to keep by her in case of need, she would be forever in his debt. She would tell him about the Game, about the Power, about the whole irrational fantasy.

"Done!" he exclaimed. "We shall be allies! Consider me your spy."

"I shall be very grateful," Kerri confessed.

Chapter 8

Honowell

The *Arcturus* slid quietly home after sunset into the dredged estuary of Honowell. The high vertical sails were wrapped snugly away as the engines shuddered to life for maneuvering through the crowded harbor. Behind rough-edged black mountains already garlanded with lights, the sky blazed.

Kerri leaned on the rail, anonymous among the eager, weary travelers. She had resumed the disguise of blackened spectacles and could see nothing clearly except the sky, the gleam of water, and lights rising beyond the shore.

She did not expect to be met. Her reply to Monday's urgent messages had preceded her by less than two days. The vagaries of overseas post made it likely that her letter would not arrive until after she had gone back to Yendys. It did not matter. She would take the cable-drawn trolley up to the heights, to the labyrinthine University district, or she would walk through the mild night. Over the pale, glassy water she caught a hint of fragrance, remotely tropical. It would be a pleasure to walk.

But no. Mother and Grandmother were there on the dock, awaiting her under one of the lamps so she would see them. They carried traditional welcoming garlands over their arms. By the way their eyes scanned the side of the ship she could tell they had not seen her. Their heads leaned together; their mouths moved. They looked normal and cheerful.

An hour later, sitting between them on the cable car, fresh flowers against her cheeks, she felt a little cheated by that same normality and cheerfulness. It was not what she had expected, yet she couldn't remember what, if anything, she had expected. She had no trouble falling in with their mood, but she felt guarded, brittle, as if they were all masked against the uninterested fellow passengers in the car. It would have been impossible to discuss the real matter of her homecoming in so public a place, but all the same she looked for hints, portents. There were none forthcoming, only smiles—proud, familiar, weary. They spoke very little.

The low white house glimmered faintly from the moon and street lamps as they walked toward it from the trolley stop. A breeze blew down from the mountains, stirring autumn-bare branches. Dry leaves rustled in gutters and in the lee of garden walls. Kerri's mother took a latchkey from her handbag and opened the front door. The cats twined among their feet in the dark.

In ten minutes more Kerri found herself seated at the scarred oak table in the kitchen. A kettle muttered on the stove, and there was lamplight. The elderly cats curled themselves around Kerri's feet, one to a foot, like animate slippers, willing to anchor her forever with drowsy, purring love.

Unaccountably, Kerri felt seventeen again, coming home for the first time from Yendys, flush with importance at being a full-fledged University student on a true course toward her proper destiny. Except this time Father was not there, grinning with shy pride, and Val was not by her side.

Sophia Bremen Nash-Dale tied on an apron and refused all offers of assistance as she put supper on the table. She was still a handsome woman. From a distance she might have been mistaken for her own daughter, except for her old-fashioned elaborate hairstyle. The piled ringlets were the same bronze as Kerri's hair, and the slender figure was the same.

Even close up, only her hands and a spray of lines at the corner of each eye betrayed her generation. She dressed smartly, the perfect professor's wife.

"We didn't tell anyone about your coming, of course," she said. "Personally, I don't think anyone here would care one way or another, but Aryel felt very strongly about it."

"Gossip travels, Sophia."

"So it does, but it *is* a legal holiday on the Mainland."

"Well, Mother, it only matters if I get held up here past Sunday. By then it would be too late to keep it quiet."

"I do see, but it still seems absurd to me. You won't be able to see any of your friends."

Kerri shuddered inwardly. Val's friends. "There isn't time anyway," she reminded her mother. *When,* she wondered, *are they going to tell me why I had to come home? We've had this conversation two times over.* She saw her Grandmother smiling at her from beyond the lamp and returned the smile. "At least I saw Timo," Kerri said. "He won't tell a soul."

Aryel nodded. "I always liked that boy," she proclaimed. "It's a pity he never went on to the University. But then, he isn't Academic born."

"He's an officer," Kerri informed her. "We had a good talk last night. That is, this morning. It was good to hear news of the marai, the children."

Aryel nodded, smiling. Although she appeared relaxed in the wooden chair, her hands betrayed a tension of waiting. They were elegant hands, as the rest of her was elegant. Not the mannered stylishness of a don's wife, but the disciplined refinement of a talented and respected Senior Fellow. Touches of gold gleamed on the rich surface of appliqued suit jacket, and rubies glowed from her ears and the heavy college ring on one finger. She wore her white hair short and expertly coiffed.

"Why don't you tell us your good news?" she asked Kerri.

"How did you know I even had any?" said Kerri. "I was saving it."

"Good news?" said Sophia, sitting down and unfolding her napkin. "Oh, tell now! Is it a baby?"

"No, Mother. I am sorry to disappoint you. It is something else." She looked down into her soup and felt color rising to her cheeks. "On Monday, the same day I heard from you, Nick and I got an invitation to the Regents' Ball at the May Revel."

"Kerri! How wonderful!"

"My dear! We are so pleased for you."

"Well, we're rather pleased ourselves. The trouble is, we have to come up with new costumes, and there isn't much time, and with me having to come here... I left Nick to cope with the shopping and getting started, but he has work to do this weekend."

Aryel said thoughtfully, "I believe I can help you with that. Let us look through my storeroom tomorrow and see what we can find."

"Oh, Grandmother, I would be honored!" Kerri gasped. Aryel Range Stewart-Nash possessed a legendary collection of festival and ceremonial costumes. Anything of hers would outshine most of the costumes in view at the Revel, even in sophisticated Yendys.

"Wouldn't they be recognized?" asked Sophia.

"Oh, Mother, as if I cared!"

"Yes, a few of the older professors might remember, but none of the younger generation..."

"And if they do, I'll simply mention the source and watch them curl at the edges. But Grandmother, you cannot really want to lend me any of your precious costumes!"

"I mean to give them to you. They will be yours in any case, some day, and I have more than I shall ever possibly wear again. All the pairs I made when your grandfather was alive are of no use to me or to Sophia. None of them have been seen in years. They should be getting some honest use. Besides they're more appropriate for young people. You shall have them. Tomorrow. Or perhaps," she added, with a look at her daughter-in-law, "Sunday.

"Now. Tell us where they're having the Ball this time. Will it be the Pavilion or the Chancellor's Palace? I suppose they can hardly have it at the Palace so soon after the poor man's death, and the new Chancellor not even chosen. I remember one year when the May Revel Ball was held in the Hall of Wings..."

They kept the talk to Revels past and future through supper. Kerri began to feel sleepy. She had given up expecting to hear anything about Father's mysterious letters until after the meal. By then, she reflected drowsily, they might just as well wait until morning. It didn't seem as if there could be anything very dreadful about the letters. Maybe there wasn't even anything very important; such a shame when she had come all this way.

"Sophia, this child is dead on her feet. We can't wait any longer."

Kerri opened her eyes. "I'm sorry," she mumbled. "It's all that sea air, I expect." She realized the table had been cleared and that her mother was pouring coffee and brandy.

Aryel got up and left the room.

"Are you all right, Mother?" Kerri asked. "I've been worrying about you since I got your letter."

"It was very upsetting at first," Sophia confirmed softly. "As if he had come back, quite irrational of me. Then, of course, I realized he hadn't, and I was crushed. And so guilty. How could I have forgotten to look there? All these years!"

"It wasn't your fault, Mother. Where did you find them?"

"There is a hidden compartment in the study."

"Mother, there are seventeen hidden compartments in this house! That I know of."

Sophia smiled a little tearily. "I know twenty-eight. Or is it twenty-nine? Your father had others even I didn't know. We looked, of course. After he...you remember. But we'll never know if we found them all. We missed this one."

"He had shown it to me once. I did remember when I came upon it. I was trying to catch a bit of paper that slipped down through a crack in the woodwork, and then it came back to me. I had completely forgotten."

Aryel returned to the room then, carrying a small bundle of papers. She set them down in front of Sophia and seated herself.

"Did Grandmother know about the compartment?" Kerri asked.

Sophia shook her head. "I found the letters," she said. "They could only have been there a few days at most when...when he died." She cleared her throat. "The dates...I'm sure he intended..."

"Let us tell Kerri about the part that concerns her," Aryel prompted gently.

"Yes. After all, that's what we made you come for, isn't it, darling? You see it turns out that he made you a Legacy after all. It's all here." Her pale fingers turned over the envelopes lingeringly and drew out a small packet which she set in front of her daughter.

Kerri saw her name lettered on the front in her Father's script. She put her face in her hands and wept.

* * *

They all recovered themselves presently. Aryel poured more brandy all round and took matters into her own hands. "The Legacy," she said, "is directed to Professor Charles Bonneville-Chatterton, one of your father's oldest and dearest friends. I delivered it to him myself and took the liberty of making an appointment for you to call on him tomorrow morning at his home. You'll find the letter of introduction there before you, no doubt. You're to see him at ten o'clock."

Kerri nodded, overwhelmed. He had done it after all. He had not forgotten this duty to her. He had provided. All the anger she had felt in the five years since his death was undeserved. She had been unable to forgive him for leaving her to the thin hope of winning a Sponsor through her own efforts and finally the ignominy of entering graduate school as a commoner. Now, instantly, everything was changed. *Forgive me, Daddy,* she prayed.

"Ten o'clock," she repeated.

"Don't worry about clothes," Sophia said. "We'll fix you up."

Kerri looked down at her sea-going shirt and trousers. "Good. Because I didn't bring anything."

"You see why we needed to have you come immediately," Sophia added. "If Professor Bonneville-Chatterton is to consider you before next year it must be now. The applications for sponsoring are to be complete by the first of May."

"You didn't apply to him this year, did you?" said Aryel.

Kerri shook her head.

"I thought not. He was willing to forego the personal interview under the circumstances, but in my opinion it does not behoove us to take any shortcuts on the formalities. This way he has no excuse to put you off until next year. We're cutting things close enough as it is. If anything goes wrong, you've still one more year to set it right. Next year you'd have no margin for error."

"I may need it," Kerri commented. "The risk I took coming here during term! I quite see why I needed to come, but I very nearly didn't." She frowned and looked from one to the other. "When I heard from you Monday, I didn't dare think it might be this. You might have given me some hint."

"I wanted to," Sophia began, "but..."

"And what if you hadn't been able to come?" Aryel challenged her. "We had no way of knowing what sort of commitments you might have had in Yendys. It might have been impossible for you to get away. You would have been wretched the rest of the term, and to no purpose, because things could still have been salvaged next year. What if someone had seen our letters? Would you want your hand tipped prematurely? Would you want to take the risk of making yourself a target before the lists come out?"

"I suppose not," Kerri replied, declining to mention that she was apparently already a target. She frowned again, considering. It was bad enough to have her course work threatened by petty acts of sabotage, but that was nothing to compare to the terror she would feel if she had to safeguard critical Sponsorship paperwork from the unknown saboteur. Up to now her enemy had left her alone on that front, and why not? She had no Legacy; she had been going through the motions, wasting her time. The Legacy would temporarily render her more vulnerable, if the word got out prematurely. Once the lists were published, on the first of June, her status would be cemented for good, unshakable. Until then not even Nick could be told.

"What makes you so certain he will have me as a Legacy?" she asked. "I applied to him the very first year. I thought as Father's friend he might take notice of me, but he refused me. I applied to him three times, and the same thing happened each time. If I wasn't good enough before, how can he accept me now?"

"It is different with a Legacy," Sophia reminded her with a sigh.

"I quite agree with Kerrith," said Aryel firmly. "It ought not to be. Every graduate scholar should be judged and chosen on her or his own achievements. This favoritism is weakening the whole caste, keeping out good blood. This family has been Academic since the Age of Dreams, and every generation has carried on graduate study under Sponsors. For at least six generations we have been in the Faculty. By heredity! But I still think it is wrong. We ought to have earned it. Every Academic son or daughter ought to earn it."

"And I haven't, have I," Kerri stated quietly. "This year will be my fifth time of asking. After next year I shan't even be eligible any more. If I truly deserved a Sponsor, I'd have got one by now. Here's the weakness you were talking about, Grandmother."

"No!" Aryel rose to her feet, so indignant she nearly knocked over her chair. "Not you, Kerri," she said harshly. "You are not one of the undeserving. You are one of the victims." She stalked to the darkened window and looked out at the invisible garden.

Kerri could think of nothing to say. Sophia looked bewildered. There was a long silence.

Finally Sophia spoke. "You are saying that if all graduates had to make formal application, if there were no Legacies at all, then Kerri would have been chosen before now."

Aryel's shoulders relaxed, but she did not turn. "Yes," she said. "That is what I meant."

"What shall I do?" Kerri asked them. "If what you are saying is true, Grandmother, wouldn't it be the honorable thing to decline Father's Legacy?"

"No, indeed," said Aryel. "Don't even think of it!"

"Perhaps the word 'victim' is a little too strong," said Sophia, "but there's no reason for you to go on being one. Things are the way they are."

"Nobody would take any notice of such a gesture," Aryel agreed. "You would not change anything by sacrificing yourself. Charles Bonneville-Chatterton will pretend that he never received an application from you until now, and I advise you to do the same."

"I shall. Don't worry. But *will* he accept me?"

"He has no choice," said Aryel grimly.

"Of course, he will," Sophia said. "Why shouldn't he? A fine young woman like you! Now, off to bed with you, young lady."

Chapter 9

The Interview

At precisely five minutes to ten the next morning, Saturday, Kerri presented herself at Professor Bonneville-Chatterton's front door. She was impeccably turned out in one of her grandmother's simplest Academically tailored jackets and a blouse and skirt belonging to her mother. Shoes, stockings, scarf, hat, and gloves were all borrowed, as was the small brooch in the knot of her scarf. She wore her own earrings and college ring.

The professor's house was more imposing than most in Honowell's University district.

Indeed, it stood on the district's very margin, on the wild heights where the homes of University officials and higher Faculty gave way to the estates of wealthy Cits and Stockholders. The house perched on a knob of the mountain, with a large garden descending all around, a lawn so perfectly manicured it bespoke professional care. A wide veranda skirted the front and sides of the house. The richly carved double front door was windowed with tall ovals of beveled glass.

The dark-suited young man who opened the door to Kerri's ring was, she realized a startled second later, an employee, not a family member. This was unexpected. Even Faculty who were very well off did not ordinarily employ household servants. Kerri had little firsthand acquaintance with the servant caste, but she was well equipped with the best training available to a Faculty daughter. She identified herself and gave up her hat and gloves with what she hoped was an air of easy self-assurance. The fellow took Kerri's cards and letter of introduction, asked her to wait in the hall and went away.

Given a moment to organize her thoughts, Kerri tried to recollect everything she knew about Professor Bonneville-Chatterton. She remembered having met him, but she had not seen him since her prep school days. He and Father had seemed very close then. It was their work that brought them together; the intimacy had never extended to families. She had never met the professor's wife, who had been dead for some years. The marriage must have been a happy one if the professor had kept her name hyphenated with his own since her death. They had no children. He and Father had ceased having very much to do with each other about the time Kerri had gone away to Yendys to University. She had a vague recollection of some quarrel or misunderstanding. It must have been patched up between them, though, if Father had felt able to make this Legacy. She wished she had been less tired the previous evening, had possessed enough presence of mind to pump Mother and Grandmother for details. Ah, too late now!

The employee reappeared. "Will you please come this way?" he requested. Kerri followed him past a graceful swoop of a staircase to another carved door. The man opened it and announced, "Miss Kerrith Nash Dale-Townsend." He bowed and departed, pulling the door softly closed behind her.

Kerri found herself in spacious room, lined with books and mellowed wood and filled with daylight from two tall, arched windows. A small fire burned upon the hearth of the marble fireplace, in front of which stood a man in a Professor's robe, her letter of introduction in his hand. He was small, slender, and balding, and he wore glasses. "Ah, Miss Dale-Townsend," he acknowledged. "Good morning. Good morning."

"Good morning, Professor Bonneville-Chatterton," Kerri replied with a slight bow.

"Please be seated." He gestured toward a brocade-covered chair near the fireplace and took a seat himself in its twin at the other end of the small, exquisite rug. Kerri sat, thankful for all those years of lessons in deportment, so many of them directed toward such interviews as this.

He took off his glasses and polished them with a handkerchief, revealing a pair of shrewd, rather close-set eyes, with which he regarded her alertly. The glasses and his quiet voice had given him an air of vagueness, but the eyes proved that this impression was misleading. Kerri waited politely, knowing better than to speak first. He studied her for a long moment, then said, "It has been a long time since I have seen you, Miss Dale-Townsend. I dare say you do not remember me."

"Indeed, I do remember you, Professor. It is a pleasure to see you again."

He accepted this conventional pleasantry with only the hint of a satirical twinkle in his eye and continued, "You look very like your mother. Astonishingly like. How is she?"

"Quite well. She asked me to give you her regards."

He put his glasses back on and looked mild and vague again. "Very kind. You must convey mine to her."

"I shall with pleasure, sir."

"Of course, I do see your grandmother often at the University. Excellent woman. Still, I must say it was unexpected when she called on me the other day. And when she told me the reason, I was touched. Most deeply touched. Your father was a fine man and a good friend. He is still very much missed among the Faculty."

"Thank you, Professor." Kerri lowered her eyes to her folded hands.

Fortunately, he changed the subject and inquired about her academic plans, nodding approvingly when she told him. As an Economist, he was not a scholar of Late Classic literature himself, beyond the usual undergraduate syllabus, but he was very well informed and seemed to be personally acquainted with almost every one of Kerri's teachers in Yendys.

He asked her to recite formally—a piece from Milne and some verses by Williams—and complimented her on her delivery. Nothing he posed to her was especially difficult or challenging, and this surprised her, especially in view of his response to her earlier application. She had been braced for a much more difficult grilling, expecting at any moment some trick question or hopelessly obscure passage to recite, some trap for her to walk into.

But he seemed almost to take her worthiness for granted, to be merely conducting a formality. And he was soon finished with it, saying that he could see she had considerable promise for an Academic career, exactly what he would expect of someone with her background, and now, if she would be so good, since she was still on her feet, would she please ring for coffee?

Almost trembling with relief, Kerri went obediently to tug on the bell-pull. Now she had time again to take notice of the extraordinary opulence of the house. Servants, let alone bells to summon them, were things she knew of only through books and plays and etiquette lessons. Although senior Faculty members were as a rule comfortably well off, few could afford to live in so grand a style as Professor Bonneville-Chatterton did. On the other hand, Regents and Chancellors and the like were said to live almost as well as Stockholders. A sudden worry bit at her: Had the professor achieved some higher post? Had Grandmother forgotten to remind her? Had she been addressing him incorrectly all this time? He had given no sign.

Newly anxious, she returned to her chair and tried to listen to the Professor's gentle reminiscent chitchat about various colleagues in Yendys. Fortunately, he did not seem to expect her to say much, though she was familiar enough with some of the names to answer intelligently from time to time.

The door opened, and a middle-aged woman wearing the demure black and white of the servant caste entered bearing a huge silver tray which she set on a low table near the Professor's chair. The tray held a silver coffee service, cups and saucers and spoons for two, and a plate of small pastries. Kerri, who had not been able to swallow any breakfast, suddenly realized she was hungry.

To distract herself, she gazed at the ornaments on the mantelpiece. There was a clock which had attracted her attention from the moment she had entered the room. Ornate with enamel and gold, small and delicate, it was the loveliest timepiece she had ever seen.

The professor noticed her interest. As he handed her cup, he asked, "What do you think of the clock?"

"It is beautiful, Professor," she said. "I have never seen anything like it before."

"I am fond of it myself," he said. "It is very old. It was made in the numbered years."

Kerri gasped. "In the Age of Dreams, sir?"

"So I was assured by an expert. Why do you look so surprised?"

Without thinking, Kerri said, "I thought such things were only possessed by..." She broke off, blushing furiously. "I beg your pardon, Professor."

He appeared to be amused. "By Stockholders?" he said with a dry laugh. "That is understandable. But, you see, I am a Stockholder myself."

Worse and worse. Kerri experienced a fervent desire that the polished floor would open and swallow her away. Somehow she managed to continue sitting primly, balancing her cup and saucer. "Please forgive me, your Excellency," she said. "I did not know."

He smiled. "Few people do," he said. "And I do not use the title. 'Professor' is good and honorable enough. It has served me well for much of my life, and I am too comfortable with it to change. You must continue to call me by it."

"Yes, Professor, if you wish it."

"I have not been a Stockholder very long," he mused, looking around the room. "It is only a few years since I inherited. I was adopted quite late in life, too, so I suppose I shall always think of myself as Academic. Born and bred Academic, you know."

He stood and walked over to a painting on the wall opposite the fireplace, a life-sized portrait of a man in rich festival garments. "My adopted father," he said, gazing at the picture. "A very noble gentleman. Your father knew him also."

Kerri found her voice. "I...I was not aware, sir, that Stockholders adopted people outside their own caste."

"Oh, were you not?" He turned back and peered toward her with an owlish stare, and suddenly Kerri felt herself struck, as if by a gust of wind, a blast of pure Power. She held on to herself and managed to keep from dropping her cup as icy panic clutched at her body. Her breath would not obey her. There was no time to summon the Veil.

Then he turned back to the painting, and the lash of Power was gone as if it had not been. He was the gentle, mild little Professor again, making an effort to chat interestingly with his old friend's daughter. *I imagined it,* Kerri told herself. *It wasn't real. I only imagined it.*

"They do from time to time." he went on with scarcely a pause. "Many of them have no offspring, you know, and yet each of them is required to have an heir."

Kerri nodded, beginning to recover. It hadn't happened. A moment of dizziness— that was all it had been—some kind of reaction to the tension of this interview, the anxiety of the past week, the changes that had come abruptly into her life.

He returned to his chair and offered her more coffee and another pastry, both of which she declined. She managed to set her cup and saucer down on the tray without too obvious a tremble. A short time later he brought the interview to a close and showed her to the front door himself.

"I shall require official copies of all your University records, of course," he told her. "You will be informed of my official decision at the usual time, and then we shall see what we can do about finding a proxy in Yendys. I have often been associated in this capacity with Professor Montgomery-Lee of the College of Mathematics. Are you acquainted with her?"

"No, sir."

"I shall send you a letter of introduction." He beamed at her. "I believe we shall deal well together," he said. "I find your qualities most impressive. Indeed, even better than I had expected. Continue to work hard and diligently, and you will have an excellent future. Good day."

"Thank you, Professor." She mustered a decent imitation of a smile as she shook his offered hand. "Good day." She bowed before turning to descend the steps of the veranda. He continued to stand in the doorway watching her, the daylight making his glasses opaque. She forced herself not to hurry. There were many stairs between the house and the garden gate. She took them calmly, back straight and head up, expecting at any moment another blast of Power from the man watching above. She felt him turn away at last and go inside, felt his conscious attention move elsewhere. Her hand was on the wrought iron gate, and she allowed herself to lean on it a little more than necessary. Her legs felt rubbery and undependable. It was over.

To give herself time to recover before facing Mother and Grandmother, she took the long way home, detouring through the Botanical Gardens. The day was fine and sunny, the best of autumn weather, but there were few people about. No doubt the parks would become crowded after the shops all closed at half past twelve. She took the hardest and steepest paths and set herself a quick pace.

She would have thought she had done well, except for her error about the clock. Oh, that was bad! She would give anything not to have blurted out those words. Had she ruined her chances right there and then? Or could she rely on the Professor's apparent amusement and mildly self-deprecating reaction to her gaffe? His kindness had unnerved her almost as much as her own blunder. And unnerved she had been, enough to hallucinate a Powerflash. *It is a long time since I've done that,* she told herself.

It had not been real. That was the first fact. She steadied herself with the old litany.

The Power is not Real. Professor Bonneville-Chatterton is not one of Them. They can't tell what I am thinking. They don't care. There is no Them. The Veil is unnecessary. It is only a Game. It is imaginary. I am grown up now. I don't need it anymore. I am perfectly well and entirely normal.

She made herself recollect his parting words. Those had certainly sounded encouraging. Why would he have spoken of finding a proxy if he hadn't already intended to accept her? *And if he doesn't,* she thought, *I shall be no worse off than I was before. Yes, they were right not to put this in letters. If he refuses me, if something goes wrong, no one will ever be the wiser.*

She came to the highest point of the Botanical Gardens. This had always been one of her favorite places. The hilltop was kept clear of trees to provide a magnificent view in all directions, and there was a little plaza with benches to rest on and a gazebo for shade. Maps were inscribed n the stone parapet so visitors could tell what they were looking at when they stood so high over the city of Honowell.

She closed her eyes and let the cool wind blow on her face. The wind always blew up here, which was one reason she liked it. There were half a dozen people sharing the place with her—a young couple absorbed in each other, a woman with a small child in a pram, two half-grown boys trying to launch a kite. None of them were dangerous. *Not Real. Not Real.* She felt the muscles of her neck begin to relax.

The noon bells of the University drifted faintly to her on the wind. Grandmother and Mother would be suffering agonies, waiting for her to come back to the house and tell them about the interview. With a quick last look around at the vista of city, harbor and mountains, she crossed to the path and descended with brisk steps.

Chapter 10

Aryel

After lunch Sophia allowed them to help with the washing up and then shooed them out of the house. She wanted to take a nap, she said, put her feet up and recover from the morning's suspense. Besides, she was sure the two of them had a great deal to talk about.

"Do you think his acceptance of me is really as certain as Mother believes?" Kerri asked as they walked to Aryel's home.

"It's the very least Charles Bonneville-Chatterton owes your father," said Aryel, "although nothing is official until the lists come out in June. He has the right to turn you down if he finds you unqualified, but there's no question of that in your case. It is very bad form to refuse a Legacy without serious cause."

"I wish I could be as sure." Kerri shivered. "I can't forget how he answered me the other times. Does it ever actually happen that a Legacy is refused?"

"There have been cases, but they are rare. And if he tries any such nonsense, he will have me to deal with."

Kerri was silent for a while, wondering how Grandmother would "deal with" Professor Bonneville-Chatterton if he did not cooperate. She was senior to him on the Faculty, but he was a Stockholder. Kerri had not mentioned this revelation while recounting the morning's trial over lunch. It would alarm Mother, and it was too close to the Powerflash. Now she wondered again how much Aryel knew.

"Grandmother," she said, "I discovered something curious about the Professor this morning. Did you know that he is a Stockholder? He was adopted, he said."

Aryel glanced at her fleetingly. "Yes, I knew that," she replied flatly. "I wonder why he told you."

"I did a very stupid thing. I was admiring a clock he keeps in his library. It was after I recited for him. I was nervous; I wasn't thinking. I said the clock looked like something that would belong to a Stockholder. I wish I hadn't said it! Oh, Grandmother, why didn't you tell me?"

"He specifically desired me not to. It was one of his conditions for consenting to see you on a Saturday. Do not worry, dear. He will not hold it against you. Indeed, if I know Charles, he wasn't offended at all but flattered that you noticed.

He hasn't enjoyed his dignities long, and few of his acquaintances have been as quick as you were. I suspect he has been bursting for *someone* to figure it out."

"But isn't it odd for an Academic to be adopted by a Stockholder?"

"Why should it be? They haven't enough children of their own. Whom else would they adopt?" She sighed. "It happens far more often than most people realize."

"I wasn't aware it happened at all. What others do you know of?"

Aryel hesitated for so long that Kerri began to feel uncomfortable about asking Perhaps it was one of those things polite people did not mention. It alarmed her that she had lived so long without learning this interesting bit of inter-caste lore.

Finally her grandmother answered. "I know of others. If they do not choose to make their status public, it isn't fitting for me to discuss it."

But Kerri persisted, suddenly remembering Monday afternoon, Arzelle on the Mall, and an old man raking leaves.

"Grandmother, Professor Edson—the one Father used to know—is he a Stockholder, too?"

"He is," affirmed Aryel reluctantly. "Why do you ask?"

"He is in Yendys. I saw him working on campus as a gardener."

"Yes. On Sabbatical." Aryel inhaled deeply. "It is just as well. He is probably the only individual in the world who could talk Charles out of Sponsoring you."

"What?" Kerri gasped. "Why would he do that?"

"He likes trouble. Stay out of his way. Tell me, Kerri, have you ever yearned to be a Stockholder?"

"Me? No, why should I? I am Academic. When I was a child, we used to pretend we were Stockholders sometimes, because they were so rich and magnificent. Mysterious, too, like people in Age of Dreams stories and fairy tales. I haven't thought about it since. There would have been no point. I had no idea it was possible to be a Stockholder without being born to the caste."

"And now that you know?"

Kerri thought for a moment. "I'm not sure it makes any difference. I cannot imagine such a life—so decorative and public and...useless. Certainly I don't know any Stockholders personally, let alone one who might be inclined to adopt me." She smiled. "You aren't trying to suggest the Professor Bonneville-Chatterton might adopt me, are you?"

"Not in the least," snapped Aryel. "He has stood Sponsor for nearly a dozen graduates and never yet showed signs of favoring one. Still," she went on more quietly, "he could do worse. And he'll have to adopt somebody soon. It is unlikely to be you. Do not think about it."

"I won't," Kerri assured her. "His house was lovely, though. It would be wonderful to have so many beautiful things like that, never to have to worry about money—and still be Academic."

"Yes. Charles is a lucky man," said Aryel. "And he owes a very great debt to your father."

Kerri smiled again, to herself. Grandmother might tell her not to think about the possibility of such an inheritance, but it was obvious Aryel had just such a hope for her only descendant. Kerri decided she herself was not tempted to cherish any such ideas—not after this morning's experience.

"Just what did Father do for him?" she asked.

"He died," said Aryel grimly.

"I beg your pardon?"

Aryel looked at her appraisingly. "My dear, I am not at liberty to discuss it—most unfortunately. You will know all about it one day, if I have anything to say. Look! There's old Miss Forsythe's house. She left to move in with her daughter, you know, and turned the house over to a young couple from the College of Fine Arts. Soon I shall be the only one of the old ones left on the circle."

"You're not old, Grandmother!" Kerri said fondly. She accepted the deliberate change of subject without question or protest, but she was shocked. *He died,* Aryel had said. How did one put a friend in debt by dying? Something about the work they were doing together perhaps? Although it was a high misdemeanor for a Fellow to appropriate credit for the work of a recently deceased colleague, it did happen from time to time. If Aryel had known about someone doing that to Father, though, surely she would have raised a loud protest in the Faculty Senate.

Perhaps she had only suspicions without adequate evidence for action. In that case she would have been forced to live in silence all this time for the sake of her own career. False accusation was regarded as a grave sin by the Academic community—as Kerri had good reason to know.

Most likely these evasions had a simpler reason. Aryel must feel uncomfortable discussing the older generations of the Faculty with her granddaughter. *She probably thinks it is none of my business,* Kerri thought. *And quite rightly.*

They turned into Browning Circle and crossed the tiny park in the center. A young woman pushing a pram smiled proudly as she passed them and nodded to Aryel. Kerri stared at the baby and wondered briefly if her turn would ever come. Nick's window of fertility was not due to open for another year or two. On the other hand, these things were not entirely predictable. It could happen any day.

They approached the seaward side of the circle where the land dropped steeply away, revealing a vista of harbor and city.

"Your view!" exclaimed Kerri. "I always forget how magnificent it is."

Aryel smiled. "I have lived here for nearly forty years," she said, "and it still makes me happy every day."

She led the way through the garden gate and across the lawn of the upper garden. At the edge of the drop a narrow twisting stone stairway descended the mountainside. The house itself was tucked into a ledge suspended above the city; only its dark slate roof was visible from the upper garden. In the spring and summer the stairway was a tunnel of flowers, but now the vines and bushes were bare, and dry tendrils of honeysuckle scraped against the stone.

The long verandah creaked in all the same places Kerri remembered. She gazed out over the city while Aryel unlocked the door. A fat black cat jumped off a nest of worn cushions on the shabby old wooden seat and landed with a thump on the boards. It stalked past Kerri without a glance and disappeared into the shrubbery.

"Old brute!" muttered Aryel affectionately.

"He's put on weight," said Kerri. "Does he still hunt?"

"He'd like you to think so."

They entered the house and went through the wide hall into the living room. In spite of the dark wood and stone of the exterior and the breadth of verandah which ran along the whole front of the house, the rooms were filled with light. The builders had incorporated clerestory windows or skylights into most of the rooms, and Aryel had chosen furnishings to enhance the effect of airiness and open space. Here there was no formal grandeur such as surrounded Professor Bonneville-Chatterton, only simple and flawless elegance: polished golden wood, brightly dyed wool, a bare branch in a clay jar against one white wall, venerable books whose gilded leather spines gleamed like jewels.

"I have always loved this house," Kerri said dreamily.

"Do you, dear?" Aryel replied softly. "Shall I turn it over to you when the time comes for me to leave? I would much rather you have it than anyone else."

Kerri gave her a quick hug. "I never dared ask. We may never live in Honowell, you know."

"That doesn't matter to me. If you want it, it shall be yours. You can find a caretaker and let the University scream as loudly as they like. But at the moment we have other business: your Revel costumes."

The costumes were stored in a room at the back of the house. The windows were shuttered. The air inside was cool. Cupboards were built along three walls, and a row of cedarwood chests stood under the windows. Aryel opened the shutters and folded them back. "We'll take things out to the living room," she said. "The light is better there." She began opening cupboards and pulling out masses of velvet, lace, and glittering brocade which she piled into the arms of her awed granddaughter.

They carried out two loads each and draped the garments over all the seats and tables. "Well," said Aryel, "That will do for a start."

Kerri was speechless. Her astonished eyes refused to separate one garment from another. She could only gape at the jumble of color and texture. She had seen a number of her grandparents' costumes, singly and at intervals, but never in profusion on all sides like this. And these were only a small part of the whole collection. There was no doubt that Aryel deserved her reputation.

"For your first Faculty Revel," said Aryel, "it would be best to dress with some restraint. You desire to impress but not to antagonize. This, for instance." She walked to the sofa and lifted a dress heavy with cloth of gold. "That would be for later, perhaps when one of you has gained a Fellowship."

Kerri nodded.

"This." Aryel gathered up a garment of pearl grey velvet trimmed in silver. "This would be much more suitable. There's the pair. We wore these for the first time, let me see, thirty-nine years ago. Your parents wore them to the first Autumn Banquet after they were married. It was cold that year. Or this." She rummaged through one shining heap and drew out a dress that shimmered with the deep blue iridescence of a paua shell, set off with crisp white lace like sea foam, black velvet and rhinestones. "Yes. We wore these...a long time ago." She became very still for a moment, cradling the gown in her arms, her eyes fixed on some distant memory, then, giving herself a little shake, she went on briskly. "Nobody would remember by now. It ought to be worn again." She held the dress up against Kerri, considering with a critical eye that glowing blue against her granddaughter's coloring. "Yes! The very thing. Spectacular but not the least overdone. And it will look very well on you."

Kerri reached out shyly to caress the shining cloth. "What beautiful brocade!" she commented. "I have never seen anything like it. See, even the weaving mimics the pattern of the paua shell—the blues and purples, and these touches of pinks and golds and greens."

Aryel grinned. "Wonderful, isn't it? I was much envied this fabric once upon a time.

"There was only one bolt of it ever imported—perhaps only one ever woven—and I got the whole thing, thanks to my kin among the Sea People. Still have a few meters left, put away safe for alterations or repairs. Here, do try it on. You may change right here. There's a good large mirror. I always like plenty of space to put my costumes on."

Kerri obediently began to shed her clothes. She had always taken an interest in the nuances of costume in general society and in the Academic world in particular, but until now she had lacked the means and the status to invest in the kind of elegance that was the ideal of that world's higher circles. As an undergraduate, and during her brief career in the Department of Public Health, her efforts toward festival clothing had always been a last minute scramble to devise something suitable, anything, or to make do with what she already had. There had never been money for more, or, indeed, the necessity. Now she would have to study the subject. Aryel's comments hinted at a whole new level of sophistication, a strategic aspect, the existence of which Kerri had never suspected. It fascinated her. Nick had wonderful ideas, but he did not think any further ahead than the next event, and his tastes were still those of an undergraduate. She could see now that the flashy, revealing blue and gold outfits he had designed for them would not have done.

Aryel, who had left the room again, returned with an armful of billowing white undergarments. "You'll have to wear it over a pair of stays, a modest hoop and a good petticoat," she said. "I trust you have proper ones at home; we'll put you in some of mine for now."

With some trouble and lots of coaching Kerri got herself into the complicated underpinnings—the chemise, the corset, the hoops and ruffled petticoat. They were of refined, modern design; in the Age of Dreams she would have required plenty of assistance to don their counterparts. The dress, however, was beyond her. Leaving the fastenings undone, she regarded herself in the mirror. The brocade shimmered where it caught the light, like moonlight on the deepest part of the ocean. Grandmother was right. It was more than suitable.

Aryel did up the laces for her and then inspected her critically from all sides. "Yes, that will do very well. It fits you nicely. Now, let me see you walk in it. Good. The length will be perfect if you wear some heels on your shoes. The costumes are both still in quite good condition; I've seen to that. But even the best cloth won't last forever, and I should like to see my good things used before they molder away. We let entirely too many things molder away in this world."

As she unlaced the dress, she made a few suggestions to Kerri about dressing her hair and finding shoes to match the costume. "Here is the matching coat, vest and breeches for Nicholas. You may have to pad the shoulders a bit for him and take in the breeches a little," she added. "Shorten them, too. He is no bean pole but he isn't a match for your grandfather in height or breadth. In fact, better yet, have him wear a pair of good black velvets with just a modest rhinestone buckle at the knee, and he'll be fine. Lucky he's got fine legs; we're seeing a lot of knee breeches again at these balls."

Placing the paua shell brocade outfits to one side, she chose two other pairs that would be appropriate to a couple on the lowest rungs of Faculty society.

"Because," she said, "now that you've been asked to the May Revel, you may expect an invitation to the Solstice Ball.

"Then there will be the Sponsoring Ceremony. These robes will be perfect for that. Thank goodness they have everyone in a group nowadays. I remember my grandmother telling me how each Sponsored scholar used to have her or his own ceremony and the family would give a lavish party afterward. They'd be in debt from it for years, she used to say, at least the new people would. They put a stop to it before my day. There wasn't time and space for all the ceremonies, all the banquets. Sophia is talking about giving a small party for you in Yendys in the spring and another here in the summer."

"I hope she doesn't mention it to anybody before the lists come out," muttered Kerri struggling with another set of hooks and laces. She extracted herself from the second gown, a pale rose velvet, and thankfully loosened the corset.

Aryel went to the kitchen and returned with wine and glasses on a tray. She placed the tray on a teak cabinet and began to fold up the chosen garments and pack them into a small metal-covered trunk which she had emptied of papers and mementos.

"You can take these on the ship with you tomorrow," she said. "It's impossible to get a carrier up here on a weekend, so we must confine ourselves to what can be managed on foot and in the cable car. I shall send more later."

Kerri stroked the rose velvet gently. "Grandmother, I can't tell you how grateful I am. Nick will feel the same way when he sees these costumes."

"It is little enough," said Aryel. There was an unfamiliar darkness in her voice. "I wish I could really help you. I wish I could tell you what you're up against. But I cannot. My hands are tied."

"Whatever do you mean? You have helped. You have always helped me. These wonderful costumes, making the appointment with Professor Bonneville-Chatterton, all the things you have done for me all my life. I owe you more than I can ever repay."

"Kerrith, there are things you do not know." She went to the cabinet and poured the wine. "So many things you cannot be told, that you need to know! But there is nothing I can do. You must find out for yourself like everyone else, and I pray you do find out before it is too late."

"Too late for what?" Kerri protested. "I don't know what you mean by 'too late'. It is never too late to learn lessons from life. You are the one who taught me that."

"So I did." Aryel smiled sadly as she handed a glass to Kerri. "And it is true. I apologize, dear. It is unforgivable of me to say such alarming things to you. Now that you are to have a Sponsor, surely the doors will open for you that should have opened long ago." She knelt again and resumed wrapping the costumes in layers of tissue paper.

"A Sponsor!" Kerri breathed. "And in the very nick of time. I don't think I've taken it in yet. Perhaps I won't until it is official. Just in case I did offend him and he takes against me. Oh, Grandmother, what if he does?"

"He can't."

"He can. You told me it happens. I am not even going to tell Nick until the lists come out."

"I *have* alarmed you. Forgive me, Kerri. Pay no attention to my foolishness. It has been difficult to stand aside these last few years, to see you cheated out of your birthright. Now that things are beginning to go as they should for you, I am allowing my feelings to get the better of me. Come. We must put away the rest of these clothes, and you must get dressed."

Soon the room was returned to its original state except for the trunk and the pile of possessions that had been turned out of it. Aryel went to fetch a basket to put them in temporarily. Kerri rescued a few sheets of paper that had escaped across the floor. One of the papers was covered with a very fine sketch of the Conservatory in the Botanical Gardens. It was signed "Ariel Range Stewart."

"Grandmother!" Kerri exclaimed. "You drew this. It's wonderful."

"You are very kind to say so, dear." Aryel's voice was calm, but she could not keep the pride out of her smile. "I did that when I was, let me see, fifteen or perhaps sixteen."

"It's beautiful! Look, there's the old west wing. It was a wreck even then, wasn't it? Mother says they pulled it down the week I was born."

"Yes. It was a scandal. Took the Council twenty years to decide, and they didn't act until someone was injured."

"Why did you write your name with an 'i'?"

"That is how I was named when I was born. I changed it not long after that."

"How curious. Whatever for?"

Aryel flushed slightly. "Oh, it was rather a fad in those days. To demonstrate that one was grown up, I suppose."

They walked back to Sophia's house together in the late afternoon, carrying the trunk between them. A raft of thin high clouds drifted in, watering the sunlight. The air was beginning to lose its warmth. Kerri scanned the sky anxiously.

"There's weather coming in," she said.

"I shouldn't be surprised," said Aryel.

"I forgot all about getting back," Kerri complained. "Now it would be even more of a disaster to be late."

"Then we had better hope that the storm passes before your sailing time," Aryel replied dryly. "It would be a shame to gain a Sponsor just as you lose your reputation."

Chapter 11

Returning

The *Arcturus* was to sail on schedule, in spite of the storm. Down at the waterfront the old hands squinted wisely at the ragged sky. It wasn't such bad weather, they said—rough, but not enough to delay the crossing. They'd seen worse, but just the same, they were glad *they* weren't setting out tonight.

Kerri had no choice. She said good-bye to Sophia and Aryel up on the heights at the cable car stop. They were worried. Sophia even hinted she should stay over a day, although Aryel said, "Nonsense! The worst is over." They wanted to come down to the harbor and see Kerri off, but she insisted on going by herself. It was easier to be brave alone under those fierce clouds. Her hunger for her home and Nicholas and the necessity of maintaining her reputation just barely overpowered her dread of a difficult voyage.

Timo pounced on her almost as soon as she entered the terminal. "I have something to tell you," he said as she shook the water off her oilskins and umbrella. "I have found out something."

"What?" Kerri had forgotten about the offer he had made during their midnight conference. She had not taken it seriously. What could he possibly find out in two days about Val's secret trip to Honowell? Unless he had marched up to Val's parents' home, knocked on the door, and asked them, and she couldn't imagine even Timo doing that.

"Not here," he said. "We'll check you in first. I got you an upgrade to second class. No charge. Don't be silly. Of course you will take it. I would have got you in first class if I could." He wrote her baggage claim ticket himself, bypassing the line of waiting passengers (half of them trying to exchange for a later sailing date), then whistled for an apprentice to take her trunk to the ship. "Be careful with that," he told the boy. "This lady is family!"

"There," he said to Kerri. "That will give us at least half an hour. You don't have to board until quarter past three. I know why Val came to the Islands. Come."

He hefted her backpack onto one large shoulder and conducted her across the lobby and through the door that led to the part of the terminal reserved for Sea People. In spite of her hereditary right to be there, Kerri felt like an intruder. She followed him nervously down a flight of stairs and across a sort of lounge where the furniture was worn and comfortable and the intricately carved woodwork was magnificent. At least two dozen Sea People sat in small groups talking. None of them so much as glanced at Kerri.

Beyond the lounge was a large room used as a library and archive. Ranks of utilitarian shelves formed bays on all sides. In the middle of the room stood a huge waist high map cabinet. A woman bent over its vast polished surface taking measurements from a chart. She glanced up briefly, without interest. There was no one else in the room.

Timo led the way to the far end, where one bank of shelves was half filled with tall, leather bound books. He selected a volume and carried it to a window where the light was good. Opening the book to a page near the end, he held it out to her. "Look," he said.

With a doubtful glance at him, Kerri took the ledger. It was a passenger log, each page documenting one voyage of one of the great ocean sailing ships of the Sea People. She had signed her name on such lists many times. No one was certain when or why the practice had originated, but the ritual of signing on and off ship was an ancient custom of the Sea People, taken very seriously by them. Having an undocumented passenger was said to bring bad luck—terrible storms, equipment breaking down, food going bad, all sorts of things. But there were so many ancient customs and rituals in the world—quite harmless, most of them, if not obviously meaningful—that nobody ever questioned or refused, although there was nothing to stop anyone signing a false name.

Val had used his real name. She scanned the page and spotted his pair of signatures about half way down, one for boarding, one for disembarking.

Timo said, "This is the voyage from Yendys to Honowell on the *Okarito* three weeks ago Thursday last."

Kerri gazed at the signature that had once been so familiar to her, now alien and distant. It was the first time she had seen it hyphenated with James instead of Dale. She decided it had a hostile look. The writing was firmer and more mature than she remembered. Her hands trembled beneath the book.

"Well," she said offhandedly. "You've convinced me he was on the ship. That is his signature."

"Now!" He leafed forward a few pages. "Here is the log from the return trip the next day. Same ship."

She found the twin signatures. "So he sailed from Yendys to Honowell on Thursday on the *Okarito*, arrived Friday, and left again on Saturday. That doesn't tell us what he was here for."

"Look again," said Timo. "Look closely at both pages."

Kerri held the book up to the light and turned from one page to the other several times, studying the four signatures. She bent closer. "Wait a moment!" she exclaimed, "They are not the same."

"No. They're not."

"He used a delimiter on the second pair. See?" With the nail of her left little finger she pointed to a tiny flourish on one of the signatures in the second log. "It is on both of these but on neither of the first pair. This is no accident."

"No," Timo agreed soberly. "It was intentional."

"Do you know what this means?" she challenged him.

"Eh, of course I do! Didn't I grow up with you Academics, go to your schools? This particular delimiter is used when a person's recognized signature is not identical to his legal name. When this fellow left Yendys, he was signing his real name. When he returned there, he wasn't"

"He changed his name," Kerri concluded. "Here in Honowell. That Saturday morning."

"He did."

"Timo, this doesn't make any sense at all. Why would he come all the way to Honowell, risk his whole reputation, to do something like that? Why couldn't he do it in Yendys?"

"He's still registered as a legal resident of Honowell. You can't change your name anywhere except your place of legal residence. Didn't you find that out when you got married?"

"I knew, but I had forgotten because it never mattered to me. My first wedding was here. By the time we were divorced, I had changed my residence to Yendys. I assumed Val had done the same. I wonder why he didn't. He probably put it off. It would be like him. I should think it would have been a lot less trouble for him to change his residence first and then change his name. He would not have to leave Yendys at all for that."

"Maybe he was in a hurry. It takes several weeks to process a transfer of residence."

"Or longer, as I do remember." Kerri closed the book and returned it to Timo. "So why was he in such a hurry? Why didn't he wait until the vacation, or at least the Long Weekend—now—when he would not need to worry about compromising himself? Why that particular weekend? It was the worst time to go. The Chancellor died, you know, and they had the Memorial on Friday. We all had to go and sign the book, in gowns and caps, no less. If Val did not put in an appearance there, it would be noticed eventually and put on his record, unless he had a very powerful excuse, like a parent dying or something. But a name change?"

"At first I thought he was only getting around to doing it from his new marriage," Timo said. "But then I realized it couldn't be that, or else he would have had the delimiter on the first pair of signatures, the Yendys to Honowell trip."

"No, he must have already taken care of that before, changed his signature, too." A tiny hope crept into her mind: *Perhaps they have divorced. Not that I have any interest in him any more, but it would serve them both right!* For an instant she pondered which would be more satisfying: Zarah leaving Val, or he leaving her.

If Timo sensed what she was thinking, he was too tactful to show it. "I can't tell you why he did it," he said, returning the ledger to the shelf, "but I can tell you what he changed it to."

"How in the name of the Dreamer did you find that out?"

"Yesterday morning I went to the Public Library and looked it up."

"The Public Library?" Kerri could not imagine anyone going to any but a university library to look up a fact. To the people of her caste, public libraries were repositories of light reading for the Cits and Peasants, of little use to a scholar.

"Naturally," said Timo, amused. "All the civic records are kept there—births, deaths, marriages, divorces, lots of things. You can find out all kinds of things in the Library. I found out Val's new name. Eh, I wrote it down for you."

Kerri accepted the tiny scrap of paper he extracted from a pocket. "But all he did," she protested, "was change the spelling of his first name." She laughed. "If that was all he risked his career for, he's...crazy!" She almost said "crazier than I am," but that wasn't the kind of thing one could say even to such a close friend as Timo. She was not yet ready to take him that much into her confidence.

"Maybe," he replied. "But if he's crazy, then he isn't the only one. I saw two other name changes like that when I was going through the civic records, people who changed the spelling of their given names and nothing else. Real peculiar spellings, too. I guess they were supposed to be pronounced the same, but you could hardly recognize them. All kinds of doubled letters, vowel changes, extra silent letters."

"How odd!" Kerri looked at the paper again. There was no change in hyphenation.

Evidently, he was still married to Zarah—to Arzelle. Valle, she read. Valle for Val. "It looks like that's what Val's done. At least you can still recognize it, and presumably you'd still say it the same way. It doesn't make any sense."

"Making sense out of it is your job," Timo reminded her. "Then telling me. Remember our bargain?"

"I did not think you were serious," Kerri laughed uneasily. "Do you really care? It is probably nothing."

He shrugged. "I'm curious. It interests me when people act strange. I like mysteries. Besides, we are family, and the man wronged you. He hurt you. I feel I have a score to settle with him."

"Timo!" Kerri was deeply touched. "There is no score to settle. *I* left *him*. But neither do I trust him. I will tell you this: I shall do what I can, short of asking him straight out."

"Unless all else fails," demanded Timo. "Or he needs a good scare. Come. I will take you to the ship."

Yendys was black and slick with rain when Kerri dragged herself ashore the next evening. A member of the crew assured her he had seen much rougher crossings, but Kerri was certain she never had. Most of the passengers had been badly afflicted with seasickness, making the compartments places to be avoided. Profoundly thankful at first for the privacy of her second class cabin, Kerri had found it too airless and confining as the ship rocked through the hours of the night. She had given up and spent most of the night in the lounge or on deck clinging to a hand hold, until midmorning when the seas calmed and she returned to fall exhausted into her bunk, where she napped restlessly the rest of the day. She had eaten nothing. She felt ill and weary and wanted nothing on earth so much as a warm bath.

To crown the experience, Nicholas was not at the dock to meet her. True, the ship was nearly six hours late. She could hardly blame him. He must have thought the sailing had been put off on account of the weather. Nevertheless, she felt abandoned and miserable. With difficulty she got her pack and Grandmother's trunk onto the shuttle carriage to Central Station and wondered if there would be any trains running this late.

There were not. She could have caught the last outbound train on the main line, the ticket vendor informed her, but the Sunday-and-holiday schedule was in effect. There would be no more local cars out of Fernly that evening. She was stranded in Yendys for the night.

Kerri sat wearily on the trunk and counted the money in her purse. She counted it twice, but there was no way to make it come out to enough to pay for a night in an hotel. She tried to think of some friend she could descend upon without warning at that time of night, but of the few she would dare to impose on, none lived nearby. She did not want to take a long streetcar or train ride to risk finding no one home and no way back because of the late hour. The prospect of spending the night huddled over her belongings in the drafty station was chilling, but there seemed nothing else to do. She bit her lip and fought the urge to cry.

Why did we ever sublet Nick's little flat? she wondered. *If we'd still got it, I could go straight there instead of sitting here. The University streetcars run until half past one.*

Suddenly she remembered. She *had* a room in the University District: her office in Paterson Hall. There was a couch there, a warm blanket in the cupboard, even a set of clean clothing suitable for appearing on campus in the morning. She was always prepared in the event of having to work all night; it had happened often enough when she was an undergraduate.

Yes! She would go. Nobody would be there to see her and ask questions. There were a tin of biscuits and some apples in her cupboard, too, and she could pinch some tea from the Common Room stock. She could even heat water in the Common Room kitchenette and clean herself up enough to face the world in the morning. Feeling newly hopeful, she got up off the trunk and returned to the ticket window to inquire about cars to the University. Luck smiled. The next trolley would leave in a quarter of an hour.

The man in the Left-Luggage Office was just preparing to close for the night when Kerri dragged her trunk to the door.

"Sure, I'll take it in," he told her. "I oughtn't. It's after closing. We was just staying open to accommodate the passengers off the *Arcturus*. You look like you've had a bit of a time, Miss. Came off the ship?"

Kerri nodded.

"Bad voyage, I hear." He gave her a form to fill out.

She nodded again, forcing her cold fingers to move the pen across the rough paper.

"How long will you be wanting to check this here trunk for, Miss?"

"I am not sure," she said. "At least until tomorrow afternoon, maybe longer."

"Then you'll have to pay the first day's charge in advance, Miss. Anything left unclaimed more than a month is taken out for auction. Here's your receipt, Miss. Good evening to you."

"Thank you," said Kerri. "Good evening."

She tucked the receipt carefully away in her pocketbook and went out to the streetcar stop. In spite of the pack on her back she felt light and unencumbered. It was good to have a plan, a place to go. It was a relief to be off the rolling ship. She felt better. She hoped Nick would not be worrying.

On the streetcar she fell into a sort of trance, looking out the streaming windows at passing street lights. Occasionally the trolley would stop, the doors would open, someone would get on or off, but she was hardly aware of it. Then there was a stop that lasted too long. There was no forward lurch or clanging bell.

"End of the line, Miss!" the driver called out.

Kerri opened her eyes. All the other passengers were gone. She was the last one. "Where are we?" she called out.

"East gate. Car doesn't go any farther up after eleven. I turn around here." He was twisted around in his seat, regarding her, cap low over his forehead.

"Oh." Kerri dragged herself slowly to her feet. The East Gate. It was a part of the campus she did not know very well, but at least it was University. Wearily, she shrugged her pack onto her shoulders and clumped down the steps into the night. The air was cold. The rain had lightened to a meager drizzle, and there was mist gathering. The trolley was halted at one side of a brick paved circle. On the far side of the circle a flickering gaslight showed cracked sidewalk and part of a fence, tall spiked bars of steel, set in a concrete wall, knee high.

There was a person standing on the wall on the other side of the fence, holding on to the bars and peering through. It was a woman, Kerri realized, a woman wearing a long white garment. She had been standing there long enough to be completely soaked; her long dark hair and the white dress were plastered dripping to her head and body. She stared at Kerri and did not move.

With a sudden upwelling of fear, Kerri recognized the place. It was the Asylum. Like a physical blow the memory of the Star Dream returned to her, the way she had dreamed it a week ago. And something else, something she had planned to remember, intended to do.

Yes. The Sisterhood of Guenevere. No, Society! The Society of Guenevere. She had meant to look it up; she had forgotten. Just a thing in a dream. Why had it seemed so significant at the time?

She turned and ducked behind the still unmoving streetcar, to be out of sight of the woman in white. The driver, munching on a sandwich, watched her uncuriously from his dry perch inside.

"Don't you mind her," he called out helpfully to Kerri. "That's only poor Miss Beckett. She always comes out in the rain."

"Oh," Kerri replied. "Thank you." She hitched her shoulders under the weight of the pack and plunged between the pillars of the gate, onto University grounds.

She had never liked this part of the campus. The buildings were old and too close together. Some were abandoned and half ruined. Worn stone and crumbling concrete monuments crowded against their foundations, thrown into vivid relief by occasional lightning. Rain dripped from the stone and from the bare trees. It was very dark except in the limited glow of the few gaslights along the broad walk. There was not a soul in sight. Kerri quickened her steps, hoping she could remember the shortest way to the livelier part of the University that she knew best.

But it is easy to lose one's bearings at night in the rain. The gaslit avenue came to an end in an unfamiliar quadrangle where an eroded fountain trickled mournfully into a lily-choked pool. Kerri passed through the quadrangle and found herself in a kind of alley that dodged between buildings as dark as tombs, forcing her to go right, left and right again, until she had entirely lost track of what direction she was going. The familiar skyline of hills around the campus was hidden in the gloom, useless for navigation. Walkways did not go through, but jogged and turned like a maze, leaving her in dead-end courtyards. The darkness was too dense to permit her to read any identifying signs, even if she had been able to find one in the occasional lightning.

She was not really frightened. She knew she would find her way eventually—the campus was no more than two kilometers across at its widest point—but she was cold and wet and tired, and this was too much like the Star Dream to be entertaining as an adventure.

Retracing her path out of a particularly frustrating dead end, she found herself at the foot of a flight of stone steps leading up to an arched doorway of an edifice she did not recognize. As she looked up, in a sudden white flash of lightning, she saw—or thought she saw—the words "Private Library" carved over the doorway. She'd never heard of such a place on campus, so the name was no help at all, but she was amused, thinking of Timo.

The bells were ringing midnight when she came out at last on a straight, tree-lined walk that seemed wide enough to actually lead somewhere. She could see lights in the distance, campus lights and city lights. Her sense of direction did a brief spin, settled to earth and told her where she must be, which was far to the east of where she had thought she was. Still, she could find her way now. On numb and freezing feet she trotted off down the avenue.

Suddenly, some thirty meters away, she noticed a glow coming from a row of windows on the first floor of the building just ahead of her on the left. The windows were curtained, but light leaked around the edges of the cloth. At the same moment she felt an edge of Power, faint and diffused...

She stopped and backed up slowly, raising the Veil with caution. The Power was located in the room behind the curtained windows. It had no awareness of her; it was intent on concerns of its own. Nevertheless, she would have to make a detour around the place.

She turned aside onto a narrower crosswalk that passed between two buildings opposite the one where the Power was. It was very dark there, but she could see another lighted avenue a few hundred meters away.

She had gone no more than ten steps when she heard the loud complaining creak of a door opening and the sound of subdued voices. Someone was coming out of the lighted building. Thanking the Dreamer that she was deep in shadow and almost out of direct sight, she sprang forward and off the path into a thicket of lilac and casuarina and pushed inward until she felt stone. She crouched down and made herself as small as she could.

The door banged shut. Voices and footsteps grew briefly louder and then receded. They had gone up the main walk, whoever they were. Kerri waited, heart pounding, until she could not hear them any more, then crept forward, gliding under the Veil. From the cover of a feathery casuarina she peered back the way she had come. It was clear. She looked to the left.

No good. Someone was coming! At least two people, with a lantern. As quietly as she could manage, she squeezed back into the shrubbery again, listening as footsteps approached. There were two people, a woman and a man. She began to make out the words of their low-voiced conversation. The woman was speaking.

"...all the arrangements already. You simply cannot put it off any longer. You must decide."

"It is going to be next to impossible. I warned you about my situation. She will find out."

Kerri's heart thudded so loudly she was sure it must be echoing across the walk. That was Nicholas's voice!

The first voice spoke again, the woman pleading. "But you are committed now. You came into this of your own free will."

They were even with Kerri now, and she could see them but not well enough to recognize. The lantern was too low to show their faces, and the woman was closer, between Kerri and the man. Kerri could not recognize her voice.

Nick said, "I know, but I never dreamed it would be this hard. I do not want her hurt, you know."

The reply was inaudible to Kerri. They passed on down the walk and away around the corner of the building against which she crouched. The only sounds left were wind and dripping rain and Kerri's own harsh breathing. Shivering, she unbent, supporting herself against the rough stone of the half-buried monument behind her.

Again, she thought numbly. *It is going to happen again. He is going to leave me. I shall die. What shall I do?*

Suddenly she ached with longing for her home, for her own airy kitchen, her own bed, her own place. It was lost, lost.

She willed herself to gather the strength she had left. *I will take care of myself,* she decided firmly. *That is the first thing. Something to eat, a hot drink, some dry clothes. Then I'll think about it, if I can't manage to fall asleep. But first I'll take care of myself.*

She was never very sure how she made her way to Paterson Hall. She managed to catch the night watchman on his round and identify herself adequately to be admitted into the building. She emerged from a fog of shock and exhaustion in her own room, safe, locked in. She leaned against the door as a puddle of rainwater grew on the floor around her boots. *I'll be all right now,* she told herself.

After stripping off the waterproof and boots and leaving them in a heap beside the door, she tiptoed to the tall window and drew the drapes. Then she lighted the lamp. She had neither seen nor heard anyone else in the building, but if They were lurking about or if Nick was abroad somewhere with another woman, she did not want to draw attention to her presence.

The room was chilly. Kerri took the blanket from her cupboard and wrapped it around her. The skirt and jacket she had worn on Thursday had gone home with Nick, but she had an old kilt and blazer in the cupboard, and the shirt in her pack would do if she pressed it with the Ladies' Room iron and remembered not to take off the blazer. Taking the shirt and lamp with her, she set off to the Common Room to put the gas fire on. She filled a kettle and, while it heated, fetched the iron and set it to heat also.

By one o'clock the shirt was pressed, the blazer and skirt brushed and ready for morning. She had extracted dry clothes from her pack and put them all on. She was clean and warm, back in her room making a satisfying meal of instant soup, biscuits, and fruit.

Next to being comfortable at last, nothing seemed very important—Nick, the unknown woman with him, Val's name, Professor Bonneville-Chatterton, none of it. Curled up in her blanket, she just managed to reach over and turn out the lamp before her eyes closed.

Chapter 12

Miss Weberly

It was not Nick.

Kerri forced herself awake at five o'clock with her mind made up. It could not have been Nick.

She had been ill from the stormy crossing, exhausted enough to imagine anything.

The proof of this was her deluded conjuring of a whole nest of Them behind a few curtained windows in an unfamiliar part of the campus. She had—name of the Dreamer!—she had hidden in the shrubbery! As if she hadn't a perfect right to be on University grounds any time of day or night. It was almost too embarrassing to think about. She had not actually seen the man with the lantern. How could she have been so sure on the evidence of a voice?

Even if it was Nick, she thought as she washed and dressed, there would turn out to be some perfectly harmless explanation. She tried to remember the exact words she had overheard, but they escaped her. She was a University Graduate; she was trained to remember things. If she couldn't bring back those few words, it was further proof that her mind had not been functioning normally last night. It was not functioning especially well this morning on less than four hours' sleep. Later she would try some of the deep memory techniques, if she felt it was necessary. And it wasn't necessary, because it wasn't Nick.

Until she actually saw him again, she would not have to know. She could go on in the suspended numbness in which she had existed since last night. She sat down at her desk and took a piece of pale grey paper from her folder. After a moment's thought she uncapped her ink bottle, dipped her pen and wrote:

> Leaving unquiet seas
> My spirit finds no still harbor

It was not wonderful, but it was the best she could do at this hour of the morning. She folded the poem in the shape of a ship and, taking a leaf of ordinary note paper, wrote, "Nick, Back safe. Busy day. K." It promised nothing. Folding the poem inside the note, she sealed both in an envelope, which she addressed to Nick at his College. She packed her book bag with everything she would need for the day and left her office. After depositing the envelope in the campus mail drop, she left Paterson Hall by the southwest door, the one that was overlooked by no window.

She was safely away before the earliest arrivals. Not even the gardeners were abroad as she passed through the empty quadrangle and turned onto the Mall. The sun was not yet up. Under a sky the color of pearl, the river ran silver between shadowy banks. It was one of the two times of the day when the whole world looked like Twilight Country, grey-lavender and mysterious.

The little coffee bar on the ground floor of the Pavilion opened at six o'clock, but a sleepy attendant let Kerri in a quarter of an hour early. She gave her order at the counter: bacon, eggs, toast, juice, and coffee with cream. She had been brought up in the belief that a good, solid breakfast was the best foundation for a successful day, and she had never questioned this precept, but she and Nick seldom took the time to put it into practice. On weekday mornings, breakfast was a slice of bread and butter and an orange, more often than not carried down the lane in the dash to the trolley circle. But today Kerri looked upon breakfast as an extra layer of armor. Her day was going to need all the help it could get.

Being the first customer in the place, Kerri had her choice of tables. She took her favorite, the corner one by the big windows with a view of both the Mall and the River, and staked out her claim with her book bag. The corner table was seldom available; this was one good omen, at least. The bells were tolling six o'clock just as she was summoned to the counter to fetch and pay for her order. She bought a newspaper from the rack and took it back to the table with her tray.

Other customers began to come into the coffee bar. They gave their orders and walked to different tables as if they sat there every day, each one alone. Some opened newspapers. The regulars, Kerri guessed. One man with thinning hair glared at her before he stumped over to take a seat in the farthest corner. Kerri, amused, realized that he probably claimed her table as his own every morning and resented being displaced.

The next person to appear was a woman in a dark blazer and short pleated skirt. She had a round, tanned face and curly brown hair tied with a ribbon. She looked familiar, but Kerri could not place her.

The woman finished giving her order, turned around and caught Kerri's eye. Kerri felt a strong desire to duck behind her newspaper. The last thing she wanted was company. The woman smiled and approached her.

"It is Miss Dale-Townsend, is it not?" she said. "Good morning. Do you remember me?"

"Miss Weberly!" Kerri suddenly recognized her acquaintance of the riverbank. She found herself returning the smile. "Good morning. Would you like to join me?" There was no help for it. It was the only polite thing to do, and she could not exist in pure solitude all day. Besides, Miss Weberly might prefer to breakfast alone herself.

No such luck. "I would be delighted," said Miss Weberly. At least there was nothing Cit-like about her appearance today. She was impeccably Academic in speech, in dress, in manners. Sitting down across the table, she said, "Every morning I hurry down here hoping to get this table, and every time Mr. Pickens beats me to it. Or nearly every time. You have put him out of temper, you have."

Kerri cast a doubtful look at the haughty back of Mr. Pickens and drew up the Veil for good measure.

"Oh, do not regard him," Miss Weberly continued in a low voice. "He is not the least bit dangerous."

Kerri stiffened involuntarily, but Miss Weberly was grinning, not looking at her.

Kerri covered her confusion by pouring herself more coffee. "You come here every morning, then?" she asked.

"Most days so far this term. My landlady's breakfasts are a horror. Her other meals are not much better, so I convinced her to let me take the room only, without board. Fortunately, she has about half Academics in the house now, so she is getting resigned to our peculiar habits."

"May I ask where you live?" Kerri inquired, with a final cautious glance at Mr. Pickens. Housing was always a safe topic with Academics one did not know well.

"In the Old Park," Miss Weberly said, wrinkling her nose. "I could not find a place any closer."

"It gets more difficult every year," Kerri agreed.

"Do you live in the District?" Miss Weberly asked.

"My husband has a tiny flat very close to campus, but it is sublet. We needed a larger place, and in the end we moved right out of the city."

"You live in the suburbs?" Miss Weberly was plainly astonished. Her small emphasis on the first word made it mean, "*You*, of all people!"

"Worse," Kerri admitted, feeling vaguely flattered. "We live in the country. An old village about two kilometers out of Fernly. It was abandoned, oh, ten or fifteen years ago. Now there are seven couples out there, all Academic."

"Evesham? You live in Evesham?" Miss Weberly tried to whisper, but her voice rose to an excited squeak as Kerri nodded.

The counter girl signaled to Miss Weberly, and she rose from her chair, but she begged, "Do stay a little longer! I want to ask you...I shall be right back. Excuse me!"

Kerri waved a hand. She was in no hurry, had scarcely begun her own breakfast.

Without meaning to, she had begun to like Miss Weberly. It wasn't just her gratifying attitude about Evesham—Kerri did not think that was feigned—or even the woman's friendliness—too many Academics were cool, suspicious creatures.

There was more, but she hadn't had time to decide what it was before Miss Weberly was back with her tray.

"I have heard of Evesham, of course," she said. "Every time anybody brings up housing—and you know it happens all the time here at the University—it never fails that somebody mentions your group and what you have done out there. Half of them think you have all willingly buried your careers, and half of them think it is a terrific idea, and all of them wish they had thought of it first. I think it is marvelous! How did you get in on it?"

"We began it, I am afraid," Kerri said modestly.

"You were the first?"

Kerri nodded.

"How? Do you mind my asking?"

"No." Kerri smiled. The Veil was beginning to thin and open up, and she could sense no flavor of Power about Miss Weberly.

"We found it one day when we were on a picnic," she said. "We had ridden out to the end of the Fernly line, on a whim, really. There is nothing there—at least, it looks as if there is nothing there—but the trolleys still have to turn around. We had our lunch and went for a walk. There were ruins, of course, as one sees everywhere. But a little farther off, there were houses still standing. In fact, several of them were in remarkably good shape. Ours, that is, the one we live in now, still had most of its glass."

"That is hard to believe," marveled Miss Weberly. "Children would have broken it. I mean, ordinary kids playing about, not necessarily yahoos."

"You would think so. We did. But there was no sign that anybody had been there, even Road People, for years. Later we found Road glyphs on stone markers at the edge of the village, so perhaps it is kapu. Local people avoid it, but nobody seems to remember why. Also, the nearest inhabited town is Fernly, and there are hardly any children there, for all it is full of Cits. They are mostly old people."

"So you decided to stay?"

Kerri smiled. "No, indeed! Not then. We began camping out there when the hot weather came. At first it was simply a lark. Then we began fixing it up, repairing the tanks and clearing the garden and cleaning. When autumn came we put in a claim on the house. That was when the others started coming."

"Who lived in the house before?" Miss Weberly asked. "Do you know?"

Kerri shook her head. "We never found out. We tried, because we thought they might still be living, and there might be a problem about the title, but the house and land were ceded back into the public domain in 63. The registry office had no record before the public domain, and we decided not to pursue it. I do still wonder who they were. They were all alone in the end, there in the village.

They held on to the place a long time and left it tidy and locked as if they meant to come back. It was the last house to be abandoned."

"How sad! I wonder what became of them?"

"They died, I suppose, or moved into town."

"Very likely."

Miss Weberly became silent then and ate her breakfast with a troubled expression.

Kerri nibbled toast and wondered if she could turn back to her newspaper. Of all the conversations she had had about the adventure in Evesham, this was the strangest. No one else had ever shown any interest in the former occupants of the house. They only wanted to know if there were any other likely houses left, and how difficult it would be to restore them.

Suddenly Miss Weberly spoke again. "Are you planning to attend the Guest Lecture today, Miss Dale-Townsend? The speaker is Professor Harkness from Dalton, a former teacher of mine. You might find him interesting."

"No," Kerri answered cautiously, trying to remember if she had heard anything about this Professor from Dalton or what his field was. She had a well-conditioned reluctance to display ignorance. "I had not expected to go. A busy schedule, you see."

"Of course," replied Miss Weberly. "Still, I recommend him, if you find that you have the time after all."

"I shall keep it in mind," said Kerri.

"Do!" said Miss Weberly. "Oh, heavens! Look at the time. I must go and practice. My recitation is this morning."

They both left the coffee bar a few minutes later, exchanging cordial wishes that they might encounter each other again, although without specific plans to meet. Kerri made her way to the nearest notice board to study the day's University Calendar. Professor Harkness of Dalton was a Historian, it seemed. However, the guest lecture was not offered by the History College of the University of Yendys but by the Drama Department of Kerri's own College.

Kerri dimly remembered reading the announcement before, but she had forgotten it, not being a student of Drama herself. The Drama faculty had a reputation as a collection of mavericks, so it was likely that some kind of controversy attached to Professor Harkness or his subject. The title of his talk was "Aspects of Theatrical Arts in the Age of Dreams," a title which might or might not suggest the kind of wild speculation that was considered somewhat improper in conservative Yendys.

Kerri wondered why Miss Weberly had thought she might be interested. She never associated herself with the more adventurous and controversial elements of

Academic society, but if Miss Weberly was that sort of person it would explain the outrageousness of her behavior the week before. She did not think any worse of Miss Weberly for it; she hardly had the right after all her years in the penumbra of failure. In her seasons of work in the City, forced to identify with the young women and men who lacked the advantage of Faculty inheritance or compensating brilliance, she had slowly and unconsciously grown a sympathy for the irreverences and tiny rebellions of some of her caste. That was all very well, but it appalled her that a comparative stranger could sense this in her, now that she was back in her correct milieu.

Yet.... She studied the notice board again. The lecture was at two o'clock, after her afternoon seminar. She had no other engagements that day, and if she went to the lecture it would allow her to postpone the hour when she must decide whether to not to go home and face Nicholas. In the meantime, there was a morning to get through. She took herself off to find refuge in the undergraduate library. Grandmother had given her some very excellent advice on Sunday; she meant to put part of it into practice without delay.

Chapter 13

Fernly Platform

The lecture by Professor Harkness of Dalton was heavily attended and extremely controversial. Kerri spent the whole hour wishing she had not gone. She began wishing it when a laughing group of History graduate students ambled in just before the lecture began and established themselves in the front row. High in the darkest corner of the lecture hall, Kerri sank low into her seat until she made sure Nick was not with them.

She had erred in trying to hide from him here. She felt out of place among the restless undergraduates in the back of the hall. What if someone from her own department saw her sitting among her academic inferiors? And the man next to her was not even Academic, in spite of an obvious attempt to dress as if he belonged. His jacket was too worn, too small, and the wrong color. His hair was overlong and looked slightly greasy. He continually pushed his thick spectacles up his long nose with nervous fingers and fidgeted with his notebook, in which he wrote voluminously in a crabbed, unsophisticated hand.

He was not the sort of company Kerri wished to be seen keeping. Yet, if she moved she would surely draw attention to herself. That would not do, for Professor Edson of Honowell, that secret Stockholder in gardener's guise, was sitting smugly nearby, among the few University secretaries and other staff who had chosen to attend. After Grandmother's warning, Kerri was even more inclined to stay out of his way.

She had invoked the Veil even before approaching the place, so she had no idea if They were present in any numbers. The Veil could not hide from her the grim disapprobation of many faculty members in attendance. Their disapproval had the bitter edge of jealousy, for Professor Harkness had actually forced his curious apparatus to work.

Even from her distant seat Kerri could make out a fuzzy image on the glowing round screen and see that it was a fair rendering in shades of grey of the face of the professor's assistant sitting on a stool in front of the immense camera. The image moved when the assistant moved, and the image changed again when she wheeled the camera around to point at an arrangement of fruit on a table. The painfully bright electric lights and the festoons of cable linking all these strange creations together gave a nightmare quality to the demonstration. In the center section the undergraduates jittered with excitement.

As strange as Professor's Harkness' apparatus was, what he had to say was far more disturbing. His speculations about the uses of electric moving pictures in the Age of Dreams went beyond any hypothesis Kerri had ever read. He gave a portrait of an alien world, frighteningly chaotic and complex, a world where people lived without privacy or silence. The faculty shifted in their seats, their hostility thickening.

I don't like it, Kerri said to herself. *I don't like it.*

Slinking out after the lecture under cover of a chattering group of natural science undergraduates—who were fascinated by the professor's machines and oblivious to the disquieting nature of the talk they had just heard—she was horrified to hear herself hailed by name. She turned back timidly and sighed with relief at the sight of Miss Weberly.

"How do you do?" she said. "I did not see you inside."

"I did not see you either," said Miss Weberly. "I looked for you."

"I found myself able to come at the very last minute," said Kerri. "Barely managed to get a seat."

They fell into step together along the walk, moving with the crowd more or less in the direction of the Pavilion.

"What did you think of Professor Harkness's lecture?" Miss Weberly asked.

"It was intriguing," Kerri answered. "The demonstration was most impressive, I will grant, but hardly practical."

"And the rest?"

Kerri took a moment to answer. "I remain unconvinced, I must confess."

"He is the first to admit that he is speculating," Miss Weberly said. "We all know speculation is not a popular pastime in Yendys. Still, they must acknowledge that the evidence all fits. It would explain many things we have never understood. The sheer quantity of television machines for one thing. What on earth did they need so many for?"

"I could not say." Kerri wished she could think of a way to change the subject. She did not like to think of the world Professor Harkness had drawn in her mind.

"Have you got time for a cup of tea or something?" Miss Weberly asked. "I am supposed to go to the library and look up some references, but I would like to put off that evil hour for a bit longer, if I can."

Another way to keep out of Nick's road. A way to put off her own evil hour of deciding whether or not to go home. "Yes," said Kerri. "I have plenty of time."

They bought cups of tea from a vendor on the terrace and sat on a bench in the thin autumn sunshine.

"How was your recitation?" Kerri asked.

Miss Weberly made a sour face. "I shall only say I have not been asked to do it over. But I have a third again as many lines for next week."

Kerri smiled in sympathy.

"Tell me," said Miss Weberly. "Have you thought about a thesis topic at all?"

"Not really," said Kerri. "It is early yet. Why?"

"Professor Greystone does not think it is too early. He asked me yesterday if I have any ideas, and I hear he is asking all his first year graduate students. I thought I might warn you."

Kerri laughed. "Horrid man! How like him. Thank you indeed for the warning. I shall have to give it some thought tonight. What a bother! Have you a topic, then?"

Miss Weberly gazed out across the dessicated lawn. "Not really. I had to tell him something, so I rattled off the first three things I could think of—all topics friends of mine at Dalton are working on. I hope he is not in touch with anyone down there, and I especially hope he does not try to hold me to what I said. I cannot think of three things I am less interested in."

Kerri smiled. "Did he write them down?"

"I do not think so."

"Then you are probably safe."

"I hope so. It started me thinking, though. I believe I should like to do something truly different, break new ground."

"Who would not?" Kerri exclaimed. "There is not a primary text in the Canon that has not been gone over with a fine tooth comb. Most of us are lucky to think of a really valid new angle on one of the commentaries."

"I was thinking of a new text."

"What? Before the Faculty and the advanced graduates wring it dry? Good luck!"

"Oh, it could be done," remarked Miss Weberly. "It *is* done. The acquisitions department of the library is further behind than most people realize. There are hundreds—thousands!—of uncatalogued books. Some of them have to be old enough. One simply has to know how to obtain one."

"And then get it approved," said Kerri. "Which might be the last one saw of it. If it did turn out to be a good one."

"Yes." Miss Weberly stared thoughtfully at the river. "Still, I know people do manage it. There must be a way to find out how."

Sponsorship, to begin with, Kerri thought. Miss Weberly had not yet spoken of a Sponsor, which made Kerri sure she did not have one. People who had Sponsors usually contrived to mention that fact very early in conversation with anyone they did not know well.

She'll realize I haven't a Sponsor either, Kerri told herself. *We are in the same fix.*

She began to feel a comradely respect for Miss Weberly.

Then, suddenly, she remembered the Legacy. How could she have forgotten? She wasn't in the same fix; she was a secret member of the elite now. The realization gave her no satisfaction at all.

It doesn't make any difference, she said to herself angrily. *I like her!*

"I would like to find out, too," she said aloud. "Let us investigate. If I discover anything, I shall tell you."

"And if I discover anything," said Miss Weberly, "I shall tell you."

"Done!" Kerri laughed.

"I am serious," said Miss Weberly.

Kerri looked at her. "I am, too," she said, realizing she was. "I must say, I do not think there is much hope for a new text, but I am willing."

One corner of Miss Weberly's mouth twisted up. "Willing to be trusted as far as you trust me? Fair enough. May I get in touch with you in the Classics College? Or could we have lunch one day?"

"Lunch? Certainly," said Kerri, thinking hard. After tonight she might be in no state to see anyone for a while, but an engagement for lunch could be canceled, if necessary, with the simplest of explanations. She agreed that Friday would do and professed herself to be looking forward to the engagement. She took cordial leave of Miss Weberly and made her escape.

She missed the five-twelve express, having dragged her feet about leaving campus and taking the time to fetch Aryel's trunk from the Left Luggage Office. She got onto the next train and found herself at the Fernly station with half an hour to wait until the next local departed. It was deep dusk. The rush hour crowds had dwindled, and the station had an echoing, melancholy atmosphere. The air had grown chilly. No insects fluttered around the lamps.

About seven minutes before the local streetcar was due to come around, the next city train pulled in, and Nick got off. He saw Kerri at once, pacing back and forth, declaiming her lines to an uninterested Cit pushing a broom across the far end of the platform.

"Hoy!" he shouted. "What intonation! We ought always to do our recitations in railway stations."

"Excellent idea!" Kerri responded. As he drew near, she dropped her voice to an ordinary conversational level and said, "Do let us get up a petition. I would adore reciting to Professor Greystone in the big chamber of Central Station. He would be down on the platform, of course, and I would be on the balcony, right under the clock."

Nick kissed her forehead. "What a sensation for all the Cits," he said. "You could improve their minds at the same time."

"Nonsense! They would just think it was some new kind of theatrical entertainment, and not very good at that." Kerri took his arm. It felt solid through the cloth of his jacket, and warm. "Unless it was Shakespeare. They do know their Shakespeare."

"What? In ordinary dress? My dear! Do not be ridiculous." His voice changed, dropped in pitch. "Where have you been all day? I sent round four notes. I called at your office three times. If I hadn't had your message I would have been sick with worry."

"I am sorry, Nick." She was. Up close, he looked exhausted and pale. "I had an awful lot to do. I never went back to my office at all."

"I skipped lunch in case you turned up. I even wrote a reply to your poem, but you never picked it up. It will be waiting for you in the morning. I didn't know what to think. You haven't written me any poetry in months."

"Dear Nick!" She put her arms around him and kissed him. "It's Grandmother. She thinks the younger generation have become too lax in the finer things, like impromptu poetry." She laid her head on his shoulder with a vast, relieved sigh. "I think I was still at sea all day. I was not quite ready to leave the islands so soon."

"Rough trip?" he asked.

She nodded. "And not just the voyage. I'll tell you about it later."

"Poor darling," he said. "I found out the ship did get in last night. What did you do?"

"I spent the night in my office," she replied, turning so he could not see her face, making a business out of gathering her belongings. "There weren't any late trains."

"I know," he said. "I missed the last one myself. I wish I had known where you were, because we could have been together. I did come to meet you, stayed at the terminal until half past nine. By that time they were saying that the ship wouldn't arrive until morning at least, and I couldn't get another word out of anybody. They closed up the information counter. The weather was terrible. I and a lot of other people were getting very anxious."

"So you stayed on campus, too," she said casually. "It's too bad I didn't know. It never occurred to me to try your office, but it was so late I don't suppose the watchman would have let me into your building."

"I wasn't there. I had the good luck to run into Patrick and Jilly when I got back to College. They put me up at their place. I dare say they would have been glad to have you, too."

"Nicholas! You didn't tell them!"

"No, of course not! I told them you were at home and that I had been too careless of the time to catch the train. I hope they didn't notice how worried I was."

Kerri was silent. Patrick and Jilly. That would be Patrick Haines-Munro and Jillian Munro-Haines, both Sponsored graduates in Natural Science and History, respectively, and long-time friends of Nicholas. She had met them several times at gatherings of History College people, and the two couples had dined at each others' homes. She had never felt quite easy with them, any more than she had with the rest of Nick's friends. She suspected they all tolerated her for his sake and thought he could have chosen better.

Could the woman in the rain last night have been Jillian Munro-Haines? Could it have been Nick after all? Could they have merely been on the way to her flat, discussing nothing more than some horrid little college intrigue that had nothing to do with Kerri at all? It was possible. But if it were true, what had become of Patrick?

She could not bring herself to ask, "Were you and Miss Munro-Haines walking in the neighborhood of the old botany labs around midnight last night?" Suppose he said yes and wondered why he had not seen her and why she had not called out. She could not very well tell him, "I was skulking in the bushes because I thought They were after me. And I thought you were betraying me with another woman and couldn't face you all day and can hardly look you in the eye even now, because I have been more stupid than you could imagine."

"I'm sure they didn't notice," she said aloud. "Oh, it is so good to be going home!"

Chapter 14

The Rose Jar

Nicholas noticed the trunk. "What is that?" he asked.

Kerri replied offhandedly, "Oh, some things Grandmother sent over. I'll show you later. What did you do all weekend?"

"Worked in the garden. Slaved over my bibliography. Sketched costumes and drafted patterns. Bought material I only half like, but it will have to do. Came into town Saturday to tryst with a lady in the library."

"A lady, eh? What's her name?" Kerri had forgotten that Nick was supposed to begin their Revel costumes. It was a shame he had bought the fabric; perhaps it could be returned. How surprised he would be!

"Anne Boleyn. She was beheaded."

"Dreamer preserve us! Whatever for?"

"Reports differ, but it seems it was her husband who did her in. He was a king," he added as an afterthought.

"That's no excuse," Kerri said. She knew all about kings, having been brought up on classic literature, and in fact she knew quite a bit about the unlucky Miss Boleyn-Tudor and her king. "How horrible," she reflected, remembering Professor Harkness and his nightmare apparatus. "People were beastly in the Age of Dreams. I suppose they must be quite sure by now she *is* history and not literature or Dreaming, or you wouldn't be studying her."

He sighed. "We are never sure," he said. "I suppose if I wanted to be sure about things I would have studied mathematics."

"You would not," Kerri told him. "It hasn't as much prestige as history."

"Wench!" he cried, chasing her toward the trolley, which was just coming to a stop. "I'll have a little more respect from you, I will."

Laughing, they picked up the handles of the little trunk. The other waiting passengers regarded them, unamused. Only one, a young man with bushy hair and spectacles, smiled on them. He was an Academic and a neighbor, a fellow pioneer of Evesham. Presently they noticed him. "Well met, Mr. Davis-Moncrief."

"Miss Dale-Townsend. Mr. Townsend-Dale. May I assist you with your luggage?"

"How kind of you." Kerri gave up her end and followed the men up the steps. They stowed the trunk behind the driver and sat down together.

"Were you away on holiday?" Mr. Davis-Moncrief inquired. Passing street lamps flashed off his glasses.

"Just overnight," replied Nicholas.

"My grandmother sent over some things," Kerri explained. "Family mementos. Books."

"Ah." Mr. Davis-Moncrief nodded. "I will give you a hand with it when we get to our end of the line. By the way, I must thank you again for all those lovely pears from your tree. We made up fourteen jars of them and had all we could eat fresh. They were delicious."

"We were happy you could take them," Kerri replied. "There were far more than we could use."

Nick said, "It is a wonder how that tree is bearing after so much neglect."

"You two have a good touch," said Mr. Davis-Moncrief. "None of the other gardens has been half as successful as yours."

"Thank you," said Kerri, "but I must say that you and Sharon have done a wonderful job on your own. You have planted so many new things. We simply tried to tame what was already there."

"We have all learned from living out here," Nick said.

"So we have!" agreed Mr. Davis-Moncrief. "And look at all of us! Seven houses reclaimed, two more being restored, and more people coming all the time. Evesham is getting to be quite the thing. Why, just yesterday a couple were out looking at the place beyond ours, that big villa. They seemed very interested, in spite of the dilapidations."

He lowered his voice. "Just between us, they were a very distinguished pair, at least the wife. I happened to recognize her. Have you heard of Arzelle Pendrake James? That is, she used to be called that; I don't know her husband's name. She is quite a favorite of the Faculty, said to be brilliant. They say she is headed for an excellent career, one of the brightest of our generation."

Kerri nodded, encouragingly, her smile frozen on a face as brittle as glass. Nick made some vague response she didn't hear for the sudden heavy pounding of the pulse in her ears.

"However," continued Mr. Davis-Moncrief happily, "I do not expect they will take the house after all, even with that size and all the advantages. It would take more than a year to set it to rights, and they seem to think they will get a residence in the District within that much time. I should not be surprised, with her prospects. So I suppose we shall not be getting them as neighbors after all. Very disappointing. They would have added so much consequence to our little settlement."

"Pity." Kerri commented through stone jaws.

"I never did think anyone would take that house," said Nick. "I suppose we shall end up having to pull it down ourselves one of these days, before some child wanders in and gets hurt."

"It cannot be all books," said Mr. Davis-Moncrief, as he helped Nicholas maneuver Kerri's trunk off the streetcar. "We could not lift it between us."

"No, it is not *all* books," affirmed Kerri.

The countryside was very dark. Sharon Moncrief-Davis was waiting at the circle with a lantern. She was seven months pregnant, living in a little cocoon of happiness. She gave no sign of having noticed Kerri's absence over the weekend and showed no interest in the trunk, although she obligingly lighted the way to Nick and Kerri's front door. Kerri fell behind to grope inside the weathered mailbox and extract the contents. There were two letters, but it was too dark to see who they were from. She shoved the letters into her pocket and hurried to catch up with the others, to light the doorlamp and unlock the door.

Mr. Davis-Moncrief helped Nick move the trunk into a corner of the hall. Then he and his wife set off into the night, the lantern swinging between them. Kerri stepped into her house.

Someone has been here, she said to herself.

She always noticed the characteristic smell of a familiar place when she returned to it after a long absence. There was always the moment of recognition: *Oh, yes! I am here again!*

This time the smell was wrong. It was there, but a thread of strangeness coiled through it. A trace of citrus? Sandalwood?

Nick was lighting the two lamps on the hall table and the rusty lantern hanging just inside the door. "I'll check the tanks now," he said.

"Yes," said Kerri. As he walked out the door with the lantern, she took the envelopes out of her pocket. They were a letter from Nick's parents and a note from one of her City acquaintances, nothing untoward. Of course. Why write, when one had all weekend to tryst in the country (with the wife safely out of the way) and waft one's perfume all over the house? Except that she wasn't sure she smelled it anymore.

She took one of the lamps and walked through the house. Everything looked exactly as when she had last seen it, barring a few small untidinesses left by Nick. The living room needed dusting, she noticed, running a finger along the lid of the piano. The cover was off the rose jar, so Nick had been in the room, at least. Perhaps it was the scent of dried rose petals she had noticed. She put the cover back on the jar.

The bedroom looked entirely innocent: no exotic scent and the bed unmade on Nick's side only. His drawers were open various degrees, and his dressing gown sprawled on the rug where he always dropped it. The study was somewhat worse for her absence, with half a dozen new piles of books and papers clumped on the floor around Nick's desk. He had left several of the books open face down, a habit she hated. She found scraps of paper in the wastebasket and marked the places, closing each book with an annoyed snap.

Of course no one had been in the house. Only Nick, working innocently— and alone!

She went into the kitchen and made conciliatory approaches to Thomas, who was noisily angry with her. As he had been left plenty of food and water by Nicholas, Kerri did not waste much sympathy on him. She started the fire, filled the kettle, and rummaged for food, observing that Nick had done no marketing and apparently little cooking or eating while she had been gone. There was some cheese left in the cooler, but very little else, no milk or bread. Making a mental shopping list for the next day, she set out cheese, biscuits, and bottled fruit. Nick came in, and they sat down to their cold supper.

"So," he said. "Tell me. What did your mother need you to run all the way to the Islands for?"

Kerri took a bite of cheese to give herself a moment to think.

"It wouldn't really be proper of me to go into detail just yet," she began. "Mother was having a bit of a crisis. She did need me. There were things to be done, papers to be signed." *Forgive me, Mother*, she thought.

"But it wasn't a life or death matter?"

"Not exactly," she lied.

He swallowed the bait and tried to smother a grin. "I have to confess I'm not altogether surprised."

Kerri had to be just. "No, she did right to send for me. And she was right not to put it in a letter. It is technically true that the matter could have waited, but it saved a lot of time and bother for everyone for me to go now. Please don't ask me any more about it, Nick. When I get leave to tell you, I will." *On the first of June*, she thought. *Or never. In the meantime, you can have your I-told-you-so, and be welcome to it.*

"Very well." He had been right. He had known it all along. It was some piddling legal technicality that could have waited. He was satisfied. He helped himself to apricots from the jar.

Kerri got up to make the tea. "I can tell you this," she offered. "I feel a lot better about Father now. That's as important to me as it is to Mother. And I did have a marvelous visit, even if it was only for two days. I had a good chat with an old friend." She told him about Timo but did not mention the business about Val. She entertained him with descriptions of both sea voyages and light gossip about the Honowell academic community.

About his own weekend, Nick had little to say beyond what he had already told her. The time was all accounted for, with witnesses for most of it. Kerri, with a twinge of proper shame, buried her earlier suspicions at the back of her mind.

Nick had been saving some exciting news.

"I didn't want to mention it in front of the neighbors," he told her a little nervously. "I had a chat with Miss Collins-Weir on Friday. They're ready to make me a full member of the group. I can't quite believe it."

Kerri stared at him. "Name of the Dreamer! That's wonderful!" She was stunned.

To be courted by a top study group was an honor every graduate student hoped for almost as much as Sponsorship. Such bodies restricted their membership to the most elite students.

They were as much social clubs as mutual help societies, and some of them were as venerable as the University itself. Since he had passed his Orals, Nick had been approached by several study groups in the History College, and Fiona Collins-Weir was secretary of the most prestigious. Her group had invited Nick on a working retreat during the summer. Kerri had been asked as well—wives and husbands were sometimes welcomed—but she had been overwhelmed with work preparing to leave her City job and had been able to decline with few regrets.

"The thing is," Nick continued, "it means I have to go on the next study retreat. I knew there was a possibility before you went out of town, but I thought I'd wait until it was certain before I told you."

How Academic, Kerri thought wryly, thinking of her own secret. "When?" she asked.

"Weekend after next. Up north at some beach. I think there's a lodge that belongs to the College."

"But Nick, that's the week before the Revel."

"I know," he answered apologetically. "And I'm terribly worried about getting the costumes done. They're even more important now because this means I'm getting noticed."

"Indeed it does! Don't worry about the costumes. I've got..."

"And the other thing is, spouses aren't invited this time. Between that and the costumes I would almost rather not go. Miss Collins-Weir said she knew it was short notice, and they'd understand if I couldn't, but you know what that means."

Kerri did. It meant there would not be another chance.

"Of course you'll go." Things were moving much faster for Nick than she had dreamed they would, even after the Regents' invitation. His acceptance into the best study group in the History College was a triumph comparable to being asked to the Revel Ball. The costumes were important but not worth refusing such an honor. She could not understand his apparent reluctance to go—unless it was an attempt to spare her feelings. If so, she did not take it kindly.

She was determined not to feel jealous, but she was aware of a little hard knot retying itself in her heart. The Legacy had melted it away for a little while. She must keep the Legacy in mind. Professor Bonneville-Chatterton. The First of June: her day would come.

Nick said, "You shan't mind being left alone for the weekend?"

Kerri smiled. "It is my turn, isn't it? And I certainly have enough to do."

Nick grimaced apologetically. "I'll try to get most of the sewing done before then, although Dreamer knows where I'll find the time."

"Nick, *do not worry about the costumes*! We shall manage. I promise. You go on that retreat. Work hard. Be with those people. There will be plenty of time for me to get to know them later. I have loads of studying to do. Maybe I shall ask one of my old girl chums to come out for the day--or even the weekend, and we'll go on picnics and read aloud to each other." *I'll ask Miss Weberly*, she thought.

"If you're certain," said Nick. He seemed very much relieved.

"Perfectly certain. I'll stock up on all the things I like to eat and you don't. Which reminds me," Kerri said, "what did you eat while I was gone? The larder was practically empty when I left."

"Oh, this and that. I used things up. I ate in town on Friday, Saturday, and yesterday. Had tea down the lane with Matthew and Sonya one evening. I daresay I forgot to eat more than once, I was so busy."

"You? Forget to eat? That's something new! You can go to market tomorrow, then. I haven't time."

"Yes, ma'am!"

They decided to leave the dishes for the moment and carried their teacups into the living room. Kerri hauled the trunk in from the hall and placed it in the middle of the rug.

"Who stopped in while I was gone?" she asked casually as she unlocked the clasp.

"What? Nobody." Nick's surprise seemed perfectly genuine. "Why?"

"Oh, I just noticed the cover was off the rose jar. You never touch it, so I thought one of the neighbors must have come by. Sharon always opens the jar when she comes in."

"No." He looked at the jar thoughtfully. "Nobody was here when I was at home, and I locked up when I was gone. I may have opened it, but I don't remember. Could you have done it before you left?"

"I suppose so." This was true. "I don't remember either. It isn't important. I'm only glad you didn't have to make any excuses for me after all."

"Now." Kerri opened the trunk. "Now you will see why I am not worried about costumes for the Revel."

Chapter 15

The Public Library

On Wednesday the four-thirty-seven express to Rainville, Fernly, and points west was canceled. "Mechanical Difficulties" the notice said.

"Nah, you won't get a place on the five-o'clock" said the woman at the ticket window. "Nor yet the five-twenty-three. She'll be full up. Your best bet, Miss, would be to go have tea someplace and take the five-forty-seven or the six-ten."

"Thank you," said Kerri insincerely. She collected her ticket and her change and retreated through the crowd.

Returning to the University would be pointless. She could scarcely get there before it would be time to turn around and come back to the station, not to mention paying out another round trip streetcar fare. She could wait in the station and try to study, but she knew from experience that she would not accomplish much. The other reason to wait was to look for Nick. If she spotted him they could pass the time together. However, he usually finished up early on Wednesdays and went home before her.

She tried the information booth.

"Were the Rainville trains running before the four-thirty-seven was canceled?"

"Oh yes, Miss. They all went out on time."

"Do they expect the problem to be fixed soon, or will more trains be canceled?"

"It's a minor difficulty, Miss. We expect to be back on schedule within the hour."

So Nicholas had probably already gone home. There was no point in hanging about here to watch for him. The crowd in the cavernous station seemed noisier and denser than usual. It was definitely damper, for the rain that had begun gently an hour ago was now a heavy downpour. The air was close and warm and almost steamy. Abruptly, Kerri made for the main doors and went out into the arcade.

Rain was still falling in premature darkness, but the cool air was a relief. Reflections of streetlights, windows, and carriage lamps gleamed on the black pavement. Kerri looked up the broad avenue that bisected the central business district of Yendys. In spite of the weather it was thronged with people and wheeled traffic. She had thought she might find a seat in a tea shop somewhere, have a cup of something hot and try to go over her Recitation for tomorrow, but, other than the opportunity to sit down, this plan did not seem much of an improvement over waiting at the station. And at this hour, on such a day, the tea shops would be so crowded she might not be able to get a seat at all.

She turned and looked to the left down the arcade where the boulevard curved between the harbor and the higher ground to the east. Shops and buildings ended at the next cross street, and on the other side stood the high stone wall of the Common with trees rising dark behind it. Beyond the trees on a hilltop nearly a kilometer away twinkled the lights of one building. The Library. The Public Library.

Why didn't I think of it before? said Kerri to herself. *It's the very place!*

Ever since Timo's revelation of Sunday afternoon in Honowell, she had felt a mild curiosity about these places. She had not been inside a Public Library since she had left primary school. She was an Academic; the University Libraries were the place for her. There was no reason why Academics could not use Public Libraries—Academics were members of the public, also—but one always took for granted that University Libraries were better.

Apparently, however, Public Libraries were more than storehouses of common novels and simple books of facts. There was information stored there that the University did not notice, lists of facts about the lives of all the people in the city. The Archives. What else might there be?

At the time of her last conversation with Timo, Kerri had formed the vague intention of going to a Public Library sometime in the future and seeing if she could find anything— oh, not necessarily useful, which Val's odd name change might or might not be, but something curious or interesting. So many things had happened in the meantime that she had forgotten this plan, but she remembered it now. True, today she had no time to hunt for curiosities; she needed only a quiet shelter to prepare for her Recitation. But she could at least have a look around. What a good thing she had left her umbrella at home and was wearing her Sea People's waterproofs over her Academic clothes. She pulled the hood of the anorak close around her face and set out toward the Common.

It took a quarter of an hour for her to make her way across the ancient park to the worn stone steps of the Library. The doors were heavy oak and iron and glass. Inside, Kerri stood dripping on the matting and stared. She stood in a vast octagonal hall three stories high. Electric chandeliers hung from the distant ceiling, a good quarter of their lights working. Elaborate gaslights protruded from the marble walls. The floor was patterned with a geometric design of polished granite and marble in many colors. Galleries railed with carved stone ringed the room at the levels of the upper two floors. The building was obviously very old. Kerri was awed. She had not realized that the Public Library was from the Age of Dreams.

Opposite the entrance doors there was a long dark wooden counter of modern build. Behind the counter stood or sat two women. One had her head down, working at some reading or writing. The other regarded Kerri with a look of boredom. Hoping she looked as if she went into Public Libraries all the time, Kerri gave her waterproofs a final shake and stalked toward the open arch on the right, one of two that faced each other across the hall. She noticed a sign advising patrons of the Library that the closing time was eight o'clock on Wednesdays.

The arch opened onto a smaller hall that housed nothing but an ornate stone staircase, going both up and down. Here the original electric lights had been converted to gaslight, and not much of that. Opposite the arch a wide double door stood propped open with wooden wedges. Beyond the doorway Kerri glimpsed books and tables and chairs, a reassuringly library-like room—not a bad place to begin.

Kerri went through the double door and found herself in a long rectangular hall, larger than the entrance chamber but only one story tall. The two long walls were lined with bays of bookshelves floor to ceiling. Tables, chairs, and card catalogue cabinets occupied the center. In one corner an elderly man in a dusty frock coat sat writing at a towering, many-pigeonholed desk behind a low railing. He glanced up as Kerri entered and then returned to his work. Some ten or fifteen other people stood or sat in various parts of the room. They were all Cits, although soberly dressed. None of them took any notice of Kerri at all.

It was not different from the University Library, not different at all, simply older and more beautiful and less crowded. A stately, dignified place. Kerri still felt like a trespasser, but she was no longer on strange ground.

She could not resist exploring before she settled down to study. She quietly backed out of the long room into the stair hall and started up the first flight. On the second floor, directly above the first reading room, there was another exactly like it, lacking only the card catalogues, and a third on the floor above. On the upper levels the central hall was ringed by wide galleries. Kerri walked around the top one to the other side of the building. Along the back wall of the gallery, there were three dark, elaborately framed oak doors, all locked. On the north side of the central hall there were three more stacked reading rooms and another staircase the mirror image of the first. She was on her way down this when a man emerged from the reading room on the second floor.

He was a tall, lanky individual with thin, mouse-brown hair almost to his shoulders and enormous hands curled around an armload of books. He wore a frock coat like the librarian in the first room, but his collar was limp and his cravat askew. His trousers were badly rubbed at the knees, and his eyes were obscured by round tinted spectacles.

Hearing Kerri's footsteps on the stairs he started and looked up. He stared at her for a second or two, and then lowered his head and plunged down the lower flight of stairs as if he wanted to get out of sight as quickly as possible.

Kerri stopped short with surprise, for she recognized him. He was the nervous man in the ill-fitting jacket who had been sitting beside her at Professor Harkness's lecture the day before. *What an extraordinary person*, Kerri thought, following more slowly to allow him time to get away. *So he was a librarian. That would explain it.* Possibly an Academic but probably not quite: one of those people in the shady borderland between Cit and Academic, with a decent high school education but no time in University.

When she reached the main floor the man was nowhere in sight. It was past five o'clock, time to settle down and study. She was on the point of entering the sixth reading room, when another notice board caught her eye. This one stood at the head of the stairs leading down to the basement. It said "Archives."

Five minutes, thought Kerri. *I'll just find out where they are, and then I'll get to work.*

Shifting her book bag to the other shoulder, she descended. The steps, though still made of stone, were steeper, and the walls that closed them in were without ornament. At the bottom Kerri found herself in a wide corridor that ran the whole length of the building. The other staircase emerged some distance to the left. Between the two stairway openings a closed door bore a sign. "Civil Archives. Hours 9:00 a.m. to 5:00 p.m. Closed Sundays."

Well, thought Kerri, *at least I know where it is now.*

She peered up and down the corridor. At each end there was a sign announcing "Exit" above a metal door. One sign was lit up; the other was dark. Cracked glass panels along the ceiling showed that the hall had once been bright with electric light. Now, only two gaslights relieved the gloom. About two-thirds of the way to the darker end of the corridor, lamplight spilled out of an open doorway. As Kerri watched, a head emerged slowly from behind the nearer side of the door frame. It belonged to the man she had seen on the stairs, the lanky fellow with spectacles.

"We're closed now," he said. "You'll have to come back tomorrow." The head retreated into the room, and Kerri heard a series of dull thumps, as of books being shifted.

"Thank you very much," she called toward the door. "I am sorry to disturb you."

The head appeared in the doorway again. "If your ship is sailing tonight, we could open up specially. That's the agreement. But only for a quarter of an hour."

"Oh," said Kerri, feeling foolish. "That is very kind of you, but I do not...that is, I am not sailing tonight."

The spectacles withdrew again, but then, to Kerri's alarm, the librarian came out of the door. Or half out. He seemed poised to dodge back inside and close the door behind him.

"Please do not bother," Kerri said, beginning to back toward the stair. "I can come another time. It is not important."

"You talk like an Academic," said the Librarian. His long hand came up to fidget with the frayed cravat. "Are you Academic?" he demanded. "I thought you were one of the Sea People."

Kerri took another step backward. She had, she decided, had enough of the Library for one evening. She would go straight back to the station. "It *is* a Public Library," she said. "Academics are members of the public."

"So they are." His voice was apologetic. "But they never come here, you know. It's too bad. Why did you come?"

"I...the Archives," Kerri stammered.

"Well, if you don't come under the Sea People's agreement, you're too late," he said. "Archives close at five."

More of him appeared around the edge of the doorway. He removed his spectacles with thin pale fingers and polished the lenses on a clean but ragged handkerchief. His long hair shadowed his face. "You've been here before, haven't you? I've seen you, come to think of it. No, not here. I know where it was! The television demonstration yesterday."

Damn! thought Kerri. "I was there," she stammered.

"Didn't like it, most of them." He shook out the handkerchief and returned it to his pocket. "Most of them didn't even listen, but I wondered if one or two wouldn't find their way over here to read up. There is a lot more about television here than in the University libraries. Nothing at all there."

"Oh," said Kerri, feeling even more uncomfortable and quite out of her depth.

"There are a lot of interesting things in the Library," he continued conversationally.

"Things they didn't know what to do with, didn't want to deal with, those University people. Now they've forgotten and they'll end up inventing a lot of nonsense, like this man Harkness. I tried to tell them once. They weren't interested."

"I am sorry," said Kerri, edging toward the stairs again.

"They'll leave it until too late," he mused, more to himself now than to Kerri. "Things don't last forever. We try, but there's only so much we can do. The paper's so bad."

Kerri stopped her retreat. "Paper?" she asked.

"You know." He restored his glasses to the top of his long nose. "The old stuff. It crumbles."

"Yes," Kerri answered slowly. "It does." She gave up all thought of immediate escape. This deserved her attention. Of course, old paper deteriorated. Especially paper from the Age of Dreams. There was tons of it left, most good for nothing but garden mulch, and anything of importance must have been recopied long ago by the University. Still....

"Do you mean that there are old things...very old things, things from the Age of Dreams, here in this library."

"Here," he waved a hand vaguely, "and in storehouses. Not enough room here. We have to serve the public, you know. That's our primary duty. Preservation doesn't get the attention it needs. We haven't the staff, even to go through all the stuff that gets turned over."

"Do you mean that nobody even looks at it?" Kerri was horrified. It was common practice for Academics to turn over family papers and books to the University Libraries when storehouses got too full to manage. Entire estates went to the University when there was no one to inherit. Everything was examined, evaluated and catalogued—copied, if possible, in case it should prove useful in future research. Now and then something valuable was recovered—a diary from the Years of Confusion or even the Age of Dreams, or a book considered lost. Non-Academics possessed books and papers, too. Kerri had never wondered what happened to those. It made sense for them to go to the Public Libraries, but surely the same procedures must be used. Surely the important things were found and preserved.

"We do our best," said the Librarian, a little stiffly. "We catalogue it and put it away. Now and then the Senior Librarians cart things over to the campus for evaluation, and they either come back or disappear. It's my opinion they throw most of it away."

"What!" Kerri was deeply shocked. The idea of throwing away old books, especially volumes from the Age of Dreams, revolted her deeply. Even if they were without value, they would be kept somewhere until they absolutely disintegrated. Nothing was ever simply thrown away. "You must be mistaken," she said.

"Well, they never turn up in any library over there. I know, because I've looked. It's their loss. It would be my gain, if people like me were ever allowed to publish anything."

"I do believe the cataloging takes considerable time," she said. What did he mean? Cits published all kinds of things all the time. Not in the scholarly journals, true, but why would they want to?

He went on conversationally, "Someday they'll find out. They'll learn. Then we'll have them overrunning the place, each one claiming to have found it first." He shook his head disgustedly. He squinted at Kerri. "They'll have to come to *me* then! Maybe you're the first. You could be. Didn't you say you wanted to see those references on television?"

"No." Kerri took another step back toward the stairs. "I wanted the Archives, but I shall come back another day."

"Oh." He sagged disappointedly against the doorframe. "Well. Although I could show you anyway. Are you a History major or Natural Science?"

"Uh, Classics of Literature," said Kerri. "Late."

"Just as well. I don't like historians. They're the ones who didn't listen. Are you certain you wouldn't like just a quick look?" He straightened up and actually took a step away from his sheltering doorway. "You couldn't check them out of the library, of course, but..."

"I am sorry," said Kerri a little desperately. "I must be going. My train...Another time, perhaps." Her heel connected with the lowest stair, and she stepped up gratefully.

"Another day, then," he said. "I know you would find it interesting."

Kerri was halfway up the stairs. "Thank you. Good evening." she replied loudly.

She wondered if he would follow her, if there was anybody else left in the basement, whether he was mad. If he was mad, he might be violent before he became demented. She had heard of such things happening.

"Any day," he called out after her. "Before five. Except Saturdays and Sundays, of course."

But he did not follow her, and she reached the main floor safely. To her surprise it was less than ten minutes since she had descended to the basement. The time was only a quarter past five, more than an hour before her train. Suddenly she longed for the familiar bustle of Central Station, the safety of crowds. Without even a glance at the watching librarians at the front desk, Kerri scurried across the polished floor and darted out the door into the rainy twilight. Pulling her hood forward and hitching up her book bag, she set off at a run toward the warm lights of the city.

Chapter 16

The Essay

By the time Kerri boarded the five-forty-seven to Rainville, she had begun to feel foolish about her flight from the Public Library. She decided not to mention the incident to Nick. She could not bear to admit she had turned her back on something so eccentrically interesting. If it had been Nick, he would have stayed to talk to the fellow, tried to find out what he thought he was offering—not that it was likely to be anything significant.

Or was it? He had said that books were sometimes sent to the University and that the University kept some of those. (She couldn't believe they were thrown away; they were probably waiting to be catalogued, as she had suggested.) Therefore, there must be some rare gleanings of interest to scholars among the stores of the Public Library. How many more of them remained hidden away, waiting to be found? And was it possible one of those might occasionally gain Faculty sanction as an accepted canonical text?

This, of course, was the other reason not to tell Nick. For a moment she was visited by a pang of guilt. She knew he was weary of hunting for a thesis topic that had a little freshness to it. If he caught wind of even the tiniest chance of a new text, he would be on it instantly, and then the whole University would swarm in like a horde of ants, and that would be the end of any possible advantage for her. Oh, he would be sorry about that, truly sorry, and he would save her whatever crumbs he could, or try to, or tell her he had tried, but he wouldn't hold off to let her have the first go. There was no rancor in this thought; she knew she would likely do exactly the same in his place.

On the other hand, she did have a pact with Miss Weberly. This recollection cost her another struggle with her conscience. At the time she had considered the agreement to be more or less in jest and Miss Weberly's hope only slightly less naive than her apparent willingness to trust a fellow Academic she hardly knew. At the time Kerri had thought no further than the opportunities she would have in gaining a Sponsor and how she might share a few of them with her new friend. Now she had to decide if she was honor bound to let Miss Weberly in on this possible treasure trove.

The next day, Thursday, the weather had retreated to a state of damp overcast with occasional drizzle. Kerri had an essay due at ten o'clock and her weekly Recitation in the afternoon. She was well rehearsed for the latter, and the essay had been finished before her trip to the Islands. She had, as usual, carried the original home with her for safekeeping and last minute revisions and left a copy in her office. Nevertheless, she experienced a moment of cold shock that morning when she set her foot on the lowest step of the entry to Paterson Hall and realized she had forgotten the original in Evesham.

Trying not to hurry, she ascended the steps and entered the building. There were a score of students in the foyer and on the stairs. Two Fellows stood talking near the stone bust of Mr. Paterson. Kerri saw no one looking at her, but They were too clever for that. She made her way downstairs to the Ladies' Lounge on the ground floor. There were two young women there—undergraduates—primping in front of the mirror and talking about the May Revel. Kerri sat down on the battered couch in the corner and began to search through her book bag. She took out a folded canvas shopping bag, the two library books she had brought to return and a sheaf of notes. She began to leaf through the notes, frowning. The undergraduates put away their hairbrushes and left.

As soon as the door closed behind them, Kerri scooped the book and notes into the shopping bag and dropped her book bag behind the couch. She stood and shoved the handles of the shopping bag over her shoulder. Even if a diligent observer noted that it was not her regular bag, well, they would think she had simply got a new one, and about time, too! She was calmly patting her hair before the mirror as the door opened. One of the college secretaries came in and went straight on to the lavatory, nodding at Kerri as she passed.

Kerri left the Ladies' Lounge and started up the stairs.

The two flights were long and had to be taken with no more than the usual hurry. Chilled and perspiring, she came to her office and unlocked the door with shaking hands. *Please*, she begged. *Let it be there. I don't have time for this today!*

The door showed no sign of tampering, nor did the office appear to have been disturbed, but Kerri knew this meant nothing. She closed the door behind her and hung up her raincoat as if nothing were amiss. As she unpacked her substitute book bag, she let her eyes take in every detail of the room. The tall wall of bookshelves was in order, dustless, the books neatly lined up. Too neatly. She always left them very slightly out of line. And she had not dusted this week; that was a Friday job.

Already knowing, she pulled the volume of Thompson essays off the lowest shelf and flipped the pages. No loose papers fell to the floor. The essay was not there.

Trembling, she lowered herself into the desk chair. Perhaps she had hidden the copy somewhere else this time. No. She had moved it there only yesterday. It was a place she had used before, but she had been in a hurry to finish several other tasks before she went home. She had not taken the time to think of a better place.

The campus chimes sounded a quarter past nine. She started out of her chair, reaching for the books next to the Thompson. There wasn't much time, but it would pay to check everything in that section to make sure she hadn't misremembered the right one. She opened three or four, fruitlessly.

There's time, there's time, she breathed to herself. *Wait. Don't show fear. Don't panic. They can't know I haven't the original.*

Then she went cold again. *I never looked to see if it was in its place at home. I checked and recopied here! I used the office copy. And someone was in my house; it smelled wrong, remember? The original isn't there. They know. Oh, Grandmother!*

She forced herself to open the curtains, to dawdle in full view of the window, to set up one of her old texts on the stand and practice some of her lines from memory in a clear, ringing voice. She made herself stay for nearly ten minutes, then wandered out idly to fetch a cup of tea and look in her mailbox. She locked the door of her office, but no one would see anything strange in that. It was both prudent and automatic. She chatted confidently with one of her fellow graduate students—another unSponsored one, probably harmless—until with a sudden gasp she broke off.

"Oh, I am so sorry, Mr. Dickson! I must run down and pick up a book Miss Chin-Gerald promised to lend me. She is going to a lecture at ten. I want to be certain I catch her before she leaves. Will you excuse me?"

Pausing only a second for his polite reply, she set down her teacup on the nearest side table—carefully, as if she meant to come back to it—and stepped briskly toward the stairs and skipped down, not a care in the world. It was the matter of a moment to nip into the Ladies' Room, fortunately unoccupied, and recover the book bag. Miss Chin-Gerald possessed an office on the ground floor, between the Ladies' Room and the southwest entrance, well out of earshot of the stairwell. She did not answer Kerri's token knock, for she had left Paterson Hall ten minutes before. Kerri had seen her from her window.

A moment later Kerri was out of the building, walking as quickly as she dared for the cover of the Milton Building. She could cut around the other side and through the rose garden and be in the Undergraduate Library quad in two minutes, with no one seeing her from Paterson, unless they happened to look out of just the right window at just the right moment. She felt cold in her indoor jacket, but there had been no way to smuggle her coat out of the building.

"Who is doing this?" she muttered savagely to herself. "What possible purpose could it serve doing this to me? I am nothing! As far as anybody knows yet, I am nothing."

Was it possible someone else had found out about the Legacy? Did the sharks of the College already sense prey? She did not believe it. The attempts had begun weeks before Mother had found the lost papers in Honowell. The perpetrator would have to have known about it before the papers were lost, five years ago, and nothing had happened until this autumn. But until this autumn she had not been in graduate school.

"I do not believe it. It must be something else. But who...?"

Who else but Them? Had They grown bored leaving her in peace? Had They decided to have a little fun with her again? Sane reality took that familiar bend to the side, but she was much too agitated to fight it or even care. She let the imaginary sense reach out through the cool mist, and then remembered it would do no good. She had invoked the Veil the moment she realized the essay was left at home and reinvoked it at least twice since. It had not had time to wear off, and it was just as effective shutting her in as shutting Them out.

Kerri forced herself to climb the steps of the library with dignified tread. Inside the first set of glass doors she turned to glance back the way she had come. There were no less than a dozen students approaching. Any of them might be following her, although she had not detected anyone tracking her through the rose garden and the quadrangle. Never mind, They could be watching for her inside.

Through the turnstile, across the high hall, down the corridor to the left, up the stairs: she came to the east wing. The unassigned study cubicles were there, row on row, facing the staircase on the south side of the stacks. Those on the first level were all occupied, doors closed. Kerri hurried past and climbed the stairs to the second level. Three doors were open there—one piece of good luck at last!—but she continued up the next flight and paused at an open door on the third level.

The cubicle was at the end of the row; it had a window. She stood just inside with her hand on the doorhandle, gazing out onto the quadrangle, as the woman who had been half a flight of stairs behind her brushed past and went into the next unoccupied cubicle, three doors down. Kerri did not remember seeing the woman before; she looked young enough to be an undergraduate.

As the door closed, Kerri turned and peered around her shoulder. The hall was empty; there was no one on the stairs. Carefully and audibly she pulled shut the door to the first cubicle, herself on the outside. She waited. No other door cracked open. No one looked out. She tiptoed to the stairs and descended softly to the second level. Four long steps brought her to the open door in the center of the row. Inside, she bolted the door and backed against the wall to the right, listening.

In less than a minute, before she heard a step outside, she saw the shadow of a person appear on the other side of the frosted glass. The handle was tried so quietly that she felt rather than heard it, and the shadow passed on with scarcely a pause and only the softest of footsteps.

Kerri went to the plain table in the middle of the tiny room and sat down upon the single wooden chair. They were a bad table and chair, unbalanced and uncomfortable, which made the cubicle unpopular. The cubicle had been unpopular for fifty years. She opened her book bag and spread out the contents: text, commentary, notebooks, pens, brushes, ink, ruler, ribbon-tied folder of formal paper. She opened her text and commentary and for a full five minutes pretended to study diligently. It was agony. There couldn't be half an hour left.

From time to time footsteps sounded outside the door, shadows crossed the milky glass. They did not stop, and no hand touched the door. Kerri laid the marker across her text and shut her books soundlessly. On the wall to her left there was a chalkboard bordered at the bottom with a narrow and excessively dusty chalk tray. She grasped this with her left hand and pushed sideways carefully. The chalktray slid about a centimeter. It made much more noise than she hoped it would.

Kerri counted the narrow boards that made up the tongue and groove paneling of the wall under the chalktray. She put her hand on the seventh and pushed downward. The board moved under her fingers. There was a tiny click. She pushed the chalk tray again.

This time it moved about two centimeters. She pushed downward on the ninth board of the paneling, which slid down a fingerbreadth and then rocked outward. The board was the front side of a long narrow box just large enough to accommodate the object Kerri drew out of it.

It was a tube of dark wood, half as big around as Kerri's wrist and as long as her forearm, closed at the ends with wooden plugs and sealing wax. She examined it carefully. Then, using a small pen knife from among the tools on the desk, she cut the wax away from one end. Fingers shaking, she pried off the wooden cap and pulled out a tightly coiled roll of paper. She went through it quickly but carefully, smoothing each page out and weighting the edges with the books. It was all there, fair copied in her own hand, secret signs to herself intact on every page. She sat back slowly in the wobbly chair and allowed herself a long deep breath of relief.

"Make a third copy," Aryel had warned her on Sunday. "Always make a third copy. Two isn't safe; they'll know you have the extra one hidden somewhere, and they'll hunt for it. But they'll gamble on you taking your chances with that much, especially the first time or two. They haven't the time to look for any more or to watch you all the time, no matter how many of them are in it; they have work of their own to do. If it's a truly important paper, make a fourth."

This time a third had been enough.

"Never stop collecting hiding places," Aryel had said. "You can't use the same one again, at least not for a long time. I'll give you a list of all the ones I knew in my day. Chances are nobody has discovered them since your father used them." No one had.

Kerri reached again below the chalkboard and tipped the panel back flush with the wall. It took both hands to raise the wood far enough to free the chalk tray again, but once the latter had been moved back to the left the hidden compartment was held firm. There was not even a hollow sound to betray its existence when a knuckle was tapped experimentally along the boards. She completed the sequence in reverse until the room was returned to its original state and dusted chalk tray, wall, and floor for good measure.

She had done all this without moving from her chair. A person trying to peer in through the frosted window of the door would not have seen her efforts. She hoped fervently there were no peepholes, but it didn't really matter now. The hiding place had saved her this time. It would not be necessary to use it again for at least a couple of terms. She could not bear to think about what she could have done if the library had been crowded and the cubicle had been in use.

Her watch had stopped. She could not remember if she had heard chimes or not. If she had been certain about the time, she would have stayed and pretended to study a few minutes longer, for the sake of appearances. Now she had the essay in her hands, however, she wanted it where it belonged as quickly as possible, before whoever-it-was had time to think of some last ditch nastiness. She smoothed the pages carefully into a clean folder and slid the folder into a waterproof envelope. Even the bucket of water trick would not destroy it now.

There was no other attempt. She reached Paterson Hall again without incident and handed her essay to Professor Tremaine-Gustafson's secretary at seven minutes before ten, looking as unruffled as if she had done no more than linger to have a chat with Miss Chin-Gerald. Her Common Room acquaintance had given her up and gone off, but her cup of tea was still there, barely cold. People were beginning to emerge and dash off to ten o'clock lectures and Recitations. Kerri looked at them all, but she surprised no knowing smiles.

The Recitation that day was not her best. Professor Greystone had a longer list of criticisms than usual, and, as Miss Weberly had warned, he asked Kerri about her ideas for her thesis. To take her mind off the matter of the stolen essay, Kerri had spent her lunch hour making out a list of possibilities, so she was not unprepared, but, like Miss Weberly, she hoped she was not committing herself prematurely. The Professor was surprisingly and gratifyingly pleased with her choices, but she scarcely listened to his comments. A new and terrifying thought had occurred to her.

The moment she was released by Professor Greyson, Kerri fled back to her office and put on her coat. She threw the necessities into her book bag and dashed to the nearest streetcar stop. There was no time to be concerned about avoiding the Asylum today. (Indeed, she made herself watch it sidelong, as the car went past, wondering if she would see that demented woman again, standing on the wall clutching the bars. She did not.) The hour was early enough that the train to Fernly was not an express, and she suffered mightily at every stop. The local trolley ride out to Evesham was a torment. Even the trolleyman's assurance that he had carried nobody out as far as the turnaround that day did nothing to allay her anxiety. Anything that might have happened could have happened yesterday, and Wednesdays were his day off. At the end of the line she did not offer to work the levers.

She got down from the car and ran all the way up the dirt road to the house.

No strange scent greeted her entry this time, nor was there any sign of disturbance or uninvited entry. There was no living thing skulking in the house except a rather noisy budgie in the kitchen. Kerri looked in every room, every cupboard and closet, to make sure there was no one spying. Only then did she dare to look into the trunk standing, obvious and vulnerable, in the center of the living room. She knelt on the living room floor and lifted the lid with shaking hands. There they were, untouched. Aryel's costumes were safe.

Kerri lay on the floor beside the trunk, breathing hard. What a horrible day, a horrible term so far! How could one live like this, year in, year out? How did Nicholas endure it, for instance? But she could not remember Nicholas ever having to defend against so many attacks in such quick succession. One or two a term, at most, and some terms with nothing at all—that was his record, at least so far as he had told her. And his experiences all seemed to belong to the general waves of petty terrorism that swept every department from time to time, hitting everyone indiscriminately. She had not dared to make inquiries in her own department, but she felt sure she would have heard if the sabotage were widespread.

What she was going through now appeared focused, personal, and absolutely ruthless.

Tomorrow she would change the lock on her office. It was illegal to have a lock that would not open to the master key kept by the Department Chairman, but she would rather face the consequences of being caught with an illegal lock than miss handing in her work on time. Clearly someone else had a key that would open her door, or else they were picking her lock, which meant they were in the building at night. There were measures she could take about that, too, tricks of her own that might teach them a lesson. She would keep a copy of each written assignment on her person until it was handed in. She would plant decoys in various compromised hiding places. She would hide or camouflage the texts she was working on, carry them too, if possible.

"Bother!" she moaned. "It's so much *work*!"

If only there were some way she could make her office truly secure. If only she could leave things there and be confident of coming back and finding them as she had left them. If only They would just leave her alone and not bother with her, as They did when she used the Veil. The Veil seemed to make her almost invisible to Them. At least it made her *feel* invisible, which was not the same thing at all but gave her, at least, some comfort. It helped. Too bad she could not Veil her office and her home!

For the first time in years she thought about what she did when she invoked the Veil.

She could barely remember how it had started; she could not have been more than ten or eleven at the time, suffering the torments of those earliest Academic rivalries with Zarah and her gang. She remembered how she had consciously and carefully imagined covering herself with a great, floating piece of silk the color of the air and becoming invisible. And how, to her surprise, it had worked. She had been able to shut out the fear, and Zarah and the others had left her alone. In later years she had told herself that they had simply moved on to other prey, but she had never stopped using the image to hide herself from people who noticed her in that particular threatening way. For years all she had had to do was think "Veil!" and it was there.

Now she wondered if there could not be some way to draw a Veil over the *places* that belonged to her, to guard them when she could not be there. She tried to imagine her office as a sort of box nestled into the building, and in her mind she wrapped it in that air-colored silk.

Maybe I have to be there in person to start it, she thought, and so she tried to create the same image for the house. She held it in her mind, lying there on the living room floor with her eyes closed, but after a moment the idea suddenly seemed very stupid.

Wearily she sat up and gently folded the seashell brocade back into the trunk. She closed the curtains before she moved the trunk to a well-concealed hiding place. Nick had suggested they go on working on the blue and gold costumes in case they needed them for some future event—after all, the material was paid for. Very well, they would do that, as if they did plan to wear them to the Revel Ball. She would talk to Nick about it tonight.

Finally she went to the kitchen and opened one of the hidden compartments she had there. The original of the essay, the one she had handed in today to Professor Tremaine-Gustafson, was there as she had left it, quite undisturbed.

Chapter 17

Alexander

Nick was in perfect agreement about the costumes. "It *has* been worrying me," he told her. "I've been careful not to mention to anybody that we've got your grandmother's creations, but word has got round that we're invited. Everyone will expect us to prepare new outfits, and it wouldn't be the first time someone had their costumes sabotaged right before an important event.

"It always seemed unlikely," he continued, "that anyone would go to the trouble to come all the way out here and break into the house, but we'd better take every precaution if someone is making a point of attacking you. Not to mention the things that have been going on in my college—definitely some loose screws there somewhere."

Kerri was relieved. She had told him about the missing essay with some hesitation, expecting him to brush off the incident the same way he had the others, but he seemed much more disposed to take it seriously than he had before. He did not question her skeptically this time—ask why she had not done this or looked in that place. She was grateful but wondered what had caused his change of attitude.

"Do you have any idea who?" she asked worriedly.

"I have some suspicions," he said, "but nothing concrete to go on. I'm hoping they'll leave me alone when the word gets around about my joining the group. Not many people dare to try anything on with that lot."

"Nice!" said Kerri. *I certainly wouldn't*, she thought. "Are things...proceeding as they should with you and them?" she asked with some hesitation. "Are you still in favor?"

He rested his chin on one hand and gazed thoughtfully at the flame of the lamp. "Yes, I think so. In fact, I've been thinking we should begin to respond to some of the social overtures. One isn't supposed to *court* these people, of course—it isn't done. But I'm getting beyond the stage where that's a problem, and I am most anxious for them to get to know *you* better. What would you think of having some dinner parties?"

"Certainly," said Kerri courageously. "I know it's a long way to ask people to come, but we must do all the right things. When would you like to begin?"

"Not before the retreat," he replied thoughtfully. "I want to see how that goes first."

"The weekend after is the Revel," Kerri reminded him. "We could hardly get anybody out here before that. They'll all be flat out getting ready, and so shall we. Maybe about two weeks after, do you think? Let's send invitations out right after the Ball."

Nick nodded. "We could manage eight at table without too much work. We'll invite three couples this time. I think that would be a good beginning gesture without constituting an intrusion, and we could always do it again soon and ask another batch."

Kerri frowned. "Would you rather have an afternoon party or something instead, and invite the lot, so as not to leave anybody out? Of course, it would be an awful lot of work, but we would manage somehow."

"I don't think so," he said. "Too obvious. Too soon. Next spring, perhaps, we'll be far enough along."

"Besides," Kerri interjected, "the garden will be at its best then."

He grinned at her, blindingly. "Well said! That thought never crossed my mind. No, truly! It didn't. Don't laugh! I keep forgetting this place has some unusual advantages. Might as well make the most of them. Well, a spring party then and dinner for eight soon. Fiona and her husband and the Soulis-Lang pair are the most important ones, and we could ask Patrick and Jilly, too, to have somebody else at my—at our level. And because we'll owe them a dinner."

"But they're not in the group."

He smiled and looked down. "I think they're going to be. They've been asked on the retreat, too."

"They?" Kerri felt her face getting away from her. "But Patrick isn't even in your college."

He looked annoyed. "I mean Jilly's been asked. They're sort of a unit, you know, like we are."

"I thought they didn't want spouses this time." She *would* ask. She could not stop herself. "Why would they allow Patrick on this so secret retreat and not me?"

"They didn't," he replied impatiently. "It was a slip of the tongue, Kerri. Jilly's going. Patrick isn't. I think he's got a Retreat of his own somewhere that weekend."

"He's been asked to join a study group in his own college?"

"Well, yes. Why not? He's very eligible."

"It's an odd time to have so many retreats," Kerri muttered. "Right before the Revel." She felt shamed that she had let her jealousy show, and it disturbed her that Jillian would be off with Nick and the others on the Retreat. In spite of all her efforts, she still had her suspicions of the woman and the designs she might have on him. Considering that, it was probably not a bad idea trying to know her a little bit better and find out what sort of woman she was. A lot could be learned from observing her and Nick together. And watching Patrick observe them. She must simply force herself not to feel intimidated.

"Give me a date then," she told Nick, "and find out where they all live, and I'll write to them after the Revel. We'd better make it formal, I suppose. What shall we serve?"

"Oh, definitely formal!" The annoyance smoothed out of Nick's face as he began to discuss possible menus. It was really too easy to distract him from one's mistakes, if one did it in just the right way.

Upon arriving at her office the following morning, Kerri sat upon the rug behind her locked door and invoked the Veil. She made it cover the outside of the door, the window—walls, floor and ceiling—like an invisible skin, a membrane of reassurance against Them. Feeling no less the fool than she had at home the afternoon before, she told herself at least it would do no harm. She renewed the Veil from time to time during the morning, learning the shape of the room, the texture of its surfaces. This afternoon she would buy a new lock.

She enjoyed her lunch with Miss Weberly far more than she had expected. They ate in Miss Weberly's office. It was pouring rain again, and there was not a seat to be had in any of the Pavilion dining rooms. They bought sandwiches and carried them back to the College of Mathematics. It was just as well, considering what they had to talk about.

For two days Kerri had wrestled with indecision. In the end she had been forced to admit that, left to her own initiative, she might never go back and face the man in the Public Library. She would intend to, but she would put it off until she finally convinced herself there was nothing in it. She needed reinforcement, and while she had not known Miss Weberly two weeks, she was inclined to trust her. Also, there was simply no one else except Timo, and he was unavailable.

Still, she did not entirely make up her mind until she was there in Miss Weberly's office. Then, suddenly, she found herself telling the tale, leaving out only her own cowardice. Miss Weberly received the news with great excitement.

"What luck!" she exclaimed. "It is something I would never have imagined. The Public Library! Every scheme I could think of began with getting into University storage somehow...."

"Which is not all that difficult," Kerri reminded her.

"No, but the idea of having to search through mountains of rubbish for something useful is too appalling."

"I am certain Public Library storage is equally appalling."

"Very likely. But perhaps this acquaintance of yours already knows something that would narrow it down. If we could only persuade him to help us."

"I think that might be possible," said Kerri, "but whether it would do us any good, I cannot say."

"Let us go directly," Miss Weberly said, "and find out. I am in terror that someone else will think of it and spoil our chances."

"Very well," Kerri agreed. "When would you like to go?"

"Now!" Miss Weberly laughed. "But how silly of me! You must have engagements this afternoon. Any time will do."

Kerri considered. Delay, she realized, would not be wise, either for the sake of her own courage or for her trust in Miss Weberly's sense of honor. "As it happens, I have not," she said slowly. "I have only to prepare for next week, do a small bit of shopping, then meet my husband for a dinner appointment. Now would be a fine time."

The Public Library was a busy place on that rainy Friday. As she and Miss Weberly tiptoed past the ground floor reading room to the basement stairs, Kerri noticed that nearly every chair in the big room was occupied. Most of the people were Cits, and most old, their colorful raincoats dripping from the backs of their chairs. She saw the swathed heads of a few Peasant women.

"Hey!" Miss Weberly had reached the bottom of the stairs ahead of her. She stage-whispered up the echoing well to Kerri, "Which way?"

Kerri descended the stairs and took the lead. The lighting in the basement was, if anything, worse than on Wednesday. In the cross corridor the door marked "Archives" was open. Perhaps there would be time to look in there afterward, if he wasn't here. She looked to the right down the hallway, toward the ancient, darkened Exit sign. One of the glass-windowed doors was slightly open and lamplight shone out as before. "I think that is the room," she whispered.

"Well?" Miss Weberly murmured impatiently. "Go on!"

There were voices in the room. They broke off as Kerri and Miss Weberly approached: there was nothing to be done about it now. Kerri took herself in hand, marched up to the door and rapped softly upon it.

The door opened so quickly it startled her, and she found herself looking up into the equally startled face of the librarian.

"I beg your pardon," she said. "I was here on Wednesday afternoon. We spoke briefly." She paused hopefully.

"Oh!" He looked at her. He looked at Miss Weberly. He looked at Kerri again and ran his fingers through the long hair that hung down over his face. "Oh, yes. I remember you. You wanted the Archives, but they were closed."

"Yes," said Kerri. She smiled.

"Well, they are open today." He half drew back as if to shut the door, which he had never opened enough to allow them a glimpse of the other person in the room. "I say," he leaned forward again, "do you need any help? There is supposed to be someone on the desk in there, but he is stone deaf. I suppose I could...."

"Actually," Kerri interposed, "I only wished to apologize for running off so quickly the other day. You had offered to show me some information pertaining to the lecture we both attended on Tuesday, and I was most interested, but I was late for my train. However, my colleague and I do not wish to trouble you if you are busy."

"No trouble," he said doubtfully. He was looking at Miss Weberly. "Are you Academic, too?"

Miss Weberly did not answer at once. "Technically," she said in a curiously flat voice. "We are both graduate students at the University."

"Please," said Kerri, mindful of the ears of the unknown person within, "please do not let us interrupt you any further."

"Not at all, not at all," he answered, looking at Kerri again. He seemed about to say something else when a voice came from beyond the door.

"Why don't you ask them in, Alex? Maybe the Academic viewpoint is just what we need."

"Oh." He looked both wary and confused. "Yes. Yes, of course. Please." He opened the door wide and stood aside. "Do come in."

"If you are quite certain we are not disturbing...," Kerri began.

"Nonsense!" exclaimed the person in the room in a hearty voice. "Not disturbing us at all!"

Kerri and Miss Weberly could see her now. She was a Peasant woman, tall, bony, and plain. Her figure was well wrapped in skirts and shawls of colorful and exotic pattern, and she wore the traditional scarf over her hair. She might have been any age from twenty-five to forty. Kerri had a vague feeling that she had seen her before, which was possible. A great many Peasants rode the Rainville train to and from the Market.

The woman had been sitting on an extremely worn leather chair in one corner of the small office. Now she got to her feet and came forward to shake hands briskly with the two visitors.

"Greta is my name," she informed them. "And this is Alexander. Alex, I call him. They aren't our real names, and you don't have to tell us yours either, just something we can call you by. We use no surnames here and no formal language. We acknowledge no caste, and you'll be welcome to study with us if you'll agree to the same."

The librarian, who looked distinctly embarrassed, bowed formally. Kerri found herself utterly scandalized and speechless, but Miss Weberly spoke up courageously.

"It is a pleasure to meet you," she said. "You may call me Loren. And it is my real name, but no one uses it in Yendys, so you might as well."

Kerri found them all looking at her. "I...ah...please, call me Kerri. I am glad to meet you."

Alexander coughed nervously. "My...my pleasure," he stammered. "Won't you please sit down?" He pulled another chair forward, gathering the pile of books and papers on it and balancing them on his large and already overburdened desk. He turned his own chair about in front of this untidy edifice and offered it to Kerri, who sat down gingerly. Miss Weberly unselfconsciously took the other chair and turned to Greta.

"What do you mean, study with you?" she asked bluntly. "What do you study? And why don't you use your real names?"

Kerri stared at her, startled. She felt miserably ill-at-ease. It was embarrassing and somehow indecent to hear so recent an acquaintance break out suddenly into contractions and informal speech rhythms. This was the Miss Weberly of the riverbank again, even to the touch of Cit accent. The whole situation was like something out of the most peculiar literature of the late Age of Dreams.

The Peasant woman chucked. "Oh, we study everything!" she said. "Whatever takes our fancy. I'm Alex's pupil. He knows more than anybody I've ever met. We meet twice a week to discuss topics of interest. Sometimes we read books and talk about them."

"Indeed!" Miss Weberly smiled at the librarian, who blushed behind his spectacles. He had found a sort of perch on one corner of the desk.

"Well, it isn't University learning," he said uncomfortably. "I haven't memorized much—never was very good at that sort of thing. I just like to find out about things."

"Alex doesn't set much store by all that memorization," Greta declared. "Neither do I. What's the point of it, if you can simply go look it up in a book whenever you want?"

Kerri felt her mouth begin to curl at one corner. This excuse was far from uncommon among those who could not pass their University entrance exams. And of course, there was a standard answer. "The point is," she offered quietly, "you may not always be able to look it up. Books get lost or destroyed. Think of how much was lost since the Age of Dreams. We memorize so that such loss will not happen again. It is our duty to preserve what little is left of the knowledge humanity once possessed."

Miss Weberly looked troubled.

Alexander protested, "If that is true, why doesn't each person memorize a different book? You all memorize the same texts, and only parts of those. Most books never get memorized at all." He spoke with such vehemence that even he looked surprised. His face grew very pink again, and he wrapped his long arms around his chest defensively.

"Well," broke in Greta. "They always say it's for training, and that they could commit everything important to memory right quick if they had to, and that's well enough. They can have that. But it isn't what we're here for. We're here to find out what we can about anything that interests us.

"As for why we don't use our real names, that's part for the fun of it, and part to leave caste out of it. We can't learn properly if we're always worrying about being different kinds of folk. So far it's just been Alex and me, but we've both been thinking we could benefit by some other minds added to the mix. Academic will do nicely, I think. Then all we need is a Road person and a Sea person. You don't know any, do you?" She shot them a skeptical glance. "I suppose not. But Academic will do very well. What do you say, Alex?"

He shrugged uneasily. "I don't know if these ladies are at all interested in our...."

"Oh, indeed we are!" said Miss Weberly, recovering admirably. "We'd be very flattered to be allowed to join you."

"It is most kind of you," Kerri said faintly. "If you are quite sure...."

"Oh, quite," said the librarian, looking at Greta. "You are most welcome. We meet here most Tuesday and Friday afternoons."

"Sometimes Alex has an old book he's found for us to look at, or some papers or maps or something," Greta told them, smiling. "Or I bring in one of my finds. I do the swap meets and flea markets, regular. We talk and read and have tea and a bite. Alex's salon, I call it!" She grinned broadly. "Do come! Next Tuesday. Three o'clock."

"Yes," said Alexander. His face broke into that sudden sweet smile Kerri remembered from two days before. "Please do!"

"We shall," Loren assured them. "We adore old books."

Chapter 18

The Card Catalogue

There was an uncomfortable moment when Kerri and Loren emerged from the library that afternoon. Having first names and informal syntax forced upon them, so to speak, Kerri had no idea how they would go on away from Alexander and Greta. It seemed silly to go back to formality, and yet they had known each other an indecently short time to do anything else.

Loren appeared to be troubled by the issue also, for as soon as they were outside, she said, "I hope you will not feel you must abide by their rules when we are not with them, Miss Dale-Townsend. I would be honored if you and I were informal friends, and I have never been one to cherish formality in any case. However, if you would feel more comfortable continuing with surnames, I have no objection."

"It seems a little foolish to go back," Kerri said thoughtfully. "I should like to go on calling you Loren, if you are willing to call me Kerri. We shall be working together, after all."

Loren accepted with a smile, and they shook hands on it. Kerri was conscious of a sense that she had overcome her prejudices in a most courageous way. She was fairly certain now that Miss Weberly was not Academic born, and she had never been quick to form friendships with people outside her own class and caste. She felt some anxiety about what Nick, for instance, would think if he found out. On the other hand, there was something rather exciting about belonging to this bizarre little group, having secrets of her own. It was vaguely rebellious, subversive—a hidden taunt to the snobs in the History College and their kind. Not to mention a defiance of Them. As long as it was *kept* well hidden!

After all, she reassured herself, in the presence of other Academics, she and Miss Weberly—Loren—would continue to speak formally.

"Will you come next Tuesday?" Loren asked.

"If I can," said Kerri. "Will you?"

"I shall need to!" Loren chuckled. "Tuesday is my Recitation, remember? It will be a refreshing antidote. But I must think of something I would like to study with them. Greta said we must come with ideas."

"Almost like choosing a thesis topic," Kerri commented.

"It isn't that bad," Loren insisted, sliding by the contraction without apparent thought. "There must be something you've wanted to learn about that you haven't had the chance."

"The Society of Guenevere," Kerri mused, without premeditation. *Why on earth did I say that?* she wondered.

"What is the Society of Guenevere?" Loren asked.

Kerri turned to her, surprised. To make such a bald confession of ignorance, Loren must be going informal with a vengeance. "Don't you know?" she exclaimed, realizing only afterward that she had used a contraction herself.

"Never heard of it," said Loren bluntly. "It sounds like an Arthurian thing, and I know all the Arthurian stuff pretty well, at least the required syllabus, but I never heard of a Society of Guenevere."

"I ran across the term recently," Kerri dissembled. "I found I could not remember much about it either, so I thought I would review it when I had the time. Which I have not," she added apologetically. "It is probably not interesting enough for you and Alexander and Greta—just something I intend to review when I get a chance. It popped into my mind just now for some reason."

They were descending toward the gate of the Common. In a few moments they would come to the streetcar stop.

"I'm surprised I can't remember it at all," Loren said. "Are you certain it is in the undergraduate syllabus? What do you remember?"

"No, I am not certain," Kerri admitted. "And in fact I rather think it is not, because I do not really recollect anything about it except the name, although I could quote you lines about Guenevere all day."

"And Arthur, Lancelot, Merlin, and Taliesin," added Loren. "So could I. It must be a more specialized thing, don't you think? In the graduate syllabus?"

"Or some Fellow's research," suggested Kerri. "Never mind. I shall think of something else."

"Oh, no," protested Loren. "I think it will do very well to begin with. We can at least find out what it is."

"The Public Library might not be much help," Kerri reminded her. "And our whole reason for going there is to try to find a new text."

"Of course," said Loren, "but I would rather not spring that directly on those two. I am quite sure Alexander does not trust us yet. It would be best to begin with something simple, don't you think?"

Kerri agreed. "I shall just look up the Society of Guenevere between now and Tuesday, shall I? Just to make certain it is not too simple to be worth our while."

They boarded the streetcar to the University and became Miss Dale-Townsend and Miss Weberly again. When they reached the campus, Kerri invited Loren to come out to Evesham for the Saturday of the weekend Nicholas would be gone.

"I thought you might like a tour of the place," she suggested diffidently. "And we could study."

Loren said she would like very much to come.

The dinner with Jillian and Patrick was a mixed experience. Kerri had seen nothing of them since the beginning of term and had no idea where she stood in their eyes. Of course, she was already on first name terms with them. They had both known Nick much longer than she had, and it had seemed silly to go on being Miss Dale-Townsend once she was married to their old friend. Still, she had never been quite at ease in their presence. She had always felt in them the same kind of condescension her father's friends had always shown to her mother: the little wife, with no Academic standing of her own.

On this point at least, her anxiety was put to rest as soon as she and Nick arrived at their tiny apartment. Both Jillian and Patrick took pains to let her know they respected her new status as an equal, or at least as a person who might become their equal if she did well by herself. Their behavior was correct in every nuance. Indeed, she ought to have expected nothing less from a couple with their background. They also seemed more genuinely friendly than before. Almost against her will she found herself charmed.

She would have enjoyed the evening without reserve, if it had not been for the small complication of Nicholas and the woman with the lantern on Monday night. As she had intended, she watched Nicholas and Jillian together, and she watched Patrick, and she learned nothing.

That night she had the Star Dream for the second time in two weeks. She woke up Saturday with a headache that would not go away all day.

It was late Tuesday morning before she was able to do anything about her promise to look up the Society of Guenevere. She was feeling harassed and behind in her work—at least partly due, she was sure, to the extra work she must do to guard herself against sabotage—and she was more than half inclined, not only to put off looking in the card catalogue, but also to cry off altogether from the meeting at the Public Library. However, she was not about to allow Loren Weberly the advantage of attending alone, however much she liked the woman, and she had to go look up some other things anyway, so at half past eleven she took herself off to the graduate library.

The lunch hour was a good time to be there. The crowds did not return until one o'clock. Kerri and two other individuals had the whole card catalogue room to themselves. This was just as well; for some reason, she did not relish anyone looking over her shoulder while she did this particular job. She took care of her work list first and then made her way over to the G section. She found the correct drawer and expertly flipped through the cards.

There was a thinnish section on Guenevere, mostly modern commentaries and monographs on the classic Arthurian texts. No "Guenevere, Society of." Nor "Guenevere, Sisterhood of," nor "Guenevere, Company of," nor anything of Guenevere. Kerri was not surprised. She had not expected the Society of Guenevere, whatever it was, to be important enough to merit a topic heading of its own in the card catalogue. Nevertheless, she noted down a few call numbers on promising sources, the ones that suggested a concern with the lady's life outside of her role as consort to the king. If Alex, Greta, and Loren felt it was worthwhile pursuing this topic (and she doubted they would), this would give them a few places to begin.

Next, she moved over to the A's to hunt through the "Arthur" section. This one was much thicker, comprising the back two thirds of one drawer and the front quarter of the next. She went through it rather perfunctorily and found a few more possibilities to note down that had not appeared in the Guenevere section.

By this time she was missing her lunch. She had done what she had undertaken to do, namely, proved to herself that the Society of Guenevere was not an entity of major importance upon which her memory had failed her. She had gathered some references she might look up at her leisure, and she was prepared to report to the others in the afternoon. At least she would not come empty handed, and she was certain that by now Loren would have thought up something that would engage their interest. There was always the possibility of suggesting television again, although the subject did not interest her personally. In fact, since last Tuesday's lecture it actively repelled her.

But Kerri was a scholar, and she was trained to be thorough. She would not leave the card catalogue room until she had made at least the gesture of looking under the S's for "Society." It was most unlikely that there would be anything there, of course. The very most she might have expected to find would be a card saying "Society of Guenevere"—See "Guenevere, Society of," in which case she would have found the reference already. On the other hand, even the University card catalogues were not totally consistent; the left hand often did not know what the right hand had filed. One never knew what one might find in unexpected parts of the alphabet. Besides, it might be a fiction title.

Accordingly, she attacked the S's—"Socio," "Social," "Socie"—"Society." This was a part of the catalogue she had rarely had occasion to use, being mostly concerned with very dry and (to Kerri) boring material from the Eighteens, Nineteens, and Twenties, along with modern commentaries on the same: endless absorption with the least interesting aspects of life in the Age of Dreams, things that might never have existed and certainly existed no longer. An ugly, sordid world, in which too many people behaved badly.

The drawer was one of the ones that had a high proportion of handwritten and temporary cards, and a lot of blank ones. These were all signs of a major cataloguing revision in progress somewhere behind the scenes. In this case it appeared to be a revision of some duration, for many of the temporary cards were in outdated colors, with faded edges.

Kerri felt annoyed, knowing by experience that it could be difficult to track references through such a process, and things tended to get lost for years. On the other hand, from the perspective of the little group of Alex's office, there was a certain amount of promise in the disarray.

She flipped past the card at first, not paying enough attention. *The Society of Guenevere.* It was one of the handwritten ones. In fact, it was calligraphed, just as she had hallucinated the words in the study at home. That was probably why she noticed it at all, for she had been thinking more about the wilderness of the cataloguing system than the job at hand; she could easily have missed it altogether.

She went back through the cards more slowly, and then again, one at a time, and then again, searching well before and behind the proper alphabetical location, in case it was misfiled. The card was not there. She saw a frustrating number of temporaries and blanks, as many as four or five in a row between any two ordinary typed cards, but there was no card bearing the words "Society of Guenevere." There was not even anything she could remotely have mistaken for it. It simply did not exist. At the place where it should have been there was a card, typed, for a "Society of Good Samaritans," pamphlet, undated, with further notations, then two pink temporaries with the same heading minus further notations, then three blanks, then a blue temporary with "Society of Grace" typed on it but no other words or numbers, then a longish run of more blanks, some marked in pencil with what looked like portions of call numbers, then "Society of International Relations Studies, Vols. 4 - 36. See International Relations." No "Society of Guenevere."

"But I saw it!" said Kerri.

Heads came up. Eyes looked at her. She realized only then that she had spoken aloud. Embarrassed, she bowed her head over the drawer and pretended to go on searching, but she knew there was nothing to find. What did it mean to have the same hallucination twice? Miserably, she flipped through the cards, not really looking at them. And hallucinated for the third time.

The Society of Guenevere.

Again.

This time she was able to stop her hands in time to go the four cards back to the place. The card felt different from the other cards in the catalogue—creamy, rich, like fine writing paper. It was quite blank. Kerri examined the card with eyes and fingers, but there was not even so much as un-inked embossing that might have caught the light at the right angle.

She glanced around quickly to make sure no one was looking and then carefully, delicately tore the card free of the rod that held it in the drawer. She detached the cards on either side of it—both blank—and stealthily palmed all three behind the notepad in her left hand. Heart pounding—for she had never in her life thought of performing such a desecration of a library—she spent a few more excruciating minutes pretending to jot down call numbers before she slipped the notepad and the purloined cards into her book bag and made her escape.

Chapter 19

The Streets of San Francisco

It turned out she need not have gone to all the trouble. She arrived at Alexander's office that afternoon to find him and Greta already engaged in some kind of research. They were bent over several maps spread out on the desk—so far as it was possible to spread anything out over the precarious heaps of books and papers which crowded that surface. The maps were all very old. Indeed, they were in pieces, mere scraps held together in places with brittle yellowed sticky tape. Even the best one was coming apart at the folds, with a number of large chunks missing altogether. In her hands Greta held another map, a new one. Kerri recognized it as the latest edition of the street map of Yendys.

"You have got to admit it, Alex," Greta was saying excitedly. "The changes run through every map we've found so far, and this last one is over fifty years old. They lead right back."

There was something very strange about Greta's words, but Kerri had no time to figure out what it was before Alexander happened to turn and see her.

"Why, good afternoon, Miss—ah, Kerri," he said. A smile seeped slowly across his face as if coming out of hiding.

"Hallo there!" Greta called out cheerfully. "You came back, did you? Where's your friend, then?"

"Good afternoon," said Kerri. "I thought I might find her here ahead of me."

She realized what had piqued her attention about Greta's voice. The woman had greeted her in the broadest Peasant accent, but she had been speaking to Alex a moment earlier in relaxed and informal, but pure, Academic.

"Not a sign of her," said Greta. "Come look what we've found."

Kerri set her book bag down in what she hoped was an out of the way place and made her way to the desk. "Maps," she observed.

Alex quickly moved aside the bits and pieces of maps on top. Some of them looked ancient enough to be maps from the Age of Dreams, which meant they were of no use, but remaining one, the largest, was recognizable.

"The city of Yendys," Alex confirmed. "Published at least seventy, perhaps over a hundred, years ago. In my opinion," he added with a nod to Greta.

"It does not look quite right, though," said Kerri. "Look at the shape of the Bay, especially on the North side. It looks distorted, angled too much northward at the west end. Look at how the shoreline is indented. It is not really like that."

"Not any more," said Greta. "The question is, was the map wrong, or has the land changed? And is it reasonable for a coastline to alter that much in seventy years or a hundred? And if it is reasonable, what about the things that aren't coastline? But that's not really what we want to show you. Do you know the North Side at all?"

"Not really," Kerri admitted.

"I know the North Side." Loren appeared in the doorway. "I used to live there. Good afternoon!"

"Hello! Glad you could come." Alex beamed.

"When was that?" asked Greta, bypassing ceremony altogether.

"Last spring. It was just for a couple of months."

"Oh, too bad. That's of no help, then."

Loren laughed. "Sorry. What have I been missing?"

Greta sighed. "You've walked into an argument Alex and I have been carrying on almost since we met. It concerns the origin of the city of Yendys, among other things."

"The origin of the city?" Kerri was conscious of a faint feeling of alarm. "It has more or less always been here, has it not?" Another part of her mind was aware that Greta was speaking Academic again. She must have attended University then, for at least a short time. But that was not especially unusual for a well-off Peasant.

"That's impossible," said Loren. "It didn't grow by itself. It must have been built some time. Funny, I never thought about it before."

"Well," said Greta, "when? And by whom? And how? Consider the towers in the city center. Consider the Hall of Wings and the bridges. Nobody knows when they were built. Nobody knows *how* they were built. Nobody could build them now. And in fact everyone agrees they were built hundreds of years ago, when people were still building large, complicated things—when they were still building things at all, instead of merely rescuing them from falling down."

"But we do know when they were built," Kerri protested. "They have dates on them."

"In numbers from the Age of Dreams!" exclaimed Alex. "Nineteen this! Twenty that! What does it mean? How can we only be on the year 71 now? Why didn't they go on using the same numbers for the years? I have always wanted to know," he mused wistfully, "how long ago the Nineteens really were."

"I think he would like to have been alive then," Greta commented aside to Loren.

"I should hope not," Loren replied with a grin. "I certainly wouldn't."

Kerri did not at all like the direction the conversation was going. One did not talk about things like this. One did one's best not to think about them.

"Seventy-one years ago," she reminded them firmly, "the chancellors of all the Universities and representatives of all the civic governments agreed upon a common date. Everybody knows that. Now it is the same date in every city—much more convenient than the old system, when every place was in a different year, not to mention a different month."

"But why should they be different in the first place?" Alex was not ready to let go of the subject. "They must have agreed in the Age of Dreams."

"We have no proof of that," Kerri replied coldly. She could not understand why he would pursue a subject so uncomfortable, and yet as she looked at the others she began to feel she was the only one affected. Loren looked slightly embarrassed, but she was at least somewhat conventional. Greta merely seemed amused, but she put her hand on Alex's shoulder before he could speak again.

"Let's have some tea," she said diplomatically. "I'm sure the kettle must be boiling by now, Alex. I'd go get it myself, but those other librarians would have a fit if they found me in that little kitchen you have here."

"Oh." His momentum interrupted, Alex allowed himself to be diverted. He pushed his spectacles back up his long nose and became the self-conscious host. "Tea. Yes, of course. Please sit down, everyone. I won't be a moment."

"Well!" exclaimed Loren when he had gone.

"I hope you aren't offended," said Greta smoothly, looking at Kerri. "You see, Alex never had any religion in his upbringing. When he is interested in a subject he becomes so involved he loses all consciousness of the beliefs and sensibilities of others. However, I must warn you no subject is forbidden here."

"I would not exactly characterize myself as a believer," Kerri said stiffly. "I was raised in the faith informally, but I prefer to think of myself as an agnostic. I do accept at least the possibility of the Dreamer."

"As do I," said Greta. "The theory does account for all our uncertainties."

"My mother was raised an Old Christian," said Loren. "In that faith there was never any attempt to explain any of it. It was as if the discrepancies did not exist, as if it were still the Age of Dreams."

"For some people," Greta commented dryly, "it still is."

Before either of them could ask her what she meant, Alexander returned with a large, heavy kettle, which he set on the floor, for lack of a better place. "Did you tell them about the maps?" he asked Greta.

The Peasant woman shook her head. "I was just about to, but let's make our tea first." She cleared the top of a packing case by moving piles of books to the floor and dusted the case with the corner of one of her shawls.

Alex opened a narrow cupboard in the darkest corner of the office and brought forth a frayed tea cloth which he spread over the packing case. Kerri went to his assistance and received from him a fat teapot, mugs, spoons and a tin of tea. Loren arranged everything on the cloth, while Greta fished about in the shapeless cloth bag that hung from her shoulder and produced a packet of sugar and a small bottle of milk. The bottle, surprisingly, was of plastic.

"Family heirloom," Greta said, seeing the other women staring curiously at the bottle.

She smiled widely, revealing an excellent set of teeth. "Genuine Tupperware."

"It looks in amazingly good condition," Loren remarked.

"That type do last," said Greta. "It's the lids that are rare. Now come and look at the map." She beckoned them to the desk again, and invited them to inspect a place on the old ragged Yendys map with its distorted coastline. "Here, on the North Side, look at this section where the streets make a rectangular grid. But see, the grid only continues for a few blocks. Now, note the names of the streets."

Kerri and Loren noted them, wondering what the point was. The North Side of Yendys Harbor was a strange and Bohemian district, inhabited (according to popular legend) by the poor, the artistic, and the mad. One took for granted that anything over there would be peculiar. It had always been that way.

"Now, compare this fragment." She selected one of the scraps of map Alex had swept aside and placed it carefully next to the place she had pointed out.

"It matches," Loren observed. "Well, some of it does. The scrap has the grid continuing on past its edges on the big map, but a few of the street names are the same."

"But the street names are upside down on the fragment," Kerri protested.

Greta beamed. "Observant, you are! Actually, they are sideways. I believe I've got it turned north to the right."

Kerri squinted at the fragment, trying to find a direction arrow or compass rose.

Loren said, "This piece is very old. Does it mean once all the streets on the North Side were straight and laid out at right angles? Bits of them are now, of course, but only on the more flattish places. Think of getting carriages up and down the hills if the roads just ignored the terrain like this. The North Side is nothing but hills."

Alex, who was making the tea, looked from one to the other of them but said nothing.

"The fragment," said Greta, "is extremely old, but it does not belong to a map of Yendys. It is part of a map of a city called San Francisco."

"What?" Kerri and Loren exclaimed in chorus. "Have you heard of it, then?"

"Certainly," said Loren. "A city from the Age of Dreams. Very famous. Historians consider it a myth, an invention. Like Oz."

"Many people believe *this* was Oz," Kerri said stiffly. "Our own country, and quite real. There are writings..."

"Well, and so it may have been," said Greta soothingly. She continued. "You see, Alex and I met because we both collect odd things. We collectors get to know one another; we help each other out. And when we find something peculiar, and we don't know what to make of it, we bring it to Alexander. If he doesn't know what it is, he usually knows someone who does. He knows more than almost anybody. Oh, yes, you do, Alexander! No need to be shy."

Alex turned crimson and busied himself pouring out the tea. He handed the mugs around, acknowledging their thanks with mumbles and nods.

Greta went on, "One of my collections is anything to do with the city of San Francisco—books, anything. I had got some bits and pieces of maps from the Age of Dreams that were said to be maps of San Francisco. I knew enough of the street names from books to satisfy me these were the real thing.

"But I started to notice something. I was spending a lot of time on the North Side a couple of years ago, and there were places over there—well, they were like places in the San Francisco books—the illustrated ones, mind. And then there were the street names, the same ones as on my bits of maps, in the same relationship, or almost. If you turned north to east and west to north and looked at them side-on. I found one neighborhood nearly a kilometer across—almost a dead match. There are others smaller. They end, and the streets curve or jog and change names, and the rest doesn't match at all."

Kerri and Loren stared at her.

Alex watched them uncomfortably.

Loren finally said, "Are you trying to suggest that Yendys is San Francisco?"

"No," said Greta. "Nor that it used to be. All I know is that some of the North Side of Yendys is very similar to bits of San Francisco, turned sideways." She swallowed a mouthful of tea and sighed with satisfaction.

Kerri suggested, "Perhaps the legend of San Francisco is based on that part of Yendys."

"Mm, possible," acknowledged Greta. "Could be plain coincidence, too. Alex has a different theory. Tell them, Alex."

"Very well." He folded his long hands carefully around his mug and cleared his throat. "I think it was done intentionally, as a sort of reminder, a copy. I think the first people who came here duplicated parts of their home cities so they wouldn't miss them so much. And some of them, at least, must have come from San Francisco."

Kerri sipped her tea and resigned herself. They were going to go right on talking about worse and worse things, and there was nothing she could do about it, short of getting up and walking out, and that would be injudicious as well as rude. She would have to stick it out and hope the subject could be changed soon.

"The first people?" Loren looked puzzled. "Do you mean the Road People? They say they were here before anybody else."

"No," said Alex. "Or yes. Maybe. I believe all the people came here at the same time, and the Road People moved away from the cities later, perhaps before anyone else."

"Then," said Loren, "you think San Francisco was one of the other cities—Urlosa, perhaps, or Crystal? Or maybe on the other side of the ocean? Only the Sea People know what's there, if *they* do. Where was the original San Francisco? If there was such a place."

Alex pointed upward. "On another planet," he said solemnly.

Chapter 20

On the Meaning of Existence

Another planet?" Kerri repeated, dumbfounded. "Alex, what on earth do you mean?"

"I mean," he explained patiently, "that this world is not the original home of humankind. We came from another world, probably orbiting another sun. What we call the Age of Dreams is our recollection of our home world."

Greta looked from Loren to Kerri and back again, a bright smile on her face as if to say, "See? Isn't he clever?" Loren looked quite stunned, but Kerri felt relieved, back on slightly more solid ground. She had begun to like Alex—indeed, she did like him; he was a gentle harmless creature in spite of his alarming enthusiasm for things from the Age of Dreams— but it seemed he was just another crackpot after all. Such people were not uncommon among those Cits who had not quite enough education. Many of them were brilliant in their way, but they were not to be taken seriously. And this was not the first time she had heard this particular theory.

"What makes you so certain of that?" she asked.

"Well, first, nothing matches, except in pieces, like Greta said. I mean, old maps and globes—the few we have—don't show the right shapes or names or anything. None of the land we know now seems to correspond to any part of the Earth of the Age of Dreams."

"There are other possible explanations for that," Loren pointed out.

Alex paid her no heed. "The calendar," he went on. "Why was it such a mess before the new dating started? Why do all the books from the Age of Dreams have the Summer Solstice in June instead of December?"

Loren protested, "They don't *all....*"

"And we don't seem to be running out of the things they were running out of," he continued. "And we can't find the rubbish they were supposed to be having such a difficult time getting rid of, and most of all, what about the sun?"

"What about it?" Loren asked with a sigh. She, too, had heard it all before.

"All the old books from the Age of Dreams—every single one of them we've ever found— have the sun rising in the east and setting in the west, exactly the opposite of the way it does now." He settled back on his perch (a stack of books) and looked around at them all with a satisfied expression. "Now, tell me, what other explanation accounts for all of these problems?"

"Alex, Alex," Loren began, half laughing in spite of herself. Kerri wondered if she was going to inform the man he was not the first to think of this marvelous theory. She hoped he would not be too hurt.

"Alex," said Loren. "It is a breathtaking idea, but there is one tiny problem. How did we get here?"

He blinked at her. "Star ships, of course. Look."

He got to his feet and, setting down his tea mug, began to root about in one of the overburdened shelves of the bookcase. "There are thousands of mentions of them." He pulled out two handfuls of ancient books and placed them on the already crowded floor at their feet. Although he handled them gently, clouds of dust rose from the crumbling volumes.

"Those are books from the Age of Dreams!" Kerri gasped accusingly.

Greta coughed sympathetically.

"Some of them may be," said Alex. "Most of them are early copies. They copied the original dates, too, you know, so it isn't always easy to tell the difference."

Loren picked one of the books up very carefully and looked at the spine. "*Planet Diabolical* by Anthea Franklin," she read.

Kerri leaned over to peer at the faded titles, forbearing to touch the books. These were all novels of a type that had been popular late in the numbered years. They were of that subclass of fabulous tale which assumed vessels capable of travel between the stars. A few such books had, over the years, been admitted to the Canon of Academe to be copied reverently, studied and have select passages assigned for memorization. The rest, however, were relegated to the warehouses, some to be copied for the public libraries, most to molder away forgotten.

About once a generation the undergraduates would develop a fad for them— Kerri remembered one from her prep school days—and even write a few, but the cult would die down after a few years. These days, except for accepted classics such as the works of Norton and Bradbury, it was not the done thing for an Academic to admit to liking, or even reading, such literature. However, the Cits perennially loved the things.

Clearly Alexander was an enthusiast. The books, it appeared, were from his personal collection, bought over the years from private storehouse breakdowns and fellow collectors. He handled the books like precious treasures and spoke reverently of authors Kerri had never heard of, although some of the names were apparently not unfamiliar to Loren.

"I cannot believe this!" she exclaimed. "You have a copy of *Flow My Tears The Policeman Said* by Philip K. Dick. Nobody I know has ever even seen a copy. We only know it exists from old lists; it was supposed lost." She added, "If I ran the world, *he* would be in the Canon, and *this*... Is it readable? Could you get it copied?"

Suddenly alarmed, Alex said, "Please, no! It isn't! That is, I couldn't...."

"Alex would consider it a favor," said Greta dryly, "if you did not mention his *personal* books to anyone."

Loren met Kerri's eyes for a meaningful second and then turned to Greta. "Oh, of course not," she said sincerely. "We won't tell anyone. But these really ought to be copied while there is still time. If it isn't already too late."

"There, Alex," said Greta. "I've been telling you. The lady scholar is right. What good are your precious books if they turn to little piles of crumbs?"

"What good are they if I never see them again?" He gathered the books gently and returned them to their shelf. "I wouldn't, you know."

"If they are your property," said Kerri, "they would be returned to you, naturally."

"Maybe," said Greta. "But we were considering Alex's theory about star ships."

"Yes." Reassured, he sat down again. "It's my opinion we must have come here in star ships. The real mystery is why there has been no contact with the home planet for such a long time."

"Alex," Loren said gently. "There never were any real star ships. They were just a literary device."

"Like heroes who could fly," suggested Kerri, "and atomic bombs."

"Like magic," Loren added, "and chocolate."

Greta laughed.

"They were imaginary," Loren continued. "A myth."

"Legends," said Kerri. "Inventions. Pure entertainment."

Alex's face became very pink. "I have seen photographs," he insisted stubbornly.

"We have all seen the photographs," Kerri said with some sympathy. "We know how they made those photographs. They called them Special Effects. But they were a fiction. There are no verifiable photographs of these vessels actually flying in far space. And, Alex, the so-called space ships, the ones that have the most claim to historical authenticity, were all quite small—room for only a few people and little cargo. We have such masses of stuff. Our largest buildings are supposed to have been built in the Age of Dreams and show no evidence of having been moved. University mathematicians have calculated how big the ships would have to have been to move everything, and it is simply impossible."

"I don't believe that," said Alex. "They had resources we can't even imagine."

Greta had been very quiet during this argument, pouring out tea as required. Now she spoke: "They did. It is true. Perhaps they did move buildings between worlds, by giant star ships or by other means. Perhaps they built copies as soon as they got here. They copied many things. Or perhaps there was no traveling at all. There is one fair truth in what Alexander has said, and it's something we all know, whether we like saying it aloud or not. This is not the same world as the world of the Age of Dreams. And that," she said, "is fact."

There was a most uncomfortable silence. Kerri stared unhappily at the floor, half expecting it to dissolve away before her eyes. She clung to the mug, solid and warm and real between her hands.

At last Loren spoke. "Something happened, Greta. Everyone accepts that. It's just that there is no record of what it was."

"That we know about," Alex muttered darkly.

"What do *you* think?" Greta asked Loren. Her eyes gleamed with excitement.

Greta was enjoying this, Kerri realized. She was actually relishing this perilous controversy. Were there many Peasant woman like her? Kerri wondered. One thought of Peasants as hardworking, cheerful souls who didn't pay attention to much beyond their lands, homes and families, their handcrafts, and the gossip of the marketplace. But this one had been to University and had time and leisure to sit talking in the library of an afternoon.

"When I was younger," said Loren, "I believed in the war theory. In the Age of Dreams, you know, they were always worried that a great war would destroy the world. They wrote about their fear of it in various ways. By all accounts, they had built terrible weapons. "

"Or knew how to build them," Kerri interrupted. "There is no proof they ever truly did."

"And it is certain there were once a great many more people than there are now," Loren went on. "Not to mention a lot more towers in cities, and that sort of thing. There seem to have been a lot of things in the Age of Dreams that are gone now. They could have been destroyed in a war, and a lot of people killed.

"And then there are the New Christians, who think that there was not only a war but a day of final judgement which had been predicted for centuries. They think the old world simply came to an end on that day, and this one somehow replaced it. All of us who are here are therefore descended from the people chosen to be in the new world."

"For all we seem to have it better than a lot of them in the old world," remarked Greta, "they do have a point. But you don't believe that either, do you?"

"No." Loren sighed. "I think I have come round to the plague hypothesis. Some disease that spread slowly, killed slowly, gave them time to learn how to manage with the people they had left. There are records of such a plague late in the numbered years."

"Which one?" Greta asked. "Which plague?"

"Was there more than one?" Loren looked confused.

Greta said, "There are suggestions that this late plague was in fact supposed to be a cure for an even earlier plague which had afflicted humanity for millennia. The intended cure went wrong somehow."

"I've heard of that," Alex said. "The original plague was supposed to have infected only males, impairing the moral functioning of their brains and causing much misery and death, although most of the fatalities were indirect."

"Oh," said Loren. "I hadn't heard of that one. Interesting! Whatever it was," she continued, "I think there must have been something that affected their ability to have children. We know they had more than we do. More, really, than they wanted. They worried about how large their population was growing, while we worried, up until two generations ago, that humanity was dying out. Until our grandparents' day, hardly anyone had more than one child. Now two is quite common." She spoke earnestly, but a blush had risen upon her face.

Greta, who apparently possessed less delicacy, laughed again. "You speak for Academics, Loren. And maybe for Stockholders. Dreamer knows *they're* lucky to have even one! The rest of us have been raising more than one child for more than two generations. City People have two more often than one. Two or three is usual in the country. You see four from time to time. Mind, we still don't have as many as they did in the Age of Dreams, and we can be thankful for that. Maybe this plague of yours has never gone quite away. Maybe that's why we have our little two to six year window of fertility, while they could build families over twenty years or more. And starve most of 'em to death or kill them in wars and such, by all accounts. On the other hand, a plague won't explain the geographic differences. I think you need to add in a touch of Great Earthquake Theory for that, or Catastrophic Climate Change. Or maybe Comet Collision. Some call it the Giant Asteroid Theory. That one's very current out in the country now and up Urlosa way."

Loren smiled and shook her head. She was willing to say no more. Kerri was astounded at how much she *had* said. Not only to think about these things, but to talk about them...! And with people who were little more than strangers. Loren must be very brave or very foolhardy. Or if she was originally a Cit, as Kerri suspected, perhaps she had less sensitivity to these things.

"And you, Kerri," said Greta. "You haven't yet told us your belief about this world. You have the faith in the Dreamer, I suppose. That our world and all of us are only the dream of Someone in that place we call the Age of Dreams, and when She awakes—pfft! we're gone!"

With extreme reluctance Kerri answered, "I do not know. As I said before, I do not consider myself a true believer, but I do hold it all to be possible. And that is because...." She paused for a moment, trying to think how best to put a lifetime of secret doubts into words without giving away too much. "My reason is that I cannot believe the other things. You all speak of some enormous catastrophe, some immense event that happened in the past. It would have to be a big one, or a lot of big ones, to change everything so much."

"Yes." Alex nodded, looking troubled. Could he finally have become aware of how much distress this discussion was causing her?

"It troubles me," Kerri continued bravely, "that we have no idea what the event was? How could such a thing be forgotten? If it was as big a catastrophe as that, or a journey so...so momentous, someone somewhere would have written it down. The survivors would have told their children, and they would have told their children and *something* would have come down to us."

"Don't be so sure," Loren advised in her Cit accent. "There's plenty of things me mum didn't tell me!"

Kerri said, "It could not have happened long enough ago for there to be no trace at all. We have too many artifacts. Surely the tales would survive at least as long as the old books and other fragile things. I cannot accept that the whole human race could develop amnesia like that."

"Ah," returned Greta, gazing thoughtfully into space. "I can accept it. In fact, I believe that is exactly what we did. That is why our learned people set such a store by memory, so we shall not forget again."

"You," said Loren accusingly to the Peasant. "You have coaxed our secrets out of us, but you haven't told us yours. What do *you* believe?"

"What, me?" She grinned at them all. "My ideas are a whole lot more frivolous and silly than anything any of you've said today."

"Come," Loren demanded. "Out with them!"

"Oh, very well. I incline to the faith of the Dreamer, myself, but like our friend Kerri I have my doubts. Mind, I don't go about in fear my doubts will wake the old lady up. She's got far too much to do without paying attention to stray thoughts of the likes of me."

Kerri felt an odd mixture of offense and relief. It was true; the world had not ceased to exist this afternoon merely for the thinking of it. The rather vague religion of her childhood did not make specific prohibitions against asking such questions; it did not make specific prohibitions against anything, as if to name the sin was to invite committing it. Still, there were unspoken understandings. For example, material reality was understood to be fragile, and it seemed overly risky, if not actually blasphemous, to take chances.

It was like thinking of becoming demented. If one did not think about it, it would not happen. Or only to other people. In fact, from the point of view of the individual involved, dementia amounted to approximately the same thing as the end of the world. The thought crossed her mind that it might be the Dreamer's punishment of blasphemers, but she had to dismiss the idea. There were far too many going unpunished, and Mr. Crockett, who had lost his mind a few years ago, was the most devoutly religious man she had ever met.

"It's not what you'd call conventional, though, my idea of the world," Greta went on. "I suppose I get some of it from the Road People. We see a bit more of them in the country."

Loren suddenly became still and watchful.

Greta said. "What I think is that the world is a living being and that She has changed Herself, dreamed the changes, if you will. We are all in Her dreaming because Her dreams are made of flesh and bone, sap and leaf, of air and earth and water, of language and music. Everything is Her Dreaming. But when Her little dream creatures turned Her dream into too much of a nightmare, then what did She do, eh? She woke up, of course. She plumped Her pillow, turned over and settled back down to dream a new dream. But because She didn't wake up all the way, the new dream had a lot of the old dream left in it, all put back together in different ways from before, with the nightmare bits left out."

The other three stared at her. Alex looked stubborn again; Loren seemed perplexed. "I suppose," said Kerri with some irony, "She dreamed our collective amnesia, too."

"Why not? Maybe they didn't even notice there was anything different right at first. Maybe it didn't happen all at once. In fact, there is something I would like to show you." She got to her feet, rearranging her draperies, and unfolded her map of Yendys, the new one. "Come. Compare the new map with the old one, here on the North Side where you looked before."

Obediently, Kerri and Loren stood up and picked their way over to the desk.

Alexander scrambled out of the way and began to gather up the tea things. Kerri stared at the maps, but she felt so chilled and shaken she did not even try to figure out what Greta might be getting at.

"It's changed quite a bit, hasn't it?" Loren commented. "The streets are a lot less straight now. That grid section is smaller, as if they've cut corners and bent to the curves. And see? They've changed some of the names to match the adjoining streets." She giggled. "Greta, I'm afraid the Department of Road Works has been doing away with your San Francisco."

Greta did not smile. She did not look at the others; she only gazed at the maps. "I have an acquaintance in the Department of Road Works," she said. "He allowed me to study their records as far back as they have them. Other than the usual repairs, there has never been any major rebuilding or moving of streets in that section."

She raised her grey eyes and looked at them each in turn. "It isn't finished," she said. "She is still dreaming the changes."

Chapter 21

Reflections

The sun was low. The light was orange-gold, the shadows long and purple. The air had grown very cold, but the icy wind felt good on Kerri's heated cheeks. She took careful note of the colors and sounds, the smells of the city, the solidity of the stone under her feet, willing them to be Real.

"Are you all right?" Loren asked. "You looked awfully pale in there."

"Yes. I am fine."

"May I walk to the station with you?"

"Of course."

They descended the steps of the Public Library and took the path down the hill to the gate of the Common.

"That was a rather harrowing experience," Loren ventured.

"Yes, it was."

"Not what I expected."

"Nor I."

"Shall you go back?"

She looked at Loren and managed a smile. "Certainly. You saw Alexander's books."

"I did. Oh, the fool! I wonder if he knows what he has there."

"You would know better than I," said Kerri. She could smell wood smoke; somewhere a dog was barking. Oh, blessed smoke! Oh, blessed dog! Oh, blessed everything that confirmed the substantiality of the world!

Loren said, "The value of his collection is fabulous to us mere readers, but none of what he showed us today looked like thesis material, I'm afraid. Some of it *would* be, if *I* had anything to say about the Canon. Still, if he could get hold of that lot, there's no telling what he has stowed away or what he has access to. We ought definitely to go back."

After a moment of silence Kerri asked, "What do you think of Greta?"

"Well, she's a case, isn't she? All cozy one minute and terrifying the next. I cannot make her out at all. For one thing, she's been to University. I wanted to ask her where and when, but there never seemed to be the right opening, and then I began to wonder if maybe Alex doesn't know. Didn't she tell us she was his pupil?"

"She did." Kerri nodded. "She does not behave like a pupil, though, does she? I would bet he has learned as much from her as she has from him. She is more than she seems."

Loren turned to look back at the ancient stone edifice. She squinted against the sun. "Do you think perhaps she is really Academic? Someone who could— um—get us into trouble? That was a rather controversial discussion."

Kerri stared at her in horror. "Name of the Dreamer! I never thought of that. Oh, Loren, she cannot be, she mustn't be! Can you imagine any Academic with enough power to do us harm who would dress up as a Peasant, talk like a Peasant, and spend two afternoons a week with a Cit in the Public Library?"

Loren laughed. "No. Yes. I can, just barely. Some of our fellow scholars play strange games. But when you put it that way, I see that we could be more trouble to her than she could make for us—if we ever find out who she really is. If she *is* anyone. I do hope you're right, but let us be careful just the same. Keep an eye on her."

Kerri felt warmed. It was good to have an ally, even better to be regarded as one. It allowed her to feel less like prey. "I like Greta," she said. "She frightens me to death, but I do rather like her."

"So do I," said Loren. "I like him, too, that Alexander. That poor sweet man with his star ships! He wants them so badly. And that old bit about the sun. How can he be so clever and so ignorant? Doesn't he realize there's nothing sacred about the names of the compass points? Has he never heard of the Great Convention?"

"I did not have the heart to mention it either," said Kerri, "on top of everything else. I wonder if Greta knows and has simply kept mum."

"Or told him, and he won't listen. In any case, I hope they aren't like this all the time," Loren said. "I am exhausted."

Their talk came round to the plan for Loren to visit Evesham on the weekend. Kerri suggested she come on Friday instead of Saturday and stay over to Sunday. Loren accepted readily. They would meet at the Public Library, have a big tea in Town and then travel out to Evesham together.

Kerri's train journey through deepening twilight was a strange, suspended time. She pretended to look out of the window as she stared at her reflection in the glass. Her face was all shadows. Did she look as peculiar as she felt? Did the other passengers see?

Grandmother, how long ago was the Age of Dreams?

Now, Kerrith, that is a question that does not really have an answer. It is not meaningful, so we no longer ask it. The important time is now, and the future....

Perhaps it had been good for her to be forced into confronting some old superstitions.

Apparently the world was not as fragile as she had always worried deep down. Of course, one thought of it as little as possible—that was part of the belief. Therefore, it was distressing to be reminded of the enormous Unknown that surrounded her world—this sparsely populated stretch of ocean coast and associated islands—in both space and time. For the first time in her life she almost felt envy for the people of the Age of Dreams, who had known their world (whatever it was) so completely and minutely, or who had at least boasted of their ability to know it. Surely the knowledge must have given them confidence and serenity.

But in the present, confidence and serenity being distant ideals, it had always been best to keep busy with the immediate demands of life, stay in familiar places, and skate very lightly everywhere else. And today she had found herself on ice a little too thin for her liking.

She had the uneasy feeling that she had been in a place where she had no business to be, consorting with people she ought not to know, doing forbidden and dangerous things. She even discovered in herself (with some shame) a vague idea that she ought to report the other three—Loren, Greta, and Alexander—to someone. But to whom? And for what? No laws had been broken that she knew about. It was not illegal to talk about the origin and nature of the world; it simply was not done. So why did she feel that she had been committing some kind of treason? And what was she betraying? Her caste? Her upbringing? Whatever the case, if there was wrongdoing she was certainly implicated. If the other three were in trouble, she was in it with them. She felt a familiar despair. She had managed to stay out of trouble for such a nice, long time!

The train was coming into Fernly before the connection dawned on her and she remembered what "trouble" meant and what that particular feeling of despair signified. Them.

She grinned at her reflection in the coach window. So! Now she was to curry favor with Them by delivering three new victims to Their mercies! The absurdity of it was so extreme she chuckled aloud. Even if They existed, which They did not—it was all nonsense! Loren was her friend, and Greta and Alexander might become friends, better ones than she had found in a long time.

To her surprise she remembered that she had met Loren only two weeks ago and the other two within days. And only a few days ago she had been uncomfortable and mildly offended at the suggestion of using given names and informal language with any of them.

Now such scruples seemed petty and ridiculous.

On the other hand, it was not a matter one could discuss with, for example, Nicholas.

He and most of the people of her acquaintance, people like Jillian and Patrick, would not understand at all.

Today Nick had planned to come home at noon and do some sewing on their decoy Revel costumes. If she was lucky, Kerri reflected pleasantly, he would have a hot meal waiting when she got there. In the meantime, she had the trolley ride out to the hamlet to get her mind out of the Public Library and in order to face him. She would not tell him anything about her afternoon. She could not even imagine what he would make of it, or of her, participating in it.

But Nicholas was not there. She came to a dark, cold house and a locked front door.

Apparently his plans had changed. Grumbling to herself, she set about lighting lamps, making up a fire in both the kitchen and bedroom stoves and putting the soup on to heat. She stopped waiting for him at a quarter past seven and had her supper by herself. When nine o'clock came and he still had not appeared, she put on her parka and gloves, took the lantern and went out to deal with the tanks. She was beginning to worry. She could not fault him for not letting her know he would be late. She had left for the Public Library before three. If he had sent a note by campus mail any time after noon, she would not have received it.

"It isn't that I mind him working late," she told Thomas. "I would simply like to know he hasn't been run down by a streetcar or something."

The bird cocked a skeptical eye at her, as if to say, "Yare? Tell us another one, then!"

"Well, I would!" she protested.

Back in the study she tried to concentrate on her lines, but it was impossible to keep her mind on the job. At every sound she would start, thinking Nicholas was at the door. She gave it up and took out the reading matter for her next essay along with her small library notebook. Three small rectangles of card fell out of the notebook and sailed off in three directions onto the floor.

Kerri stared at them stupidly. She had absolutely forgotten about the cards purloined from the card catalogue. Newly horrified at the desecration she had committed upon University property, she sprang out of her chair and snatched the cards up again. Quickly she thrust them into a random cubbyhole of her desk.

A moment later she found herself staring at the cards in the cubbyhole. A fact had dragged itself to the front of her brain. When she had picked up the cards from the floor and put them away she had had the impression there had been writing on one of them. Possibly more than one. Slowly she reached into the cubbyhole and pulled the cards out again. She looked at them carefully in the lamplight. They were blank. One by one she held them close to the light and examined them minutely on both sides. She even tried to look through them; they were barely translucent. There was nothing.

She thought she would be able to tell which of the cards was the one upon which she had seen the phantom lettering in the catalogue room. At the time it had seemed slightly thicker and creamier in color than the others, which she had supposed to be some kind of blank spacers. (There were all too many of the latter in the library card files.) Now she could not be sure which was the right card. In this light, at least, and to her fingers' touch, all three of the cards seemed to have a slightly different weight and color, no one of them standing out. Each time she examined one, she would find herself thinking, *no, not this one*, while at the same time one of the other two lying on the desk, seen at the edge of her vision, would seem to be surely the one. It was always the one farthest from her eyes' center of focus that seemed to flicker with the ghost of script. With a cry of frustration she threw the cards at the door of the study. They winged mindlessly down to the carpet, looking as innocent as ever.

At that moment she heard the front door open and the unmistakable sounds of Nicholas opening the front door. "Kerri? Are you here?"

"In the study." Kerri scrambled out of her chair and gathered up the cards, jamming them into the pocket of her cardigan just as Nick appeared in the door of the study. "Where have you been?" she asked. "It's after ten."

"Oh," he said, kissing her absentmindedly on the forehead, "I suppose you didn't get my note."

"No. What note?"

"To let you know. There was a meeting." His eyes flickered with something wild, a shadow she could not read. He did not quite look at her.

"Was there?" said Kerri. *He is lying*, she thought.

"The study group. I didn't find out about it until this midday. You know how they are with new people."

She did not know, but she said, "Yes. I see. Well, I went to the library this afternoon and never stopped back at my office, so I must have missed your note. I'm just glad you're home safely." She was conscious of the catalogue cards still in her hand inside her pocket. "Have you eaten? I left the soup on the back of the stove."

"Ah, thanks!" He looked ordinary again, the wild look as nonexistent as the writing on the index cards. "I had a sandwich at tea time, but I'm starving now. It's miserable cold out."

He went off toward the kitchen. Kerri waited behind long enough to move the cards from her cardigan to the pocket of her parka, hanging over the back of her desk chair. Then she followed him.

"Were there many people there, at your meeting?" she asked as she cut him some bread. She wondered, *Who is she? Who were you with?*

He had already got himself some soup and was tucking into it hungrily. "Quite a lot of people," he said. "There were some from other study groups, even other colleges, I think. People I didn't know except, in a few cases, by reputation. Rather important, some of them."

I'll bet, thought Kerri. "What were they doing there?" she asked, and then realized, *I am asking too many questions.*

An odd, tiny smile appeared on his face. He didn't look at her. "I'm not entirely certain," he said, "but I think we were being vetted. We new people."

"You and Jilly," said Kerri.

"Yes, and Morgana. All three of us. We had to speak to the assembly, introduce ourselves, summarize what we're working on, that sort of thing. There was some last minute stuff about the Retreat, too. Very tedious."

"Who is Morgana?"

"Miss Lewis? Haven't I mentioned her before?"

"I don't remember," Kerri said. "Very likely you have. I haven't met her, have I?"

Nick said, "I don't think so. Not formally. You may have seen her about in our common room."

"Ah," said Kerri. "You'll have to introduce me then. It's a job keeping track of your associates."

"It is," Nick agreed, grinning. "Come around to lunch tomorrow then, and meet her."

"I'll do that," said Kerri.

So, she thought, there's Jillian Munro-Haines and now this Morgana Lewis. Not married—very interesting! Which one is after him? Or is there somebody else I don't even know about?

She did meet Nick for lunch the next day. They went into his department common room, and he introduced her to a number of people, one of whom was Morgana Faith Lewis. Miss Lewis looked vaguely familiar, but she was not an individual Kerri remembered taking particular notice of before. She was a tall pale-eyed woman, very plain, bespectacled, with severe features and greying hair tied back in a bun. She had a direct manner and a deep resonant voice. Kerri had to acknowledge privately that she had a kind of charisma, but there seemed to be nothing about her that might attract a man like Nick. On the other hand, it struck her that except for herself she could not have said what type of woman Nick might be attracted to. She felt no wiser than before.

Chapter 22

Retreat

Kerri said good-bye to Nick in the lobby of Central Station on Friday afternoon. This was his choice. She guessed he did not want her to come to the platform and take leave of him in front of the rest of the group, and at first she felt inclined to be hurt. However, upon reflection, she decided it was wiser to avoid being visibly left behind. Even the smallest appearance of forlorn-ness might take root in the mind of some influential onlooker and do her damage at some future time. So Nick went off to his train, and Kerri made her way across the crowded lobby in search of her own Retreat.

Loren was sitting on a bench in the arcade, trying to fit a pile of parcels into a large carry basket. Her book bag and a worn canvas duffel lay at her feet.

"Can I give you a hand?" Kerri called out as she approached.

"Oh, hooray!" exclaimed Loren. "I had to reorganize twice on my way from the market, and I was beginning to think I would never make it all the way to the library."

Kerri took the duffel. "What is all this?"

"Provisions for our retreat."

"How very kind! But Loren, it was quite unnecessary. We are well stocked up."

Loren contradicted her happily. "Sausage!" she promised, waving one fragrant bundle under Kerri's nose. "Cheese! Pastry from Hagars'! Grapes! Sunflower seeds!"

"Sunflower seeds?"

"For your bird. Does it eat sunflower seeds?"

Kerri laughed. "Do not worry. Something will."

"I know," said Loren cheerfully. "Country people always have neighbors dropping by."

They got to Alexander's office ahead of Greta that day. Alex was genuinely glad to see them both, and slightly surprised, is if he had feared they would not come back. (As well he might after last time, Kerri reflected.) His office was noticeably tidier than on Tuesday. The shelves were stuffed fuller than ever, but a number of the piles on desk and floor seemed to have been eliminated altogether. An effort had been made to dust. He explained apologetically that he had not yet been able to find a fourth chair, but there was a small stool--he would just go put the kettle on, wouldn't be a moment.

Some of Loren's groceries were for their little party: tea, sugar, milk, and a raisin cake. "Because," she said, "I think it's only right if we take turns."

Kerri agreed. "I shall bring the goodies next time."

Greta came in then, Alex returned, and they all settled down to a cozy and completely uncontroversial afternoon tea. They spent the whole time talking about food. Alex was an expert on dietary practices of the Age of Dreams (and very strange some of them were, too!), Kerri was keen on fancy cookery, and Greta collected ancient recipe books, so there was plenty to discuss.

Kerri and Loren left the library at five o'clock. They were so full of raisin cake and some little sandwiches cleverly provided by Greta that they decided not to have an evening meal in town but go directly out to Evesham before it got any colder.

"How quiet it is," Loren said as she followed Kerri up the dark lane from the trolley circle. "One is almost afraid to speak at all."

"Voices do carry here," Kerri affirmed.

The air was bitter. They were glad to get into the house, to lamplight and shelter from the wind. Kerri showed Loren the spare bedroom (hastily cleared the day before of the Revel sewing) and the bath, and went to the kitchen to build up the fire in the stove. In a few moments Loren joined her and met Thomas Aquinas, who decided to have nothing to do with her. She set about unpacking her basket, while Kerri put the kettle on and rearranged things in the cooler.

"Tomorrow the ice man comes. I hope he's early so we won't have to hang about the house. We could tour the village, if you like."

"Yes, please! Is there pleasant walking here? I'm longing for a good tramp."

"A good tramp you shall have! And we'll stop at Sharon's and buy some eggs. They have hens."

"Hens!" Loren exclaimed. "Imagine!"

Kerri giggled. "We could have them, too, if we fixed up a place for them. It is one of the many things we haven't got round to yet."

Loren accompanied Kerri on her inspection of the water tanks and listened with unfeigned interest as Kerri explained the catchment system and showed her the windmill-driven pump that lifted water from the storage tanks to the cistern and solar heaters on the roof of the house.

"What if there is not enough wind?"

"We can pump by hand," Kerri said, "or foot, rather, like a bicycle, but it is a lot of work. And hardly ever necessary. There is almost always wind here, even more than this. They even ran an electrical generator by wind in the old days. It's still here. It doesn't work."

"Ah! Could you fix it?"

"Well, I couldn't. Nick couldn't. I don't know if it could be fixed. We haven't got anything electrical, anyway, except the old light fittings. But they are probably unsafe, and we have no light bulbs...."

Back in the kitchen, Kerri made supper and coffee. They sat at the table talking and studying until midnight.

The ice man did come early Saturday morning. They helped him shoulder the week's block of ice into the cooler. "Weather's going to turn," he commented as Kerri paid him.

"He says that every week," she muttered to Loren as he climbed up on his seat and clucked to the horses. The wagon lumbered on up the lane to the next house, and they were free for their walk.

Fortunately, the ice man was wrong, and the weather held fine and cold all morning. Walking through the overgrown ruins was less melancholy than it might have been in the rain. They strolled past the remains of the shops and the post office, the roofs long since fallen in. Loren admired the restored houses and peered curiously in the windows of the empty dilapidated ones that still stood.

"This is a big one," she remarked as they waded through an abandoned garden. "It doesn't look too bad. Have you ever been inside?"

"Once," said Kerri. "There's water damage. The roof's bad."

They made their way through tall weeds to a set of steps which led up to a stone paved terrace. The stones were broken and overgrown with vines, skeletal now in winter. The trees which had once provided civilized shade had gone wild, ripping at the pavement and steps with their roots. A pair of French doors were visible in the facade of the villa, nearly covered by a mat of ivy. Amazingly, only two panes of glass were broken. Loren looked through one opening.

"It was beautiful once," she said. "Has anybody got a claim on it?"

"They'd have to occupy it first. It's been tried a couple of times, but nobody has ever lasted more than a month. You weren't thinking of giving it a go, were you?"

She spoke in jest, but Loren did not return her grin. "You know," she said, "I am."

"You cannot be serious," Kerri said. "Not a person has come out here who hasn't been tempted. Some of them even brought builders to look at it. It isn't worth it."

"It would be to the right person."

"The right person would have to be a Stockholder, then. It isn't just the work; the place would cost a fortune! Oh, it would be delightful to have you living out here, but, believe me, that house is a heartbreaker I would not wish on anyone."

Suddenly she remembered Mr. Davis-Moncrief's tale of Val and Arzelle looking at the place. She chuckled. "On the other hand, I just thought of somebody I would wish it on, if only the house were a long, long way from here. My ex-husband," she explained to Loren's inquiring look.

"Oh," said Loren. "You were married before."

"Yes."

"You are not on good terms with him, I take it?"

"Not on any terms at all. But he and his wife were out here looking at the house, according to a neighbor."

"Oh dear!" said Loren. "Then I had better claim it at once and come to your rescue!"

They laughed and wandered back across the ruined terrace. As they pushed through the shrubbery to the lane, Loren looked back wistfully.

"I haven't got a home," she commented.

"In Dalton?" Kerri inquired.

"Oh, my mum and dad have a little house there. It's not where I'd like to live, though, and they're still young." Loren shrugged. She seemed half-embarrassed. "Also, I never felt much like settling down in one place, you see. Even if I did, there's my career hanging in the air. But if I could settle," she glanced at the sagging roof of the villa, "I'd fancy a place like that."

Kerri did not know what to say. In most families she was acquainted with, the issue was owning too many homes, some of which had to be given up in each generation in order to comply with the legal maximum of two residential properties per person. She already had her allowance, the Evesham house and the old family cabin down in Twilight Country, deeded to her when she had first gone to University. But Sophia and Aryel owned three houses between them, the two in Honowell and a country cottage on one of the other islands. Nick had only one home in his name, the flat in the city, but he also was an only child, and his parents also owned three homes. Unless the law were to be changed, which was unlikely, they would eventually have to decide which houses to part with. It was a sadness she did not like to think about, for she loved all of her family homes.

They stopped for the eggs. Loren was introduced to the neighbors and duly admired their garden and the hens. Back at the house, she and Kerri took a vote between themselves and decided it was just warm enough for a picnic lunch—if they had it in the greenhouse porch, which could be very pleasant on a sunny winter day, with a fine view out over the garden and, beyond its bounds, the rolling land that had once been farmed. They shared a bottle of Kerri's own home-brewed cider and got slightly silly dissecting the personalities of every mutual acquaintance they could discover.

Loren proved to be a gifted mimic. Her imitations of the more pompous Fellows and notorious students kept Kerri helpless with laughter through most of lunch.

"I can't believe they have not thrown you out of college," she gasped after on particularly deadly imitation of a certain student they both, it turned out, despised. "You have got him down perfectly, the pompous beast!"

"I do not show this to everybody," Loren assured her with a grin. "See if you can guess this one. Another pompous beast, a she-beast."

She stood up and minced toward the window, tossing pantomimed hair back from her cheeks. "It is *my* opinion, Miss... ah, Miss...Whoever," she drawled, "that you have not got a gram of authority behind your argument. And why not? Because *I* have all the authority there is! And do not bother to try to find any, because if you do *I* will take it away from you."

Kerri stopped laughing and sat up. The color drained from her face. "Arzelle Pendrake James," she said, "to the life."

"Oh." Catching sight of Kerri's face, Loren abruptly became herself again. "Is she a friend of yours?" she asked anxiously. "I hope I did not offend."

"Arzelle and I both grew up in Honowell," Kerri explained. "We went to school together. And do not worry. Friend is not what I would call her."

"Thank goodness!" Loren flopped down on her cushion. "You had me worried for a moment."

"Do you know her well?" Kerri asked cautiously.

"Not I. Only from a distance," Loren said. "I have had the good fortune to escape her notice almost entirely so far."

"Lucky you." Kerri smiled.

"Then I was born lucky. I do not quite belong to the class of people she deigns to notice, you see. Tell me, is she as much of a bitch as people make her out to be?"

"What?" Kerri gasped, wondering who these people were who could have such courage. "Do they? I've never heard anybody call her that."

"Perhaps you haven't been listening to the right people."

"Perhaps not," said Kerri doubtfully. After a moment she asked, "Do you know her husband?"

"No. I've seen him. He lurks in her shadow, rather. Nice looking chap, fancies himself a bit of a Romeo."

Kerri admitted hesitantly, "I used to be married to him."

"Ow! *That's* your ex-husband?" Loren sat up, wide-eyed. "The one you'd wish the villa on? Now I understand. Had you already separated when he—forgive me! I know it is no business of mine."

Kerri shrugged. "It is all right. We all grew up together, but Val never seemed to like her when we were kids. He and I married very young, the year we came to University. We were not...it would not have lasted anyway. She was married to someone else, but right after graduation she got rid of him and scooped up Val, all in one economical effort. Once I took the situation in, I was very glad to be out of it." She managed a lop-sided grin. "I did flee, rather, at the first inkling."

"To Nick?"

"No. I met him later. He is from Urlosa, but he did his undergraduate work at Dalton. Say, I wonder if you ever met him there?"

"Not that I remember. I suppose I may have set eyes on him, but I don't recollect hearing his name. Well, now I understand why you don't number Miss Arzelle Pendrake James-Dietrich among your friends."

"Actually," said Kerri. "It goes a good deal further back than that. We were... rivals, from very early on. When we went through Preliminary Exams at the end of Year Eight, she accused me of cheating. Publicly."

Loren stared at her. "My god! How dreadful! Why?"

"A crib card was found taped to the underside of the table I was sitting at," Kerri said. "Zarah—her name was Zarah then—swore she had seen me put it there."

"But you didn't, of course!"

"No. There was another witness, a boy in our class. He had seen Zarah tape the card there herself, and he told the authorities. She knew he was in the room watching her, but she did not take any notice of him because he was of the Sea People. Ordinarily he would not have come forward, but, you see, I am related to the Sea People through my father's mother. They take care of their own."

Loren nodded. "Like the Road People. I know."

Kerri continued, "Also, the Graphology Committee determined that the writing on the card was hers."

"So *she* was cheating!" Loren gasped.

"The case against her was dropped because there was no information on the card that would have been helpful on the exam."

Loren shook her head amazedly. "I don't understand. She must have known what could happen to her if she couldn't prove her allegations. She ought to have been ruined for life. False accusation is punished very severely, in Dalton anyway, and in Yendys too, I'm told."

"It is everywhere." Kerri sighed. "Sometimes I think it is one of the few protections we have, although it seems to protect the guilty more than the innocent. I suppose the consequences are less severe for thirteen-year-olds. And Zarah comes from a very important Faculty family in Honowell. All that happened to her that I ever knew about was that she was sent away to live on the Mainland, here in Yendys where nobody knew about the scandal. I never saw her again until the third year I was here."

"And did you do well on the Prelims?"

"Highest on the island that year," Kerri admitted. In fact, her score had been sixth highest among all examinees everywhere that year. "I always got very good marks, so it wasn't an anomaly, I would have thought, only it seemed to make some people more ready to believe I had done what I was accused of."

"Some of the mud stuck, too, I'll bet," Loren said sympathetically.

"Some."

"What about Arzelle's exam score?"

"It was high. She was about eighth on the island-wide list."

Loren hooted, "Not even close! She was stupid to try on such a trick. What did I tell you? The woman is a bitch—and a fool!"

"Arzelle Pendrake James is no fool," said Kerri. "She is a very dangerous person."

"I know." Loren nodded, becoming sober again. "She is one of Them!"

Chapter 23

The Watchers and the Game

Who?" Kerri whispered. The world had come to an abrupt stop.

"Oh, you know." Loren looked away, suddenly ill at ease. "Them. The people who—well, maybe it's just me and my imagination. Or one of the those things that simply isn't talked about. Never mind." Her face took on its stubborn Cit look, as she nervously brushed back her hair.

"Please," said Kerri, following this confused explanation with no trouble at all. She swallowed. "What do you mean—isn't talked about? What people?" With conscious effort, she refrained from engaging the Veil.

"People like Arzelle." Loren grimaced and downed the rest of her cider.

"Like her? How?"

"It's hard to put into words. Fortunately, there aren't too many like her! Or there are, only not so bad. Sometimes I imagine, you see, that they're all watching me, waiting for me to do something wrong. Wishing it. Willing misfortune on me and then judging me for it. I *am* aware," she continued, avoiding Kerri's eyes, "that I have a tiny problem about not having been born quite Academic. I try not to, but there it is. And people *will* behave—well, you know how they behave."

"Yes," said Kerri, remembering behavior, other people's and her own. And there was enough of the latter she was not proud of, thinking back on how she had often spoken, behind their backs, of not-quite-born-Academics like Loren. In a small voice she asked, as much of herself as of Loren, "Am I one of Them?"

"You?" Loren grinned. "No, not you! You *could* have been—you were born for it— but you're not. I could tell right away. I always can."

"How can you tell?"

Loren thought about it. "How can I tell? I don't know. I just can. They have...." She stopped, frustrated. "It isn't simply arrogance. I mean, They're all arrogant as hell; that's part of it, but many Academics are arrogant as hell. Pardon me."

"Oh." Kerri waved a reassuring hand. "I agree. They are. We are."

"But not all the arrogant ones are...the people I'm talking about."

"Them," Kerri prompted.

Loren nodded. "Well," she sighed. "Now you know I've got too much imagination."

"Not at all," said Kerri. "I do know what you mean. But you are the first person I've ever met who, ah, articulated it so well." *I am not the only one*, she thought, stunned. *I am not the only one.* She cleared her throat. "Have they, that is, Them—have They ever actually *done* anything to you? Has Arzelle?"

"I don't think so." Loren frowned in thought. "No. At least, nothing I could put a finger on. Maybe I haven't made the sort of mistake they're looking for, yet."

"I have," muttered Kerri.

Loren continued, "I decided long ago I could more or less ignore them, and I would have been able to, if it hadn't been for the Watchers."

"The Watchers?" Kerri's mouth felt dry. She took a large gulp of cider. "Is that what you call them, the people like Arzelle?"

"No." Loren flushed slightly. "Not all of them. Just the first two I noticed. And they aren't really like the others exactly. Dangerous, perhaps, but not in the same way. It is difficult to explain."

Kerri asked hesitantly, "Are they anybody I would know? Anybody I should watch out for?"

"Oh, they aren't in Yendys. I hope. At least, not yet. I haven't seen them. And I have no idea who they are." Loren smiled crookedly. "And it's all a lot of nonsense, anyway. Just ghost stories from my childhood."

"I like ghost stories," Kerri offered, untruthfully. She scented Information, the real stuff, useful.

"Oh...I don't know. It's all just stupid and boring." She glanced up. "I've never told anybody about it."

"You needn't tell me, if you would rather not," Kerri assured her regretfully, "but if you did, I would not repeat it to anyone. And I would not think it is stupid and boring, and I would not laugh," she added.

Loren considered. "Swear you won't," she demanded. "Swear it by your membership in the Gang of Four."

"I beg your pardon?"

"The Gang of Four." Loren blushed faintly and smiled. "I hadn't told you. It's my private name for our little library group. I hope nobody minds. It's from the Age of Dreams. A group of musical performers, I think they were, or revolutionary anarchists, or something."

"Revolutionary anarchists!" Kerri repeated, not knowing whether to be amused or affronted. Suddenly she thought of dear Alex, fussing over the tea, and she giggled. "I like it! Let's tell the others. Only I suppose we had better look it up first. In any case, I do solemnly swear, by the Gang of Four and on my honor as a scholar, never to tell anyone anything you divulge to me here today." She filled up both glasses to the brim.

Loren looked impressed.

Kerri felt surprised by Loren's willingness to trust her. Surprised, touched, and a bit awed. *Maybe this is someone I could trust,* she thought. *An exchange.* "Sometimes," she offered hesitantly, "just talking about things puts them more in perspective."

Loren nodded. "Very well," she began. "It goes back to when I was in prep school, maybe sixteen, seventeen. I used to have these dreams. They were ordinary dreams, some pleasant, some not, except there would be a person away to the side of what was going on, watching. He never did anything, never spoke, but always I felt...judged."

"He? Always male?"

"I think so. Yes."

"Old? Young?"

"About my own age. Maybe a little older."

"You said there were two?"

"Yes. They never appeared in the same dream. I called one the Dark Watcher because he had dark hair. He was the more stern, the more condemning. The other had fair hair, so I called him the Bright Watcher. He was more sympathetic, but always rather sad, as if I'd let him down, failed to live up to expectations. I think I dreaded him more than the other."

She downed another swallow of cider, looking out over the garden and into her memories. "Those were difficult years. In our school the lines were rather rigid. Between who I had been and what I was trying to be, I didn't have a clue who I was. It was hard. I was always in a worry. Had I done something I shouldn't? Had I failed to do something I should have done? Had I misspoken?"

"I know," said Kerri. "It was like that for all of us, no matter how we were born. You need to believe that."

Loren snorted. "Not everyone! Not for the ones who made it difficult. Them!"

Thinking of the Star Dream, Kerri asked, "Do you still have the Watcher dreams?"

"Oh, yes," said Loren, "but the dreams are not the problem. It's not dreams I'm afraid of these days." She hesitated. "This is the worst part. You will think I am crazy."

"Here." Kerri divided the last of the cider between them. "You are not crazy. I am not crazy. We are not crazy." It was a pledge.

"Do not be so sure. I haven't told you yet. I saw the Watchers, and it was no dream. I was awake."

Kerri frowned. "You saw them?"

Loren nodded. "Not long after I started University. First I saw the Dark Watcher. Afterward I thought I must have been mistaken. Then, the very next day, I saw the Bright Watcher. I became frightened."

"Are you certain," Kerri inquired carefully, "that they were the same people from your dreams? Dream people can be rather vague."

"I cannot explain," said Loren unhappily. "I just *knew*. It was one of those inner certainties one simply cannot overlook. Besides—they watched me. That is, they knew...they were aware of my existence. They shouldn't have taken any notice of me. I was no one in particular."

In spite of herself, Kerri smiled. "Isn't it possible they simply found you attractive to look at? Young men do watch young women, you know. And vice versa."

Loren looked at her blankly. "Oh, no," she protested. "That isn't possible. They were not of my caste."

"But that doesn't matter, not once you've entered University." Even as she said the words, Kerri knew they were untrue. Of course, it mattered, and never more than in those early undergraduate months.

"It was impossible," Loren insisted stubbornly. "In any case, I found it no trouble to stay out of their way. They were in different colleges from mine; we had no mutual acquaintances; our paths did not cross. I got over being so terrified. I would have forgotten all about it, if I hadn't gone on having the dreams."

"So you never even found out who they were?" Kerri felt a little let down. From the way Loren had begun her story, she had expected something quite as strange and perverse as the Game. She had almost made up her mind to tell Loren about the Game, a kind of exchange of confidence. But now she suspected that this personal mythology of Loren's was mostly the working of an overactive imagination, combined with coincidence and simple misinterpretation of ordinary events. On the other hand, the same thing could be said about the Game. Who was she, after all, to pass judgement?

Loren shrugged. "I never really tried to find out their names. I was certain, though, that there was no connection between them. At least, I had no reason to think so until I saw them again.

"It was later, after I graduated and left Dalton. I traveled, as I told you last night. I got up to Urlosa, and then I needed some money, so I found a job there and stayed on. Then, one day I saw the Dark Watcher.

"It was at an outdoor concert, very crowded. I turned around, and there he was. Watching me. I was so unnerved, I left the concert. The next day on my way to work I passed a newsagent, and there was the Bright Watcher, calmly buying a paper. He looked up and saw me. I know he recognized me. It all came back to me then. I was terrified. I can't quite believe now that I could have been in such a panic, but I was."

"Why didn't you speak to him? To either of them?"

Loren looked shocked. "Speak to them? You don't understand. With Watchers the object is to escape being noticed, not to draw attention to oneself. I couldn't, and anyway...well, I simply couldn't."

Kerri found this entirely plausible. She wondered if Loren had something like the Veil. It seemed unlikely. Maybe if she knew about the Veil she would find it useful. It might be an act of great helpfulness to tell her. *Although I can't,* Kerri thought.

"I do understand," she said. "You are certain it was them?"

Loren squinted out at the sky. "Oh, there have been a lot of times since then that I've wondered if it wasn't a mistake. At the time, though, I was dead certain. I left Urlosa. Please don't think they scared me away; I was startled, but I was not that frightened. I had been thinking of leaving for some time. I missed the traveling, you see. Their appearance seemed a kind of sign that the time had come."

"I see," said Kerri, who did see. Signs and Portents were something she believed in and understood the importance of. She also suspected Loren was minimizing the fear she must have felt. "So then you came here to Yendys."

"No. I went to the Islands. I'd never been there. I had always wanted to go, but I kept putting it off because I get terribly ill on boats. There was a job I could have for the asking in Crystal, so I went there. The voyage was dreadful, but the island was bliss."

"Lovely town," Kerri agreed. "My mother has a cottage on that island. We used to go in the holidays."

"Lucky you!" Loren sighed. "I might still be there, except six months after I got there the Dark Watcher turned up."

"What? Again?" Kerri did not know what to think. This was stretching coincidence too far.

"I know, I know," said Loren sadly. "I did not believe it either. I was in a public place, and I am sure he didn't see me. I thought I made myself stay long enough to make certain it was him, but later I wondered if my mind was playing tricks on me. By then it was too late. I had already left Crystal. I didn't wait for the other one to turn up.

"I came here to Yendys, applied for a place in the graduate school. I've been here a year and a half now, and there hasn't been a sign of either one of them. I don't really expect them to appear. It must all have been mistakes and coincidence. People who happened to share a resemblance. That is what I think when I look at it logically. And yet, I am always on my guard. And I seem to have grown a sort of sensitivity to people who have that kind of predatory awareness, like our mutual friend."

"Arzelle?"

"Yes. It began in those Dalton undergraduate days. It was as if the Watchers were a kind of catalyst: They changed me. I began to notice people like our mutual friend and...other things. For a while reality got all wobbly. It was frightening. I thought I was going demented, but somehow I got through it all right."

"How?" asked Kerri.

"By focusing on my work. I...just turned my mind away from it all. I made it...unimportant. It worked until...well...I told you. Urlosa. Here I do not worry about the Watchers—that is all over long ago—but They are all around me here, and They are much worse. And by now you must have no doubt that I belong in the Asylum. This is wonderful cider!"

"Thank you," said Kerri. "And you do not belong in the Asylum any more than I do."

Loren studied her for a moment. "You've noticed Them, too, haven't you," she said.

Kerri nodded. "All my life."

The decision was sudden: *Yes. Now. Quickly.* Like diving into cold water.

She took a deep breath. "When I was little, I thought of it as a Game, a kind of hide and seek...to escape Their notice, to outwit Them. I did not always succeed, it seemed, but I could never under any circumstances allow Them to find out I was on to Them. That would be the worst thing."

"Yes, exactly," Loren agreed. "One must never look at the Watchers, because to look is to become visible. I know."

"Of course," said Kerri, hastening to redeem her credibility. "I never thought any of it was real; I still don't. I never really believed They could read my thoughts or cause me to make mistakes or do wicked things to me, although Arzelle claimed she could. She and the others are simply people I cannot trust, people who make me nervous, who have been unkind or rude to me, who have made me feel small and seemed to enjoy it."

"Some people are like that," said Loren. "I don't know why." She gazed out the window thoughtfully. "Maybe it's these times we live in. Don't you be so sure it isn't real. There's something real in it, anyway. And I wouldn't be surprised if we're not the only ones. By the way, did you know there is a unicorn in your garden?"

"Blast!" Kerri jumped to her feet. "Not again! Those damned pests will jump any fence. They're worse than the kangaroos, and they eat everything!" She charged toward the outer door and ran out, waving her arms. "Go on! Get out of here, you rascal! Shoo!"

Loren followed, laughing. The beast lifted its head out of the lilac hedge, whose next year's buds it was stripping, and blinked innocent eyes at the advancing humans.

"Get out!" shrieked Kerri. She picked up a stick.

The unicorn backed away from the hedge, still chewing. Then it suddenly turned, gathered itself, bounded over the fence and trotted off down the field toward the trees.

"Oh, look at this," Kerri moaned, examining the munched place in the hedge. "They make such a mess."

"Do you get a lot of them?" asked Loren. "I didn't know they came this far north."

"There are a couple in the neighborhood." Kerri threw her stick across the fence and started back to the house, brushing her hands together. "I think they wandered up last summer when the boundary shifted. I never saw any around here until last December. They're a real nuisance, but I don't know what we can do to drive them off."

She was glad the unicorn had come into the garden. She was stunned at what she had done, still trembling from the shock of it. She had actually Told someone. And not even a friend anciently trusted like Timo; she had given her secret to someone she had not known a month. But Loren had not judged or looked at her as if she were losing her mind. No, Loren had accepted every word. Loren had nodded and so much as said, "Yes, I understand. Me, too."

Suddenly Kerri remembered Greta's bizarre theory about the Dreamer and the world. She realized over the intervening week the idea had somehow become not so bizarre. *Perhaps*, she thought, *when the Dreamer went back to sleep, when things were put back together, there was something put a little wrong in all our minds, something that appears to some of us like craziness waiting to happen, so we feel threatened and shamed, and we keep it secret. Maybe it has something to do with our memory problems. Maybe it's the reason why some people go demented: the thing that is waiting to happen happens. Will it happen to me? Is that what Zarah can see, why she gloats? Is that what They see when They look at us?*

The two of them wandered back into the house, but the confidential mood was broken. They talked of unimportant things, like Unicorns and the unstable boundaries of Twilight Country. They both needed to settle down to studying, they told each other. It would be tea time soon.

Chapter 24

Thomas

The last week of April blew in gusty and unsettled. The city's pulse began to quicken in anticipation of the May Day Festival. In the central district, crews from the Department of Public Works labored to put up decorations that would remain in place until after the Solstice. At the University undergraduates hurried to complete the illuminations they had designed for the annual competition among the colleges. The weather seemed to change by the hour—now fine, now grey and wet—and planners of balls and parties tried anxiously to provide for every possible contingency.

Nick came home from his Retreat in excellent spirits. He had cemented a number of valuable contacts, it seemed, and enjoyed himself besides. He was willing to chatter on about the whole thing at such length and in such detail that Kerri was nearly able to convince herself that he was not carrying on a flirtation with anyone, let alone something more serious. He was certainly affectionate towards her, which she appreciated, although she knew from experience with Val that it was not necessarily a good sign.

He was pleased to hear that she had passed a productive weekend and enjoyed the visit of her friend. He expressed hope that he would be able to meet Miss Weberly soon. Maybe the three of them could have lunch together some day, he suggested. Not until after the Revel, though. Which reminded him that Kerri ought be sending invitations for their dinner party. And he had better do some work on those false costumes. Even if they were not to be worn for the Faculty Ball they would still come in handy for some other holiday event.

The *real* Revel costumes were complete and ready in their hiding place. Nicholas had altered his to fit and bought a new dress shirt, to which he had added a quantity of fine inherited lace. Kerri had bought shoes and a new petticoat and rehearsed the best way to dress her hair. They had booked a hotel room in town for the night of the Revel. They had been lucky about the hotel. It was only a few blocks from the Palace where the Ball was to take place, with no steep hills to climb in between. Walking would be possible if the weather turned out fine. This was an advantage because by the time they had received their invitation there was no hope of engaging a private carriage, even if they had been able to afford one. Just in case, they reserved a place on the omnibus laid on by the hotel.

On Tuesday, Kerri ventured again into the Public Library. The group had agreed to meet at lunch time that day because Alex had a staff meeting in the afternoon. Kerri brought bread and cheese and milk for the tea. Greta, who apparently never came empty handed, contributed pears and a cake.

With a bit of prodding, Kerri persuaded Loren to tell the others about the Gang of Four. Mirthfully they all agreed to adopt the name and reminded each other that they really *must* look it up. Nobody could agree on the source. Greta thought she remembered that the Gang of Four were a band of Outlaws in the Old West, while Alex was sure it had something to do with Sherlock Holmes.

"There was something else you thought of looking up," Loren said to Kerri. "What was it? Something about Guenevere?"

"The Society of Guenevere," Kerri affirmed. "I did look it up. Well," she admitted as she saw their expectant looks, "I got as far as the card catalogue. No luck there."

"What is the Society of Guenevere?" asked Alex.

How refreshing it was, Kerri reflected (not for the first time in this company), to be among people who had no fear of revealing ignorance and asking questions. Half the peril and confusion of Academic life seemed to stem from people pretending to know things they did not. Or pretending not to know things they did. At the same time she was guiltily conscious of a small sliver of contempt for Alex, that he did not think to protect himself.

"It is very silly of me," she admitted, "but I cannot seem to remember. That means it is overdue for review."

"I can't remember it either," Loren told them, frowning. "That may be a reassuring sign. If *two* graduate students can't remember something, it shouldn't be very important. But one never knows."

"It's an Academic thing, then?" mused Alex. "I don't believe I've ever heard of the Society of Guenevere. Although I know who Guenevere was, of course. I haven't read any of that King Arthur stuff in a while. Not since I was twelve."

"You found nothing in the card catalogue?" Greta asked. "That was at the University, I suppose. We might try here."

"There were no direct references," Kerri replied. "I noted down a few sources that I might follow up." Guiltily she remembered the stolen cards. What had she done with them? Put them in her desk, no, her maroon cardigan, in the pocket. Or was it a jacket?

"You know, it just occurred to me," Loren said to Kerri, "that it might be from a poem. There are so many Arthurian poems. Nobody learns *all* of them, unless it is their specialty."

"A line from a poem! That sounds very likely. Yes, of course! Williams, do you think? It cannot be Tennyson. We would have recognized it right away." Kerri felt relieved. It must be a poem, not in the undergraduate syllabus—that would account for her not knowing it. It also meant it would be easy to find, given a little time. So much for the Society of Guenevere.

The only remaining puzzle was, what had it to do with Nick's research? The History College had not yet declared King Arthur historical, so far as she knew. On the other hand, if they were getting ready to do so, it would be a major breakthrough. If Nick was involved in something of that magnitude, he was indeed entering the inner circles! She would have to think of a way to try to worm the information out of him. And she had worried about doing him out of some hypothetical treasure trove in the Public Library!

"The Society of Guenevere," Greta repeated. "Now where have I heard that name? I'm sure it wasn't something I read on a page. It was something I heard spoken of."

"You do remember it then?" asked Loren.

"It's just coming back to me. Not long ago it was, neither. As you might say, overheard somewhere. But I don't recollect the occasion."

"A public recitation, perhaps," Kerri suggested.

"Aye, that'll be it." She dug out a little notebook and a pencil and wrote down the words in bold, angular block letters. (Kerri, always interested in other people's graphological styles, watched out of the corner of her eye. Authoritative, she decided, but unrefined.) "If I remember where I heard it, or if I come across it again, I'll tell you."

Where Greta might come across a reference to an obscure literary subject, Kerri could not imagine, nor did she place much faith in Greta's having heard anything but the most popular of poetry. Nevertheless, she appreciated the offer. One never knew: Look at Timo and his brilliant detective work over Val. "That would be very helpful," she said.

"We've all got it on our list now, anyway," said Alex.

"Along with the Gang of Four!" Greta remarked.

They all laughed.

It was agreed that they would not meet on Friday, on account of the festivities. Kerri acknowledged diffidently that she and Nick were to attend a private party, although she was vague about which one. Greta also had a set engagement. She was going to a dance with some chums, she declared. Loren thought she would probably join the crowds for the public celebrations on campus and wander about looking at the illuminations, maybe dropping in on a college open house or two. Alex said he intended to watch the fireworks over the harbor but had no other plans.

Kerri left the public library at two o'clock and caught the streetcar to the River Market to do some shopping. They needed meat and fresh fruit-and-veg at home, and Thomas was literally out of birdseed. What he had in his feeder was all there was, and it would be gone by tomorrow.

The mask sellers were out in full force. Kerri was not a collector, but she enjoyed looking at the splendid display. One mask caught her eye, a confection of white lace, black velvet and rhinestones. It was so perfect a complement for her Revel costume that she bought it immediately.

By three o'clock she was on the train for home. At that time of day the trains stopped at all the stations, but Kerri did not mind. She was in very good spirits. She was well prepared for her recitation Thursday. Her work was caught up, another essay turned in this morning without incident. It was two weeks since her unknown saboteurs had succeeded in playing any kind of trick on her. Perhaps the new lock on her office door had stymied them for the time being. It was a very good lock with a dummy hidden catch and a combination knob, and she was unlikely to be caught for a while, having arrived at an understanding with the cleaning staff. The gratuity involved was so reasonable that Kerri was sure most of the office locks in the building must be illegal by now.

Best of all, this morning she had received a brief but cordial note from her Sponsor-to-be, acknowledging the receipt of all requested transcripts and other materials. Her paperwork was in good order, and he was writing to Professor Abbot-Remarque about standing proxy for him in Yendys. As soon as he had the reply from that Faculty member, he would send Kerri her letter of introduction.

One month! Kerri thought gleefully. *I shall be In at last! How surprised they will all be. Although they shouldn't, they ought to have realized I deserved it. I can't wait to see Nick's face, and those snobbish friends of his. Then, of course, I can hint about how it was only a tragic oversight all along, a grave injustice. I* should *have had a Sponsor from the beginning. It will be fun to watch them backpedaling and pretending they always respected me, truly.*

This kind of happy reverie occupied the whole of the long journey to Evesham, and Kerri arrived at her front door without ever once feeling the weight of all the parcels she carried. She went straight to the kitchen to set down her burden.

"Food is here for starving budgies," she called out gaily. From the cage there was silence. "Thomas?"

He was lying cold on the floor of the cage, a pathetic ball of yellow and green fluff.

Kerri took him out and cradled the tiny fragile body in her hands, but it was too late to bring back the warmth and the song. He weighed next to nothing, smaller than he had ever been in life.

When Nick arrived half an hour later, she had already wrapped Thomas in a piece of soft cotton flannel and found a box.

"Oh, Nick," she said, when he walked into the kitchen. "Thomas is dead." She began to cry again.

They buried him in the garden. Nick dug a hole among the skeletons of the lilies. "I can't understand it!" he exclaimed angrily as he shoved the spade into the heavy soil. "He was in perfect health."

"He was getting old, Nick." Sometimes Kerri forgot that Thomas had been Nick's bird, that they had had each other longer than Kerri had known him.

"Not that old." He cast the spade aside and brushed the dirt off his hands. There were tears in his eyes. "Not that old."

They carried the cage out to the shed, and the stand and all the bird toys. Neither of them could bear to have any of those things in the kitchen.

"And you had just given him a new treat," Kerri mourned.

"No, not I." Nick detached the molded stick of choice seeds from the wires of the cage. It looked new, almost untouched. "Didn't you put this in for him?"

"No. I bought seed today because I thought he had nothing at all. I thought of buying him a treat, but I didn't. I didn't notice he had that one until just now."

Nick looked puzzled. "I don't remember it being there last time I cleaned the cage. That was Thursday. I had a lot on my mind. Oh, well, it looks like he didn't fancy it much." He crumbled the treat and scattered the pieces across the pavement, along with the seed remaining in the feeder. A sparrow fluttered down from the shed roof and hopped cautiously toward the gift. "Enjoy," Nick said to the sparrow.

"Nick. I am so sorry."

He didn't answer for a long time. "So am I," he said finally, as he closed the door of the shed.

They washed their hands and had a cup of tea, and then Nicholas went to work on the sewing, while Kerri tidied up and began a pot of soup. Presently he returned to the kitchen and asked her, "Did you move any of the sewing?"

"Not since before the weekend." Kerri thought for a moment. "I haven't been in there since Sunday afternoon, when I made up the bed again. Is something missing?"

"I can't find a piece of the collar of one of the capes. I had them all cut out and marked and pinned together, I thought, but it's not in the stack."

"Maybe it got mixed up with one of the other piles when I put away the sewing before Miss Weberly came. I tried to be very careful to keep things in the order you put them, but it might have happened. Did you look through everything?"

"Not very carefully, I suppose." He was already on his way back to the guest room. "It'll turn up, no doubt. If it's really gone astray, I have a big enough scrap to cut another piece. It's just frustrating. Makes me wonder if I made a mistake and didn't cut out enough pieces in the first place. Which is possible."

"Work on one of the other garments for now," Kerri called out to him. "That's what I'm going to do."

Ten minutes later he was back in the kitchen with a strange and dangerous look on his face. He went to the window and stood looking out, wordless.

"Nick? Did you find it?"

"Half the back of your bodice is missing." He bit the words out one at a time. "It is a big piece. I cannot cut another out of the remnants."

Kerri stared at him. "You cannot be implying *I* did something to it!"

"No." He turned to her, ice blue eyes glaring under black brows. "I know you did not. Someone has been in this house."

"What...?"

"They killed my bird."

"Thomas! You don't think..."

"I *do* think."

She followed his gaze out the window to the stone-paved kitchen yard, saw the dead sparrows among scattered bits of budgie treat. One, still dying, fluttered convulsively against a geranium pot. Her hand went to her mouth. "Name of the Dreamer!" She met his eyes, horrified. "Nick. What else is missing?"

She reached the study a second before him. After a brief and frantic survey of both their desks, the file cupboards, the bookshelves and the currently important hiding places, they met in the middle of the room and leaned together shivering.

"I can't tell if anything is gone," said Kerri.

"Nor can I." Nick held her tightly.

"Maybe they just wanted to sabotage the costumes—it's almost the last minute and they'll know we're desperately behind in the making. We'll be all right, thanks to Grandmother. The real ones are untouched."

"Thomas," Nick reminded her.

"And poor Thomas. What kind of person would do such a thing?"

Nick was silent for a moment. Then he said, "Your friend, Miss Weberly—how well do you know her?"

Chapter 25

The Veil

"Miss Weberly?" Kerri stared at him. She felt ill with shock. "No! Not a chance! I will not believe that of her."

"She was in the house," Nick reminded her. "She spent two nights in the room where we keep the sewing. She must have been in the kitchen at least once when you were not with her. She had the opportunity."

It was true. Horrified, Kerri thought back over the weekend, everything they had done, Loren's movements. "I cannot believe it," she repeated unhappily.

"She knew we had a bird. You said she brought seed for him."

"Sunflower seeds, Nick. She didn't know what kind of bird he was. We fed them to the rosellas." Could she have been taken in by Loren? Deceived, betrayed—after she had given her trust, something she never did easily. Why, they even called each other by their given names! And she had Told Loren about the Game. "There's no motive," she whispered.

"You told me she recites in your college."

"Yes, but she doubles in math. I think that is her real interest. And she isn't that kind of person—she is totally forthright. And absolutely not a rival. She doesn't seem to be making any effort to compete or make a name for herself. I've never seen her in the Common Room; nobody ever even mentions her name. I only met her by accident..."

Kerri closed her mouth abruptly and looked down. Unless forced to, she would much prefer not to admit to Nick that she had known Loren less than a month or that her new friend was a Cit—although the latter fact was in Loren's favor in this case. Scholars of Cit background were seldom implicated in the kind of sabotage Kerri and Nick had been subjected to. Too few of them had anything to gain by it, and all of them had everything to lose. She stepped apart from Nick and sat down dispiritedly at her desk.

Nick remained standing in the middle of the room, hard faced, arms folded. He had no reason to trust Loren, whom he had never met, who had been in his home not at his invitation. He raised an eyebrow. "Perhaps it was not so accidental. What if she is the person who has been harassing you this term? Or in league with someone who *is* a rival? What if she is doing it for someone else? A lover, perhaps?"

"I don't know if there is one," Kerri admitted. "But I do not think so. Not anybody in College, at least, or I'm sure I would have heard. Maybe nobody in Yendys at all. She hasn't been here long. She's from Dalton. I've never seen her with another soul on campus. Indeed, I've suspected she hasn't any friends yet but me."

She was becoming angry—at herself for trusting Loren so easily, allowing herself to be inveigled into all sorts of dubious activities and acquaintances, at Loren for being so vague and evasive about her background. She realized she knew nothing at all about the woman, beyond the facts that she had grown up in Dalton and gone to University there; her parents were still living (and probably City People); she had traveled the country after graduation, working at odd jobs before resuming her education. Oh, yes, and the Watchers. That *was* peculiar, especially thinking about it here in Nick's sane, normal presence. Most of all, she was angry at Nick for throwing shadows upon a friendship she had come to value more than she realized.

Nick went to his own desk, looked down at the papers there. He said thoughtfully, "Maybe there's someone who owes me a grudge from my Dalton days."

Then, suddenly, facts added themselves together in her mind. She almost laughed with relief. "Wait, Nick! No. The rosellas weren't harmed at all, but the sparrows died at once. If Miss Weberly had put the treat in Thomas' cage any time while she was here, he would have been dead by Monday. And you worked on the costumes last night, without missing anything. It had to have been done today while we were gone.

"And if you are thinking she could have come back today, I know she couldn't. She recites on Tuesday morning. We lunched together, and after that she was in the library the whole time I was, under my eye. She had no time for a quick run out to Evesham."

"An accomplice..." Nick began, unwilling to part with his prized suspect.

"So whose accomplice?" she interrupted angrily. "Any number of people know where we live, know about Thomas. It's no less likely to be any of them than Miss Weberly. If she didn't do it when she was my guest, there's no more reason to suspect her than lots of other people. Less! It could as easily be somebody in your study group." she ended stubbornly.

He looked as horrified as she had felt when he had suggested Loren as the culprit. "Kerri! The idea! I refuse to believe any of them would do such a thing. They don't need to. They're miles ahead of me, most of them."

"You're moving up very fast," she reminded him. "Even someone who is ahead of you now might not always be. You could be seen as a threat."

This argument was irresistible. "You're right." He sighed. "We don't know enough to rule anybody out, not even our neighbors here in the hamlet—although I can't imagine it being one of them! I don't mean to treat your friend unjustly; I only want an answer. Who has done this? How did they get in?"

"Any one of a number of ways," Kerri told him. "Remember, *we* got in with no trouble that first day. Most of the windows have no bolts. The others we've never bothered to lock. Why should we? The lock on the greenhouse door is a joke. It must have been easy. But to come all the way out here! I can't believe it could be anyone from here in Evesham, either."

"Nor can I." He sat still for a moment looking out the study window. His face looked pinched and tired. "The hardware shop in Fernly will be open until six. I'll borrow a bicycle and go buy some new locks and bolts. I suppose we'd better start locking the ones we've got."

"I'm going to throw out every bit of food I didn't buy today," she said, glad to think of something definite to do. "Except the sealed jars, and I'll examine every one of them to make certain they *are* sealed. Damn!"

Nick got to his feet. "I suppose you had better do that," he said. "Before I leave I'll go through the outbuildings and see if there are any other signs. You search inside. Find out if anything else is missing. While I'm gone, don't leave the house."

Kerri nodded. *The Veil*, she thought. *I'll try it over the house, like I thought of that other time. It may be a silly game, but it can't hurt.*

As soon as she had seen Nick pedaling off down the road on Mr. Leigh-Ibarra's bicycle, she opened all the interior doors in the house, including all the cupboards and drawers. She took herself to the spot in the hallway that was as near as she could tell to being the exact center of the building. There she sat cross-legged in a posture of meditation. She closed her eyes and did the slow breathing for relaxation. She tried to empty her mind.

The Veil. She pictured it rising, the color of air, from ancient brick boundaries of the flower bed, arching domelike over the house. She imagined it again, another layer arising from the fenced boundaries of the garden, taking all the yard and the outbuildings under its shelter. She imagined it strong and safe and lasting. Malice would look elsewhere for a target. Trouble would pass by this place. Inside the Veil the house would be guarded and protected.

How I do wish the Veil were real, Kerri said to herself.

They talked of nothing else that evening. There was one puzzle they kept coming back to. Toward whom was the attack directed? Both their costumes had been sabotaged. However, the capes were nearly identical, and the materials had been laid out in such a way that the unknown saboteur could have thought he or she was damaging only one costume, and that a woman's. That would mean Kerri was the intended victim; therefore, the intruder could be the same person or persons who had been persecuting her earlier in the term.

On the other hand, the poisoning of Thomas argued an enmity against Nicholas, provided the assailant knew that Thomas had originally belonged to Nick. Furthermore, anyone who knew Nick well enough to know about Thomas would know that it was Nick who made his and Kerri's festival costumes and that ruining either of them constituted an attack against Nick. Certainly Nick had rivals in his College who knew all these things, and he, too, had been subject to several attempts at sabotage this term.

Or was this act directed at both of them together? Could their separate troubles on campus be linked somehow? Or was this invasion of their home something separate and unrelated to the things that had happened at the University?

The poisoning had to be premeditated. There was no substance in the house that would have done the job, nothing anyone could have seen and poured on Thomas' treat in a momentary impulse of spite. And both of them were sure they had not purchased the treat.

While they were trying to study after supper, Nicholas said, "I have been wondering if there is someone who hates me for being invited to the ball and for getting into the group. Someone who was passed over."

"Have you a suspect in mind?" Kerri asked.

Nick thought for several moments. "There are several possible," he said doubtfully, "but none of them...I can't believe any of them would go to these lengths. No, I won't tell you who they are. We may need your unbiased observations at some point."

"I am at your service," said Kerri, feeling unexpectedly comforted at his use of the first person plural. Then she frowned. "But I just thought of something. Who knows you've been invited to the Ball? Who have you told that isn't invited?"

"Well, the only people I've told myself are a few in the study group, and those few are going, but I'm sure it has got round by now. I doubt there's anybody in my department who doesn't know."

Kerri said, "Doesn't it seem to you that if a person knew we'd been invited to the Faculty Ball, they'd realized we couldn't be planning to wear the blue and gold costumes? Not only are they too far from finished, but they are completely inappropriate."

He pondered that for a moment. "I'm not sure they would realize it. A lot of the people who imagine themselves as contenders do not have very sophisticated taste, when all is said and done. Or the person might not have cared one way or the other about the Ball, as long as damage could be done in some way."

It was as frustrating as it was mystifying. Because there were no leading suspects, they were in the uncomfortable position of having to suspect everybody. Except each other. Kerri was thankful for that at least. It was the first time in some weeks she had felt solidly allied with Nicholas, since the beginning of term, in fact. And if they were to be allies, they must share relevant information.

"I've just remembered something," she said. "Something else you should know." For the first time she told Nick about her feeling that someone had been in the house the weekend she had gone to the Islands. She reminded him of the rose jar and told him of the faint perfume she had smelled when she walked into the house. "I thought I must be imagining it," was the reason she gave him for not mentioning it at the time. "It seemed so unlikely, and I was so tired I could scarcely think. I am still almost certain I imagined it, but let us consider the possibility that someone did come into the house then. You weren't here; you spent a lot of that weekend in town. Who knew about that?"

"I don't think anybody did," he answered. "I was avoiding everyone so as to cover for you, remember?"

"But you did run into people—you told me when I asked what you'd been doing while I was gone. You even spent a night with friends. And there was that dinner at Lucia's Thursday night. By your account most everybody there was a member or prospective member of the study group. You could have mentioned to someone that you'd be in town Friday or Saturday."

"Kerri, I carefully told everyone that you were home laid up with influenza. I delivered your letter of apology to Lucia most publicly. They may have known I wasn't home, but they didn't know you weren't."

"Oh. I had forgotten about that. Well, if someone *was* here, it could just as well have been the Tuesday—we'd both have to be in town then. Everyone would know that. They could have seen Thomas and the material for the costumes and planned to come back later."

"Hmm." Nicholas leaned back in his chair and tapped the end of his pencil against his chin. "Tuesday again. We might look for someone on campus who has an opportunity to get out of town for several hours on Tuesdays."

Suddenly Kerri remembered she had told Loren that very morning where she lived. She had seen Loren again after Professor Harkness' lecture, but there was plenty of time in between for someone to go to Evesham, reconnoiter the house and return to campus, even with a morning recitation. The round trip could have been done in about three hours. And she had only Loren's word for it that she had actually attended the lecture. She had not actually seen her until afterward. Of all the people in her acquaintance, Loren, having known Professor Harkness at Dalton, would be the one best able to fake attendance at the lecture.

There had been no sign-in book. And there was no overlooking Nick's suggestion that more than one person could be involved. Loathsome as it was to entertain these suspicions, Kerri had too much experience to dismiss them out of hand, as miserable as they made her.

She said, "What a bother it is, not having any idea. If only we could narrow it down somehow. Let's ask the trolley men if they remember anyone, any strangers coming out on those days. If it would help," she offered, "I shall keep an eye on Miss Weberly."

"I wish you would," Nick said, "at least to clear her." He volunteered then to be especially observant of the study group people also. "It's only fair," he added. "And we might see if we can find out anything from the neighbors. One of them may have even seen something."

"I wish one of us could stay home on guard," Kerri said. "I won't be easy in my mind any time we're both away from the house."

"Neither will I. We can't, though. We have department daybooks to sign Wednesday and Thursday; we have lectures and seminars. We have to appear in our common rooms. You have recitation. But, Kerri, we shall find out who has done this," Nick promised. "They are going to regret it very much indeed."

The next morning, while Nick was bathing, Kerri did her new Veil ritual again. And as if the Veil really worked, there was no invasion on Wednesday, nor on Thursday. But by then, the attacker, like everyone else in Yendys, must be getting ready for the May Revel.

Chapter 26

The Ball

"Seventeen," declared the woman in spangled blue tulle. "Seventeen in the receiving line. Thirty-two altogether out of fifty invited."

"Fifty? Oh, nothing like fifty," the man behind her commented with a little deprecating cough. "The Regents never invite fewer than two hundred, although it is rare for even half that many to attend."

His wife (in cherry brocade) added reprovingly, "According to *our* information, there will be at least seventy appearing at some time in the evening and twenty in the receiving line." With white-gloved fingers she kindly picked an invisible piece of lint off Blue Tulle's shoulder.

Blue Tulle lifted an eyebrow and looked Cherry Brocade up and down. "The receiving line is one thing," she declared frostily. "*Dancing* with a Stockholder is quite another." She managed to suggest by her tone of voice that she had done this a great number of times, which, if true, would lend her a prestige with which it would be unwise to meddle. The Cherry Brocade couple retreated into silence.

Kerri glanced at Nick and saw him roll his eyes in mock despair. She had to bite her lip to keep from breaking into giggles. It would surprise her very much if the woman in blue tulle had ever danced with a Stockholder or if anyone riding the hotel omnibus was in a position to know how many Stockholders were invited to the ball.

The omnibus rumbled slowly over the pavement toward the gate of the Palace of the Arts. It was a showy vehicle, leather, oak and polished brass, all hung about with garlands of greenery and glowing lanterns, but it was damnably slow. The coachman was no doubt paid by the hour! They almost could have gone on foot and got there sooner. Kerri vowed they would walk back to the hotel, unless it happened to be outright raining. She would never tolerate hearing the evening dissected verbally by these deadly boring people, some of whom were still arguing about how many Stockholders would be in the receiving line, the consensus being somewhere between twelve and twenty.

Twenty Stockholders in the receiving line, along with all the Regents, the Vice Chancellor, a quantity of Deans and assorted other important personages!

She hoped fervently the number was exaggerated. Otherwise, she and Nick would never get to dance.

As first-timers they had no choice; they *must* be formally introduced in the Reception Hall by Nick's Sponsor. Next time they would be allowed simply to be announced by the herald. No, they wouldn't, bother and damnation! Next time, *she* would have a Sponsor, and they'd have to be presented all over again by Professor Bonneville-Chatterton's proxy. *If* they got invited next time, which would be the Solstice Ball, less than two months away.

It's the first two curtsies that are the most risky, she reminded herself. *Get the footing and the weight distribution right on the first two, and then I'll find a rhythm to carry me through the rest. If I manage it correctly, I should be able to come up without grabbing a handful of skirt. I must resist the temptation to do so—what an awful gaffe! At least, only Stockholders get curtsies—Dreamer be thanked! The rest will get that silly pretend handshake and maybe a bow or demi-bow. Take the cue from Nick's Sponsor and Nick, because I'll never hope to hear the introductions from behind them. Bother, I wish it were over!*

"I could do with a beer," Nick muttered next to her ear.

"Me for champagne," she whispered back. "As soon as we get ourselves free."

In spite of the funereal pace of its horses, the omnibus arrived at the Palace in good time. The building (a museum on ordinary days) was ablaze with electrical lights. Tiny bulbs by the thousands outlined the doors and windows and clustered twinkling in the trees. Ranks of burning torches lined the walkway and the broad steps. It was an enchanting sight.

Nick and Kerri joined the crowd thronging up to the door, trying to hurry without appearing to be in haste. Nick's Sponsor, Professor Thornwood-Bly, and her husband, a distinguished physician, caught them just inside the entrance hall and bore them off to the lengthening line of people awaiting presentation, sending a footmen off with their cloaks.

The Professor inspected them with an experienced eye. "You will do very well," she said approvingly. "Very well, indeed! Most impressive for your first presentation."

"I quite agree," said Dr. Bly-Thornwood. "Very beautiful. Did you make these costumes?"

"For this occasion we are endowed with family treasures," Nick said. "The costumes were created by my wife's grandmother, Professor Stewart-Dale of the Faculty of Honowell. They were also worn by her father, Professor Dale-Nash of the same Faculty, and her mother."

"Ah!" exclaimed Professor Thornwood-Bly, beaming at Kerri. "That is excellent! Of course, I was confident you would do us and yourselves credit, my dear young people."

Kerri smiled gratefully at Nick. His deft reminder of the respectability of her lineage would firmly establish her social equality to the senior couple. Not that the Professor was much of a stickler, she was more the type to simply overlook people unless they were specifically pointed out to her as worthy of notice. Now Kerri would not be left out of conversation as they waited their turn.

As the line progressed, Kerri had her first real opportunity to look around her. The decorations were magnificent. Most of the artworks had been moved into storage for the occasion and the walls hung with great wreaths and swags of flowers and greenery, in which were nestled thousands of the tiny twinkling electric lights like those decorating the exterior. Where the decorators had contrived to procure such a quantity of lights Kerri could not imagine. She supposed the electricity must have been wired into the Palace in the Age of Dreams. The chandeliers and other lamps were all the usual gaslight, although there were banks of candles here and there.

She also studied the costumes. Professor Thornwood-Bly was right about her and Nick doing themselves credit. Until that moment Kerri had not fully appreciated the magnitude of Aryel's gift. Everyone in sight was dressed appropriately, but few costumes were as well-designed or beautifully crafted as hers and Nick's. The students tended to be a little too gaudy and cheap, the Faculty respectable and unremarkable, if not downright dowdy. This shocked her. She had always known her grandmother was talented in this respect, as in so many others, but she had never realized that such excellence was not a common thing, even among the revered Faculty. She saw people looking at her and Nicholas, sidelong covert glances, assessing, envious. Their attention did not ease her nervousness.

To their collective relief, the wait was not so long as they had feared. The line moved quickly. The Professor barely had time to brief them (unnecessarily) on the protocol, before they found themselves at the entrance of the reception hall. Then Kerri heard their names announced and found herself being presented to the Dean of the College of Natural History, the honorary chairman of the occasion.

A name, a handshake, a bow. A name, a handshake, a bow, a smile. It was going well. They were making a good impression, she thought; they were receiving compliments on their costumes. She risked a glance up the line toward the more glittering end. There were Stockholders indeed; looked to be dozens of them. A smile, a name, a nod, a handshake. More bows. And here was the first Stockholder, an upright elderly man in a coat heavily embroidered with silver and what looked like sapphires. *Where are my feet? Sink gracefully to the floor (without touching the skirt). Rise up again (hands off the skirt!). It worked, thank the Dreamer! Step back with another little bow, weight on the other foot, turn, two small steps along the line. Another Stockholder—are they all*

elderly men? (Descend, rise, hands off the skirt. It's like a dance, really.)
No, the next few are women, looking like dowager empresses. Good heavens,
look at all those opals!

As her deportment teachers had promised, Kerri found her rhythm. And
of course, she and Nick had rehearsed as often as they could, but she had never
been confident she would be able to carry it off on the night, and it was years since
she had been presented to so many people of so many different ranks. Now,
everything was going perfectly, and they were nearing the end of the line where
the Stockholders were younger, though no less dazzling. Here was one, third
from the last, who could not be over thirty, an extremely fine-looking fair-haired
young man in the exact opalescent blue brocade Kerri and Nick were wearing.
It was even trimmed with black velvet and white lace like theirs, but the design
recalled a slightly earlier period of the Age of Dreams. *His* diamonds, Kerri was
certain, were real.

Charming he was, too. Instead of the usual glazed-eyed polite murmur of
acknowledgment, he looked Kerri straight in the eyes and smiled. "I am delighted
to meet you," he said, not loudly, but as if he meant it. His glance brushed over
her as if to point out the extraordinary similarity of their dress. "Clearly it was
meant to happen."

She was so astonished she nearly lost her balance. Only the rhythm and the
practice saved her from tripping as she rose from the curtsy. "The pleasure is
mine, your Excellency," she gasped, seeing his smile deepen to a grin. Her face
felt so warm, she knew she must be blushing. She thought he winked at her, but
then she was away to the next introduction. *I shall have to tell Grandmother,*
she was thinking confusedly.

"Your Excellency, I beg to present Master Nicholas Andrade Townsend-Dale
of the College of History and Mistress Kerrith Nash Dale-Townsend of the College
of Classic Literature. Her Excellency, Margarethe Girrawang Fairchild."

A memory trickled into Kerri's mind: Central Station, the day she met Loren,
the day she got the letters from home that changed her life, the day the invitation
came for this Ball. A tall Stockholder in black, surrounded by entourage, striding
through the echoing crowded chamber. Margarethe Girrawang Fairchild.

She wore black again, some unusual matte fabric, fluid and clinging, elegantly
draped into a slim pillar of a gown reminiscent of Age of Dreams fashions of
the Nineteens, both daring and distinctive. Masses of diamonds, of course, and
long black gloves. Her dark hair was swept smoothly back and piled into a high
intricate knot. In keeping with her Age of Dreams style, her eyes were heavily
painted, but they glinted with amusement as Kerri and Nick made their bow
and curtsy.

As Kerri rose, the Stockholder Fairchild leaned forward and said in a low voice, "Take care. The tigers are on the hunt tonight."

Profoundly startled, Kerri raised her eyes and met ironic grey ones. Nick, who had apparently heard nothing, was already turning away to follow his Sponsor.

Her Excellency laid a gentle hand on Kerri's wrist. "Don't be frightened," she muttered. "You'll knock them dead!" With a minute jerk of her chin she sent Kerri, speechless with surprise, off to catch up with Nick.

The last presentation over—Kerri never did remember it—they found themselves at last in the ballroom, a vast chamber normally housing large sculptures (removed for the occasion). Professor Thornwood-Bly and Dr. Bly-Thornwood were most pleased with the performance of their protegees and said so. Nicholas expressed his hope that the Professor would honor him with a dance later in the evening; the doctor gallantly asked the same of Kerri. They settled on the second dance and penciled in their names on each others' cards. Then the elder couple politely excused themselves, and Kerri and Nick, liberated at last, snagged champagne from the tray of a passing waiter and went in search of a place to sit down.

"That tall woman in black near the end," Nick said when they had collapsed (gracefully) onto an out-of-the way-bench. "The Stockholder—Oh, I cannot remember the name. Did you hear what she said to me?"

"She spoke to you?" Kerri stared at him. Had Nick caught that strange comment after all? And she, herself, was she finally going completely mad? Of course not. It was a trick of her imagination, nothing more.

"Yes. She said, 'Hold fast. They do not take prisoners, you know.' What do you make of that?"

"*Who* do not take prisoners?"

"I have not the slightest idea. I nearly tripped over my feet, I was so shocked. But she smiled in the most pleasant way. I mean, I did not get the impression she was making fun of me or anything like that. It was more like an odd pleasantry than a warning."

Kerri thought for a moment. Taking prisoners did not sound much like hunting tigers. It might be this Stockholder made enigmatic pronouncements to every raw, unsuspecting graduate student who came through the line. This Stockholder. "It sounds like a quotation," she said. "I have read that some Stockholders affect little personal idiosyncrasies and fads. Perhaps it was something like that."

"Possibly." Nick nodded. "What did she say to you?"

"To me?" Kerri felt her face reddening. "She told me not to be frightened. She said, 'You will knock them dead.' She meant I would impress people."

"She meant the costumes, most likely," said Nick, satisfied with this conclusion. "I have heard the expression. Age of Dreams slang. Stockholders are very strange."

"Yes, they are," Kerri agreed. *I must have imagined it*, she said to herself. *It is quite impossible. Tigers?*

Suddenly Nick straightened and peered through the crowd. "Look! There is Professor Hayley-Garcia. I must pay my respects and see if his wife will give me a dance. And I see Jillian and Peter and the others! Give me your glass. It is time to start filling in our dance cards."

He placed their empty champagne glasses on a nearby table and helped Kerri to her feet. Hand in hand, they left the alcove and set off across the vast floor. She felt suddenly shy. This was her first venture as an adult into the society she had been groomed for since birth, and it seemed to her as if her newness and inexperience must show on her like some peculiar adjunct to her costume. But other than a few sidelong envious glances at their dress, she and Nick seemed to attract no untoward attention—and, of course, there was no reason why they should. They belonged here as much as anyone. *I belong*, Kerri reminded herself. *No one knows yet, but I am here as much by my own right as I am as Nick's wife.*

She had no idea of the time. They had left the hotel at half past six. Long as it had seemed, the ride to the Palace must not have taken much above half an hour. They had been among the earlier arrivals, say, soon after seven o'clock. Another forty minutes meeting the Professor and his wife and waiting in line, ten minutes being presented, another ten recovering. Make it a quarter past eight. The dancing would not begin until half past nine, which left them about an hour to get partners organized.

She had been a little worried about that. These formal faculty affairs subscribed to an ancient tradition, Dreamer knew why, that the men did the inviting of dance partners, except for Stockholders, who did their own asking. This left the ladies rather helpless, in theory.

Among the students, however, things usually fell into place more casually, friends trading off cards until they were all full—always with the understanding that any such arrangements could be superseded by ranking Faculty or, rarely, Stockholders. But Kerri, still without confidence of her welcome among Nick's friends and lacking allies in her own department, worried that she might find herself sitting out partnerless more than once. This was not supposed to be any disgrace, but it certainly wasn't a mark of success.

Therefore, she felt reassured when, half an hour later, her dance card was filled. She had seven dances with Nick (some of which could be traded off if necessary), four with various Faculty or their spouses, including her auditor, Professor Graystone. The remainder were parceled out among graduate students, mostly from among Nick's colleagues, with a few, rather surprisingly, from her own college. From here on, she could relax and expect to enjoy the evening.

Her equanimity did not last long. Across the crowded floor she caught sight of a familiar profile, and her heart sank. Yes, of course. Why should he not be here? How had she ever expected to come to the Faculty Revel of May Eve and not run into Val?

Chapter 27

Change Partners

He was wearing a skirted coat of terracotta velvet, heavily appliqued with gold braid and sequins. The hue did not flatter him, although it was extraordinarily becoming to Arzelle's dark coloring. Her gown, of the same terracotta velvet, was a near imitation of a very famous and widely copied Age of Dreams garment (originally manufactured, according to legend, of window curtains), more usually seen in dark green. It was ornamented with cock feathers and cascading gold cords and tassels, the skirt spread over wide and inconvenient hoops. Not, on the whole, a felicitous choice for either of them, Kerri decided.

The pair of them were deep in conversation with an older man in brown satin, a colorless, unassuming individual, the sight of whom chilled Kerri to the bone. What was it Grandmother had said? "The only person in the world who could talk Charles out of Sponsoring you." Professor Edson of Honowell. Well, there was this to be said for his presence: If he was here in Yendys for the May Day holiday, he was not in Honowell talking anybody out of anything. And with any luck at all, he could be avoided this evening, and so could Val and Arzelle.

With that in mind, she shifted her position in order to put people between Val and herself and turned her back to make herself less noticeable. For good measure, she renewed the Veil, although there could be no need yet; she had last done it only a few minutes before. Unfortunately, she and Nick were involved in conversation with several acquaintances and there was no polite way for her to draw him off quickly to a safe distance. And then it was too late.

"How delightful it is to see all of you here!" caroled an exquisitely modulated voice behind Kerri. "My dear!" Arzelle was kissing cheeks with one, shaking hands with another, Val grinning in her wake. "Why, Kerri, darling! How wonderful to see you here at long last! Look, Val, here is our Kerri."

Kerri found herself seized by Arzelle, enveloped in a cloud of heavy exotic scent, felt the air next to her cheek kissed as Val said, "This is an unexpected pleasure, indeed. How are you, Kerri?"

At long last! Kerri fumed to herself. *An unexpected pleasure, indeed!* "Quite well, thank you, Val," she replied, sounding rather feeble in her own ears. *Disaster,* she thought: *Val and Nick.* She gathered herself together. "Good evening, Arzelle. I do not believe either of you have met my husband...."

"Oh, Mr. Townsend-Dale and I are great friends," cooed Arzelle, bestowing her hand upon him in such a way as to invite him to kiss it. "Are we not, sir?"

Nick took her hand but merely bowed over it. "Yes, we have met. It is a pleasure to see you again, Miss James-Dietrich. Good evening, Mr. Dietrich-James." Kerri was disturbed to witness that he was blushing.

To her infinite relief, Arzelle then proceeded, with ebullient affection, to greet the other students present, most of whom seemed to be acquainted with her, including Jillian and Peter, who looked about to faint with awe.

"Nicholas," Kerri said in a low voice near his ear, "I did not know you had met Val. You never told me. Or Arzelle, either."

"It was not an event of much consequence," he whispered back. "I shall tell you about it later, if you like."

If she hoped to get away at that point, Kerri was disappointed again, for all too soon Arzelle turned her attention back to them, exclaiming joyfully that she was certain Val and Kerri had a great deal to catch up on, and it would be the least she and Nick could do to permit them to have a dance together to do so. And she simply longed to have a chat with Nick; she and he *always* had *so* much to talk about. Yes, of course, she knew their cards must be booked up—*hers* was, naturally, from the minute she walked in the door—but surely there was one they could trade off. Gaily, she plucked Nick's card out of his hand and scanned it.

Before Kerri knew what had happened, it was all arranged. The fourth dance, the one before the first intermission, she would dance with Val and Arzelle with Nick. There was nothing to be done about it except to agree with grace, but she felt disheartened. She had particularly counted on that dance as a kind of safe harbor early in the evening, when the two of them could compare notes and take stock of how things were going, bear each other up. Now she might be stuck with Val through the intermission and not see Nick again until the seventh dance, three-quarters of an hour later.

Worse, she was feeling altogether alarmed by Arzelle's implied claim to friendship with Nick. Arzelle leaned on his arm, gazed warmly into his eyes—she positively glowed for him. It did not look like "a matter of little consequence"; it brought back bad memories. On the other hand, Val did not appear at all bothered by it. No doubt he realized, as should Kerri—as she hoped Nick did, that Arzelle was simply being Arzelle. And Val did seem sincerely delighted to see Kerri again, no hard feelings (if he was entitled to any). Perhaps, if they just behaved themselves, it could be got through with civility and no damage done.

Fortunately, at that moment the orchestra began the overture that signaled the beginning of the dance. Groups broke up, and couples gathered around the margins of the ballroom ready to join in the Grand Promenade, led by all the important persons from the receiving line and a number of others. As lower ranking students, people like Nick and Kerri only watched the parade and then found places for the first dance, a waltz.

"I hope you do not mind my dancing with Val," Kerri began hesitantly, when they were waltzing and there was opportunity for halfway private talk.

"I am not exactly enchanted by the prospect," Nick replied, to her satisfaction, "but I really did not see any way out of it, did you?"

Kerri shook her head.

"And of course, I must dance with Miss James-Dietrich," he continued. "She has a lot of influence, and she is charming as well. I do not like to subject you to this awkwardness, but I know you will handle it splendidly."

"Thank you," said Kerri. "You need have no fears on that score. But, Nick, I am surprised that you have not mentioned knowing them. You know what they were in my life. I do not like to think you have been concealing this acquaintance on that account."

He looked embarrassed. "I was not concealing it. It was simply not important enough that I remembered to mention it, although I certainly would have eventually." He sighed. "I met Miss James-Dietrich last spring when the study group began to scout me seriously. It was just an introduction at a large gathering, of no moment. I forgot about it completely, and in fact I did not remember her connection to you at the time. Since then I have run into her from time to time at group functions. Her husband was present once quite recently, and she introduced us."

Kerri frowned. "She is in your study group?"

Again, his face colored. "No. She is a member of another one, in her own college, but there are a lot of doings back and forth between groups, as you know. She seems to be on very close terms with a number of the people in my group." He looked closely at her face. "Please, Kerri, I know you dislike it. I understand, completely. I do not greatly like it, myself. But there is nothing to be done about it. She possesses a great deal of influence, and I need her good will. We must make the best of things like this."

"I know," Kerri said unhappily. He was right, but she had the feeling he was not being completely frank with her about the situation. It was hard to believe, for instance, that he had found the whole thing as forgettable and unimportant as he claimed. On the other hand, people in study groups liked to affect a loftily secretive manner when it came to group business. Maybe Nick was not yet sure what things he could tell Kerri and what he could not. Certainly, he had been somewhat evasive about the study group matter, although she had been worried off and on that he was using the whole thing as a cover for something else. She recollected suddenly her suspicions about Jillian, or that other woman, Miss Lewis. She had not thought about that in days, not since before the incident of Tuesday.

The bits and pieces came together into a cold certainty, glittering with logic. It was Arzelle. Arzelle was the one. *Nick and Arzelle.*

She wanted to cry out her fear to him then and there, her suspicions, accusations, beg him to reassure her that there was no truth in any of it. But she was frozen, dumb, going through the movements of the waltz, while Nick chatted on about some trifling bit of gossip they had heard earlier. The roaring in her ears was so loud, she could hear neither him nor the music. The air seemed to blacken around her.

"Kerri, are you all right?" He had noticed.

"Perfectly," she gasped, and the world miraculously righted itself. "It must be the corset. I am not accustomed to dancing in it. I feel a bit out of breath."

"Would you like to rest?"

"For a moment, if you do not mind."

They danced their way off the floor and strolled into the hall beyond. Kerri declared she was feeling much better. She had had time to get a grip on herself. Arzelle being Arzelle did not mean that Nick was being Val. If Arzelle was trying to play that sort of game with Nick, it must be putting him in a very delicate position, especially if, as he said, he needed her good will. What he needed from Kerri was her love and trust and no silly hysterics. Very well. Nick had won her love and earned her trust. But she did not have to trust Arzelle one inch!

By the time they found Professor Thornwood-Bly and her husband for the second dance, Kerri had recovered her equilibrium and was able to be a pleasant companion to the doctor, who turned out to be a delightful partner. Then she had her dance with her auditor, Professor Greystone, who was less fun (and not nearly so fine a dancer) but perfectly courteous. She had hoped to find Nick afterward, hoped the two of them would be able to seek out Val and Arzelle together, but Val approached her as she was taking leave of Professor Greystone. He told her he had left Arzelle with Nick—they were somewhere about—and asked if she would like any refreshments. She declined and exerted herself to find pleasant and innocuous things to talk about until the music began again.

It was one of those slow, mannered dances which allow plenty of opportunity for conversation, the figures being simple and little exchange of partners taking place. Kerri wondered what she and Val would be able to talk about for the ten minutes of the music. They had already exhausted the weather, the Revel decorations, and each others' costumes. She would not stoop to gossip about personalities. In desperation, she asked him about the progress of his studies, certain that he would be happy to expound at length on the fascinating subject of himself. All she would have to do would be to look interested, make appropriate noises of appreciation and ask leading questions when he appeared to be running out of momentum.

Unfortunately, this tactic turned out to be less than successful. He seized upon her gambit as if it were an opening he had been waiting for, but instead of taking advantage of the invitation to talk about himself he immediately turned the subject around to Kerri and her belated entry into graduate study.

"I hear," said Val pleasantly as they stepped around each other, "that you have been having some trouble getting your work in on time."

Kerri laughed merrily. "Nonsense! Where can you have heard such a thing?"

The figure of the dance separated them briefly. Torn between anger and relief, Kerri thought, *Stupid, stupid man! You could not resist, could you? And now I know!* They came back together and joined hands for the next figure.

"My source is unimpeachable," he assured her with a smile.

"Your source is misinformed." She chuckled. "Or pulling your leg. Or both. I am surprised you do not know better than to trust these gossips—who are only making mischief for you: Depend upon it. I have had no trouble this term, nor do I expect to have."

They circled again. Val echoed her laugh, softly. "It is early yet," he commented. "You will no doubt find the work more than you bargained for as the term goes on."

Is he warning me? she wondered. *Doesn't he care if I figure out what he is hinting at? What a fool!* "Ah, Val! You always did expect other people's experiences to validate yours in a given situation—how well I remember! Not all of us find graduate study burdensome, I assure you."

"Who finds it burdensome? Not I!" Val's expression of pleasant attentiveness had acquired a hardness about the mouth that she remembered well. "But I am surprised *you* have put yourself to the trouble. You have all the entree you could ever hope for."

His double insinuation—that she had married Nick for his position and that she had no other hope of Faculty status, being unSponsored—made her want to slap him, but she merely batted her eyelashes at him. Here was one nose she would relish rubbing in it when Sponsors were announced in a month's time. The thought improved her humor immeasurably.

"There you are!" she exclaimed. "You are doing it again. Exactly what I was talking about!"

It took him a minute to unravel that one. She saw his jaw clench with anger and wondered if she had gone too far. Then his face smoothed into amiable amusement. He did, after all, have a Sponsor and was thus nominally on the same footing as Arzelle, in spite of her more dazzling reputation. "You are making no sense at all, my dear," he informed her. "I was used to your vagaries once. No longer, I am afraid."

Again the dance parted them as they moved through the next figure. Kerri smiled graciously at the gentleman who nearly stepped on her foot. She bestowed a nod on an acquaintance in the next set whose eye she happened to meet. Nick and Arzelle were nowhere in sight, but the room was very large. She tried not to look about for them too obviously, but she felt more anxious than ever. Another turn and she was again hand-joined to Val, who looked in perfect good humor.

He said, "I want you to know that I do admire you for making the attempt to continue your studies. It must comfort you to know that no one will think the worse of you if you withdraw at the end of the year. Or even the end of term, if things prove too difficult."

You beast! Kerri thought. Her increasing anxiety about the whereabouts of Nick and Arzelle left her no room for patience. She felt a hair away from losing her temper publicly. Val obviously did not care a whit if she understood that he was involved in the campaign of sabotage against her; he knew she had no proof, and he was confident there was nothing she could do to stop it. Otherwise he would never have been so stupid as to give himself away in such a crude fashion. The ego of the man! He couldn't bear to have her suffer in ignorance. He wanted her to know who was making her life miserable.

She adopted a slightly puzzled and distracted look. "Forgive me, Val. I was not attending. You were saying?"

"Oh, nothing of consequence. Are you trying to catch sight of our spouses?" He was, for a fool, all too perceptive. "It is very likely they are sitting out the dance. My wife was feeling a touch of fatigue."

"Is she?" she asked him, wide-eyed. "Poor thing. Never had much stamina. No, I was merely wondering if there is any substance to some talk going around during the reception." In response to his inquiring look, she continued. "It was speculation that the name of the new Chancellor would be announced tonight."

"Ah!" He lifted his chin wisely, a man in the know. "There is nothing to it. Much too early. The committee have met only once."

"That is what I understood," Kerri said, nodding. "It seemed impossibly premature, the poor man gone hardly more than a month. The memorial convocation was beautifully moving. It is a pity you were not able to be there." She managed a look of sad sympathy.

"Of course I was there!" He had not been able to conceal the flash of alarm in his eyes. "It was indeed a fine and moving remembrance. You may not have seen me, but my signature is in the book."

"That," said Kerri mildly, "would be quite a feat, considering the other places your signature was recorded that day. However, *I* will say no more about it, if *you* will put a stop to this ridiculous nonsense you have, ah, heard about me."

She had the pleasure of seeing all the color leave his face. He lost track of the dance utterly and stood staring at her. The lady on his other side, finding him out of step, gave him a prompting nudge. Kerri took the hand of the man on her right and crossed the set to the change. By the time she returned to Val, his face was dark with rage. He opened his mouth as if to say something, then abruptly turned and walked away off the dance floor, leaving her stranded partnerless and the set one gentleman short.

"How charitable of your friend to grant me my heart's desire." The voice at her side spoke even as a gloved hand took hers and guided her smoothly into the turn. The dance continued with scarcely a break. The other people in the set, who had barely begun to notice something had gone amiss, realized all was well and, with a few covert looks at the gentleman at Kerri's side, returned to minding their own business.

Too stunned to speak, Kerri recognized her rescuer. He was the fair-haired Stockholder in seashell brocade, the one she had met in the receiving line, whose costume so inexplicably matched hers and Nick's. Knowing her face to be crimson, she managed to complete the figure without fainting or otherwise disgracing herself, finally daring to say, when they got to the promenade, "Your Excellency, I am honored."

"And I," he said with a grin, "am damned lucky."

Chapter 28

Enter a Hero

"Lucky, your Excellency?" Kerri said, trying to return his smile. Her thoughts were racing madly in at least three directions. *Val abandoned me on the dance floor—such a scandal!*

How embarrassing! People will think—but no, they won't, because I am dancing with a Stockholder! However did that happen? My, he is gorgeous! All gold-colored and sort of shining, and those eyes...! But where has Val gone? What have I done? I should never have provoked him. He looked angry enough to do anything. And Nick's off somewhere with Arzelle. I've got to find him. No, let him find me. I am dancing with a Stockholder.

"Yes. Not only have I the opportunity to dance with a lovely lady, I may have also found a clue to a longstanding mystery in my family." His dancing was faultless. His manner, while not overly familiar, was relaxed and friendly, calculated to put her at ease.

"A mystery, your Excellency?" Kerri was intrigued in spite of her confusion, as well as ridden by a new anxiety: she did not remember her new partner's name. Frantically she began to dig through her memories of the reception, hoping that he would say something to jar the proper association out into the open.

"A trifling one," he said, "but a longish tale. Perhaps you would allow me to tell you in the intermission."

"It would be a pleasure, your Excellency," she said with complete sincerity, tossing Val and the others mentally to the winds—at least for the moment.

She turned away to circle the gentleman on her other side and then followed into the ladies' star in the center. This was the last figure. There was no sign of Val, nor of Nick, nor Arzelle, although she saw half a dozen people she knew looking at her and her partner with astonishment. And she still did not remember the Stockholder's name.

The music ended. She sank into her deepest curtsy, imitated nervously by all the other women in the set. Then the blond Stockholder offered his arm and led her off into the lofty entrance hall, where there was slightly less crowding and more air. *He's not as tall as I thought*, she noticed dazedly, *no taller than Nick anyway.*

"These receptions are such a whirlwind," he said with a grin. "I hope you will forgive me, but I do not remember your name. I am Andrew Kianga Ryan."

Kerri turned to him with a relieved, and for the first time completely genuine, smile. "I am Kerrith Nash Dale-Townsend, your Excellency," she said. "And I am most grateful for the rescue."

As if in appreciation of her double meaning, his grin widened. "Who is the ill-mannered gentleman?" inquired Master Kianga Ryan. "Is he a friend of yours?"

"Not a friend," Kerri replied, "although we have known each other from childhood." He raised an eyebrow.

"Ah, an old quarrel?"

"Exactly so, your Excellency." *He's older than I thought,* she said to herself. *No, he isn't. He's younger. It's his eyes, so wise, as if he's seen a thousand years, lines at the corners, he's been in the sun a great deal, and his face is tanned. But he can't be more than a year or two older than I, if that.*

"His loss is my good fortune, then," he commented with a smile. "Let us sit here. Champagne?"

They seated themselves upon a wide sofa next to the wall, and a waiter, responding to a signal Kerri had not seen, hurried to them with wine. Aware that champagne was the last thing she needed in her dazzled state, Kerri accepted the glass with murmured thanks.

"Now I shall tell you about the mystery," said her companion.

"Yes, please," said Kerri. "I am much intrigued, sir."

He leaned back and settled himself against the cushions, preparing to enjoy the telling of his tale. "Long ago," he began, "When my father was a young man, he had a close friendship with a woman who was slightly older than himself. She made for him this costume I am wearing. They both said it was the forfeit of a wager between them that she had lost, but naturally there were rumors that it was a token of another kind. She made a matching outfit for herself, and accompanied him to a ball rather like this one, where it is said they made a very pretty couple.

"There was a great deal of speculation about the two of them, not all of it kind—many of his friends and hers did not approve of the relationship, and people can be rather cruel. In the end she married another man and went to live far away. My father put up a good front, but those who knew him best believed him heartbroken. It is certainly true that he remained single for many years. He never spoke of her and he never wore this costume again.

"Later, my mother, who cared little about these old rumors, decided such excellent workmanship should not go to waste and desired a matching gown to be made for it so that she and my father could make good use of the pair. She went to every cloth merchant, every tailor, every dressmaker in this city and several others, but there was no more of the brocade to be found. One merchant remembered seeing the stuff before, and he said only the one bolt was ever imported. He had made a very high offer for it, but it had gone to a daughter of the Sea People who had taken a fancy to it. How it got into the hands of my father's friend—that was the mystery. Or if it was not the same, how did she come by it and what became of the rest of it?

"My mother made a few more inquiries, but there was no trace of the cloth. She is not a woman who enjoys being thwarted, and so when the costume came to me, she told me always to be watchful for the brocade or for the one gown known to have been made from it. And now, you see, I have found it." He smiled triumphantly.

An astonishingly lucky guess or the truth? Kerri wondered mildly if he had made up the whole thing for the sake of conversation, although it seemed far fetched and silly to suppose such an awesome individual should desire to prolong this interlude with her insignificant self. However, it would be an experience worth remembering, so she was willing to play along for the moment, especially as Nick was nowhere in sight. Various people who knew her passed by from time to time, trying not to stare. She saw them stealing envious glances at her and whispering to each other. This was gratifying.

"A most interesting story, your Excellency" she said. "I wish I could be of help, but I am afraid I can shed no light on your mystery. This costume and my husband's have been in my family for several generations. They were made by my grandmother, who lives in the Islands. Perhaps there was more of the brocade after all."

"Perhaps." He lightly touched the lace that billowed from her sleeve. "But do you not think it odd that not only the brocade but the lace should be the same? And both are trimmed with black velvet."

"I am certain it is a coincidence," she told him, wondering in the back of her mind why she should feel it all the way up her arm when he had only touched her lace with a fingertip. "And, you see, the historical referents are not the same at all. My costume is of a much later period."

"So it is," he agreed with a sigh. "Although costumes have been remade before, especially ladies' gowns."

"May I ask if you know the name of your father's friend?" Kerri inquired.

"I was not told," he said, "but I believe her given name may have been Miranda. When he gave me the costume, my father made a cryptic reference to himself as Caliban. It was my impression that he was remembering his friend and reliving his sadness about losing her. That is all I have to go on."

"Oh," said Kerri faintly. "Shakespeare's *Tempest*. I see." Which she did. It occurred to her that it was probably not her place to enlighten him with any of her speculations. The best thing to do would be to change the subject. She decided she had had more than enough champagne.

"Andrew! Here you are! I have been looking for you." A slight, dark, elegant young man in ruby velvet approached them. Kerri saw at once that he was a Stockholder, although she was certain he had not been among those at the reception.

"Marius! Well met, my friend! I should like to present Miss Kerrith Nash Dale-Townsend. Miss Dale-Townsend, this is Marius Warralonga Campbell, a very old friend of mine."

Immediately Kerri got to her feet and executed a deep curtsy. "Your Excellency."

"I am pleased to meet you, Miss Dale-Townsend." He bowed, smiling radiantly. "All of Andrew's friends are going mad wondering who his exquisite partner is and how the two of you contrived the matching costumes. Please, please sit down again."

Kerri did, blushing, while her companion laughed heartily. "We had come to conclusion that it is a coincidence," Master Kianga Ryan said. "A most happy one, though. Marius, have you spoken to Margarethe?"

"I have just come from her, and I have my orders. I stand ready if needed, which duty will prove a pleasure, I am certain."

"Excellent!" exclaimed Master Kianga Ryan. "And you have my personal assurance that it will so prove." He grinned at Kerri.

Kerri, feeling entirely lost in this conversation, said, "Your Excellency, I ought to return to the ballroom. My next partner will be looking for me." People were beginning to drift back toward the ballroom.

Master Warralonga Campbell smote his forehead in mock anguish. "Alas! I knew it was too much to hope that such a lovely creature would free for the next dance. Perhaps he will not find you, Miss Dale-Townsend, and then you would do me the honor."

"The honor would be mine, Sir," Kerri replied, feeling terribly out of her depth. As a Stockholder, Master Warralonga Campbell could claim precedence over her student partner (some acquaintance of Nick's), but she was bound in courtesy to make contact with the latter so he could formally yield the dance. And she was uncertain whether or not Master Warralonga Campbell was really asking her to dance or just being gallant. She had been taught what to do under these unlikely circumstances, but theory, she found, had not truly prepared her for the practice.

A few moments later she found herself re-entering the ballroom arm in arm with *two* Stockholders, and when her student partner did not present himself—perhaps he felt too shy to approach her in such company?—she was led into the round dance by Master Warralonga Campbell, who proved to be every bit as charming as his friend, although (she decided secretly) nowhere near as interesting, nor as blazingly good looking. As the circle dance came to an end, Master Warralonga Campbell presented her to yet another of his Stockholder friends, who whirled her into the waltz when her *next* student partner failed to materialize.

After that she was to dance the schottische with a professor of Nick's, who, to her relief, did turn up in good time, allowing her an interval in which to come back down to earth. (It did strike her as odd that she should find it a relief to dance with a member of the Faculty.) The gentleman was kindly and courteous but had little to say, being one of those people who can both dance and converse, but not at the same time. This suited Kerri quite well, because she felt far too distracted to make polite conversation.

It was very odd that two partners in a row had stood her up. She did not know either of them well, but if they were here, they were people who ought to know better. One such incident could be easily understood as an oversight, an accident, a case of shyness, but *two*...! It was provoking and worrisome, and there was still no sign of Nick. She was beginning to feel anxious, for the next dance was to be theirs, and it was over an hour since she had seen him. On the other hand, she had met and danced with *three* Stockholders, one after the other, which was three more than most ladies of her caste were likely to meet at any ball in their lives. In the glow of such a success, she could easily sit out for a while if Nick did not turn up, and no one would think the less of her. She watched the passing dancers for a glimpse of paua shell blue brocade, until she realized with a guilty start that it was not Nick her eyes were seeking.

At the end of the schottische, Professor Hayden escorted her to a chair, chatted politely for the regulation five minutes and then excused himself to go find his next partner. He had scarcely turned his back when she was pounced upon by three women she knew, including Jillian Munro-Hanes, eager to pump out of her every detail of her Stockholder adventures. But here at last—Dreamer be thanked!—was Nicholas, who whisked her away to the other side of the room before she had to think of what to say.

"Where have you been?" Kerri exclaimed. "What has happened? You look absolutely harrowed! Are you all right?"

"It is Miss James-Dietrich," he told her. "Not only did she keep me by her the whole of the last intermission, but she somehow arranged to trade off dances with people so that I ended up with her again for Number Five. I only got away for Six because I had to go to Professor Paley-Norton's wife. Then she arranged to snag me again for Number Seven. It was all I could do to get away from her in time to find you. She seemed to think you would not mind being stood up. I am afraid I had to be rather abrupt."

"Indeed," said Kerri, feeling the glow of her triumph beginning to seep away at this news. "Well, I should not let her do it again, if I were you, or people will talk." It was bad enough for Arzelle to monopolize Nick so blatantly, but she almost resented more that hearing about it should steal from her the exalted state she had been in. "I was stood up twice," she told him tartly.

"What?" He seemed to focus on her for the first time. "When? Tonight? By whom?"

She showed him her dance card. "Numbers Five and Six. Fortunately, I was not left abandoned. I met several gentlemen who were more than happy to take up the slack."

"Oh." He frowned at the names on her card. "I am glad you were not left on the wall. How very peculiar, though. I think I had better have a word with these two fellows."

"Oh, Nick!" she sighed wearily. "What would be the good of it? Never mind. We had better find a set, or would you prefer to sit out now?" The music was beginning.

"Yes, I could use a rest. Let us get out of the ballroom anyway. It is frightfully hot. I would prefer that we not encounter Miss James-Dietrich for awhile."

"Well, put on your smiling face," Kerri said as they emerged into the hall. "Here she comes!"

Nick groaned when he saw Arzelle hurrying toward them across the marble floor, her hoops swaying like a bell.

"Oh, Mr. Townsend-Dale," she cried, "I do need your help! Kerri, do be a lamb and let me borrow him for a few minutes. Val is missing, and we cannot find him."

"Calm down, Arzelle," said Kerri. "He must be in the ballroom. The eighth dance is starting."

"Do not tell me to calm down!" Arzelle snapped. "He was seen leaving the building, and I had to fob *my* partner off onto Janelle so she would not raise a fuss about Val leaving her on the wall. Oh, do come, Mr. Townsend-Dale. We are going to search the grounds, and I need your help."

"He has just gone for a breath of air; depend upon it," Kerri said. She suddenly felt afraid. There was a thing Val might do about what she had said to him during their ill-fated dance. It was a criminal thing but something he could well get away with if nobody stopped him. Did he feel threatened enough? *Oh, but surely not tonight, not during the Ball.* Yes, he had left the building, according to Arzelle, who seemed genuinely anxious. She tried to think.

"Listen, Nick," she said. "I shall not mind if you give a few minutes of your time to Miss James-Dietrich, although I am certain Mr. Dietrich-James will turn up any moment. I shall meet you here during the intermission. Now I beg you both to excuse me." She sketched a bow and left them, Arzelle already leading Nick away toward the foyer stairs.

Nick might return during the break, or he might not. Kerri could worry about that later. Now she walked as fast as she could in her high-heeled shoes and billowing skirt to the ladies' retiring rooms on the second floor. There was writing paper there, and pen and ink.

There were professional messengers lurking about outside the palace; there must be. They would always be found wherever important people might need them. Kerri was not important, but she had an errand that would not wait. She prayed it would not be too late.

Chapter 29

Derring Do

The ladies' retiring suite was empty except for one attendant in servants' black, standing arms folded at her station near the dressing tables. "May I help you?" she asked Kerri.

"I wish to write a letter," said Kerri breathlessly.

"Up there." The attendant pointed to a spiral staircase of gilded wrought iron that ascended to a kind of loft or gallery at one side of the room, over the door to the lavatories.

"Thank you." Kerri slipped her shoes off and gathered her skirt—no one who mattered could see her now—and clambered up to the loft. It was wider than it looked, a cozy retreat furnished with a couch or daybed, in case of fainting guests, no doubt, and a small, elegant writing desk, upon which a tiny lamp shed a dim light. Beyond the desk a glass-paned door led out onto a minute wrought iron balcony with moonlit treetops beyond. From desk or couch one would be quite concealed from anyone below.

Kerri sat down at the desk and dropped her shoes on the carpet. In a drawer she found pens and writing paper with the Palace of Arts crest embossed in deep blue. Selecting a pen, she dipped it into the inkwell and wrote:

To any officer of the Sea People at Yendys:

I am Kerrith Nash Dale-Townsend, born in Honowell, granddaughter of Aryel Range Stewart-Nash of Honowell, a daughter of the People.

I send an urgent warning. I have just learned that there may be an attempt to damage, steal, or destroy passenger logs from the month of March of this year. This attempt may take place tonight, even as I write this letter. I urge you to take immediate steps to protect the logs from harm.

Also I beg that you will forward this message with all possible speed to Timo Range Tomore of Barr Landing, presently serving aboard the *Bright Bird*. He can confirm the danger to the logs, and he can vouch for my identity and character.

Respectfully,

Kerrith Nash Dale-Townsend

She folded the message and tucked it into an envelope. She had turned it over and was beginning to write the address when the door opened below and several people came into the lounge.

"...left the ball altogether, but it is *my* belief he is tucked away in a dark corner somewhere with one of his lady friends."

"Or she sent him on some errand and made the whole thing up in order to go off into a dark corner herself with the beautiful Nicholas!"

The unseen women passed on into the lavatory, and Kerri could no longer make out their words, although she could still hear the sound of their voices. Quickly she finished addressing her letter and lit a match for the sealing wax. Then, letter sealed and ready, she still hesitated.

She should leave now. If she got herself down the little stair this minute, she would be gone before the women came back out; they would not see her. But they were talking about Arzelle and Nick and Val, and her curiosity was overpowering. Perhaps Val had not actually left the ball; perhaps there was no need for this panicky note to the Sea People. In the end she turned out the lamp and stayed where she was.

"Yes, she has had her eye on him for a long time. Oh, it is no secret. Everybody knows."

The women emerged from the lavatory and went to the dressing tables to sit and repair their faces and hair. Kerri craned up to see them better as they sat before the tall mirrors. There were two of them, but she recognized neither. The attendant hovered silently. Suddenly she glanced up and her eyes met Kerri's in the mirror. Her face remained expressionless; she looked away again immediately. Kerri shrank back, her heart pounding. The two ladies went on with their chatter, seeing nothing beyond their own reflections.

Their language lapsed carelessly into the informal.

"And does he seem susceptible? I thought he didn't look very happy."

"Oh, he has been coy in public, but he looks to be coming round. Since the beginning of term she's put pressure on him he'd be hard put to resist."

"Used her, ah, leverage, you mean? I'm surprised she'd have him on those terms. By force? Not of his own accord? How shame-making!"

"Not to Arzelle. She likes it that way." There was laughter. It was not kind.

"Well, if she's made it an alliance matter, he's no choice, poor lad. He might as well give in and enjoy himself."

"Indeed, I hear he already has. She's not so smugly triumphant lately for nothing!" There were more giggles.

"What about Val?"

"Oh, Val—I'll give you odds she dumps him off on the little ex-wife. Soon to be double ex!" There was snort of laughter.

"Not if Emily gets at him first!"

They laughed again. Kerri heard them get up and move toward the door, their voices returning to formal cadence.

"No," continued the second woman. "You keep your odds. I shall not take your money so easily. You must not have heard what else is going on tonight. Everyone is talking..."

The outer door was opened, the voices lost in a sudden intrusion of sound, then cut off altogether as the door closed.

Kerri crouched at the desk in the darkened loft, taking slow careful breaths. To some extent she had been prepared for a long time, but it made no difference. She still felt numb and sick. In some dispassionate part of her mind she was aware of a sense of relief: she was not mad. She had not imagined it. The threat was real, had always been real. On the other hand, it chilled her to discover it was real. She decided she would rather have been secretly a little mad, imagining impossibilities, than lose Nick.

But had she lost him? Could it be true that he had already betrayed her? Somehow she could not quite bring herself to believe that, in spite of months of suspicion, in spite of what she had just overheard. She acknowledged there was hope in the fact that Nick was apparently not altogether willing to be pursued by Arzelle. She could not imagine him pretending a reluctance in public that he did not feel in private. He was not subtle in that way. It would be more like him to be openly friendly toward any woman with whom he was having an affair, concealing only the fact of the affair.

Whatever the answer, there must still be something Kerri could do to head off disaster. *What? Me? The "little ex-wife"?*

Kerri seethed with the insult. For that was what truly galled her, far more than the unsurprising revelation of Nick's possible betrayal. The truth was out. All their smiles, all their supposed acceptance of her for Nick's sake—all lies! They held her in contempt, just as she had always suspected. They were laughing as they watched Arzelle cut her out with Nick and prepare to "dump" Val. Well, let them laugh now. She would find a way to get back at them all.

Not that Val did not deserve to be dumped. Not that she had not expected Arzelle to do it sooner or later. She had never believed in her heart that Arzelle had wanted Val for any other reason than to take him away from Kerri. Certainly, this was the only reason she was interested in Nick. Or perhaps not; Nick was a much better prize than Val.

He was also cleverer. Surely he would see through Arzelle, if he had not already.

And when Kerri told him what she had discovered tonight...!

She whispered a few rude words to the darkness. She could not tell him. She had no proof at all. None. Nothing Val had said to her could be taken as actual confession, nor would it be taken so by Nick's logical mind. If Kerri took her suspicions to Nick, he would naturally have to consider them in the light of her old grudge against Val and Arzelle, and especially after tonight the tale would sound even more like shrewish jealously. No, until she had better proof than Val's needling, Kerri's position would not be improved by saying anything to Nick.

Kerri found herself staring at the sealed letter in her hand. It would have to be delivered, no matter how irrational and panicky it might seem in hindsight. She had to take steps to protect the one piece of evidence she had against her antagonists, evidence that implicated them in a crime against the whole University community, not just herself. If only she had some ally. She felt too much alone. If only Timo were here!

Below, the door opened again, and a glittering crowd of ladies spilled into the room, talking at the tops of their voices. The eighth dance was over; the fifteen minute intermission had begun. It was too late to get down from the loft without being noticed and whispered about. Kerri pounded her thigh in frustration. She could not even simply hide here in the loft and wait out the quarter hour until they were all gone. Someone was sure to come up for a look around. And she *must* find a messenger.

Half crouching, she crept the short distance to the balcony door and peered out through the glass. From inside, the balcony looked like nothing more than a piece of architectural whimsy, but it was more: It was a sort of catwalk, probably a fire escape, that followed the side of the building as far as she could see in both directions. She couldn't go to the left; that would take her past the very tall window in the main part of the lounge, but to the right there might be another window through which she could get back into the building, or a stair or ladder to the ground. Very likely, she warned herself, it would turn out to be a dead end, and she would have to come back. She found herself reaching for the latch.

The door was unlocked. In a moment she was out on the balcony in the moonlight, the letter in her pocket, her shoes in her hand, her skirt hiked up around her waist. The wrought iron structure looked fragile and probably was hideously dangerous, to judge by the long rust stains that ran down the stone wall from the bolted supports. It was barely wide enough for one person *not* wearing a ball dress, but it passed a number of windows, at least one of which had light showing.

Kerri edged along, trying not to look down through the corroded iron filigree. The ground was a long way below on this side of the Palace, falling away in a steep tree-covered hillside. There were no lights; the formal gardens did not extend this far.

The first two windows were dark and locked. The third glowed with light. When Kerri looked cautiously inside, she saw a crowded and untidy office, a harassed-looking middle-aged woman huddled over a desk piled high with ledgers of some kind. The woman looked very cross, as well she might. It must be hard to have to work when the rest of the world was celebrating. Or perhaps the woman disapproved of revelry and was taking refuge here. In any case, she didn't look as if she would sympathize with Kerri's plight. Kerri crept past the window.

She was beginning to shiver. The night was cold. Kerri began to think she would do better to go back. Up ahead the catwalk seemed to come to an end in shadow where the wall met a massive round tower at the corner of the building. The next three windows were unlit and, when she tried them, unyielding. But here at the end there was a more substantial balcony, a pocket of stone in the bend between facade and tower, and an opening in the parapet just wide enough for her to scrape through. With relief she stepped off the shaky wrought iron onto the solid surface. She let go of the bundled skirt and petticoats and made an attempt to smooth them; no doubt they looked hopelessly crumpled. Thankfully, she put her shoes back on her chilled feet. She did not look forward to returning the way she had come.

As her eyes adjusted to the darkness, she saw two possible exits. There was a narrow stair curving down around the outside of the tower, and there was a low door into the tower itself. To her despair the door was locked. There was not even a handle or knob on the outside. She gave a few half-hearted raps upon the door, knowing it would do no good, and turned to contemplate the stairs. They must lead to the ground. Once she got down, surely she could find her way back around to the entrance. And how would she persuade the guardians at the door to let her back inside?

Suddenly there was a grinding sound from just within the door, the sound of a bolt being shoved back. Kerri descended two steps and flattened herself against the wall. The door opened with surprisingly little noise. Amber lamplight poured out to mix with white moonlight on a pale head, on a costume that became a composition of grey, black and white, on tiny stars of diamonds.

"Hello?" He took another step forward and looked out along the iron fire escape. "Miss Dale-Townsend? Are you here? Oh, please be here! I am near despair trying to find you." His voice did indeed possess a note of despair. It was, Kerri noted, an extremely pleasant and resonant voice.

She stepped away from her concealment. "Master Kianga Ryan?" (Never again would she forget his name.) "How did you know I was here?" She was so astonished and so absurdly glad to see him that she forgot to feel any consciousness of the difference in their castes, or much embarrassment at being caught in such a ridiculous predicament.

"Miss Dale-Townsend! Thank the Dreamer!" He held out a hand. "Do come into the warm. It is bitter cold out here."

She took his hand and let him lead her into the tower. Once inside, she recognized the place immediately, a spiral ramped gallery four stories high, open from top to bottom. The walls were covered with paintings, and an enormous sculpture of cord and dyed silk hung suspended in the open interior. She was standing on the small platform at the top of the ramp, where there was a life size bronze statue of a young girl kneeling, holding a toad on her palm. Kerri recollected the statue, but she could not remember ever noticing the door.

She turned in some confusion to her companion. "Your Excellency, I thank you for coming to my rescue again. I was exploring...it was very foolish. "

Master Kianga Ryan smiled disarmingly. "It is my pleasure, Miss Dale-Townsend, but I know what fun it is to have the run of the Palace of Arts. It is a dream labyrinth—all too tempting, especially if one can find a way to get up onto the roofs. Have you ever seen the penthouses? No? They are like a fairy tale village up under the stars. Perhaps I could show you—but no, it is too cold. Another time. Let us leave that door unsecured in case someone else goes exploring." He did something to the latch mechanism so the door did not quite close, took off his coat and laid it over her shoulders. He offered his arm. Dazed, Kerri took it, and the two of them started slowly down the ramp.

"You see," he continued, "I thought you might be there because the only place you could have gone was out onto that fire escape. I saw you retire into the ladies' rooms, but I did not see you come out, and I know the Palace quite well. I was afraid you might attempt to go down those stairs onto the grounds. It is all brambles and loose gravel down there, and there is no way out except through a locked gate in a very high wall."

"I am most grateful for your thoughtfulness, your Excellency," Kerri said. The coat was warm from being on him, and the warmth seemed to seep into her body like a drug. It was exceedingly odd, but she was finding it very difficult just now to be concerned about Nicholas and Arzelle and Val. They would keep until later. Her eyes fell on a bit of silver embroidery on the coat sleeve, a tiny monogram entwined in a motif of leaves: "A. R. S." She seemed to see it from a great distance, without surprise.

"I was hoping you might honor me with another dance," the Stockholder said. "The one we had was too short to count, and there is a waltz coming up. Marius was hoping to beat me to it. I left him watching the door at the other end, hoping you would emerge. He is probably still there."

"Master Warralonga Campbell?" Kerri asked.

"The same."

"How delightful." Kerri felt as if she were being tossed about in a small boat on a very choppy sea. "I am much obliged to you both about the waltz, your Excellency, but I am afraid I have another partner."

"If he insists, I shall relinquish you too him with regret," said Master Kianga Ryan, "but in the meantime I hope you will allow me to take you near a fireplace and procure you a warm drink."

This sounded like a heavenly idea, but with a start Kerri remembered her errand. It had seemed so pressing only a few minutes ago. "Your Excellency, forgive me," she began, "but I cannot accept your kind offer. I must go down to the front door and find a messenger immediately. I have written a letter. It is most urgent."

"Oh, in that case," he said, "we shall send my personal messenger. He waits in the foyer in case I have need of him. I put him at your disposal."

"Sir," Kerri protested, "I cannot—it would inconvenience you too much."

"Nonsense!" He grinned. "It would inconvenience me far more to track you down again. After all, I am your appointed protector. And I am determined to have that waltz, you see."

"My appointed protector?"

"That is, Marius and I. Both of us."

Kerri had to laugh then, helplessly. "Very well, your Excellency. I shall be very glad of your help in finding any messenger at all. But you must enlighten me. Who appointed you?" They reached the bottom of the ramp. She took his jacket off her shoulders, not without regrets, and pressed it into this hands. A footman materialized to assist him into it.

"We appointed ourselves, Miss Dale-Townsend, although I confess you were pointed out to us by a mutual friend, who prefers to remain anonymous."

"Indeed?" Kerri wondered, thinking vaguely of Arzelle and Professor Edson, of various Faculty members, and strangely, of Loren and Alex. "A chum, in short," she murmured under her breath.

But he heard her, and the lines at the corners of his eyes deepened with amusement. "Exactly so," he said.

Chapter 30

No Such Thing

Quiet reigned on the omnibus as it rumbled back to the hotel at three o'clock in the chilly morning. No one seemed inclined to talk. The two dozen Revelers dozed or gazed out the windows, lost in private contemplation. Thus, it was not immediately obvious that Kerri and Nick were not exactly speaking to one another.

Nick had elected the dozing option, although Kerri suspected he was only pretending. She tried window staring at first, but soon found her head leaning against the glass and her eyes closing, as the coach swayed hypnotically along the pavement.

She had the cold satisfaction of feeling herself on higher ground, morally, than Nick, although knowing this did nothing to make her feel less bruised or less guilty. Why did it seem that by spending the evening dancing with one Stockholder after another she had committed some kind of impropriety? That it would have been somehow more fitting to have lurked dismally in a corner being stood up by partner after partner while her husband allowed himself to be pursued openly by Arzelle Pendrake James-Dietrich?

She sensed that Nick did not approve of her success. He had been oddly ungenerous about it; in fact, he had affected to ignore it, making no comment at supper and behaving, when presented to her new acquaintances, with a stiffness and lack of geniality that were quite unlike him. If she had not known him so well, she would have thought he was either embarrassed or jealous. He ought to have been gloating with her, but he displayed, instead, every symptom of a man with his nose put badly out of joint. Under ordinary circumstances, that might have been understandable, but these were *Stockholders*!

Yes, it was a little disconcerting that Master Kianga Ryan's costume matched theirs, and it was possible some people might suppose that this was planned, and that there was some kind of scandal behind it—although it was unlikely anyone would have noticed who did not know them all well or see the three of them together at some point. But Nick could not seriously suppose that Kerri was responsible for the coincidence. Nor could he imagine there was any substance to the light flirtation Kerri had carried on with the Stockholder or any of his friends. That would be ludicrous. He had no cause to disapprove, and his attitude was painful to her. Did he think it was her duty to be a failure?

And if flirting at the Ball were cause for guilt, Nick had reason to feel guiltier than she did. He had bobbed back and forth like a tennis ball between her and Arzelle all evening. Not until the supper intermission had Kerri been able to find the courage to bring up the matter with him. Even then she had made an effort to conceal the magnitude of her distress, only daring to admit that she had overheard people talking. To her dismay, that fact had not surprised him, and she felt it did not alarm him as much as she thought it should.

She had the impression he did not quite know what sort of response he ought to be making to the whole matter, either publicly, or privately to her, or within himself. To her alone he had claimed to be uncomfortable about all the attention Arzelle was giving him, and yet he seemed sincerely worried that hinting her off would get him into some kind of trouble. He had made no more than a token effort to put a stop to the business. Or perhaps Kerri wronged him in thinking this, for Arzelle had backed off, apparently of her own accord, later in the evening. Perhaps she had finally taken the hint from Nick.

Or else Val had made her do it. The two of them had been seen quarreling heatedly during the supper break at midnight, which was about the time Val had reappeared—or, at least, the first time Kerri had seen him since he had abandoned her on the dance floor. If Val had been able to make Arzelle back off, Kerri reflected grimly, it was the first time she had ever known him to have any influence over her behavior.

At least her student partners had begun to approach her again around supper time, which had greatly relieved her anxiety. Someone—possibly Nick; she *must* be charitable— could have pointed out to them that it was rude not to do so, no matter how many gentleman of superior rank surrounded her. Except for the individuals from her own college, she had turned them all away without a qualm, silly idiots! She owed them nothing, even if she had a choice about the matter, which she did not, etiquette being firmly on her side. Besides, with...Master Kianga Ryan and his friends she'd had fun—glorious, intoxicating fun. They had danced, they had talked, they had laughed, they had drunk quantities of champagne and told each other outrageous stories. She would never forget it.

She knew better than to suppose for one moment that there was anything significant about the attentions of Stockholder Kianga Ryan and the others. She cherished no expectation of any continued acquaintance with any of them. It would be foolish and self- destructive to do so. No doubt they had singled her out more or less at random—or maybe not, considering her costume—to amuse themselves. Yes, that must be the explanation. She could not take seriously His

Excellency's talk of "protectors," whatever strange illusions she had experienced in the receiving line. If their original object had been to terrify her with their grandeur or fluster her into some kind of embarrassed collapse, they had not succeeded. She had held her own, she thought, with as much dignity and poise as anybody could reasonably expect from someone of her age and experience. Perhaps she had even entertained them a little better than they had expected. And even if they had intended nothing more, at least at the beginning, than to make fun of her, they had never treated her to her face with anything but propriety and gallantry. They had made her feel, indeed, protected. She was grateful to them. Without them she would have had a dismal evening indeed.

Very dismal. Catastrophic, in fact. Disastrous. Heartbreaking. She found herself staring at Nick's sleeve, at the cuff, at the embroidery in the corners. She would never have noticed it if she had not known it would be there: a tiny device of an entwined monogram, camouflaged in vines and leaves. "A. K. R."

She was on the narrow iron catwalk, clutching at her endless skirt, trying desperately to keep from dropping her shoes into the abyss below as she inched her way along. She must hurry! At any moment one of Them would think to open the fire escape door and look out, and then They would be after her. The ancient metal groaned dangerously. At any second it would part from the wall and drop her to her death.

No, she was safe on the stone now, hammering frantically on the tower door with no handle or knob, but it did not open. No one was there, and voices were coming behind her, voices that whispered and judged and accused. In the moonlight she could not see Them, but she could feel Them coming. There was no more time. She turned and threw herself down the stairs, careening from parapet to wall and back as she leaped, three, four steps at a time, her full, layered skirts melting away like smoke. Her shoes were lost, and the letter. She would have to deliver the message herself, if only she could remember to whom she was supposed to deliver it. If only she could remember what the message was.

The stair went down and down, and then she was lost in a wilderness of monuments, great blocks of brick and stone, cold under the moon. She dodged among them, running along a pavement of slate, leaping from shadow to shadow, her breath burning in her throat. They were old monuments, these, worn so smooth that all carven letters were effaced by the elements. Old, and shabby, and yes, filthy with black dirt, with soot, lazy tendrils of smoke winding up from the pots on top. They were chimneys, not monuments. She was on the roof.

He had said, he had said the roof was safe. He had told her, *go to the roof.* He would be there. He would help. But she could not find him among the chimneys, among the shadows, and the voices whispered ever closer behind her.

She had done it this time. She had really done it! Now They knew, and They were going to make her pay. She should never have... never have... something. She should never have done it, whatever it was. This time she was truly in for it.

But if only she could find him, he would help her. He could stop Them. He was on her side. He could protect her. No. No protection. She did not need protection. She would turn. She would fight Them. Whether she found him in time or not, if he was on her side, she could fight Them.

She found an avenue between two vast roof-peaks, a gutter of slate slabs, a sharp valley between tiled mountains. She ran out of the chimney wilderness and up the valley, through an arched gateway and into a garden, a maze of hedges and topiary and night-blooming roses with silver rimmed petals. Their perfume drugged the air. In the distance lamplight glowed in the windows of the village, safe and warm. He would be there; he had said so. If only she could reach the village before the voices caught up with her, before They took her, she would be safe.

But the moon had already turned the color of blood and began to go out, eerily, like a dying coal, like the fading windows of the fading village, leaving the windy sky in possession of the stars, coming out of all directions in the void, muttering and whispering. The treacherous roses dissolved into stars and snickered among themselves in the echoing void.

"Soon to be double-ex, poor thing!"

"He has no choice. It is a matter of alliance now!"

"Poor thing."

Kerri said, "Damn. And damn and damn." She whirled blindly upon unseen gravel and shrieked at the stars, "What do you want from me? What do you bloody want?"

The voices ceased, astonished, and in the sudden silence all Their cold attention turned to focus on her.

"Hush. Hush. Kerri, hush. You're dreaming. It's all right. It's only a dream. Hush."

Nicholas was holding her in the dark. She was in bed. The room took shape around her, the unfamiliar room, with windows in the wrong place, windows dimly lit by the earliest light of dawn. She was in the hotel. Nick said, "You're all right. It was a dream." He pulled the comforter up over them both. It smelled of dust and lavender.

"Oh." She rubbed her face stupidly. "Did I make a noise?"

"You called out, 'What are you doing?' or 'What do you want?' or something like that."

"Loud?"

"Woke me up. Probably woke up the people next door."

She groaned. "Sorry, Nick. Nightmare." She wondered why he wouldn't let her go back to sleep so she could meet someone on that rooftop.

"So I gathered. Do you remember it?"

She tried to think, shifting the pillow under her head. She was supposed to be mad at Nick about something, wasn't she? It couldn't have been important, whatever it was. "I don' know," she mumbled with effort. "The Ball, I think. Lost in the Palace." She heard her sleepy voice say, "The Soci'ty of Guenevere. I don' know."

For three seconds Nick was motionless. Then he patted her on the shoulder. "There's no such thing," he said. "Go back to sleep."

"Yeah," she sighed. "Sorry."

"It's all right," he repeated, turning over. "Forget about it."

She was wide awake, turned to stone. *Did I say it out loud?* she wondered, terrified, her heart thudding against her nightgown. She could hear the words echoing in memory. *The Society of Guenevere. I said it, I did. Aloud.* She forced her body to relax, forced her breath to come and go, deep and even, knowing Nick was still awake. She could feel the tension in his body, even though he was no longer touching her, and she knew he had heard her words.

Just a dream. They would both have forgotten about it in the morning. *Breathe in. Breathe out. Shift like a sleeper, arms and legs falling all unconsciously, and breathe in, out.* It seemed a long time before she felt Nick drift off, heard his breathing change. For much longer she lay open-eyed in the icy dawn, breathing.

Chapter 31

Telling About It

Kerri woke with the unexplainable sensation of having evaded some tremendous disaster. In those first moments of drowsy consciousness she could not remember what the disaster was, only that it was big and dark and vague, like bad weather, and she had come through it somehow without getting wet. Then memory came back to her: the Ball. She had survived her first Faculty Ball.

How odd it was to be thinking of the experience as a survival, a disaster averted, almost as if it had been a war or something, and not a party. (Not that Kerri knew very much about War; one studied the Age of Dreams examples, of course, in school, but it was a cursory overview, an unpleasant little necessity, like vaccination. One was not obliged to become familiar with the details.) True, the Ball had not been at all what she had expected, and indeed it had turned out very strangely, but it had not been as bad as all that, she told herself sleepily. In fact parts of it had been simply glorious.

She was visited by the sudden sharp recollection of the shape of planes and shadows around the eyes of Stockholder Master Andrew Kianga Ryan. She heard in memory a voice that made her very bones resonate, and a sensation both wonderful and excruciating tore through her like an arrow. One last time. She let the arrow fall and die. There was no other choice. Certain glories could be disastrous; such dangers were best evaded, averted, avoided. Much better and more to the purpose to think about old, familiar, manageable catastrophes like Arzelle and Val and whatever they were up to, and what Nick might be up to, with Arzelle or somebody else.

She was beginning to doze again when the memory came to her suddenly, chillingly— having the Star Dream at dawn, waking Nicholas. The words she should never have said: The Society of Guenevere. Had she truly uttered them aloud? Could Nick really have heard? It must have happened, for she had lain awake so long. She wondered if he would remember. Probably not. She hoped not. She willed him not to, and she wondered why she felt so horrified and frightened at what she had done. It was not as if she had murmured the name of some other man, which she might easily have done under the circumstances—but that thought must be dismissed instantly. The Society of Guenevere was a dream thing, an hallucination, a phrase from a forgotten poem, of no consequence. That is what she would say if Nick should chance to mention it. "Oh? I said what? Something in my nightmare, I suppose. I don't remember now." But he would not mention it; he would have forgotten, he had not heard.

Then she recalled what he had said. "There is no such thing."

Not "What's that?" Or "What are you talking about?" Or "Never heard of it." Or even "I see."

There is no such thing.

The room was warming at last, radiators gently clanking in the corners. Kerri wormed her way out of bed and made for the bathroom as Nick stirred and grumbled softly under the quilts.

"What time?" he mumbled.

"Quarter to ten," she said. "Our brunch reservation is in forty-five minutes."

"Mm," he replied.

She decided then that she would take her cue from him. If he preferred to behave this morning as if nothing had happened, so would she. As long as he did not speak of her dream and her words, she would say nothing. She would not even think about it. And, she reflected, whatever he was up to with Arzelle or whomever, however badly he had championed his own wife at the May Revel Ball, however silent he had been on the way back to the hotel, his behavior afterward in the privacy of their room had gone a long way to make up for all of it. She felt inclined to forgive both him and herself and chalk up the rest to her notorious imagination.

The hotel dining room was full of Revelers, all dressed in their May Day best. For Kerri and Nick this gala brunch was a great extravagance, but then, it was May Day, and they had long promised themselves this treat as a reward for securing the ball invitation. Because they had made an early reservation in order to get back to Evesham while something remained of the day, and because most people who attended the ball would not emerge until at least noon, they had made no arrangement to meet any friends for brunch. Kerri was glad of this. She did not care to face anyone she knew this morning and felt vastly relieved when their little table for two turned out to be situated in a relatively out-of-the-way corner of the restaurant. Nor had Nick made any protest, although he seemed to be spending more time gazing distractedly out over the dining room than conversing.

Halfway through brunch Kerri recollected her letter to the Sea People. She choked on her croissant, causing Nick to look at her with concern and the waiter to approach with the water pitcher.

"I am all right," she told them. "It is nothing."

Taking refuge behind her coffee cup, Kerri tried to compose herself. She felt her face flush scarlet with the mortifying knowledge that, not only had she succumbed to an attack of paranoid silliness, she had committed the gross error of making her hysteria public, had put it in writing, a stupid, stupid thing to do. It did not help to reflect that she had sent the letter by private messenger. Such documents were always being intercepted, messengers bribed.

Did not the plots of countless popular novels and plays depend upon mishaps of this kind?

On the other hand, a Stockholder's personal messenger ought to be less corruptible than the average agency messenger. Unless His Excellency was in league with Them, which she refused to believe. And an enigmatic letter to the Sea People was not exactly a public document. The People were notoriously close-mouthed to outsiders about family business, and she, Kerri, was more or less family, as Timo had been pointing out all her life.

Yet, even if the letter remained private, she realized with renewed agony, it had been an exercise in futility. The ships' logs were not even kept in Yendys; they were in Honowell. There was no possible way Val could have run down to the waterfront and destroyed the critical pages, because the pages were a day's sail across the ocean. *Stupid! Stupid!* Kerri railed at herself, her appetite completely gone. Val might even yet try to get at those records in Honowell, and she had not thought to warn the People of that, unless Timo happened to think of the possibility when he received the message. She wondered how long that would take and where Timo was. She had better write to him at once care of the shipping office and give him some kind of explanation—nothing too specific: coded, making reference to their discussion at sea that night, promising to explain everything in person when they met.

She hoped that would be soon. Timo always understood, always took her ideas seriously, always respected her hunches, allowed her flights of fancy open wings. Even when the idea was a silly, hysterical, adolescent overdramatization built on failed love, candlelight, and champagne.

In the early afternoon they went home to Evesham. Homecoming was still a melancholy thing with no Thomas to greet them, but at least the house was untouched. Everything was exactly as they had left it. Nick went off to see to the water tanks and the woodpile, and Kerri set to work inspecting and brushing the Ball costumes and setting them to rights for being put away. She found herself able to handle the fateful brocade with equanimity, directing her mind firmly toward the question of how to tell Grandmother Aryel what should best be thought of as an amusing anecdote, a trifling coincidence: his Excellency's costume.

It would be some time, she decided, before she and Nick would wear this pair of costumes again. In the meantime she would take the first opportunity to convey to Aryel the hint that more such bequests would be very welcome, now that she had so vividly experienced the value of her Grandmother's talent.

As the afternoon wore on, nearly every one of the Evesham neighbors dropped by to give May Day greetings and pass the time of day. Somehow the word had gone round that Nick and Kerri had been to the Faculty Ball, and since they were the first in the hamlet to achieve that distinction, everyone wanted to know all about it. They ended up having an enormous community potluck tea at the Moncrief-Davises', Sharon having cooked a great pot of beans for the vegetarians, roasted a turkey for the non-, and baked pecan pies. All Evesham came, nineteen counting the children. Someone brought a barrel of home-brewed ale, Nick contributed four bottles of his blackberry wine, and they all got merry.

Kerri and Nick were able to satisfy everyone's curiosity about the Revel without mentioning Arzelle at all. In fact, there was a surprising amount to tell—the decorations, the food, what everybody wore, the music, what a bore it was to observe protocol and formal language for so many hours—and they had great fun telling it. Nick seemed to take an especial delight in relating Kerri's surprising adventures. She was toasted and teased for dancing, not once or twice, but a *dozen* times with *eight* different Stockholders. Amid all the affectionate laughter of good neighbors she saw on Nick's face the pride that should have been there last night, and Kerri knew that no ball in any palace could be finer than this.

"We need to set a date for our dinner party," Kerri said to Nick on Monday morning as they gathered their things to leave for the City. "I ought to send the invitations today," she added. "I was thinking of a week from next Friday, if that would suit you. Any later in the term we shall be getting awfully close to Finals. We would have to leave campus as early as we could, and it would be a bit of a rush to get ready, but the streetcar runs late enough there'd be no problem for people getting back to town. It shuts down at nine, you know, on Saturday and seven on Sunday. If we get most of the work done during the days before, I think we could manage it. We might even hire in someone from Fernly for the day to help out."

Nick considered this seriously for a moment. "That makes a good deal of sense," he said. "This Friday would be even better, but it's much too close and last-minute. I'll tell you what." He shrugged into his coat and shouldered his book bag. "I'll feel them out today in a casual way and send you word one way or the other this afternoon. Then you can write the invitations and post them before you leave campus. Have you got decent writing paper?"

"Always," Kerri assured him smugly.

Accordingly, when she received his terse note in the mid-afternoon University mail ("Go ahead. N.") she got out the box of "best" writing paper she kept in her desk at her office, prepared her most reliable pen and set herself to composing dinner invitations in her finest calligraphy to the three selected couples. It took the better part of an hour. She had just sealed the last envelope with a relieved sigh and begun to clean her pens when there was a soft knock on her office door.

"Oh, Miss Weberly!" Pleased, Kerri admitted her friend. "How delightful to see you! Do come in."

Loren's eyes were gleaming with mischief and curiosity. She only waited for the door to be closed behind her to exclaim excitedly, "I overheard Mr. Ladner tell someone you and your husband were at the Faculty Revel Ball last night and you danced with every male Stockholder under the age of fifty. He said your student partners were all quite cut out, and somebody or other—I didn't catch who—were all in an uproar about it."

Kerri grinned and sat down again at her desk. She felt a bit guilty now for not having the courage to mention the Ball to Loren before. She had assumed her friend would be envious. Kerri would have been, in her place. She ought to have known Loren well enough by now to understand that the other would see it all as an enormous lark.

"Come!" pleaded Loren. "Tell! One hears outrageous stories after these affairs, but this does beat them all. It cannot be true. What really happened? Unless," she drew back a little, suddenly mindful of Academic protocol, "you would rather not."

"Well," Kerri began, trying not to grin, "it isn't exactly true. That is, it wasn't *every* Stockholder under the age of fifty. And one of them was probably sixty, if he was a day. The best dancer of the bunch, too, and extremely amusing."

"No!" Loren gave a delighted crow and threw herself onto the couch. "God, how delicious! Was Arzelle there? What I wouldn't have given to see her face!"

"She was there," Kerri conceded. "I haven't a clue what she thought. She seemed too busy with her own concerns to pay any attention to my doings. But see here! Are people really talking about me?" She could not be surprised, but she did not like it. And who was in an uproar? No doubt her rivals here in the department. It was an alarming thought; she had given them little enough cause to take notice of her before. Now they would not know what to think, and she could not blame them. She did not know what to think, herself. At least her experiences at the Ball inclined her to acquit the lot of them of persecuting her.

"There was a buzz in the Common Room," Loren replied. "It isn't all over campus, if that is what worries you. That is, it may *be* all over campus, but *I* wouldn't know about it."

"Most reassuring," Kerri commented.

"Oh," said Loren, "you aren't unhappy about it, are you? No one thinks ill of you. In fact, they all seem most impressed. Indeed, Mr. Ladner and his companions appeared to consider it all a well-deserved pie-in-the-face to some of our snottier colleagues. Who are probably in terror over all the snubs they've given you, never dreaming you had such connections! It's fabulous!" She collapsed into laughter again. "Of course, I never dreamed you had such connections either, but it is still wonderful to see them sweat."

"I assure you I have no 'connections'," Kerri said. "That I know of," she added. "For sure," she continued almost under her breath. "My best theory is that the group of them adopted me, so to speak, as a kind of pet. There was nothing unkind in it. They were charming and friendly—treated me from first to last like one of their own. It was quite a lot of fun."

"I'm sure you rose to the challenge beautifully," said Loren.

"If I had not," Kerri admitted, "I am certain they would never have kept it up. They would have dropped me at once."

"But if you haven't got connections, then why *you*?"

Kerri told Loren about the matching costumes and how Master Kianga Ryan had rescued her when Val abandoned her (which was even juicier a story than Loren had heard in the common room; apparently that part of it wasn't generally known). Delighted at the foiling of Val, Loren swore herself to secrecy on the Gang of Four and listened raptly. Kerri took so much enjoyment in at last having someone with whom to share her adventure wholeheartedly that she remembered only just in time to get her envelopes stamped and into the outgoing mail before the last pick-up of the afternoon. She had regretfully to turn Loren out, but she suggested meeting for lunch the following day.

"Yes, let's!" Loren agreed. "How is your schedule tomorrow? I have nothing pending after lunch, and I was thinking it might be interesting to go root around in Alexander's library and see what there is to see. Ever since that first day I have had visions of forgotten texts simply sitting in the stacks for the finding. Impossible, I know, but I will not rest until I have looked." They emerged into the corridor; her language changed abruptly. "I have not yet had the opportunity to do so, and I have so looked forward to it. Would you care to join me?"

Kerri considered this as she locked her office door. "I have a paper to finish. The weekend put me a little behind, all the festivities...." No shame in admitting this; the Faculty Ball being the best of excuses, worthy of flaunting in the corridor, in fact. She continued, "If I am well enough along, yes. Otherwise, I shall just meet you at the usual time and place." Conscious of surrounding eyes and ears, she knew she could say no more, but Loren nodded in understanding, said a polite farewell and departed sedately in the direction of the stairs.

Kerri posted her invitations and her letter to Timo, written earlier in the day, and returned to her office to prepare to go home. She remembered that she had yet to make her planned visit to the Archives. Life would only be busier as final exams and the holiday season approached. There would probably be no better time than tomorrow. She had always intended to have done a little detective work of her own in the Archives of Yendys before she next met Timo, something concrete to tell him, even if it had no significance. It could do no harm to spend an hour in the Archives if she had nothing better to do, but she suspected it would be a waste of time.

With luck, she would be hearing from Timo soon. A pleasant thought occurred to her. Perhaps she could tell him about the Gang of Four, even bring him to one of the meetings, with the others' permission, of course. Alex and Greta had implied they wanted diversity; Timo was of the Sea People. They could not help but like him. Loren, too. He would like them. He would fit right in! And Kerri would be keenly interested to hear his take on Greta. She would never have expected it when she had last seen him in Honowell, but she had a great deal to report.

Chapter 32

The Archives

"You do not have to do this," Kerri whispered. "Honestly. It is *my* little project. I am not sure it is not going to be a complete waste of time."

"Not at all," Loren whispered back. "What else am I going to do in an hour? Barge in on Alex early? Find a place to sit down and study my lines? Now *that* would be a waste of time! I just had Recitation, and believe me, I am *not* in the mood."

Loren had already spent all her afternoon since lunch working her way through the dismayingly vast collection of books in the upper floors of the Public Library. While she had unearthed many intriguing volumes, none of them showed any promise as a possible thesis text, and by the time Kerri had arrived and hunted her down, she had been ready to take a rest from the search. Upon Kerri's hesitant announcement of her intention to do some research in the Archives before knocking on Alexander's door, Loren had offered to come along and help, desiring, she said, a "different flavor of dust" for a change.

"Very well," said Kerri. She drew a large breath and opened the ancient heavy door into the Archives of the Yendys Central Public Library. "Oh my!" she exclaimed.

"Good heavens!" said Loren.

A great cavernous space stretched away before them, dimly lit and faintly musty.

Beyond a sort of foyer separated off by high oak counters stood ranks of metal shelves, filled floor to ceiling, marching away into the gloom. To the right an opening in the counter gave onto a cluster of tables and chairs, mostly covered with stacks of papers. Beyond them, a metal staircase descended to a lower level. Another opening on the left led to a small office alcove occupied by the Archivist, the librarian on duty, sitting at the regulation massive, cluttered desk and glaring at the two intruders over the tops of his spectacles.

He ignored Kerri's polite attempt at an ice-breaking inquiry and shouted in the toneless bellow of the hard of hearing, "Rules posted on the wall! No materials to be taken out of the department! Leave used materials in the shelving basket on the counter! No lamps or candles to be carried by hand. If you light one of the jets, do not turn it out when you go; leave all lights on! Archives close at five o'clock!" He then turned back to his own business at his burdened desk and benefited them with no more of his attention.

Kerri let out the breath she had been holding. "It is bigger than I expected," she said to Loren in a low voice.

Loren hovered just inside the door, apparently entertaining serious second thoughts about her offer to help. "What are we looking for, exactly?" she inquired.

What indeed, Kerri said to herself as she gazed in dismay at the tottering stacks of dusty files and ledgers. Here she was in the Archives, all these weeks after first acquiring the notion, and she had only the vaguest idea what she was doing here.

"Anything," she replied to Loren. "Anything unusual or peculiar." She ventured into the nominal reading area and looked in vain for a place to put down her book bag.

Loren risked a step farther into the room, one hand still yearning for the door handle as if to facilitate instant escape. "Perhaps you could be more specific. If you would."

"For instance, name changes." Kerri, thinking frantically, could not remember any reason for coming into the Archives other than Timo's fateful discovery about Val's name change. And that, while decidedly peculiar, seemed insufficiently important to inspire digging in this tomb of official records. However, she had persuaded Loren down here, and she had to give some reason. "My first husband changed his name not long ago. I found out about it rather by accident. He is keeping it secret; I do not know why. He does not know I know—I do not *think* he knows I know."

"And the record is here?" Loren nodded at the wilderness behind the counter.

"No. At home. That is, in Honowell. I shall tell you about it another time. But the person who told me made the discovery in the Archives in Honowell—a place it would never have occurred to me to look—and I thought, well, there might be other discoveries to be made. You never know." She spotted a small reading table, inexplicably clear of piled papers and triumphantly dropped her book bag on it.

"I see." Loren drew a deep breath and abandoned the exit. "Very well." She marched over and set her book bag down next to Kerri's. She pushed up her sleeves. "Name changes. Anything else?"

"Marriages. Divorces. Oh! And adoptions! Especially adoptions." Suddenly she remembered that her Sponsor-to-be and Professor Edson had been adopted by Stockholders. Perhaps there were more such adoptions to be found. It would be helpful to know who among the Faculty were secret Stockholders.

"Children?" asked Loren, puzzled.

"Not necessarily. Adults can be adopted, too, you know." Kerri began to warm to the subject, to think creatively. "Names you recognize."

"Ah!" breathed Loren, suddenly enlightened. "*Them*! You're looking for information about *Them*!"

"Well, as a matter of fact...." Surprised, Kerri realized that this was so. She had not quite got round to looking at it that way, but now that Loren had said so in plain words, she understood that she had intended all along to look for nothing else. Naturally. Perhaps because Val ("Valle") was the original seed of this dubious quest, and Val was now, at least by virtue of marriage (if one could call it virtue where Arzelle was concerned), firmly allied with Them.

"Anything at all about Them," she repeated with renewed confidence. "Anything that might be..... "

"Useful?" Loren suggested helpfully.

"That sounds terrible!" Kerri protested. Then she met Loren's eyes, and they both burst into laughter. "Hsh! Hsh!" hissed Kerri, with a horrified look at the librarian, but the man took no notice. He continued to scratch away with a tall feathered quill in his little island of lamplight.

"So," Loren continued between giggles, "anything *useful* about Them. I like it!"

"*Any* mention at all," Kerri amended, trying to regain her composure, "but especially anything that suggests a pattern. We don't know what might turn out to be, um, useful, eventually. And business transactions!"

"Business transactions?" Loren looked puzzled. "Would that sort of thing be here also?"

"I do not know," said Kerri. "Perhaps nothing more than the establishment of partnerships or corporations." Her knowledge of business was somewhat elementary, her City job having been in the administration of the Health Department. "Bankruptcies," she suggested. "Inheritance. Wills and things."

"So," Loren said thoughtfully, "we are looking for any patterns, any peculiarities, either personal, professional, or financial, to do with Them. Going how far back?"

"At least eight years," Kerri decided. That would extend the search back to well within the time she had still been with Val, before Zarah-Arzelle had come back into their lives with her new name. "Or, say, ten. It doesn't matter. No need to be methodical about chronology, at least at first. Let us dip in at random and see what we find."

"Agreed." Loren took out a pencil and notebook and flipped open to the first blank page. "There is one small problem, though."

"Yes?"

"I need names. I do not really know who *They* are. Oh, I can think of dozens of people in Dalton, but that won't do us much good here. Beyond Our Mutual Friend, I can't think of more than half a dozen possible names here in Yendys. I haven't been here long enough. You're going to have to help me by giving me a list."

"You cannot mean written down!" Kerri objected.

"Of course I do. How else shall I know what needles to look for in this haystack?"

Kerri looked around them, peering into the shadows on all sides. "Very well," she said. "But let me write them down, not say them out loud. And mind you do not lose the paper!"

"Most definitely not!" Loren said, handing her the notebook. "I shall commit it to memory and destroy it after! Eat it, if I have to."

That set them giggling again, while Kerri dashed off as many names as she could think of, using the crude hand known as "Runestick," a style appropriate for "lists written in haste." Quickly, she filled the page with a single column of names.

"These go all the way back to my earliest undergraduate days," she told Loren. "Nine years ago. I could think of more if I took my time on it, but this will do to go on with."

Loren scanned the list, nodding slowly. "Two or three I've heard. The rest, no. I think I shall start back in time and work forward. Nine years, you said? Ten? I'll start at ten. I shall call out if I find anything. Or if I get lost. If I don't show up to tea, send a search party."

Grinning, Kerri watched her go, then dug into her bag for her own writing materials.

Equipped, she set off down the nearest aisle, only to encounter Loren coming back. "Matches," said Loren. "It's dark as pitch back there. You have to light the jets as you go along. And there wouldn't be a map, would there?"

There was, mounted on the wall just inside the entry door—a huge diagram drawn in faded ink on heavy parchment, stained and curling at the corners. The original labels were much embellished with numerous corrections, scratchings out and long sinuous arrows indicating that various sections had been moved from here to there in the labyrinth. Five minutes' diligent study of this artifact revealed several helpful items of information. First, records here went back no more than seven years, due to lack of capacity. According to an attached notice, everything older had been moved to the "Archive Annexes" at another (unspecified) location. Second, everything was recorded in duplicate. For instance, the record of a birth would be entered in the chronological register of the District in which it took place, with a copy of the actual certificate filed in the separate "Births" section. Finally, the Archives were separated according to the administrative districts of the City. This would narrow down the search considerably, for the areas inhabited by Academics were fairly well defined. Although the so-called "University District" overlapped four separate civic districts, searching through four sets of records was much less daunting a prospect than searching through all twenty-four.

"You don't have to do this," Kerri repeated to Loren as they studied the map. "It is probably not worth it."

"I shall think of it," replied Loren firmly, "as an adventure in research, a discipline. It's worth half an hour, anyway."

Which, Kerri discovered looking at her watch, was cheating, as Alex would not be expecting them for forty-five minutes yet.

Leaving a trail of feeble gaslight behind her, she made for the area labeled "Name Changes" on the map. It took several false turns and a bit of backtracking before she found the right bank of shelved binders. Dumping a litter of manila envelopes and dusty papers off a convenient chair, she dragged it to her chosen station under the nearest gaslight. Ten minutes later the light shone upon the page she had been looking for. February 28 of the year 66. Zarah Pendrake James (then James-Wallace) had changed her given name to Arzelle. There, in black and white.

All right, she did it. I already knew that. Now what? Kerri took a blank sheet off her notepad and tore a strip to mark the page. Idly, she began to turn over the pages of the ledger, the certificates bound into the book, without more than half looking at them. She was more than ever convinced this whole endeavor would be boring and futile, but at least she would give it until the three o'clock rendezvous down the hall at Alex's. It would keep her from worrying about things, like the imminent prospect of having to talk about the ball in front of Greta and Alex—Loren would not fail to mention it—and having to face the ironic grin of that enigmatic, so-called Peasant woman.

It surprised her a little how seriously Loren seemed to take the whole "Them" nonsense—almost as if she truly believed They were a real force of malevolence and not merely the persecution fantasy of a couple of struggling, second-rate students. (Not really second-rate, she reminded herself, merely unSponsored and therefore having some legitimate cause to feel slighted, if not actively persecuted.) As for herself, she had not given much thought to Them in weeks, not even at the Ball, where They had been in abundance. She had renewed the Veil at regular intervals throughout that evening—or she had done so whenever she had remembered, amid all the distraction—and that had always been a fool-proof way of blocking at least the mental emanations of Their malice. And she had been rather busy....

In fact, she had scarcely considered Them at all since the day she had told Loren about Them. Or, to be more accurate, the day Loren had told her. The day Thomas was murdered was the only time in weeks she had imagined Them intruding upon her life. Now that she had evidence that Val was behind the break-in and all the other sabotage since the beginning of term, she realized she had dismissed the whole campaign as some kind of unfinished business of the old triangle, a personal thing, not part of the long mythology of Them, in spite of Arzelle being implicated.

And more: Finding out that, yes, Nick *was* being pursued by another woman (Arzelle! Surprise!), she had been able to dismiss also her fantasies of Nick's infidelity. At least, dismiss the fantasy part of it. To the extent there was truth in the rumors, she had—she and Nick had—a problem. The problem was real, not delusion or madness on Kerri's part, no figment of her imagination. And, like the fact of Val being behind the sabotage, a reality was much easier to confront than a phantom, than fear of madness, sheer not-knowing. She had yet to confront Nick straight on about Arzelle, but if it became necessary, she could do it with the assurance of having concrete observations, not to mention public witness, on her side. He would not be able to put her off on the grounds of "imagining things".

In the wake of all this, the old stuff about "Them" had dwindled to an anecdote of childhood and adolescence. It was almost as if she had relinquished the whole thing to Loren, turned it over to her to worry about. She felt a small guilt about this. It was not quite fair of her to let Loren carry the burden alone. Certainly she had no right to look down her nose at Loren—as she had almost caught herself doing just now—for persisting in a complex of imaginings which she, Kerri, had left behind.

Between the problem of Nick and the fading of Them, she almost missed the first familiar name.

"How very, very odd," she muttered to herself.

John Hennessy Garibaldi had changed his given name to "Johnn" on 4 April of the year 66. She remembered John Garibaldi, although she had not known him personally— handsome, personable (perhaps a bit too personable), two years older than she. Sponsored by a Dean, no less. One of Them, without a doubt. She tore another strip of paper to mark the page.

The very next certificate held yet another familiar name, Mary Franken Ostley, also a couple of years older than Kerri. They had been in a lecture class together Kerri's second year, but she had no other memory of the woman. On the same day Mr. Garibaldi had changed his name, Miss Ostley had added an extra "M" at the beginning of "Mary". *Rather striking, I suppose,* thought Kerri. *I don't care for it myself. Like Val—they only changed the spelling, and Timo did say there were more such in Honowell. Does this constitute a pattern? What on earth were they doing it for?*

She closed that volume and, without enthusiasm, picked up another—dated April, 68 —from the stack she had brought to her chair. This time she began at the beginning and leafed through the certificates with more attention. The greatest number of name changes recorded in the ledger were the usual sort due to marriage—hyphenations, mostly. There were also shockingly many cases in which one spouse had adopted the other's surname outright. Kerri assumed these must be Cits of the more old-fashioned type; The better educated classes of City People had long ago abandoned the practice as outmoded and adopted the Academic system of hyphenation: Not only did it suggest higher status, but it was so much easier to change back. Of course, Peasants neither changed their surnames (when they had them) nor hyphenated, and Stockholders were not required to leave personal traces of any kind in the public record. And then there were, almost as common as marriage name changes, the un-hyphenations for divorce.

Within the first two dozen entries, however, she found three more peculiar spelling changes. The third was a name she knew, Fiona Collins-Weir of the College of History—she whose approval was all important to those who, like Nick, would belong to the most elite study group, who would have the juiciest thesis topics. She, for whose favor Nick and Kerri planned a most important dinner party. Fiona had always, definitely, been one of Them; now, in the eyes of the law, she was "Fiyona".

A hand touched Kerri's shoulder. It was only Loren, whispering, "Found anything?"

"I'm not sure," Kerri whispered back. "But one item you will find interesting." She picked up the first binder and opened to Arzelle's change of name.

"Oh ho!" said Loren, forgetting to whisper. "Our Mutual Friend!"

Kerri smiled. Loren had taken up the epithet out of an apparent reluctance to pronounce Arzelle's name aloud. Soon, no doubt, she would make it a acronym—"OMF," as the Gang of Four were already becoming "The GOF." Loren read the certificate carefully, as if she were committing it to memory. "What are the other markers for?" she asked.

"More people whose names I recognized."

"They changed their names? Or just got married or divorced?"

"It's a little odd. All five of them only changed the spelling, otherwise kept the same name." She showed Loren Fiona's page.

"Hm," said Loren without enthusiasm. "Strange. I rather like the look of it, though. More...what? Distinctive? 'Fiona' is such a common name."

"I suppose," said Kerri, suddenly horrified as she realized she had addressed Fiona's (Fiyona's) dinner invitation with her old name, a grievous mistake. *But how was I supposed to know?* she worried silently. *Nick never mentioned it. In fact, he gave me the names and addresses written down, and he wrote 'Fiona' with no 'Y'. Does he not know, or was he just supremely careless? I had better ask him, maybe in general: Is he certain he gave me the right addresses and spellings of everybody's names? Because I don't think I want to explain how I found out about this spelling change.* She said, "I understand some people on the Islands have been doing this too—changing the spelling of their names. My ex-husband did. I cannot imagine why, unless it was a fad in certain circles."

"Makes sense," said Loren. "Less radical than a tattoo." She snickered at the notion of anyone with Academic ambitions getting a tattoo. "I never heard of it, though, but I am not the sort of person to be up on all the latest fashions."

Kerri frowned. *But I am*, she thought. *Or I try to be.* "I have not heard of it either," she said. "Did you find anything?"

"Possibly," said Loren. "Something worth showing you anyway."

"Excellent!" Kerri closed the binder without regret and noted gladly that it was less than twenty minutes to teatime.

Loren knelt on the floor next to Kerri's chair and opened the book she carried, a ledger marked "Farhill Jan - Mar 64". Several pages were marked with long strips of torn paper. She turned to the earliest marking and laid the open book on Kerri's lap.

The smudged and blotted pages of the ledger were full of the events of other peoples' lives: marriages, divorces, births, deaths. All were entered in the regulation copybook hand of the regulation civic clerks—the names, residential addresses, fees paid.

"This one," said Loren, tapping one entry with a fingernail. "A change-of-address notice. He is not particularly high on the list you gave me, but he is the first one I found at all."

"I did not know change-of-address notices were included in the civic records," said Kerri.

"Nor did I. The Post Office must forward them. As you can see, the entry is backdated." Loren grimaced at the page. "I don't much like the idea. But is this useful? I don't even know where these addresses are."

"They would both be flats, not houses. He moved about half a kilometer closer to campus," Kerri said. "I don't think it is significant, but now we know the city keeps this information. It may turn out to be of use someday. What are the other marks for?"

"Two divorces and a marriage," said Loren, rising to her feet. "Those were the only name changes I found. Two more address changes. Nothing suggesting a pattern. There seem to be no business transactions of any kind, unless you count things like wills probated, real estate taken up or relinquished by individuals, that sort of thing, and not concerning anybody on my list. Anyway," she took the ledger and stumped off the way she had come, talking over her shoulder, "I've had enough of this for one day. Let's go bully Alex into putting the kettle on."

Chapter 33

A Quarrel

Greta did not come to the Public Library that afternoon. Kerri did not know whether to feel relieved or anxious about her absence. The more she knew or guessed of Greta, the less she knew what to make of the woman, although she was coming to suspect a large capacity for mischief. She had tried not to think about it in advance, but this time it had taken more courage than usual to knock on Alex's office door, to face his mysterious colleague. Alex told them Greta had sent her apologies; he did not elaborate, and Kerri could not bring herself to ask for details. She politely echoed Loren's regrets at the news and braced herself against the next meeting.

It could not be denied that the conversation seemed a bit flat without Greta, although it was pleasant. Alex served them tea and biscuits and chatted as amiably as ever. He had a pile of things to show them, mostly novels of very dubious origin. His special prize was a badly damaged book on television, which he persisted in believing to be a topic of intense interest to Kerri. He actually pressed her to borrow it, which would have been quite improper as it was yet to be catalogued—which impropriety seemed to bother Alex not at all. (He expected it to be discarded, he said.) She tried to put him off, pleading the pressure of work and the end of term looming, but just in time she remembered a wisdom of her Grandmother's: "Never reject out-of-hand information that is freely and openly offered. You may judge its value after you know what it is." She accepted the book with slightly embarrassed thanks and promised to return it Friday, hoping that she could trust his assurances that it would not be missed.

Loren expressed interest in several of the novels and easily persuaded Alex to loan them to her for a few days. Kerri watched her closely during this transaction, wondering if Loren had seen in any of them the potential for thesis material (Loren being more informed than she about literature of dubious origin), but Loren did not indicate by so much as the flicker of an eyelash that she was interested in anything more than curling up with a "good read."

Kerri shyly raised the subject of inviting Timo to a future "afternoon." She told them what an old and trusted friend he was, dwelt on his tolerant and inquiring mind, his curiosity, and love of mystery. She emphasized that, as a son of the Sea

People, he would add yet another fresh point of view to their circle. Both Alex and Loren seemed cautiously receptive to the idea, but neither of them would give a committed assent without hearing Greta's opinion.

"We wouldn't be the Gang of Four anymore," said Alex, troubled.

"We shall always be the Gang of Four!" Loren reassured him with a warm smile. "But we might have guests, with your consent. Remember, as one of the Sea People, this man is not in Yendys regularly."

"True," Alex agreed. But he would wait to hear what Greta had to say.

By prior agreement, the foray into the Archives was not mentioned. If they ever actually found anything of importance, Kerri had remarked, *then* it would be worth sharing —the same kind of oddity as Greta's maps. They had decided that each of them would spend further time looking at the records whenever they had a few moments to spare in the Library, their only disagreement being over whether it was necessary to take notes. Loren wanted to; Kerri disliked the notion of writing anything down, although she felt foolish trying to give a reason. Loren might believe in Them, but she was not ready to believe that They had the leisure (or the motivation) to pry through other people's personal papers.

However, Loren's office had never been burglarized, her texts never hidden, her papers never destroyed. Nor did she have a spouse who might accidentally come across a cryptic list of names and ask, "What's this?" Or just see it—that would be bad enough.

In the end they had compromised: Anything written down must be encoded somehow and kept hidden. Loren's eyes sparkled at that; she thought it would be a good game!

On Wednesday, Kerri came home to find in the mail box responses from the three couples she and Nick had invited to their dinner party. All three declined.

She could not believe it at first. She read the formal calligraphed notes several times over before the words sank in. All three. There had always been a chance that at least one of the guests would have a prior engagement, but all six of them! And after Nick had gone to the trouble of finding out if the date would be appropriate.

Or she assumed he had gone to the trouble. Could he have sent the note of confirmation to her before he had actually got round to making inquiries? That would not be like him, although it could not be ruled out. Could he have misinterpreted their responses?

Or could he have asked in such an indirect way that they had misunderstood about the date? All of them? It did not make any sense.

Kerri made a pot of tea, but it didn't help. She went outside and poked at the garden for a few minutes, came back inside and poked at the fire in the stove. She even took up Alex's book about television but could not force herself to read even one page of the fragile volume before she buried it in a desk drawer. She found herself pacing distractedly around the house, feeling more and more angry and depressed by the moment.

When he came home half an hour later, Nick was as mystified as she was. "But I thought it was all settled," he protested, after reading the notes over as many times as she had. "They definitely gave me to understand—all of them—that they were free that evening."

"It's me, isn't it?" Kerri couldn't stop the words from bursting out of her.

"What?"

"It's me. I'm the reason they won't come." She made another tense orbit of the kitchen, her hands clenched in her pockets.

"Kerri, what in the name of the Dreamer are you talking about?"

"I'm not good enough for them. They've never thought so. They're making it as plain as they can. They will not dine in my home." She was appalled at herself, hearing the words she was saying, hearing the child's voice saying them, but she could not help it.

"What rubbish! I can't believe I'm hearing such nonsense from you."

"Is it nonsense, Nick? Is it really? I may be unSponsored, but I'm not stupid, nor am I blind and deaf. They've done nothing but patronize me from the moment they met me. They don't think I'm good enough for them, and they don't think I'm good enough for you." To her horror, she began to cry.

"Have you gone completely round the bend?" Furious, he began, like her, to pace the kitchen. They circled each other suspiciously.

"I've heard them. I've heard what they say about me. 'The poor little wife' they call me, as if I were some kind of mentally deficient child. And they make wagers on how soon you will leave me for Arzelle James-Dietrich. If you haven't already." Ugly, nasty sobs forced themselves out of her, and she hated them. And he wasn't going to comfort her and tell her it was all right. He was going to stand there and shout at her and call her names and belittle her and, yes, treat her like a mentally deficient child. And he would deny everything, which would make her believe him even less.

He stood there, and he shouted at her. "Leave you for Miss James-Dietrich? D'you think I'm crazy? Where are you getting these ridiculous ideas?"

"I saw you. The whole world saw you. At the Ball. You spent half the night with her. You ditched a dance with me to go off with her."

"Kerri, you practically pushed me into her arms that one time, and you ran off.... You never did explain that one to me. Was it your Stockholder you were running to? How do you think I felt with *that* going on in front of everyone all evening? Hearing my wife gossiped about everywhere I turned!"

"I suppose you would rather they had sneered at me and pitied me for being a wallflower. Apparently that was the alternative, thanks to all those friends of yours who stood me up. And you wonder where I get these ridiculous ideas!"

"So what did you expect them to do? Challenge a Stockholder? And besides, not all of them were my friends. I never heard of half of them!"

"They put their names on my card! It doesn't matter whether I was talking to a Stockholder or a kangaroo. They should have come; it's the rule. It is simple decent behavior."

"And how long did you give them to get to you when the music started? I never noticed that you waited at all. You could have given them a chance."

"How could you notice? You were off with Arzelle! I waited. I waited long enough the first few times. Then I didn't care. Why should I? You didn't seem to."

"*I* didn't? Me, pursued by a harpy from one side, and on the other side people are taking bets on how soon *you* were going to leave *me*..."

"Were they?" Kerri was arrested in mid-pace, the momentum of her temper suddenly derailed, confused. Calling Arzelle a harpy! That was a good one. That was promising.

"Well, I don't *know* that they actually did, but I felt as if they were, behind my back." His fury seemed to evaporate. He had come to a stop with his back against the cooler and now he slid down limply to the floor.

Kerri found her handkerchief. She was conscious of an absurd desire to giggle through the tears. She sat down on the nearest chair. "They were Stockholders, Nick. Talk about ridiculous ideas!"

"So," he said, "where *did* you go when you dashed off and left me to Miss James-Dietrich's tender mercies?"

Images wheeled through Kerri's mind: the letter to the Sea People, herself on the fire escape, Andrew Kianga Ryan with the moonlight on his hair. "The Ladies' Lounge," she said in a small voice.

"Oh." The eyes that had been glaring at her with anger and suspicion became unfocused. "The Ladies' Lounge," he repeated blankly.

Kerri nodded. His suddenly enlightened gaze returned to her face. He blushed.

Suddenly they were both laughing.

"You should have said something," he gasped.

"I thought I did," Kerri prevaricated. "You must not have heard me."

"Or Arzelle drowned you out. I thought...I don't know what I thought." He ran his hands through his hair and took a deep and somewhat shaky breath.

"I know what *I* thought," said Kerri, sounding a bit trembly herself. "And then when I was in there, that's where I heard them talking about you. And Miss James-Dietrich."

"Who?" Nick frowned.

"A couple of women. I don't know who they were."

"Silly gossips!" he exclaimed. "I suppose I do understand why there was talk, but truly, Kerri, you mustn't give it any credit. There's always talk—about everyone and everything. About me. About you. I have no intention," he continued earnestly, "of leaving you for Arzelle James-Dietrich or anyone."

Kerri regarded him sadly. "Then why didn't you just tell her to get lost?"

"Finally, I did," he said, with a gentle gasp of bemusement. "More or less. It wasn't easy, Kerri. Like heading off a charging buffalo, in fact. And she's...she's not a person one wants to offend."

"I know," said Kerri with feeling.

He chuckled again, "I simply could not get it into her head that I would not allow myself to be appropriated. It took the whole damned evening. I don't know if she is incredibly dense, or what."

"Not dense," Kerri assured him. "Incredibly determined. Be careful of her, Nick."

"Oh, come now," he scoffed. "She may be important and influential, but she's not dangerous."

Kerri found herself unable to reply. She took a deep breath. "About the dinner party," she began.

"The dinner party," Nick repeated thoughtfully. "That's off, for now, obviously." He considered for a moment. "I can't imagine how I misunderstood them. They said they were free. That is, Fiona did and Jilly did, and Marvin made more or less positive noises. I didn't talk to their spouses."

"Why not?"

"Why would I? I'd have had to hunt them down in their own departments, which would have been a bit more obvious than I liked. If one were going to invite the two of us to dinner, would one feel it necessary to talk to both of us? No, one wouldn't. And then, suppose I had already agreed to an engagement and hadn't yet told you about it, and you *thought* we were free that evening, and we weren't. That could happen."

"I suppose," Kerri agreed glumly.

"Depend on it. That's what did happen. I just find it hard to believe—*all* of them."

"So do I," said Kerri. She gave a last swipe to her nose and stuffed the handkerchief back into her pocket. She got up to see to the fire. "You did tell them to expect a dinner invitation from us?"

"Well, not in so many words." He was annoyed. "To what purpose? I only asked if they were free that evening. If you're going to invite someone formally, you invite them formally. You don't ask them verbally first."

"Of course, you do," Kerri protested. "Especially for a dinner party like this when one or two people coming or not coming can make a big difference. Especially on such short notice." She rattled the stove lid back into place and got the soup to put on.

"Doesn't make sense," he muttered.

"Makes perfect sense. Ask your mother."

"Anyway," he went on, "I hope we've heard the last of that nonsense about them all refusing to dine in your house and not approving of you and all that."

Kerri felt deeply ashamed of herself for the outburst. She had never intended to let Nick see that she noticed or minded, but now that it was out in the open (for the first time in several months) she intended to stick by her convictions. "I'll allow that the dinner party may be only bad luck," she said firmly, "but I do not believe it. And I am not mistaken in how they treat me. It has been better since I returned to the University this autumn, I do admit, but it is still there. And there is no other accounting for what they did to me at the Ball. I did not imagine that, and you know it. They do not regard me as an equal. They do not treat me as an equal. They treat me exactly the way my father's colleagues always treated my mother. I know what I am talking about. I grew up with it. Set the table now, if you please."

His face stubborn, he moved to find mats, plates and cutlery. "I still think you've built it far out of proportion," he insisted, but without force. "And if there is any truth to what you say—mind, I'm not saying there is—surely, it will be different now you're back at University."

"I hope so," said Kerri tonelessly, cutting the bread.

"Well," said Nick. "We will simply try them again for another day."

By the end of supper he had talked Kerri into a better mood (at least outwardly) and coaxed her to make new plans. It was rather a relief after all, he pointed out. The end of term was a terribly busy time to be putting on a fancy dinner party. They would wait a few weeks, pick a new date right after finals or, better still, during the holidays—invite a larger group.

All would be well.

Although Kerri did not believe a word of these reassurances, she went along with it all, let him talk on, agreed with everything he suggested. He was right about one thing: it was a relief to put off entertaining and trying to impress these people she did not like very much, try as she would. She did not even much care at the moment whether Nick's people ever came to dinner at all, although she knew they would have to eventually, if he was to succeed.

She was still appalled and stunned by the sickening row with Nicholas over the whole thing. She had never given way like that before, lost her dignity, behaved like a child. He had never lost his temper toward her like that, except—oh, that time he thought he had caught her snooping in his desk, and that wasn't really directed toward her at all but a reaction to stresses at work. Or so he had said.

"And there's the next retreat to work around," Nick reminded her. "This is the really important one, the one where I shall get a chance to talk thesis topics with the people who have some influence."

"Oh, yes." Kerri had, in fact, forgotten all about it. Now she remembered, with the old familiar knot tying itself in her chest. This was more than an informal weekend working party for a small, select group of students. This would be one of the big Retreats, a convocation of the esteemed, the powerful, the leaders and masters of the University. They gathered after Finals in some holiday place, skiing or surfing, drinking and dining, negotiating and dividing up research territories and vetting the hopeful younger individuals who had been invited, the lucky ones deemed worthy of consideration for Fellowships and, someday, Faculty seats. Without inclusion in these events, there could be no advancement,

Kerri remembered resentfully, and without a Sponsor, a student would never be included. Sometimes, however, spouses were invited. "Where is it, Nick? Am I supposed to go with you?"

He looked unhappy. "I don't think so. I'll have to make sure. In any case, I don't know how you could because it starts while exams are still going on."

She frowned. "Sounds inconvenient for a lot of people."

"Most people who are going don't have exams this term or have arranged to take them early," Nick assured her. "There will be a few who have to come down late, but things will be starting up as early as the Wednesday evening."

"And how long does it last."

"Until Monday afternoon, officially. Most people are staying on until Tuesday morning—one last evening..."

"That long! We'll have to put off our own holiday," Kerri said, deliberately casual.

"You wouldn't see much of me if you did come," Nick said. He got up to clear the table, a signal that he was impatient to drop the subject and get to work. "The negotiations over thesis boundaries will go on for hours. I am *not* looking forward to that, although I've yet to get into the worst of it. I hope there will be *some* free time, or I shall be ready for the Asylum by the time it is over. There should be recreational opportunities. It is a famous resort, after all."

"Famous? I don't believe you've mentioned where this retreat is to be held."

"Haven't I?" He poured hot water into the dishpan. "It's at The Lodge."

"*The* Lodge? You don't mean in Twilight Country? On the Lake?"

Bent over the sink, he nodded without turning around. "The very one."

"But isn't that rather expensive? Not to mention public? For a private retreat?"

He shrugged. "I suppose it won't be as quiet as we might like, but the prices are very reasonable. There's some sort of special deal. The University is more or less taking over the town for the duration, getting a discounted rate, and it's off-season anyway. I don't suppose the whole thing will cost me half what we spent on the Ball."

"Oh," said Kerri, "I'm not objecting to the money, Nick. How could I mind, when it's something this important? If it were really beyond our means you could always stay at my cabin; it's only a short walk to The Lodge, not even two kilometers. I could go down with you and keep to myself, off out of the way, while you're busy. I wouldn't intrude; no one would know I was there. That is, I could go after I'm done with Finals and meet you. We could stay on afterward for our own holiday or travel to some other place."

He did turn around then to look at her. "That's an idea!" He considered for a moment, then shook his head. "No, the arrangements are already made. If we'd thought of it sooner...but then, I'm probably better off being right there in the thick of things. Less likely to miss something, more chances to talk to the people who count. That sort of thing. You would be too much of a distraction." He grinned. "I might get in trouble. Better wait until it's all finished and join me then." He turned back to his dishwashing. "Thanks for the offer, though."

"Any time." *The people who count*, she said to herself. *Them. Arzelle?* Not that she would mention that name again tonight for anything in the world.

"Besides," he reminded her, "I would not wish to be away from town on Tuesday, when the lists come out. When this is all out of the way, we can get on with our own holiday. Go to the Islands, if you still want to, or down the coast."

"Yes," said Kerri. "We'll talk about it tomorrow." It was kind of him, she thought, to imply that he believed her name would be on those lists. He did not really believe it would be. He would be surprised.

She finished the last of her tea and rose from the table. Tomorrow was Recitation, and she had a quarter of her lines still to learn. On her way out of the kitchen she scooped up the letters of refusal and took them with her to the study. She would rather have burnt them to ashes than look at them or even touch them again, but there was something she needed to find out. At her desk, holding the paper close to the lamp she studied the signature of Fiona Collins-Weir. Yes. It was there. A delimiter. So Fiona still kept the new spelling of her name—new five years ago—but she did not use it in public and had not incorporated it into her signature except for the tiny extra curl that signified a disparity between signature and legal name. And Val had also signed his name with a Delimiter.

Frowning, she picked up the note in which Martha Lang-Soulis regretted that she and her husband were unable to accept the kind invitation of Miss Dale-Townsend and Mr. Townsend-Dale, etcetera. Miss Lang-Soulis' signature clearly showed a delimiter. *Has she changed her name, too?* Kerri wondered confusedly. *Has Jilly?* But Jillian Munro-Haines' signature possessed no extra sign; her name was apparently unaltered. *The fashion must have changed*, Kerri reflected. *Maybe They are getting tattoos these days.* In spite of everything, she smiled.

Chapter 34

The Influenza

She slept very badly that night. Toward morning she had the Star Dream, but after waking she could remember none of the details. Although she and Nick had achieved a kind of truce after the dreadful row the evening before, he seemed cool and preoccupied in the morning.

On the way to the City he barely spoke—he must get some reading done, he said—and spent most of the ride immersed in his book. She felt most uneasy about him. It was all her own fault. How could she have lost control so badly? She would have given anything to turn back time and undo the scene she had made.

And the dinner party. She had not been looking forward to it. She ought to feel glad that it was postponed. (Surely, only postponed!) In fact, she *was* glad. Why couldn't she have seen that yesterday?

She had not had a good feeling about the project from the moment Nick had suggested it, but she had been too obedient to her sense of duty to him to marshal any arguments against it, even in her own mind. Now she could think of several. To begin with, the timing was inconvenient. It would have been a lot of work, a lot of trouble, especially with finals looming.

As for why the invited guests had all refused, she still had her suspicions, and every right to them. Call them suspicions, although they felt more like certainties, even in the cold light of day. In the cold light of this particular morning, however, she found she did not much care. Let them affect to shun her now. Everything would be different when she got her own Sponsor. Far better to venture out upon the social stage *then*. Less than a month to wait, now. The thought did not improve her spirits much.

When she arrived at her office she discovered that she had left home several library books that were due. In the ladies' lounge she overheard Charlotte Danvers, a fellow student, make a slighting comment to another about "Miss Dale-Townsend's pedestrian handwriting"—an outrage, considering that Miss Danvers had the worst penmanship in the department. No one could possibly respect *her* opinion on the subject; still, Kerri found it immensely aggravating and unavoidably depressing. She simmered about it for hours. There was a graduate student meeting called at short notice in the Common Room at half past twelve, which meant she got no lunch or meditation time before her Recitation. So frivolous was the matter under discussion—should they or should they not have a department holiday party before Finals?—she found herself suspecting someone had called the meeting on purpose to deprive her of prep time. By the time she was due at Professor Greystone's office, she felt cranky and exhausted and had a headache coming on.

In spite of every other possible thing seeming to go wrong that Thursday, the Recitation went well, including a surprise review of earlier materials. The Professor always asked for excerpts from previous assignments as the term drew to a close, a tactic that had been known to send the unprepared into a dead faint. However, Kerri had been expecting the testing and performed adequately. She had never had any trouble retaining her lines in long term memory and even now could recite most of her undergraduate pieces with only minimum cues.

This was the one arena of academic achievement in which she had always had firm self-confidence. Recitations were set, known, immutable on the printed page. No one could say, "You are wrong. You are thinking illogically. You are taking unwarranted liberties. You are making unjustified conclusions, You are mistaken. You are wrong." The words were there, independent of argument, opinion, prejudice, likes or dislikes, independent of who you were and what people thought you were capable of. If you delivered the words properly, your delivery might be criticized, but no one could say you were wrong.

And what in the world it was good for, she commented glumly to herself, nobody knew. *I've been corrupted by Bad Influence*, she noted: *The Gang of Four. I'm becoming a Revolutionary Anarchist.* She felt like Subverting the System. It was that sort of day.

By the time the Professor dismissed her, her headache had got to the throbbing, nauseating stage. She had intended to go hunting again in the Archives at the Public Library after her Recitation, maybe pop in and say hello to Alex—she had looked forward to it as an antidote—but instead she returned to her office, locked the door, took two aspirins and lay down on the couch.

When she woke, it was dark, nearly six, according to the clock. She groaned and sat up, feeling no better than she had before her nap. The headache seemed to have moderated by the process of spreading evenly over her entire body. Paterson Hall was silent; nearly everyone would be gone by now. She had missed all the express trains; she would never get home before seven. Nick would be wondering where she was by now. "If he comes home at all," she muttered. "Couldn't blame him if he didn't."

She packed her book bag, put her coat on and dragged herself down to the ladies' lounge to wash her face. The cold water helped to clear her mind just enough to remember a book she had intended to bring home as reference for next week's essay. This meant dragging herself back up two flights of stairs, unlocking the office again, relighting the lamp. She found the book and was just extinguishing the lamp, when it occurred to her that it had been days since she had tried the Veil on her office—since the Ball, in fact.

Well, it couldn't hurt. She tossed her possessions on the couch, locked herself in, and sat down in her meditation posture, which, oddly enough, seemed to ease the ache in her back and legs. *Veil,* she thought, letting the air-colored shield slide around the space of the office like a glove. There was something so comforting about the old ritual that she felt eased and found herself tempted to drift off to sleep again, right where she was.

"No!" she commanded herself. "Put the coat on, lock up and go home!" Veil or not, she took her usual care in locking and sealing the office.

Out in the cold, bracing air, she began to feel better and clearer-headed. A cup of tea from a vendor at Central Station helped even more. By the time she got on the Fernly-Evesham streetcar, the headache had retreated to a kind of dull fog, although the rest of her still felt as if it had been trampled by horses in the not too distant past.

Nick took one look at her, when she let herself into the house, and ordered her off to bed. "Sign in tomorrow, get a waiver, and then come straight home," he suggested, concerned. "You've got no lectures or anything due on a Friday, and I think you have got influenza. It's going around my college. Don't worry about supper. I'll fix myself something and make you some broth and toast." If he was still cross at her over the previous evening's outburst, it did not show.

"Flu," said Kerri feebly. "I think you're right. For real this time. Too bad we used it as an excuse last month."

Nick chuckled. "Then I won't mention it to anybody."

Safely tucked in under the quilts, she invoked the Veil over the house and garden. She had meant to do this every day since Thomas died, but, like Veiling her office, she had forgotten since the Ball. Fortunately, nothing untoward had happened in the meantime. It was not a proper Veiling, with centering and doors open and so forth; it was much more like the quick invocations she used to protect her person from Their attention. But she was in bed with influenza, and Nick was up and about. It would have to do. Besides, it was merely the Game, so what did it matter?

Immediately, she felt comforted, as she had in her office, like a small child wrapped at long last in the one favorite, beloved blanket. Not only did her aches seem to ease, but she felt her mind relaxing as well. It had been a bad day, but no wonder, if she was sickening with flu. Everyone had bad days from time to time.

Things were going to be all right with Nick. "Oh, and I have to take those library books in tomorrow," she reminded herself sleepily.

Then, suddenly, she remembered: Fridays were Gang of Four days. She groaned and opened her eyes. How could she miss tea at Alex's? Greta had to be asked about Timo. And there was a tentative plan to lunch with Loren. Not to mention the Archives. *That* was one endeavor that *should* be put off. Waste of time.

I have to go to Town tomorrow, she thought. *Get a waiver. Might as well go to the Public Library. Why? Don't be silly. I'm sick. I've got the flu. No, I have to go. I'll miss something. They'll do something important, and Loren will have an advantage. Unworthy thought. So what? She will, even if she doesn't use the advantage. I would use it, if I were in her place. Would I? I'd keep track of it anyway.*

If I don't go, I don't have to face Greta. Put that off a few more days. Don't be silly. Why should I worry about facing Greta? What harm can she do? Got to keep track of her in any case. I've got to go.

But it's not until three o'clock. That's the whole day on campus to pretend I'm fine.

Feel like perfect hell. Just want to turn in my library books, check in at the department, get my waiver, go home and rest. Not stay all day. Could lie down on the couch, pretend I'm not there if anybody knocks. No, then I'd sleep too late and miss it anyway. Tea at Alex's.

Best not to try. Send a note to Loren. Explain. Say I'm sick. Give my regrets to the Gang of Four. Long live the Revolution!

But the next morning, Friday morning, she felt better than half alive: A bit weak and shaky, still aching in muscles and joints, but only a little feverish. She thought she might last the day after all, she told Nick, if she took things very easily. He had his doubts and said so, but they both knew she must make the trip to town to sign the department Day Book. She promised him she would go home early, that she would stop in at the Infirmary and get a waiver for Monday, in case she didn't get better over the weekend. Nevertheless, he looked so concerned when their ways parted in the Main Quad that she wished she had come down with the flu two days ago. Then he would have made allowances for her on Wednesday and they would not have had that dreadful quarrel. Indeed, maybe she had been sickening even then, and that was why she had let go in such a shame-making way.

In the interests of conserving her energies, she returned the library books first and then went directly to the Infirmary. Apparently the influenza had attacked the University on a broad front, to judge by the number of miserable-looking people in the waiting room and the number of waivers being carried out the door. Kerri got hers, when her turn came, without any trouble.

Although she had not requested it, the nurse wrote the waiver through to Wednesday. "Go home!" she said firmly to Kerri. "Do not come back until you are really better. We cannot have the lot of you infecting everyone else on campus."

"But by next Thursday..." Kerri began.

"Next *Wednesday*," interrupted the nurse, "if you are still not on your feet, write to the Infirmary. We will extend your waiver to Friday and post it to you and your department secretary. Do not come in person! When is your Recitation? Thursday? I shall give you a waiver for that also. Notify your auditor today."

"Yes, ma'am!"

"Pity there are no telephones any more," the nurse grumbled. "People could stay at home in the first place, and we would not have all of this nonsense and everyone infected."

"Yes, ma'am!"

Kerri accepted her waiver with some guilt, for she did not feel as ill as she had last night, nor as miserable as all the other waiting victims looked. If it had not been for the long round trip between Evesham and the University, she would never have bothered. In her undergraduate years, living in the District, she had never asked for a waiver, no matter how ill she had been. It was always possible to totter the few blocks to campus to sign in.

On the other hand, she thought as she trudged up the stairs of Paterson Hall, *it's a bloody long trip from the country, and maybe I won't feel so fine by Monday.* The walk from the Infirmary had exhausted her. Her headache had returned, and the other aches and dizziness and the rest. Feeling worse by the moment, she signed the Day Book and unlocked her mailbox. There was a note from Loren, folded in the shape of a penguin; nothing else.

"Eureka!" said the note. "News from P.L.! Lunch off? West Gate half past twelve? Please confirm. L." This was lettered out in the form of a haiku.

At first Kerri was too much befogged to make sense of this missive. She sat stupidly at her desk, coat still on, counting the syllables to make sure they came out to the right number. Then the meaning began to take shape. News from the Public Library. Did that mean Loren had gone back to the Archives and found something? Or had she received some communication from Alexander? (A worrying thought. Why should Alex write to Loren and not to her? How could Alex write to either one of them? He had never been told their surnames.) No, "eureka" suggested a discovery. Loren wanted to meet at the West Gate at twelve thirty and go off campus somewhere to lunch so they could discuss whatever she had found.

"Damn!" muttered Kerri. "She would! Lunch, then, and straight afterward I'm off home."

She burned the note and wrote a post card in reply: a single enigmatic word—"Confirmed."—with no signature or even an initial. "Let the College spies have fun with that!" she said to herself as she dropped it in the post box. She returned to her office, wrapped herself in her coat and the blanket from her cupboard, and started to read over next week's lines.

"You don't look very well," said Loren.

"Influenza," croaked Kerri.

"You poor thing! You ought to go home. Get a waiver."

"I did. Then I got your note."

Loren grinned fiendishly and said nothing.

"Very well," said Kerri. "Don't tell me. I don't care. I'm dying anyway."

Loren laughed. "Let us stay on campus then. I've no intention of hauling your corpse back up this hill."

They returned to Kerri's office, since it was more comfortable than Loren's, although Kerri decided she seemed to feel worse in Paterson Hall than she did anywhere else, even outside in the cold. Maybe there was something wrong with the ventilation. Loren tucked her up on the couch and went out in search of chicken soup for Kerri, a sandwich for herself and tea for both. While she was gone, Kerri invoked the Veil over the office. She had been doing it at all day at frequent intervals—completely illogical, but it seemed to help.

"I shan't tease you any more," Loren said, when she returned and the door was safely closed. She kept her voice low, conspiratorial. "I went to the Archives yesterday—just for a few minutes; I had an appointment in that part of the City—and this time I really found something. The Society of Guenevere!"

"What?" Kerri sat up, forgetting all about her aches for the moment.

"I did. I found it. I opened a ledger at random, started looking, and there it was. It was pure luck, nothing else."

"Tell me!"

"On June 30, year 66, a house in Glen Eden was transferred from the estate of a Miss Wilma Hinchliffe Beckett-Martinez to a Society of Guenevere."

"So there *is* such a thing!" Kerri murmured. She thought for a moment. Miss Becket-Martinez must be Academic, by her name, and Glen Eden was one of the most desirable neighborhoods in the University District—hillsides with heavenly views of the city and harbor, enormous houses on large lots that invariably passed from parent to child and rarely came into the Public Domain. "What is the Society of Guenevere, then? Did it say?"

"No," said Loren. "This was the third to last entry in the Rosewood District registry for the second quarter of that year—just the bare bones. There might be more information on the document itself, but I did not have time to hunt it down. Perhaps this afternoon or next week."

Kerri nodded. "Well," she said. "At last. I do not mind telling you I am relieved to know the Society of Guenevere does exist and that it isn't something we should have remembered from the Syllabus. Whatever it is—or was; this was five years ago, after all—it is some real entity, not a literary or historical reference."

"You know what I think?" declared Loren. "It is a tontine!"

"Ah! Of course. That does make sense. In that case, there must be at least one surviving member."

"Perhaps not. Remember, this Miss Becket-Martinez died five years ago. They may have all been quite elderly. By now the Society of Guenevere may no longer exist. Glen Eden. That is a rather elegant area, isn't it?"

"Rather." Kerri sneezed suddenly and a wave of dizziness came over her. "I have coveted each and every one of those houses. A tontine. Of course." She leaned back and closed her eyes.

"We can talk about it Monday," said Loren, gathering up the remains of lunch. "You go home and go to bed! Now!"

"But it is Friday," Kerri protested. "The Public Library. I wanted to get an answer on whether I could invite Timo. And—damn!—I forgot to bring back Alex's book!"

"Did you read it?"

"No", she sighed.

"Well, there you are," said Loren. "You *can't* go to tea at the Library. You weren't meant to. Don't even think of it! I'll make certain we take a vote about your seagoing friend." She grinned mischievously. "I shall give them your regrets. And I promise you, I won't let them discuss anything important while you're not there. You'll not miss a thing."

"Long live the Revolution!" Kerri whispered, reaching for her handkerchief.

Chapter 35

Gossip

If one had to be confined to bed with influenza, this was not a bad weekend to choose. The weather turned nasty that Friday evening, wave after wave of cold, wind-driven rain blowing in from the sea, a perfect Saturday to stay inside, close to the fire. Unfortunately, Nick had to go into town. He had an appointment with his dentist and needed to look up something in the library. He worried aloud about leaving her alone, but there was no question that he would go. For one thing the laundry needed picking up or both of them would be in a pickle by Monday. For another, they needed supplies—Kerri had not done her usual marketing before the weekend. He did not like to leave her alone, he said, but he was afraid he must go. Kerri told him not to be silly, go on to Town, she would be all right.

It was plain to see that he was preoccupied. He was kind and attentive, bringing Kerri tea and broth and hot lemonade, but more than once he did not respond when she spoke to him, his eyes looking far away into nothing. When she mentioned his abstraction, saying that she hoped *he* was not coming down with the flu, he told her, no, it was only the dreaded thesis topic negotiations. Of course, with his ancestry and his standing at the University, there could be no doubt that he would get something with a little meat on it, but life would be so much more livable for the next two years if he could also achieve a topic that interested him, better still if he could ingratiate himself well enough with the right people to be given a subject, no matter how small, on the frontiers of scholarship—a passage from a recently approved text, something not already picked clean, analyzed to death and weighed down by generations of scholarly commentary.

Therefore, she kept her unworthy misgivings to herself and said again he must go and not worry about her. If he would just enlist one of the neighbors to get the ice in, she would manage very well, would not even have to get out of bed. *You are protesting too much,* she thought peevishly; *I am not going to die if you go to town. What are you really going for? Perhaps to drop in on Miss Collins-Weir and apologize for your "little wife's" presumption of inviting her to dinner? Or to have lunch with Arzelle?* She felt too ill to be ashamed of herself for thinking such things.

Nick stoked up the kitchen stove and lit a fire in the little bedroom stove that also warmed the study—it was the first time that season they had needed more than one fire— and went out to see if Tim Moncrief-Davis would do the ice. Tim was willing. Nick went off on the nine-forty-five streetcar.

At midday, Sharon Davis-Moncrief came over with a pot of freshly made chicken soup for the invalid. She ran a bath for Kerri, re-filled the kitchen boiler, and made up both the fires. When Kerri, bathed and fed, was tucked up in bed again in a clean flannel nightgown, Sharon sat with her for awhile to keep her company.

"Only until Tim comes to do the ice and fetch me home," she promised. "If I'm making you tired, only tell me at once, and I shall go." She took out her knitting and set to work on yet another garment for the baby.

"Not at all," said Kerri. "Please do stay a little while. I've hardly seen you since the beginning of the term, and I miss our chats. I only hope you don't catch this flu. We can't have you ill now."

Sharon and her husband Timothy had lived in the abandoned hamlet almost as long as Kerri and Nick. Although they were graduate students, they were bound for City careers, not the Faculty, and seemed contented with their lot. Neither had a Sponsor or hope of one. They were good, decent, amiable people. Sharon and Kerri had become fast friends in the early isolated days, and had long ago fallen into informal speech when they were alone.

"Oh, I never catch anything," Sharon said calmly. "Healthy as a horse! As the saying goes. I don't mind telling you, though, I shall be awfully glad when Her-or-His Highness is born. I feel like a very ripe pumpkin. And look like one in this pullover. Vile color. I say that even though I dyed the wool myself, and proud of it I was, too. Ah well, pride goeth, etcetera."

Kerri laughed weakly. "How much longer now, one more month?"

"Please! Three and a half weeks!"

"It seems to have gone by so fast."

"Says you! Sometimes I think I have always been pregnant, and I always shall be pregnant. Any other kind of life was just a dream. The University. These days it feels a million kilometers away."

"You miss it?"

"Not a bit. Sometimes I even wonder if I shall go back next year. Or ever. I'm having such fun here—the dear cozy little house, the garden, my hens and sheep, the baby, the blissful quiet. I was a scholar. Whoever would have thought I would become like this?"

"I can imagine it," said Kerri thoughtfully. "There are times when it seems a heavenly idea."

"On the other hand," said Sharon, placidly knitting, "it is probably just brain chemicals, arousing my nesting instincts. By the time the baby is crawling I shall probably feel I have been buried alive out here, ready to get back to the old grind—join all you slaves to tradition on that miserable early trolley every morning."

"Miserable is a good description, now that winter is on," said Kerri.

"Winter, indeed!" Sharon affirmed. "Did you know there is snow on the mountains?"

"No! Snow! This early?"

"You could see it this morning from the other end of the village, before the clouds closed down again. I would not be surprised if it snowed here. Seems cold enough. Oh, look! That was Tim just passing by the window. The ice must be here."

She put away her knitting and got ponderously to her feet. "I'll go let him in."

In a few moments she returned. The ice was in, she told Kerri, and Timothy was filling up the woodboxes, and there was a kettle on the back of the kitchen stove in case Kerri needed any hot water.

"Oh, and I've got news from Tim," she said, with some excitement. "There's a party of workmen at the big villa. Tramping all around, in and out. They've got the key."

"Oh, no!" exclaimed Kerri.

"Oh, yes. Someone's taking the place."

"No! They can't be. This has happened before. Remember?"

"I know. The inspection will put them off. But listen to this! You'll never guess! Young Elizabeth walked over and asked them what they were up to, and she said they told her a Stockholder is interested in the place. It's a Stockholder!"

"What? You must be joking!"

"That's what they told Elizabeth *and* Elizabeth's mother!"

"A Stockholder. Here."

"Boggles the mind, doesn't it? We're going to wander casually over that way on our way home and see what we can find out. Is there anything else you need before I go? No? Then I'm off. Take care, now."

After Sharon had gone, Kerri lay under her quilts thinking of the news she had just heard. A Stockholder taking the villa! How on earth could that happen? How could any Stockholder have even heard of the place? True, there was no denying that only a Stockholder, or someone almost as rich, could afford the fortune needed to restore the old house to a livable condition. Someone like Loren could never have done it. Still, Kerri was saddened that Loren might not even have the option now. She did not look forward to telling her friend about this. On the other hand, it would be some compensation that the lovely old place would not have to be demolished, and that Arzelle and Val would never get it. Not to mention what a resident Stockholder would do for the reputation of Evesham, which might go from quirky and interesting to fashionable and desirable. Yes, *that* was compensation! Strange, a month ago that would have been the first thing Kerri would have thought of.

And there was another thought in the back of Kerri's mind, one she did not want to acknowledge at all. All the same, there it persisted, quite stubbornly, despite her firmest resolution. *Who is this Stockholder? Could it be someone I have met? Could he have heard of the hamlet because I live here? Could he have investigated because he was curious about the place where I live? Could he have discovered the villa then and decided to acquire it?*

After all, Stockholders are not limited to two residences.

No! Do not be ridiculous! A thousand times no! Impossible. Don't even think about it for a minute, because it simply cannot be true. In any case, it will be another false alarm.

All the same, Kerri found her mind wandering into strange and beguiling fantasies that afternoon—all proper and chaste, to be sure, but nevertheless entertaining. No doubt it was the fever.

Not until the early dusk was falling and Nick was letting himself in the front door did she remember that some Stockholders were also Academics. Professor Bonneville-Chatterton, her Sponsor-to-be, was such a person, also Professor Edson, her enemy, if there was such a thing. How many others? They were all adopted into the Stockholder caste, and they kept it secret. It could be anyone. She felt a sudden chill: Arzelle?

Against her own better judgement and over Nick's strong protestations, Kerri took herself into Town on Monday morning. She did feel better, she told him (and herself) after the benefit of a weekend in bed. She had two lectures she could not afford to miss. It worried her to leave her office untenanted for so long. She kept on justifying the idiocy of the trip until they were on the streetcar and it was too late to back down. Nick had already given up. He was distant this morning, admitting that thesis negotiations were becoming stressful and, no, he did not want to discuss it.

Kerri knew she had made a mistake as soon as she reached Paterson Hall. A wave of dizziness hit her the moment she set her foot on the bottom step of the front stairs, and she thought for a moment she would have to sit down on the cold stone until she could gather the strength to totter to the Infirmary—all the way back to the river. She would never make it that far. Without thinking, she raised the Veil. It seemed to help.

Somehow, she managed to put one foot in front of the other until she found herself on the second floor in the Late Classics Department. The open area by the mailboxes and the receptionist's desk seemed more crowded than usual this morning. People stood in small groups, talking in low, urgent voices. Most of them looked frightened.

Marya Chin-Gerald spotted her. "I thought you were home with a waiver," she said, frowning.

"And so I should be," Kerri retorted. "Yet here I am. What is going on?"

"You do not know? But you went home at midday Friday, did you not? You would not have heard."

These were ominous words. "I have not heard what?"

Miss Chin-Gerald was apparently too shocked to play games. "Two people in this building demented on Friday. They did not find the second one until yesterday."

"Name of the Dreamer!" Kerri gasped. "Who?"

"Mr. Grahame-Skovanek and Miss Rippinger."

"Name of the Dreamer!" Kerri repeated. Miss Alice Rippinger had the office next door to her own. Kerri had not liked her very much—she was a shrill and uncongenial person—but still...! This was too close. This was devastating.

She started to ask, "Which..."

Miss Chin-Gerald said, "It was Mr. Grahame-Skovanek they found yesterday. He had not been home, and his wife insisted the watchmen search the whole building. He was not in his office, you see. They found him in the third floor men's lounge in one of the cubicles."

"And Miss Rippinger?"

"She happened to leave her office door open Friday afternoon. She was lying on the floor. Someone walked by and noticed."

Kerri let herself into her office with shaking hands. She averted her eyes from the open door beyond her own. Several people were inside, talking in low voices. University officials, most likely, someone from the Health Department, perhaps a relative or friend packing up the victim's personal effects. She had no idea whether Miss Rippinger had any living relatives. So few people did, besides their parents and perhaps a child, and Miss Rippinger had never been married. She had not seemed to have many friends. And now she was in the Asylum for the rest of her life.

I should have been friendlier, Kerri thought guiltily. *At least more civil.*

She invoked the Veil around her office as soon as she stepped inside the door. It was a habit she intended to cultivate, and this morning, of all mornings, she was not likely to forget it, not with the department seething in fear and horror around her. Unsurprisingly, she felt better immediately, truly protected. She exhaled deeply and sat down to recover.

She was glad she had forced herself to come to Town today. She had known there must be a reason for feeling so, yes, *compelled* to be here. As frightening as these dreadful tragedies were, it was much better to be here, to find out, than to be outside the lines of communication even for one more day. Two people were gone. This would change the dynamics of the department, change everyone's position. She had done right to come.

After a few minutes, she stirred herself to take off her coat and begin examining the room for signs of tampering. She found none. The new lock was apparently still working, or else Val (if it really was Val) had taken her threat to heart. Perhaps he was simply too busy these days.

She had finished her examination and arranged her work on her desk when there was a hesitant tapping at her locked door. Kerri opened it to find another first year graduate student she knew slightly. The woman seemed surprised.

"Oh!" the woman said. "I did not know anyone was here. I want to have a look."

"At what?" asked Kerri.

"The office. Before I put my application in. I see they have not moved her things out yet."

"These are my things," said Kerri. "This is my office."

"You have already moved in?" The woman spoke accusingly. "I understood applications were still being accepted."

"I beg your pardon?" Kerri inquired coolly.

"The office," the woman explained. "I did not think it would be reassigned so quickly, but I see I am too late." She looked annoyed.

"Reassigned?" asked Kerri. "I do not understand. I have been in this room since the beginning of term. There is no reassignment pending."

"But," protested the woman, "is this not the office where..."She broke off in confusion.

"I believe," Kerri ventured reasonably, "that you must be looking for Miss Rippinger's office. That is next door, and I have no doubt it will be reassigned, as Miss Rippinger will no longer require it."

"But I am sure I was told it was *this* room," said the woman stubbornly. Kerri could understand her disappointment. Her office was larger than Miss Rippinger's, with a bigger window and a better view.

"Next door," she said with no sympathy and just the right amount of condescension. "This office is mine. Good day." She shut the door firmly and found herself trembling.

What if I had been here Friday afternoon? she wondered. *What if I hadn't taken ill and gone home? Might it have been me?* But that was absurd.

Dementing was not like lightning striking whatever person happened to be in the right place at the wrong time; it was an illness, a seizure of the brain. The cause was unknown, and there was no known cure, but it came from within its victims. It was not inflicted upon them from outside, and it was not contagious, so far as anybody could prove. It would not happen to Kerri.

A memory: Thirteen years ago. Zarah circling her like a bird of prey. "You see, I know all about you. I know what is going to happen to you some day. You are going to lose your mind. You will be demented. I can tell. I know how to see the mark of it, and the mark is on you. There is nothing you can do about it. You can not escape. Some day it will happen."

Someone knocked at the office door.

"What now?" Kerri muttered savagely. "Another vulture?" She threw open the door.

Loren stepped back, startled. "You *are* here!"

"Oh," said Kerri. "Miss Weberly. I thought.... Never mind. Come in."

She locked the door behind Loren and turned to face her friend.

Loren stared at her with a pinched and anxious face. "You've heard, I suppose," she said.

Kerri nodded. "Just now. Can you believe it? People are already trying to get their offices. Vultures! Predators!"

"Disgusting," Loren agreed. "Actually, I put my name in Friday afternoon."

"What?"

She shrugged. "Well, I do have that little tiny cubby in Mossfield Annex, no window to speak of. Wouldn't you?"

Kerri thought about it. Loren's office was tiny, dark and badly located. Of course she wanted better. Why not? It would be fun to have her next door. Not that it was likely to happen.

"I suppose," she said. "But it is most depressing."

"Yes, indeed," Loren said. "How are you feeling? I didn't really expect you to be here."

Kerri sat down at her desk again. "I have been better. I probably shouldn't be here, but I got very well rested over the weekend, and I felt I must come to campus today; I did not know why. Just as well, as it turns out. I've got a couple of lectures to go to. I shall go home early."

Loren nodded. "Good. Don't work yourself into a relapse. We missed you Friday."

"At Alex's? How was it?"

"Pleasant." Loren grinned. "You will be glad to know that Greta thought it would be great fun to meet a 'Sea Person', as she called your friend, so we are all agreed that you may bring him along to tea any time he happens to be in town on one of our afternoons. No notice required."

"Thank you," said Kerri. "What did you all talk about?"

"Architecture mostly. Old buildings. Abandoned homes. Greta was telling us about restoration, about which I'm beginning to take an interest, as you know. She's had experience on at least one restoration. She did not exactly say so, but I suspect she may have worked on a contractor's crew once. It wouldn't surprise me."

"It would surprise me," said Kerri thoughtfully. "Then again, maybe not."

"I told them about the big house in your village," Loren continued. "The one I took a fancy to."

"Oh, about that," said Kerri uncomfortably, "I am afraid someone else has had a look at it. Just on Saturday. A whole crew of inspectors were out. Or so I was told."

"No!" Loren cried. "My house! They can't!"

"In fact, they probably won't," Kerri assured her. "However, I must tell you this time gossip says it is a Stockholder."

This brought Loren up short. "You cannot be serious! How very odd. Evesham is not exactly a Stockholder sort of place, is it?"

Kerri shook her head. "Yet, who else would have the money? Truly, Loren, I shouldn't worry. Chances are it will come to nothing. If you are serious about the house, perhaps you ought to make inquiries of your own."

"Take up squatter's residence. That's what I should do." Loren sighed. "In winter. Cheering thought. I don't know if I am that serious." She got to her feet. "I must be on my way. Ah! I nearly forgot. There was something else we talked about on Friday."

At Kerri's look of alarm, she chuckled. "Do not worry! As I promised you, we discussed nothing important, although Alex had something he was burning to share with all of us. In fact, he was the one who insisted on postponing it until you could be with us."

"Really?" Kerri felt flattered. "What is it?"

Loren pulled a paper-wrapped parcel out of her book bag and handed it across the desk. "You are to read this book. I had it over the weekend, I am to pass it on to you, and we are to discuss it next time. Well, I suppose not tomorrow, as you will scarcely have had time to read it. Maybe Friday."

Kerri reached for the package and began to unwrap it. "You do not mean this is a possible text, do you?" she asked sharply. "You did not tell Alex we were looking for one?"

"Oh, no," said Loren. "This is just something of Alex's that he wants to talk about because it interests him. Or because it interests Greta. It may have been her idea."

The book was ancient, fragile and heavy. Kerri looked at the faded lettering on the spine. *Dreams.* She lifted an inquiring eyebrow at Loren.

"Whatever you do," Loren instructed, "don't lose it. It doesn't exactly belong to Alex. In fact, I think he may have extracted it temporarily from the acquisition process. It doesn't have a catalogue number on it, or even the library stamp."

"Oh dear!" said Kerri. "Not again!" No library would loan out a book, even to an employee, until that book had been officially stamped and catalogued. If Alexander had waylaid this volume from Public Library acquisitions, she was holding what might as well be stolen property, and not for the first time. This was much worse than the case of the television book, about which she could say, if confronted, that she had accepted his loan in good faith, assuming that the book had been his personal property. "Perhaps we had better take it straight back to Alex and make him return it."

Loren said, "He swears it won't be missed, and I believe him. He says it came from a box of books they got out of a warehouse at least three years ago. The backlog over there is worse than at the University. It will be months before anybody can process that particular box. And even if they processed it tomorrow, nobody would remember what was originally in it. I don't think it is a valuable book."

"Not Canon," Kerri agreed, turning over a few brittle pages. The author's name was unfamiliar to her. "Old, though. Age of Dreams?"

"Well, maybe." Loren shifted her book bag to the other shoulder and moved toward the door. "Shall you read it?"

Kerri hesitated. She was an educated person, intimate with many great books, long passages of which she had committed to memory. But she very seldom read anything she had not at some time been told to read. Even the books she read for relaxation were invariably from the Syllabus of Study—old friends, such as Dickens, Kipling, Sayers, Tolkien, who could be revisited again and again. She had always realized that finding a new text upon which to base her thesis meant that the text would have to be *read*: new territory, entirely uncharted. However, it had never occurred to her that in the search for this new text, she might have to read other new books that had no ultimate purpose at all, so far as her Academic career was concerned: books that were not Canon. Yet, how else could a new text be found?

"Yes," she said. "I will read it."

Chapter 36

Dreams

Not five minutes after Loren had gone, Nick appeared, pale faced and out of breath, in Kerri's office doorway. When he saw her, he sagged against the door frame with a deep sigh.

"Nick?" Kerri stared at him, startled. "What is wrong?"

"You..." he panted. "You are...Are you all right?"

"As right as I was an hour ago, when you last saw me," said Kerri. "Which is to say, not tip-top, but I shall survive."

She hastened from her desk to pull him into the room and shut the door against the stares of the curious in the corridor. To her surprise, he put his arms around her and, trembling, held her tightly.

"My dear!" she said. "What has happened?"

He did not answer immediately. He released her and, taking one of her hands in his, dropped heavily onto the old couch. Hesitantly, Kerri sat down beside him.

He took a deep breath and said in a voice so low she could scarcely hear him, "The first thing that happened when I got to my college this morning was a chap I know came up to me and offered me his condolences."

Kerri blinked.

"Took me a few minutes to figure out what he was talking about. Finally I got it clear that he thought you had demented over the weekend."

Kerri blinked again.

"Well, I set him straight. Told him I'd just left you in the quad and you were perfectly competent. He seemed quite confused...embarrassed. Somebody'd told him, he said. Must have been a mistake, he said. Said he was glad it wasn't you after all."

"It was Miss Rippinger," Kerri whispered. "In the office next door to mine. I found out when I got here. Poor woman! I feel dreadful about it. It happened Friday afternoon, apparently."

He looked at her. "Oh. Name of the Dreamer! The woman next door."

Kerri squeezed his hand. "And you came running up here anyway." She felt deeply touched. Nick rarely showed his face in Paterson Hall; she was not sure why. And she had never, never heard him speak informally anywhere on campus.

"That's not all," he continued, keeping his voice down. "By the time I reached the door of my office, three other people had offered me their sympathy. It was *you*, not just some woman in your building. They mentioned you by name."

Kerri stared at him. "By name. Me?"

He nodded. "At that point, I panicked. I dropped my stuff, locked up and ran straight over here. But you're well, you're fine." He took her in his arms again. "Oh, Kerri, Kerri! This is a hell of a place!"

Kerri huddled bewildered in his embrace. "I don't understand this, Nick. Somebody came to my office a while ago, wanted to move in. A friend even looked in to assure herself I was all right. Why does everyone think *I* was one of the demented? Or is this mere wishful thinking on somebody's part?" She added irritably, blowing her nose again.

"I don't know. I don't know. But it wasn't you. Thank the Dreamer! Thank God! All it takes is just one person getting the story wrong, and it can spread all over campus, and it was the weekend, so nobody would see either of us to refute it. And I started worrying because I hadn't gone straight to the College. I'd dashed over to Vickson's to buy some writing paper, and I started to think there had been time; something might have happened to you..."

He was babbling. It was unlike him to babble.

"...and so I came straight over. But here you are. And you're all right."

"Well," said Kerri, digging into her pocketful of extra handkerchiefs, "I wouldn't go so far as to say I'm 'all right.' Decidedly under the weather, in fact. But I'm certainly not demented." She blew her nose dismally. *At least*, she thought, *not yet.* "Miss Rippinger wasn't the only one, unfortunately. Mr. Grahame-Skovanek demented also; they do not know exactly when, sometime late Friday or early Saturday."

"I hadn't heard that." He stared at her, horrified. "Two in one weekend in one department. Did you know him?"

Kerri shrugged. "Not really. It is devastating, nonetheless."

He sighed and shook his head. "I'll be so glad when this term is over! Sometimes I hate this place. Sometimes I hate this whole..." He waved a hand helplessly, but Kerri knew exactly what he meant.

"Sometimes," she said. "So do I. But mostly you love it. You do, Nick. And you're good at it." It was unnecessary for her to say she did not mean his studies. "Much better than I am."

He shook his head again. "I don't know. I don't know." He buried his face in his hands. "Sometimes I have no stomach for it."

She laid her cheek on his shoulder and put her arm around him. "The holidays are coming," she reminded him.

"Yes." He straightened up and took a breath. "Let us just get through what we have to get through. We shall survive."

"Of course," she patted his shoulder.

"Kerri?" He took both her hands in his and looked down at them. "I want you to remember one thing."

"Yes?"

"I love you. No matter what it looks like. No matter how strange things seem or what anybody else says, I do love you. Will you remember that?"

Touched, puzzled, wondering if she ought to be terrified, Kerri replied, "Of course. I love you, too. You remember that."

"I always do." Still not looking at her, he stood up and visibly collected himself for the return to the public corridor. "Back to work. I must go."

"Me, too," said Kerri. She unbolted the door and let him out. She watched him down the corridor, dodging around the lingering knots of traumatized students. At the top of the stair he suddenly turned, looked back and met her eyes. He gleamed a smile at her, and then he was gone. She smiled as she closed her office door again.

She was frowning by the time she sat down at her desk. How could this mistaken story have spread so widely around the University? A dementing was big news—although this term there had been so many one might think the community should almost begin to take them in stride. But she could not remember another case in which so many people, a *lot* of people, had got the victim's identity wrong. Or could it be she had never paid particular attention because it had never happened so close to her before? The fact that there were two incidents must have added to the confusion, and she *was* right next door. She remembered what Nick had said: it would only take one person to get the offices mixed up, someone who didn't really know who was in which room on this floor, someone who liked to blab. Yes, she could quite see how it must have happened, spreading over the weekend.

She did not like it, though. She did not like it. *Wishful thinking on somebody's part.* She leaned back in her ancient creaky chair and invoked the Veil over her office, over her life.

Two lectures, five cups of tea and a dozen and a half handkerchiefs later, Kerri sank gratefully onto the seat of an early afternoon train. She was finished for the day. Bed was waiting. Tomorrow, perhaps, she ought to use that waiver and not be such a fool.

During her brief morning visit Loren had said nothing about the Society of Guenevere. Surely, she would have mentioned if she had found anything new. Most likely she had not had time to go to the Archives and hunt up the duplicate document of the real estate transfer from that woman—what was her name? Miss Beckett-Something...Beckett- Martinez! The name caught at Kerri's memory; she had heard it in some other connection. But the woman must have been someone of note to have owned a house in Glen Eden, perhaps a member of the Faculty in earlier days.

It might be interesting to trace the history of the house during the last ten years, if only to try to discover a few more names of individuals connected to the Society of Guenevere. Kerri was more than half inclined to accept Loren's hypothesis that the Society of Guenevere was a tontine. Such affiliations were far less common nowadays than they had been two generations ago, although unmarried and childless Academic people still occasionally formed them, to give some illusion, at least, of family.

The remaining mystery was how the name had come into Kerri's consciousness, to be hallucinated at odd times since. Had she heard it or seen it written down? The hallucinations had been both visual and auditory, although the latter happened only in a dream and after the first seeing. And had the original contact happened long ago or only recently, perhaps even the day of the first hallucination? That day was not difficult to remember; so many important things had happened, yet even the best memory could not call up every detail of a whole day nearly two months before.

Kerri unfocused her eyes and let her breathing fall into meditation rhythm in order to allow that day to return, gently, unforced. Somewhere in her memory of the events of that day she might find a clue. Perhaps it was something she had not been especially aware of then, something overshadowed by those things that had seemed most important at the time—the sabotage attempt, the letters from home, the invitation—or by encounters that had proved significant later on—meeting Loren, for instance. As she let her mind float lightly, in no particular order, over all she could remember of that day, several avenues of possibility began to open before her, threads that might be worth following, at least one that was definitely worth watching closely.

Or could the Society of Guenevere have come from a more distant memory, called up by some obscure association on the day of that first sighting? On that April Monday she had been thinking of her mother, of her father, of her grandmother. She had been looking for her grandmother's letter on Nick's desk in the study when she had seen the invisible words. Was it possible that Aryel herself was the connection? Could she in fact be a member of the Society of Guenevere?

Aryel belonged to the so-called "baby boom" generation, that awakening time leading up to the Great Convention, when the birth rate had begun to rise again at last, for no apparent reason. It had been a time of optimism: The species was not going to die out after all, or at least, not so soon. Many of the sad social bulwarks against the coming night of extinction had been cheerfully allowed to fall from use, although some people, especially the childless, had continued to form tontines and still did. It was unlikely but possible that Aryel belonged to one. In that case Kerri could have heard of the Society at any time during her life. It might have been spoken of openly, no secret, a dull grown-up thing of no interest or importance to a child, forgotten until that day.

Abruptly, a memory came to her: "He owes a very great debt to your father." "Just what did Father do for him?" "He died."

Her father and Professor Bonneville-Chatterton. Her Sponsor. Her father and his friend, whose friendship had ended under a cloud, under circumstances never explained nor alluded to. Could it be Father who was involved with the Society of Guenevere? Was it possible? Suddenly certain of Aryel's dark pronouncements began to make a murky kind of sense. Of course, a tontine contract would supersede the inheritance rights of any member's spouse or child to any property owned by the group. No wonder Aryel was bitter on Kerri's behalf. Her son had died young and most untimely, cheating Kerri out of an inheritance to which she might have had reasonable expectations. Furthermore, there was a Stockholder adoption at issue somehow in this tangle of secrets. Recollecting that, Kerri felt herself drawing back, wondering if perhaps, after all, she would really rather not know. There were some losses of which it might be better to live in contented ignorance.

She hugged her book bag on her lap, and when her nose collided with it suddenly, she realized her eyes had forgotten to stay open and her neck was not paying attention. The vibration of the moving train was putting her to sleep; she would miss the Fernly stop if she could not rouse herself.

What is this book I've smashed my nose into, she wondered sleepily. Alex's book, brought by Loren, stashed in the top of her bag just as she was leaving, an afterthought. She sat up and took the book out of the bag. *Dreams*, said the faded gilt lettering on the threadbare cloth-covered spine.

Or not Alex's own book, but Contraband. She put the book back into her bag, put it at the very bottom of the bag, and looked around her to see if anyone had noticed. Nobody was paying the least attention to her.

She rubbed a clear space on the fogged window and peered out through grimy glass, trying to figure out where the train had got to by now. They had left the City proper and were winding into the residential neighborhoods, the suburbs. Suddenly the train shot out of the alley of trees and buildings and launched itself onto one of the bridges that spanned the many rivers and inlets of the Harbor. In the brief clear vista, Kerri could see distant mountains, white with snow, half shrouded in cloud.

There was snow on the ground at Evesham too, just barely—a lacy, almost melting crust over the flattened grass at the side of the lane, on the ragged lawns. It must have snowed during the morning; nothing was coming down now, and the wind, for a mercy, had dropped. Kerri thought, a little foggily, that if she were not at death's door she would enjoy going for a walk out beyond the village where she could really see the countryside and the mountains.

Now, that is a thoroughly revolting idea, she said to herself as her chilled fingers turned the key in the front door. (*Veil,* she thought, drawing her protection over the house as she stumbled into the front hall.) *A nice cup of something hot is what you need, my girl!*

As it so often happens when one finally gets to bed after hours of longing for a nap, Kerri found she was not sleepy any more. She had changed her mind about the Society of Guenevere: Ignorance was never better than knowledge. If there was anything to find out about this mysterious entity, she would find it, if only to satisfy herself it had nothing to do with her. Besides, she had remembered something else. Nick, the morning after the Ball, saying, "There is no such thing."

Yes, she thought, *the tontine might be wound up, with everything passed to the one survivor and perhaps by now to that person's heirs, but how would Nick know anything about it?* Was the Society of Guenevere something his family was mixed up in, something she might have heard mentioned by his parents or seen written somewhere in their house? He had received a letter that day, the one with no return address on the outside; he had been unusually secretive about it.

The simple, logical thing would be to come straight out and ask Nick about all of it.

She had no intention of asking.

She piled up the pillows behind her, poured out another cup of tea on the bedside tray and opened up the book *Dreams.*

An hour later, even more awake, she got out of bed, went to the study and rummaged for an unused notebook and pen and ink. She carried these back to the bedroom, made room for the ink on the tea tray, and got under the quilts again. She opened the notebook and wrote at the top of the first page, "The Star Dream."

The book, *Dreams,* was unlike anything she had ever read before. From internal evidence it was clearly not a book from the Age of Dreams; on the other hand, it was very old. Not thesis material by any stretch of the imagination— she had known that from the first page—yet it fascinated her, in a guilty sort of way, like some modern, lightweight, trashy novel one was not supposed to admit to reading, much less enjoying. It seemed to be a sort of manual for the interpretation of dreams, set in a context that pretended to be some kind of research in the Academic style. (And wouldn't the Faculty howl at the very idea of someone researching dreams? Worse than television!) There was extensive citation of other so-called "dream researchers"—Kerri wondered if the author had made them up—and enough footnotes, appendices and indices to satisfy the strictest formalist, but the essence of the thing was the idea that one should try to remember one's dreams, write them down, try to understand what they meant. This understanding, the author implied, would help one make better sense of things in waking life.

That, by itself, was enough to hook Kerri: Her waking life had always made so little sense. She was willing to try almost anything (short of admitting her bewilderment publicly by asking for help) to impose some kind of rational structure on things. Hadn't she made up the Game for that very purpose? And as crazy as it was, had it not worked? At least, well enough to get her by. It crossed her mind that what she had found here, what Alex had found, was someone else's Game. This writer, this Miss Marks-West, had somehow been able to write *her* Game down, to get it published, an incredible thought.

Of course, she had disguised her intent somewhat by pretending that the whole thing was a commentary on, and further development of, the works of a person named Faraday, who had supposedly written extensively on the same subject in the Age of Dreams. It was all hedged about with the proper language and stylistic trimmings. Kerri didn't imagine for a moment that she would find in the University Library anything by Professor Faraday or any of the other people cited in the book. The fact that the book had been published at all led her to conclude that it dated back to the so-called Years of Confusion, that vaguely defined period (no one knew how long it had really lasted) following the end of the Age of Dreams, when all kinds of bizarre, undisciplined things were thought to have happened. Publishers would have printed anything at all in those days, with or without Approval.

The thing that excited her the most, that sent her barefooted to the study, was the fact that the book did not tell the reader what the interpretations of dreams were to be. There were no tables, lists, indexes of symbolic meanings according to subject matter— nothing like that. Instead, the reader was encouraged to find her own interpretations, according to what made sense to her about what was happening in her own life. "You have the answers," the author said. "You are the only one who has the answers for you."

If I have the answers, thought Kerri, *I am going to waste no time discovering what they are.* Thence, the notebook, because the first step was to write the dreams down.

Recurring dreams were important, the book said, so Kerri would begin with the one recurring dream that haunted her the most, the Star Dream. She wrote first a quick description of the general pattern, how other dreams turned into the

Star Dream, how it always ended the same way—in that vast dark place among the whispering points of light—and then she would wake up. Funny, on paper, in the light of afternoon, it did not look so daunting. Nor did it look any more meaningful, written down, than it had ever seemed when she woke sweating in the dawn.

The book said variations in the recurring dream could be interpreted in relation to the meaning of the repeating pattern. Therefore, Kerri set out to make a list of all the variations she could remember, but there were few particular ones over the years which remained in her mind in any detail at all—some of the earliest ones, back in her childhood, and the versions of the last few weeks since the Star Dream had begun to come back. There was the night after the Ball invitation and the letters from Mother and Grandmother—that was the "Society of Guenevere" version. There was the time after the ball—the village on the roof of the Palace of Arts. There had been at least one other time. She struggled to remember.

What was it? Something about being lost on campus in the rain. Lightning. The Private Library. Yes! Eagerly she wrote it down at the bottom of her list.

Then remembered, cold as ice: That one was not a dream.

Chapter 37

Timo

After such a Monday, there was no question of staying home on Tuesday, waiver or no waiver. Kerri did feel better, or at least she told herself she did at intervals of approximately five minutes, all the way to Town on the train. This day there was no worse surprise waiting for her than a note from Timo pushed under her office door some time the previous afternoon. It was unsealed but unsigned, in an acceptable Academic-style hand; he knew the University environment all too well. He was in Yendys, the note said. He would call at half past eleven on the hope of taking her to lunch.

Promptly on time, he appeared at her open office door, resplendent in a deftly tailored blazer and his best Academic accent. He had dressed himself to pass as Academic, wanting, he told her when they were safely out of the building, to "blend in" when he called for her.

On the way to the restaurant, they talked only of family matters, personal news, especially Timo's most recent promotion.

"Off the shuttle run for good, I hope!" he said happily. "The cargo trade is the real thing! Of course, it is less predictable, and Malia isn't very happy about that. But when I'm home I get to stay longer, and she does like that part. So do the kids." Timo's wife Malia, owner of a profitable farm, had never been interested in going to sea, in spite of her ancestry.

They went to a restaurant off campus, a stylishly decorated place frequented by genteel Peasants and younger Cits in business and the arts. Except for Kerri there was not an Academic in the place, but, she reflected looking around her, that could only be because her own caste had yet to discover it. The food was supposed to be quite good, according to Timo's informant; the ambiance was undeniably up-and-coming.

They did not discuss Kerri's situation until they were seated at their table and had given their order. Her original message the night of the Ball and the following letter had taken a week to reach him, he explained. He had been "away." He did not say where; Sea People did not. He would have looked her up in any case for her own sake and because he had been dying to hear if she had made any progress on their little mystery, especially since receiving her message, but he also came as a representative of the People, who would appreciate an explanation.

"I feel such a fool," Kerri began. "It was the fruit of a moment's panic, nothing more. I cannot imagine what they thought at the terminal, and I am grateful for their courtesy in sending you. The records you showed me that day—I believed there was reason to think that someone would, that Val would try to destroy them or alter them. At the time I forgot the log books were not even on the Mainland. I realized almost at once I was making a fuss over nothing."

"Hold on!" said Timo. "Maybe not. There was an attempt."

She stared at him. The table attendant came with his beer and her hot lemon tea and went away again.

"Someone tried to get into the private sections of the Yendys Terminal twice that weekend. Cheers!"

"Cheers!" replied Kerri faintly, lifting her cup with an unsteady hand. "Val?"

"Not the first time. It was a man in his twenties, identity unknown, just before dawn on May Day. They had received your letter by then, but they didn't know what to make of it. Then someone noticed this character trying to get into the room where the records and charts are kept. It happened to be locked at that hour. Fellow said he would come back later and ducked away before anyone thought to hold him. Dark haired like Val, but not tall enough. Dressed right, walked and talked wrong. Could have been Cit or Academic. Sound like anybody you know?"

Kerri shook her head, thinking, "Who?" Could there be anyone else involved besides Val and Arzelle?

"After that," Timo continued," they set up a watch on the records room and alerted everyone in the building."

"The second attempt?"

"The next day in the afternoon, just before the Island shuttle sailed. Eh, it was a madhouse around there, the day after the holiday. This time they had their eyes open, but he still got upstairs before somebody stopped him. Different fellow, taller, had the clothes and the walk. When asked his business, he said he was looking for somebody. He mentioned a name. Mine. Only he used the wrong form of my title, the one used by a female when speaking of a male relative not present."

"Val!" said Kerri with a triumphant grin.

"According to the description, he could have been." Timo grinned. "If he hadn't been above learning a little more about us in his youth he might have got away with it."

"Did they hold him?"

"No, they escorted him out. There was no reason to be sure he wasn't in fact looking for me. I am known there, and my ship calls regularly. He talked Island enough that they thought they better give him the benefit of the doubt in spite of his mistake on my name. All they really had on him was that he was in a restricted part of the building, a plausible blunder. On the other hand, he was attempting to impersonate one of the People, a discourtesy we do not look on kindly. It doesn't happen often. Twice in two days is enough to get everyone's attention. Since they didn't know what your letter was about, they worried what they might stir up if they held him, so they let him go, kept the watch on the records and sent word to all the other shipping offices, especially Honowell. I gather there are messages waiting for me in over a dozen places, urgent summonses to get back here at all speed. The decision was to take precautions but otherwise sit tight until I could get here and talk to you."

"I had no idea." Kerri shook her head slowly. "It is serious, then?"

"The People are taking it very seriously," Timo replied. "We are grateful to you for the warning. We don't like outsiders snooping around our private spaces, let alone messing with our documents. It is my charge to convey our gratitude to you and get an explanation. What is the story?"

She covered her flushed cheeks with her hands and took a deep breath. "That weekend," she began, "the one you told me about, when Val went to the Islands, the Chancellor of the University had just died. All classes, lectures, recitations—everything was canceled the next day, which was Friday, and there was a memorial convocation in the Arena that morning. Waivers were available to anyone who had a good excuse not to be there, but one could not simply skip it and go to the beach. Everyone was expected to attend, to sign the book. Well, Val's signature is in the book."

"But he could not have been there," exclaimed Timo. "He was at sea from Thursday afternoon to Friday evening."

"Exactly."

"Forgery!"

"One place or the other. It had to have been."

"And that is a crime."

"Not technically, I suppose. Not a civic crime, anyway; it was not a cheque or legal document, merely a Record of Presence. However, under University rules and by University traditions it certainly is a serious offense. Not as bad as cheating or plagiarism or false accusation, but a very black mark to have on one's record. In fact, he would be in much less trouble if he had skipped the convocation with no excuse and gone to the beach."

"She did it for him."

"Possibly, but we cannot be certain. Remember, there was that other man who tried to get into the private section of the Terminal the first time. We do not know who he is or how he is connected. I suppose you are certain it was Val on the ship and not someone else forging his name there? Are you sure the man on the ship was not this other man?"

"Dead sure. Eh, I recognized him first and looked for the name later." Timo shook his head in disbelief. "Why didn't he use a false name on the ship? Nobody would ever have checked."

"That is just it," said Kerri. "Nobody would have, ever. It would never have occurred to him to use a false name on the ship. Who would have known? I would be willing to wager he did not make contact with anyone he knew in Honowell while he was there. It was sheer accident that you saw him, you recognized him, you told me, and I happened to know he was supposed to be elsewhere." She paused, bleakly. "And I let him know that I knew."

"Ah!" Timo folded his hands, perceiving progress. "I figured you must have told him somehow."

Their soup arrived at that moment, but as soon as the server had gone, Kerri told the tale of what had happened between her and Val at the Ball. It meant that she had to let Timo know about all the term's sabotage, attempted and successful, including the suspected invasion of her home and the murder of Thomas. She was most reluctant to do this; it made her feel like an hysteric, not to mention ashamed of her own caste before a member of another. Fortunately, the bare facts sufficed. Timo was familiar enough with Academic life to require no long explanation, no convincing, but when she got to the part about Thomas, he could not contain his alarm.

"Poison!" he said. "I do not like this at all." With a grave expression he let her continue as they finished their soup and went on to the main course.

"Hinting to him that I knew about the forgery was the only weapon I had to hand at the moment," she concluded. "I regret not still having it in reserve, but I was so angry at him I would have done anything to make him stop. Or at least sit back and think before the pair of them tried any more nasty tricks."

He nodded slowly. "It may not have been the wisest thing, but it's done. In your place, I probably would have done the same. And it may slow him down at least for a bit."

"If it is him," said Kerri.

"Do you have doubts?"

"I have no proof, but I am certain he is implicated. If he is not doing these things, he knows who is."

"Could it be *her*?"

Kerri hesitated for a moment. "Very well. I shall tell you honestly what I think. Until I spoke with Val, I assumed it was someone in my College. Now I believe both of them are actively involved, possibly with one or more accomplices in Paterson Hall. But I would have said this is not in Val's style. I have known both of these people for many years. Most of the mischief that has been done to me this term is the sort of thing Arzelle would think up. Perhaps she hatches the ideas, and he carries them out. What I cannot figure out is their motivation. Why would they bother? How can Arzelle possibly have any further reason to hurt me? She won. She got Val. She is on top of the world, and I am no threat to her any more. What possible purpose could she—or he!—have?"

"I cannot imagine." Timo shook his head. "Perhaps she thinks you won. You let Val go without a fight and moved on with your life. Married someone even more eligible, according to my Great-Aunt Aryel. But let us set aside the question of motivation for now. What happened next?"

"My very next thought," Kerri took up the tale, "was that he might try to destroy the evidence. It would be like him to do it immediately. That is why I sent the letter right away by messenger during the Ball."

Timo pondered a moment. "Wouldn't it be easier for him to destroy the forgery in the convocation guest book?" he asked. "Get hold of the book, tear out that page? He wouldn't care about the other signatures lost. Does anybody ever look in those things anyway?"

Kerri sighed. "Rarely. Hardly ever. But he could not get hold of it easily. By the time of the Ball the signatures would have been transcribed onto an official list that is available for public viewing in Memorial Library, even though the names are not the actual autographs. The original book—or books; they had at least ten lines going—would have been sealed and locked away in a vault somewhere."

"Then could you get at it to prove the forgery?"

"Oh, easily. Especially if I could get a Faculty member to back me up. Even on my own, with a charge that serious. Of course, if the proof turned out not to be there, I would be in very big trouble for false accusation. I would certainly check the open list before I did anything, and it is possible he could get at that. Still, even those pages are numbered and embossed across every name with the University seal, so only a very sophisticated job of tampering would pass. It would have to be done under the nose of the librarian on duty. They watch like hawks; they are the most suspicious people in the universe! Or else breaking in at night somehow. And even the open lists are locked up in cupboards when the library is closed. It would be an immense operation to try to cover that end of it, far easier to try to go after the ships' logs."

"Yes, I see," said Timo thoughtfully. He was silent for a moment. "Nevertheless, do you think it is something he is capable of? And if it is, would he go to the trouble?"

264 Deborah K. Vleck

"I do not know," said Kerri. "Val is a very clever man, sometimes too clever for his own good. The simple, honest and straightforward was never quite good enough for him. Bored him, at least when he was younger, when I knew him best. It would be entirely in character for him to have arranged the forgery, the clandestine trip to the Islands, the name change, all of it, for no particular reason except the thrill of it. For a bet, perhaps. He was always doing things like that in prep school, almost always got away with them, too. He left off that sort of thing when we came to University, had less time to play, and he was with me all the time, not his playful chums. Maybe he is at it again. Maybe Arzelle encourages him, or does not care.

"Certainly he could—and would!—think through all the aspects of covering it up, if he felt he had to. Whether he has the resources and the skills to carry it out, that I do not know."

"We know he has a male accomplice," said Timo. "I would sure like to find out who the fellow is. I wish you would try to."

"I shall keep my eyes open," Kerri said. "If I think over his old friends that I knew, perhaps one of them will ring a bell. I wonder if this man is the one who committed the forgery in the convocation book. Not that it lets Arzelle out. They may have decided that she would be too conspicuous to get away with it. She is very widely known, and she would have had to sign her own name and then either forge Val's on the spot or else get back in line. She would be noticed. Either way, it might have seemed too risky."

"Is there someone who would do her bidding like that? Take such a risk?"

"Undoubtedly. Dozens of people. Trying to suck up to her or afraid of her. And it might have been his bidding. Val has his friends, too. Arzelle might not have had anything to do with this part of it."

Timo grinned mischievously. "But you would rather she did."

Kerri returned the grin. "Let us simply say, I would not be the least surprised if she did."

"So, then," Timo said, "This fellow, whoever he is, has a stake in concealing the forgery, so he agrees to make the first attempt on our shipping records. Eh! Here's another thing I just thought of! The name change. There is a record of that in duplicate in Honowell. It would not do them any good to destroy or alter the ships' logs if they didn't do the same thing to all the records of the name change."

"But that would defeat the whole purpose of doing it in the first place," said Kerri, "going to all that trouble at a most inconvenient time."

Timo thought for a moment. "If Val was only changing it for a bet or something," He suggested, "it wouldn't matter, after the bet was won. Kerri, do you have any idea why he did it?"

"Actually," Kerri confessed, "I may be making some progress on that investigation. I was planning to tell you the details after I found out a little more. The only concrete thing I have discovered so far is that other people have changed their names in the same fashion, but you knew that already from your original search of the Honowell Archives."

"You mean, people *here* have been doing it also?"

"Yes. I am going to see if I can find a pattern, but I have not had time to pursue it. It may not mean anything."

Timo agreed. "Some kind of joke or stunt, maybe, like climbing up the bell tower on the outside. A fad."

"That is what I was thinking."

They ate their lunch silently for a while, each deep in thought.

"Here's an idea!," Timo ventured. "Suppose he did get into the Honowell Archives, not to destroy the record of the name change but to alter the date. It would be simple! Easy! Archives are so casual—you know if you've been there—nobody would care. A pen knife and the right color of ink, that's all you'd need. He could change the date on all the copies, including his own, and the district register—like in that book about the woman who wasn't dead after all..."

"*The Woman in White*. Wilkie Collins. Yes," said Kerri. "Go on."

"Say he changed it to a time when he was on the island for legitimate business, the last time he was there, eh? Like in the summer. He must have gone over to visit his parents." Timo became animated over his new theory. "Eh, he back dates it to when he was there earlier, he gets his name out of the ship logs somehow, he doesn't need to do anything about the convocation book, because there's no proof he was ever elsewhere at the crucial time, he's got his name change for whatever reason, and he's home free!"

Kerri considered this. "Yes. That would cover it. I think he would go for that plan first because it would leave his attendance at the convocation unquestioned. He would have it all. It is the only way he could have it all. And I would have nothing on him. I would no longer be a threat to him. However, he would have to go to Honowell to take care of it. Timo! He may have already gone!"

Chapter 38

Fools' Errands

"I could find out," said Timo. "But this time you can be sure he would not use his own name for the journey."

Kerri frowned. "On the other hand, he could hardly have had the time to get away yet, not even this last weekend. He would have had to sign in on campus Friday, so, leaving Friday afternoon, he would arrive Saturday evening at the earliest. The Public Library would have been closed until Monday morning. Say, he hits the ships' logs Sunday— supposing he could get at them—does the Public Library on Monday, takes the next ship, which is Monday afternoon. The earliest he could return would be tonight, which means he would miss two days' attendance. Under the circumstances I cannot imagine he would take the risk of having someone forge his name in the day book. It would only compound the offense. Tell me, did the people at the Terminal do or say anything to him that might have let him know that they had been warned?"

He was not sure. He would ask. "Why?"

"Because as long as he does not realize that I am on to him and have cut off his access to the ships' logs, he might think he just got caught through bad timing. He might believe he will eventually succeed, with enough care. He knows me well enough to gamble that I will not go to the authorities and foment a big scandal unless there is another act of sabotage. Therefore, he probably thinks he is safe until the end of the term, as long as he and Arzelle leave me alone. Over the holidays he would have freedom and time to carry out whatever plan he has in mind."

"Unless...oh, damn! Unless he got a waiver for having the flu! I got one. I have not used mine, but they were giving them out with a liberal hand on Friday, no questions asked. He could even have got his earlier in the week and sailed off with plenty of time to spare."

"Is there some way you could check?" Timo asked.

"I suppose so," said Kerri, with a sigh. "I could go look in his department day book. I would rather not show my face over there if I did not have to, though."

"Okay," said Timo. "I shall go look. They do not know my face at all, and I shall take care he does not see me."

"Such a lot of trouble, Timo! I am not sure it is worth it." She sighed again. "If he has already made the journey and carried out the plan, there is nothing I can do. If he intends to go at some later time, there is no way I can stop him."

"Ah!" said Timo. "But if he can't get at the ships' logs—and I know for a fact he hadn't as of last Friday, and therefore he can't, because I have seen to it the particular documents are specially hidden—it would not avail him to go to Honowell at all. Eh, it would be even less to the purpose if he got there and found that the record of his name change had been, um, mislaid somehow."

"Timo!" Kerri was scandalized. "Tell me! *Has* it been mislaid?"

"Not yet," he allowed with a smile. "But I am certain it will be by, say, Thursday. Of course, it will turn up eventually, if needed."

"Of course!" Kerri laughed.

They both declined dessert. Timo paid the bill and they went to the saloon for coffee.

With some hesitation Timo asked, "Eh, what does your husband have to say about all this? You haven't mentioned him since we began to discuss this business."

"I have not told him," Kerri confessed. "Oh, he knows all about the sabotage. Thomas Aquinas was his bird, after all. Indeed, he has had a few attempts made on him alone this term, although we do not know if they are connected to the attacks on me. What I have not told him is that Val, and very likely Arzelle, may be responsible."

"Why ever not?" he hissed. "You've got to tell him! You need to be standing together against these people!"

"It is complicated." Kerri tried to explain. "I am not confident that he would believe me, for one thing. He thinks I have too much imagination, and he may be right. All of this rests upon some vague remarks Val made at the Ball, when he was trying his best to needle me in general. *I* am not even confident any more that he implied what I thought he did. There is no real proof, and Nick requires a good case to be made in such a situation, or he withholds his belief. He has an historian's skepticism. How could I make my case without telling him about Val's little trip and the forgery? I have not told him about that either."

She paused. It was not easy to explain, now, even to herself, why she had kept this from Nick, unless it was to avoid giving him a reason to patronize her. Which was not doing him justice, she supposed. At least he was not as much inclined to be patronizing as most graduate students. He had no need to be. "Certainly I would not tell him without talking to you first, and this is the first chance I have had."

"Yes, I see," mused Timo. He shrugged. "I'll leave that up to you. It is fine with me if you tell him. If you don't, eh, your business."

"For another thing," Kerri added, "he knows I have a history with these people. It would not be unreasonable to suppose that I carry a grudge against them, that I would jump to conclusions because of prejudice, a readiness to blame them for what might be my own carelessness and absentmindedness. Also, I found out at the Ball that Arzelle has been, well, pursuing him...."

"What?" Timo exclaimed. "No! Kerri, are you saying she got your man, right? So now she's going after your new man? Is that what you're telling me?"

In spite of herself, Kerri chuckled. "It looks that way."

"Woman's got problems!"

"Tell me about it! It would be funny, except..."

"He's not going for it, is he?" Timo's brows pulled together ominously.

"No. No! He seems unable to tolerate her at all, at least since the Ball." She described Arzelle's behavior on that occasion and Nick's reaction. "He is afraid of offending her, though. You know, she has enormous influence, has a lot of important connections within his College, his department. Until he gets his thesis topic confirmed, he cannot afford get himself on anyone's bad side. No. If Nick ever had inclinations in that direction, he seems to have been well and truly driven off." *Or else*, she thought, *he is putting on a very good act.* "So, you see, I did not feel comfortable trying to convince Nick that she and Val are behind the sabotage. It seemed...petty. I would rather deal with it by myself."

"Eh! You've got *me* to deal with it, too!" he said with emphasis. "You are not by yourself, and I think you are making a mistake not to tell Nicholas. I want you to promise me that if they try anything—anything!—you tell him! Write to me, but first you tell him!"

Kerri nodded solemnly, realizing she had no intention of keeping such a promise and hoping a nod of the head did not count as a pledge. To be on the safe side, she crossed her fingers under the table.

But Timo paid no heed to her equivocation as he went on, "I've got to go away today. We sail this afternoon. I'm going to be gone, oh, at least two, three weeks. Maybe a month. I don't want to find out when I get back that somebody poisoned you...!"

"Timo!" Kerri exclaimed. "Name of the Dreamer! Poison me? Can you honestly imagine they would actually do me physical harm? This is not the Age of Dreams, you know. Do not be absurd."

"Well," said Timo, momentarily brought up short. "They did poison your bird. At least, be careful, won't you? Be mindful. I wish I could stay around here and keep an eye on you, but I can't. Do you have anyone else besides Nick you can trust to watch your back?"

"Oh!" said Kerri. "I was forgetting! Yes, I do. I have made some interesting new friends. They are unusual people, but I think, yes, I do believe they can be trusted. They would like to meet you."

"Eh, Kerri, you know I don't care much for hanging around with Academics. They act like I don't exist."

"You have just been exposed to a few bad ones, that is all. Most of them have better manners than that, especially the older ones. And anyway, these are not Academics, or only one of them is, Miss Weberly. The other two are a Cit and a Peasant. And even Miss Weberly is not your typical Academic."

"Are you kidding me?" he asked with a grin. "With you? Miss Twelfth Generation Faculty Daughter?"

"Not kidding." She smiled in reply. "I always had time for *you* and your folk, so I could not have been such a snob as you make out, *and* it is possible that I have matured, you know. I like these people. You would like them. We are all having tea together this afternoon. Could you come?"

He shook his head. "Not this time, sorry. We're sailing, as I told you. I have to be back on duty by three. Some other time?"

"Yes, please," said Kerri. "Any Tuesday or Friday. We meet in the Public Library on the Common. One of them is a Librarian, an Archivist; we have tea in his office."

"Some day soon," Timo promised.

"I think I'm going to ask them to put me back on the Island-Mainland shuttle run so I can keep an eye on you," Timo said. They had left the restaurant and were walking slowly toward the nearest trolley stop. "Can't do it right away; I'm on contract for this long trip."

"Don't you dare do any such thing!" said Kerri, too indignant to mind her language. "You have been working for this promotion all your life."

He shrugged. "Eh! There will be another time."

"I will not have you believing I am in any real danger. That is absurd!"

"I don't care," Timo said stubbornly. "I am more than worried. I'm angry. I don't like these sharks harassing you. Anyway, you are family, so it is a clan matter."

"It is an Academic matter!" she hissed. "It is a personal matter. If you start telling people...!"

He raised a hand in promise. "I will use discretion. I have to tell them something at headquarters, but I will keep the personalities and the history out of it."

"Very well."

"I shall come to see you the moment I get back. In the meantime, always remember you have the People at your back."

He put her on the trolley to campus and stood waving farewell as she rode away. She could have walked, but today, still weak from the flu, she was ready for the self-indulgence of the ride. Of course, it was farther by car—pedestrians could take the shortcut along the river, while the streetcars had to follow the power line around the perimeter of the campus, past the Asylum.

The Asylum. Kerri stared at it looming on the hillside ahead. Miss Rippinger was there now, and Mr. Grahame-Skovanek. Forever.

In spite of the raw windiness of the day, some of the inmates walked aimlessly out in the gardens behind the high barred fence. Half a dozen of them stood on the knee wall, grasping the bars and looking out with dead, expressionless faces. Kerri remembered standing like that in a dream, fingers cramped around rough iron bars.

What if, she thought in sudden horror, *what if they are not unconscious after all?*

What if they are still there, trapped inside, looking out, unable to speak or respond? Imprisoned in their bodies? And no one could tell, no one could know. No one could help them. And they live on for years, years!

No, it was too dreadful an idea. It could not be. Yet, now that she had thought of it, she could not make the idea go away. Worse than death itself, a life like that. She told herself it could not be true: there would be some way to communicate. Surely the eyes could speak. Someone would have discovered the truth by now, or at least thought to ask the same questions. As far as she knew, no one ever had, so there could not be anything in it.

Her racing heart began to slow. Her breathing eased. Life was already difficult enough without inventing things to be terrified of. She had done quite enough of that in the past. She made herself look dispassionately at the demented ones clinging to the fence.

There was no light of awareness in those dead eyes. She remembered the woman in white in the rain, the night she had returned from the Islands. She remembered fleeing from that haunting figure to lose herself on campus in the darkness. She remembered the Private Library.

The trolley drew to a stop at the East Gate. On a sudden impulse, Kerri jumped up and got off the car. It was farther to walk to Paterson Hall from here, but, flu or no flu, she would walk it, she would retrace her steps and find again the place called the Private Library.

She found the old fountain and the lily pool. She found, she thought, the first alley between buildings, and the next turning, and the next. After that, nothing seemed to match her memory. There were too many little walkways, too many courtyards and galleries and turnings that she did not remember seeing in the dark that wet night. Then, she had followed what seemed to be the only path. Now there were choices at every step, and nothing looked familiar. Even if she had been willing to ask for directions, which she never considered doing for a moment, there were very few people about. The place felt almost as creepy by day as it had by night.

Her memory picture of the building, revealed in a single lightning flash, was no help, for the architecture in this part of the campus was all of an age. Several of the buildings had stone steps and arched porches, but the most likely one had no words carved on the lintel.

No structure announced itself as a library of any kind. Most of them appeared unused.

She went so far as to ascend to the porch of the one building that best matched her memory, to try the door and peer in at the windows. But the door was locked, and the windows that were not boarded up showed nothing more than dusty stacks of boxes and old furniture. Whatever it had originally been used for, the building was nothing more than storage now.

I am wasting my time, she decided. What would such a place be: a Private Library?

Private for whom? She had an amusing mental image of a gaggle of doddering old Professors, keeping a secret collection of literary treasures in some locked room, not noticing that the volumes they guarded so jealously were crumbling to dust. *I imagined it,* she instructed herself, *because I had the Public Library on my mind that night—one of those little tricks of the brain.*

Her aching bones reminded her she had been flat on her back less than two days before; the foolishness of continuing was manifest. Therefore, half an hour after beginning it, she abandoned the hunt with little regret, glad to make her way back to the bustle of the Mall area and the Main Quad. If there really was a Private Library—could she not have read it wrong or hallucinated the lettering, like the "Society of Guenevere?"—it would keep for another day.

By the time she returned to her office, it was nearly time to go to Alex's, or else decide not to go. But she had not been on Friday, and she had not seen Greta in two weeks. She must go. She worked on the week's essay for half an hour and then set off for the Common, stopping along the way to buy some seed cakes for refreshments.

As Kerri approached down the dim corridor, Greta's raucous voice rang out from Alex's office, relating an amusing anecdote about something that had happened at a flea market on Sunday.

"Hallo, it's Kerri!" she exclaimed without pausing for breath. "How's the invalid? How're you feeling? Better? You don't look so good, dear. You should've stayed home in bed. But come sit down right over here. You've got to see my finds from the weekend! Put the kettle on, Alex. Kerri needs her tea, poor lamb."

Alex hastened to give up his chair to Kerri, greeting her less loudly but with obvious pleasure. "Did Loren give you that book?" he asked. "Did you read it?"

Kerri accepted the chair with a smile of thanks. Greta was only an eccentric Peasant woman, after all. *What can I have been thinking?* Kerri said to herself. *Name of the Dreamer, she goes to flea markets!*

She replied to Alex. "She did. Thank you very much. I read some of it, not all, but I am finding it most interesting. Oh, and I have brought back your book on television."

Alex's eyes brightened as she pulled this unsavory relic out of her book bag. Clearly, he was all too ready to launch into discussing the subject so near to his heart. Kerri made up her mind to bear it nobly.

"Later, Alex!" charged Greta. "The tea."

He departed regretfully. Out of one of her canvas bags Greta produced her finds—old magazines, plastic charms, a pottery mug, half a dozen rainbow disks, and various other objects that might or might not date to the Age of Dreams, curios and baubles to add to Greta's seemingly innumerable "collections." Kerri dutifully admired the lot. "What do you make out of the disks?" she asked politely.

"Make out of them?" Greta looked mildly shocked.

"A lot of people used to make mobiles out of them when I was in prep school, although I suppose mobiles are not really fashionable any more. What did they call them? Suncatchers! Someone is always thinking up new uses for them; they are so pretty. I have even seen them applied to costumes, although personally I think they are rather too big and ungainly for decorating clothing."

Greta shook her head. "I just collect them," she said. If Kerri was not imagining it, the Peasant looked faintly scandalized. "They kept information on these, you know. Music, too."

"Yes, I *do* know," said Kerri firmly, raising an eyebrow. But Greta, not being Academic, surely meant no offense.

"They ought to be preserved," insisted Greta, "not *used* for things."

"As long as we can't get the information *off* them," retorted Kerri, "we might as well use them for something."

"Not these," said Greta. "Eric Clapton! Etta James! The idea! Might as well burn your precious books!" As if to make certain nobody had ideas of making wind chimes or some other such project, she gathered the shiny disks, wrapped them carefully and tucked them back into her bag. A sudden grin quirked one corner of her mouth (to Kerri's relief; one did not want to offend Greta, whatever she was). "However, The Smudgepots you can have to do with as you like. Target practice, perhaps. It would sound better than their so-called music!"

Eric who? Kerri wondered uneasily. *The what pots? What sort of practice?*

Returning in time for this last exchange, Alex diplomatically diverted their attention to the charms. Loren arrived, breathless and red cheeked, and they all made tea. The talk broadened to plastics in general and then somehow to antique costume jewelry and old furniture.

Fortunately, there was no further mention of the subject of television. Kerri had read the book lent her by Alex—to be honest, she had skimmed it; it was opaquely technical and assumed all sorts of lost, arcane knowledge on the part of the reader—but, finding herself profoundly uninterested in the subject, she carefully did not call attention to it again. She took advantage of the tea preparations to shift some papers on top of the book, hoping Alex would not remember to bring it up again before she left. He did not.

Chapter 39

Numerology

The book *Dreams* did not come into discussion until they were on their second cup. Alex wanted Kerri to finish reading it before they talked about it in any depth; therefore, they agreed to bring it up Friday or the following Tuesday. Greta declared they should all try to record some dreams and analyze them, just to see if they could get anything out of it.

"We do not have to tell our dreams, do we?" Kerri asked.

"Only if you want," said Greta.

"In the meantime," said Alex with his usual eagerness, "I have another book to start around the circle. Something that turned up in the latest warehouse the Acquisitions Department cleared out. I realize we may not be finished with *Dreams*, but perhaps we'll want something to talk about next." From the bottom drawer of one of the file cabinets he extracted a small bundle wrapped in calico cloth. He unwound it reverently and held out to them a small volume with a stained green cover.

"Ew!" Loren screwed up her face in distaste. "That wasn't a dry storehouse exactly, was it?"

"Numerology." Greta read the nearly effaced title on the cover. "What is numerology?"

"Sounds mathematical," Kerri remarked, holding out her hand.

Alex let her have the book. "It is," he said. "That is, there are numbers in it. I thought I knew something about mathematics, but I've never heard of anything like this. I thought maybe you University people could tell me more about it, that it might be some Academic thing they don't teach in our schools."

With care, Kerri turned over the first few pages. Loren peered over her shoulder. The name of the author was unknown to them both. The book looked old enough to be a relic from the Age of Dreams, although it had been printed on good acid-free paper. The pages did not crumble, and the mildew on the cover had not yet inflicted much damage inside.

"The way it works is, they take the letters of the alphabet," Alexander explained, "and assign them values between one and nine."

"How do they do that?" asked Greta. "There are twenty-six letters."

"They start with 'A'—that's one—and continue to 'I', which is nine, and then start over again. So 'A', 'J', and 'S' all have the value of one. 'B', 'K', and 'T' are all two, and so on."

"There is a chart," Kerri observed. "Each number has three letters under it except nine. Zero is not used."

"Well, I am a graduate student of mathematics," Loren declared, "and I have never heard of anything like this before either. To be honest, I think it is some kind of parlor game, possibly from the Age of Dreams. Long forgotten."

With a crestfallen sigh, Alexander said, "Very likely you are right. I haven't had time to read it all, but the object seems to be to take words and turn them into numbers by adding up the values of the letters. You keep adding up the digits of the result until you end up with a one digit number, and that is the number of the word. Each of the nine digits has a special meaning; I don't remember what any of them are."

"But words already have meanings," Kerri protested. "What is the point?"

"It's just casting out nines," Loren said, taking the book gently out of Kerri's hands.

"I only noticed them doing names and dates, actually," Alexander said, "not ordinary words."

"Oh, I remember that, casting out nines!" Greta exclaimed proudly. "We used to do it to check our addition and things. When I was in school," she added by way of clarification. "You cast out nines to reduce a word to a one-digit number—Alex is right; only names and dates seem to be used—and that one digit number gives the character of the name or date. Oh, this is absurd!"

Loren rolled her eyes. "It *is* a parlor game. 'One' means 'Unity', a soul at one with itself. There's a lot of other 'one' stuff, but 'two' signifies a dual nature, among other things. Every number has its own Great Significance. Oh dear!"

"No wonder nobody remembers this game," Kerri commented. "One would run out of entertainment very quickly."

"But someone found it interesting enough to write a whole book about it," Greta pointed out, "and print it on good paper."

"There is that," Kerri agreed. "On the other hand, any number of books have been written about chess and how to play solitaire."

Loren leafed back to the title page. "The date's in the very late Nineteens," she said. "As we know, they published books about anything at all late in the Age of Dreams. They had no taste or discrimination. It doesn't mean it is important. It doesn't even mean it is really a book from the Age of Dreams. All during the Confusion they made up dates more or less at random."

"Oh well," Alex sighed. "I thought it might be something. Or at least entertaining, like the *Dreams* book."

"And why not? We could do our own names for fun," Loren suggested. "Where's a piece of paper, Alex? Let's see what your number is."

"But does one add up only the first name?" Kerri asked. "Or the whole thing? And what happens to people's numbers if they get married? Do their numbers change? Do their characters?" She thought about it for a moment. "I suppose they must," she decided in a quiet voice.

Alex looked perplexed. "I didn't read enough of it," he confessed.

"That's not like you, dear," said Greta, suppressing a smile.

"I've been busy," he explained with a warning frown at her.

"It looks as if full names are used in the examples," Loren said. "No, here are some with only a given name. I think the idea is that each part of the name means something different, and the full name means something else again. Oh, and here they've added up the vowels and consonants separately. This Numerology seems to be quite complicated," She had printed out "Alexander" in block letters and written the proper digit over each letter. She began to add them, muttering under her breath.

"Greta is a one," said Greta, pleased. "I figured it out already, in my head," she explained. "I am a unified soul."

Kerri glanced warily at the Peasant woman. *The hell you are*, she said to herself.

"You are a three, Alex," Loren announced. "At least, 'Alexander' is a three. Oh, but I forgot. That isn't your real..." She broke off, reddening.

Kerri had forgotten also that Alexander was not his real name. Fleetingly, she wondered what it was. "What does three mean?" she asked, reaching for the book.

"Hey, if you don't like your number," joked Greta, "you can always change your name!"

"What?" Kerri stopped, her outstretched hand arrested in mid air.

"You could change your name," Greta repeated. "Say, you don't want to go on being a stodgy old Four, you change your name and become an exotic Nine." She chuckled.

"Is Nine exotic?" Alex wrinkled his forehead anxiously. "How do you know Four is stodgy?"

Kerri looked at her hand and withdrew it to her lap before the others could see it shaking. She felt wrapped in ice. She felt Loren looking at her, unsmiling.

"What?" said Loren softly.

"Just a guess," Greta replied to Alex. "Four as in 'four square', and all that."

"Nothing," Kerri murmured. She drank all the rest of her tea in one gulp. It had cooled; it did not warm her. "We'd better do this again another day. I need to catch an early train today."

"Heavens, yes! Look at the time," exclaimed Loren. "And you barely on your feet again. I'll walk you to the station." She closed the book. "This is rather fun after all, Alex. If you will allow me, I should like to borrow the book for a couple of days. I could learn the system and try it on all our names."

"Well, I wasn't planning..." Alex was obviously of at least two minds about her request. On the one hand he could hardly be reluctant to allow his friends liberties with either his personal collection or Public Library property (unauthorized by the Main Desk upstairs) after the other times he had urged his latest enthusiasm on them all. On the other, he had as much as admitted that he had yet to read the whole thing. It was unlike him to let any book out of his hands before he had mastered the contents himself. However, this particular book seemed to be nothing more than some silly game after all, no new science from the Age of Dreams. And Loren's interest was undoubtedly flattering.

Greta looked back and forth from him to the Academics. She had dropped her open Peasant face, Kerri noted. Someone wise and calculating looked out of those grey eyes.

Kerri breathed evenly and resisted the Veil, but there was no Powerflash, no apparent Power at all in Greta, and her face suddenly went Peasant again, as if it had never been anything else.

"The thing is," Alex went on, "that book isn't my own, you see. It hasn't been catalogued, but it was counted and marked..."

"Since when did you care about that?" laughed Greta.

Alex reddened but went on, "...and Miss Fine seems unusually anxious to get at this particular batch—I think because of the damp. There's a lot of conservation work to be done."

"Oh," said Loren. "I do understand. It's bad luck for us, though, because the University might take it, and then we'll never get another chance to play with it."

"You think they would?" Alex ran bony fingers through his long hair. "But if it isn't serious, historic, or literary, it isn't their kind of stuff at all. We get all the games and curiosities."

Kerri cleared her throat. "We haven't looked at the whole thing. There might be something more valuable later on, some real mathematics, something valuable, forgotten. You never know. Why not let Loren have a crack at it?"

"I suppose it will do no harm," Alex decided reluctantly. "I can't believe they'll even begin on the batch before the holidays. I know Miss Fine is setting nearly everything aside to prepare for some conference she has to go to. That's why I borrowed it in the first place. Very well, take it. Only be sure you bring it back next time."

"Don't worry," Loren assured him. "I shall not let you down, Alex. Thank you."

Greta looked at her. She said nothing while Loren and Kerri gathered their coats and book bags.

"By the way," Kerri said, in haste to create a distraction. "did Loren tell you? She found the Society of Guenevere."

"Oh, that!" Alex remembered, vaguely embarrassed at letting Kerri's "discussion topic" fade from the group agenda. "Did she?"

"Where?" Greta asked.

"In the Archives," Loren replied. "Inheriting a house. I believe they are a tontine."

"Ah," said Greta wisely. "That would explain it then."

"Explain what?" challenged Loren.

"Why you weren't having any luck with the poetry angle," said Greta with a grin.

Alex dismissed the subject. "So much for the Society of Guenevere."

"What is it?" Loren asked her breathlessly. They were alone on the stone-paved pathway across the Common. Since leaving the library they had not spoken.

"Names," Kerri croaked. "They changed their names."

"Who?"

"Val. Arzelle. Fiona. Lots of other people. I don't know who. Remember? I found them in the Archives."

Loren frowned. "I know you found Arzelle."

"There were others. And listen! They changed the spelling, *only* the spelling, of their given names, except for Arzelle."

Loren shrugged. "You thought at the time it was a sort of fad in certain circles. Perhaps they think it is dashing."

"They use delimiters to hide the changes from the world," said Kerri. "What kind of fad is that?"

"They use delimiters?"

"Some of them do, at least."

"You didn't tell me that. I thought it was something about the Numerology book that set you off," Loren complained. "That's why I went to all that trouble to talk Alex into letting us take it out of there. Now he'll be expecting me to have read all this boring nonsense, and all the time you were intent on the Archive business."

"No! It *is* the numerology!" Kerri almost hissed, whispering. She spun around on the path to assure herself no eavesdroppers lurked nearby. In the distance a dozen screaming schoolboys played a rough game of soccer on the open grass; there was no one else. "I could not understand why they did it? Why just change the spelling? Why hide it? It is the number! Greta said it. She said, 'if you didn't like your number, you could change your name.'"

They came to the brow of the hill between the library and the gate, in the open lawns, away from trees.

"Are you trying to tell me that those people changed their names to get them to add up to a different number?" Loren sniffed. "People you have known for years have done this, people on the Islands have done this, and you and I have never even heard of numerology? It doesn't add up. If you'll pardon the expression."

"Very well," said Kerri. "Let us add them up and see what we find."

"Now? Here?"

"Why not?"

"Couldn't we go to a tea shop or something and sit down where it's warm? I mean, you've been ill. And what about your train?"

"I lied about the train. I shall take a later train. Of course we can't go inside. Do you want to sit in some public tea shop with a contraband book on something that may be, well, not respectable?"

"Not respectable!" Loren rolled her eyes and grinned. "Contraband? Are you sure you're not—never mind. I beg your pardon. Very well." She trotted over to the nearest bench. "I'll give you until I begin to freeze," she called back over her shoulder. "Then I am going home."

Kerri followed her to the bench, which was, she noticed gladly, in the open with a good view in all directions. No one would be able to approach unseen. She sat down and rubbed her gloved hands together. The low sun gave no warmth at all.

Loren found a scrap of paper and pencil in her book bag. "Who shall we do first?"

"Val," Kerri decided. She had already worked half of it out since leaving Alexander's office. "His old name, the given name, is an eight. He added another 'L' and an 'E'. That is another three and a five, makes sixteen, makes seven."

"Right," said Loren, scribbling on her paper. "So at least he did change his number. But shouldn't we be doing the whole name?"

"Later. Let us check the part they changed first. Now, Arzelle."

"What was her name before?"

"Zarah." Kerri spelled it.

Loren wrote it down and calculated quickly. "Nine. A strong number. Magisterial!" The both giggled. "But 'Arzelle'...let's see...mm, and five makes thirty-four...is a seven. Like 'Valle'. They match. Cute! I wonder if it is a coincidence."

"Go on!" Kerri urged. "Do Fiona. She added a 'Y'. And John Garibaldi."

"Fiona. She was a...a nine before, and afterward...a seven." Loren stared thoughtfully at the scrawled numbers, her ironic smile gone. "You know," she said, "maybe this is not cute."

"Nor a coincidence," mused Kerri. "What does seven mean?"

Loren thumbed through the book. "There's a whole chapter, but in brief, seven is the number of mysticism, scholarship, introversion...."

"Sure!" Kerri snorted. "Arzelle is such an introvert!"

"...introspection," Loren went on, "Magical power."

"Power," Kerri repeated.

They looked at each other.

"John What's-his-name," said Loren slowly. "What did he do?"

"An extra 'N'." She watched as Loren reduced the name.

"John. A two. Add one 'N'. That's five. Seven. I think," Loren said, "we have found ourselves a pattern. And all of these people are...*Them*?"

"Every one," Kerri affirmed.

"But what does it mean?"

Kerri shook her head. "Maybe nothing. Just some silly fashion, as we thought in the first place. Perhaps it is nothing more than how to tell for sure...."

"To tell who is one of *Them*," Loren finished thoughtfully. "Ah! Well, I do call that useful. Should we go back and tell Alex and Greta?"

"No!" Kerri scanned the Common anxiously and lowered her voice. "No. Not yet. We have never mentioned Them before in the Gang of Four, and I don't much care to bring it up and explain it all from the beginning. I am not ready for that, and I suspect you do not trust Greta that much. Nor do I, come to that."

"I suppose not," Loren admitted, troubled. "I certainly do not want to look ridiculous in front of her or Alex. Especially Alex. On the other hand," she continued slowly, "I shouldn't mind having someone else—how shall I put this?—on our side." She grinned suddenly. "Lord, I do sound a fool!"

It was an appealing notion, Kerri admitted to herself, for a moment weighing the hope of allies against the terror of sharing this, her oldest, most personal secret. Terror and caution won, for now. "Here is what we shall do." She felt within a pocket of her book bag and brought out a small box of matches. "Tonight you will take the book home and read it, as much as you have time for. It has to be you, because I shall not have the chance with Nicholas about." In a windless moment she got a match alight and touched it to a corner of the paper Loren still held. "We can think about telling Alex and Greta later, when we know more."

Loren held the burning paper until the flames approached her fingers; then she dropped it on the path. "You mean, find out how many of Them there are. In the Archives. I will go. Tomorrow."

Kerri nodded. The paper had burnt to ashes; she ground them into the gravel of the path with her foot. "There is someone I must tell, though," she said. "As soon as I can."

"Your grandmother?" Loren asked, having been told enough about that redoubtable old woman to sense a kindred spirit. She wrapped the numerology book in her scarf and stowed it carefully into her book bag.

"No," Kerri answered. "The friend I told you about, my cousin Timo of the Sea People, the one I wish to bring to the Gang of Four. I trust him, and he can help us. He already...." She broke off and stared at Loren. The pink light of the setting sun could not warm the paleness of her face.

"What!" exclaimed Loren. "What is it?"

"My grandmother." Kerri shivered. "She changed her name."

Chapter 40

Nightmares

She left Loren, still confused and half alarmed, at the streetcar stop just outside the Common and hastened, by the first shuttle, to the sea terminal, but she was too late. Timo's ship had been gone for nearly an hour. Knowing it would be weeks before he could receive a letter, Kerri wrote him one anyway, saying only that there was a new development in the subject they had been investigating together and that she must talk to him as soon as possible. She left the letter in care of the Sea People at Yendys, as well as a copy to be forwarded to his first likely port of call in the Islands.

Then the Commandant's assistant took pity on her and told her it might be possible to send a message to Timo by other, quicker means. It was not made clear how this would be accomplished, only that the message must be brief and would pass through many hands.

Having chosen her Academic heritage over her Sea People blood, Kerri could not be made privy to all the People's secrets, but she had long been aware they had mysterious ways to communicate quickly over long distances. She had hoped the opportunity would be offered, and, fortunately, Academic life had prepared her well for the task of conveying private meaning in a few, well-chosen, enigmatic words.

"Names news. Very urgent. K."

She thanked the Commandant's assistant profusely and ceremonially, leaving him smiling with surprise at her correct form. Then she caught the train home, for she had done all that she could do. There was no other immediate action she could take to hold off the sick feeling of worry and depression that loomed over her like bad weather coming down.

She could put it off no longer. She must add up the letters A-R-Y-E-L. One plus nine plus seven plus five plus three. Twenty-five. Seven.

Not Grandmother! Aryel had never been one of Them!

But how do I know? Kerri asked herself. *I have grown up close to her; everything about her is familiar to me. If she were one of Them, might I not be so accustomed that I would never notice? Might it not simply blend into all she is? And she loves me; she would never act against me. She is family, not a rival. She is on my side, so how could I ever know?*

The answer was as quietly obvious. Yes, Aryel might in fact be one of Them—the Them of her own day. By all accounts during her long career she had been every bit as formidable as women like Arzelle or Fiona. She had rolled over her rivals like a typhoon, but she had never shown anything of that side of herself to her granddaughter. Kerri had only known her to be loving, amusing, supportive, and wise.

And who were They, anyway? Soberly Kerri reminded herself of the reality she knew, had always known, deep down, behind the Game: They were simply people. They had no magical powers, nor could They read minds. It might seem to Kerri and Loren and others less self-assured that They had acquired some special secret about how to succeed in life, how to intimidate, how to clear others out of their juggernaut path, but if there was a secret, it was no more than this: They were individuals who had an extra zest for competition.

Simple, honest, straightforward achievement was not enough for them; They must prove themselves in the vanquishing of others, by any means possible.

Kerri remembered an old folktale of the Age of Dreams when people had possessed vehicles capable of moving as rapidly as the fastest trains, more than one hundred kilometers an hour. Some of those who controlled these fabulous carriages had never been able to believe they were getting anywhere, no matter how fast they were going, unless their vehicles were overtaking and passing other vehicles. When they could not overtake, they followed perilously close behind. They forgot all common sense, let alone common courtesy, going faster and faster, following closer and closer, until they put themselves and other people in great danger. Many had died because of this. Kerri reflected that They were like that—driven, unable to perceive any achievement, any progress that did not come at someone else's expense.

Not that They would go so far as to make that expense fatal—this was not the Age of Dreams, after all! Or would they? And were there not fates worse than death?

Deliberately, she did not let her mind open that door again. *Surely not.* Then, suddenly, sickeningly, she remembered Thomas. Yes, he was only a bird, but to her and Nicholas, his death had felt no less than a murder. It was horrible and unforgivable, and if Kerri had been able to find a shred of evidence identifying the killer, she would not have hesitated to take the matter up with the civil authorities. Unfortunately, at the time she'd had no idea whom to suspect.

And yet Thomas's death was not properly relevant to the issue of Them at all; it was part of Val's vendetta against Kerri. Why he felt he must still torment her, she could not fathom. *Is he sorry he chose Zarah?* she wondered. *Is he punishing me for letting him go so easily?* Intriguing thought!

Val's torments were obviously personal, not professional, but Kerri had never doubted that, in general, the sabotage which made life hazardous and miserable for younger members of her caste came, if not from Them, then from people who aspired to be Them. What a dismal way to live one's life: never able to take joy in any accomplishment for its own sake.

And the changing of names to sevens? Surely nothing more than marking oneself as a member of a certain (perhaps desirable and influential) clique—one of those fashions that came and went periodically at the various Universities, reviving about once a generation, like platform shoes and wearing one's hair in elaborate braids. It must have spread from Yendys to Urlosa and Dalton and then to the Islands, as usual. Perhaps many years ago, numerology had had something to do with it, but Kerri had no doubt that the connection was long forgotten and the significance of the number seven quite lost. Otherwise she would have heard about it. *Surely*, she would have heard about it. Things were tense enough without the worry that she had missed out completely on an important fad or—worse!— that she had already unknowingly betrayed her ignorance in some chance conversation.

There was one simple way to settle the whole business: ask Grandmother. Not now, not by letter. During the holidays, when she and Nick went over to the Islands, she would look for the opportunity to bring it up in a casual way. Aryel would probably laugh. "Oh, that!" she would say with a chuckle. "Great heaven, are they still doing that? Well, you never know what silly fad is going to come round again."

Sometimes she told herself the whole trouble was simple stress—final exams, thesis topics, Sponsor announcements, study group politics, the usual horrors of the end of autumn term. Then, suddenly, she would remember the Gang of Four, her father's Legacy, the Ball, the dementings, Thomas, the sabotage and how suddenly the acts of persecution had ended. She remembered a voice, a hand laid lightly on her sleeve, the angle of a cheekbone—all of the things, both large and small, that added up to make this season the most peculiar she had ever lived through. She could not even call it a "bad time," for she had endured worse. For instance, this was nothing like the torture of being accused of cheating on Prelims. And it was, despite certain emotional resonances, completely unlike the anguish of ending her marriage to Val.

In a dream between Tuesday and Wednesday she fancied she saw a pattern in all the recent strange twistings in her life, a way in which everything began to come together into a meaningful whole, but when she awoke only a glimmer of that pattern remained, blowing away like smoke as she tried to hold on to it. For some reason she kept thinking of something Greta had said, one of those library afternoons—it seemed ages ago now. "She is still dreaming the changes." *What changes are these*, Kerri wondered, *which have come upon my life so furtively, so confusingly?* She had the uneasy feeling that even achieving a Sponsor would not make things right, not any more.

Wednesday morning brought a brief note from Loren: "Pursuing further research as time allows, which is not much. Exam Thursday."

By Friday Kerri's health was much improved, in spite of a week of doing most of the usual things and never taking advantage of her infirmary waiver. She spent many hours under the quilt on the couch in her office, alternating work with napping, emerging only for lectures, a seminar or two, her Recitation and the most essential errands, then going home as early as possible. She and Nick kept the fire going in the bedroom and subsisted on soups and bread and bottled fruit.

Nick was pale, preoccupied, and out of sorts that week. He had little appetite and complained of headaches. Kerri wondered if he was sickening with the flu himself. He did not deny that he felt worn and tired, but he could not afford to have the flu, he said, not with thesis topic choosing so close.

The week had been a tense and bitter time on campus. The holiday season notwithstanding, the end of Autumn Term was the most stressful part of the Academic year, with thesis topics and Sponsorship declarations pending, not to mention stipend work assignments for the coming term. The traditional pale blue envelopes had begun appearing in mailboxes Monday, setting everyone grumbling. Kerri felt she had no business complaining about her assignment: to begin July the first—six hours a week typing and filing at the Public Health Department. True, it would mean serving as an underling to her own replacement. Yes, it would be boring, but it could have been much worse. Still, she wished she could have put off being reminded her one term of grace was nearly at an end.

To make matters worse, there had been four more dementings since Monday, two in the College of Philosophy alone. This college, Val's, had known more than its share of dementings the last year or two. The third victim was a Junior Fellow of the College of Natural History, at home on Wednesday evening, which made the seventh person in Arzelle's College to go down since the beginning of term, practically guaranteeing (according to gossip) that Arzelle would succeed to the Faculty much sooner than she might otherwise have expected.

Kerri's own College of Literature was not spared. One of two men who shared the office directly upstairs from her lost his mind Thursday morning. Kerri had been over to Mossfield Annex for her Recitation, Professor Greystone being temporarily located there while his offices were repainted. Returning, she walked in upon all the uproar, saw them carrying out the unfortunate victim, saw the greyed faces of her colleagues lining the foyer and stairs. This third incident in Paterson Hall in less than a week left everyone in the building shaken, grieving, and terrified, not least Kerri, who spent that hour after her Recitation sitting at her desk, shivering, renewing the Veil over and over again.

She did manage to write down four dreams. In the first, she wandered through what she thought was the campus, although she recognized nothing. The only light came from a feeble, flickering candle she carried in her hand. She remembered that she was supposed to be looking for the Private Library. "You need a better light than that," said Greta, who walked up and blew out the candle. Suddenly it was morning. Kerri saw that she was in the center of the Honowell campus in its high cirque of mountains, not in Yendys at all. She realized she had been searching all night, she had missed her ship to the Mainland, and she was going to be in all kinds of trouble. That was the end of the first dream.

In the second she was supposed to meet Nick for lunch, but either she had forgotten where they were supposed to meet or else he had never told her. She had come to his College to try to find out where he had gone, but everyone she asked gave her a different answer, none of them helpful. She never did manage to find him. It was one of those miserable, wandering-around, fruitless search dreams that so often turned into the Star Dream, only this one did not, because she stopped it. When the light started to dim, as it always did, and the noise of whispering to rustle under the wind, Kerri exclaimed in irritated disgust, "Oh, please!" and woke up. It was not until she wrote it down that she realized how odd this was.

She dreamed she was at the Ball again. Stockholder Andrew Kianga Ryan was there, but he never approached her. She kept looking for him, but there were so many people in the way she could only catch a glimpse of him now and then. His costume was festive Peasant garb of an old-fashioned style—a wide-sleeved white shirt, like a poet or a pirate, tall cuffed boots and a bright scarf around his waist. Very dashing but entirely inappropriate.

Sometimes he seemed to be watching her from a distance; at other times she felt quite sure he had gone home and abandoned her for good. At least she had Alex to dance with—he was dressed as a librarian. She herself was draped from head to toe in veils of iridescent gauze.

Suddenly Loren ran up to them and seized them both by the arm. She wore the shocking yellow jumpsuit in which Kerri had first seen her, the worst possible choice, not only wrong for a ball but hideously conspicuous. She was out of breath and looked distressed and frightened. "We have to get out of here!" she pleaded. "Hurry!"

"But I have an invitation," Kerri protested. Then she realized she could not remember whether she had an invitation or not. But, of course! Nick had it. Only, she had no idea where Nick was and, in fact, did not remember coming to the ball with him. At that point things became very confused. She was either trying to find Nick (whom she kept getting mixed up with Stockholder Kianga Ryan) or trying to leave the ball with Alex and Loren, except they could not find their way out of the building, or even up onto the roof, where Kerri seemed to remember they ought to go, although she could not recollect why.

The fourth dream was particularly disquieting. Nicholas had left her for Arzelle, and everyone expected Kerri to get back together with Val, which was the last thing she wanted. Then she found out somehow that Arzelle was pregnant, and she felt doubly betrayed. Nick was only twenty-five; most men did not enter their window of fertility until they were at least twenty-eight. She had always assumed they would be together when the time came; she, Kerri, would bear a child with him. Now she would never be able to get him back from Arzelle. The two of them would be bonded for at least twenty years, and, worse, she was certain that Arzelle was lying, that Nick could not be the father.

In the dream, Kerri felt cheated. She felt consumed with anger. She went searching for the two of them with a thirst for vengeance worthy of the Age of Dreams in her heart. In the vague, abrupt manner of dreams she found herself at the Asylum and saw Nick there, inside, standing at the fence as the inmates did. And yet he was not demented. He was alive, frightened, desperate. He reached through the fence toward her and called out to her piteously, "They will not let me out! Please make them let me go." As she ran up to grasp his hands, she realized that the whole tale about him and Arzelle and the pregnancy was nothing but lies. She woke in a sweat from that one and did not shake off the feeling of doom and depression all morning.

Chapter 41

A Dinner Party

Fortunately, that cold morning was Friday, 14 May, and there was the Gang of Four to look forward to, a fine antidote to the creeping tensions of the University. Kerri fled earlier than usual to the Public Library and took refuge in the dusty reaches of the Archives, where she was unsurprised to find Loren, leafing patiently through the chronological record of name changes.

It was her second visit since Tuesday, Loren explained, apparently having taken on the investigation of anomalous name changes as a personal quest. In spite of Kerri's continued nervous objections against keeping anything in writing, Loren had already amassed quite an impressive dossier on peculiar spelling changes in names. She had established the existence of several general patterns. First and most significant, of all the people on the list Kerri had originally given her, all but four had changed their names. Loren had every expectation of finding the missing few in the records of other districts of the city. Second, the phenomenon was definitely not a passing fad. Although the number of changes fitting the pattern varied widely from year to year, there were never less than thirty in any of the years covered in the Archives and usually a far higher number. The practice appeared to be exclusively Academic, but, as Loren freely admitted, name forms and University District addresses did not constitute reliable proof. Finally, and most odd, the occurrences fell into well-defined clusters each year.

Loren had made a graph of the number of cases by month and then, as her dossier grew, by quarter month. She found few occurrences or none during the summer months. The frequency increased during the autumn and peaked in winter, with the highest number occurring in May and June, tapering off during the following months, except for a second brief, lesser rise during the first two weeks of September. Then, after the Spring Equinox, the number of name spelling changes fell off rapidly, with almost none after the end of October. Furthermore, the few cases she found of known Academics who changed their given names to normally spelled but different names also fell within these yearly clusters. Arzelle had changed her name from Zarah at the beginning of her first Autumn Term as a graduate student.

"Then, if it is happening this year," Kerri mused, "we would be into the peak season right now."

"Yes," said Loren. "But I can't confirm it because the districts hold their own records for as long as a year. There is nothing more recent than October. Why don't you have a look at the names and mark any others that you recognize?"

"Very well," said Kerri. She began at the end of the list and worked backward. "Are they all sevens?"

"The few I have taken the time to add up. What about your grandmother?"

Kerri nodded. "Seven."

"Are you going to write to her?"

"No. I will ask her when I see her next. But I've known her all my life, so I cannot imagine this is anything sinister."

Loren shook her head. "I don't know what to make of it at all."

"Neither do I. Did you bring Alex's numerology book to give back to him?"

"I returned it yesterday," said Loren. She turned away from Kerri's raised eyebrow to busy herself putting things back into her book bag. "He was on duty in here when I came in, and I had the book with me. I took plenty of notes," she added reassuringly.

"Did he ask why you were here? Did you mention the name changes to him?"

"No. Of course not! I said something about finding a friend's new address." After a quick glance at Kerri's frowning visage, Loren added guiltily, "I needed to return the last bunch of novels that I borrowed as well. And ask if he would loan me more to read over the holidays."

"So you've been going to visit him on other days? Alone?"

"Only twice, yesterday and May Eve, and just for a few moments each time. We didn't really talk. He seemed very busy, more shy than usual. Got rid of me as fast as he could."

"And the old novels," Kerri said, trying not to sound suspicious, "any possible texts there?"

Loren laughed. "Not so far. I know what you are thinking." She got to her feet and dusted herself off. "If I found anything, I would tell you right away. In fact, I know Alex would be pleased if you would read them, too. Why don't we take turns? You might enjoy some of his books; they're really very entertaining."

"I shall think about it," said Kerri soberly, half ashamed of herself and only half appeased. She disliked being put in this position: She must either trust Loren or else waste a lot of valuable time reading uncanonical, if not trashy, novels. Entertaining or not, she could imagine what Nick would say if he caught her with such books!

She continued to run backwards through Loren's list of names and dates, occasionally ticking one with a pencil. "Eh! Here is one you missed," she said.

"What do you mean?"

"A name you should have recognized. You were the one who brought it to my attention before."

"How could I have done that?" murmured Loren, squinting at the name. "I've told you I do not know anybody in Yendys."

Wilma Hinchliffe Beckett.

"O-oh," said Loren, suddenly connecting. "I did miss it. Oh, my goodness! The Glen Eden house. The old lady!"

"We do not know that she was old. And she was married by the time she died. Or widowed."

"Or widowed," Kerri agreed. "Let me see. This name change was scarcely two years before her death." She frowned. "I had assumed all these name changing people were students, young people, but perhaps they are not. On the other hand, perhaps she died young."

"We could look her up right here in the Archives," Loren suggested. "Find the death certificate. Shouldn't be difficult. We know the approximate date and which district to look in. Her age would be on it."

Kerri closed the dossier and handed it back to Loren. "Is it worth the bother?" she wondered. "I cannot believe that any of this is at all important."

"What else are you going to do in half an hour? Besides, there might be further trace of the Society of Guenevere. And the record of her marriage. I wonder if her husband minded Them getting the house instead of him. I know *I* would have minded!"

"It is none of our business," said Kerri.

"I know," Loren answered brightly. "Look, it is like a puzzle. I am a mathematician. I like puzzles and patterns and connections, even if they have no significance in the greater world. This woman was a connection between the numerological name changes and your Society of Guenevere—both unimportant, perhaps—but I am intrigued, and I am going to look her up!"

"A coincidence," Kerri countered as she helped Loren to replace the name change ledgers on the shelves. "And it isn't *my* Society of Guenevere."

Loren grinned at her sidelong. "I think you do not *want* a connection. You do not want any significance!"

"I simply desire to keep things in proportion. It is too late in the term, and we have far too much work to do to let our imaginations run away with us, especially over something this..."

"Silly?"

"Trivial. Ephemeral."

"Well." Loren dusted off her hands and picked up her book bag. "I think you need to let your imagination run away with you from time to time. It would do you good." She set off down the aisle, bound for the district registries.

Kerri stared after her. "Indeed!" she retorted. "Like the Watchers."

Loren stopped abruptly and turned around, her expression suddenly sober. "No!" Then, more quietly but very deliberately: "Not like that. This is different. This is not imaginary. This is on paper. And it will still be on paper if I come back tomorrow to look again."

"Quite right," Kerri agreed grimly, thinking of vanishing script on Nick's desk and illusionary cards in the university library catalog. "I apologize," she said. *Name of the Dreamer, I am in a foul mood!* she thought. *What is the matter with me?*

There was no death certificate for Miss Wilma Hinchliffe Beckett. She was not dead. She had been committed to the Asylum, demented, at the age of twenty-six, the widow of Mr. Craig Powell Martinez-Beckett, deceased the year before. She had no survivors. Her sole heir was an entity called the Society of Guenevere, of which no further word was written in the registry entry.

It was nearly three o'clock; Alex and Greta would be waiting. As Kerri and Loren made their way out of the Archives, Loren said, "Next week I intend to look up the death of Mr. Martinez-Beckett. And the marriage. You are very quiet."

Kerri said thoughtfully, "I think I have seen her. At the Asylum. One night there was a woman holding onto the fence, in the rain. Staring out, like they do sometimes. I was on the trolley, and the driver said her name was Miss Beckett."

"Very sad," Loren commented. "I was thinking, it might be interesting—when I have the time, of course—to go to the Bureau of Housing Properties and Public Domain and look up the history of the house."

"It might," Kerri agreed.

At the first opportunity, Kerri asked Alex, "Do they keep records of corporations and partnerships in the Archives, too?"

"No, those go to the North Annex. Why?"

"I thought it might be another good place to look up the Society of Guenevere."

"Thought you'd already found it," Greta commented, pouring out the tea. "A tontine, you said."

"We're just curious who was in it," Loren explained.

Later, they all shared their dreams: Alex's dreams of finding wonderful, forgotten things buried in ruined buildings and old refuse piles; Greta's dreams of gardening and dinner parties and trying to rescue small children from drowning; Loren's dreams of perpetually trying to catch a train, of being late to an exam,

Deborah K. Vleck

of fleeing either to or from something. Each had made some beginning of interpretation, following the practices described in the book.

They found themselves cautious and reserved about commenting upon one another's dreams, even Greta seemed a trifle uneasy in this new, more intimate territory.

Kerri's uneasiness was more than a trifle. She could think of no graceful way to refuse to take her turn, and so, last of the four, she told her dreams in barest outline, omitting details, emotional overtones and all mention of Arzelle: She had been hunting by candlelight on the Honowell University campus for a particular building that did not exist; Greta had blown out the candle because it was morning. She had tried unsuccessfully to find Nick to keep a lunch date. She and Loren and Alex had been looking for a way out of the Palace of Arts at the same time she was, again, trying to locate Nick. Nick had been trapped in the Asylum.

"I can guess what inspired that last one," Loren commented grimly. At Alex's querying look, she said, "There have been rather too many dementings this term. The latest one was yesterday morning, upstairs from Kerri's office."

"How dreadful!" exclaimed Alex, a shade disapprovingly, as one who felt himself a safe distance from such dubious goings on.

Greta clicked her knitting needles together more briskly than usual. "Sometimes I think that University of yours is a woeful unhealthy place," she declared.

"Well," said Kerri, smothering a sneeze, "nobody can argue with that these past two weeks! A third of my department is out on waivers."

"At least," Loren commented, "since it was Nick trapped and not you, you must not be worried about your own sanity."

"Indeed," replied Kerri noncommittally.

"Those other three dreams, now," Greta said thoughtfully. "They are all about a search of some kind."

"I did notice that," Kerri agreed. "And I have had such dreams before. It would seem to mean that perhaps I am searching for something in waking life, but I do not know what that thing might be. In the dreams the object of the search varies. It might be a person or a place, as in the examples I have just told you, but it is just as likely to be a mislaid book or a paper or an item of clothing." She wished she had never agreed to be part of this uncomfortable discussion and tried in vain to think of a graceful way of leading the conversation away from the subject.

Alexander asked shyly, "Have you tried using any of the techniques in the book?"

"Not in any depth," Kerri admitted. "I have not got round to it. I shall try, though."

"If you can discover what it is you are looking for," said Loren, "perhaps you will realize where to find it."

* * *

I am searching for something, Kerri told herself as she made her way through the bustling streets of central Yendys. *What am I searching for?*

A disturbing question—more disturbing than it ought to be—and for that reason, in some perverse way, it was also a promising question. She felt poised on the edge of discovery. Perhaps there was something of value in this dream business after all.

She was in no hurry to go home that evening. Nick had told her he planned to stay in his office and work late, she must go ahead and have supper without him. This would have been the night of the dinner party; obviously, he did not care to be reminded by a quiet house. Neither did Kerri. She considered hunting him up and proposing dinner in town before they went home, but she did not feel energetic enough to go back to campus. It was too late to visit the Bureau of Housing Properties and Public Domain to investigate the Glen Eden House. She decided to dawdle for a while in town, look at the shop windows glittering with holiday merchandise, perhaps do a bit of shopping, have a bite to eat somewhere.

At a quarter past seven she found herself standing in the warm gaslit entry of the Brandon Arcade, shaking out her umbrella. The working week was ending; the crowds were thick. It took her some time to make her way up to her favorite stationer's shop on the topmost floor. She and Nick shared a fondness for fine writing instruments, and she thought she might buy him a new fountain pen as a Solstice, "good-luck-on-your-thesis-topic" present. There was one she'd had her eye one for some time, hoping each time she went in that the price would be marked down. It was not, but she bought it anyway.

Afterward, she wandered out to the gallery that ringed the great atrium of the arcade and leaned over the railing to look down at the crowds of Friday evening shoppers and pleasure seekers. Montague's, a fashionable and elegant restaurant that occupied a quarter of the ground level of the arcade and as much of the atrium floor itself, bustled with early diners. One particularly well-turned-out group—the men in formal black, the women sparkling with jewels—stood enjoying cocktails on the small balcony of one of Montague's private banquet rooms.

With astonishment Kerri recognized Jillian and Peter. And wasn't that Fiona and her husband? One by one, she picked them out, the intended guests of her failed dinner party, laughing together, obviously dressed for a special occasion. *Oh,* she thought, *they did have another engagement after all. Here they are.* There were two or three other people she recognized. The Morgana woman. One of the men who had stood her up at the Ball.

Name of the Dreamer, she said to herself, suddenly cold all over. *It is Them. Veil!* she thought.

Suddenly, the group broke up and began to drift back through the open door to the inner room. As they moved aside, Kerri caught sight of Nicholas in his tuxedo, conferring with a waiter. The waiter nodded as Nicholas spoke, nodded again, receiving instructions. With some final comment, Nick gestured toward the inner room and turned back to his colleagues. For some reason he happened to glance up across the atrium. He saw Kerri.

For two long seconds they stared at each other. Then he turned his head. Jillian was waiting by the door, smiling, saying something to Nick, holding out a wine glass to him. He took it and followed her into the private dining room. Kerri caught a glimpse of him shaking hands with someone before the waiter closed the doors and set off purposefully toward the kitchen.

High above she leaned on the polished brass railing and gazed down upon the elegant diners at Montague's, the candles, the silver, the crystal, the white linen.

Chapter 42

Lies and Evasions

He returned to the house a little before eleven o'clock to find her in the study, sitting at her desk.

"Where is your tux?" she asked. "I hope you did not wear it home in this weather."

"In my office." He stood in the doorway of the study, slowly unwinding his scarf from his neck. Melting sleet dripped from his coat. "I tried to find you, but you weren't there when I came back out."

"I wanted to catch the seven forty-five," she informed him.

"I see." He began to take off the coat. Under it he was wearing the same workaday clothing in which he had gone to town in the morning. "Whatever possessed you," he asked, "to spy on me?"

"What?" She gaped at him, half laughing with surprise. "Spy on you? Are you mad?" On the other hand, she realized, he couldn't very well accuse her of imagining things. Not this time. She took a small, bitter pleasure in being the one to suggest madness for a change: *his* turn to be unreasonable, irrational, illogical, unbalanced.

"Then what were you doing there?"

"What were *you* doing there?"

"What did it look like I was doing?" he asked irritably.

You're in retreat, my sweet Nicholas, she thought. She widened her eyes at him. "What did it look like? It looked like working late, of course. I hope you accomplished everything you wanted to."

He opened his mouth and then closed it again. Abruptly he turned and disappeared from the doorway. She heard him walk back to the front hall, hesitate there, return to the study, without coat and scarf. She watched from her chair as he walked to his desk, took the chimney off his lamp, hunted for matches.

"What did it look like?" she repeated calmly. "It looked like you hosting a dinner party in one of the city's finest restaurants for a group of people who refuse to dine in your home with your wife."

"I was not the host," he snapped.

"And how you are going to pay for it out of your stipend, I cannot imagine," she continued. "Maybe your mother will loan you the money. I certainly have better uses for mine."

"I was not the host!" he shouted.

"I am not a spy," she replied quietly. "You were watching me!"

"I happened to see you. It was completely unexpected."

"You did not follow me to the Arcade?"

"Mercy, no! What have you been imagining?" *Take that!* she thought. *Delicious*, she decided, trying to ignore how small it made her feel to get her own back for once, aware in one tiny corner of her mind that getting back at Nick was always mostly getting back at Val. *I will stop behaving like this*, she commanded herself sternly. *Whatever tale he tells.* "I was coming from afternoon tea with a friend and some shopping," she said. "Minding my own business. Which had nothing whatever to do with you. It is a public place, Nicholas. If one of us owes the other an explanation for being there, it is not I."

He lit his lamp, waved out the match and replaced the chimney. Sullen-faced, he sat down heavily. "I *did* try to find you," he said. "I ran all over the damned arcade. I was going to make you come and join us. They couldn't have..." He broke off and stared at the glowing lamp wick.

"They could not have what? Turned me away? Why not? If there is a limit to their rudeness toward me, I have yet to encounter it." A sudden horrifying possibility occurred to her. "I hope you did not tell them you had seen me."

"Of course not. I excused myself for a few minutes. I doubt I was even missed." He slumped back in his chair. "You've got it all wrong. I was asked to join the party almost at the last minute. Someone had canceled, the booking was all made...."

"And by a stroke of good fortune you just happened to have your tuxedo handy!"

"It has been in my office for weeks, since I fetched it from the cleaners. I simply never got round to bringing it home. Name of the Dreamer, Kerri! This party was the reason they couldn't come to dinner here. It was planned long before we sent our invitations. They weren't rejecting you when they declined to come. I told you so at the time."

"So. They were lying in the first place when they told you they were free this evening."

He lifted one shoulder, equivocating. "Not exactly. Maybe. One of those polite little social lies, perhaps. I did not make it clear just why I was inquiring about their plans. I was trying to be, you know, subtle and roundabout so our invitations would be fresh. No doubt, they were just trying to keep me...us... from feeling left out."

"Ah. I see. Then how kind of them it was to relent and include you—'almost at the last minute.' Pity you did not persuade them to relent far enough to include both of us."

He could not meet her eyes. "There was just the one cancellation. They only wanted one man to make up the number, and in any case I'm not sure I am on such terms with that group that I can invite along extra guests. Although," he added, "if I had been able to find you in the Arcade, I would have."

Not at all mollified, she reopened her text to the place marked by her finger. "Oh, *that* would have helped the case, forcing me on them! Without proper dress. I would not have allowed you to do that."

"Then what do you think I should I have done?" he cried out. "It seems I am damned whatever I chose to do."

"I never said I wanted to crash this party I was so clearly not invited to. And if you want my opinion as to what you ought to have done, you ought to have declined. They had no business asking you in the first place. They had no business asking any married person if they could not include the spouse. Not to an occasion like this!" For the first time her voice rose. That would not do. She took a deep breath. "There are plenty of single men in your college. They should have asked one of them, if all they needed was someone to make up their numbers at the last minute."

"Maybe they did ask all of them, and they were all unavailable."

"Or had enough presence of mind not to let themselves be used in such a fashion. In fact," she went on bitterly, "if I were you, I would consider it a very bad sign that Jilly and Peter and Miss Lewis were apparently included from the start, but you were only good enough for an afterthought. Has your status in the History College slipped so badly?"

"Of course it hasn't slipped," he replied tartly. He drew himself up straight, face reddening. "This wasn't that kind of a party. It was a simple social occasion."

"Indeed. A very simple little private black tie dinner at Montague's, planned weeks in advance, if what you tell me is true. In other words, they only despise you socially, not professionally—if that is possible. Name of the Dreamer, Nick! For all they knew, we were still having our dinner party without them. You as good as told them we knuckled under and canceled it because they couldn't—or wouldn't—come." She thought about this for a second, unhappily aware of all the mistakes that had gone into this evening. "That is what we should have done. We should have invited some other friends, our neighbors, people we can count on, people we don't have to impress, and given the dinner anyway."

He considered her words for a long moment. "Yes," he conceded finally. "You may be right about that." He looked at her accusingly. "Why didn't you suggest it in the first place?"

"Why didn't you?" she countered.

"It never entered my mind." He pondered a moment further. "If I'd had time to think about this affair tonight, I probably would have declined, for exactly the reasons you cited. But I wasn't given time. They put me on the spot, rather, and at the moment it seemed to me that it was better to be included as an afterthought than to be left out entirely. It seemed that declining would give them the wrong sort of message."

She glared at him. "Oh, don't be dense, Nick! It would give them the message that you are in demand, that *we* are in demand, that we are not the sort of people who are available at the last minute. All you had to do was to say we had other plans."

"Yes. Well," he replied with a small shrug. "It can't be helped; it's too late now. Perhaps this has been a small strategic error, but I can't believe it is a serious one or that it will do any lasting damage. And I do think you are making far too much of the whole thing."

She rolled her eyes. If the first line of defense—she was "imagining things"—proved untenable, he must fall back on "making too much of things."

Looking somewhat abashed, possibly recognizing that he had trotted out this particular admonition too many times in the past, he tried again. "You must realize I walk a very narrow path these days. After the retreat, after the holidays, after I get my topic, I'll be in a much stronger position. Until then, I am rather at the mercy of the way things are done."

"Indeed!" she muttered with an irritated snort.

"You have the upbringing to know what these matters are like," he said. "I thought you would understand."

"I understand as well as you would in my place," she told him stiffly. "You ask understanding of me. I ask the same of you. Our caste is notoriously cruel to marriages. You know this. Think of what your parents went through, and mine. You expressed concern about the messages, the signals, you are sending to your associates. Do you wish to send the message that you are the sort of man who doesn't mind if his wife is excluded from his company and the company of his associates? Or do you want it known that you are committed to your marriage and that you regard a slight against me as a slight against both of us?"

"Of course I am committed to our marriage!" he exclaimed angrily. "You know I am."

"I would be a lot happier if you would not keep it such a secret from your colleagues," she retorted. "Otherwise, we are fair game to those who would break us up for the fun of it. And do not tell me such things don't happen, because you know perfectly well it is only more of 'the way things are done.' I should not have to be telling you this." They stared gloomily at each other.

Finally he said, "You do not have to tell me. I know. I do battle for you more than you realize, but I don't always have that option. Sometimes I must make the best of a bad situation." He leaned forward upon his elbows and spoke earnestly, "Look, Kerri, I regret very much that you were hurt by what you saw tonight. Causing you pain was the furthest thing from my intention. I knew even before I saw you that I hadn't used my best judgment, but by then it was too late, and I never thought...well, I can only apologize to you. I am sorry."

He looked genuinely regretful. She took another deep breath. "Very well," she said. "I accept your apology. But next time, *think*!"

"Yes. I will." He smiled wanly at her and opened a book.

As he looked down at his desk, she studied him silently. His face, in the lamplight, looked thin and pinched, more exhausted than she had ever seen him, but there was a complacency about his mouth, a satisfaction, relief. Facing her had gone better than he had expected. The crisis had been handled. She had been reasonable. If she had not seen him in the Brandon Arcade, she realized, if he had not seen her watching him, he never would have told her about this evening. He would have lied. She wondered if anything he said to her was the truth any more. She closed her book, tidied her papers and stood up. "I am going to take a bath and go to bed."

"All right." He leaned back in his chair, affectionately watching her. "I have some things I must finish yet. Good night."

"Good night."

Locked in the bathroom, she ran herself a nice hot bath and let her mind simmer gently.

You looked like a host, my duck, she thought. *You did.*

A truce seemed called for. They spent the weekend in apparent amity, doing the usual Saturday chores together, studying companionably in the evenings, taking care to preserve a normalcy neither of them felt. In the darkest moments, she knew she was losing Nicholas—to Arzelle, to someone; it did not really matter whom. Or losing him to no one but to some irredeemable flaw in her own character. Sometimes anger overtook her, and she vowed she would not let Them break up her marriage without a fight. More often she felt herself pulling away from the pain, as she had been all term, creating a distance between herself and him, so that she would not have to feel when the time finally came. Letting him go, as she had let go of Val.

Finally, late on Sunday afternoon when they were at the far end of the property mending the fence and the silence had grown too long, she said to him, "Are you going to leave me? If you are, I wish you would just leave. Go. Don't draw it out. It is doing me no kindness."

The low sun threw his face into stark relief as he stared at her. It seemed to her that he looked shocked, terrified.

"*Leave* you," he whispered. "What do you mean?"

"Make up your mind," she said grimly. "Go. Or stay. But do it *now*. So I know."

"I'm not going to leave you." He sounded stunned. Slowly, he put down the wire cutters and took off his heavy leather gloves. He walked to her and put his arms around her.

"I am not going to leave you," he repeated. "Are you going to leave me?"

"No," she said.

They held each other for a long time, until the sun was below the horizon.

"I am afraid," she said as they walked back to the house.

"I know. I am sorry. I am afraid, too."

"Are you?" She looked at him.

"Sometimes." He opened the door to the shed and placed the tools inside on the bench. "I just keep telling myself, things will be easier soon." He came out of the shed and touched her shoulder gently. "Can you hang on a little longer?"

"How long?"

"A couple of weeks, a few days more."

She hung the coil of wire over its nail and pulled the shed door closed. "Yes," she said slowly, "if you don't..." She could not finish the sentence.

"I won't," he said.

She nodded, but so remote had she become that she did not know—or care—whether she believed him or only pretended to believe him.

Chapter 43

The Find

Monday came and went without incident: No dementings on or off campus, no tampering in Kerri's office. She renewed the Veil night and morning over her small room in Paterson Hall and over the lonely house and garden at Evesham hamlet, but her heart was not in it. Something had happened over the weekend, something sobering, saddening. She was too old, Kerri realized; it was time to let go of the Game forever, time to go Real and stay there, to deal with her marriage, her career, the real behavior of real people.

On Tuesday she left the campus at half past two, slipping out of the building by the southwest door. The day was sunny, windy and quite cold, the very sort of blustery winter day Kerri liked best. It was more pleasant to be out of doors than in, and in any case she felt not the least bit guilty. If anyone in the department missed her, let them think (as they always must, of a Tuesday or Friday afternoon) that she had gone off to the library or over to meet Nick, trying to curry favor with his formidable colleagues. Let them think so. After all, they were right. Not about Nick—he and the formidable colleagues were having some kind of last minute meeting about the coming retreat; he would (again) not be home for supper. But she *was* going to the library.

She pulled open the heavy door of the Public Library a few minutes past three and entered the ancient octagonal hall. Without a glance at the watchful librarians presiding from their oaken lair she went directly to the north stairs and clattered down to the basement. Today there was no stopping at the Archives. Let Loren pursue such trivia if she wished. The Veil, Kerri decided with a cool, rational maturity, would be the next thing to go. Except that the Veil was so easy and so simple. And such a habit.

They were all there. Loren was making the tea, and Greta, bundled in colorful shawls, was cutting up a raisin cake. Alexander was trying to find space among the piles of books to fit a fourth chair, a rickety object, loose jointed and dusty, unearthed from some neglected lumber room. Kerri eyed it with misgiving. "Another relic from the Age of Dreams?" she asked.

They all turned toward the door with pleased exclamations. Alexander beamed at her with his quick smile. "It's quite safe," he assured her. He pulled an enormous and rather grubby handkerchief from one bulging coat pocket and dusted the seat of the chair. "Anyway, *I* am going to sit on it." He did so. The chair creaked threateningly but remained whole and upright. They all laughed. Alex stood again, still beaming at Kerri, and ushered her to his own lopsided desk chair.

"Thank you," said Kerri, smiling back with real gratitude. "What news?" she asked of them all.

"No news," said Greta with a grin. "Nothing's new. It's all old."

"Very well, then," said Kerri. "What's old?"

"Alex has found another book," announced Loren.

"Alex has found another warehouse full of books," corrected Greta, "but he has brought one especially to show us. He might have the decency to wait until we've finished the last one, but no!"

"You have all seen it already." Kerri tried not to sound accusing.

Alex reddened and Loren explained, "He wouldn't even get it out until you arrived. Nobody's seen it except him."

Merry with relief, Kerri laughed. Of course, they would not! These were true friends. She accepted her mug of tea and a slab of raisin cake and wondered what bit of weirdness Alex had unearthed this time. She asked with some anxiety, "Another uncatalogued library book?"

"No, indeed," Alex assured her eagerly. "This one is mine, bought and paid for! I don't know what you all will think of it. It's a little unusual, a change of pace." He had already read it, naturally. As a matter of course, he passed it to Greta.

"Well, by rights, it's Kerri's turn to have first go at it," Greta declared.

Kerri hastened to protest that Greta should go first, as by her seniority in the Gang of Four. With Finals bearing down on her, the very last thing she needed, she said to herself, was another of Alexander's extremely odd finds to read. Television! Dreams! Numerology! She had no room in her life for this sort of nonsense these days.

"Very well," said Greta. "If you insist. Me first, then you, since you went last before, then Loren. But next time you go first. No excuses!" She held the new book up and peered at the worn and faded spine. It was a thin book, leather bound, printed on thick paper. "What's it, a novel?" she asked. "*In Watermelon Sugar*. Odd name for a book."

Loren's head came up.

Kerri held out a hand kept from shaking only by sheer surprise. "May I have a look?" she asked.

"Sure." Greta handed her the book casually.

"It's more what they call a novella," said Alex with a grimace. "I'm not even sure I would call it that. A series of short little vignettes. Very strange. Seems to be some kind of story of the Years of Confusion. I don't go for novels much," he informed them unnecessarily, "except for certain kinds I like, but this is out of the ordinary."

Delicately, Kerri opened the cover and turned to the title page. She met Loren's eyes. "Yes," she said, dazed. "Brautigan."

A grin materialized slowly on Loren's face. "Eureka," she murmured as Kerri passed the book to her to look at.

"You know the author?" asked Alex. "You've heard of him? I never did, but then, you two know more about literature than I would, being Academic. From the story I never supposed he could be from the Age of Dreams. Or maybe he's not the right kind for the University. Not literary enough, or something. Still, it struck me when I came upon it, and I thought it might be worth a read."

"Oh, yes," said Loren, turning the pages with apparent indifference. "We've heard of Brautigan. And he is probably from the Age of Dreams—mid to late Nineteens—although that's in some debate. He's not one of the Great Names—in fact he has been fairly obscure until recently." Without obvious reluctance, she returned the book to Greta's outstretched hand.

Name of the Dreamer! Kerri thought. *What have I done? I could have been the one walking out of here with that book, and I turned it down.*

"So you've read this already." Alex looked a bit crestfallen.

"No," said Loren, admirably deadpan. "Not this particular work."

"I haven't either," said Kerri, hoping her face was under control. "Um, few people have. It is not in the Syllabus," she explained, trying to put just the right tone of offhand dismissiveness into her voice.

Greta looked from one of them to the other and back again, very quickly. Not much got past her, Peasant or not.

"I certainly do look forward to reading it," Kerri added with a hopeful and longing look at the book in Greta's firm grasp.

With wholehearted sincerity, Loren said, "So do I! Tell us, Alex, what piqued your interest about this one? Have you had it in your collection a long time?"

Alexander shrugged, grinning. "Not long. A couple of months ago there was a warehouse going, a big one—an old one!—tons of books. The Acquisitions Office needed every hand they could get to box up the collection and take it to library storage. They usually ask me; they know I'm willing. It'll be years before they get through it all. I was keeping my eyes open, like I always do, and I spotted a few things that looked interesting, spaceship stories and...."

"And they just let you pull them out and keep them, I suppose," Loren remarked.

"There was an old woman there," he continued. "She was hovering, watching, touching things. It was cold in the place, frightfully uncomfortable. I offered to bring her a cup of tea. Turned out she was the owner...."

"Uh huh!" said Greta, who had seen it coming and who knew Alex's ways of old. "And she offered to let you take anything you fancied, right?"

"From under the nose of Acquisitions? I doubt it! No, she knew better than that, gave me a signed receipt, blank. Said to take what I liked and fill in the particulars later. She wouldn't let me give her much money, said she could see that I loved books, that I cared about them the way she did, liked the ones she liked. She could tell by the two she saw sticking out of my pocket."

"How embarrassing!" Loren laughed.

"All she wanted was to know they would be cared for," Alex went on. "She wanted them to be read and enjoyed, not gathering dust in a warehouse for years—which, even donating to the library, was the best she could expect. It's happened to me before." He grinned again suddenly, but his eyes were sad. "You would be surprised how many times. An old person, the last of her family, inheriting the possessions of generations. The time comes when they're ready to let go of everything that doesn't hold a personal memory. Some try to sell it off. Some simply turn their backs on their inventory, abandon it; when they die, everything reverts to the Probate Department for the usual agencies to pick over. Sometimes, the old folk make an effort to find decent homes for their possessions while they still can. Not for money, just to see that the good old things with use still in them don't go to waste."

"I know," said Kerri gently. "Too many old things, not enough people to remember or care. I am glad you are there sometimes to buy their books, Alex. It is kind of you to trust us with them." She could not restrain herself from glancing anxiously at the prize resting in Greta's careless hands.

Alex flushed slightly. "Oh, not at all," he said happily. "My pleasure."

"All the same," Greta admonished him sternly, shoving the Brautigan ungently into her bag, "I hope you've got that bill of sale properly filled out and put away safe. You know them upstairs will raise a stink if they ever catch you. I've said it before, and now I say it again in front of all four!" She jerked her chin toward Loren and Kerri. "And I'll also say, as I've said before, you need to be getting your own personal books away from here, because if they find out upstairs what you been up to, they won't stop at confiscating what properly belongs to the library. Mark my words."

The color drained out of Alex's face, and he replied placatingly, "Yes, I know. You are quite right. And I will, very soon. I've been looking for a place. It's just, there isn't room where I live."

"Well," grumbled Greta, "maybe I can give you a bit of help there. I'll ask around, see what I can find." She resumed knitting fiercely.

Alex's next order of business was to pass "Numerology" to Greta. For a hopeful moment, Kerri thought she might relinquish the Brautigan, but she cheerfully accepted this second assignment without hesitation. He also pressed the television book on Loren, Greta having read it after Kerri, in the hopes that they could finally discuss this subject so close to his heart as soon as the next meeting. Although Kerri groaned mentally, Loren accepted the tattered thing with every appearance of eagerness, and Kerri remembered that Loren had actually been enthusiastic after Professor Harkness' disquieting presentation. *We are in for it now!* Kerri thought. *I should have buried the book a little deeper on his desk, or tucked it onto some shelf, behind something.*

And now that he was launched, Alex enthusiastically pursued the regrettable topic of ancient electrical wonders, speaking with reverence of telephones and computers and something called "modem." He interrupted himself every few minutes to remind them all that they would "really" discuss all this after Loren had read the book; then he continued merrily to tell them all about it. It seemed to Kerri that even Greta's grey eyes were glazing over with boredom. She had just decided she had spent a decent interval in the company and could politely take her leave when Loren put down her teacup with finality and began to reach for her coat. "I must be going," she announced, with a meaningful look at Kerri. "And don't you have a train to catch?"

"Oh, yes! Look at the time!" Kerri got to her feet in a hurry. "The, um, new novel does not look a long book, Greta. If you finish it by Friday and hand it along to me, I am sure I can pass it to Loren in time for her to read it before the next Tuesday."

Greta cocked an eyebrow at her. "Sure. What's the hurry?"

"Finals," Loren (with admirably quick thinking) reminded them all. "And after Finals the University goes on holidays."

"Ah!" said Alex.

"True," said Kerri, surprised by a sudden sharp regret. "Indeed, next Tuesday may be my last day with you for a while. I shall be out of town at least part of the holidays. Will the rest of you continue to meet?" she asked with some hesitation.

"Not me," said Greta. "I'll be out to the country until after Solstice. Next Tuesday's my last day as well for a while. Tell you what. I'll pass the book along Friday whether I've finished it or not, unless you think neither of you won't have time to read, with your exams and all."

"We have to take a break now and then," Kerri countered, hoping she was not making too much of an issue out of it.

"And it does look like a quick read," Loren added, putting on her gloves. "What do you say, Alex? Shall we let this one go until after the holidays?"

"No, no," he protested. "Read it now. I've lots more books I want to share with you."

"Fine!" Greta beamed cheerfully at all of them. "Friday, then."

Kerri and Loren managed to take their leave then and escape, followed by Greta's smile and the sound of Alex fussing nervously with the teapot. Kerri, dropping behind Loren to settle her book bag more firmly over the shoulder of her winter coat, heard Greta say to Alexander, "My friend, the time has come to do something about that matter of which we have so often spoken. You cannot leave it any longer. I have a proposition for you."

She did not hear Alex's reply, for one of them shut the office door. She waited, quivering. No Power, no menace. She raised her eyes to see Loren, frozen at the bottom of the stairs, looking at her gravely.

"I cannot believe I did that," Kerri moaned for the fifth or sixth time.

"I cannot believe you did that either," Loren agreed darkly. "But how could you have known? With all of the things he's tried on us so far!"

They had gone to "Maud's," a little restaurant in an alley off Market Street, not far from Central Station, where the food was good and fast and cheap. Over a hearty lamb ragout and some excellent fresh sourdough bread, they shared their mutual shock (guardedly—it was a public place) and tried to make some kind of sensible plan.

"Not knowing doesn't matter," Kerri continued. "My grandmother always said, do not reject information out of hand, whatever the source. And the one time it counted, I forgot her wisdom." She sighed heavily. "Of course, it might be a fake."

"No!" Loren cried out intemperately. "It can't be! It mustn't be! I won't let it!" She lowered her voice. "We have to think of what to do," she said.

A lost Brautigan! Missing since the Age of Dreams, known only through mention in other texts, old bibliographies, and one crumbling eight-page fragment of disputed origin, divided scrupulously between locked vaults at Yendys and Urlosa Universities. If Alex's copy was genuine, it was the kind of discovery that could fuel the careers of a whole generation, the very thing for which they had cultivated Alexander in the first place—although in her heart Kerri had never believed that anything would come of it. She felt dazed at the suddenness and unbelievability of the find. It could not have happened just like this, so easily, so soon.

"And Greta," Loren went on, remembering to keep her voice low. "D'you suppose she has any idea? She was watching us like a hawk, but then she always does. Remember, back in the beginning, when we wondered if maybe she wasn't really a Peasant, if she might be Academic? Today I saw her take that book, and—I feel terrible for saying so, or even for thinking it—but I wondered even then if we'd ever see it again."

"You do not trust her," Kerri observed, in a neutral tone of voice.

"I do. I did. I should like to. I think I do. But now I am wondering about her again. And then, what you heard her say when she thought we'd gone...."

"I really do think," Kerri said, "that she was referring to something else, something going back a while between the two of them." She ran her fingers through her hair distractedly. "We ought to have been honest with them. We ought to have told them straight away. Now they'll feel they can't trust *us*."

"I agree. Alex would have seen to it that we all had a fair go. She would have been forced to give it up or else unmask herself and share. At the very least, she'd have been put on notice. Although if she is really a somebody, she'll do whatever she likes without giving a damn about Alex or us or anyone else! Or am I being totally uncharitable and ridiculous?"

"No, you are not," Kerri replied. "Do you want to go back to the Library and tell them now?" She looked at her watch. "Greta has probably gone, but Alex might still be there if we hurry."

Loren stopped, frowning. "No. Damn! I can't help it. I keep remembering that a secret shared by four is less of a secret than when it is shared by two. Perhaps we should wait at least until we have some kind of a plan before we say anything."

Kerri grimaced, half relieved, half shocked. It seemed Loren was a true Academic after all. "Then perhaps our only alternative is to give her the benefit of the doubt for now," she said slowly. "See if she comes back on Friday and lets it out of her hands."

"If she knows what she's got, Friday will be too late," Loren sighed. "But I suppose there isn't anything else we can do. If it's gone, it's gone. You're right. We should have said something. I hate deceiving Alex, even for a few days. Bother!" Kerri stared broodingly at the flame of the lamp on the table. "I feel like a thief," she said.

"So do I," lamented Loren. "And we haven't even got the goods."

Neither of them said anything for some time. It was not particularly edifying to realize that their need to make things clear among the Gang of Four came at least as much from fear that the horse might already be out of the barn as it did from scruples of loyalty and honesty. Nevertheless, Kerri reflected, the loyalty was there. If anyone had told her six short weeks ago that she would feel so firm a solidarity with such an odd, outcaste lot of people, she would have thought them cruel or mad.

"Suppose she does bring it back on Friday," Loren said finally. "What do we do then? I mean, besides telling the two of them the truth?"

"Convince them to keep it quiet," Kerri answered. "If we can. And even if we can enlist their...support, this is going to take some time."

For she was beginning to see a second and potentially greater problem. Neither she nor Loren had any idea how to go about breaking the news of their discovery to the proper authorities. It had to be done in such a way that the two of them retained, if not control, at least rights of study of the book, and that would not be easy for two obscure persons without power and with few important connections. The whole weight of Academia would be against them. Seven years had passed since the last time a lost text had been recovered into the Canon, and by now only the most privileged graduate students were getting their first look at it.

"We might look up the details of what happened before," Loren suggested. "Old newspaper files. Find out the official protocol."

Kerri nodded. "We must lay the groundwork very carefully. Keep it secret at least until we have taken our Orals."

"Perhaps one of us will have a Sponsor by then," Loren said hopefully.

"That would be helpful," Kerri agreed, old habit winning out over new solidarity and a temptation to tell.

"Of course," Loren muttered glumly for at least the tenth time, "it would help even more if we had the blooming thing in hand! Next time Alex offers you one of his books, for heaven's sake, take it!"

"No matter how moldy or boring!" Kerri vowed.

I ought to feel elated, Kerri said to herself. *I have found a text!* And yet many questions troubled her mind. How well could she trust Loren? Did Loren trust her, and did Loren have reason not to trust her? What was Greta up to, if anything? Was it conceivable that she would appropriate the text? Would Alex be on Greta's side if she took scholarly possession? Might Alex sell them all out to an outsider with a lot of influence and cash?

Even if the four of them could stick by each other, their lives would change forever once this discovery came out.

Not elated, she felt oppressed. What would become of them all now? What would happen to the Gang of Four and the cozy afternoons in Alex's office? What would become of their solidarity? To her surprise, she was sorry the book had appeared; she wished mightily that it had not. Or that it could have waited until, say, next year. She was not ready.

Chapter 44

Promise

For once, Kerri was thankful the end of term was bearing down upon her. If she had not been overwhelmed with papers, examinations and recitations, she would have had time to worry about Greta and "The Find" (as she and Loren had taken to calling the Brautigan novel when they needed to mention it between them). The three days of waiting would have been even more excruciating. Nor could there be any question of digging about in musty old records to unearth trivial facts about strangers, even if they were neck deep in the "Society of Guenevere."

This last week of classes she had two essays due Thursday, not to mention her last regular recitation of the term. There was a departmental student meeting on Friday, to be followed by an end-of-term luncheon party that would, with luck, take her right up until time to leave for Alex's. And Nicholas wanted to take her out to dinner that evening, not to Montague's—he had too much sensitivity for that—but to some equally special place. He was, she admitted grudgingly to herself, making an effort.

They scarcely saw each other that week. He had no written exams to prepare for, only one essay and a final interview with both his tutor and his Sponsor, but there seemed to be numerous meetings about the coming retreat, a lot of bustle. She knew he was having a costume of some sort made by a seamster in the City, paid for by his mother, and Kerri knew it was for some sort of gala planned during the retreat, but that was all she knew about it. He spoke about it as little and as vaguely as possible, appeared embarrassed, and always turned the subject as soon as he decently could. She put the best interpretation upon this—he wished to save her from feeling excluded—and she tried not to feel embittered at the suggestion that she was, in fact, excluded. Fortunately, the press of work and study made it possible to distance herself from this also, most of the time. And she had one other, very effective antidote.

"I have a Sponsor," she would say to herself. Then, more wonderingly, "Possibly, I have a text!" This was a most powerful litany, banishing her bitterness and anger like magic, for she realized that in a few months' time nothing They had done to her—no rejection, no victimization, whether intentional or through oversight—would make a bit of difference. No one would be able to touch her.

No one would be able to hurt her. *If* she played all her cards perfectly. And *if* she and Loren got the Brautigan.

The student luncheon party was not the trial and bore she had been dreading but strangely and unexpectedly amusing. She found herself the object of significantly more male attention and courtesy than had been her usual experience since returning to school.

Obviously, the word had gone round that her marriage was not expected to last out the year, and she was, she realized belatedly, not such a bad prospect from the gentlemen's point of view. This was a novel concept. She had been paired with Val from a very young age, and then there had been Nick, and in between she had been too shocked and damaged to notice anyone, in particular or in general. So her new popularity came as a pleasant and flattering surprise. It meant nothing, of course, but it lightened her heart and reminded her that if, Dreamer forbid, things did not turn brighter with Nick after he got his thesis topic, it might not be the end of the world. Life would go on. *(Moonlight on black velvet. No. Do not think about it.)*

"You could have had it Tuesday," Greta said, casually tossing the Brautigan into Kerri's lap, "for all the time it took me to read. I finished it before I got home. Peculiar book. Realized I'd read it before."

"Thank you," said Kerri in a faint voice, not daring to meet Loren's eyes. They had only just arrived, had scarcely sat down, had made no concrete plan.

"You have read it before?" Alex sounded disappointed.

"Right!" Greta paused a moment. "It was the bit about the tigers, made me remember."

Kerri, studying a page of the precious object with a sudden and apparently complete absorption, did not look up, but Loren wondered aloud, "Tigers?"

Greta chuckled. "Read it years ago. Have a copy, in fact, somewhere among the family books. Not in so good a condition as this one here. Probably crumbled away by now."

"You have a copy," Loren repeated blankly. She and Kerri glanced at each other at last and exchanged the tiniest of nods.

"Somewhere," said Greta with a shrug.

"If you do," Kerri said slowly, "I should find it and hang on to it, if I were you." Gathering her courage, she closed the book and looked Greta in the eyes. "We think it is possible that this is a rather special book. We ought to have said so Friday, but we weren't certain."

"What do you mean, special?" Alex wondered.

"It's been missing," Loren enlightened him. "Lost. Since the Age of Dreams."

"Lost." He blinked at them from behind his glasses.

"This book," Kerri explained, "if it is what it appears to be, is a lost work by a writer who was only recently accepted into the Canon. He is still very controversial."

"Why?" asked Greta.

"Because," Kerri continued uncomfortably, "it has been suggested that he lived and wrote on the very cusp between the Age of Dreams and the Years of Confusion."

"I see." Alex frowned, trying hard to grasp the relevance of all this. "And that would be significant?"

"It would," Kerri replied. "If he wrote both in the Age of Dreams and during the Confusion, his work might shed some light on those times. However, external references, at least, place him firmly in the Age of Dreams, and in any case he is in the Canon now. Every effort is being made to find his work, with mixed success so far."

"This particular book," Loren told them, "may be one of the Brautigan works that have never yet been found complete. If it is genuine, that is."

"In other words," said Greta, leaning forward intently, "what you're saying is that the University wants this book!"

Kerri nodded. "Yes. It would be regarded as a major discovery." *What have we done?* she asked herself. It would have been so easy to say nothing and bring the book away at the end of the afternoon. But there! It was done.

With a sudden unfolding of knees Alex rose to his feet. He put his hands in his pockets, bowed his head, and, lacking room to pace, rocked back and forth, heel and toe. They all watched him. Finally he spoke. "I always dreamed," he mused, "that someday the University, the people who care about learning, would realize that there are things of value here, important things, that this place is more than a dumping ground for their castoffs, for the slight, flimsy literature of the uneducated public. And I would be ready to show them all the treasures they have overlooked, not only here in the Public Library but everywhere, in the collections of ordinary people, like me and Greta. All of the things they've forgotten because someone, at some time, decided they were not worth remembering. All here, waiting.

"They might...they might begin to see that knowledge is more than memorizing a lot of words. Knowledge is...a journey. A puzzle to be solved. A garden to be planted and nurtured and harvested. All it would take would be something, the right book, that would get their attention, somehow. And maybe, finally, here it is! I always dreamed they would come to me. The day *you* came...," he shot a swift, luminous glance at Kerri, "I said to myself, 'It is beginning!' And now...and now...here it is!"

He broke off suddenly and looked at them unhappily, at Loren and Kerri and Greta in turn, at the concern on their faces, at the tears in Loren's eyes. "But you tell me about my book as if you're breaking a piece of bad news. I suppose I should have realized things were not going to be quite as simple as I suspected."

"Hush!" said Greta, with a soothing pat to his sleeve and a knowing look at Loren's woeful countenance. "There's nothing to fret about yet. Listen. Hear Kerri out." She challenged Kerri, "Have you told them at the University?"

"No!" exclaimed Kerri. "Absolutely not! For one thing, we do not know if the book is genuine. There have been so many false alarms about various lost texts, so many forgeries; it seems unlikely this could be the real thing. And it would only be right to tell both of you our suspicions first."

"Suspicions," repeated Alex, looking disappointed in spite of himself.

Loren said, "There is a fragment in one of the special collections at the Graduate Library. Only a few pages, very fragile, but supposedly genuine. They keep it in a special glass case with some other rare fragments. I went and had a look at it this morning and memorized what I could, so we could compare."

"Name of the Dreamer!" Kerri said in alarm. She thought, *what a mercy we did not run into each other there. It would have been too suspicious. Why did I suppose she would not think of going there, too?*

"I did not have to sign anything," Loren assured her. "There must have been three other people looking while I was there, and I made a point of examining everything in the case."

"Good," said Kerri. "You see," she explained to the others, "if either of us displayed any new or undue curiosity about this fragment, it might be noticed and we'd be watched."

"Watched?"

"I think I understand what they're leading to, Alex," Greta said. "If the book is real and the University powers find out about it, they'll be on it and on you like a duck on a beetle, and them who found it won't never see it again and won't get a look-in for studying the thing. Am I right?" she challenged the two other women.

"Yes," Kerri admitted. *You do forget your speech, Madame Greta, she said to herself. You forget for awhile, and then you remember, and then you spread it on much too thickly.* She said, "Oh, they would make promises, which would never be kept. And they would surely make a fuss over all of us at first, but the wrong sort of fuss, patronizing, and then we'd be forgotten. And if the book turns out not to be the real thing—which is a strong possibility—we would be the ones to get the blame for crying wolf, even if we had tried to keep them from finding it. The powers that be might even proclaim the book a fake at first, simply to discredit us, then later, when they've got rid of us, turn around and find it authentic after all. No retractions or apologies would ever be offered. This has been known to happen. Loren and I are common students. We have no Sponsors. We have no influence. We have no people of importance to stand behind us and back us up. And you, Alex, are not even a member of the University." She hesitated an instant over whether to include Greta in this characterization, decided quickly that it would be most diplomatic not to mention her at all at this point.

"We'd be ruined," Loren said bluntly. "The little people are always the easiest to blame. Kerri and I would be finished at the University, and you might very well find yourself out of a job eventually for some excuse. Some unconnected reason. I doubt they'd ever let you near another warehouse. I don't know what damage they could do to *you*, Greta, but I guarantee you would not relish the experience."

"So you see," said Kerri, "we cannot simply go and *tell* them."

Loren said, "Most important to us is that it is your book, Alex. It belongs to you, and you are the only one who should decide what becomes of it."

"They would take it, wouldn't they? Bill of sale or no."

"I am afraid they would," Kerri told him gently. "The University has rights of eminent domain in such cases. They would give you the amount you paid to purchase it. That is all."

"And you would never see them or the book again," Loren added. "Oh, there might be a lot of flattering attention at first—or there could be if Kerri and I were not involved to be a problem for them—but I do not think you would be able to accomplish the goals you just spoke of so eloquently."

"Then, what is the point?" he declared unhappily. "If that is the way they're going to behave, they can't have it."

"If they find out you have it," Kerri told him, "you will be forced to give it up."

"Why didn't you say something on Tuesday?" Greta demanded. "For all you knew I might've lost it or something."

"I did not believe it on Tuesday," Kerri answered, trying to convince herself it was more or less the truth.

"There didn't seem to be any need to alarm you on Tuesday," Loren added soothingly. "But now that I have seen the fragment, perhaps we can be more certain one way or the other."

Alex looked from one to the other. "All right," he said.

Kerri gave the Brautigan into Loren's waiting hands. She watched Loren leaf carefully through the brittle pages to the page Kerri had already found, unobtrusively, while they were all talking. Loren wore that look of concentration one saw on the faces of students going into their weekly Recitation, the remembering trance.

"Here," said Loren suddenly. She read, "'On my way to the shack, I decided to go down to the river where they were putting in a new tomb and look at the trout that always gather out of a great curiosity when the tombs are put in.'

"That is it," she said, continuing to scan the pages. "The typeface is the same, too, or very close. And the layout of the page. Of course, I'd want a look at more of the pages in the fragment before I could say one way or another, but these two are identical to what I saw in the case. Obviously, this copy has been rebound; the original editions were not of high quality. But the binding is very old, could be from the Age of Dreams. Also, if the book is genuine, the paper must have been neutralized at some point to have lasted so well. An expert would be able to tell. If it is a forgery, it was brilliantly done."

She closed the book and gave it back to Kerri. Kerri handed it in turn to Alex. They all looked at him.

"Well, my friend," said Greta. "You must decide what you are going to do about this."

He stared at the slim leather-covered rectangle in his hands. "Right now I wish we could pretend it's just an ordinary book," he said mournfully. "Forget all about the University and just read and talk the way we planned, the way we did before."

"We can," said Kerri tentatively, "if that is your decision, but you need to know that if any one of us ever so much as hints at the existence of this book, well...."

"All hell will break loose?" Greta suggested. "Are you saying, if Alex decides he wants to keep this quiet, you two won't go tell the University?"

"That's exactly what we're saying," said Loren firmly.

"By whatever oath you like," Kerri declared.

Alex sighed deeply and shook his head. "But I don't know if that's what I really want, either. If this book is as important as you say, it would be the right thing to make it known, whatever the consequences to me, personally. Who am I to keep such a thing hidden? It would go against all my principles."

Greta cleared her throat. "I don't know much about Academic life and all," she said, "but I do know one thing. When these book discoveries happen, the ones who benefit most are the ones in University who get to study them first."

Alex looked anxiously at Loren and Kerri. "It would mean a lot to both of you— professionally, I mean—if they let you use it and not just take it away. Wouldn't it?"

"It would mean everything," Kerri said.

They fell silent and drank their cooling tea. Finally, Alex put down his teacup and picked up the Brautigan again from the desk. He cradled it in his large hands for a moment and then held it out to Kerri. "The two of you are my friends," he said, "and I trust you. If this book should be made known, then I want you to be the ones to benefit from it."

Gravely, shyly, Kerri accepted the precious volume. She fumbled for words. "Your generosity," she began, "is...."

"Humbling," Loren finished for her.

"My only condition," Alex continued, "is that you both share equally in whatever comes of this."

"Or else," Greta added in a velvety tone, "you will regret it very much. And I'm putting another condition on the two of you, myself. When the day comes you tell the world about this little book, mind you see to it that Alex gets the credit for it he deserves."

Kerri and Loren nodded solemnly. "Absolutely!" Loren promised.

"With courtesy and honor to him," Greta said. "As an equal, in intelligence and dignity. You will not allow those high-nosed sticks to make him look the fool."

Kerri raised her right hand in pledge. "By the Gang of Four!" she said. "We will do what we can."

"The problem," said Loren, "is that we don't have the first idea what to do about the book. As you know, taking it to the authorities now would be utterly fatal. We need to find out what the official procedure is, whom to approach and how."

"It may take years," Kerri said. "It may have to wait until one of has—or both of us have—achieved a position of some strength in our careers. At the moment we are not...advantaged in that direction. In the meantime...." She sighed.

"In the meantime," Greta suggested practically, "we shall take turns reading it, as always. We shall have a lovely discussion about it after the holidays, and then Alex can put it away safe while you two start preparing for the day. Mind you don't wait too long. If Alex has this book and if I have it, there's no telling how many copies are in the world. Even now, someone up the hill there could be fixing to steal your glory, all unbeknownst to you."

"That's true," said Loren, with a worried frown and a flicker of a glance at Kerri.

Kerri, fighting a sudden stab of worry brought by Greta's words, kept her silence.

"And what about you, Greta?" Loren asked innocently. "You must share in this discovery as well. You found the book before Alex did, even if you did not know what it was."

Greta ducked her head and waved a hand in denial. "Me? Lordy, no! Not me. I don't want no part of it."

Indeed! thought Kerri, lifting an eyebrow.

"But that wouldn't be fair," Alex protested. "After all you have done for me, all you have given me, I could not let you be left out of this. You know how long we have had this dream."

"Your dream, dear, not mine. No, I'll not be a part of anything public. No mention at all, understand! Oh," she assured him, "if there's any help I can give you, I'll give it, no question, so long as you leave me out of it when you tell the tale. Indeed, here's what I can do. That copy of mine I told you about, I'll go hunt it up and make sure it's the right book, and if it is, I'll put it some place safe, just in case anything happens to yours. Then you'll have a bit of insurance, so to speak, in case," she shot a sharp look at Kerri and Loren, "anything goes amiss."

Alex took Greta's outstretched hand and clasped it sincerely. "You are a good friend!" he told her. "I thank you, and I—in fact, all of us, I'm sure—will respect your wishes." He looked questioningly at the other two.

"Yes, of course," said Kerri.

"Me, too," said Loren. She spoke willingly enough, but she did not look entirely pleased.

She still thinks Greta is up to something, Kerri decided. *Which may be true, for all these promises.* "Perhaps we have no right to ask anything in return of the both of you," she said soberly to Alex and Greta, "but we can only plead for your secrecy on this matter. If you tell anyone at all, no matter how little interest they have in Academic things, rumors of this discovery will eventually reach the ears of someone who understands the importance of this book."

"True enough," said Greta with a wry grin. "Fair's fair. I pledge not to tell anyone, by the Gang of Four."

"You have my pledge also," said Alex. After they had shaken hands all around, he said with obvious relief, "It is settled, then."

Kerri placed the Brautigan in her book bag with careful reverence and, she hoped, not too obvious a haste. They had been right and wise to tell; she was certain of that now. Of Greta she was almost certain.

Chapter 45

In Watermelon Sugar

"I need a break. I am going for a walk," she had said to him. "A long walk. I may not be back until sunset."

Deep in books and notes, barely attending, he had nodded and said, "Take care."

And after a circuitous ramble around and through the ruins of the ancient village— roundabout enough to make sure no one followed—she had ended here, in the remains of the upper story of the "Tower," the tallest ruin standing. The steel beams still held up sections of floor here and there, large enough to sit on and whole enough to bear the weight of one person, and from the windowed landing at the head of the stair, now open to the air on two sides, she could see or hear anyone approaching over the tall weeds and tumbled rubble outside. Cross-legged on old concrete, Kerri sat and read "In Watermelon Sugar the deeds were done and done again as my life is done in watermelon sugar."

She had kept the book on her person from the moment she had left the Public Library, not trusting her office or any hiding place in her home. Through the very pleasant dinner with Nick, it had lurked between her feet in the handbag that was just a little too large to be right for an evening bag—but he had not noticed. Thank goodness the book was no larger! (Thank goodness she had been able to find the purse for sale, very cheap, reasonably matching her dinner dress, at a flea market stall on the way back to campus to change clothes and meet him.) Through Friday night, she had slept on it, literally—tucked it inside the pillow with the zip cover, safe from any stealthy hand under the mattress or along the headboard. And this morning in the house she had carried it in the large inside pocket of a loose jacket, traded now for her grandfather's immense greatcoat, worn over enough layers of sweaters and woolen pants to keep her warm as she sat reading long into the winter afternoon.

A peculiar book with a peculiar title. A disturbing book. Eerie, and at some level, all too comprehensible.

She closed it finally and took a deep shuddering breath. Out across the derelict village the shadows were growing long and the light golden. A magpie floated down and landed on a bare branch of an apple tree in one of the abandoned gardens.

318 Deborah K. Vleck

From somewhere over by the road a meadowlark caroled, counterpoint to the hiss of light wind through the dry grasses.

How could this writer have known, she wondered, *what the Years of Confusion would be like?* People still talked about those times, even though no one was left alive who actually remembered them personally—if memory could be relied upon. Aryel had always said that there were many Confusion survivors alive when she was a little girl. Or people who claimed to be survivors. (And in the present there were still people who were indisputably Confused.) Aryel's own grandmother had told her tales which Aryel had repeated to her son and granddaughter, and there were many other stories in circulation. Never consistent, barely coherent, yet they all possessed a flavor that was immediately recognizable. This Mr. Brautigan had somehow captured that flavor exactly. He was established as a writer from the Age of Dreams; there were reliable accounts of his death in the numbered years, long before the Confusion. How could he have known?

And what must they have thought of this book, those original readers in the Age of Dreams? She could not even begin to guess. But she could see that this one slim volume contained enough oddity and controversy to ignite the Academic world and keep it bubbling for years. This book, this very book, here, in her hands.

And yet, outside of an ingrained reluctance to dwell upon the question of what the Confusion might have been like to live through, it was not the prophetic phenomenon of *In Watermelon Sugar* that disturbed Kerri so much as the story itself. In it, a woman is betrayed and abandoned by her lover and ostracized by her community for committing an error of taste—an error of which she is entirely unaware. The community regards her subsequent suicide as "for the best" and celebrates her death with great pomp. The unfairness of it, the hypocrisy and duplicity of the lover (who was perhaps not so much offended by the unfortunate woman's mistake as eager to drop her in favor of a new love) left Kerri fuming with anger.

One of Them, she decided. *He was one of Them, the snake! And so were all those heartless friends of his.*

"I did not get that out of it at all!" said Loren, somewhat plaintively. "Of course, Margaret's death is sad, but it didn't affect me particularly or strike me as the central event of the story. If anything, the mass suicide of the gang of hooligans is the central event—if the book has one, a debatable point. There isn't much of a plot. Or did I simply miss it?"

It was Tuesday midday. They had met for lunch at Maud's (of the good bread and comforting lamb ragout), ostensibly to celebrate the completion of Loren's

Final Recitation of the term and Kerri's one written exam, in reality to talk about *In Watermelon Sugar*.

Kerri had handed the book over to Loren first thing Monday morning, torn between worry that Loren would not protect the treasure adequately and relief to be rid of the responsibility for a while. Loren had managed to read the book twice in spite of the work she had to do, keeping it, as Kerri had, on her person the whole time. The task of guarding the secret gave her considerable anxiety, she declared; she would be glad to hand it back to Alex.

Unlike Kerri, Loren professed herself charmed by the curious story, by the whimsical, gentle world of the protagonist. "I thought it was rather delightful," she said. "The various tragedies—the way they were told—gave it just enough bite. But whether there is much substance there from a scholarly point of view...." She shrugged.

"I don't think it matters whether there is substance or not," Kerri countered. "That is, *we* give it as much substance as we choose, we scholars. I do not know about you, but I definitely see enough there for many theses."

"Especially ours!" exclaimed Loren. They touched glasses in a toast.

"Why do you think you identified so with the character of Margaret?" Loren asked.

Kerri shook her head, wondering if it was wise to have made this confession. "I am not sure," she said. "Now, after some time has passed, I am not certain I still do identify with her. I shall have to read it again, more analytically. I did not admire the character particularly. It was the unfairness of the way she was treated that struck me so strongly, I think. She thought she was living according to the rules of her community, but she discovered, too late, that those were not the real rules. She was judged and found wanting and condemned by the real rules. I do not know whether the real rules were kept hidden from her intentionally, or whether she was merely dense and stupid, but I know how she felt. It reminded me of Them and how They operate."

Loren nodded soberly. "I see what you mean," she said. "I am beginning to think this may turn out to be a chewier morsel than I thought on first reading. Or second. It will be interesting to find out what Alexander and Greta think."

But they were not to be enlightened that day. They took their time over coffee, wandered slowly to the Common, looked at all the shop windows on the way, and got to the Public Library just on three o'clock, to find Alex's door locked, his office dark. On the door an unsigned note told the world that he had been called away by a family emergency and would not be in until Wednesday morning.

"Oh!" Loren could not conceal her disappointment. "I wonder what is wrong. I hope he is all right."

"Did he write the note?" Kerri wondered, frowning.

"That is definitely his handwriting," Loren affirmed quickly.

"Ah," said Kerri, vaguely surprised. It had never once occurred to her to examine (or even notice) Alexander's writing. She refrained from commenting upon how ill-formed it was—crude and immature—but of course, Alex did not possess the graces of a real education. It was not his fault, she reminded that inner critic, nor did it detract one whit from his many fine qualities.

"No sign of Greta," she observed, looking anxiously up and down the corridor. "Should we wait for her, do you think? Might she want to go to tea with us elsewhere."

"Tea? I am still full of lunch," said Loren. "And Greta is almost always here when we arrive. I think she usually stays the whole afternoon. She'll have come and gone ages ago, I reckon." She sighed. "Botheration! I did want to get this book off my hands."

"Perhaps we could try tomorrow," Kerri offered. "Or," she added generously, "*you* could. I shall not have the time. I need all day to prepare for my Final."

"I could," Loren agreed. "But I would rather not. Oh, I do not mind visiting Alex any day of the week; it's the blasted book I mind. I've no safe place to put it, and I'm weary of carrying it."

"I could find a safe place," Kerri offered. "I do not know when I might be able to return it to Alex, but I believe I could store it safely for the time being."

"Very well. You take it then!" Loren rid herself of the Brautigan without the least sign of regret. "Now. How about we pop into the Archives and see if we can add anything to our meager information about the S.O.G.?"

"You pop," said Kerri, carefully placing the wrapped book into her bag. "I want to go home and study. Tell me if you find anything."

I oughtn't to have told her about my gut reaction to In Watermelon Sugar, she said to herself. *Too revealing, even if it is Loren, who doesn't seem to be out to gain every possible advantage, unlike most of my so-called peers. Funny how much I've come to trust her. Things I'd never tell another soul. I hope I don't have cause to regret it.*

I do know why I identified with Margaret, though. It's the way things are going with Nick. And the way Val treated me. And Arzelle. And the others. And the feeling that the rules I've always lived by, the rules I was taught, are not the real rules. What are the real rules?

She had a hiding place in mind. There was a place in the old village, the cellar of what had once been a shop or business of some kind. The structure had been built upon sloping ground, with the ground floor dug back into the hillside. This shallow cave, filled with rubble, and a few sections of wall were all that remained of the building. Kerri thought she might find a dry hiding place under the overhang in which to secrete the waterproof metal box that now held the Brautigan. Or perhaps not. Everyone in the village knew about the cave, had gone at least so far as to clamber up to it and peer inside. Perhaps it was too obvious, too open, but it was the first place she thought of trying, admitting that nowhere on her own property was safe enough, an intruder having entered at least once and probably twice.

Once again she made her way carefully and quietly through the ruins, stopping often to look and listen for anyone following—as if anyone would; they were not a nosy lot, the neighbors, and in any case it was getting dark and nearly dinnertime. She approached the hollow obliquely across the slope, coming down from a thick stand of gum trees and ragged pines at the border of the overgrown cemetery. As soon as she came up to the remains of the old walls she saw that the cave could no longer be considered as a hiding place. Someone had cleared out most of the fallen masonry and rotting wood from the interior of the ruin and built a new wall across the opening of the cave. It was a fine strong wall of thick timbers, filled in with stonework at the top and sides. In the middle of the wall was a wide, heavy door, elaborately hinged and fastened in wrought iron, with one small window, high up, barred on the outside and shuttered on the inside. The door was locked with two sturdy bolts, high and low.

"Name of the Dreamer!" Kerri exclaimed under her breath.

Gingerly, she made her way into the cleared area before the door. She heard nothing from within and nothing outside except the usual evening noises, the intermittent warbling of birds. Now she could make out a mark upon the door, centered below the window, a circular device about as large as the palm of her hand, shallowly carved out and painted over —a Stockholder's household crest. She did not recognized the sign, but she did not doubt that it belonged to the Stockholder who had made claim to the large house (which Kerri still thought of as Loren's) in the inhabited section of the village. The house was said to be nearing readiness for habitation—a large crew of workmen had been going at it feverishly for two weeks now—but no one had yet laid eyes on the mysterious new neighbor.

Kerri surmised that he or she had annexed the cave for storage, although the house was a significant distance away, up and over the rise. By the width of the door, it might be a carriage house, although she wouldn't have thought the overhang deep enough—not to mention the ground would have to be cleared much more before anything wheeled could drive in here! Couldn't be a stable— too airless. Kerri could only trust the arrangement was legal, Stockholders not being bound by the same estate laws as other people, but she was not pleased by such a proprietary act in *her* ruins. Gently she tried the handle of the door. It did not give a millimeter.

"Very well," she said to the door, "but no more."

The light was failing fast when she finally found a hiding place that met her strict requirements: a narrow space between stones high up in one of the walls of the "tower" where she had first read the book. It was near the farthest corner from the stairs, deeply shadowed even in daytime. She stuffed some loose stones in front of the box to camouflage it further, made one last careful reconnaissance of the area, and slipped away home through the darkening ruins. When Nick arrived from Town she was innocently in the kitchen, getting supper together.

"How is it going?" she asked, when he kissed her cheek in greeting.

"There is a light at the end of the tunnel," he told her, smiling. "I got all the loose ends tied up—picked up the laundry, did all my other little errands—so all I have to do now is pack and sign out of the Department for the holidays. How about you?"

"Everything is done except my final recitation. I gave myself a little time off today, went to lunch and window shopping with a friend."

"Oh, that's nice. Have you any plans for when I'm gone?"

She smiled. "Catch up on my sleep. Clean the house. Maybe have some of the neighbors over to tea. Go for some long walks."

"Sounds restful," he said with a trace of wistfulness. Then, after a pause, "I wish this were over."

"So do I." She smiled again benevolently, hoping he would take it as a sign that she wished him a good time, that she hoped he would enjoy himself. She could not very well say, "I hope it is tedious and political and boring and miserable. I hope you find all the women crass and charmless. I hope you realize how much you miss me and how much better it would be if I were there."

"As soon as I get back," he said, "let's go up the coast. I have to start training for my stipend job middle of the month, and Dreamer knows I shall need a good rest before that."

"To the beach house?" she asked. "Do your parents know we'll be wanting it?"

"I mentioned it." He yawned wearily. "A few weeks ago. They said, yes, whenever. But I'll write again tomorrow before I leave and remind them."

"I hoped we could spend a little time in Twilight Country, at the cabin," she ventured.

"Maybe we could do that, too," he answered noncommittally.

"Any news about Sharon?"

"Not yet. Not since they went into Town on Sunday for the duration. Tim was back to take care of the chickens yesterday. I'm certain he would have stopped to tell us if she'd given birth. And she isn't due for another week, after all."

"Yes," said Nick, "but you never know."

In view of everything that had happened, it came as no surprise when the Star Dream visited her in the early hours of the following morning. She was in the ruins of the old village whose surviving remnant was now called Evesham. The sky was that particular luminous violet of the hour after sunset, the sky of Twilight Country. She was searching for a place to hide Alex's copy of *In Watermelon Sugar*, and she was worried, because the book gave off so much light that small gleams leaked through the joints of the metal case.

For some reason the weeds and stones, the overgrown trees and fallen timbers provided no impediment to her progress. She seemed to float over the ground, hovering at last before the cave-cellar where she had vaguely intended to hide the book. For the first time she perceived that the building which had once stood there had been a bank and the cave a vault—an entirely appropriate spot to place a treasure for safekeeping.

Only now as she came to the cave itself she saw that it had been transformed, walled over. Just as the light faded she recognized the facade of the Private Library, the double doors closed and immovable. When she turned, the stars were there, distant and coolly glowing, and their whispering rose like a night wind. There was another glow, surrounding her, and to her horror she realized that light was seeping from the box she still held, the box with the precious text. She must hide it!

She looked down and suddenly she remembered something she had read in *Dreams*: If the dreamer becomes aware that she is dreaming, she must try to look at her hands, concentrate on the hands, try to gain lucid control over the dream.

I am dreaming now, she realized.

She looked at her hands, looked at the box. She did not wake up.

When she raised her eyes again, the darkness had lifted. The sky had resumed a twilight purple, and she saw everything with an unnatural clarity, except the whispering stars, which had faded and grown large and fuzzy, as if out of focus. No gleams of light now came from the Brautigan; the metal case had become impenetrable and smooth as marble.

She turned again to face the facade of the Private Library and saw that the double doors stood open under the arch. More floating than walking, she passed through the doorway and found herself in a room that looked exactly like one of the reading chambers of the Public Library. Upon the ranks of shelves there were books of all sizes and conditions, from heavy jeweled folios bound in gilt filigree to disintegrating paperbacks. She reached for a book and opened it. The pages were blank.

Oh, she thought, *this must be where they moved all those blank books that used to be in the regular libraries.* She reached for another book. It, also, was blank from cover to cover. A third, blank. And yet she thought she saw, as she flipped through the pages, a fragment of writing upon one of them. She leafed back a page at a time, looking for the writing, but she could not find it.

And then suddenly she remembered this was only a dream and found herself in her bed in the house, Nick breathing quietly beside her. She got out of bed and found her way by the earliest dawn light to the study where she stood confused on the carpet, wondering why she had come. There was an envelope lying on top of the clutter on Nick's desk. She went to the desk and looked down at the envelope. She recognized it: the letter he had received the day the ball invitation came, the envelope with no return address. But this time, upon the flap where the return address should be, the words were penned clearly and with elegance: The Society of Guenevere. Even as she realized what she was seeing, the line of calligraphy faded into the paper and vanished. Without conscious intention found herself picking up the envelope, opening it, taking out the folded paper inside. There was nothing written on the paper. It was blank.

I am still dreaming, she realized, and then she was truly awake, lying in bed. Her eyes were sticky with sleep and she could feel the weight of her body pressing into the mattress. In the dreams she had been weightless. Nick stirred and stretched and lifted his head to look at the clock. With a pleased and drowsy sigh—it was not yet six o'clock—he turned over and reached for her.

They parted ways in the Main Quad, Kerri to Paterson to sign in for the day and put in a brief appearance before burying herself in study, Nick to sign out for the term, to meet his friends and catch the train to Twilight Country and the retreat. It was an affectionate farewell, matter-of-fact, cheerful. He was nervous, but he had every right to be with his thesis on the line. *That's his top priority*, she reflected, *whatever the women there may try.* She walked off to Paterson Hall thinking, *it will be all right.*

As she crossed the campus, she thought about the morning's double dream, how she had managed to make it lucid for just a moment. She had actually managed to cancel the stars, and not for the first time, but this morning she had been able to go on dreaming, and she had found, not what she was looking for, but something. The Private Library, filled with empty books. Except for one book, one page—a fragment barely seen and not found again, as if it had evaporated from the paper.

And then the letter for Nicholas, also empty of words, blank but for the writing upon the envelope, until it, also, had vanished. The Society of Guenevere.

In her office she took out of her book bag a pencil and the small notebook in which she had been writing down her dreams. She had already written today's dream in brief, all she could remember. She added a few more notes and considered what the dream might mean. According to the book, a literal interpretation should always be considered first.

Perhaps the disappearing writing meant that she needed glasses and her waking mind was not aware of it yet. It would bear looking into. It would also explain the earlier hallucinations—a species of waking dream, possibly. "Make appointment with optometrist!" she wrote.

The anxiety about hiding the Brautigan in the dream was obviously connected to yesterday's quest and her discovery in the ruins. She was certain the building with the cave had not been a bank; they had always thought that the bank had been in the "tower." Could the cave building have been a library? This was possible, although if any books had been left there they would have been finished off by mice, insects, and rot long ago. Unless they had been properly stored in the cave. She had never tried to get very far inside; no one had, to her knowledge. It was not safe: snakes, spiders, splintery and rotting wood, falling earth.

Besides, she had assumed the space did not go very far back, a couple of meters at most. It might have been worth taking a serious look if the Stockholder had not walled it all up.

Whatever had been left there was gone now.

Impatiently, Kerri tossed the pencil and notebook into her bag. She had no time for this nonsense. Her final recitation was less than twenty-four hours away.

Chapter 46

Finals

Kerri went to her Final Recitation of the term with a familiar feeling of dread. It was Professor Greystone's practice to have his secretary give out his replies to any of his pupils who might have applied to him for Sponsorship that year, the chosen time being the end of each student's Final Recitation at the close of Autumn Term. He seemed to feel it was more humane than keeping the unfortunate candidates waiting for the answer to arrive by post, and yet he could never bear to hand out the fateful envelopes himself. It was said that one could tell what the answer would be by the way he conducted the exam. He was always easiest on the unfortunate—but only Autumn Term.

Kerri knew she would get a refusal. Had she not asked him four times? Not that it mattered a whit, she told herself firmly. Professor Bonneville-Chatterton's official written confirmation of Sponsorship—signed, sealed, incontrovertible—lay in her safe deposit box at the bank. Her letter of introduction had been duly carried to Professor Montgomery-Lee. Kerri had met briefly with her again that very morning to pick up the signed, sealed Proxy confirmation, which she had also taken straight to the bank. (She had high hopes of a cordial relationship with the Professor, a straight-forward, easy-going sort of woman with a sense of humor and, obviously, much experience of mentoring.) All the necessary documents had been registered at the appropriate University offices, with the receipts collected and, likewise, safely banked. Everything was in place except the public announcement on the traditional date of June the First, five days away. Kerri did truly have a Sponsor, at last.

Still, no one likes to be rejected, even where it does not matter. Kerri loathed facing the half-hearted exam she knew she would get, out of pity, from the Professor. Like being forced to cheat: it would leave a bad taste for a long time. And so undeserved! It would be all she could do to refrain from letting him know somehow that his condescension was not only unwelcome and insulting but entirely unnecessary. However many tart remarks rose to her tongue, she must confine herself to the words he asked of her. One did not antagonize one's Auditor, especially at exam time, whatever the provocation.

Almost worse than facing the Professor was the knowledge that she would have to walk back to her office with that conspicuous white envelope in her hand, braving the gauntlet of students who enjoyed loitering in the corridor during Autumn Finals Week— jackals and hyenas!—watching for the victims to emerge from Professor Greystone's rooms. She felt sick to think about it, in spite of being able to rub all their noses in her triumph at the beginning of next term. Just for today she must go on pretending.

Therefore it took the first ten minutes of the exam and a few near stumbles in her memory before she caught on to the fact that she was, after all, getting a decent grilling from the professor. His examination covered the entire syllabus, requesting passages she had not recited since Freshman year, since prep school, not to mention all the most torturous bits from this past term. He asked complex questions, quizzed her on the Commentaries, demanded analyses. With mounting surprise she let her well-trained memory reel out the words, and then suddenly it was all over, and she was back in the anteroom, being handed The Envelope by the secretary, who actually met her eyes and smiled.

Dazed, she made her way back to her own office, almost unaware of her watching colleagues, hoping she looked properly dejected. She did not know what to think.

Behind her locked office door she tore open the envelope and read the letter. But what a farce! She sat down upon the couch chuckling in spite of herself. Professor Greystone was pleased to accept her as his Sponsored Graduate Student—or he *would* have been pleased, he wrote, except he understood that one of his distinguished colleagues intended to Sponsor her pursuant to a prior arrangement. Therefore, he would, with reluctance, relinquish his hopes to help further her career in this official way, although he looked forward to continuing to hear her Recitations. It only remained for him to congratulate her, etcetera, etcetera.

Liar! Kerri thought. *Liar! A cheap acceptance, sir, wasn't it? But how did you find out?*

Somehow Professor Greystone had got wind of her change of fortune. Would she get similar hollow tributes from all the Faculty who would otherwise have turned her down? She wondered how far the news had spread. Not, apparently, to the hyenas in the corridor, judging by their grins when she passed by.

But there was no need to think about it any more for four whole days. Her final papers were all handed in, recorded in the daybook, and receipts given. The Recitation was the very last thing she had to do this term, and now it was over. She put the letter back into the remains of the envelope and tucked it into her book bag. Thank the Dreamer Nick was already off to his retreat and not there to ask questions! She packed up carefully, locked her office and sealed the door. Once she signed out on the Finals List today, she did not have to appear officially on Campus again until the first day of winter term.

Downstairs in the foyer she found Loren waiting for her. "I did not want to come up," Loren explained. "Was it nasty?" She knew better than to ask directly if Kerri had applied to Professor Greystone for Sponsorship and what the outcome had been, but asking about the exam was an oblique way of making the same inquiry.

Kerri shrugged. "It is over," she said with a noncommittal grimace. "And I am all signed out for the term!"

They passed out of the building and walked in silence down the steps.

Loren said suddenly, "I am going to the Public Library. I thought I should tell you. I need to talk to Alex." She looked troubled. Kerri noticed that she carried both her book bag and a well-stuffed travel pack.

"What is it?" Kerri asked. She looked around to see if anyone was close enough to overhear. "Is it about The Book?"

"No," said Loren, frowning. "You are welcome to come with me if you want." But she went on striding up the Main Quad, straight away from either the streetcar stop of the River Gate.

"I suppose I could," Kerri agreed, hurrying to keep up, puzzled. "Is it about the S.O.G., then? The name business? Perhaps it is time we told him about all that. He is one of the Archivists. Maybe he knows something."

"Yes," said Loren. "Yes, that too."

Kerri looked at her curiously. "Have you found out something?" she asked.

"Yes. No. I don't know!" Loren moaned.

"Hush!" said Kerri, looking around them furtively again. Fortunately, no one was nearby. By this day, the Thursday of finals week, the campus population had thinned considerably. She and Loren had walked the length of the Great Quadrangle; the Pavilion loomed before them.

Loren stopped and stared up at the brick and stone facade, at the windows on the upper floors. "I saw the Bright Watcher yesterday," she said.

"You did what?" Kerri took her by the arm, turned her about and marched her back up the Quad, angling toward the streetcar stop. "Are you certain?"

"No," Loren wailed. "Almost. When I saw him, I was. Five minutes later, I wasn't."

"Where?"

"Here. Right here. On Campus. In this Quad. Talking to one of the gardeners."

"Name of the Dreamer!" Kerri said. "Did he see you?" *One of the gardeners,* she repeated to herself, unsurprised.

"I don't think so. I turned right around and went away. I walked all the way to the Public Library. All I could think of was to go see Alex. He is the sanest person I know, and I feel safer there than anywhere else."

"I do not understand," Kerri said. "If you went to the Public Library yesterday, why...?"

"He was not there. His office was closed and locked. I looked into the Archives, but he was not there, nor the deaf man. Some woman I have never seen before." Her accent veered unconsciously from Academic to Cit and back again. She continued, "I did not have the courage to ask, so I went home. Then I thought: they'll find me there. I packed a few things and took the ferry over to the North Side. My old landlady gave me a room for the night. I woke up this morning feeling like a complete fool. But I still have a bad feeling about something, and I don't know if it's Them, or what. Kerri, what is the matter with me? Am I going demented?"

"No, of course not! Stop it!" She gave Loren's arm a brisk shake, mindful of the cluster of people waiting for the streetcar. "Do not say such things. We will go see Alex and have a nice cup of tea. Here is the trolley stop. For heaven's sake, be careful what you say."

"He is still the sanest person I know," Loren lamented. "Except you."

In spite of herself, Kerri burst out laughing. Every person at the streetcar stop turned to look at her.

They could hear the voices as they descended the stairs to the library basement. Someone was talking, and someone was crying. They rounded the corner into the hallway of Alex's office and saw two women in front of his door. No light shone from the office, and the door was closed.

In spite of the darkness in the hallway, Kerri could see that the taller woman was one of the librarians, an important one, by the look of the Academic style robe she wore over a correct charcoal grey suit and bow-tied white blouse. She sounded annoyed and looked put out. The other woman, the crying one, was small, thin, dressed as a Cit. She looked and sounded quite desperate.

Spotting Kerri and Loren, the librarian hastened forward to intercept them. "May I help you?" she inquired with icy politeness.

Kerri, never more glad to be dressed to the teeth for her Final Recitation, drew herself together, looked the woman up and down, and replied with hauteur, "We are looking for the Archivist who uses this office. We have an appointment." She remembered suddenly that she had no idea of Alexander's real name.

The sobbing women broke off her crying and stared at Kerri with near colorless eyes.

Loren, motionless, stared back at the woman. She began to make a small thin noise, a keening.

"Then I regret to inform you," said the librarian, with apparent satisfaction, "that Mr. Albertson died yesterday morning. Therefore, he will not be keeping any appointments."

Loren's thin moan ceased abruptly. Her book bag hit the ground with a crash.

"Mr. Albertson," Kerri repeated stupidly. "The man in this office."

"Yes," said the woman impatiently. "A heart attack. Quite sudden and unexpected."

Kerri said, "It cannot be. You must be mistaken."

The City woman broke into sobs again. She fell to her knees against the closed door.

Suddenly Loren was on the floor next to her, holding out both hands. "Are you a friend of his?" she asked.

"This is his wife," said the librarian gesturing with her chin. "I cannot make her understand that the room has to remain sealed until the investigation is complete."

Loren froze. "His wife," she repeated.

"All I want's his personal things," the woman cried out. "They're not library property. They're his. They've no right to keep 'em. It's not right!"

"Of course it isn't!" Loren put her arms around the widow. "I am certain there is some misunderstanding."

"What investigation?" Kerri inquired numbly.

The librarian looked down her nose at the Cit woman on the floor. "Mr. Albertson," she enunciated, "is suspected of borrowing library property without proper authorization. Or taking it outright! Including some particularly sensitive and valuable materials. Until we have had the opportunity of searching his office thoroughly, the room must be kept sealed."

Kerri's heart gave a thump she was certain must show through her scholar's robe. She met Loren's startled eyes for the tiniest instant. "I am sure," she said to the librarian, "that the gentleman would not do such a thing. There must be some simple explanation. Depend upon it; the items have merely been mislaid. Surely there can be no objection to allowing his family to recover his personal effects. Under supervision, of course. *If* there is... an investigation."

Alex is dead, she thought. *It is not true.* She did not have any understanding of it, any feeling of it. He could not be dead. Not Alex. It was ridiculous.

"Please," Loren said. Mechanically, she got to her feet and dusted off her skirt, trying to recover an Academic dignity to match Kerri's, but she could say no more. Her mouth trembled; she gazed, horrified, dazed, into Kerri's eyes.

Kerri looked away. She continued, "What can be the purpose of causing so much distress to his nearest survivor? It is not necessary. Will you not give her just a moment?"

"I am sorry," said the librarian, looking anything but sorry. "It is out of the question while here is the possibility of theft."

"Theft!" Kerri exclaimed with half a laugh. "Surely not!" She continued in her most clipped, formal Academic accents, "And this lady is quite right about her husband's personal effects. The only theft I can see is your denial of her rights to her property. Watch her if you like, but if you persist in denying her access without good cause, she could be well justified in bringing a legal action against the Public Library and the individuals involved."

For the first time the librarian looked less than certain of herself. She said, "The room cannot be opened without permission of the Head Librarian."

"Then," said Kerri, with a quelling politeness, "we will have a word with the Head Librarian."

The librarian sniffed. "I regret to tell you that she is gone for the day. If you care to make an appointment, you will have to apply to her secretary, but I assure you there will be no opportunity of doing anything before Tuesday. She is gone for the long weekend."

"I see," said Kerri. "Then will you please direct us to her secretary?"

"Very well." With a suspicious look at the City woman, the librarian turned toward the stairs. "This way."

"Come," Loren said gently to Mr. Albertson's tearful widow, helping her to her feet. "We will get it all cleared up. I am sure it is only a misunderstanding."

"Well!" said Kerri bleakly to Loren. They stood at the top of the steps just outside the main entrance to the Public Library, watching the small forlorn figure of Alexander's wife as she walked away across the Common.

An appointment with the Head Librarian having been made for Tuesday afternoon, there had seemed nothing further that could be done. A private memorial and burial had apparently already taken place, and Mrs. Albertson could only shake her head and weep when Loren asked her where her husband was buried. However, she had managed to write her address down for Kerri and thank them both for their help. She had no idea who they were or why they should be kind to her. She accepted their help with timid thanks, too shy and too overcome with grief to question it.

For a long time Loren said nothing. Her face still looked stunned, lost, dizzy—round-eyed, without a tear.

"I cannot believe it," Kerri said. Her mouth, her face, her whole body felt numb and icy. "He cannot be dead."

Loren did not seem to have heard.

"A heart attack," Kerri tried again. "But he was so young." *Like my father*, she thought. *Exactly like my father.*

Deborah K. Vleck

She started slowly down the steps, hardly knowing what she was doing. Loren followed. They walked along the path in the general direction of the Station.

"His name was Mr. Albertson," Kerri said.

At last Loren spoke. "He was married," she commented in a voice without expression. "He had a wife."

"Loren?" Kerri stopped walking and looked inquiringly at her friend. "You weren't in love with him, were you?"

"No." Loren stared down at the path. "But you know...." She looked up to the treetops and took a deep, shaky breath. "I had almost made up my mind I was going to be. A day more, a week, perhaps, and I would have been."

"I am so sorry," Kerri said. She could not remotely imagine how Loren could have been attracted to Alex in a romantic way. To be sure, he was a perfectly sweet person—a dear, dear man—but he was not at all handsome or attractive in any way that Kerri had ever perceived. And he was not even an Academic. "I am so sorry," she repeated inadequately.

Loren shrugged, staring at the trees. "I was not in love with him. Truly, I was not. But I was very fond of him. I shall miss him." Quite suddenly, her face went to pieces and she stood on the path weeping piteously.

It was more than Kerri could bear. "So shall I," she said, in tears.

"I don't know what to do now," Loren said.

They had come to the edge of the Common and stood under the arch of the gate in the cold winter sunlight. A brisk wind was blowing off the harbor. A ferry hooted, setting out for the North Side over the glinting water.

"I'll tell you what," said Kerri. "Why don't you come out to Evesham with me? Stay the night. Stay the weekend. Nick's gone on Retreat. We'll neither of us have to face anybody, and we neither of us should be alone. The Watchers won't be able to find you out there."

"The Watchers!" Loren exclaimed. She managed a small, teary smile. "I had quite forgotten about the Bright Watcher and all. How little I care about all that now. It doesn't seem to matter. I think I could walk right up to him or either of them and pass the time of day without a qualm. Pity he's not here. What an opportunity to get it over with, that first dread moment! Me, neither caring nor afraid." It was the longest speech she had made since they had come to Alex's office. She put her damp, crumpled handkerchief back into her pocket.

"Will you come?"

"Yes, I will. Thank you, Kerri. I have to go somewhere, and I'm all packed, after all. I shan't be good company, but I do not much want to be alone."

"I don't care if you are good company or not," Kerri assured her. "Neither will I be, very likely. I had better go to the Market before we get on the train. How absurd it seems to think of food at a time like this!"

They strolled toward the station, the ferry terminal and the marketplace. There was no hurry.

"I don't like this investigation business," Kerri worried aloud. "We have taken out some of those books, you know. This could be trouble."

Loren frowned. "How could they know?" she asked. "There couldn't be anything to identify *us*! Could there?"

"I don't know," said Kerri. "He never knew our surnames. I never saw him write anything down, which isn't to say he didn't when we had gone. All the same, I wish there was some way to get a look at that office before they 'investigate' it."

"It would help the...his...*her* as well," Loren added. "I would like to do something to help her," she went on restlessly. "They are not treating her fairly at all. She *could* bring an action. And he was always so worried about his own books, what might happen to them if anyone, the wrong people, got hold of them. Now it is probably too late."

"We did the best we could," Kerri reminded her. "If we can't get in, there seems to be little likelihood anyone else can before that Head Librarian comes back to Town."

"I know. But I wish there was something we could do. You have *me* worried now, too."

"I hope so," Kerri commented dourly. "We probably *should* be worried."

They walked on, past the station, past the terminal, past the Sea People's building, to the Market.

"He might have told us!" Loren protested suddenly. "You think he would have mentioned her at least once."

"Yes. Well, I suppose it simply never came up." Kerri smiled. "I never mentioned Nick, now that I think of it."

"I suppose Greta knows about her," Loren said. They stopped and stared at each other.

"Greta," Kerri said.

"Good heaven!" Loren said. "I wonder if she's heard about this. We've got to let her know, and we don't have an idea what *her* name is either."

Kerri looked pensively into the distance. "Maybe we don't," she said. "Maybe we do. Maybe there is something that can be done before Tuesday."

Suddenly she turned on her heel and veered off toward the street at the edge of the market, walking quickly and with purpose.

Loren ran after her. "What is it?" she cried. "Where are you going?"

"The Messengers'" Kerri called back over her shoulder. "Come on!"

The Message Agency on Waterfront Street was a very tony place, used to sending all kinds of messages and parcels, for all kinds of occasions, anything that must be hand carried to a special destination. At the service counter, Loren watched in puzzlement as Kerri chose a sheet of paper and matching envelope of the finest quality the place could offer.

"And I shall need a candle for the sealing wax," she told the impressed attendant, "and a liveried messenger."

She sat down at the writing desk and chose her most reliable pen, conscious of Loren looking over her shoulder. After a few practice strokes on a piece of scrap, she put the thick creamy sheet of writing paper before her, dipped her pen, and wrote in her finest copperplate hand:

> Your Excellency:
> I pray your forgiveness for this intrusion. If the following makes no sense to you, then I beg you will disregard this missive and dispose of it at your convenience.
> Alex died yesterday morning. He is being investigated for possible theft of materials. His associates may be vulnerable. The office has been sealed. They will not let his widow recover his personal effects. Her address is below. Can you do anything to help?
> Gratefully yours, K.

After writing Mrs. Albertson's name and address at the bottom of the page, she blotted the letter, folded it carefully in half and enclosed it in the square envelope. She turned the envelope over and stared at it.

"But who is it for?" Loren asked in complete bewilderment as she helpfully lit the candle for the sealing wax.

Kerri gave her a terrified look but said not a word. Dipping her pen again, she wrote upon the smooth surface of the envelope:

> To Her Excellency,
> Stockholder Margarethe Girrawang Fairchild

Chapter 47

Gambit

Loren stared at the envelope. "Are you out of your mind?" she hissed.

Kerri shook her head. "Not yet," she murmured hopefully.

"Then would you please tell me what you think you are doing?"

"I will explain," Kerri said with an expressive glance toward the watching clerk. "Later. Not now."

She dripped sealing wax on the envelope, waited the precisely correct amount of time, and impressed her personal seal. "There," she said. She blew out the candle and rose from the writing desk.

The clerk raised his eyebrows when he saw the name on the envelope. "I do not know the present location of the addressee," Kerri informed him gravely, "But I do not require delivery to the person herself. Household representative is sufficient."

"No problem, Miss," he assured her in an impressed voice. "We can deliver to any Stockholder on the name alone. The messenger is just getting his coat on now. Will there be a return?"

"Just the receipt," Kerri told him. "You may hold it here for me to pick up later." She did not write her name or address on the form, which caused the clerk to raise his eyebrows again, but he made no comment as he handed her the stub. He must deal often enough with people who allowed themselves to be identified only by the serial number on the sending form. He handed the receipt half of the form to the messenger, who had just emerged from the back room, splendid in full livery.

Kerri then proceeded to pay the fee, which was high enough to give her pause, even with Loren paying half, which she suddenly insisted on doing.

"Thank you," Kerri said to Loren when they were safely back outside. The messenger was already on his way, white gloved, on horseback.

"Don't mention it," said Loren doubtfully. "Now, enlighten me. What was that all about?"

"Trying to get help," Kerri replied. "For Alex's widow. For us, too—if it works."

"Am I to take it that you know this Stockholder personally?"

"I was presented to her at the May Eve Revel Ball," said Kerri. "But I had met her before under less formal circumstances. So have you. I think. I hope."

Light dawned suddenly in Loren's eyes. "No!" she said. "No!"

"Yes." Kerri nodded. "Yes."

"You are trying to tell me," Loren said carefully, "that this Stockholder is *Greta*?"

Kerri nodded again.

Loren exhaled a long low whistle. "Greta," she said, shaking her head slowly. "I don't believe it. How do you know? Are you sure?"

"No," Kerri said with a sigh. "When she is present, I am absolutely certain. Everything fits. But later I think, it cannot be. And I was a great deal more sure two weeks ago than I am now. It is just like you say it is with your Watchers: you are certain it is them, and then in five minutes you are not."

"Like that? I hope not!" Loren rolled her eyes. "Greta, a Stockholder," she mused. "Yes, I know they occasionally dress as Peasants when they want to go unnoticed, but it never occurred to me. I suspected she was Academic—even though there were things about her that didn't make sense if she *was* Academic. But this...! How did you think it? What put you on to her?" They strolled slowly back toward the Market. No one paid any attention to them.

"At the Ball," Kerri began in a low voice. "When I was presented to her, in the receiving line. I would not have recognized her. You know, we have never seen her hair uncovered at the Library. I would hardly have looked at her clearly if she had not spoken— but it was the voice, the eyes. I was in such a state of shock I couldn't say a word, and then I never got near her again the rest of the evening, which was just as well. I would not have known what to do."

"She acknowledged meeting you before?" Loren asked.

"No. Not in so many words. But she spoke to me as if she knew me. She gave me a warning, and then...I am not absolutely certain, but I think she saw to it that my evening was...memorable. And successful. You see, I think it was her doing that I had all those Stockholder dance partners."

"Ah!" said Loren. "Her friends."

"They must be. The Stockholders all know one another. There are not very many of them, and they do not have much to do with outsiders. And a couple of them said some things that gave me the impression they had been asked to look out for me. I cannot imagine anyone else there who could have done this, who might have had my interests at heart."

Loren considered this. "All right. We'll take that as evidence. What was the warning?"

"Her words to me were, 'Take care. The tigers are on the hunt tonight.'"

"The tigers?" Loren repeated, puzzled. "Wait! She mentioned tigers recently. They're in the book, The Find!"

Kerri nodded. "I could barely keep my countenance when she said that the other day. At the Ball Nick told me that she spoke to him also. She said, 'Hold fast. They do not take prisoners, you know.'"

"Who? The tigers? The Stockholders? I don't understand. Why would she talk them into asking you to dance, and then warn you against them?"

"I do not think she was warning me against her friends," Kerri said. She gave Loren a significant look. "I think she was warning me—and Nick—against Them." She turned in at the doorway of a tiny grocery shop and picked up a basket. "Let's see. Rice, sugar, tea, what else?"

"Them?" Loren exclaimed excitedly, hurrying in behind her. "What has Greta to do with Them? Or this Stockholder person, if she is Greta." She helped gather the things on Kerri's list and, again, insisted on adding a few treats at her own expense, but her curiosity had to wait until they were back in the open again. They had stopped at the butcher's, the greengrocer's, and the bakery and turned back toward the station before Kerri would say any more.

"You see, I have not told you," she said, "there are other things that have been happening, that happened that night. For one thing, except for my own husband and my ex, all my student partners stood me up, until nearly the end of the Ball. They did not even go through the formality of approaching me to relinquish their dances. Now, one or two may have felt too shy, seeing me in company with Stockholders, but I could not credit for a moment that they are *all* so ill-bred."

She looked around them again quickly, guarding against eavesdroppers. "I do not know how many people are aware of this aspect of what happened that evening, and I implore you not to say a word about it to anyone."

"I won't," Loren promised. "How awful! But how peculiar. They had to have known better, even if you were surrounded by a dozen Stockholders. Do you think it was intentional?"

"I do," said Kerri. "Perhaps it was planned in advance, and Greta got wind of it somehow. Considering the number of people involved, it is not beyond reason that she could have overheard some talk. She also said to me, 'Don't be frightened, you'll knock them dead.' Reassuring me, you see, because she had taken steps to protect me. And I did 'knock them dead' with the help of those gallant chums of hers."

Loren frowned at her. "'Don't?' 'You'll?' She couldn't have said it that way, not at a formal Ball."

"Those were her exact words. In Greta's voice, I swear."

"You know," Loren mused, "it would be just like her, to say something outrageous, *with* contractions—or even slang!—in the middle a stuffy proper occasion, with the lords of the University and City looking on. It's a very Gang of Four thing to do. Still...a Stockholder!"

Further discussion became impossible, for the late afternoon crowds were thickening about them as they neared the station. They bought their tickets and boarded the train.

Loren stared morosely out the window all the way to Fernly. Thinking about Alex, Kerri decided. She thought about Alex also, all the way home. She still felt blank. The feeling was familiar; she took some time to identify the occasion when she had felt the same. It was the voyage home to the Islands her Senior Year, just after her father had died. The disbelief: *This is not real.*

"I don't hear Thomas," Loren remarked as Kerri let them into the house. "Oh! I had forgotten about Thomas. I am sorry."

"That is another thing I did not tell you," Kerri said. "Not the whole story. But there are a few small chores I must do first, if you will excuse me."

The first, not so small, chore she must do was make certain the house and grounds were secure, that no one had broken in to do any mischief. Since Thomas's murder, both she and Nick had been very careful to see that the house was locked up tight when they left in the morning and to inspect for evidence of intruders when they came home at the end of the day. And, of course, she must renew the Veil, night and morning. She resented the necessity. It angered her to think of how the intrusion had poisoned her home. How dare they? While she made her rounds, Loren helpfully built up the kitchen fire, put some water on to heat, and unpacked the groceries.

Grandmother's costumes were untouched in their hiding place. There was no sign that anyone had been in the house or even tried to get in.

Come to think of it, Kerri said to herself, *there hasn't been any sabotage at all since that day, neither here nor at the University. It's been nearly a month, and nothing has happened. I couldn't go a week the first part of the term without some little trick being played against me. Does this mean it was Val—and her!—doing it all, and that I got to them with my little threat?*

The thought pleased her, but she felt it was unlikely she could have such power. She had known them too long to believe they would give up so easily.

Kerri and Loren sat long over their tea that evening, and, later, over a bottle of wine, talking of Alex and Greta and the University and life. For the first time, Loren spoke at length of her family, of the not quite comfortable boundary they occupied between Cit and Academic. Her father was the one, it seemed, and her mother the other, and there had been, astonishingly, an uncle! Loren's mother had a brother, and this brother had actually achieved a Sponsor and the beginnings of a career on the Faculty. And then, on the verge of taking a Senior Fellowship, he had abandoned the University and "gone off somewhere," as Loren put it. He had married out of caste. They had had very little contact with him since, and, of course, there was no Legacy to come to Loren, a disappointment to which she alluded with wistful disappointment rather than bitterness. She had been brought up not to count on it, she explained, since he would very likely have had a child of his own someday, but she had not been able to prevent herself from cherishing a tiny hope.

Kerri, in her turn, gave Loren a more complete story of her history with Nick, Val, and Arzelle than she had done so far. Finally, she took Loren into her confidence about the sabotage, and told how Thomas had been deliberately poisoned, although she did not mention how Loren herself had come under suspicion.

"I had no idea." Loren shook her head gravely. "I have heard of this sort of thing, of course, but I have always thought it was highly exaggerated, a few isolated incidents. It has never happened to me."

"Keep on doing well in school," Kerri said flatly, "and it *will* happen to you. There are precautions you should take."

"I know," said Loren. "I know all the things one is supposed to do, the hiding places and so forth, but I never took them seriously. I shall have to begin. Tell me, do you know *who* has been doing this to you? It goes without saying that it must be Them, but *which* Them, if you follow me?"

"Who do you think?" Kerri sighed. "Val, for certain, and probably Our Mutual Friend, plus at least one other person on one occasion. Val as good as confessed to me the night of the Ball. Arrogant fool! He knew I wouldn't be able to prove anything against him, and he couldn't resist crowing. But you know, I think I may have stopped him, at least temporarily."

"You threatened to sic your Stockholder chums on him!" Loren guessed.

"No, this happened before I met the chums. I happened to discover a thing Val didn't want known, and I let him understand I could expose him if he kept it up."

Loren grinned. "How intriguing! Might I ask what it was?"

Kerri considered for a moment. "I don't think it would be wise for me to tell you, at least not yet. It is enough to get the pair of them in a lot of trouble. *And* me, if I could not prove it. You'll be interested to know it was peripherally connected to his name change, but that is all I can say for now.

"Anyway, when I told him, he became furious and abandoned me on the dance floor, and that was when Andrew...when the first Stockholder came to my rescue. And it was after *that* my partners began to stand me up. I am inclined to believe he and Arzelle were behind that too, although I cannot think how they managed it. I have not been able to decide if they intended it all along or if it was organized on the spot to pay me back for threatening him."

"If it was organized on the spot," Loren said, "then Greta's warning must have been about something else, or nothing at all."

"True. That is why I think it was planned, and I have other reasons. Later, I looked at the names my dance card again, and they were nearly all people from Nick's study group, and Arzelle's and Val's colleges, all men over whom Arzelle could have some influence. Only two students from my own department got dances—and those late on the list— although several expressed regret that my card was full before it got to them. One of them told me the card was actually snatched out of his hands. Of course, it is safe enough to say a thing like that *after* the fact, and none of *them* made an attempt to rescue me during the evening, so I do take it with a grain of salt."

"Uh-huh," Loren said skeptically in Cit accents. "It sounds a wee bit far fetched to me, it does."

Kerri chuckled. "It does. It *is*, but there is more. Later in the evening, Arzelle and Val were seen having a heated argument, and after that, my partners began turning up again."

"Aha!" Loren exclaimed. "They called it off!"

"I think so. And I realized tonight that there hasn't been a single incident since then."

"Well! It looks like you fixed them!"

Kerri sighed deeply. "I wish I could think so, but I don't. I'm afraid they'll be back with worse."

"So sic your Stockholder friends on 'em!" Loren suggested. "What if it isn't Greta after all, though? What will you do?"

"I didn't sign the letter." Kerri shrugged. "I didn't put anything in it that could identify any of us or leave my name at the messenger shop. If she isn't Greta, she won't understand it, and she'll just throw it away."

They fell silent again. It was past midnight. The tank had not been checked, nor the fire banked for the night. *How absurd that everyday chores still need to be done,* Kerri reflected, *even though someone has died.* Loren stared vacantly at the lamp. Most likely she had not stopped thinking about him even for a moment, in spite of all Kerri's efforts to distract them both from that sickening emptiness.

He could not be dead.

"I think I'll take off in the morning," Loren said at last. "Take to the country, go walkabout. I need to get away for a bit, out of this City."

"Where will you go?"

She shrugged. "I don't know. South, maybe. I haven't been to the Emerald City in a long time."

"What about our appointment with the Head Librarian Tuesday morning?"

"Oh, that! Damn! And *her* to face as well." Obviously, she did not mean the Head Librarian. "I suppose I can't leave you to deal with all that alone, can I?"

"Not if you value your health! Couldn't you stay out here over the weekend? You'll be quite welcome, and the Watchers won't find you. Help me outnumber the Head Librarian and *then* go walkabout."

Loren laughed faintly and laid her forehead on the table. "The Watchers! I keep forgetting about them. It's awfully kind for you to ask me, but I've got to go home, at least to get some things. I wasn't thinking very clearly when I packed. And all I really want to do is get out on the road and keep walking until I'm too tired to think."

Kerri said, "Look, if you like, I'll escort you into Town tomorrow and you can pick up what you need, but then you must come back out here. Or...wait! I've an even better idea! I have a holiday home, a little house, a cabin down in Twilight Country. It's quite near the Border and right on the Lake, about a kilometer from the Lodge. Let's go there! Before all this happened with Alex I had half an idea to hop a train down for the weekend. Nick's there. Well, not at the cabin, He's at the Lodge on one of his retreats. A lot of the study groups have gone there on some big mass retreat, but the cabin is far enough around the lake that it would be easy to stay out of their way, and from what I understand they're politicking, not holidaying, so they won't be wandering over our way. We could catch a train back Sunday night. It's not walkabout, but it is out of the City, and Twilight Country can be a good place to go in...difficult times. We could even stop at the Emerald City, if you like. It *is* on the way."

Loren sat up and rested her chin on one hand. "You must have been thinking your husband would join you there," she said. "I don't want to intrude."

"He might," Kerri agreed, "but he's been saying he'd like to meet you." With some regret, she let go of the romantic little reception she had been planning for him, with candlelight and wine, the enigmatic note she would have sent him at the Lodge. It was a small enough sacrifice to make for her friend in the wake of Alex's death. Loren should not be left alone to brood, and she had no other friends in Yendys now except Kerri.

"I'd like to meet him," Loren replied. "I just wish the circumstances were happier." Suddenly she yawned. "I am so tired. Could I decide tomorrow morning?"

"Of course," said Kerri, getting up from the table.

"I suppose," said Loren, "that he never told her about us either."

Chapter 48

Yellow Brick Road

"I saw your unicorns again," said Loren, when Kerri stumbled into the kitchen at half past seven. "I made coffee. Milk and sugar?"

"Just milk," Kerri yawned. "Please. Where were they?"

"Lurking in an old garden out at the far end of the village. There's a shed or something still standing, more or less. Apple trees, raspberries gone crazy."

"Oh, there. Yes. Decent apples, actually. Excellent raspberries. We all pick there. Thanks. Good coffee. How long have you been up?"

Loren shrugged. "Since before sunrise. I didn't sleep much. I went walking in the ruins."

"Mmm," said Kerri, thinking back to that horrible moment, on awakening, when she had suddenly remembered that Alex was dead. Would it be more real today? "You'll see a zillion unicorns down in Twilight Country," she said.

"A zillion? Feeling slangy this morning, are we?"

"Long live the Revolution!" Kerri sighed into her coffee mug. "What will become of the Revolution now?"

"Don't!" said Loren, less sharply than she might have. "Just don't." After a moment she added, "I went to look at my house."

"Your house?" Kerri rubbed her eyes and blinked. "Oh, your house. Yes. Quite a transformation, isn't it?" She began to rummage for bread and oranges.

"He didn't wait his month out," Loren said bitterly. "It isn't fair. Here, let me do that." She cut the bread while Kerri put plates on the table.

"He's a Stockholder," said Kerri. "They don't have to wait at all if they don't want to, nor occupy the place."

"I don't suppose you know who he is?"

"How could I? Some Stockholder—that's all anybody knows, even the workers. I assure you the neighbors have been trying night and day to get some information out of the crew, but they truly don't seem to know who has hired them. It's all being done through an agent."

"I thought he might be one of your new friends."

"Well," Kerri said casually, "he could be, for all that. No doubt he'll show his face eventually, and then we'll know. Not that any of them would remember or recognize me, nor am I certain I would remember any of them well enough to recognize."

"I am going to think up a plot to make him lose interest in the place," Loren decided. "As soon as the coast is clear, I'll move in. I rather like what they've done with the garden," she added thoughtfully. "You don't suppose," she said, "it might be Greta."

"It is possible." Kerri poured them both another cup and passed the milk. "That would be convenient, wouldn't it!"

"Supposing you're right about Greta being this Stockholder Fairchild," Loren added doubtfully. "Speaking of houses, I never told you what I did Wednesday before I had my little shock in the Quad. I took myself up to Glen Eden to have a look at Miss Beckett's house. Did a fine little piece of detective work."

"Ho, Sherlock! Any clues?"

"Yes, indeed! I thought if I could find out who lives there now I could get some clue to the membership of the S.O.G. Oh, I was brazen, thought up an excuse, went right up to the front door. Gorgeous house by the way! But it's unoccupied. Looks like it has been since late summer. Garden's unraked and neglected looking. I even peeked into some of the windows. Saw dust covers over all the furniture."

"It seems a unlikely such a place would remain empty for more than a couple of weeks," Kerri pointed out. "I can't believe some opportunist hasn't attempted a squatter's claim."

"Quite right! The thought passed through my mind that I might go for it. Then I thought, no, there must be some reason. So, I took me down the hill to the nearest pub and ingratiated myself with the proprietor. And I did get a bit more information about the house, for what it's worth. It seems the right to occupancy has been in dispute since the last resident demented."

"That long? But Loren, that was years ago...".

"Not Miss Beckett. The one after her."

"After her? Name of the Dreamer!"

"Yes. Unlucky place, that. The publican immediately figured I was looking to try for squatter's rights, and he warned me off, good and proper. Said I wouldn't want to go across the people who own the place. Formidable group, he called them. Said he wouldn't be surprised if anyone brave enough to squat the property ended up demented. He meant it as a joke, but I think he was half serious. Apparently, the house has acquired enough of a reputation to scare off potential squatters.

"Anyway, I asked him what group he meant. He knew only that they are some club of University people, associates of Miss Beckett. Beckett-Martinez, he called her. He spoke of her with respect. I guess she came into the pub several times when her husband was alive, and it was the husband who was best known in the pub—and fondly remembered. 'Regular all-round bloke' the publican called him. 'Generous and open-handed.' It seems he was the original owner of the house, which had come down through his family. I gather he was rather well off, somewhat older than his wife, and had no other relations."

"Thus the house passed to her, and then to the S.O.G."

"Yes, but here is the real kicker. I found out the identity of one of the parties vying for occupancy of the house, and you'll never guess who it is!"

"I cannot imagine," said Kerri.

"Our Mutual Friend."

"No!" cried Kerri with a startled laugh. "This is too weird! But, Loren! This must mean that Arzelle belongs to the Society of Guenevere."

"Well, she is definitely mixed up with it somehow. The odd thing is that he—my friend, the proprietor—implied the dispute is between her and the group that owns the house, as if she is an outsider with some claim of her own. That was all I got out of him. It was getting on toward midday, and he had lunch customers coming in."

Kerri shook her head. "This is unbelievable! You have almost got even with me for surprising you about Greta. And yet...you know, I am not as surprised as I might have been. Somehow it all fits together. I hope you gave the gentleman a nice tip."

Over breakfast Loren announced that she had decided to accept Kerri's invitation for the weekend. She decided there was no need to go back to town to get more of her things— she had enough for a weekend in a cabin, if not an extended trip into the bush—or to rescue those books of Alex's still in her possession. It was the Watchers she was worried about, not the library authorities. She had brought the name change dossier with her and gladly availed herself of the opportunity to conceal it in one of Kerri's secret compartments.

Kerri suggested they forego the long roundabout journey into town to catch the train on Main Line South. Instead, they could hike across country and board at Hampton Forest, the first country stop outside of Yendys, about eleven kilometers southwest of Evesham. "It's an easy walk," she told Loren. "There's a very good track between here and there. The Road People keep it open. They use it."

Loren looked interested. "Oh! Do they? All the better."

They set off just before ten o'clock, knowing they would miss the train that left the City at noon, not caring. The day was fine and mild, the very last tag end of autumn. All the trees that would shed their leaves had already shed them. The golden grasses of summer were beaten down and weathered grey. Still, the sun shone cheerfully, and Kerri could not help but feel a lifting of the heart, in spite of Alex. Even Loren's spirits seemed to rise as they walked. Neither of them had much to say.

The Road People's road was a well maintained dirt track about four meters wide, ditched on both sides, and recently graded. Every now and then it passed between a pair of standing stones inscribed with the mysterious glyphs of the Road People, their secret written language. The stones always made Kerri nervous when she walked the roads, although she knew the Road People had no objection to the public use of their highways.

"I wonder what they're for," she remarked as they passed the second pair of stones. "Kilometer markers," Loren said.

The third pair of stones had just come into sight when they heard the sound of a vehicle overtaking them. Not horse drawn, it possessed an engine. They crossed the ditch on the right and climbed up the bank to wait for the vehicle to pass.

Around the last curve came an ancient lorry, swaying on fat rubber tires. A full load of something bulged beneath khaki tarpaulins tied down with a net of thick rope under a layer of dust. Reflected sunlight flashed blindingly from the windscreen. To Kerri's astonishment the conveyance skidded to a halt opposite the two of them, and the driver leaned out the open window of the cab. He was clearly of the Road People, a young man stunningly beautiful after the fashion of his kind. His dark skin, broad nose and curly sun-bleached mop of hair marked him as a member of one of the northern clans.

"Want a lift?" he shouted.

Kerri looked at Loren. "Is he serious?" she wondered.

"Sure," said Loren matter-of-factly. "I've ridden with the Road People before."

"Is it safe?"

"Quite safe, and we'll be able to catch that train after all. Come on!" Loren bounded down the bank and over the ditch to the lorry. She said something Kerri could not hear to the driver, who grinned, showing dazzling white teeth. He glanced beyond Loren to Kerri, following more slowly.

"I can take you to Hampton Forest," he called out. "Get in."

They went around to the left side of the cab and climbed up onto the worn leather seat, putting their packs on the dusty floor of the cab.

"You'll have to slam that door good and hard," the driver told Kerri with a friendly smile. "And then flip that hook over the ring there, just in case. The catch don't work too good, and we wouldn't want you falling out when I go around the next curve."

With some difficulty and a little assistance from Loren, Kerri managed the door, but before she was quite settled, the driver did something noisy with the pedals and levers in front of him and off they went with a roar of the engine. "Name of the Dreamer!" Kerri muttered under her breath as she righted herself.

Shouting over the noise, Loren introduced the two of them. The driver told them his name—Kerri could not make out what he said—and shook hands with both of them. Then he and Loren carried on a spirited conversation at the tops of their voices. Kerri soon gave up trying to hear what they were saying and concentrated on not becoming giddy, riding so high up and so fast over the dirt road.

In less than fifteen minutes, they were in Hampton Forest, bouncing down a rutted lane in much worse condition than the Road People's road. The lorry slowed to a crawl, and the conversation became audible to Kerri.

"Of course," the driver was saying, "what you folks call the Age of Dreams isn't the real one. It's yours, but it's not the original, the Road People's. Ours is always with us. Our memories are there. Yours is far away; your memories are lost."

"Or hidden," said Loren.

"Hidden pretty good!" he remarked.

"And what if we could find them?" Loren asked recklessly.

Kerri shuddered and braced herself for the end of the world.

The driver looked at Loren appraisingly. A moment went by before he answered. "Let them stay lost," he advised. "Keep them in your Age of Dreams. You have everything you need."

Loren nodded thoughtfully. Nothing more could be said because they had arrived at the station, and the driver was much occupied making his way through the traffic of wagons and pedestrians. There were four other lorries, too, all as dusty and decrepit as the one in which they rode. Kerri had rarely seen so many motorized vehicles in one place. Seeing as how the world had not ended and the ride hadn't been the death of them all, she began to relax, to loosen her cramped fingers from the inadequate grips she had been able to find.

When they got down from the lorry, the driver called out to Loren, "Any messages?"

Loren grinned. "Just say I'm well. Everyone is well. School is going fine."

"Okay!" shouted the driver.

"Tell him to write!" Loren added, slamming the cab door.

"Right-oh!" The driver laughed and waved. "Nice to meet you, Miss Dale-Townsend!" he called to Kerri who smiled and waved back. With a crash of gears, the lorry moved off slowly toward the freight loading gate.

"What was that all about?" Kerri inquired as they shouldered their packs and turned toward the ticket window. "What a gorgeous young man! Did you know him?"

"Never met him before," answered Loren, still chuckling. "But he is, rather, isn't he? It was about my uncle, actually."

"Your uncle?" Suddenly Kerri remembered Loren's mother's brother, the one who had married out of caste, abandoned a Fellowship and not left a Legacy.

"Oh," she said. "Your uncle."

Loren shrugged. "Well, at least I do get rides," she said. "Makes traveling in the bush a lot easier. Faster, at least. And interesting!"

"So I should imagine!" said Kerri. "You expected to be picked up, didn't you? I've never heard of the Road People taking up outcaste passengers unless they're in distress, but you weren't even surprised he stopped."

"I didn't know for certain that someone would come along," Loren confessed. "But if someone did.... They all know me; I don't know how. And they always stop and offer a lift."

"Does he write to you—your uncle?"

"Sometimes. Not often. He sends messages."

They bought sandwiches and apples to eat on the train and then purchased tickets for Twilight Country, taking the Main South Line as far as the Emerald City, where they would transfer to the spur line to the lake towns and the Lodge. There was over an hour wait between trains, not a bad thing, Kerri decided. She always enjoyed walking in the Emerald City, with its cloistered estates and vast gardens, its sinuous lake and fresh mountain air. *We could have afternoon tea there*, she thought. *One of those old cafes with tables out under the trees.*

The chill of the afternoon—the Emerald City, being higher in elevation that the coast cities, was even colder in winter—forced them to have their tea indoors after all. They sat at a booth by the front window of a venerable tea bar in the ancient shopping district near the station. The tea bar was run by one of the strange ethnic sects of the City, less isolationist than some, whose members wore the ancient folk dress of a people who no longer existed outside the Age of Dreams or some land only the Sea People had seen, across the world. The shy brown-skinned girl—she looked no more than eleven years old—who brought them their tea and cakes wore layers of brightly dyed silks and masses of silver and gold jewelry. She spoke with a flawless Academic accent. Everyone in the Emerald City spoke as an Academic. The place scorned the concept of castes, at least outwardly, and prided itself on the easy mingling of its many disparate groups. Perhaps it was no accident that nearly every Stockholder kept a home somewhere in the region.

"Have you ever been to the University here?" Kerri asked Loren.

"I crossed the campus once on my way through," replied Loren. "Why? Is it full of Them?"

"I don't know," said Kerri, looking out at the leafless trees. The low sun threw long shadows across the brick plaza. "I cannot tell. It is different here. One never hears very much about the place, but whenever there is an opening in the Faculty, the Senior Fellows from every other University apply in droves."

"Might be for the eight room houses with two hectares of garden," Loren commented.

"Might be," Kerri agreed. She had never thought much about it before. *They* were in Yendys and Honowell. This she knew from personal experience. According to Loren, They also infested Dalton. Might They not be everywhere? Or at least in every locale with an Academic population? A most disturbing idea, this. She had always felt safe and at peace here.

And still could, she reminded herself. It was only the Game. Even now, when it was played by two, it was still just a Game, and a stupid Game, at that. *Funny,* she thought. *When someone one cares about dies, one suddenly realizes how stupid and silly and frivolous some things are. There's nothing like a death to remind one of what is really important...family, good friends, good health, a good home.*

Nick should be here, she thought suddenly. He shouldn't be on his stupid Retreat; he should be here with me, on our way to Twilight Country for the holiday we've been promising ourselves so long. I could tell him, yes, I'd tell him about Alex—not everything, not about the meetings and Greta and all. So he'd understand why I feel so sad. Just say that a friend died, an acquaintance. Just say I knew him—from where? The Public Library? I couldn't. He'd wonder what I was doing there more than once. Then where? The Market? The train?

I couldn't tell him.

Chapter 49

Twilight Country

The little train to Twilight Country squatted hissing on the track of the spur line when the two women returned to the station. Behind the bulbous steam engine, self-consciously resplendent in brass fittings, seven wooden cars glowed in slick bright colors, painted like circus wagons. The sun was just setting, about a quarter to five by the station clock, and lights were coming on at the station and all over the city. The Emerald City was the only town of any size still lit entirely by electricity, and the inhabitants took great pains to keep the system in good repair.

Kerri had walked all the way down to the end of the platform, trying to keep warm, resisting the heated, well-lit waiting room. She wanted to board the train and be on her way. It would be well after dark before they could reach the cabin—or as dark as it ever got in Twilight Country. She looked to the south, searched the sky, as if the border could be seen from here. She knew better. This time of day, all the world looked like Twilight Country, and the real Twilight Country was never apparent until you were in it. She turned to walk back up the platform, to find Loren, who was inside looking at magazines.

Suddenly she sensed Power, oozing onto the platform from the station house. She snapped the Veil into place. At the same moment, Loren shot out of the door and ducked into the nearest shadow. Her eyes gleamed in the light from the windows as she spotted Kerri. "Look!" she warned in a whisper.

Through tall windows Kerri could see clearly into the brightly lit, high-ceilinged waiting room. At the far side, among the tubbed palms and varnished benches, a group of at least twenty men and women milled about, chatting in a loose group. Each was carefully dressed in tweed, denim, leather, long coats of dark wool—the very essence of Academic-in-the-country. Each carried luggage. From them the aura of Power shone almost visibly, as if it could drown out the electric glow from the stained-glass lanterns. Even with the Veil at full strength, Kerri could feel that energy beating against the boundaries of her shield.

"Name of the Dreamer!" she exclaimed softly. "Them?"

"If ever there were such a thing!"

"I believe it! My hair nearly stood on end when they walked in, and I wasn't even looking at them at the time. Do you recognize any of them?"

"Not from here," Kerri answered cautiously. "A couple of them look familiar, but I cannot say I know them by sight. They were not here when we got back to the station, so either they are Yendys people who came in on the later train and went out for tea like we did, or they are E.C. people just setting out. I say, you didn't attract their attention, did you?"

"I hope not. I don't think so. They seem very absorbed in their own company. They aren't going where we're going, I hope!"

"I am afraid they must be. They look definitely *en route* instead of arrived, and this is the only train departing to anywhere for hours."

"I was afraid of that," said Loren. "Bother! What are we going to do?"

"They won't ride in the front car." Kerri indicated the boxy blue and purple carriage directly behind the tender. "Only local people take that one...the Peasants."

Loren nodded. They gave the lighted station windows a wide berth, making their way down the platform toward the lightly-hissing engine. Kerri, still Veiled, put her head in the door of the first carriage and inspected the interior, dimly lit by a pair of oil lanterns. Aside from an elderly Peasant woman snoozing on the blue plush, surrounded by covered baskets, the carriage was empty.

They sat in the back as far out of the light as possible and watched anxiously out the carriage window until the group of Academics straggled out of the station and into one of the rear cars. Their shrill chatter never stopped. Not a one of them glanced toward the front of the train.

Loren sat back heavily with an exaggerated sigh of relief. "Isn't it wonderful," she remarked, "how much we depend upon people behaving predictably?"

Kerri thought about this. "But to do otherwise," she reasoned, "would attract undue attention."

"I think," said Loren slowly, "that this is one way you and I are different. You use conventionality as a disguise, for protection. I use unconventionality for the same purpose— to escape notice, to hide, perhaps because I've never been good at being conventional. I don't quite know how. You, on the other hand, are very good at it."

Kerri frowned. A lifetime of doing exactly what was expected of her, she reflected, had not only earned her what success she had gained in her world but had also afforded her vital protection against those who would have used her mistakes as weapons against her.

Indeed, she had exceeded expectations whenever she could. She liked to think of herself as correct, accomplished, possessing an instinct for the appropriate, doing the right things well. But...conventional? The word had a connotation that was so...common!

"For instance," said Loren, "I could never have cut that librarian down to size the way you did yesterday. Or whipped out a letter to a Stockholder in one try, no mistakes, not to mention actually sending it off."

Appeased, Kerri said, "But I would not have been there at all if it hadn't been for you. In fact, I probably would not have had anything to do with the Gang of Four in the first place if you hadn't dared me to go back. I would still be putting it off. And I would certainly never have had a ride with the Road People!"

"True," said Loren with a grin. "Perhaps we'd better not depend upon *your* conventionality any more."

Kerri lifted her chin toward the rear of the train where They lurked. "At least we can depend upon theirs! So far."

The conductor stumped aboard just then, making about twice as much noise as one man ought to, even one so solid with a crisp blue cap and a watch on a gold chain. He punched the Peasant woman's ticket, tucked between the slats of one of her baskets, without waking her. He punched Kerri's and Loren's tickets without more than a glance at either woman and stumped off to the next car. A few minutes later the train began to move, to slide out away from the incandescent lights of the station, between warehouses, cranes, and small manufactories into the dark marshes at the end of the long lake. The Light Bulb Factory flashed by, lit like Revel Night as the train curved south toward the high country, along the slopes of the mountains. The old woman woke up briefly, looked about her, and settled herself to sleep again.

"How did you do that?" asked Loren thoughtfully, as if continuing a conversation.

"How did I do what?" returned Kerri, wondering, puzzled, if Loren thought she had awakened the Peasant—or put her back to sleep.

"That thing you did on the platform, when you saw Them in the station just before I got out the door. It was as if you suddenly went invisible. I mean, I could still see you, but also I couldn't. Or rather, I didn't."

Kerri turned to stare at her, expressionless. She blinked.

"It's difficult to explain," Loren went on, in some confusion. "As if I would never have noticed you at all if I hadn't already known you were there. Like a light going out. Bother! How absurd it sounds now. I must have imagined it."

"I did sort of freeze...." Kerri ventured, helpfully.

"That was probably it," said Loren. "Like an animal in the woods. They hold so still you simply lose sight of them. Good instinct!"

"Not conventional." Kerri commented with a smile.

"No," Loren laughed.

Kerri laughed with her, but she felt torn. Of all times, this was the perfect opportunity to tell Loren about the Veil. Loren needed to know about the Veil, especially if the two of them were to be ducking Them in Twilight Country. She *wanted* to tell Loren, but somehow she could not make the words come out. There had never been any words, other than "Veil." Now she could not think of a way to describe it that did not sound far more absurd than merely disappearing on the station platform. The moment went by; she said nothing.

Loren inclined the back of her seat and settled herself to take a nap. The train ran out in the country, the electric glitter of the Emerald City vanished into its surrounding hills. Not even the light of a farmhouse pierced the solid darkness of the land. And they were entering the forest now; the ragged black silhouettes of the tops of pines and gums fringed the edges of a sky still pale with the last of twilight. Kerri stared out the window at the passing night, stared at her own reflection in the window glass.

Loren was quite wrong about her. She was wrong about herself. She had never been conventional. Witness the Veil, the Game, the countless little stratagems she employed to guard herself, to force some intelligibility on the world. But these were private things.

Publicly unconventionality was another matter. She had always fancied herself as Loren saw her: skilled at avoiding strange, unAcademic, outlandish behavior. And yet she had done her share of it before she had met Loren: the illicit trip to Honowell, for instance—and in disguise, no less!—although, strictly speaking, she had *met* Loren before that. And very likely she would have gone back to the Public Library on her own and might have met Greta sooner or later through Alex. It certainly *felt* as if she had done more unconventional things than usual since she had met these people. Her life had certainly changed.

What had changed the most, she decided after some thought, was her perception of things that were not, for lack of a better word, *safe*. They no longer terrified or offended her. Clearly, unconventionality had its advantages. If used intelligently, it could be most effective. The trick, obviously, was to be able to tell when to use it. Enlightenment struck her suddenly: This was Arzelle's secret! Arzelle used the unconventional when it suited her, used other people's expectations.

But I do not want to be like Zarah! she said to herself, shocked. *Zarah. Arzelle. She cheats. She lies. She steals.* Remembering Thomas: *She kills. I do not want to be like Arzelle.*

Arzelle's unconventionality, in fact, had no boundaries. It went all the way to the unethical, the malicious, possibly the harmful, but her conventional behavior did the same. It, also, could be nasty, and no thought of other people's suffering had ever slowed her down.

Kerri found herself suddenly on the brink of a dark mental territory into which she did not care to venture, as if she had brought herself right up to the edge of the Age of Dreams somehow, pressed her nose against its very windows. She drew back, looked at the reflection in the glass instead of the dark forest beyond, speeding silently past. Expectations and conventions could be understood, manipulated, used, without actually doing evil.

It was not necessary to be like Arzelle.

They got off the train at Lashings, the market town that was the last stop before Twilight Country. It was a bit farther by road from there to Kerri's cabin than it was from the Lodge station, but there would be fewer eyes to recognize a pair of students in search of solitude.

Also, Friday was market day in Lashings, and Kerri wanted to pick up milk, eggs, bread, and other edibles. They were only just in time, for the town square clock had already struck six when the train came in. Vendors had closed their stalls in the square, and the shopkeepers were beginning to put up their shutters. One of them, remembering Kerri from childhood, was willing to accommodate a pair of late customers when asked prettily.

By half past the hour, Kerri and Loren were setting off southeast from the town on the high road toward the coast, carrying the full basket between them and their packs on their backs. They needed no lantern, the moon being full. As they walked, farmers' carts passed them, homebound at a leisurely pace. One of the locals offered them a ride, which they accepted with thanks, glad to cut even a short distance off the hike.

The farmer dropped them a little more than two kilometers beyond the outskirts of Lashings, where the track to the lake turned off to the right, southward past one last farm and into the forest. By then they were thoroughly chilled and looking forward to moving again. The temperature was falling; they would be the warmer for the walk.

After they left the road no more traffic passed them, and the world became very quiet. Their feet crunched in time on the packed earth of the track. An owl called from somewhere nearby. From time to time a light wind sighed gently through the pines. The women spoke in whispers when then they spoke at all. Loren seemed lost in thought, and Kerri had thinking of her own to do as well as a respect for the silence.

Last time the moon was full, I was at the Ball, she said to herself.

"Oh!" said Loren suddenly. "We've crossed!"

Kerri raised her head and looked around her. As usual, she had not noticed the exact moment of crossing the boundary into Twilight Country. Indeed, at night in winter, especially the night of the full moon, there was little difference to be seen. Only in the shadowy places where the moonlight could not reach was the faint luminosity visible, seeming to come from within leaf and stem, from every growing thing. She looked down at her hands, but the silver patina of moonshine overpowered the glow her body would show in more darkness.

"And there is the lake!" she whispered.

They had just come over a low fold of land, and now before them an easy slope descended to a dark, still expanse of water glimpsed through the trees. The track angled downslope, bending to the east, meeting up at last with the lake shore, which it followed for about half a kilometer before crossing a bridge and climbing up again. There were few habitations on the north side of the lake, but away in the distance to the south, across the water, a line of lights flickered along the far shore and reflected down the water in sparkling lines, marking the more populated recreation area, where the Lodge stood, the resorts, the little hotels and rooming houses and cabins.

"How far?" Loren asked quietly as they stopped and traded sides of the basket for the third time.

"We've come about half way to where we're going," Kerri answered. "We've another couple of kilometers to go, say, two and a half, and then it's as far again to the Lodge. Well, maybe not so far. It depends on which way you go, whether you follow the shore, go by the track, or go straight across by boat."

"Have you got a boat?"

"Three. A canoe, a rowboat and a little sailboat. Very little. Racked up in the boathouse for winter."

"Do you sail?"

"In summer. I like the canoe best."

"Ah," said Loren. She fell silent again.

As they continued east, clockwise around the northeast arm of the lake, their view of the lights became cut off by the shape of the land, and they could see the more scattered lights of the private dwellings on the western shore. A number of Stockholders held large estates over there, Kerri explained, handier to the train and the good road. She herself preferred the wilder east side, where the cottages were more humble and rustic.

After the path turned more or less south again they began to pass isolated cabins, all shuttered and dark at this season. The track widened and became a proper road that showed signs of regular maintenance. Out of habit, Kerri peered at her watch as she passed through a patch of moonlight, but she could not make out the time, and, in any case, the hands would have halted the instant she crossed the Boundary. It must be well past eight o'clock by now. She was beginning to be very hungry, and her feet were freezing.

"Not far now," she murmured.

A few minutes later she halted abruptly and said, "That's odd!"

"What?"

"Lights."

"One of your neighbors has come out for the weekend?"

"I don't think so." Kerri moved forward again slowly. "No," she said after a moment. "That is my place."

"Someone is there?"

"It must be my husband. He does have a key."

"Maybe he came to check on the place."

"He must have. It's a little late at night. You'd think he'd come during the day."

"Maybe he didn't have time."

"Perhaps."

As they drew nearer, Kerri began to make out what she was looking at. The door lanterns were both alight, and someone had hung a third lantern on the gatepost. Lights also burned inside the cabin, both in the front room and in the bedroom at the back, although all the curtains were drawn and no person could be seen. Smoke rose from both chimneys. She felt a touch of Power, instantly invoked the Veil, then felt like an idiot. There was no such thing as Power. It was nothing more than her own anxiety, and no wonder. Someone was inside her house without her leave.

Chapter 50

Unexpected Company

"You *are* sure this is your place?" Loren asked doubtfully.

"Of course," said Kerri, turning in at the gate. "I've been coming here all my life." She walked boldly up the path, up the front steps, across the deck to the front door.

She could hear voices now, many voices—it sounded like a party—and Nick's voice not among them. *I do not like this at all*, she thought, opening the unlocked door.

The voices gradually fell silent as she stared at the familiar shabby sitting room, now crowded with people and luggage, clothing everywhere. Academic robes and other shimmering costumes hung from the curtain rods; mattresses and bedding covered the floor.

"What in the name of the Dreamer is going on?" she asked, outraged.

Loren hovered wide-eyed behind her in the doorway.

"A local," muttered one of the men to the woman beside him.

A woman stepped forward confidently and set herself as a barrier before Kerri. "May I help you?" she asked in a chill voice, her chin raised haughtily.

"What are you people doing here?" Kerri demanded.

"We are guests of the owner," the woman announced coldly. "May I inquire why you invade our privacy without even the courtesy of knocking?"

"You are no such thing," Kerri blazed back. "This is my house. I am the owner. I invited no one, and I do not knock upon my own door."

The woman's mouth fell open. She retreated a step in spite of herself, even as a new voice sounded from the kitchen doorway.

"Oh, my gracious! It is Miss Dale-Townsend." With astonishment, Kerri recognized Fiona Collins-Weir emerging apron-clad from the kitchen, wiping her hands on a dish towel. "Kerri! This is such a surprise. Nick never told us you were planning to come down this weekend."

Kerri could only stare at her. *These are Nick's friends*, she realized, belatedly beginning to recognize them. *The students from his department. The study group.*

"It is all right, everybody!" Fiona called out gaily, picking her way across the room. "This is Nick's wife, Miss Dale-Townsend. Kerri, dear! You must not have received your husband's message before you left town, but I can explain everything. Please come into the kitchen; it is a little more quiet." Her eyes widened as she discovered Loren. "Oh? And this is...?"

"Miss Weberly," said Kerri, unsmiling, "of the Classic Literature *and* Mathematics Colleges. Miss Weberly, may I present Miss Collins-Weir of the College of History?"

Fiona and Loren exchanged polite nods.

"Where is my husband?" Kerri asked bluntly. She had not seen him yet, nor, she realized, did she see Jillian anywhere. There were some ten or a dozen people in the room— about half men and half women, some known to her, all of them staring—plus luggage for at least that many. She could hear more voices in the kitchen.

"It is a long story," said Fiona apologetically. "Please come. I will tell you."

Loren stepped back to retrieve the market basket from the front porch, then followed Kerri through the cluttered room. Kerri thought there was something wolfish about Loren's defiant smile, teeth bared. *She is terrified of these people*, Kerri realized. In the kitchen two men and a woman were preparing a large quantity of lasagna, salad, and garlic bread. Kerri was distantly acquainted with all three and greeted them in good form, introducing Loren. Hoping the rumblings of her stomach were not too audible she relieved Loren of the basket and set it just outside the kitchen door in the tiny back porch. They shrugged their packs off in a corner as Fiona resumed cutting vegetables and explaining.

"You see, when we arrived Wednesday, we discovered that there had been some kind of mix-up in our reservations at the Lodge. No need to go into all the details, but the end of it all was they had no rooms to put us in. The other hotels and houses are all closed for the season or filled with private parties. The manager of the Lodge sent a message to the owner of one of the closed rooming houses pleading with him to open up and accommodate us, but the soonest he could arrive here is Saturday. We had no place to go. No place at all. So Nicholas very kindly offered us the use of your cabin until we could get into the rooming house. I am certain he wrote to you straight away to explain, but the letter must have missed you. He said you would not mind, under the circumstances, and no one expected you."

"I am afraid I do mind," said Kerri, unmoved. "And it is irrelevant whether I was expected. I do not notify anyone in advance if I decide to use my own house. The cabin was not my husband's to offer, and I have need of it. Tonight."

"But you must understand, there was nowhere else we could go. Could we not prevail upon you to let us stay, just for tonight? You would have our undying gratitude. And we would be most happy if you would join us for dinner before you go."

"Before we go?"

"Well, you can see for yourself there is hardly room for two more," Fiona said with a regretful smile.

If the mention of dinner had made Kerri suddenly ready to say, "Yes, of course, do stay!" this last comment evaporated every particle of sympathy she had been feeling for the intruders' plight.

"We are not going elsewhere tonight," she explained, as if to a dull child. "You do not seem able to grasp the essential point of the matter. This *my* house. There is always room for *me*. There is always room for my *invited* guests, so there is room for Miss Weberly. If there is lack of space, the persons who must be inconvenienced are those who are only willing to avail themselves of my hospitality when it is not offered."

For a brief instant anger flared in Miss Collins-Weir's eyes, but she masked it immediately with another of her deprecating little smiles. "Forgive me, I am tired; I was not thinking. Of course you are not going. And we cannot force ourselves on you, but..."

"You are certainly making a good effort!"

"...but we can only appeal to your kindness. Truly, our only other alternative is to sleep in the open, and you must know how cold it is tonight. We shall be gone to the Lodge first thing in the morning! And if the rooming house man opens up for us tomorrow, we shall move in a flash, because grateful as we are to Nick—and to you!—for this shelter, it is most wearyingly far to walk."

Kerri sighed deeply. She was furious at being put on the spot like this. She hated it—being forced to accommodate all these people who had never been better than condescending to her, people who had refused her invitations, stood her up for dances at the May Eve Ball (yes, there at least two of those in the sitting room), done their best to come between her and Nicholas, and who did not see anything wrong with putting *her* out in the cold. She hated being forced to subject Loren to their sneering ways and false politeness, when Loren most needed—they both needed—peace and solitude to grieve for Alex. It was monstrously unfair. For two cents she would toss the lot of them out and let them freeze, if it were not for the fact that it would inevitably make things worse for her and probably for Nick, too.

"Where is Nicholas?" she asked.

"He is in a meeting. It is expected to last until quite late, so we were not expecting him back to dinner. Most of us have to go back to the Lodge for various business later this evening, so we can tell him you are here."

"Where did the bedding come from?"

"Borrowed from the Lodge, from those unheated cottages they only use in summer. And the sleeping porches, I think. They very kindly sent mattresses and blankets over in a cart."

"How are you getting it all back?"

"The workmen will come back with the cart and get all of it, and our luggage as well."

Kerri sighed again. "Very well," she said, with what grace she could muster. "You may stay tonight. Miss Weberly and I shall use the bedroom, so we should appreciate your clearing out anything you have in there."

"Yes, of course," said Miss Collins-Weir, breaking into the closest thing to a genuine smile Kerri had seen since she arrived. "I know I speak for all of us when I tell you how very grateful we are and how sorry we are to inconvenience you. Thank you so very much! And you must join us for dinner! Unless you have already eaten?"

Her relief seemed so genuine that Kerri realized she could indeed have turned all these people out into the cold; she had that power. But she decided she was glad she had not, in spite of the anger that had subsided only a little. She was beginning to feel slightly ashamed of her bad temper. And famished! "That is very kind," she said. "We shall be happy to join you. Thank you."

"Most kind," Loren echoed—the first sound she had made since entering the kitchen.

She hoisted her pack back onto one shoulder and lifted Kerri's by the shoulder straps, waiting.

A few minutes later, in the hastily cleared bedroom with the door safely closed, she whispered to Kerri, "Perhaps we ought to just leave and let them have it for the night. I think I would rather sleep out in the cold than spend the night surrounded by Them. They're all Them, aren't they?"

"Yes." Kerri dropped her pack on the old day bed and collapsed beside it. "Do not worry. We shall survive. I am damned if I shall let anybody, especially Them, drive me from my own house! And you may be sure that is what Fiona had in mind."

"You don't seem to be at all afraid of them. They give *me* the utter creeps."

"No doubt I shall be afraid later. I am too furious at the moment."

"Is that *the* Fiona with a 'Y'?"

"The same." Kerri unzipped her parka and shrugged out of it. "I suppose I have truly antagonized her now."

"I am afraid you're right," said Loren. She lowered her pack tentatively onto the floor. "Can she...can They do anything to you? To us? For revenge, I mean."

"More of the usual," muttered Kerri bleakly. "Although my backing down would have been much worse, believe me. Not only would it have increased their contempt, it might have left me vulnerable to a squatter's counterclaim on the house, which for sheer spite I would not put past any one of them, so I had no alternative. What a mess! I should like to strangle Nick. How could he?"

"It sounded as if he had no choice either," Loren suggested.

"True," Kerri admitted. "That is, he probably thought so. But there is always a choice. Speaking of which, you can have first choice of whichever bed you like." The room, which was large, had four, accumulated during the days of her father's youthful house parties. Besides the brass daybed, with a truckle bed under, there were a vast four-poster on the kitchen side and a narrow cot under one window.

"We didn't need to throw them all out," Loren observed anxiously. "This room could hold five easily."

"True," Kerri acknowledged with a sigh. "But I can tell you I was in no mood to make any more accommodations. Besides, they have the loft, which is bigger than this room, and the whole sitting room. The bathroom is going to be the real problem. Although, for the hardy, there *is* the outhouse."

"The one by the window," Loren decided. "I believe I shall not unpack."

As there was no table in the cabin large enough to seat seventeen, the people ate wherever they could find a place to sit down. Kerri, as the nominal hostess, got a seat at the round kitchen table with Loren and four others—Fiona, Marta Lang-Soulis and her husband Harry, and a Mr. Ratsavong-Woodman, all of whom—to judge by the deferential way the others treated them—were major powers in Nick's study group. Loren would much rather have dined in the front room, sitting on the floor with the "peasants," she informed Kerri in an undertone, but there was no help for it. They must weather the ordeal somehow, be on their best behavior in spite of everything.

Kerri had met Mr. Ratsavong-Woodman very briefly once before. The first and last time she had seen him had been when he put his name on her dance card at the May Eve Ball. She decided not to mention this, as he showed no sign of remembering her, which was just as well. She felt far too outnumbered to give herself the satisfaction of telling him how very much her good friend, His Excellency Marius Warralonga Campbell, was obliged to Mr. Ratsavong-Woodman for being unable to claim his dance with her, due, no doubt, to some sudden indisposition. Too outnumbered, and much too hungry and tired to be reliably clever in front of these people. Best let it go and eat, for the food was very good indeed, as was the wine, a heavyish, fruity red.

Among so many people, two bottles of wine did not last long. Half way through the meal Fiona got up to open another, a green bottle with no label. She poured for Kerri and Loren first. The wine was unusually dark in color, almost black in the lamplight.

"I think you will like this," she said. "It is rather special." To the others she gave smaller portions. "Remember," she told them, "*we* still have work to do tonight and a couple of long hikes. After this, it is coffee for us!"

"You *would* remind us," Harry grumbled. "Another day like this and I shall be utterly done in."

"Nonsense!" Marta exclaimed. "It is good for you. Keeps you fit."

She had a point, Kerri thought. Harry looked as if he could use a few more long walks than he was accustomed to getting.

"This is interesting wine," Loren said. "I have never tasted anything quite like it before." This was almost the first thing she had uttered at dinner, a sign that she had, finally, relaxed a little—although none of them had been talkative, the conversation limited to small chat about the weather and the scenery around the lake.

"Yes. It is wonderful, is it not?" Fiona beamed at her. "A friend of mine makes it. Not much, maybe twenty dozen bottles in a season, parceled out to a few friends. It is not easy to get, but I have been among the lucky the past few years."

Kerri picked up her glass—a chipped and ancient family relic—and took a small sip. Smooth, lighter than one might think from the extraordinarily dark color, a complex of fleeting flavors among which she was able only to pin down a hint of raspberries. And Fiona was right; it was quite wonderful. And something else.

Kerri frowned. "I had this before," she said. "I cannot remember when, but I know I have tasted something very like this in the past."

"Impossible!" Fiona exclaimed. "As I said, only a few people. well, on the other hand, I suppose it is possible, now that I think about it. And it is so good, one would remember." She smiled benevolently and lifted her glass. "To generous friends," she said.

"Hear, hear," said Harry, who drained his glass with one gulp and returned to attacking his third helping of lasagna.

Kerri took a larger sip, trying to think of where she had tasted the wine before.

Memory did not yield up any clues. It must have been long ago, and she was more tired than she had realized. Loren, she noticed, was almost nodding off in her chair.

Fiona noticed. "You two must be quite exhausted from your journey," she said sympathetically. "Do not feel you need to linger and be sociable, for we must finish up and be about our business. Go on to bed as soon as you like. We shall do the washing up, and I promise you there will not be a trace of dinner when you get up in the morning. And we plan to have breakfast at the Lodge, so we shall be on our way early."

"Very good," Kerri acknowledged, trying to suppress a yawn, thinking, *I'll just finish my wine and be off to bed.*

Loren got carefully to her feet. "Then I shall excuse myself," she announced, eyes half-closed. "It was delightful meeting you all. Thank you for dinner. Good night." As she turned toward the door, she nearly stumbled, to be caught by Mr. Ratsavong-Woodman, who gallantly helped her out of the room.

Kerri watched them go, watched him return, realized she had not moved a muscle in several minutes, lacked even the energy to get out of her chair. *I am exhausted,* she realized. *All that walking and no sleep to speak of last night. And Alex.* Mustering all her strength, she dragged herself upright and cast what she hoped was a bright smile at the group around the table. Mr. Ratsavong-Woodman still stood behind his chair, watching her alertly. *In case,* she realized, *I need help, too. Which I may.*

"Thank you very much for dinner," she said. "And a good evening to you all."

"Will you not finish your wine?" Fiona asked. "It would be such a pity to let it go to waste." Helpfully, she put Kerri's glass into her hand.

"Indeed," Kerri replied vaguely. *Not that I need to,* she reflected. *I believe I am drunk as well as tired, but the wine is much too good to go to waste.* Obediently, she drank the last of it and wondered again, *where have I tasted this before?* With careful precision, she set down the glass on the table. "Good night," she said.

"Good night," they called in chorus as she made her way almost competently and quite unaided to the hall door. At the last second she glanced back and saw them watching her, silently, warily. Except for Mr. Ratsavong-Woodman who pointedly did not look at her at all.

He sat down again and sighed.

He knows perfectly well who I am, she realized with dull and bleary resentment. *I should have let him have it, outnumbered or not.*

Chapter 51

The Calling

In each layer of sleep she dreamed she was awake. Sometimes she was in the forest, her body dark of Twilight's gleam, sometimes in the cabin bedroom, struggling feebly with the locked door. And then she would remember that the door could be locked only from the inside, that someone else should be in the room with her, that—at the very least—her hands should glow softly against the scarred oak. And, remembering, she would swim up through another layer and dream again of waking.

There was a sound, a heavy vibration she could feel in her back teeth, like something immense being dragged across the corrugated roof or like the thunder of ancient machinery inside the generator station of Emerald City. There was a light, hurtingly bright, spearing in under the door, up the sides, along the top, through every crack, until she made one last immense effort—"No!"—and broke surface. The vibration ceased.

Half sitting, half lying on her side upon the daybed, she opened her eyes and saw no more light than the vague and dubious undarkness of night in Twilight Country, heard no more sound than her own breathing and the creak of the springs beneath her as she struggled upright. Over by the back window, someone slept beneath a huddle of blankets. Kerri became aware that no blankets covered her shivering self.

I woke up because I was cold, she told herself. I am still dressed. I never went to bed properly. Why?

Her parka was half under her. She tugged it free and put it on, pulling up the hood and trying her best to do up the zip with her numbed fingers. All her movements had the curious feeling of being performed under water, slow and weightless, and her mind felt the same, suspended, without any sort of passion or interest in anything. And yet some part of her had the sense to put on the parka. She recognized this as a good thing, probably.

From this curious remoteness, she began to recognize certain facts: She was in her cabin at the lake. Her last meal had contained more than a little garlic. The person asleep on the cot was Loren. She began to remember: The two of them had come here in the night, not many heartbeats ago. Others were here, many people, Nick's study group from the University, and they had fed her and Loren exactly the same wine she had drunk years ago, the night Val had betrayed her with Arzelle. Perhaps a different vintage, but Arzelle's wine for certain, seductively delicious and surely drugged. Or a drug of itself: no difference. And she had been trying to fight it, trying not to fall asleep. The last thing she remembered was locking the bedroom door from the inside. She smiled. They would not have been able to check up on her if they had wished to, and undoubtedly they had wished to. None of it seemed to matter in the slightest.

She considered this detachment she felt, if one could call it feeling. There was something familiar about it, something more immediate in memory than that long ago evening with Arzelle and Val in the old flat up by the University. *The Veil.* It was like the Veil, and it was not like the Veil. It was more, somehow, and less. Crude: heavy canvas compared to fine silk. She frowned and tried to raise the Veil. The Veil did not come. Or did it? She could not tell. She could not be certain she had ever been able to tell. *This is bad,* Kerri said to herself; *I should be alarmed.*

Loren sat up suddenly, hooded with blanket, and looked out at Kerri with the owlish stare of the abruptly wakened. "What was that?" she said.

"What was what?" Kerri asked.

"That sound. That chanting." Her eyes lost focus. "No. It's gone now."

She is dreaming, Kerri thought, but she became still, listening. She could hear a faint tapping, like water dripping into a steel sink. Had it been there all along, or had it only begun now? It stopped. Several seconds passed. There was a muffled bang, and then the tapping began again, neither nearby nor far. She could not tell if the sound came from inside the cabin or outside.

"There it is again!" said Loren.

Kerri held her breath, listening. Tapping. Another bang. Metallic, tinny, like an empty water tank being hit with a stick, or two rubbish can lids being struck together— children playing at marching band. Then, far in the distance, an airy whistling or vocalization, high, unnatural.

"There," said Loren.

The sound gave Kerri gooseflesh, as might a badly rusted hinge or fingernails across a chalkboard, but she could recognize no words or even be certain she was hearing a human voice. Perhaps it was only a hinge: the boathouse door? Had they got into the boathouse?

Damn them! She stood up, or rather, she found herself on her feet with no recollection of having got there. She could hear nothing now because her own pulse pounded so loudly in her ears. She became aware of a heavy thudding in her chest and realized, *I am afraid. I have never been afraid before; I have only pretended to feel fear. This is real fear.* She felt as if she had become two people standing side by side in the cold room. One was desperately afraid; one felt nothing at all.

She watched Loren carefully unwind herself from her cocoon of blankets. Loren was still fully dressed, even to the boots. She groped for her parka, tangled in the blankets, and put it on, fished for her gloves in the pockets. When she had covered her hands, only her face showed and her eyes, glimmering with the luminescence of Twilight Country. Kerri looked down at her own hands. They glowed with a healthy normalcy, not lifelessly nonluminous as in her dream.

"What is happening?" Loren whispered.

"The wine was drugged," Kerri whispered in reply as she realized they had been whispering all along.

"I know. I've been fighting and fighting it. What time is it?"

"After midnight. Getting on for one o'clock." Kerri did not bother to look at her non-functioning watch.

Loren nodded. "Not as drugged as it could have been, then," she commented.

"Or we are not as drugged as we were meant to be," said Kerri.

"Or we are fast recoverers. Have the others gone?"

"I don't know. I can't tell. I can't hear them. There were some noises, but they could have just been the wind blowing things. No talking."

"I heard someone chanting," said Loren. Her teeth chattered. She picked up one of the blankets and wrapped it around her. "I want to get out of here."

"I won't leave," Kerri protested.

"You're afraid to open the door," Loren told her.

"Absolutely!"

"I'll open it then." But Loren continued to stand where she was, staring at the door, as if she could open it by will alone. "Light a lamp first," she said.

Kerri's frightened self could not move, but her detached self found matches in a drawer and put flame to the wick of the bedside lamp. Loren, visibly regretting her bargain, tiptoed to the bedroom door and put her ear against it. "They've gone," she announced.

"They're asleep."

"No. They are not here." She leaned against the door as she turned the bolt silently and lowered the door handle. The door squeaked thinly as she eased it open, and both women flinched, but lamplight shone out upon an unoccupied room. An empty room: the luggage, the litter of sleeping bags, the shining ceremonial robes hanging from the curtain rods—all were gone. Except for a few embers shining redly under the fireplace grate and lingering smells of smoke and cooking, there was no other sign the room had been inhabited at all since autumn.

Kerri pulled her parka more closely about her and ventured cautiously away from the shelter of the bedroom into the tiny hallway, past the bathroom—empty—to the threshold of the kitchen—clean and swept, with only the lingering aroma of garlic to tell of the dinner a few hours before.

"Ah!" she exclaimed as three more quick steps brought her to the kitchen table.

Triumphantly, she snatched up the key lying there, Nick's key to the cabin on the key ring she had given him, the key she had had cut at the locksmith's in Fernly.

"The cabin is safe," she whispered. "They can't get back in. Unless they cut another key. Even so...."

"Where is that light coming from?" Loren had followed Kerri into the kitchen. There the curtains were thinner than the heavy drapes so carefully pulled across the sitting room windows. A pale, rosy light flickered upon the walls. "Can't be the door lamps. Wrong direction." She tiptoed to the nearest window, one that overlooked the lake, and pulled the curtain edge a scant centimeter aside. "There is a fire," she said. "Come, look."

"The boathouse!" Kerri cried. "Damn them!" She ran toward the door.

"Don't go out there! Wait!" But Loren followed, carrying the lamp, through the sitting room, out the door, down the steps and onto the wide lawn sloping gently down toward the water. She caught up with Kerri at the stone circle where a campfire burned merrily upon the ashes of countless years of campfires. More than a campfire, almost a bonfire. "I could have told you it wasn't the boathouse," Loren urged. "Let's go back inside."

"Go on, if you want. I need to check the property."

"Can't it wait until morning?"

"No." Kerri turned, scanning the lakeshore and the forest with worried eyes.

"Then don't go down there alone. What if someone's in there? I'll go with you."

Kerri considered this. "Very well, but first, take Nick's key and go lock the door. Make sure all the doors are locked."

"Right!" said Loren. "No squatters!" She exchanged the lamp for the key and dashed back to the cabin. Kerri examined the ground around the fire ring. The grass, cut short at the end of the summer season, had been further beaten down and greyed by winter, but it was still possible to see signs of trampling feet—several people, more than two or three, coming down from the house, milling around by the fire ring, leaving the fire ring. One trail angled off to join the road to the Lodge, another led toward the boathouse. The woodpile next to the fire ring was visibly diminished, but no more than one fire's worth.

She stood very still and listened, but all was silent now except for the wind through the pine forest, punctuated by the slam of the door as Loren re-emerged and bent to turn the key in the lock. Kerri did not hear anything like the strange tappings and bangs, the eerie whistling or creaking she had heard upon awakening. Could she have imagined those sounds? Could it have been the wind banging a loose shutter somewhere on the house? Or could she have heard the very sounds of Nick's people leaving? Someone had been here, very recently. The fire was testament to that. *Where are they?* she worried. She blew out the lamp.

Loren rejoined her in the moonlight and firelight. "All right," she said, somewhat breathlessly. "Your castle is secure from squatters, and here are your gloves." She took the lamp so Kerri could cover her hands against the cold. "Why did you put the light out?"

"Did you see anything?" Kerri asked. "Out any of the other windows? Did you hear anything? Voices? Noises?"

"I didn't look," Loren replied, startled. "I didn't listen. Why? Those sounds we heard—I haven't heard them since...."

"Since we lit the lamp," Kerri finished thoughtfully.

Loren glanced around nervously. "Do you think those people are still here?"

Kerri nodded. "Wherever they are, they haven't gone far. The wood on top had barely begun to burn when we came outside. So unless someone else made the fire—in which case, who?—they cannot have gone far. But from here we should be able to see lanterns from time to time along the road at least half way to the Lodge—this time of year with so many leaves down. There are no lights. I've been watching. Are they walking in the dark? I know it's moonlight, but with all that luggage? Where are they?"

"In the boathouse?" Loren gazed dubiously upon that structure, squatting darkly against the water.

"Not enough room. Not for all of them. Besides, it's supposed to be locked. But some of them went down there at least. Come on. No, keep that key in your pocket, just in case. I've got mine safe." She set off across the grass with Loren close behind. Away from the fire her eyes began to adjust to the moonlight again, a cold silver on the flattened grasses, the weathered shingles of the boathouse roof, the rippled water of the lake. By the time she came down to the boathouse door she could make out the hasp in place, the padlock firmly fastened. Nick had possessed no key to this lock or any other but the door of the house.

Relieved, she let out her held breath. *We'll put the kettle on,* she thought. *Make some cocoa. If they left any.*

"Uh oh," muttered Loren.

Kerri inhaled again sharply. "Uh oh, what? What?"

"On the dock." Loren stood on the decking beyond the boathouse, pointing down toward the water. When Kerri joined her, she could see an irregular mound at the end of the dock, a pile of objects. "Their luggage, if I'm not mistaken," said

Loren. "And those mattresses and things from the Lodge. To be fetched by boat in the morning. Didn't she say a cart would come?"

Kerri peered out across the lake toward the Lodge and wished she had not. "Not tomorrow," she gasped. "Tonight."

Across the silvered water a dark shape was gliding, growing larger by the second, rocking gently in the light wind: a boat of some kind, under sail, heading straight toward Kerri's dock.

"Come on!" squeaked Loren, but even as she spoke, a torch flared alight on the boat, and another, and half a dozen more. *That is the yacht from the Lodge,* Kerri realized.

The two women fled back up the slope, only to be confronted by more lights. A double procession of masked figures carrying torches and lanterns came around both sides of the house, marching toward the shore. They wore long ceremonial robes and garlands of evergreen boughs and gum leaves. They marched to a sound that could be heard now, a metallic drumming, a tapping. There was no doubt in Kerri's mind who they were, and yet she was newly filled with a terror she seemed to remember feeling long ago, a pain and sorrow from childhood—the days of watching and worrying, of Zarah and Zarah's unkind friends, Zarah saying, "You will be demented some day. You have the signs. I can see them."

Loren turned, wide-eyed. "What is going on?"

At that moment all light vanished. Struck blind, Kerri dropped to her knees, felt grass beneath her frantic hands. She heard Loren scream once. The drumming kept on and on. *Oh, what have they done to me?* Kerri cried silently. She heard the sound of the drumming and that high whistling again, definitely a whistle, too harsh to call it a flute, only the resonance of the sound was changed, as if heard inside a large echoing room, as if a giant box had been clapped down over them all, quenching the fire and all the torches and the moon and every living cell in Twilight Country.

Abruptly she remembered: *I have been here before. I know this place.* On her hands and knees feeling the grass, feeling the twigs and stones digging into her flesh, she looked up and began to see amid the blackness dim unfocused blurs of light, elongated, egg shaped. As she watched they grew brighter—ovoid forms of light, a cluster of them beyond where the campfire should be and another cluster in the opposite direction, smaller in size, possibly farther away. She saw now that the globes of light were linked with a web of fine, barely visible filaments of light which sparkled minutely. *The people,* she realized. *I am seeing the people.* At the same time, the sensation of being in a box changed, as if the walls of the chamber and the ceiling were receding into an unimaginably vast space.

And just as suddenly she recognized: *This is the Star Dream. The Star Dream. But I am awake.*

From somewhere deep within her, or within the earth itself, something immense and dark welled up and rushed toward the surface. And it filled the absent sky and gathered itself over her head for her demanding. Anger.

A voice spoke in tones of authority from one of the lights. "Sisters and brothers, our rite has been invaded." A woman's voice. "What judgment shall we pronounce upon these intruders?"

Kerri rose to her feet and faced the lights and shouted, "No! We will not be used this way!" From above and below the anger-summoned strength poured into her, called down from the sky, called up from the earth as she cried out, "No!" At the last moment she found Loren's arm and grabbed it with her left hand as light exploded about them both in an immense shattering of the cocoons of darkness that held them, a rending of the very air.

There were screams, and when Kerri's sight cleared again she could see the campfire circle, flames still burning heedlessly. She could see herself and Loren, who was just getting to her feet, and the robed people, and beyond them the house, unharmed. But the light was strange, a pink-orange glow that seemed to come from everywhere and nowhere in particular, as if Kerri's eyes had changed their function somehow, some shift apart even from the shifted sight of Twilight Country. She looked down at the lake which was coal-dark, like a lake of nothingness instead of water. The yacht had arrived at the dock. Half a dozen people, also dressed for ceremony, lined the railing looking up at the land, but they did not move.

I did this, she realized wonderingly. We did this. Loren and I, for this thing that happened came from her also. We called on...something. And it came. Out of us. To us.

And we were stronger than They were.

On the lawn, some of the robed ones were sitting on the ground holding their heads. The others looked about themselves uncertainly. Most of them had dropped their torches, and their masks lay broken on the grass. Kerri recognized them easily—Fiona and Harry and Mara and the others. And, among them, to her astonishment, she saw Jillian robed in white. And Nicholas, staring at her with shock and grief. One of Them now.

Her anger turned to ashes. The power from earth and sky and soul wavered and melted and bled out of her. Kerri ran. She turned away from all of it and ran away across the lawn, across the road and into the forest, the dense enchanted forest of Twilight Country.

Chapter 52

Flight

"And what in the name of the Dreamer was that?" Loren panted as she climbed the last few meters up the hill. She dropped to her knees on dry pine needles and bowed her head, breathing hard.

Kerri shook her head. "I don't know." This was somewhere in the neighborhood of the truth.

Beginning to catch her own breath, she leaned back against the outcropping of rock against which she had propped herself and looked up at the stars, no sign of dawn. A few ragged clouds sailed fast along the upper wind, although at ground level there was just enough breeze to keep the pines talking. She was glad it was Loren following her when she was forced to stop and rest. There was no sign of anyone else. Not yet.

She wiped the tears from her cheeks with her sleeve and looked about her for a likely spiderweb stick. She had blundered through at least one web on her thoughtless flight. Even at such a time, she had no desire to crash through any more. She found one and waved it absently. "We have to go on," she said. "They'll be looking for us."

"I doubt it," Loren gasped.

Kerri did not reply. The light had changed again, she realized. The strange ruddy glow had faded away except at the very outer edges of her vision. Night had again become what passed for normal in Twilight Country. Perhaps there had been no glow. Perhaps it had been no more than some illusion of firelight and terror. She rubbed her eyes. Half drunk, terrified, exhausted, still in shock from Alexander's death—how could she trust her own perceptions? When had she ever been able to trust them?

"Come on." She pushed herself away from the rock and set off upward again, ducking under low branches. "Just a little farther. There is a better place to stop."

Loren, wise herself to the hazards of the forest, provided herself with her own spiderweb stick and followed with a sigh.

Presently they emerged onto a kind of plateau at the crest of the ridge that overlooked the eastern shore of the lake. The pine forest gave way to grass scattered with gum trees and with pinnacles and squat towers of stone, protrusions of the rocky spine of the ridge. In the moonlight the place had an eerie resemblance to the tumbled ruins of Evesham or even to pictures of legendary Stonehenge. Kerri had always imagined it as some kind of ruined city, the remains of long abandoned temples to forgotten gods. She never came to the cabin without climbing at least once to "The Acropolis" and standing upon "her" rock, her Lookout Tower. She ran to the familiar humped shape and clambered up the side.

She could not remember the first time she had climbed this ridge and stood upon this rock. She had done it so many times, so many summers, that she got to the top without thinking and stood gazing down over the trees while Loren fumbled for hand- and footholds.

From here Kerri could see down over the trees to the lakeshore and the cabin, and beyond, across the old reservoir to the Lodge and resort village, to the large estates on the western shore. Down below by the lake the bonfire still burned. Tiny points of light—they must have rekindled their lanterns and torches—swarmed around the fire, gathering in several clusters or moving about singly. Kerri could just make out the boat from the Lodge, sails furled, tied up at the dock. It was easier to pick out the corrugated metal roofs of the cabin and boathouse, which appeared, from this distance at least, to have been undamaged by...whatever had happened. Nor did there seem to be any lights inside the buildings, one thing to be thankful for.

"It looks like they are putting the luggage on the boat," Loren observed, having finally reached the vantage point. "They're leaving, thank goodness!"

"Perhaps," Kerri agreed. "I hope so."

"Do you have any idea what happened?" Loren ventured. "When I saw them coming around the side of the house, I went completely blind all of a sudden. Then there was that great lightning flash, or explosion or something, and I was sure I was going to die, but I didn't, and then I could see again." She paused. "Which isn't an adequate description, but it will have to do. And then you ran off, which seemed like a good idea at the time, judging by the looks I saw on their faces, so I ran, too. I got the impression," she continued, "they all supposed it was our fault, the flash or blast or whatever it was." She paused again. "But that is ridiculous."

"Maybe," Kerri said. After a moment she added, "Nick was there."

"Oh, was he? I had a feeling that might be why...I mean, I had a feeling he might be there, but I didn't see him. That is, I wouldn't have known who he was, anyway, would I? Would you like to borrow a handkerchief? I'm sure there's one in one of these pockets somewhere."

"No, thanks." Kerri, having finally found her own handkerchief, made another futile pass at her face. She was getting to the hiccup and deep breathing stage, some detached part of her mind marveling over how it was possible to cry and run at the same time.

Loren, tactfully keeping her eyes on the distant activities by the lake, said, "They are definitely doing something at the boat. I'm sure they're putting the luggage on. How clever of you to find this place where we could watch and see when it's safe to go back down."

"Oh, this was always my rock." Kerri blew her nose and stuffed the handkerchief back into her pocket. She pulled her parka hood up over her head and tied it on firmly. "I think we had better not count on going back down right away. See that group of lights to the left? I'll give you odds that's a search party."

"You may be right," muttered Loren as the cluster of lanterns elongated and began to move toward the ridge. "Did Nick see you? He must have insisted they let him come looking for you. Does he know about this place?"

"Yes."

"Maybe they think we're hurt."

"If we were hurt, would we be running? I think they know we were not injured."

"Then why would they bother?" Loren fretted. "Why don't they just let us go. That's all they wanted, isn't it? To chase us out so we wouldn't pollute their precious exclusive retreat?"

The two women watched for several minutes as the lights moved under the trees, winking in and out but always moving closer—eight, ten, at least a dozen of them. Now they began to climb the slope.

"Perhaps we had better move away from here," suggested Loren, already beginning to scramble down from the lookout. "Not that I want anyone to worry about me needlessly; I just don't feel like a social encounter right now."

With one last look at the approaching lights, Kerri followed her. "Let's go on up the ridge," she proposed, "south, toward the Lodge. It'll keep us on higher ground, and we can see better what they're up to."

"Right," Loren agreed.

They set off jogging through the grass, but they had gone no more than twenty meters when they came to the remains of a campfire ringed by stones. The fire had burned so recently that wisps of steam still rose from carefully doused ashes.

Loren took off a glove and held her hand over the fireplace. "Warm," she confirmed.

"You know, I'll bet this is where they went when we thought they'd gone. This is where they were with their robes and masks and their chanting."

With effort, Kerri pulled herself together. "One of them said something about a 'rite,'" she recalled. "I wonder if they were having some kind of initiation ceremony up here."

"For the study group?"

"I suppose it must have been."

"I've never heard of such a thing," said Loren as she replaced her glove. "Not for a University graduate study group. The Road clans do, of course. The trade guilds do, and I've heard the Faculties do something of the sort, but it seems a little over the edge somehow for a study group, if you know what I mean. Silly and affected. I should have thought they would fancy themselves above that sort of thing."

"I never heard of it either," said Kerri. It was one more thorn in her heart. Why had she not known? "Maybe it's only a peculiarity of this group," she suggested, "or something they thought up just this one time. Either way, I don't like it. We—the lake kids, the families—used to come up here for picnics and cookouts. They have no right!"

"Well, you don't own it, do you?" reasoned Loren. "It's park land. What's to stop them? At least they put out the fire."

From the next stopping place, higher on the backbone of the ridge, they could not see the cabin any more, but they could look down over The Acropolis and see clearly as the pinpricks of lantern light emerged from the pines below.

"Close," Loren commented. They crouched in the lee of a fallen tree, as much for shelter from the chill breeze as for concealment.

"They were awfully fast," Kerri agreed. Was that calling she heard, over the roar of the pines? Or did she only imagine it? "Why did I run?" she wondered aloud. "Was I crazy to run away? Should we go back?"

"No," Loren replied. "I do not think you are crazy. You ran because you were frightened or because you were embarrassed. Or both. Which?"

"Both," Kerri decided. "This is very stupid."

"Perhaps."

"So why did you run?"

"Because you did. And because I was frightened. Now I am embarrassed. And not quite over being frightened. So if you can think of a logical, reasonable explanation for all of this, we can go back. Otherwise, no, thank you."

The group of lights had broken up and scattered through the stone pinnacles, moving slowly now.

"Well," Kerri began slowly, "there must be a logical explanation. We were barely awake, it was dark, we'd been drinking. A lot of things have happened to us lately. I'm sure we were primed to imagine all kinds of...."

"Imagine! They drugged us, for pity's sake!" Loren hissed. "They took over your house and tried to throw you out. Did you imagine that? And I don't know about you, but I know I did not imagine going blind, and I did not imagine being struck by lightning. Or something. I don't know why it didn't kill me, and maybe

I'm only imagining I'm alive, but I do not want to go back while there is any chance of encountering those worthies. Yes, I know our packs are there. We can get them later." With an angry snort she rose to her feet and tucked her hood more closely around her face.

Kerri sat back on her heels and rubbed her face with her hands. "I have to talk to Nick," she said. "Even if he is...one of Them, I have to talk to him."

Loren's eyes narrowed. "I hope he isn't, for your sake. But if I were you, I would not run down just now and take it up with him in front of all those witnesses. On the other hand, what *are* we going to do? Is there some other place we can go to get out of the cold, short of hiking all the way back to Lashings? Should we lurk around up here until they leave—which they may not? If we do, we had better keep moving to stay warm."

When Kerri did not answer, she continued, "Very well, if you insist on going back, I'll go with you, but I do not like it. I have a very bad feeling about all of this."

"You're right." Kerri rose slowly to her feet at last and took a deep breath. "We have to move. I need to talk to him, but I can't face Them now, Loren. I can't. Not yet. I only wish there was some way to let him know I'm all right."

"Serve him right if you didn't! But decide, because they are coming this way."

"Are they tracking us?" panted Loren some minutes later. "How could they have any idea which way we went?"

Toiling ever higher up the ridge, they had lost sight of the Acropolis, but not of the cluster of lanterns that followed them. No closer, fortunately, but no farther away. They stopped to rest a moment and saw the lights appear again through the trees, first one, then another, then more. There were seven altogether. Some of the search party must have gone back or remained on the plateau, but more than half of them were clearly approaching.

"They spotted us back there," Kerri decided. "Or else they've made a lucky guess. They're just following the trail like we are." Indeed there was no choice, if one wished to travel with any speed in this terrain.

"How could they have seen us?" Loren protested. "We're totally covered except our faces, and I can't believe we're bright enough to show at this distance. Not in moonlight. After all, *we* can only see the lanterns, not them. Unless they can see us moving somehow."

"Or heard us. Do keep your voice down." Wearily she followed as Loren resumed her slow jog up the ridge.

"They shouldn't be able to hear us with the pines rustling like this. But why pursue us at all? I don't understand this!"

"Unless," replied Kerri, "they do believe we were hurt after all."

Which would be laudable of them, she thought, *but I do not buy it. They're not behaving like rescuers.* She was conscious of a growing alarm. Nick must be with the search party, or someone else familiar with the rough country around the Lake. How else could they have known where to begin looking? And how had they picked up the trail so quickly and unerringly? One would have expected them still to be spread out across the Acropolis— plenty of hiding places there, including several small caves where an injured or frightened person might take shelter. Yet, here they were, not ten minutes behind.

She found herself fighting the temptation to stop and look back every few steps, to wait until she could count all seven lights. Experimentally she tried to calm her mind and open it to the Power-sense. Not a reaching out for it—the sense did not work that way—but waiting for Power to reach out to her. And she felt something, perhaps. A vague, diffuse pressure. Or she imagined it.

All she could really be certain about was the sensation that she had quite lately been rung like a bell. Her whole body still reverberated with the echo of the incident by the bonfire. And now after a little time, she realized there was a flavor to the echo that she recognized, a flavor she remembered from somewhere else. As if this thing, or something like it, had happened before, but when? When? The Star Dream? No, not that; something real. *What happened to us back there?* she wondered for the twentieth time. At least she felt almost clearheaded again. The drug must be wearing off, none too soon.

"If they're following the path, we should get off the path," Loren suggested in a low voice the next time they paused for breath. "Maybe we should try to go down to the road and double back. Even if the rest haven't gone, we might be able to nip inside without them seeing us. Lie low until they've gone, or at least get our packs and a few more warm clothes."

"Too late," Kerri whispered back. "We've come too far. There is an escarpment between here and the road along this stretch. It's a sheer drop, ten meters or more. There are a few places we might climb down, but even if I could find one, I shouldn't like to try in the dark."

"What about the other side of the ridge?"

"Not much better, and then we'd have to climb up and over again. We have two choices—go on or go back."

"What if we go on?"

"The escarpment ends just this side of where the lake shore curves west. We can get down there, but by then we'll be closer to the Lodge than to my cabin. And when we take the road back we'll be on a long stretch between cliff and water with no cover, so if there is anyone at all coming south along the shore, we'll be forced to meet them."

"Well, that's jolly! What do you propose we do?"

"We could stay up high and circle around the back of the village and come down behind the west wing of the Lodge."

"And then what?" muttered Loren. "Walk into the Lodge dining room and order breakfast?"

"Very funny!" Kerri retorted. "No, here's an idea. The grounds are rather overgrown on that side. There should be plenty of cover, and I don't think there are many guest rooms at that end—just laundry and workshops and the like. From there, we try to make it to the station. The first train pulls out just before daylight. If we time it right, we could hop on it directly and ride to one of the private stops along the western shore and walk back around to the cabin. By that time, they'll surely be gone."

"Have you got any money?"

"A little. Enough. And I've got my return ticket in my pocket."

"So do I." Loren sighed. "If I didn't want my pack for the holidays, I'd say let's just stay on the train and go on back home. But where's home? I can't go home."

"Home," repeated Kerri bleakly. Like the ripples of a stone dropped into a pool, her thoughts spread outward to all her homes: the cabin, the house in Evesham, the University, her parents' house in Honowell. And suddenly she remembered with crystal clarity: standing upon the heights of the Honowell Botanical Garden, looking down at the city, her mind and body still thrumming with the aftereffects of the Powerflash in Professor Bonneville-Chatterton's study. It was the kind of memory Sophia called a "body memory," the truest kind—powerful, wordless, and undeniable.

It happened, she realized anew. *It did happen, the Powerflash. That day. I did not imagine it. It was real, and it felt like this, like tonight. Tonight by the lake. A Powerflash. Only tonight's was bigger, much bigger. And it wasn't done to me. I did it. I! Loren and I. She helped. She...channeled it somehow. Otherwise, who knows what would have happened. It might have killed us both!*

As they set off again she looked over her shoulder. "Oh, gosh! Look! They're closer!"

"They are! Damn! They can see us! They must be able to see us. Look at you! Look how bright your face is!" Loren whipped off a glove and stared at her hand. "Look at my hand. We're a couple of beacons. No wonder they don't give up. They can see us."

Here in an exceptionally dense stand of pines the shadows were dark enough that there could be no mistake. The faint luminescence of the plant life was clearly outshone by Loren's hand.

"We can't do anything about that," Kerri exclaimed. "This is Twilight Country. Life glows in Twilight Country." She quickened her pace. "Put that glove back on, for pity's sake!"

"Well, *you* stop turning back to look at them! You might as well be waving a torch." The moon was low in the sky now, winking in and out of the clouds. The wind had picked up, booming through the pine forest. No need to speak softly now; they must almost shout to make themselves heard. The path began to drop down below the top the ridge, which was narrow here, and spiky with stone. As she stumbled onward, Kerri began to catch glimpses of stationary lights, not far off, below and up ahead to the right: the resort town.

She could see the long mass of the Lodge, surprisingly lit up for this time of the night. Or morning.

She wondered if the boat had returned from the other end of the lake by now. And what a tale they would have to tell, whoever was aboard!

Impulsively she pulled off the glove from her left hand, stared at the gently glowing flesh. *Veil*, she thought, and like a cloud passing over the moon the glow of her hand dimmed and went out. It was gone, as if she had died, or turned to stone under the sunless sky of Twilight Country. At the same moment, something else happened. The sensation of being followed vanished utterly.

Here the trail had dropped well below the top of the ridge. The pursuers, if they had not turned back, would be hidden by the angle of the land for a minute or two. Kerri risked a quick glance back. No points of light. Perhaps she and Loren had gained a little distance. The two of them loped across a small clearing into a deeply shadowed dell.

"Stop!" Kerri gasped, catching Loren's sleeve. "Just a moment. There is something we can try, a way we can hide from them."

Loren was staring at her face. "Name of the Dreamer! You're dark! What happened to you? Are you all right?"

"There's no time to explain. Just try this. Imagine you are covering yourself with a...a veil that will make you invisible. Concentrate on it. Pretend you're pulling it up and over yourself and wrapping it around you."

"What?"

"Just do it! Focus! Believe it will hide you. Believe!"

Her face a study in bewildered skepticism, Loren apparently tried. There was no change. "Should I close my eyes?" she asked.

"If it helps. Try again!"

Loren closed her eyes and took a slow deep breath. But again, nothing happened.

"I should have told you weeks ago," Kerri lamented. "I should have had you practicing. Even if I thought it was just a game, we should have tried."

"Tried what?"

"Come on! One more time. Just try!" She gripped Loren's shoulders and willed Loren to understand. *Veil*, she said to herself desperately, *Veil!* To her astonishment, Loren's ungloved hand went dark.

"Name of the Dreamer!" Loren repeated, staring at the hand. "I felt that. Did you do that?" She turned enlightened eyes—in a darkened face—to Kerri. "I don't know if I could do it by myself, but I feel it. A Veil, like you said. As if it flowed over me when you touched me."

Experimentally, Kerri stepped away from her friend, one pace, three. Loren did not brighten. "Maybe it can cover us both," she said. "Or maybe I've somehow given you your own. I don't know. I've never done this before. Or, anyway, not... under these circumstances."

"This is very weird," Loren replaced her glove, "and I trust, whatever you did, it will wear off at some point. For now, it may help. Let's go."

They had scarcely set off again when the first lantern came into view behind and above them. Too close. Ahead the path divided. The right hand path turned sharply downhill; they had come to the end of the escarpment.

"Keep left." Kerri whispered. "Upper trail."

A few minutes later they stopped again to look back. The cluster of lanterns had stopped moving, hesitating at the fork in the trail. Then, one by one, the lights moved down the hill, following the right hand path.

"They don't know which way we've gone," Loren exulted. "They can't see us any more."

"It works!" Kerri breathed, mostly to herself. "It's Real, and it works."

Chapter 53

A Timely Encounter

In Twilight Country, one does not look at the sky in daytime, nor at the horizon at dawn or dusk. The sun might be invisible to the eyes, but it is still there, and it can burn or blind.

Nevertheless, it is easy to forget and try to catch a glimpse of the sunrise, the sign that one has crossed the Boundary in the night. Sunrise and Sunset are the most dangerous times.

The women kept their eyes resolutely away from the west as they came down the steep mountainside toward the Lake and the Lodge. The moon was down, and grey light grew under a pearly sky. Amid its vast lawns and gardens the ancient hotel appeared to snooze peacefully, stone and white clapboard in the dawn mist. As Kerri had promised, the grounds were overgrown and unkempt on the western end, past the croquet lawns, the tennis courts and rose gardens, and here the fugitives could slip across to the train without attracting any attention.

She felt unspeakably weary.

"Why are you running?" Loren had asked. "Because you are afraid or because you are embarrassed?"

Because I am stupid, Kerri thought.

For the last hour or so, she and Loren said very little to each other. They had fallen silent after losing the search party, unwilling to spend any of their waning energy on talk when they still had so far to go. Unfortunately, there had been energy to spare for thought, and Kerri had wrestled in circles with her own thoughts. Most immediately, she deplored her own judgement in suggesting this roundabout route back to the cabin. It was an idiot thing to do. Even with the train, they had a full day's tramping ahead of them and nothing to eat, no bath, and no certain rest at the end. And what was the fuss about, after all?

In the cold pale dawn, the incident at the cabin was rapidly losing its power. She had gone over it scores of times in her mind, and she could find no way to reconcile what she thought she had seen and heard in her wine-befuddled state with everything she knew of reality. People did not call down flashes of unnamed power out of the sky and blast everyone in sight. It was ludicrous to have thought so, even for a moment. In that case, why had she run? Nicholas?

Well, if asked, she could say she had not seen him. She could say she had not recognized any of them. She could say she and Loren had been setting out to leave anyway, and they'd just gone. They hadn't run away. Of course not. Absurd idea!

Perhaps she could say one of them had been feeling ill, and they had decided to go back to town. No, that suggested weakness or even impending dementia. It had the ring of an excuse. What about an appointment in the City, suddenly remembered? Suspicious, but it might do. Or—better!—a spur of the moment notion to do something silly and dashing, such as breakfast in the Emerald City. Brunch in one of the famous restaurants! Yes. It would even cover for their being in the vicinity of the Lodge, should anyone see them. The resort village station was the closest and easiest to get to from the cabin; returning to Lashings would have made no sense. As for why they had followed the ridge instead of the road, why they had not waited for the lantern bearers, well, she would think of a story to cover those things also. She must relate all this to Loren when they had put a safe distance between themselves and the Lodge.

Without incident they slipped through one of the lesser gateways on the mountain-ward side of the Lodge grounds, behind a ramshackle gathering of garages and maintenance sheds. They circled the abandoned tennis courts and entered the rhododendron woods, finding their way blocked finally by a high brick wall, remnant of the wall that had once surrounded the whole property. Further along, Kerri knew, there was an opening in the wall, a gateway through which the supply wagons passed going to and from the station. So the two of them followed the wall as best they could, avoiding fallen trees and bramble thickets and finally coming unavoidably near one of the older and less desirable guest wings of the Lodge, a three story wood frame annex far from the lounges and dining rooms. In summer the rooms were generally used by youth groups and tourists who did not know any better. They were seldom occupied in winter. Even considering Fiona's tale of the Lodge being overbooked—and Kerri had good reason to doubt that now—it seemed unlikely that any Lodge guest would consent to be housed in such out-of-the-way, badly heated quarters, especially when reputations and futures were at stake.

So firm was she in these reassurances that Kerri did not see the man sitting at the bottom of the fire escape until she had already stumbled into the clearing, Loren close after her.

"Good morning," he said. "Fine morning for a walk."

"Good morning." Kerri recovered herself. Lodge employee, he must be, in scuffed boots, denim, plaid flannel, and a grubby old anorak of no particular color, taking a few moments to eat his breakfast in the fresh air. Beside him on the step there was a tray with a plate of buns half covered with a linen cloth and a good-sized pot of something hot. It was coffee; Kerri could smell it. "Yes, it is a fine morning," she said.

He brushed crumbs off his hands and smiled as he rose to his feet. He was quite an attractive young man, Kerri noted, rather the same physical type as Val—dark-haired, hawk-nosed, broad-shouldered, about her own age. His eyes were kind, although she detected an ironic twinkle in them now.

"I wonder," he said, "if you would both care to join me for breakfast? The kitchen sent far too much for one person, and it seems a waste to send it back."

Kerri's heart sank as he spoke. His inflection was pure Academic, and the kitchen did not send breakfast trays to the hired help. Moreover, the aroma of coffee made her almost sick with longing. "That is most kind of you," she stammered, "but we are trying to catch the early train."

"Well, you are too late. I heard it pull out a quarter of an hour ago."

"No!" exclaimed Kerri. "It could not be as late as that."

"Difficult to tell the time in Twilight Country," the man replied with a pleasant smile. "There will be another train later in the morning, but now you have plenty of time, so you might as well accept my invitation. You must be hungry after walking all night."

"I beg your pardon?"

He glanced up beyond them through the woods. "They are still searching, you know, although they will have to call it off for a while this morning to take care of business. Must have been over a hundred people out in the wee hours after the news came back."

"Forgive me, sir." Kerri managed to say. "I have no idea what you are talking about."

"The search parties. You two. Last night's adventures. Word travels fast, and I have exceptionally quick ears. I know who you are. Oh, do not be distressed. I have no intention of turning you in. Arzelle Pendrake James is no friend of mine. It amuses me beyond anything to behold this pickle she has got herself into over this. Nor do I have any direct connection with the Society of Guenevere." He sat down on the step again and gestured at the tray. "Please. I would be honored if you would join me."

Totally at a loss for words, Kerri could only stare at him. At her left shoulder she could sense Loren, frozen immobile, would break any second and dash in terror into the woods. And there was nowhere to go.

"Do I know you, sir?" she asked finally. (When all else fails, one must fall back on a frosty formality.)

"No." He stood again. "Please allow me to introduce myself." He hesitated, laughed, and said, "On second thought, I shall not. Then I shall be telling the truth when I say we have never met. But that leaves me with an unfortunate advantage since I know your names. For now, if you have to call me anything, call me Domenick. It is my given name, although my oldest friends call me Nick."

In spite of herself, Kerri felt a smile twitch the corner of her mouth.

He continued, "Later on, if necessary, we shall all introduce ourselves properly and be appropriately formal. Now, do come have a bite. I shall go up and get two more cups. Better still," he stopped and gazed again out towards the trees, "why not come inside to my rooms? Sooner or later someone is bound to come along down here, and we do not want you to be seen. Come." He bent to pick up the tray and opened the screen door, holding it politely for them.

Kerri turned and looked at Loren, but Loren was looking at the ground. Her brown face had gone a ghostly grey.

"Truly," said Domenick. "I shall not betray you. You have no reason to trust me, I know, but I can offer you a hiding place for now and something to eat, and then, if you insist, you can go and catch the next train. I do not recommend it, but I will not stop you. Your way will be clearer later, anyway, because they will have to give up looking for you in another hour or so, and none of the staff will give a damn if they see you. This is my private entrance. I always request these rooms if I can get them because I can come and go without anyone watching, and so can you, when it is safe. So do come up."

At that moment a voice called out somewhere in the rhododendron woods, and another answered from the direction of the tennis court. Abruptly Kerri took it upon herself to decide. "We have no choice," she whispered to Loren. "Someone is coming!" Loren did not reply, or even look up, but she followed Kerri to the door and inside to the fire escape.

It was not a proper fire escape, in spite of the Lodge management's designation.

Rather, it was an outdoor staircase in a screened enclosure that climbed three stories up the end of this southwest wing of the building. Made of wood, it was surely more of a fire trap than a reliable exit, but it was indeed private. It ended at the top in a kind of open air sleeping porch screened on three sides and furnished with four bare cots, two chests of drawers, a couple of low tables and half a dozen assorted wooden chairs. Beyond this, Domenick's rooms were inside the building proper—a bedroom, a bathroom, and a sitting room, all decorated with a frayed elegance which suggested they had seen better days. Yet, the suite was homey, comfortable, and undeniably appropriate for a person who cherished his quiet and his privacy.

There were books everywhere. In twos and threes, they lay on the small writing desk, on chairs, even on the floor. More books spilled out of a worn carpet bag lying beside the sofa. Clearly they were not Lodge amenities but the property of the room's occupant. Kerri noticed that not a single one showed a title on cover or spine.

Domenick laid the breakfast tray down upon the table in the sitting room. "I shall just go down the hall to the maid's pantry and see if I can find some extra cups," he said, smiling. "I must lock you in, but do not be alarmed. Nothing will prevent you going out the way you came in, if you must go. Please make yourselves at home." He bowed formally and let himself out into the corridor. Kerri heard the key turning in the lock. Thoughtfully, she began to take off her gloves.

Loren had remained out in the sleeping porch, where she stood anxiously at one of the screened openings, looking down anxiously at the woods below.

"Do you see anyone?" Kerri called out softly.

"No." Loren turned for just a moment with a look so bleak, so terrified, that Kerri felt utterly taken aback. Not ever in everything that had happened during the night had she seen Loren looking so frightened.

"What is it?" she asked. "Loren?"

"Is he gone?"

"He went to find some coffee cups...."

"We have to leave. Now."

"We can't leave. They're looking for us out there, and we've missed the train."

"We can't stay here. Not with him!"

"Well, it is true we don't know him, and he is one of Them, and we can't exactly trust him, but...."

"I know him."

Kerri stared at her.

"He is the Dark Watcher."

Chapter 54

Domenick

"Are you sure?" asked Kerri.

Loren gave an exasperated sigh. "Tell me," she said, "what does it mean to be *sure* about anything?" Hands in pockets, shoulders hunched, she wandered to the threshold of the sitting room, the farthest she had dared to come so far. "How do we *know* we know what we know? All I'm sure of is, I'll have one of those buns, if you please."

"Come and help yourself," Kerri suggested mildly, following her own advice. "Listen, we cannot go back out there until the coast is clear. If we have to take cover, it might as well be here. Besides, I want to talk to this gentleman. He knows about the Society of Guenevere. He knows about Arzelle, and he knows what is going on. I want to find out what he knows."

Loren uttered a sound that could only be characterized as a growl. With an expression close kin to a snarl, she stalked into the room, snatched one of the buns, and retreated to the porch just as a key turned in the lock of the door to the corridor.

"Here we are," said the man Domenick cheerfully. He held the door for the uniformed maid, a diminutive, grey-haired woman who balanced a tray with two coffee cups on one hand and clutched a stack of towels and bed linens with the other.

"These is they, eh?" she said, handing off the tray to Kerri, who had jumped to her feet, dropping the remains of her breakfast behind the coffee pot. "Need training, don't they?"

"No fear, it will all be taken care of," he said soothingly. "Mrs. Haggarty, may I present Miss Holmes..." he waved a hand at Loren, backed carefully against the porch window with the daylight behind her and the bun out of sight in a pocket, "...and Miss Watson." He indicated Kerri, who nodded, nonplussed. "I am certain their luggage will arrive later today, but I need them to commence their duties this morning, and, as you can see, they cannot appear as they are, even in the back halls and stairs. I know that you, resourceful woman that you are, can suggest something."

Hastily, Kerri laid the tray upon the table and with a murmured "By your leave," relieved Mrs. Haggarty of the sheets and towels.

"Do not run off, Miss Watson," said Domenick. "Stay and listen."

"Well, sir," began the maid, rubbing her chin and squinting suspiciously at each of the younger women in turn, "I could borrow a pair of uniforms from the Lodge stock—just for the day, mind!—and they're to be laundered and returned fresh and ironed on the morning."

"Excellent idea!" exclaimed Domenick. "Then go and bring them, if you please. I shall be gone when you return, for I have duties of my own to attend to, after I finish giving my staff their instructions for the day. I would be very grateful if you could personally bring them up some lunch on a tray before the staff lunch time. A little indulgence, just this once while they get themselves sorted out. Then we shall put you to no more trouble today."

"Very good, sir," said Mrs. Haggarty, folding her hands over her aproned waist. "And will they be joining the rest of the staff for supper tonight, sir?"

"We shall see," he replied. "One last thing, Mrs H. Under the circumstances, we shall have to pretend that I am unattended, at least until the luggage comes and my staff learn their way about. Appearances are important, you know."

"I quite understand, sir." She nodded wisely.

"I have every confidence in you, Mrs. H." He dropped a handful of coins into her palm.

"That will be all, thank you."

"Very good, sir," she repeated, pocketing the tip, and with a last skeptical look at "Miss Watson." she departed from the room.

"Just set those down anywhere," he indicated the towels in Kerri's arms, "and come have some breakfast. Listen carefully and save your questions for later. I have very little time." He sat down and poured out two cups of coffee.

Kerri placed her burden on the nearest empty chair and picked up both cups. As she carried one to Loren, he continued speaking, "The story is that you are here to serve as my personal staff for the duration of my stay, but that you are on loan, if you will, from an associate. Thus, you arrived after me, quite late last night, in fact, and your luggage was delayed in the Emerald City by mistake."

As she took her cup and saucer, Loren gave Kerri a dark look and jerked her chin a fraction toward the stairs. With a minute shake of her head, Kerri returned to the sitting room and deliberately took a seat opposite their host, looking him level in the eyes. *I am in no one's service by my own,* her action said. Casually she recovered her half-eaten bun, and placed it on her saucer.

He seemed only more amused. "Also, you are new in service, which means two things—first, that you have had an experience... well, similar in some respects to what you went through last night, which I can safely say without knowing the details," he added with a hint of a smile at Kerri's look of affronted innocence. "Although

I look forward to hearing them. This means that you are members elect of a very proud caste—next thing to family, so far as Anna Haggarty is concerned. She will be disposed to protect you. I have known her for many years, and I trust her.

"Second, you are clearly not trained yet and therefore it will seem perfectly right and natural that you will not appear outside these rooms except on such errands as I send you, and those only to service areas. Although the staff will be aware that you are here, they will leave you alone until you are officially introduced in the employees' dining room, which will not be until I am satisfied you will not disgrace me. Or," he added with a grin, "that is the way it would be if you truly the Misses Homes and Watson, newly arrived to my service."

Kerri raised an eyebrow and sipped her coffee, every gesture coldly formal. Behind her, Loren made no sound. Kerri doubted that Loren could hear everything being said in the sitting room; Kerri would listen for both of them. *The man is an incurable blabbermouth*, she realized. *In love with the sound of his own voice. If I could keep him talking, what how much more could I learn?*

"So," said Domenick. "You are quite safe here, for the time being, as safe as you could be any place." Suddenly, his smile vanished and he sighed. "Which is not very safe at all, I am afraid. I must be plain. Your situation is very dangerous."

"I can be dangerous myself, if necessary," Kerri informed him. There was information here. She could almost smell it.

"I have no doubt of that!" he replied seriously. "But you misunderstand. I was not referring to anyone here being a danger to you. I am talking about the natural, physical consequences of last night's incident. It is a wonder you survived at all."

He sipped his coffee and went on, "From what I heard, you are lucky to be alive and mentally intact. Of course, the drop-off will protect you for awhile. Indeed, I have never encountered such a drastic instance of it. You seem drained beyond anything I have ever encountered—quite blank, in fact. That is probably just as well. It means you still have a little time."

"Perhaps more than you suppose," Kerri commented coolly, trying to look as if she knew exactly what he was talking about. *Drained?* she wondered. *Drained of what?*

"Perhaps." He nodded. "I hope so. Because it would be much more to all our advantage if I could delay stabilizing the two of you until after this morning's business."

"Or refrain altogether," she replied dismissively. *He has lost me*, she thought, her alarm growing. *What is he saying? Stabilize? Does he mean to imprison us somehow? To turn us over to the others? Is he only delaying us here until they come? He did leave the room; he could easily have sent a message. It could be that every word he has said to us is a lie.*

She put her coffee cup down on the table and rose to her feet. "You have been very kind," she said, "but we cannot impose upon you any longer. Thank you for your hospitality."

"No! Wait! Please!" He stood up.

In the porch doorway she turned to look back at him. "Good-bye," she said. Loren was already half a flight down.

"Please hear me out," he called after them. "No one is coming. I have told no one. Please! You need my help. It will kill you next time!"

"I do not think so," said Kerri from the top of the stairs.

"Listen!" He came as far as the sitting room door and extended both hands, pleading. "I swear, Mrs H. is the only person who has even an inkling you are here, and she is safe, I promise. I have known her all my life. She thinks of me as a son. She thinks you are working for me. That is all."

"We are not working for you," Kerri informed him icily. "We are not even pretending to work for you."

"Of course not," he said. "I am trying to help you."

Loren paused and looked up through the dusty gloom. "Are you coming or not?" she asked, low-voiced.

"Just a minute," Kerri whispered. At that moment she heard the piercing moan of a train whistle. "You lied to us!" she accused him. "That is the early train."

"No, it is not. It is the second train coming in. I told you the truth. You are free to go, if that is what you wish—I cannot stop you—but you are only walking to your death or dementia."

"And you can prevent that."

"I can. I can remove the immediate physical danger."

"How?"

"It is a simple process, but it requires a specified amount of time, and Dreamer knows I am late already." He sat on one of the porch cots. It creaked and sagged under him. Out of the corner of her eye, Kerri saw Loren descending silently, one cautious step at a time.

Against her better judgment, she remained on the top step, regarding Domenick, and thinking, suddenly and inexplicably, of her grandmother. *Stay and listen*, Aryel's voice said in her mind. *Learn something!*

I am going to find out at last, she said to herself. Until now, I did not really want to know, but here it is. I am going to find out about Them. Even if I die, I will know.

"What is your recommendation?" she asked neutrally.

"Stay here," he said. "At least until I can get back to these rooms. No one will expect you to be here. No one will come looking. You can get cleaned up, and you can rest. I have to leave for a few hours, but as soon as I can, I will come back and make certain you are stable. After that we can talk about what to do next. I can begin instructing you in the immediate essentials."

Instruction. This had a promising sound. "And what is in it for you?" Kerri asked. She noticed that Loren had crept back up within listening distance.

He laughed faintly as he stood up, wringing another squeal of protest from the cot. "Next to the fun of putting the twist on...certain deserving individuals, nothing else signifies much," he said. "But I do admit I will not disdain the...ah... prestige, this rescue will lend me. And you also, do not doubt it! Eventually, anyway. For the present you are in for a difficult time, whatever you do—I will not lie to you about that. That is why you had better rest and recruit your strength. But it will be well worth it in the long run, I assure you."

Why, Kerri wondered, *do we have this idiot cultural taboo against showing ignorance? If I were not so well brought up and so well trained, I would simply ask him what the hell he is talking about.* And at the same time, in another part of her mind, where the Game still laid out patterns and rules and far-fetched logics, every word he spoke was beginning to make a terrifying kind of sense.

"Think about it," he said. "I can say no more. I must go and change. I am late. Just one thing. Do not get separated. Whatever you choose to do, you must stay together. A hundred meters apart at the most, especially while you remain in Twilight Country. It is the only hope you have. Now, I pray you will excuse me." He turned and went into the sitting room and beyond to the bedroom. Kerri could hear him moving about, opening and closing drawers and cupboards.

She looked down at Loren's drawn face. "Wait," she pleaded softly. "Play along. Just for a little while. I think something very big is going on here, and I must find out as much as I can."

Some ten minutes later Domenick emerged from the bedchamber wearing a long robe of maroon wool with gold piping and silk facings of a deeper maroon. Over this he wore a hooded stole of silk in a blue and black chevron pattern. He carried a soft four-cornered cap of maroon velvet. It was the very exact kind of costume a junior member of the Faculty or an upper level graduate student would wear during morning hours to an official ceremony, to some occasion of mild festivity and moderate importance—a Convocation, for instance. To someone of Kerri's upbringing, It spoke eloquently of his position in the world and his plans for the next few hours.

She had returned to the sitting room and resumed her chair by the breakfast table, where she was slowly sipping her second cup of coffee. Loren remained on the fire escape, although she was no longer poised for instant flight but perched on the top step nursing her own coffee cup. When Domenick entered the room, Kerri put her cup down and rose to her feet.

"We have decided to stay for the time being," she told him.

He nodded, pleased. "I am relieved to hear you say so." He crossed the room and stood with his back to the fireplace, from where he could easily see Loren on the porch.

"You see," he explained to Kerri, "your being here puts me in rather a delicate position. I can tell you have not been stabilized—that is my particular talent—but I do not know how much you know. Given your good condition and...various comments you have made, it is apparent that someone has told you...things.

"According to the Society of Guenevere, none of them got a chance to touch you or talk to you. Considering the circumstances, I suspect they are not telling the whole truth. Obviously, the more they can do to salvage the situation themselves, the better it will be for them and those linked to them. Or perhaps someone spoke to you earlier—a family member, possibly. It would not be the first time the rules have been bent or broken in such a way. *I* prefer to follow them as close to the letter as I can, which means I must be extremely careful what I say to you at this stage."

"And," Kerri drawled, "you intend to help them...ah, salvage the situation?" Inside, she felt stunned. Right in front of her all along!

He gave a short, sharp laugh. "Me? Not in the least. I—and any number of others— will be only too glad to see those who have been...shortsighted reap the consequences of their shortsightedness. That is why I am delighted to help you, myself." He turned to the mirror over the fireplace and positioned his cap carefully on his head.

"Of course," he added, "it would be far more interesting, and, I do admit, far better for you in some ways, if you could find an outside third. There has not been a stable independent cell in three generations. It would be worth sacrificing the link just to watch what it would do to the Alliance. If there were any way I thought you could find someone in time, I would happily sit back and watch the fun. But I do not think you have enough time to go back to the City, and there is no one here."

Satisfied with the angle of his cap, he began to gather up the scattered books and stuff them into the valise.

"Can I give you any assistance?" Kerri asked.

"No, no! Not with these. I would rather you not handle this little private library of mine. If you require something to read, there are some novels on the shelf by the fireplace and a few periodicals on the other table. I am sorry I cannot offer you more to pass the time, but I suspect you will be wanting sleep most of all. I shall tell them to bring sheets for the cots when I order your lunch. You can find blankets in the chest beside the door." He spoke that last words as he took the books into the bedroom, out of sight. There was a sound of a door opening, thumps, the sound of a door closing.

"Thank you," said Kerri, trying unsuccessfully to crane her neck far enough to see into the bedroom. "For your help. You...have been very kind."

"It is my pleasure." He emerged from the bedroom smiling. He had, Kerri noticed again, an extremely attractive smile. "Please make yourselves at home. Now I must leave you. Until after lunch. I shall not lock the door, but I recommend you bolt it and open it to no one but Mrs. H. or me."

"Yes," said Kerri.

With another smile, he was gone. She took a deep breath and sat down again. Had she done the wise and prudent thing, she wondered, or simply placed herself and Loren in a worse scrape than the one they were already in? And if the two of them did not stay and face whatever had to be faced, what would they do? Where could they go?

Maybe it would be best to run away after all. Or not to run, but deliberately to turn her back on a world that despised her. There were other worlds. The world of the Sea People had always been open to her. At any time, without notice, she could walk into any of their communities and be welcomed as a sister, as a person of a respected lineage, as a full equal. Tears of grief and self-pity dripped slowly down her cheeks as she thought of Timo, of the unjudging warmth he and his people, her grandmother's people, had always given her.

And then there was Nicholas. Her heart ached when she thought of him.

"Here," said Loren's voice, from behind her. A handkerchief appeared over her right shoulder.

"I've got one," she protested, beginning to hunt through her pockets.

"No problem. It's his, anyway. Well, maybe it's not his. I found it in a drawer on the porch. Take it!"

The handkerchief, a pastel plaid cotton square of a type no gentleman would willingly buy for himself, looked clean and ironed and smelled of dust. Kerri took it and used it gratefully.

"Did you hear any of that?" she asked.

"Enough." Loren sat down in the chair opposite. She looked much less frightened than she had before Domenick's departure, but no less determined. "So, the Society of Guenevere is your husband's study group. Mystery solved. I had no idea study groups gave themselves names."

"Nor did I," Kerri admitted. She shook her head slowly. "But then, obviously, they are not simply just a study group. We do not have the whole story yet by any means."

"Do you still think there is anything to be gained by hanging about?" Loren asked. "I mean, if we can't leave this room—and I'm more than willing to take him at his word about that—what can we do?"

"Look very carefully at everything he brought with him, for one thing," said Kerri. "Those books, for instance. He went to a bit of trouble to put them out of sight, and he seemed quite anxious that we not touch what he called his 'private library,' which arouses my curiosity for reasons I can explain, if you like.

"And another thing! From everything he said and from what he was wearing, I believe there is some kind of formal event this morning, some kind of Convocation. Something They all have to attend. He told us to stay here, but I have no intention of obeying him in that, either. After Anna comes back with the uniforms, I intend to dress up like a maid and get out and take a look around to see what I can see."

"Didn't he say we should stick together?"

"He did. If we can believe anything he said. I assumed he meant we should both stay here at the Lodge or both go. Anyway, I am sure it will do no harm to go just a little way further into the building. While I am gone you could search the suite, find out what you can. Or you can go and I can stay, if you would prefer. Let us give it a try, and then, whatever happens, we shall clear out and make our way back to the cabin or back to the City, unless we find a really good reason not to go."

Loren considered this. "We'll never catch that train that just came in," she pointed out. "When is the next one?"

"Early afternoon, I think," Kerri said.

Loren glanced at the clean white towels piled on the sofa. "I certainly wouldn't mind a bath."

"Nor would I! We can stand guard for each other, and the door is bolted. Oh, damn! No, it's not. I forgot."

And, as if on cue, there was a knock. They only had time to exchange startled glances before the door opened and Mrs. Haggarty put her head in.

"Why, you lazy things!" she exclaimed. "You've too much to do to be lolling about there. And you've no excuse now I've brought you something proper to wear. Get up and look lively, now. There's the beds to make up and this mess to clear. And we need to have a little talk, you and I."

Chapter 55

Alliance

At Mrs. Haggarty's direction, they made up two of the cots on the porch and cleaned the bath while she set Domenick's bedchamber to rights. Then she herded them into the sitting room, where she made them stand while she proceeded with her "little talk," which began with a thorough catalogue of rules and procedures for Lodge staff. During the whole lecture she bustled about tidying and dusting the room, discovering under a chair several books Domenick had overlooked. She gathered them up unceremoniously and set them down on an empty bookshelf, thumping them into place briskly and without respect.

Catching sight of Kerri's scandalized expression, she said, "Oh, I know he'll fuss. He always does, but he knows I won't let things be left strewn about like this in any of my rooms. They're all blank, anyway, every one, first page to last, so what he carries them about with him for, I can't imagine. To impress the others, I suppose, like them robes and costumes they all wear. Now if he tells you to leave 'em be, you'd best do as he says. Your position's not the same. But he knows me.

"Of course," she added, "I can see you're not in domestic service as a regular position in life. You've got that refined way of speaking. City girls! You'll just be doing this as part of your connection to the Alliance, as the occasion demands. Well, you're not alone. There are plenty like you, especially on these retreats when they have to send most of the regular staff away and bring in their own people. You'll make lots of friends, I dare say. Just remember you're not here on holiday.

"Don't expect the staff here to be waiting on you and treating you like guests. When you're here to work, you're just like us, so don't put on any airs, or you won't be back, and you'll be getting a bad name with Them, which you don't want, I guarantee!"

"May I ask a question?" Kerri dared to interrupt.

Mrs. Haggarty fixed her with narrowed eyes, but she did pause and listen.

"You said there were others like us. Are they Academics?"

The woman laughed. "La! No, child! Academics, indeed! If they was Academics they'd be in the Alliance proper, now, wouldn't they? Put your mind at ease! They're mostly City People like you. Maybe even some you already know. You'd be surprised."

"Yes," said Kerri, nodding. "I see."

"And then," Mrs Haggarty went on, "there are a good few country folk like me. But we all follow the same rules and treat each other equal, and we all get protected the same. Why, I haven't ever had another attack since the first one, and though it's been thirty-four years, I'll never forget that day if I live to be a hundred, nor ever take the risk of going through that again!"

She paused again and regarded them this time with some sympathy. "I gather the two of you are still recovering, yourselves. Nick told me it happened only lately."

"Not long ago," Loren agreed.

Mrs. Haggarty nodded. "Ah, well. You will feel yourselves again soon, and as I said, if you do right, you'll never have to go through it again. Your patrons will see to it, as long as you keep your side of the agreement. It's no burden at all, and you'll find yourselves very well paid into the bargain. The rules are simple. Keep your mouth shut about Alliance business, and help out when called upon. And when you're here, you abide by staff policies and do your job just like the rest of the staff. Is that clear?"

Kerri murmured, "Yes, ma'am." Loren echoed her. The housekeeper seemed satisfied. Straightening one last chair, she said, "Well, now! I've other rooms to do, and the guests should all be out of them by now. But before I leave you I'd better take you down the corridor a bit and show you the bathroom you can use and a few other things. Get those uniforms on quickly, and meet me in my little pantry. It's about four rooms along. You can't miss it. Quick, now. I haven't got all day. Did he give you a key? No? I shall get you one from the Head Housekeeper. Bring the tray when you come." Then she was out the door and gone.

"So we're not even allowed to use the suite bathroom," Loren grumbled. They had retreated to the sleeping porch, where Loren had taken up her watching post again after wrapping the remaining buns, putting them into her anorak pocket, and dividing the remaining coffee between their two cups.

"Very shabby," Kerri agreed as she pulled the maid's dress over her head. "I intend to use it anyhow."

"So do I. What in the world is this Alliance? He spoke of it, too."

"I'll see what I can find out," said Kerri. She swallowed the rest of her coffee, now barely warm, and smoothed the front of the dress. "Goes well with my boots, doesn't it?" she commented.

Mrs. Haggarty's pantry was indeed easy to find, for the door was open and the housekeeper was there loading soiled crockery onto a cart. "Here you are," she said. "Or one of you. Where's your friend?"

"She is feeling very poorly," Kerri lied placatingly. "Not recovered yet, I suppose. I made her lie down. I can show her later."

Mrs. Haggarty shrugged. "Very well. Take care of those breakfast things first, and then come with me."

A moment later they were making their way along the bends and turns of the third floor annex corridor toward the central section of the Lodge. Mrs. Haggarty pointed out the nearest service stair and the two small windowless bathrooms reserved for staff use, one for women, one for men. "Always leave them cleaner than you found them," she said. "Remember, the blue doors are staff doors, white doors are guest doors. And here's another pantry and the main service bay for this floor. Service elevator there. Don't use it unless you have a cart with you. It's for heavy loads, not to save your feet. Take the stairs, in general."

Kerri acknowledged everything with respectful nods and murmurs, seeing no reason to dispel her mentor's impression that she had never set foot in the Lodge before. But when they came to a pair of heavy fire doors that marked the boundary between the annex and the Lodge proper, she balked. "I do not think I should go any farther," she said. "I do not want to be seen."

"Oh, no worries!" Mrs. Haggarty exclaimed. "They've all gone downstairs by now for the procession. Don't you want to have a look at them? It's a sight! Just come have a peek, and then you can go back. I can't take but a minute myself. I've got my rooms to do."

Kerri followed her through the fire doors into the much wider and more lavishly appointed hallway beyond. As promised, there was no one in sight. Nevertheless, she was relieved when Mrs. Haggarty turned aside to pass through one of the blue doors. Beyond it, a narrow uncarpeted side corridor led to a little tangle of pantries, washrooms, and closets at the head of another service stairway. At the very end there was a small room fitted out as a kind of lounge or sitting room, and here, to Kerri's discomfort, were gathered at least a dozen uniformed women and men clustered at the one large window. They all turned to stare as Mrs. Haggarty led her in.

"This is Miss Watson," Mrs. Haggarty announced. "She's come to do for one of my gentlemen in the Annex while he's here. She's a City girl and new to service. Watson, this is Miss Martin and Mr. Haines and Mr. Charles and Mrs. Lamb...." She continued rattling off names which Kerri would never bother to remember, while Kerri nodded shyly at each and smiled as she thought a City girl, new to service, might nod and smile. They seemed friendly enough, but clearly they were more interested in what they had been looking at outside.

Politely they made room for Mrs. Haggarty and Kerri at the window.

"You're just in time," one of them said. "The procession's about to begin."

Kerri found herself looking down on the wide flagstone terrace at the back of the Lodge. It was crowded with figures wearing ceremonial robes and hats in rich, dark Academic colors—burgundy, navy blue, forest green, and more black than anything else. Jewel tones of hoods and facings added accents of brightness—sapphire, scarlet, white, emerald green, every color of the rainbow, and glints of gold and silver. She recognized no one, but at this angle she must not expect to unless one of them happened to look up. She could hear the murmur of voices.

"It looks like a Convocation," she said without thinking.

The woman next to her replied, "Oh, aye! It is. They're off to the amphitheater in the forest. See? There's the Silver Rose Society. They're on my floor. And the Eagle Clan with a new banner, looks like."

"The Brotherhood of the Blue Book," one of the men pointed out. "They're the ones with those funny peaked blue hats. The Glory Tigers are right next to them."

"Look!" said someone. "Here we go!"

A double line of dignitaries—dozens, perhaps more than a hundred men and women —approached along the terrace. These had more gold and silver trim to their robes than the general crowd, and most of them carried wands of office or tall decorated staffs. Some carried banners furled and tied around their poles. The crowd opened up for them and fell in behind them four or five abreast as they turned and processed down the wide steps to the lawns.

"Are those the Alliance?" Kerri dared to ask Mrs. Haggarty in a low voice.

"Who? Do you mean the ones in front? Silly child, those are just the Council and the other important ones. Everybody down there is Alliance, and not the whole thing, by any means."

Kerri thought she recognized Arzelle in black, scarlet, and gold, her dark hair swinging beneath a red plumed cap, a gold staff in her hand. Not at the head of the procession but near the front: she was, apparently, important here. It was no surprise. Kerri looked for Val near her, but she could not pick him out. Perhaps he was less important. She spotted someone in maroon who might be Domenick.

The servants watched in silence from their high window as the terrace emptied and the procession made its way across the wide lawn and into the trees.

"Well, what did you think of that?" the woman next to Kerri asked.

"Most impressive," Kerri granted.

"Wait until tonight!" the woman said. "You haven't seen anything yet!"

"Enough," Mrs. Haggarty called out, catching Kerri by the sleeve. "There's work waiting. We're off."

"Later then, Miz H!" several of them said. "Ta, Watson! You'll be welcome here."

"Thank you. It was lovely meeting you all," said Kerri. "What happens tonight?" she asked when they were back out in the main corridor.

"Saturday night's their big do," Mrs Haggarty replied. "It's like a ball, but not quite. He will explain."

As they passed back through the fire doors, she took hold of her courage with both hands and asked, "Mrs. Haggarty, do you know anything about the Society of Guenevere?"

"La, yes! Who doesn't? One of the stronger societies in the Alliance, for all they're on the younger side. Well connected to the Council, I hear. Nick mentioned them, did he? No wonder. Everybody's talking about them this morning."

Kerri could not help starting when she heard the name, even as she remembered, no, only Domenick, not Nicholas. "He did not say much," she admitted. "Only that something happened last night. Do you know what it was?"

"You'll have to ask him, if he'll tell you, and most likely he won't, as it's no business of yours or mine. Late last night it was, and something big, I heard. Some kind of accident, with people injured, although I gather all the members were able to be on their feet for the Procession. There's a rumor that a couple of outsiders got killed, a pair of tramps, but I don't give it any credit. Tramps won't cross the Boundary, especially not at times like this."

"So the Society of Guenevere is part of the Alliance," Kerri ventured.

"Aye, a small part. One of many. There must be, oh, thirty or forty societies and brotherhoods and sodalities and what-all here this weekend, and that's not the whole of it, not at all. Just the Yendys bunch, or the parts that are in favor, plus a few from Emerald City and points farther away. But it's your patron you should be asking, not me. Here we are. I hope Holmes feels better. Your lunch tray will be in my pantry in about two hours for you to fetch."

"Thank you, Mrs. Haggarty," said Kerri with genuine gratitude. She knew when not to put pressure on a source. The housekeeper might be useful and informative again in the future, if she was treated carefully.

She let herself into Domenick's suite and bolted the door behind her. Loren was seated at the writing desk, bent over a book. She looked up at Kerri with a puzzled frown.

"They're not blank at all," she said. "His books."

Chapter 56

Private Library

"They're not?" Kerri stopped fumbling at the buttons on the uniform and went to look over Loren's shoulder. While she was gone, Loren had closed the door to the sleeping porch and built up the fire in the fireplace. The sitting room was already much more comfortable.

"No," Loren replied. "There is some kind of writing in them, but it is very hard to make out. As if the letters are moving about somehow. I can't seem to focus on them properly. I can make out a few words when I look just a bit to the side, but it's giving me quite a headache."

"Let me see," said Kerri. She took the book from Loren's hand and walked to the west window where the morning light was as bright as it would ever be in Twilight Country. She opened the book to a random page.

It was true. The book was not blank. There were letters, words, paragraphs on the page. She could see the forms, but they seemed to swim and waver as she tried to look at them. Any spot she managed to focus on clearly was blank—the spaces between lines, between words, the indentations of paragraphs. Yet, when she did concentrate on the white spaces of the page or let her gaze relax entirely, she could make out scattered words. The book seemed to be beautifully calligraphed by hand, with ornamental capitals and flourishes and a fine attention to proportion and design of the page.

She remembered the envelope on Nick's desk: blank except when she did not look directly at it. The Society of Guenevere. Dizzy and faintly nauseated, she closed the book and rubbed her eyes as the dominoes fell and fell and fell.

"Do you see it?" Loren asked.

Kerri nodded.

"They're all like that," said Loren. "I looked at the these two first. Then I picked the lock of the armoire and got at the rest of them. And do not be alarmed! I shall put them back exactly as I found them. Steady! You'll feel better in a moment. If you try again, sit down first."

"I will," said Kerri. "I am all right." She returned the book to Loren and sat down on the sofa. "I have seen this kind of thing before," she said. "I thought it was an hallucination. I thought I was going crazy. Maybe I am. Maybe we both are."

"Or maybe not," Loren replied. "Where did you see it before? When? What did you see?"

"The Society of Guenevere. That's how it all started. That day in April when Nick and I got our invitation to the May Eve Ball. The day I met you, in fact."

"It was written on the invitation?"

"No. On the envelope of another letter Nick received that day, on the flap where the sender's name and address should have been. He was so...furtive about the letter when it came. Spiriting it away to his desk, not opening it in front of me. It made me suspicious at the time, although I never suspected anything like this...! But then he just left it lying there among his other papers, and that is where I saw it. I saw the words for only a flash, less than a second. He was angry with me for looking on his desk, but he pretended it was about something that had happened at the University. It wasn't, though; it was about this."

"And that is where you got the Society of Guenevere?"

"Yes. I swear I never heard of it before that day."

"And all that blathering about Arthurian poetry...?

"Sheer invention and lies."

"Whew!" Loren uttered a low whistle. "You! You had me convinced I should be remembering it from the Syllabus. You put on a good act there." She chuckled. "Well, now we know better. Did you find out anything more when you went on your little reconnaissance?"

"Some. Not enough." Kerri took a deep breath. "I saw the Alliance."

"So who is this Alliance?"

"Them. Everybody here. That is who They are. That is what They call themselves. The Alliance. They were all gathered behind the Lodge on the Terrace, decked out in their best Convocation robes. Mrs. Haggarty took me to a place where the servants were watching Them from an upper window. Hundreds of Them, Loren."

"What were they doing?"

"Getting ready to have a procession."

Loren shook her head. "It sounds awfully formal and official for a retreat, even a working retreat. But who? Students? Faculty?"

"Yes. No. Both." Kerri frowned. "It cannot be any official University function in the usual sense—that's a line of thought I really do not want to follow right now—but it was archtypically Academic. And, according to Mrs. Haggarty, this Alliance only allows Academics. If you're a Cit or a Peasant, you only get to be 'in service.'" She grimaced. "A few months ago I would not have blinked at that. Before the Gang of Four."

Loren raised a meaningful eyebrow. "And the Society of Guenevere?"

"I am getting to that. This morning we learned, courtesy of Domenick, that the old S.O.G. is, in fact, Nick's study group. But after last night I do wonder whether it is only a study group, or whether the study group identity is a...a mask for something else. The Alliance seems to be some kind of... collection of smaller groups, and the Society of Guenevere is one of those groups. They're not only students. Many of the people I saw looked too old. And these groups all have pretentious names—oh, like the Silver Rose Society, for instance—and banners and robes and colors and whatnot. Whether they are all taking themselves much too seriously or simply having fun playing elaborate, pompous games, I cannot tell you, but it is all supposed to be huge secret. Mrs. Haggarty tells me we 'in service' people are supposed to keep our mouths shut and do as we are told. Or else we'll have another...um, attack."

"An attack? An attack of what?"

Kerri shrugged. "She did not say. But I suppose we know."

Loren stared at her for several long seconds. Then suddenly, unexpectedly, she began to laugh. "So in we stumble and make them look all anyhow," she gasped.

"It is not funny!" Kerri protested ineffectively, as the absurdity of the situation reduced her to giggles also. When she could speak, she continued, "There is more. Because of us, the S.O.G. are now entirely notorious. The story Mrs. H gave me is that there was some kind of horrendous accident, and two tramps were killed or injured...."

"Tramps!"

"That is what she said. And there are other injuries alleged, although apparently not serious. If anybody had really been hurt, I'm certain Domenick would not have behaved toward us as he did. If They were shaken up a bit, it serves Them right, in my opinion. I think the whole uproar and the S.O.G. being in hot water with the rest of them is over our merely being there last night and what we did."

"And what did we do?" Loren cried out, abruptly serious again. "What did we do? I remember it, but I don't understand what I am remembering. It makes no sense. It has no meaning, except I was afraid, and I was angry, and...it was like a rage, a storm, like every fit of bad temper I ever had in my life rolled together in one gigantic flash."

"That is exactly what I felt," Kerri said. "Except I felt as if I pulled in even more of that energy from outside of myself, as if I were a tall tree in a thunderstorm, just asking to be struck by lightning."

"A pair of trees," Loren added. "A pair of lightning rods. And generating a little electricity of our own. They did not expect it."

"Whatever it was," said Kerri, "it was something Domenick recognized, for all he only knew of what happened to us by hearsay. He is familiar with such events.

By implication it must be something They all recognize. Something They know, something we are not supposed to know about or to do."

"Well, we did it." Loren got up and began to pace back and forth across the hearthrug.

"We did it big. An attack, indeed!"

"We did," Kerri agreed. "That is why they followed us. That is why they did not want to let us simply go away, why they need to find us now. Domenick implied there is some kind of aftereffect of the incident that will do us serious harm eventually, but I wonder if he is lying. Maybe we are the danger, and they need to stop us somehow."

Loren stopped pacing and frowned thoughtfully. "That idea did suggest itself to me when he was dropping all his pregnant little hints. What is this stabilization? A lobotomy or something?"

Kerri said, "I don't like the sound of it either. He said something about 'an outside third,' as if he was suggesting an alternative. My impression was that he meant a third person, somebody without any connection to all of this."

"Third in relation to what?" Loren wondered. "To us? To him and some other party he had in mind? To perform this stabilization, do you think? But he could not have meant someone entirely outside this Alliance. How would they know what to do?"

"I do not know," Kerri replied. "Perhaps I should go back out and look for more clues."

"No!" Loren protested. "We have to go," she said intensely. "I have to leave this place. Truly. I need to get out of here. If you must stay, stay, but I am going."

"Because of him?" Kerri grinned at her. "Relax. He won't be back for a while. They all went off in procession to some amphitheater in the forest. They'll be gone for hours. And you cannot still be afraid of the gentleman. After the way he helped us, fed us, hid us from the rest of Them? I think he's rather intriguing. Not to mention good looking."

Loren snorted. "He may be partly rehabilitated, but I still do not trust him. I'm sure he is serving his own interests and no one else's."

"Are you still quite certain he is your Dark Watcher?"

Loren closed her eyes and rubbed her temples. After a moment she answered, "Yes. Yes, I am. He recognized me, you see. He knew me. Instantly. There was a...connection. Later on I made myself really look at him, watch him, when you were talking and I was out on the porch with my back to the daylight—clever of me, don't you think?—and there is no doubt in my mind it is him. Older, of course. It has been...several years. Also, the name is right."

"Domenick? I thought you said you did not know the Watchers' names?"

"Not officially, not for certain, but once I overheard someone calling out to him, and the name was Domenick or Damian. Something like that." She returned to the writing desk and brushed her fingertips gently across the leather binding of the book she had been examining. "It's funny, though," she added gazing down at the book. "Here I am, and here he is, and nothing horrible has happened. The sky may have fallen, but not by his agency."

"Maybe he offered to help us on your account," Kerri suggested provokingly. "Perhaps you have been mistaken about him all these years. I wonder if his interest in you wasn't always of a less menacing nature than you thought."

Loren shot her a scornful look and gave a last dismissive tap to the book. "I know what you are suggesting," she said impatiently. "It is nothing of the kind. Now or then. Back in Dalton, of course, it would not have entered my mind because of the caste difference. It should not have entered his. He should never have even noticed my existence in the first place. But he did. Goodness knows why." She sighed. "All of that old Watcher business seems completely dead and irrelevant now. In fact," she added with some surprise, "if the only issue was facing him, I would stay, and gladly. Get it over with. Un-demonize him. Break the spell. Establish that he has no power over me.

"But it's not him. It is this place. It feels...I don't know how to describe it. Wrong. Dangerous. Like a sound I can almost hear...a buzzing...in my mind. As if the walls are filled with angry hornets. Any minute they'll find an opening and come pouring out. It seems hard to breathe." As if to underline this, she took a deep breath. "And everything you told me about what you discovered makes me feel the danger more."

Kerri yawned and stretched. "The buzzing feeling—I know what you mean, although I suspect it has something to do with too much coffee and not enough sleep. But there are hundreds of Them and only two of us. I dislike those odds. Also, he told us to stay put, and I find myself strongly disinclined to do as I am told. You're right," she said. "We'll go."

She stood and gathered up the clothing she had discarded earlier. "I hoped I'd get a bath before I got back into these. Do you think you could stand it long enough for me to get cleaned up a little? Don't you want a wash yourself? We'll both feel better for it. And I would like to have another quick look at those books."

"Suit yourself," said Loren. "But you're wasting your time with the books. You'll see." She seized a pair of towels and disappeared into Domenick's bedchamber, headed for the bathroom beyond.

And she was right. Kerri did see. She put her parka on over the maid's dress, still half unbuttoned, and took a random armload of books out to the marginally better light of the sleeping porch. She sat for her study in a venerable wicker armchair cushioned with a folded blanket, trying to keep her exhausted mind on the task of focusing her eyes on the pages.

She could tell that the books were of diverse ages and qualities, written in several different hands. She could make out a word or phrase here and there, but not enough to form a sense of the content of any volume, except one, which seemed to be a cookbook. The fifth book she opened was a real beauty, with its soft buttery cover of purple leather and thick, creamy pages—as much a delight to the hands as it was a frustration to the eyes. She flipped through it without truly looking at it, and suddenly a whole page became clear for an instant. She read, "...were chartered in the year 34 with a core of six initiates from the College of Architecture at Yendys and master links to..."

Startled, she looked again at the sentence, only to see the letters begin to swim and fade before her gaze. Too weary to be frustrated, she closed her eyes and thought about how good it would feel to sleep for awhile. The chair was not uncomfortable. With an effort she opened her eyes again and read, "...and master links to the Brotherhood of the Wren and the Fractal Society. Secondary links were formed to...." One line she was able to read, and then she lost focus again.

Not the books, she began to realize. Our eyes. Something to do with our eyes. As if there is something about the writing that forces us to not quite look at it. Almost as if it were Veiled somehow, with the Veil beginning to wear off.

She remembered her own personal Veil and realized it, also, had begun to wear off.

In fact, it was gone. She had last renewed it, for both herself and Loren—when was it? About the time Domenick departed for the procession. That was long enough. She would not renew it just yet, she decided. She would wait until they were ready to leave the lodge.

She thought of the hundreds of blank books scattered throughout the libraries of the University. Place holders. That is what she had always been told they were. Reserving space for books that were forthcoming. If I looked at those books now, she wondered, would the pages still be blank?

Loren opened the door from the sitting room and put her head out into the porch. Her curls had been brushed and tamed under a bandanna, and she looked visibly cleaner and happier. "Well?" she inquired.

"There's a sort of knack," Kerri told her. "I'm beginning to get the hang of it. With enough practice, I think I could read this stuff, although everything I've made out so far is dismally dull."

"Oh?"

"This one seems to be a sort of chronicle or journal about Alliance groups. Something about 'links.' The calligraphy is well done, very clear. When you can see it."

"I don't want to see it," said Loren. "I want to go."

"Yes." Kerri closed the book and got to her feet. "If you will kindly put these books back where you got them, I'll clean myself up a bit, and we'll be off."

Chapter 57

Walkabout

The time must have been nearing midday when they crept to the bottom of the fire escape and slipped out into the twilit overgrown garden. The sky looked no different than it had at dawn: a glowing, even periwinkle scattered with wisps of windblown cirrus, glowing brilliant white in the sunless daylight. Away from the encircling hills and forest, the horizon would show a band of bright silver, a reflection of sunlight outside the boundaries of Twilight Country, but here by the lake the illusion of twilight was unbroken. Only the natural rhythms of the body, the smells and sounds of the forest gave any clue to the time of day.

They crossed the few hundred meters to the wagon gate at a dead run, expecting all the while some kind of outcry, Mrs. Haggarty's shrill voice, at least, summoning them back or calling down the chase. But only the mourning doves called, and a distant crow, not even a kookaburra. Bursting through the gate, they plunged down into the shallow ditch that ran alongside the dirt track and waited for a tense moment. No footsteps followed, nor wagon wheels on the gravel. Back, then, onto the track they ran, slowing only when the trees thinned, and the lesser establishments of the village—the shops, restaurants, and minor lodging houses—began to come into view. There they left the track, vaulting over the low fence to the west and setting out across country, circling around behind the little railway station. From that side they could make their way along the edge of the woods, hidden from the town by the grade of the railbed.

Kerri's plan was to cross the tracks again as soon as they were out of sight of the village and go back toward the lake, following the shore as closely as possible. This meant taking the dirt road that served the estates along the western side of the lake, the shore itself being closed to the public right of way. The railroad pulled away at such an angle that the track was only intermittently visible from any train, and there were plenty of places to take cover should anyone pursue them by the road itself. Eventually, they would come to one of the whistle stop platforms that served the western shore. At that point they must decide: Would they continue on around the lake to return to the cabin, or would they signal the next train to stop for them and carry them back to the Emerald City?

And what purpose would be served by either alternative? If the Alliance had as much interest in them as Domenick implied, then surely there would be someone left watching the cabin and its approaches. Equally certain, there would soon be no safe refuge in the City, not even Evesham, especially not Evesham. Nor on the Islands. The thought of losing all her homes, losing, indeed, all the life she had ever known, filled Kerri with misery and despair.

What was left? Get through to the Sea People somehow and beg for shelter? She could do that. She did not know if the Sea People would receive Loren, but Loren had her own resources—the Road People. For that matter, the Road People would probably take both of them in. This thought gave Kerri no comfort. She did not want to spend her life in the wilderness, living rough and moving with the seasons. She was a city-dweller, a scholar. She had never had the least desire for any other life.

The last alternative was to turn and face Them, to stand before whatever judgement the Alliance passed on those who trespassed upon its secrets. Perhaps there would be mercy; Domenick's kindness almost lured her into believing that, informed as it undoubtedly was by his own self interest. But she could no longer hide from the core of her fear. She knew in her heart what the punishment would be. *Will I know I am demented?* she wondered bleakly. *Will I be unaware of everything, or will my mind be blank like Domenick's books, chasing little wisps of consciousness around my brain?*

Deep in this black despair, she had no warning when Loren grabbed her by the collar and hauled her into the nearest turnout, the driveway into one of the west shore estates, gated with a fine brick arch and filigreed wrought iron.

"Climb!" Loren hissed at her. "Horses coming!" She was already halfway over the gate herself, and Kerri, moving more quickly than she would ever have thought she could after a sleepless night on the run, was right behind her. On the other side they shoved through the dense line of columnar junipers that lined the drive, pressed themselves behind the masonry of the gate support and held their breaths. For good measure, Kerri laid her hand on Loren's sleeve and invoked the Veil.

She could hear the hoofbeats now, pounding rhythmically, coming from the direction of the Lodge, now slowing as they approached the gate. Someone spoke in the lane, but she could hear only the voice, no clear words. *Did we leave footprints?* she wondered, remembering the hard-graded surface of the track. Another voice answered in low tones, as the horses, two of them, clopped past. They slowed but did not stop and soon picked up a trot again, fading into the distance.

"So much for our head start," muttered Loren. "They've finished whatever they were doing, and now it's time to hunt. I hope they had to miss lunch," she added in an ill temper.

"They may not have been looking for us," Kerri answered hopefully. "They may have simply been some Stockholders out for a ride."

"You did your Veil thing again, didn't you?" said Loren.

"Yes."

"I thought I felt it. If you hadn't, we might have been able to tell it was Them."

"And They would have been able to tell it was us!" retorted Kerri.

"So now what do we do?" asked Loren. "You know this bit of country better than I do."

"Keep your voice down! We have two choices. We can go back out and make for the country on the other side of the railroad, try to move along that way to the next stop."

"But if they've already passed us by the road, they may be waiting at the platform," Loren protested, "Or they may have warned someone, told some kind of lie about us so we'll get detained. What's the other choice?"

"Cut across this property to the lake and follow the water for awhile. The houses are far apart and few of them are likely to be occupied this particular weekend. There's plenty of cover, lots of places to hide and spy out the land. With luck we won't be spotted, and even the Alliance would not dare trample over Stockholder territory looking for two lost lambs. I hope! We might even borrow a boat and take off straight over the water."

"Sure," responded Loren. "Might as well be hung for a sheep as a lamb! Let's do it." They emerged from their hiding place and crossed the pebbled driveway, plunging through a matching row of junipers into a deceptively wild-looking rhododendron wood through which they could catch glimpses of a great house, redbrick and half-timbered gables. No smoke rose from any of the half dozen chimneys; the house appeared to be unoccupied.

The two women skirted its vast green lawn and climbed the fence to the next property without incident. Here they dodged around a cluster of outbuildings and greenhouses and found themselves in a beautifully laid out formal garden. The beds were covered over and tidied down for winter, but a few late roses still bloomed along the sheltering wall. On the other side of a hedge, a voice was raised in song of a loud and tuneless sort over the regular scraping of a rake.

Kerri gestured right, toward the lake, and Loren nodded. They tiptoed back in behind the nearest greenhouse and set their course downslope toward the water. There were trees between the garden and the water, and Kerri had hopes of a boathouse, perhaps a small canoe that might not be missed for a while. Once she and Loren got to the other end of the lake, they could let the borrowed craft drift. Eventually someone would see that it got back to its owner.

There was indeed a boathouse. It was unlocked and quite empty, but far down the edge of the lake, beyond a patch of rushes and a nice sandy beach, a little dock stood out over the water. At its end bobbed a dinghy, with not a living soul in sight. That was well and good, but in order to reach the dock, they would have to cross the open beach or the lawn above it. There was almost no cover between the lake and the many windows of the manor house that looked down from the rise.

"Now what?" whispered Loren. "We can't assume there's nobody home. We've already heard someone in the garden."

"We could swim," suggested Kerri, at the price of an elbow in the ribs, "or we could just walk brazenly across. What's the chance of someone looking out one of those windows?"

"Yes, and what would they do to us if they caught us?" Loren wondered. "What do Stockholders do to trespassers? I've never heard. Don't you think they might just let us go with a warning?"

"More like lock ye up in the dungeon!" remarked a voice behind them.

Kerri whirled about so quickly she found herself sitting in the mud beside the boathouse, staring at the elderly man on the path. A bald, angular fellow of remarkable height, he leaned on a large, very sharp looking scythe and grinned as he sized up the two young women he had caught trespassing. Loren was frozen in a half-crouch, her hands in front of her as if to fend off attack.

"Now, now," he said mildly. "We don't do any beheadings without a proper trial. Madam wouldn't stand for it."

Loren straightened slowly and lowered her hands. "We didn't mean to trespass," she said, sounding as much the Cit as she ever did. "We got in accidentally. We'll go."

"That would be an interesting accident, it would!" said the man. "Ye'd have to fall out of the sky or come across the water, and I'm thinking ye'd be in much worse shape than ye are, either way."

Kerri picked herself up and dusted off bits of grass and mud. "Truly, we apologize for the intrusion," she said. "We mean no mischief." In spite of his mention of "Madam" she had more than half a suspicion she was addressing the owner of the estate himself, not some mere gardener. Stockholders were keen gardeners themselves, as a rule, and in the country there was not much to tell them apart from Peasants, unless they chose to put on trappings of state. He would indicate somehow if he expected to be addressed in proper form; in the meantime, the best thing to do was to address him as he presented himself and not try to deceive him about her own caste. As for "Madam," she was probably his wife.

She gestured toward the far shore of the lake. "I own a house over there. We are only trying to get back there, and we thought it might be faster if we could follow the shore."

"Ye'd go much faster by the track," he countered, his suspicion visibly increasing. "There's no public right of way here. All this side is private right down to the water, except the boat landings next to the railroad halts."

"That's what we were making for," Loren lied. "It seemed better to keep to the water until then than to cut across someone's property and find no way out. You see, we came from all the way down the end of the lake."

"Aye, you've trespassed a good bit of ground, haven't ye?" He was losing patience.

"Look," said Kerri desperately. "We are trying to escape from someone who is looking for us. They mean us harm. I cannot explain, and I know it is difficult to believe, but it is true."

"They are searching for us on the road," Loren explained. "We could not go that way."

"We have done nothing wrong," Kerri added. "We had the misfortune to make some influential people angry at us, quite by accident. If we can only get away from them, they will lose interest in us, and all will be well. It is all very silly, actually, not worth a tenth the fuss, and we are most embarrassed to be caught like this. Just let us return to the road, and we will take our chances and bother you no more."

"Well," he rubbed his chin. "It might serve ye right if they caught you, these folk ye're running from. I'll let you out the garden gate, but mind, if I catch you in here again, I'll lock you up and send for the magistrate, I will."

"Have you really got a dungeon?" Loren ventured, made bold by relief.

He laughed then. "Sure! Deep and dark as a well. Rats, too! You'll want to stay clear of it. Come along."

He made them go ahead of him up the path, directing them to the side of the formal garden through a hedge-lined passage. Through gaps in the shrubbery Kerri snatched glimpses of the house, a big rambling structure made of some kind of golden stone. There was a wide flagged terrace along the lakeward side, white tables with green umbrellas, white chairs and lounges with green cushions. In the middle of the terrace reposed a swimming pool, a jewel of flawless blue. *What a lovely place*, she thought. *Pity it never sees the sun!* In Twilight Country, sunshades seemed ridiculous, until one remembered the unseen sun could burn here as well as it did in ordinary country.

Noting her lagging, he said, "Move along now!"

They came to the end of the hedge avenue and turned left to follow a pergola hung with brittle vines and the dried shells of wisteria. Suddenly, a figure appeared at the other end of the pergola and stood in the twilight, slowly taking off its garden gloves as it watched them approach. It was a woman, tall, angular, her head tied closely in a kerchief. She wore rough pants and a loose smock and vest, but her upright carriage and the bean-sized ruby winking on one finger left no doubt that this was "Madam," in the flesh. She tucked the gloves under her arm and removed her tinted glasses.

Kerri came to a stop some ten meters from that chill and curious grey-eyed stare. She felt Loren make as if to duck behind her, heard the exasperated sigh of the gardener.

"Well, Lawson," said Greta, beginning to smile. "What *have* you got there?"

Chapter 58

Greta

"My dears, my dears," said Greta, "what are we going to do without him?"

An arm around each of her comrades, she walked them slowly to the house past rows of bare, pruned rosebushes. Kerri and Loren did not reply; there was nothing to be said in answer.

"How on earth did you find me?" Greta continued. "My people never caught up with you. They're still looking."

"You received my letter, then," Kerri stated.

"I did. It was a shock in more ways than one. You kept me guessing right up until that moment—but we can talk about all of that inside over a cup of something hot. And perhaps lunch. Have you eaten? No? I shall take care of that. The important thing is that you got here somehow."

Loren asked anxiously, "What did you mean about *your people* looking for us? Do you mean people at the Lodge?" She remembered then to whom she was talking and blushed deeply. "Your Excellency," she added hesitantly.

"You mean, *the* Lodge, up the end of the lake? Goodness, no. What has the Lodge to do with anything? I haven't been there in months. Hardly ever go up there, as a matter of fact, except to dine now and then. I set my City agents and a friend or two on your trail first thing yesterday morning. At least since May Eve I had some clue where to start, which I wouldn't have had a month ago. And don't you dare, either of you, start getting ceremonial on me! I won't have it. No titles! I'm Greta, your friend, and we're still the Gang of Four, however many of us are left."

"And this is your home?" asked Kerri. "You traveled a long way to the Public Library twice a week!"

Greta shook her head. "No, this is only a weekend cottage. Most of the time I live in a house in a suburb of Yendys. I also have a flat connected to my offices in the central city and several other homes. I come here as often as I can."

They came to the house and entered through a glassed-in, wicker-furnished porch that faced the rose garden. This would be a pleasant place, Kerri reflected, in the summertime—even more so outside of Twilight Country in the real sunshine. She followed the others into a corridor where they hung their coats on pegs. Greta removed her head scarf, and for only the second time—the first time since the

Ball—Kerri saw her hair uncovered, dark brown, nearly black, wavy and thick. She wore it done up in a loose coil on the back of her head, and it made her look abruptly like the Stockholder she was, in spite of the rough corduroys she wore.

As Kerri put her gloves into the pocket of her parka, she felt about to make sure her return ticket was still there. Reassuringly, her fingers found the rectangle of card at once, even as she realized she had chosen the left pocket, the wrong one—she always put her tickets and her keys in a right-hand pocket—and the card was the wrong shape, to broad to be a ticket. She pulled it out from beneath the wad of gloves: a white rectangle pierced by one hole at the center of one of the long sides, torn through to the edge from that hole.

"Name of the Dreamer," she muttered. She remembered now, hiding this and its two fellows in her pocket that night when Nick had come in suddenly, the evening of that first afternoon in Alex's office when the world had not stopped.

Greta and Loren, waiting patiently, looked at her curiously. Hastily, she found the other pocket, confirmed the presence of her return ticket and joined them.

"What is it?" asked Loren.

"A reminder of my sins," Kerri said with a small laugh. "From the card catalogue in the University library."

"You *stole* a card from the card catalogue?"

"I did, but do not fear for the future of the library. This card is blank."

"No," said Loren. "It's not."

Kerri looked at the card, and read plain as day, "The Society of Guenevere." The inscription was hand-lettered, no fine calligraphy but neat and businesslike. Below the title there were some other notations, numbers, dates, initials, all in the same hand. To be sure, the letters did show a regrettable inclination to jump about on the surface and the eye to drift away, but the effect was much less than it had been on the pages of Domenick's books. She handed the card to Loren, who stared at it for a long moment.

"But it is blank," said Greta, looking over her shoulder.

"You do not see anything?" Kerri asked her.

"Nothing."

Loren met Kerri's eyes. "Never mind, then," she said.

"I want to tell her," Kerri decided. She took a deep breath. "It is time we got some allies of our own."

"By all means, tell me," invited Greta, clearly perplexed, "but do come in and sit down by the fire while you do it."

She led them into a small sitting room that looked out toward the terrace and the lake. The furnishings were homey chintz. The walls were hung with

pleasant landscape paintings and, remarkably, a few framed photographs, and a
fire blazed cozily on the hearth. "Make yourselves comfortable," she told them. "I'll
just dash back to the kitchen and tell Mrs. Lawson there will be three for lunch."
Following Kerri's gaze to the bell pull next to the fireplace, she laughed. "Yes, it
works," she said, "but it's no more trouble to go to her than make her come to me.
I'll only be a moment."

Loren sat down heavily on the nearest sofa. "You were right," she gasped. "About
Greta. I can't get over it. I never dreamed.... And the card! From the University
Library? You never said a word. Why didn't you tell me you found the Society of
Guenevere in the library? When did this happen?"

"The card was blank," said Kerri with a shrug. She went to the fire and warmed
her hands. "I had forgotten all about it. I stole three cards from the catalog that
day. I had never done anything like that in my life before. I wonder if the other
two are still in my pocket. I don't remember feeling them just now."

"And what are all these letters and numbers?" Loren, still in possession of the
purloined card.

"I do not know. They were invisible before."

"I wonder if we couldn't decipher a few of them, knowing what we know now,"
Loren suggested.

"*I* wonder about the other blank cards in the catalogue. What would we see
if we looked at them now?"

Loren's eyes widened. "And all those blank books on the library shelves. Name
of the Dreamer!"

And lintels over doorways, said Kerri to herself. *And goodness knows what
else!*

Greta returned just then, bearing a wide and heavily laden tray. "Lunch will be
along directly," she announced. "But tea is ready now. Or coffee if you prefer—I
do, myself, before noon. If 'noon' means anything here. Or sherry, which might
do us all even more good! I hope you haven't plans for the rest of the day, because
I shall burst if I can't get you to answer all my questions, and I have the feeling
they can't all be answered in the time it takes to eat lunch."

She placed the tray on a low table and dusted off her hands. "You can begin,"
she continued, "by telling me how it was that Lawson found you by the boathouse.
He is terribly confused, said you gave him some story about being hunted by
people from the Lodge. Why didn't you tell him you were friends of mine? And
how did you get into the grounds without ringing at the gate? I supposed you had
come across the water, but Lawson says there's no sign of a strange boat." Taking
a seat next to Loren, she began to pour out sherry with quiet efficiency. Nobody
wanted tea or coffee.

Kerri came and sat down facing them. "It is difficult to choose a place to begin," she said. "In the first place, we did not know this was your house. We were not looking for you. We only found you by accident."

Greta frowned. "Then you weren't coming to me about Alex?"

"No," said Loren. "We came from the Lodge. We had to leave the road because we did not want to be seen by anyone. We climbed in over the gate of the house next door. We knew we were trespassing, but it seemed the best thing to do at the time, and we meant no harm. Oh, this sounds very stupid!" She gave up for the moment and sipped her wine.

"Maybe it would be best to back up a bit," said Kerri quickly, "beginning from when we found out about Alex."

"Yes, do. And may I say how grateful I am that you found a way to let me know? I would not have found out for days." Greta pulled a handkerchief from her sleeve and dabbed at her eyes and nose. The gesture, while certainly genuine, was schooled and refined, just the sort of thing Peasant Greta would never have done in Alex's office.

"You have known him much longer than we have," Kerri acknowledged sympathetically. She felt tears in her eyes yet again, but they were on Greta's account. She seemed to have finished her own crying for Alex, she realized. She had been fond of him, but she had known him too brief a time and held herself too detached to need much grieving, unlike the other two.

"Not all that long, really," Greta replied with a deep sigh. "I became distantly acquainted with him three or four years ago. We met at the flea market and got to know each other as fellow collectors, but I only tracked him down to his library lair about a year ago. I would stop in to visit him from time to time, and we fell into the pattern of Tuesdays and Fridays. He would offer me tea. He seemed to enjoy the company so much. He seemed such a lonely man, in spite of all the people who knew him around the swap meets. So shy! Few people knew his real name, although I had found it out. I think he was afraid he might lose his job if the Library administration found out about his other interests. I couldn't imagine why they should care, but perhaps he knew better than I."

"Did you know his wife?" Loren asked.

"I've never met her, and he rarely mentioned her or anything about his personal life. But I knew he was married. My agent was able to contact his wife yesterday—frightened her half to death, I gather."

"Is she all right?"

"She was *not* all right. That is, she is absolutely shattered, of course, and on top of that she is terribly worried about this business at the Library, the accusations against Alex. She has no idea what it's all about and thinks she's going to be held accountable. My representative had a deuce of a time getting any information out of her at all. But her mother was with her and another older woman, some family friend, and they were taking care of her in their way. I've got one of my legal people looking into the Library matter, but she wasn't able to find out much on Friday. Of course, all the library staff who know anything had taken off for the weekend. Nothing can be done until Monday at the earliest. Or, more likely, Tuesday.

"As for your plan to confront the Head Librarian, she—Alex's wife—told my agent about that. She is very frightened about it. I can take care of it, if you wish. You need not go at all. I think I can put some heavy pressure on them for Mrs. A. I can be formidable, if I choose."

"I'll bet you can," Loren declared. "I wouldn't miss it for the world."

"We shall all go," Kerri assured her. *Or maybe not,* she said to herself, remembering their confrontation with the Alliance. She asked Greta, "Do you know how he...how it happened?"

"Alex? Heart attack. Or so I assume. I don't know what else it might be to kill a man so young—he wasn't above thirty-two or three—so suddenly. His wife said he went without warning Wednesday morning, not long after he'd arrived at work. I know City People are jealous of their privacy, but she was extraordinarily evasive. Wouldn't even reveal where he is buried, but we can find that out later." She stopped and shook her head. "I was with him only the day before. One last time; I'm so glad. Although I never dreamed it was the last time."

"No," said Kerri. "You could not have been with him. That was the day he was gone. Tuesday. We found a notice on his door saying he'd been called away on family business."

"That was me," Greta confessed. "I persuaded him to move his personal collection of books and things out of his office at the library to a more secure place. I met him at the Library with a horse and wagon and a man to help out late Monday night, and the three of us got everything out and away well before dawn. You'd never recognize that office now! He had no idea the hiding place was in a house I own. In fact, I acquired the house for the very purpose. To be a sort of clubhouse for the Gang of Four."

She grinned at Kerri. "You'll find it conveniently close to home. I was going to give all three of you keys...."

"My villa!" exclaimed Loren. "The Evesham house. It was you! You're the one who took it."

"I am, but I hope you'll consider it your own, as well. Indeed, you are welcome to live in it, if you want," she said to Loren. "I have no intention of taking residence myself, and I would rather not leave it vacant. It really is a marvelous house. You can even come to call without the neighbors' seeing you." She smiled at Kerri. "There's one especially curious feature, a tunnel from the basement to the ruins of an old building nearby. I had it shored up and cleaned out and put a good stout door on it."

"Ah," said Kerri. "I noticed that."

"But it was to be a place for all of us," Greta continued. "An alternative to meeting in the library. I suspect it was only a matter of time before we would have had to stop that in any case."

"What did Alex think of all this?" Kerri asked.

"He did not know. I didn't want to tell him until I could tell all three of you, so I told him it belongs to a friend of mine who lets me use some of the space for storage. He didn't question it, and he seemed very relieved. He always said he kept so many of his books in his office because he had no room for them in his house, but I think he was also concealing the size of his collection from his wife. She'd have thought he was spending far too much, and no doubt he was. I know he'd been anxious about the safety of his treasures. Lately, I think he was afraid that someone on the staff suspected he was unofficially borrowing a book here and there, and apparently he was right. We all know he was not guiltless in that respect. He was worried that if he got caught, everything might be confiscated, even his own possessions. I think we were not a moment too soon."

"Is it possible that some of the books you removed were library property?" Kerri asked guardedly.

"There's no doubt of it. We didn't have time to go through them all, and he was never as careful as he should have been. He tried to catch them, but I'm sure he missed a few, and he might not remember where some of them came from, he's had them so long."

"And we've had them also," Kerri regretted. "The dream book! I am so thankful I returned that, at least. And the Brautigan! But that belonged to him. Or so he said."

"It was his," Greta assured her. "He was always honest about the provenance of his literary finds, and he always put the borrowed ones back eventually. I think you should consider the Brautigan his gift to you both. His bequest to you. His wife did not know he had it, and it would be of no value to her. It is yours. I hope one of you has it in a safe place."

Kerri briefly met Loren's eyes. "We do. But beyond that there are certainly grounds for them to be suspicious at the Library. This is very bad. Maybe we could find the library books and smuggle them back somehow."

Greta smiled. "That would be a job! But, yes, we might, if it would ease your mind. However, I'm not sure we could tell by looking at his books which ones are library property. You know he always insisted he never took anything that had been catalogued, so there is no way to prove anything in his possession was not his own. They could make a fuss, but they couldn't even fire him on mere suspicion. And I cannot imagine there is any way the missing materials—if there are any—could be tied to any of us."

"Unless your inquiries, and my meddling with the Head Librarian, set their backs up," worried Kerri. "I wonder if that was not a mistake."

"I don't see why it should be," Greta responded. "Why shouldn't his friends take his part, especially in view of the widow's distress?"

Kerri met Loren's eyes. "Well, it might be more complicated than that. This may not have been the best time for Loren and me to draw attention to ourselves. Or to serve as any kind of character reference for Alex."

"Do you think...?" began Loren.

"Whatever do you mean?" asked Greta.

"We seem to have run into a bit of trouble," Kerri went on, wondering how to begin to explain.

Loren broke in, "Do you belong to the Alliance?" she asked Greta boldly.

Chapter 59

Safe Refuge

"What is the Alliance?" Greta looked genuinely puzzled.

"It does not matter," Kerri tried to tell Loren. "It is too late. Whether she does, or whether she does not...."

"Have you ever heard of the Alliance?" Loren persisted. "Do you know anything about it at all?"

"No, I...."

"And how am I...how are we supposed to trust you when you have misled us all this time about who you really were?"

"Misled you!" Greta gasped, half laughing. "I suppose I did, but I assure you...."

"I know I should not speak so disrespectfully to a Stockholder," Loren broke in again, doggedly, "but it is important. There has been too much deception in my life lately, too many shocks. I do not trust anyone anymore. Maybe you," she shot at Kerri. "Maybe not."

"Loren!"

"They're *your* people, after all. I'm finding it hard to believe you didn't know something about it. Even an inkling. You're married to one of Them, for heaven's sake. Were you hiding it all this time? Lying to me? Are you one of Them after all? Or were you willfully blind? Or just stupid?"

"Loren!"

"I'm sorry!" Loren groped for and found her grubby and much-used handkerchief. "It's just...first the Watchers, and then Alex, and last night and this morning. I don't know what I'm saying any more. I don't know what I'm thinking." She wiped her eyes and blew her nose despondently.

"I was stupid," Kerri reflected calmly, staring into the fire. "I was willfully blind. I had enough pieces of the puzzle, but I never put them together. I just thought I was crazy. But if I deceived anyone, it was myself."

"Them?" Greta looked from one to the other. "Who? What are you two talking about, and what is going on here? This is not about me, is it? Or even about Alex. What on earth has happened?"

Kerri turned her gaze to the Stockholder. "Something did happen last night," she said, searching for the simplest, shortest way to tell the bare essentials. "The two of us stumbled onto something we were not meant to know about, and now we have got a lot of people upset and angry at us—trying to find us for goodness knows what purpose. They are based at the Lodge. We suspect drugs were given to us. We have been running away all night—most of the way around the Lake and up into the hills. We have had no sleep and little to eat, and we are both too tired to think properly or give a very coherent account of ourselves.

"Finding you was sheerest accident, coincidence. Whether it was a good thing or a bad thing, whether we can trust you or not, I do not know, but at this moment I do not think I am capable of running any further. Not just yet. If ever. So if you are part of this business at the Lodge, if you already know about it and you are simply holding on to us until They get here, have mercy and call Them in at once, before we can dredge up the strength to run again."

"Drugs? The Lodge?" Greta stared at her, shaking her head. "I have no clue what you are talking about, either of you, but I could see at once that you are not your usual cheerful selves. You look done in, both of you. I wondered if there was more to it than Alex. If you are in some kind of trouble, I will help you as much as I can.

"It is true you have reason to distrust me, but truly, I never intended to deceive you. My Peasant persona goes back years and years, even before the swap meets. Most of us who grow up in my world have these disguises. We do it almost without thinking; it is part of our lives. It does not seem dishonest to us but a kind of courtesy, a civility. It allows us to get about the country or the City without a lot of fuss and bother, to make things easier on other people and on ourselves. Alex would never have allowed me to befriend him if he'd known. I was terrified you would give me away to him. You did not. *That* gives me reason to trust *you*. But that's neither here nor there, now." She set down her glass and rose to her feet.

"The thing is, I do not have any connection with these people you are worried about. I swear it. You can believe me or not, as you choose, but right now I shall go to the Lawsons and tell them to deny your presence and mine to any callers. As soon as lunch is ready you are both going to eat something. And then you are going to have nice warm baths and go to bed. You shall be my guests for today and the night, if I can persuade you to stay. I want you to sleep out the afternoon or sleep the clock around, if you like, and when you are rested and feeling more fit, you can tell me all about it. Or not, if you choose. No arguments. I shall be right back."

She went out of the room, closing the door behind her.

Loren, giving her nose one last wipe, returned her handkerchief to her pocket. "I'm sorry," she repeated, looking numbly down at her hands. "I did not expect to... give way like that."

"Never mind," said Kerri. "I understand. I've given way myself more than once in the last few hours while you held up like a champion. Are you all right? What do you want to do? Do you want to leave? If you want to keep running, I shall go with you, if you want."

"You said you couldn't."

"I know I said so, and if we decide Greta is dangerous, it is just as well I did say so. But I can go on if I must. I admit I could use a rest. I should never have had any sherry. It makes me want to sit here forever in front of this fire. Although a bath would be utter heaven."

"I was rude to her," said Loren. "And to you."

"She doesn't mind a bit. Nor do I. I'm feeling rude myself, if it comes down to it."

"But you don't show it. You're so much better brought up than I. Did you hear yourself talking to her? Formal. You never dropped out of it, not once until just now. I almost threw my glass at you."

Kerri laughed, and after a few seconds Loren joined in.

"I'm glad you restrained yourself," Kerri said. "Well, what shall we do?"

"Stay. Even if she *has* gone to fetch Them, I don't care any more. It's either face Them now or run away to the Road People forever."

"And if Greta's all right," added Kerri, "you can run away to the Road People later."

"What will you do?" Loren asked bleakly. "I'm certain the Road People would take you in. They are a very warm, accepting people, but you have much more at stake than I do. And you have a connection with the Sea People."

"Another place to run," Kerri agreed. "I *have* thought about it since last night. Many times. I do not know what I shall do. Get through today first, I think. Accept shelter from Greta, if she turns out to be on our side, or at least not on Theirs. I'm so tired, and...Name of the Dreamer, I want so badly to trust her! She has already rescued me once. Why would she have done that if she were one of Them? She could so easily have left me to twist in the wind at the Ball. And she came up trumps over the Brautigan. Even if she does turn out to be one of Them, this Alliance thing doesn't seem to be exactly monolithic, does it? I mean, look at Domenick. They must have Their factions, Their differences. If we pick the right one, we may save the day yet. We may not be in as much trouble as we thought."

"That's the sherry talking," Loren commented.

"Very likely. So we stay?"

Loren nodded. "For now. I could sleep and sleep!"

"And so you shall," remarked Greta, coming back into the room. "Lunch is served, and the Lawsons have been alerted to keep the gates closed to all comers. Come along now. I'll show you where you can wash up."

The meal was put before them in the dining room, which, like the sitting room, looked out over the terrace, the lawns and the Lake. Carved wood paneling, a Turkish carpet, and ruby red hangings added to the warmth of the fire on the hearth, hearty soup, and bread fresh from the oven. The housekeeper, Mrs. Lawson, was introduced with proper ceremony. Small and round as her husband was long and lean, she obviously had status as a household retainer of long service, fussing over Greta as she might a daughter and beaming at her charge's new friends. Kerri, conscious of a lingering uncertainty in herself about how to relate properly to private servants—fostered by that infamous upbringing Loren complained about, as well as reading too much literature from the Age of Dreams, no doubt—was glad the housekeeper did not show any inclination to hover over them after the introductions were made and the food served, but took herself away, leaving them in peace once the cider was poured into their glasses.

There was little conversation over lunch. Loren ate quietly and deliberately, sitting very straight as if she might fall out of her chair from weariness if she let herself lean in any direction. Greta kept things going with light commentary on the weather and the work she'd been doing in the garden, while Kerri tried to listen and nod and say a suitable word now and then. Lulled by food and warmth, she soon found herself beginning to yawn uncontrollably.

"I'm putting you in the blue room," Greta told Loren as she led them up the stairs, "and you, Kerri, in what I call the rose room, although it isn't as twee as it sounds. Each one has a private bath, so there's no need to take turns, and the beds are all turned down and clean nightgowns laid out, and if you'll just drop your clothes in the corridor, Mrs. Lawson will pick them up and get them washed and dried for you. You're not to worry about a thing."

The rose room turned out to be a comfortable bedroom done mostly in cream with a rose motif on the wallpaper and the fabrics, dried roses in glass bowls, fresh hot house roses in a vase beside the bed. The room was at the corner of the house overlooking the rose garden on the south and facing the road on the west. There was working electric light, called up from a switch next to the door, and warmth pouring from two radiators. Not twee at all, and the bath was heavenly. In the interest of staying awake long enough to fall into bed, Kerri resisted the temptation to sink into the tub and chose the shower instead, washing her hair twice with rose-scented shampoo and wrapping herself afterward in thick cream-colored, rose-scented towels. She even found a comb and ribbons to tie her wet hair after she had put it in a loose braid.

She donned the nightgown, a plain no-nonsense garment in soft white flannel, and bundled up her discarded garments to put them out in the hall for the housekeeper. It gave her some hesitation to do so (A genuine country-house housekeeper! Fancy!), but she reflected that she had been given a direct order by Greta, and one might as well do these things the proper way, if offered the hospitality of a Stockholder. At the last moment, she remembered to go through the pockets and remove her bits and pieces, including the purloined library catalogue card, the writing still perfectly visible upon it. Then finally she could put out the light and get into the delightful soft bed and pull up the cloud of a coverlet.

Her last thought before she fell asleep was, surprisingly, of Andrew. It startled her, and obscurely reassured her, that he had not crossed her mind until now, all the time she had been in Greta's house. She wondered vaguely if she would see him again, if he might be one of the friends Greta had set looking for her and Loren, and her mind drifted away into a dream in which he was riding a horse up and down the road outside the estate, calling and calling her name. She did not think of Nicholas at all.

When she woke, darkness had fallen. There was no way to tell, here in Twilight Country, whether it was early evening, the middle of the night or near morning, but someone had come into the room while she was sleeping. On the round, lace covered table by the window, a lamp had been lit, an ordinary oil lamp, and there was a tray with a cup and saucer, a fat little tea pot under a quilted cozy, a plate of lemon slices, a tiny pitcher of milk and dish of sugar. Kerri felt her hair. The braid was still quite damp: not morning, then.

A tartan dressing gown was draped over the chair next to the table, and folded on the seat lay her own underwear, freshly washed and dried. A pair of fuzzy slippers lay on the floor neatly side by side in front of the chair.

A note on the tray said, "When you wake up, do not bother to dress. Come down as you are. I shall be in the sitting room. G."

How good she is! Kerri said to herself. And how wonderful it was to be pampered and sheltered, after everything she had been through. It was like finding oneself in one of those wonderful Late Classic novels about legendary England Between the Wars, quite the most beloved period of literature from the Age of Dreams because (barring things like telephones and automobiles) it was the most like home—or like one's idealized version of home and everything familiar in post-Confusion society. Civilized, elegant, not too formal. Somehow, one expected Stockholders to put on more of a show, live in more state, but it stood to reason they would not bother if they did not have to, if they were not directly in the public eye. *I could live like this,* Kerri thought, regretting for the first time that tenuous possibility of her father's lost inheritance.

She put on the slippers and dressing gown gratefully and made a visit to the bathroom. Refreshed, her face washed and teeth brushed, she poured herself a cup of tea with lemon and went to stand by the window, looking out at darkness. The wind was up, the sky thickly clouded over. She wondered if anyone from the Lodge still hunted for her and Loren. This would be a bad night to do it in, and tonight, Saturday night, They had something special going on at the Lodge, by all accounts.

What could They be up to, this Alliance? Who were They, exactly, and how did Their doings relate to the shocking burst of earth-sky energy that had struck Kerri and Loren the night before? That there was some kind of relationship, Kerri had no doubt, and she was certain it linked together all the puzzling elements of her life, new and old. The illusionary writing on Nick's letter, in the card catalogue, in Domenick's books—not an illusion, it seemed. The mysterious procedures by which some people received fellowships and professorships, and others, equally talented, did not. All these mysterious name changes. The crafty, judging watchfulness of Arzelle and people like her, their influence over others. Her two experiences with the drugged wine. Poor Miss Beckett in the Asylum. Even the Veil. All knotted together somehow with the Alliance.

Is this what the Veil has always protected me from? she wondered. She shivered: the thought that this Power might be real! Worse, it might be malevolent, even deadly. How much did They control it? What did They use it for, besides keeping Their secrets? She felt then a thread of the terror she had so resolutely banished from her mind the last few weeks, the nearby tragedies that now looked like nothing so much as near misses. *Name of the Dreamer!* she said to herself? *How far are these people willing to go to protect Their secrets and get what They want? What do They want? And why on earth should They bother about me? What threat can I possibly be to Them? Do They know I have the Veil?*

Deliberately, she did not invoke that protection but tried to relax her body and mind, to feel about her for any wisp of the mysterious energy she now felt certain she would recognize. Yes. Yes, there it was, but soft, diffuse, unfocused, without any specific location, like the rain that now beat against the windows. She felt no sense of danger, threat, or evil. Nothing personal. More like a force of nature manifesting itself in a faint vibration that seemed to rise up from the earth into her bones, to come from everywhere at once, gentle, constant.

And then, suddenly, she was no longer sure she felt anything at all. *I've imagined it,* she told herself. *These people are nothing more than silly secret societies calling themselves study groups or literary clubs or what-have-you, parading around with their robes and banners when nobody's looking. Doling out thesis topics to the chosen elite. How dare they!*

And now, of course, they'll never choose me! I've gone and busted it good and forever. Unless they have to take me in now, and Loren, too, to keep us from blabbing our heads off. A pretty shameful business all round, and I'm not sure I'd even want to be part of their ridiculous games, even if they asked me nicely. Perhaps that's all they wanted, at the cabin, at the Lodge. Perhaps they don't know what hit us and them any more than we do, and they're truly worried about us and want to help and take care of the mix-up. Perhaps nothing did hit us, and it was all some kind of drunken dream, and Loren and I have been perfect fools and idiots and scared a lot of silly but well-meaning people half to death by running away. Not to mention ruined our careers for good and all.

Then, belatedly, she wondered about Nicholas. Where was he now? What was he doing? How was he feeling about what had happened? And how did he feel about her, Kerri? He must be finding himself in an awful spot, worrying about his wayward wife, possibly trying to make all kinds of excuses for her, nervous about his own future. He could not be very far into this Alliance thing. Every troubling and evasive thing he had done since the beginning of term, or even since last spring, now appeared in a different light as the actions of a man getting himself into something new and uncertain, something he was required to conceal. She had thought it was a love affair, but it might have been this. In any event, there would have to be some kind of a reckoning with Nick before she could say whether or not she still had a marriage.

And do I want this marriage to continue? she wondered. And wondered again at her own dispassion. It seemed as if all the lies, all the betrayals, had taken place long ago, in some far away place, had happened to someone else. *This has happened before,* she realized. *It was like this with Val, yet not like this.* The break with Val had taken her by surprise; there had been intense pain, followed by a period of numb lucidity that allowed her to complete the business of separating herself from him, then pain again for many months. This time she had been expecting, anticipating disaster for weeks, had already gone through the pain in bits and pieces. Presently, she must be in the numb stage. She hoped it would last as long as she needed it.

She drank off the rest of her tea and set the cup back on the tray. Greta might still be in the sitting room. Greta must be faced—if possible, eventually, alone.

Chapter 60

Imagination and Belief

"You recognized me at the Ball," Greta ventured. Wrapped in a worn velvet dressing gown, she knelt in front of the sitting room fire, rearranging logs with the poker. With her dark hair uncovered now, lying down her back in a thick braid, she looked younger than Kerri had thought her before—perhaps Kerri's own age, surely no more than thirty. Oddly, she also looked more like the Stockholder Fairchild at the Faculty Revel than Greta of the Swap Meets and the Public Library, yet, in spite of that, unfrightening.

Perched on the sofa with her feet curled beneath her, Kerri nodded. "When you spoke to me," she said. "I recognized your voice."

"Why did you never say anything about it?"

"First, there was never a good time, when the others were not there. Second, I was not convinced it was true. I thought I might have imagined it. And finally, it seemed to me that if you were—who I thought you might be, it was not my place to speak first."

"I understand." Greta nodded. "And I would have spoken, except, as you said, there was never an opportunity that one of the others wasn't there, and until I received your letter I wasn't absolutely certain you knew, especially since you hadn't told Alex."

"Did you expect me to?"

"I didn't know what to expect." Greta gave the logs one last shove, set the poker aside and dusted off her hands. She resettled herself on her cushion to face Kerri. "But then, I didn't know you then as well as I do now. I was unable to come to the library that first Tuesday after the Ball—it couldn't be helped; I had another appointment—but I was in such agonies of suspense I dropped in on Alex first thing the following morning on some excuse or other. And he was none the wiser, so I knew you had kept silent. And then, the next time we were all together I began to doubt that you had, in fact, recognized me. You were very cool, upon my word. I would still be guessing!"

"It was not my place to say anything to Alex," said Kerri. "Or even to Loren. Until I was forced to. She did not believe me," she added.

"Well," said Greta after a few seconds' pause, "now that things are out in the open,

I hope you and Loren will not hold my masquerade against me."

"I can only speak for myself," Kerri replied. "And *I* do not hold it against you. But there is one question I must ask. What did you mean when you warned me about the Tigers? At the reception, before the Ball, you said to me, 'The Tigers are on the hunt tonight.' And then you said, 'Don't worry, you'll knock them dead.' Those were your exact words."

"Heavens!" Greta protested faintly. "You people *do* remember things, don't you? Well, that is an interesting story, as a matter of fact. It had reached our ears that one of the graduate students had cooked up a plan to humiliate a rival by packing the other woman's dance card with her own handpicked cronies and having them all snub her for the dances they'd signed for."

"So you *did* know!" Kerri exclaimed. "And it was planned in advance. And I did not imagine it," she added after a few seconds' pause.

"No, you did not. Ordinarily we do not involve ourselves in Academic rivalries— we've enough of our own!—but we were in the mood for *some* kind of a diversion to make the evening interesting, and this plot was so low and spiteful, we decided to do what we could to foil the scheme...."

"We?" Kerri interrupted.

"Oh, my friends—Marius, Andrew, the others who danced with you, some of the women you were presented to—near every Stockholder in the place, I reckon. And every servant in the place—that is, all of ours, not the Academic ones! They were our eyes and ears, hovering to find out the identity of the intended victim. You had a lot of people looking out for you that night!"

"I had no idea," Kerri said soberly.

"After the reception had begun," Greta continued, "one of the footmen came to me and said he had learned that the woman in question was being presented with her husband, and he knew what they were wearing and would point them out. Then you were announced, and I saw it was you, and on top of that, here's the servant giving me the signal! I was quite stunned, and so was Andrew, for reasons of his own. Even if you hadn't been a friend of mine, I think he would have appointed himself your champion. *That* is a story I wouldn't mind hearing one of these days, but it's beside the point now.

"Anyway, my anger against those miserable students was doubled on your behalf. It became a personal matter as well as an issue of civility and honor. I wanted to warn you somehow, and to let you know things were in hand, not to worry. I wanted to warn your husband as well—very pleasant-looking chap, by the way!—to stick by you and not let them get away with it, but I'm afraid I only ended up puzzling you both. There wasn't time to explain or even think of what I ought to say, so I said the first thing that came into my head."

Deborah K. Vleck

"Tigers."

"From that old book you and Loren are so excited about, believe it or not." She grinned.

"The Brautigan." Kerri smiled back, shaking her head slowly. "Life is very strange. At least now I can thank you properly. I wish I could thank all of your friends, as well."

"I will be happy to convey your gratitude to them," Greta replied. "Although it is unnecessary. I know they considered themselves well rewarded by your manners and presence of mind. You played along as well as if you were in on the whole plan—ours, that is, not that woman's nasty trick. Total poise, Marius said. You rescued him from what he expected to be a deadly boring evening, dancing with elderly ladies from the ranks of the Regents and upper Faculty. As for Andrew, he was enchanted! His only regret was that you were a married woman."

"How gallant!" Kerri commented with an admirably level voice and just enough of a smile, she hoped, to convey that she took neither Andrew's enchantment nor his supposed regret over her married state seriously. She could give them no weight. He was a Stockholder. Not of my caste, she repeated silently to herself. She remembered Loren saying those very words of the Watchers, but Loren had been making excuses. This barrier was true. Anyway, she was still married and had no desire to be otherwise, if she had anything to say about it. And if she repeated that idea over to herself often enough, she might stop questioning it.

"What I should like to know," Greta went on, "is, who was that woman, and what reason did she have to employ such a mean-spirited plan against you? And how does she come to have the power to do such a thing?"

"In answer to your first question, she is a childhood acquaintance and schoolfellow of mine named Arzelle Pendrake James-Dietrich. For the second, she is married to my first husband, whom she took from me, and she wants my second. As for the third, I can only guess."

"Then...guess!"

Kerri was silent for a long moment, staring into the fire. "I cannot do that," she said at last, "without reference to the adventures that brought us here, and I cannot tell you those, not properly, without Miss Weberly being here."

"Then," Greta scrambled to her feet and reverted abruptly (and, so far as Kerri could tell, unconsciously) to Peasant accents, "how about I have a listen to see if she's stirring? And look up a bite of supper for all of us? Are you hungry? Not very? Well, you may be later on, if the tale's a long one. I'll just see we have everything we need to hand, and then Mrs. Lawson can go to bed. Please excuse me."

She went from the room, leaving Kerri to gaze into the flames, lost in thought.

* * *

"What time is it?" Loren stifled a yawn and rubbed her eyes as she shuffled across the carpet. "No, this is Twilight Country. What was I thinking? Silly question." She cast herself into a large high-backed armchair beside the fire and blinked sleepily at Kerri.

"Between nine o'clock and half past, by my guess," said Greta, coming into the room bearing a tray laden with dishes, cutlery, various covered plates and a bottle of good brandy. She set this down on the coffee table, muttering, "The milk. The milk," and went out of the room again.

"How long have you been up?" asked Loren. She sounded a bit cross. "How much did I miss?"

"Not long," said Kerri. "And very little. We were talking about the Ball."

"Ah!" Mollified, Loren tucked herself more comfortably into her chair. "That was a good sleep," she said. "I needed that. How are you?"

"Better for the bath and the sleep," Kerri replied.

"The milk!" Greta announced from the doorway. She held an immense jug in one hand and a bouquet of mugs in the other. Kerri got up quickly to close the door and take the mugs. Greta returned to her cushion in front of the hearth, setting the jug on the fender to keep warm. "If we need anything else, we shall have to forage in the kitchen. I've sent Mrs. Lawson off for the night."

"Do they live here in the house?" Loren asked.

"No. In the Gatehouse, up by the road. Well. Here we are." She uncovered the dishes on the tray, a plate of cold ham and cheese and another of assorted cakes and sweet biscuits, a cottage loaf, fresh baked. There were a bowl of tawny apples and a basket of muffins covered with a checked cloth, a tall pot of coffee— to Kerri's approval; tea would have been quite redundant, in her opinion—and assorted other supplies for a long evening of light or hearty nibbling. Greta settled herself cross-legged and prepared to secure a muffin on the tines of a long-handled toasting fork. "Since you're the closest," she advised Loren, "would you mind very much pouring out the hot milk or coffee or both, whichever anyone wants? Your reward will be the first muffin, and I am an expert toaster! I'll take both, if you please, half and half with just a smidgen of brandy."

"Certainly." Loren unfolded herself and reached for the jug. "Kerri?"

"The same, thank you."

"And do help yourselves to whatever you fancy. Now," she commanded, "it is time for the story. No more dark hints and rolling your eyes at each other. I want to know everything that happened."

"Now, let me see if I understand this." Greta leaned forward and pressed her hands together in front of her. "After you sent the letter to me about Alex, you decided to come down to Twilight Country, just to get away for the weekend. When you arrived at Kerri's place, over across the lake, you found it occupied by colleagues of Kerri's husband. They treated you rudely, asked you to dinner, drugged you, and then left you alone. But they came back in the middle of the night, all dressed in robes and masks and the like. When you saw them, you both went blind. Then there was a great flash of some kind, and you could see again, but you ran away. Never mind why. You felt yourselves in danger at the time; we'll leave it at that.

"Some of them followed. You kept running. They kept following. But Kerri somehow dimmed you both out so they couldn't see you, and you lost them. You were making for the train, but when you passed the Lodge you encountered this individual, this man Domenick, who hid you from the search that was apparently still going on. You discovered that the Lodge was crawling with secret societies of Academics who have changed their names to add up to seven, that Kerri's husband's friends constitute one of these societies, and they're all after you because of what happened at Kerri's cabin.

"You decided their intentions were not kind, so you ran away again, but not before you discovered that you could see writing on what had been apparently blank pages. You both claim to be able to see writing on a file card that looks blank to me.

"You did not get on the train but followed the road, where you were so afraid of discovery you trespassed on the grounds of the place next door, and then, by sheer coincidence, on my property. Lawson caught you, and here you are. Have I got it?"

"More or less." Loren gloomily cupped her chin in her hands and gazed into the fire.

"In a nutshell." added Kerri. "And leaving out a lot of the important bits. Sounds incredibly stupid, doesn't it?" She put down her mug and reached for another tidbit from the table. She'd had just enough brandy, she decided, to give her some objectivity. Pity it wouldn't last. "Stupid, stupid," she repeated.

"No, not at all," said Greta, surprisingly. "You'll be interested to know someone did inquire at the gate this afternoon for two females answering your description. A dark-haired fellow. Could have been your friend Domenick. Lawson sent him away none the wiser. You said this Domenick told you he was going to neutralize you or something...."

"Stabilize us."

"Stabilize. Whatever. I don't like the sound of that. I'd've run, too. And all this as consequence of what? Your interrupting their party at your cabin? No. Not worth it. They were leaving, anyway. Because you found out they like to style themselves in these little secret clubs and parade around in ceremonial robes and so forth? Well, that might be embarrassing for them—although they're not as secret as they suppose; I've had some inkling about it myself forever— but they could hardly be out for your blood on that account. If we were in the Age of Dreams I might entertain the possibility. Goodness knows people did terrible things on much less provocation in those days, but this is not the Age of Dreams. They might more likely invite you to join in, flatter you into silence, for what it's worth. Perhaps that is what they had in mind, why they were trying to track you down.

"But no," she answered herself. "You do not think that is the reason. You think it is because of the thing that happened at Kerri's cabin, this so-called flash. What your various sources told you at the Lodge suggests that you are right. And I, myself, keep coming back in my mind to this strange phenomenon. I keep asking myself, what was it? It could not have been lightning. Last night was windy but clear. I heard no thunder. Besides, if you'd been struck by lightning, I doubt you'd be here to tell about it. So." She paused. "What happened? What really happened to you over there last night."

"I didn't say it was lightning," Loren began. "I said it was *like* lightning. It seemed to come down from the sky..."

"And up from the earth, too," Kerri broke in. "It was like a wind passing through me. Like a huge soundless blast of noise. But like none of those. I could talk about it all night and not be able to describe what it was really like. If it really happened," she added after a moment. "Perhaps it didn't."

"What do you mean?" protested Loren. "It damn well *did* happen! I don't begin to understand what it was, but it was real. Don't you dare tell me it wasn't!"

Kerri stared at her and felt a flush rising to her face. She felt as if she had been slapped. One always withheld one's official belief from these things. To do otherwise was to step right up to the edge of the abyss. But she had stepped right off that edge long ago. And if Loren thought it was all real....

"Very well," Greta continued in a deliberately reasonable voice. "I shall not tell you so. We shall take the reality of the thing as read and grant that we do not know what it was. My next questions is, how was it done? Did these people have some kind of electrical apparatus? An explosive device? Fireworks?"

"You don't understand," Loren said. "*They* didn't do it. *We* did it."

Greta raised one eyebrow and looked to Kerri for corroboration.

"It felt as if we did it," Kerri explained reluctantly. She felt cornered; then, quite suddenly, a calmness descended upon her. Something within her abruptly stilled, something that had turned and twisted and hid and lied for as long as she could remember.

"So," said Greta, clearly and slowly, "what, exactly, did you do? I mean," she went on, "if I were them and someone blew my nice mask off with a great blast of something-or-other, I should jolly well want some kind of an explanation. No wonder they ran after you!"

Loren spread her hands irritably. "I don't know what we did. All I remember is, I was afraid and I was angry. Mostly angry." She seized another sweet and popped it into her mouth defiantly.

"And you?" Greta directed her grey gaze at Kerri. "You know more than you're telling," she accused. "I think, something like this has happened to you before. That is why you ran."

"That is one reason," Kerri affirmed. From that still, calm place, the words, finally, began to come. "I was angry," she said. "I am still angry. I feel as if I have always been angry. Last night, I took my anger, and I borrowed Loren's anger, and I made of it, we both made of it, a great concussion. That is what it felt like. And it felt like...a thing I've sensed before, yes, with some people. Certain people. A power they have. Or that I imagined they had. Oh," she paused in confusion, "I don't know. I don't know what the truth is." *I've said too much*, she thought.

"A power they have," Greta repeated, frowning.

"I know what she's talking about," Loren offered. "We have spoken about it a little, the two of us. We discovered we've both always had this uneasy suspicion—no, more than a suspicion—a sense that certain people, mostly in our own caste, have a kind of—how can I describe it?—a kind of extra awareness, a knowingness, and the capacity to influence things to go their way. I am not putting this very well."

"Oh, I know exactly what you are saying," declared Greta. "I've had the same sort of sense about certain people, too. People of your caste. And mine. But the latter...." She broke off, frowning.

"Domenick knew," Kerri went on. "He knew what had happened. And he seemed...pleased. As if we had done something very clever, something special. Something he could put to use for his own benefit."

"The man who took you in at the Lodge? Is he one of the people who have this knowingness?"

"Oh, yes!" said Loren meaningfully.

"Loren thinks she might have met him before," Kerri explained evasively. That part of it was Loren's truth to tell, after all, or not tell.

"So," Greta pressed on, "you are suggesting that there is some kind of link, or at least some similarity, between this power you've sensed in other people and what you did across the lake last night?"

"It felt similar," Kerri affirmed.

"Then," said Greta, "presumably you both possess this magical power also!"

Loren gave a sharp snort of laughter. *"Magical* power! Who said *magical* power? That's absurd!"

"Why?" asked Greta.

"Because there is no such thing as magic," Kerri reminded her crisply.

"How can you be sure?" Greta argued. "If something happens, and it seems magical, and there is no other reasonable explanation, why not call it magic?"

"Because you'd look a fool if you did. Because there *is* a reasonable explanation. There must be. Or else we did imagine it all in some drug-induced state. That is more likely than magic. This is no Age of Dreams fairytale. This is Real Life. There is no such thing as magic. Greta, what are these wonderful dark confections? I've never tasted anything like them in my life, and I cannot stop eating them."

"Yes, they are exquisite," Loren agreed. "What are they made of?" She helped herself to another.

"Chocolate," replied Greta with an eldritch smile.

They stared at her, and then, as one, turned astonished eyes to the greatly depleted assortment of smoothly shining brown confections on the silver tray.

Finally Kerri found her voice. "But chocolate," she said slowly, "is just another myth from the Age of Dreams." She licked her fingers thoughtfully.

"There is no such thing as chocolate?" Greta mocked softly. "Oh, but there is. If one knows how and where to find it."

Loren's eyes narrowed. "And you do?"

"I do. So do most people of my caste. We do not...make much noise about it. There isn't a lot of it to be got, you see. It is not easy to come by."

"A Stockholder secret," said Loren disapprovingly. "But now we know!"

"For whatever good it will do you." Greta shrugged. "There's no official secrecy about chocolate. Not that I would share my supply with just anyone. It is one of those quiet things. If you know about it, you know about it. If you don't, you don't. One doesn't make an issue of it."

"Like the Alliance," Kerri mused, almost to herself.

"Or like magic," said Greta.

"Very well," said Kerri. "I will believe in chocolate. I have eaten it. I will believe in the Alliance. I have seen it. But you cannot persuade me to believe in magic. You cannot persuade me to believe that what we did by that fire last night was magical."

"Then what was it?" Greta asked intensely. "Don't you want to know? Don't you want to find out."

"How?" Kerri demanded. *I don't, though,* she told herself. *I do not want to know. Yes, I must know. Now. Or die.*

Greta grinned widely at both of them. "I think you ought to try to do it again!"

Loren looked at her as if she had lost her mind. "Do it again? We can't do it again?"

Deborah K. Vleck

"Why not? Why not *try?* Try to recreate the phenomenon. If you could make it happen again, you could observe it this time. You might begin to understand it." Greta clapped her hands together eagerly. "Let's do it!"

Chapter 61

Storm Cell

Outside, the rain had stopped. Fitful gleams of moonlight shone through growing rents in the rapidly tattering clouds. Crossing Greta's rain-drenched lawn with an armload of dry firewood, Kerri wondered how she had ever allowed herself to be persuaded to try this mad experiment. She could not banish the unhappy suspicion that this was the very thing Domenick had warned against.

On the other hand, who was this Domenick, that she should believe anything he said?

How could she ever again believe anything any one of Them had ever said to her? She regretted that she had not done a better job of pumping him for information when she had the chance. Or—perhaps even better—Mrs. Haggarty and the other servants. If only there had been more time....

Down on the pebble beach, Loren knelt on a bundle of sacking and fashioned a cone of kindling with expert fingers. She looked up and grinned as Kerri dropped her armload of wood beside the fire ring. "More than that," she said. "It was a big fire. Remember?"

"I'll fetch another lot if you'll fetch another lot," Kerri replied curtly. "It doesn't need to burn all night, you know. Just long enough. However long that is."

"Sure, I'll go," Loren replied cheerfully. "Good thing it's warmer than last night."

She was right. The rain had been the herald of a warm change, bringing a deceptively springlike softening to the air. "I hope it is a good thing," Kerri said, glancing uneasily at the sky. "We want the conditions to be as much the same as possible."

A lantern appeared up at the garden door of the house, and Greta, holding it. Her hands and face glowed dimly; the rest of her, clothed in black, blended into the shadows. They watched her cross the lawn, leaving darkened footprints in the silvered grass.

"I found some wine that might do," she said somewhat breathlessly as she came up to them. "It is an Island vintage, a red, on the heavy side but quite good, as I remember. Of course, it doesn't have the secret ingredient, but since we don't know what that was, we shall have to do without."

"We might do without the wine," Kerri worried. "We'd had it hours before. Well, a couple of hours. And we drank all that brandy earlier tonight. We might do better with clearer heads."

"It wasn't that much brandy," Greta replied. "And by all accounts your heads were anything but clear last night. Still, I think a wee glass might help set the stage, so to speak. I propose it more for symbolic than practical value." She set the basket containing tumblers and wine bottle carefully down upon the beach.

"Now," she shook out the bulky bundle she had carried under her arm, "robes and masks were more of a problem. I don't keep much in the way of costume at this house, just a few odds and ends in case of last minute invitations to receptions and things. But I did find some old cloaks in the wardrobe in the blue bedroom. I think my mother used to wear them to the opera. Frightfully gaudy, but the gowns were supposed to be absolutely severe to show off one's jewels. They've got nice hoods, though, the cloaks, and they're surprisingly warm. Masks I do not have, but I brought some scarves. We could improvise."

Loren grimaced. "Do you really think we need these? We did put on the same clothes we were wearing...."

"And *They* were the ones in ceremonial dress, not we," Kerri added.

"Perhaps not, then." Greta shrugged. "Just trying to think of every possible thing."

"It would be rather fun," Kerri agreed. *And if it isn't real*, she thought, *if it's just a game, it wouldn't matter. And isn't it just a game?* "But perhaps we ought to try first without. They're beautiful, though," she added, reaching out shyly to caress the spangled velvet.

"A bit old fashioned, but I like them, too," Greta agreed. "Some other time, perhaps. I'll just put them on the porch, out of the wet." She left the lantern on the beach. Loren moved it closer to the fire ring.

"This feels ridiculous," she said. "I hope to heaven nobody sees us!"

Kerri laughed. "That sounds like something I would say. Thank goodness there's a bit of breeze blowing. No one will hear us either. Very well, what else do we need? Torches? Garlands? They were wearing garlands of some kind—in winter."

"No, I think you were on the right track before," Loren said. "We should not try to assemble all the things They had, They wore, They did. If *we* performed the magic, we have to duplicate what *we* did."

"Don't call it magic! It wasn't magic!"

"Well, it wasn't chocolate! I shall call it magic if I please."

"Chocolate," stated Kerri meditatively, "*is* magic. Let us go bring more firewood."

When they returned, Greta was waiting for them. She had uncorked the wine. "Are we ready?" she asked. "Have we got everything? Can we light the fire? Or shall we drink a toast first?"

"I think the wine first or not at all," Loren commented, "then the fire." She fetched the glasses out of the basket and held them while Greta poured.

The wine looked black in the darkness. Kerri held her glass up against the moon to awaken a deep ruby ghost of the summer sun that had ripened these grapes seasons past in the Islands.

"To success," Greta offered her salute.

"To magic!" Loren added.

"To the truth," said Kerri and took a sip. It was not the same as Arzelle's dark smoky wine, but that, she decided, was not necessarily inappropriate. And the wine was a good wine, mellow, full-bodied, and honest. She felt curiously nourished and strengthened by it, as if drinking from the very earth. From the earth the power had come, and down from the sky.

She gazed up again at the sky, splotched now with broken, silver edged clouds. *Where is it?* she wondered. She steered her thoughts away from the Veil. This time she needed its opposite, the thing she had always used the Veil to hide from. That thing might be Real, or it might not. Always, always before she had decided in favor of Unreal. She considered herself a rational person. Here, now, under the wild stars, the cold moon, it struck her for the first time that rationality—and indeed, to an extent, Reality itself—was a matter of choice. That choice could be made, must be made, repeatedly. And there was no rule or necessity that the choice must always be the same.

She decided: *Real. Game, Veil, Power. All real.*

And it was easy. Had she not always believed? Standing on that belief, she tried to reach out with her mind, with that special sense, real or unreal, to find that Power. Nothing answered. Under ordinary stars, an unexceptional moon, the wind blew innocently.

What else? she asked the sky. *What else did we have? What else is needed?* "Anger," she said aloud. "We had anger."

"Anger." Greta lifted her glass in another toast.

"Anger," Loren repeated as she set a match to the kindling.

"And where do we get anger?" Greta asked.

"Remember," said Kerri. "Remember last night."

Loren said fiercely, "Remember Alex!"

"No," commanded Greta coldly. "Not for this."

Loren shrugged. "Not for this," she agreed.

Kerri thought, *this is getting too serious and grim. What fools we shall feel!*

"Remember anything," she told them.

Greta offered the wine around again, but nobody accepted any. She packed the empty glasses and the bottle back into the basket and stood with her arms folded, wearing the expression of one trying not to look disappointed. Loren poked at the fire, now burning well and brightly. They fell silent then, looking into the flames, searching for anger.

As the fire grew, Kerri found herself thinking of the Ball. Not of Andrew, not of moonlight on black velvet, but of the malice of her colleagues, of Val's sneering contempt and open rudeness, of the petty, disgusting childishness of Arzelle's nasty little plot and how easily she had got people—got Them!—to go along with it. An ember, a satisfying spark. She thought of Arzelle and Val, and blew gently on that tiny ember of fury. She fed it memories of Nick's haughty friends, of every slight, every veiled insult, every false smile, and felt the anger blaze up, hot and bright. She remembered the dinner party at Montague's from which she had been so pointedly excluded. She thought of Thomas, cold and still in the bottom of his cage. She thought of saboteurs stealing her essays and hiding her books, of strangers invading her own special lakeside home and trying to cast her out of it. And suddenly, inexplicably, she thought of the empty faced woman in white, Miss Beckett standing at the Asylum fence, gripping the iron bars with pale-knuckled hands.

At that moment she felt it, coming as if from a distance, like a fast, heavy freight train or an earthquake, pouring toward her through stone and soil, water and trees, gathering overhead in a vortex of wind. She met Loren's wide, frightened eyes above the fire. "What is it? What is it?" Greta cried out, and Kerri knew with an abrupt certainty that whatever was coming would surely kill the three of them.

"Join hands!" she shouted, reaching out. "Don't let go for anything!" And around the fire, which was, fortunately, not so big as it might have been, she clasped Greta's hand on her left and Loren's on her right. The other two joined their free hands, and as circle was completed, not a second later, the gathered power poured down and up through them. Kerri felt her hair lift and stand out from her head as her eyes suddenly looked out upon another place, a darkness, and she was standing in the darkness, and the others were with her, and light was rushing toward them from all directions at once.

She saw the light flow into her body and beyond it until she became an ovoid cocoon of light. Before her two other eggs of light bloomed, the three glows linked with fine cords of light that snaked between like lightning. If it was death, she decided, it was spectacular, and it did not hurt. And at that same moment she knew she was not dying, that she had come somehow to a place she had seen only once before outside of the Star Dreams. Yet, not a place, a "where," any more than it was a mode, a condition, a dimension. *And I have become a star, she realized. No, I was always a star. Only now did I learn how to shine.*

The rushing energy, as it spiraled into the circle of joined hands and wills, somehow found focus and resonance, circling and settling into a kind of humming vibration flowing around and around, potent and dangerous still, but now captured and controlled, understood, possessed.

Kerri's vision cleared, and she was again standing next to the little campfire, hand-linked with her two friends, meeting their astonished eyes, feeling the astonishment on her own face. As the roar of power faded to tameness, she became aware that her hands ached from gripping tightly. Her whole body hurt, as if she had tensed every muscle at once, which, no doubt, she had.

"I think...it might be safe to let go," Greta ventured, her voice barely more than a whisper. The others nodded, and, carefully, they released each others' hands, aware that in the other place the cords of light still bound them together into a kind of molecular being. Nothing happened. No harm came. The Power still hummed within them, potent but tamed. And Real.

Greta spoke again. " I understand now. I understand many things now."

Kerri rubbed her hands. "That's what he meant by a 'third,'" she said wonderingly.

"We would have died," Loren agreed. "It needs three to be stable."

Kerri nodded, knowing this to be true. A cell of two—or one alone—would not stand, would fail, would burn, but three would hold, like the truss of a bridge, rigid and strong.

This is how it works, she realized. This is what They have. The knowledge came to her, whole, perfect and elegant, and she saw it in her mind's eye: a network of interlocking triangles of stars, nodes of Power connected by filaments of Power, whose avatars in the world of daily life chose to express their connection in the form of societies, brotherhoods, guilds with trappings of color and ceremony and secrecy. Each society, each cluster of stars, was linked to others. No part of the net could be disturbed without disturbing all.

But we are not in that net, she realized. *We are outside of that structure.* A thought teased at the back of her mind, something Domenick had said, but she could not remember what it was, only a vague impression that being on the outside might work out to be a very good thing. An advantage, like finding a new text! Something to be hoarded and guarded until one learned how best to make use of it. She smiled.

Loren took a deep breath and let it out. "Well," she said to Greta, "I hope you're satisfied!"

Chapter 62

Nicholas Redeemed

"You're all right. You're...here." He stood in the kitchen doorway, braced against the doorframe as if exhausted. He was playing the part very well, Kerri decided, observing the stubble on his chin and the smudges of darkness under his eyes. Or perhaps he was not playing a part, after all. Turning her back on the grey light of the winter afternoon, she closed the front door carefully behind her, keeping her hand on the handle, just in case.

"I am quite well," she said. "You are back early. I did not expect you until tomorrow," she added untruthfully.

"What did you expect?" he replied, a shade irritably, "after you...well, that's in the past now. You're here. You're still alive. That's the important thing. I've been sick with worry." He did look it. He rubbed his eyes wearily. "Thank the Dreamer you're all right! Where have you been? And your friend, is she well? Is she with you?" He straightened and moved a step closer, looking hopefully at the door behind her.

"She is not with me." Kerri tightened her grip on the door handle. "I do not know where she is." *Not exactly where,* she added to herself. *Upstairs, downstairs. Who knows?*

Nick took another cautious step and raised his arms as if he would embrace her. "Then we need to find her," he said. "You don't realize it, but you are both at great risk of severe damage to your health and sanity." His concern looked completely genuine, and probably was. "I can help you. I know what to do...."

"Do not touch me!" Kerri barked. "Do not come one step closer. It will not do you a speck of good. She is not here. And I am gone," she warned him as he took another step, "if you come any closer."

He stopped and lowered his arms uncertainly. "You don't understand," he said. "There is very little time. I know this must be terribly confusing for you, but everything will be put right if you let me help you."

"Everything is already fine," Kerri replied. "And I am not in the least confused." She opened the door.

"Very well, I shan't touch you yet." He raised his arms again beseechingly. "Just don't run off again. That would be the worst thing." He looked genuinely frightened now. "Please. Don't leave. You might die out there. You have to believe me. I am telling you the truth. I promise I won't come any closer. See?" He backed toward the kitchen until he stood again in the doorway. "Just don't leave. Let me explain."

Looking past him, Kerri could see almost nothing of the kitchen. The living room was empty, but the study door was half closed and the bedroom was out of her view. Since she had entered her home, Veiled, she had listened and watched with every ordinary sense, but she could find no clue, either in his behavior or in her observations of the house, to tell her whether or not he was alone. She was fairly sure by now that there was no army of Them lying in wait, but there might be someone, one or two, the advance force. The Veil would wear off soon—she had raised it at least a quarter of an hour ago, before coming into the village—and then she would know. In the meantime, she would stay at the door, ready to run if she needed to. But only then. This was her home, and she was tired of running.

When Kerri did not move, Nick spoke again, more confidently. "Now, we have to find Miss Weberly as soon as possible. It is very important. Something has happened to both of you. I know you don't understand it, but you will. Everything will be explained, but first you both urgently need help. There is a treatment. It is a simple procedure; it does not hurt. I promise. In fact, it will be wonderful! It will make everything right," he promised, "for you, for us, for our future. But if you don't let me help you, you could die or go demented at any moment—please believe me. I was terrified I'd already lost you, that you were suffering out in the wilderness somewhere, where no one would ever find you. But now you're here, and everything is going to work out as it should. I've been taught exactly what to do, how to take care of you, but it won't work unless your friend Miss Weberly is present, so please tell me where we might find her."

"No," said Kerri.

"Please," he begged, but, keeping his word, he did not come closer. "You both need to be..."

"Stabilized?" she inquired.

Mouth open, he stared at her.

"I don't think so," she said casually.

"It's too late, isn't it?" He saw the truth suddenly, and relief and resentment struggled with each other in his face. "Someone already took care of you? Nobody informed me. Well!" He took a deep, shuddering breath. "At least you're not going to die or dement on me!" He managed a small crooked smile. "I wish I could have been the one to link you in, but it's probably just as well. I'm not exactly experienced, and being told *how* to do something is not quite the same as actually *doing* it, is it? To be honest, I was scared to death I'd do the wrong thing."

She said nothing, watching him relax.

He leaned against the kitchen doorframe and folded his arms, nodding. "Things aren't so serious, then. We can talk." He met her eyes and smiled more easily. "How much have you been told? Who was it? When did it happen? Which group? If it was *us*, I would know by now, so it must be someone else. But that is not a problem. All we need is one other person in either group, and we'll be properly linked up in no time. *Then* we can get on with our lives and get rid of all the nonsense. Nothing to worry about. It's going to be marvelous!"

He looked at her so hopefully, so expectantly, that she went as far as to close the front door again and return his smile. She was almost certain now that there was no one else in the house. Nick by himself she could handle. He would want to do things the right way; it wouldn't be like him to try to force anything. She wondered if she dared to take off her heavy backpack.

Encouraged, he went on, "It's been damnable for you, I know, and I've been in agony about it from the beginning, but there was nothing I could do. I tried, you know. I need you to believe that. I tried everything I could think of to get them to take you, too."

"Did you?" Kerri inquired neutrally.

"I did. Not necessarily in the S.G. I don't think I could have pulled that off. But somewhere. There are plenty of groups in your own college. You'll never know what I went through! Against all advice—they said I was putting myself way out on a limb, but I didn't care. I kept trying to get you in all the way up until the Retreat—even after I got there— but someone up the line kept turning you down."

"Really?" said Kerri. *Do I need to ask,* she said to herself, *who it was that kept turning me down?* "Why?" she asked.

"I didn't understand it." Nick shook his head, remembering. "They kept telling me you were not qualified. Imagine! You! With your background! I knew they were wrong about you, and I was in agonies because I couldn't convince them. I knew it had to be a mistake, and it was!"

"Yes," Kerri agreed. "It was."

"I knew it couldn't be about your not having a Sponsor. That seemed like such an excuse! I mean, there are others who don't—well, not many, but some—and they knew it wasn't your fault. And anyway, they were wrong about that too!" He beamed at her. "I would give anything to just hug you; I'm so delighted!"

At her blank look, he said, laughingly, "The lists! They came out this morning, or had you forgotten? The lists! Your Sponsorship. Congratulations! I can't tell you how happy I am. I nearly wept when I saw your name. All those years of waiting, and you'd finally made it, and you weren't here to enjoy it, and I was so afraid something terrible had happened to you...."

"Oh," she said faintly. "The lists. Today is Tuesday, the first of June. I *had* forgotten." *I have a Sponsor now,* she told herself. *It is official, and now everybody knows. I've waited all my life for this day, and it doesn't seem to mean a thing. I feel nothing. How very odd.* "So...my secret is out."

He nodded, grinning. "Very sly, you were! That trip to the Islands—I never suspected a thing. I should have, I might have if I hadn't been so distracted by the Society of Guenevere and the Ball and everything."

"Well," she came to a decision and swung her pack to the floor, "it's hardly to be wondered at. You had a great deal on your mind, after all. I *did* notice."

"I know you did. I know you realized something was up, and I felt like a complete villain, not being able to confide in you, forced to let you make all kinds of wrong assumptions, but what could I do? You know now what restraints I had to deal with. The rules are strict. I was tempted to break them many times, believe me. But now I don't have to. *You* have a Sponsor. *I* have a thesis topic. We're both in the Alliance. We have lots of reasons to celebrate. I can hardly bear to wait until we can do it properly."

"A thesis topic," she repeated. "Congratulations. What is it?"

His face clouded. "To be honest, I don't exactly know. I was sent here to wait for you, in case you turned up, and I hadn't been informed what the final decision was. We'd narrowed the list down to five or six, and I could live with any one of them, although none of them are what I would have chosen if I ruled the world. But I'm not complaining. In fact, we might find ourselves very pleasantly surprised. The Committee took a sudden renewed interest in me on Saturday, as you might imagine. I don't have to tell you, I certainly owe that to you." He chuckled, shaking his head. "I can laugh at the whole thing now, but it was no fun at the time."

"I can indeed imagine," said Kerri, wondering how to answer his earlier questions, if he ever stopped to listen.

"But what are we doing still standing here?" His attention returned suddenly to the present. "Here I've been, doing all the talking, and you haven't even had a chance to tell me your story or settle in from your journey or anything. Would you like a cup of tea? The kettle's good and hot. Are you hungry? Would you like a bath? I say! Here's an idea. Let's get cleaned up and go into the City for a festive dinner. I can find out my topic—they'll be posted by now—and we can look up someone to link us. Then I can touch you again," he grinned meaningfully, "and then we can really celebrate! What do you say?"

Kerri, free at last to get in more than an edgewise word, found herself speechless, but Nick had already whirled away to make the tea. She ventured slowly as far as the kitchen doorway where he had been standing and stopped there, watching him bustle cheerfully. He looked completely happy. Kerri felt completely depressed, emptied of anger like a spent balloon. If only things could be as he thought they were; then both of them could be happy.

Did he really try? she wondered. *Can I believe him? If he told the truth about that, then he is not one of the enemy. I can forgive him and go on loving him, and we can be together again when all of this is over. If it ever will be over, whatever 'over' means. I've let him talk and talk, and tell me more than he realizes, but in a moment it will be my turn, and I shall take his happiness away again. Will he still want me, then?*

Nick paused in his clatter of tea preparation and looked at her expectantly. "So tell me," he invited. "Where on earth have you been the last couple of days?"

"With friends," she told him. "In the country."

"And who got you stabilized? That was a prize, I'm told! Was it anyone we know? Who?"

"I can't tell you," she said.

"Well then, what is their affiliation?"

"What do you mean, affiliation?"

"You know what I mean. What group, what society do they belong to?"

"You don't understand," said Kerri with grim satisfaction at being able to use the words on him for a change—unjustly, for he did suddenly understand then, finally. She saw it in his eyes.

He became perfectly still, halted in the act of lighting the table lamp, staring at her.

"Oh," he said. "You're not...it wasn't...."

"One of yours," she finished for him. "No. It wasn't."

"You found a third." He remembered the match, waved it out at the last instant before the flame reached his fingers. "You found someone outside."

She nodded.

He fumbled with the glass chimney, got it in place somehow and sat down abruptly.

"Oh. Then...this is different. They told me it can happen, but they said...oh, my!"

"Yes." She left the doorway then and came as far as the table, but she did not sit down. She watched his face as something in him went as far away from her as he had ever been in those secretive days before the Retreat, farther.

"But how did you know? How did you...?" He looked at her as if she were a stranger. "I can't stay here," he said.

"I'm afraid not," she confirmed, "for the time being."

"For the time being," he repeated dully. After a moment he continued, "Well, it never lasts forever. They tell me these outside nets always attach to the Alliance eventually. We'll...Wait!" His face paled. "I shouldn't even be talking to you. Oh, what have I been saying? I'm in trouble now. I'm not supposed to tell you anything."

"Why not?" she protested.

"It's the rule." He glared at her, angered and disappointed.

"Break it. You said you wanted to."

"I can't." He looked down. "I just can't. Damn!"

"Nick, I really need to know what is going on. I am entitled to know. I have proved it."

"I can't tell you," he said. "And I can't stay here."

"Where will you go?"

"Into town. My flat is vacant."

"Oh. Decent of you to get around to mentioning that." She frowned. How long had he had this little bolt hole in the City? Since the Ball? Before? A few minutes ago she had been prepared to forgive him, and now they were back where they had been, facing each other across an abyss.

Reading her thoughts, he gave a small, irritated shrug. "It only happened during Finals. They got a better place, all of a sudden, moved out Thursday. Their notice was waiting when I got here."

"I see," said Kerri. "What happens next?"

"There will be someone coming to talk to you—just one person, you don't need to be frightened...."

"I am not frightened. This person will answer my questions?"

"I don't know," he said. He looked down at the table for a long moment, then up at her, sadly. "Why don't you have that cup of tea?" he said. "I need to go pack a few things. I want to catch the next trolley."

"By all means," said Kerri. She tightened her grip on the back of the chair. "Nick, does this mean we are finished? Are you leaving me?"

"No. It doesn't mean that. I don't think it does. I don't know what it means, but I do have to stay away until—well, I can't do any more harm than I already have done—until the Alliance decides what to do about you and Miss Weberly and this other person." He grinned hopefully. "Can't you just tell me who it is? Sharon? Someone in Evesham?"

"I'm not going to tell you," she said. "*We* also have our rules."

He nodded, accepting. "Of course. Well, maybe this will all be cleared up soon."

"Can we at least keep in touch?" she asked.

"I don't see why not. Let's try anyway, whatever They say."

"Yes." She watched him walk out of the room, giving her plenty of distance. When he returned to the kitchen, scarcely ten minutes later, she was sitting at the round table, pouring her second cup.

"I'm off, then," he said. "Write to me, will you?"

"I will," she promised.

"Maybe we can clear everything up by the holidays, and I can come back."

"I hope so," she said. "Nick, I have to ask you one question. The Society of Guenevere...what does it have to do with King Arthur?"

Mildly startled, he replied, "Nothing, so far as I know. Not a thing. Please stay here and wait. Truly, there's nothing to be frightened of. Someone will come. It will be all right."

"Yes, I'll stay. This is my home."

He nodded. "I do love you," he told her.

"I believe you," she said. "I love you, too."

After he had gone she sipped her tea and wondered if she could carry this off without reinforcements, if it wouldn't be better to abandon ship and dash up the lane to Greta's villa, to have a real tea with Greta and Loren—cozy, safe. But no. If They had any intelligence at all, They would be watching the house. If she attempted to leave, she would be followed. No point in exposing her own bolt hole until she truly needed it. She did envy Loren, getting to use Greta's marvelous secret tunnel—such a piece of nonsense but distinctly useful under present circumstances—and being allowed to see first what Stockholder resources could do to the dilapidated old estate. But Kerri had made her decision, and she must hold to it now.

Nick's words had confirmed her suspicion that Greta's identity was a powerful card, perhaps as powerful as the Brautigan. Each one must be saved and played at the proper time.

She had not even finished the second cup of tea when the knocker sounded at the front door, sooner than she had ever expected.

Chapter 63

The Existence of Meaning

A misty drizzle had begun to fall into the afternoon. Aryel shook out her umbrella in the front hall and commented that it was dismal out, simply dismal, made her remember why she quite preferred living in the Islands. She allowed her granddaughter to help her off with her coat and accepted the offer of a cup of tea. As usual, she was elegantly dressed, impeccably groomed, no trace of being rumpled by travel. Kerri wondered if she had in fact made her way to Evesham by trolley or by some more exotic means. She thought back to her own morning ride in Greta's sleek black motorcar, the first and only time she had ever been driven in a private automobile.

"You got here very quickly," Kerri commented as she led the way back to the warm kitchen.

"As quickly as I could," her grandmother replied.

"Is this a family visit, or are you here to represent Them?" Kerri asked bluntly, unwilling to waste any more time.

"Both, dear. Both." She sat down in Nick's chair, folded her hands upon the checked cloth and smiled pleasantly.

So much for that last bit of hope, Kerri thought as she fetched another cup and saucer from the cupboard. Silently she set them before her grandmother and poured the tea. She sat down opposite. "Well," she said at last. "I am listening."

"First off, I am delighted to see you so well. You cannot imagine how worried I was." Aryel reached across the table to pat her hand.

Startled, Kerri exclaimed, "I thought you weren't supposed to touch me!"

"Oh, nonsense," Aryel chuckled. "Of course, I can touch you. It makes no earthly difference now."

Kerri's eyes narrowed. "Nicholas was not supposed to touch me. He tried when I first came, but I would not let him. Later, he said it was forbidden, under the circumstances."

"Nonsense," Aryel repeated. "I suspect your Nicholas has been misled a bit, and it is just as well. You will both be better off apart until things are more settled."

"What things?"

"Many things. Most of them do not concern you at all except as a catalyst. Old issues. Political things. Other people's old, worn out quarrels that do not have anything to do with you. Your primary concerns just now—and mine—are your health and well-being and your position at the University."

Kerri got up and paced a turn about the kitchen. "I am well," she said. "My position at the University is not the issue. My primary concern is information. I have questions. I want answers. If you cannot give them to me, you might as well leave." She made her hands busy, pumping water, refilling the kettle, stoking the fire. When Aryel did not reply, she added, "I suppose it is against the rules for you to tell me anything. Nicholas said so. Be assured I shall not tell you anything either. I cannot think why you bothered to come."

"You have every right to be bitter, my dear. You have been treated abominably, and it has gone on much too long. You have every right to be angry with me, for I let it go on and did nothing to stop it or to help you. Yes, there are rules, and I followed them, because I have always believed myself to be an honorable person. I have watched cheating all around me—and protested in the proper quarters, of course—but I would not cheat, even when it involved my own flesh and blood. Perhaps it is more honorable in the end to choose family ties over one's solemn vows; I do not know. Yet, I did not so choose, and now things are coming right, and in a way I never expected in my wildest dreams. You are quite correct. It is not permitted for me to tell you anything. That is, I cannot give you information. Unless it is specifically asked for. And even then, there are considerations...I should have to use my best judgement and endeavor not to step over boundaries."

"Unless it is asked for!" Quickly Kerri returned to the table and faced her grandmother. "Are you saying that you will answer questions?"

Aryel cocked one eyebrow but said nothing.

"You will answer some questions?" Kerri tried again, too excited to conceal her hope. "If I ask the right questions?"

Aryel smiled. "To the extent that I can."

"I see." Kerri took another restless turn about the kitchen. Her first impulse was to reject sullenly even this qualified offer of help. There was certain to be a price for asking even the right questions. It was not fair. She was owed the truth, the whole truth, especially from one who had always professed to cherish her. They had been clever to send Aryel, someone she loved, someone she had always trusted, the one person in the world who knew best how to ferret out her secrets, put her off her guard. And yet... *Never reject information:* this she had been taught, over and over again, by the old woman sitting here in her kitchen. *Wherever the truth lies, it does not reveal itself in ignorance.* And family love and trust, if real, could work both ways. She might have to pay something for knowledge, but surely she herself was bright enough to see that the price was no higher than she was willing to pay. Surely, now that she knew with whom she was dealing, she could guard her own tongue. There might be room for negotiation. She thought of her fellow conspirators, not far away, and how they had allowed her to persuade them she must return home for this very purpose: to find out the truth!

Suddenly, she was conscious that she was starving, that she had offered her Grandmother nothing to eat, and it was close to tea time, starting to get dark. She began to look through cupboards, found a new loaf of bread, peanut butter, apples. While she hunted for provisions, Aryel sipped tea and watched her calmly, refraining even from small talk about home. When the simple meal was on the table, Kerri sat down again and began her interrogation.

"First," she said, "what happened to me? What happened to us out there by the lake."

"I am sorry," said Aryel. "That is a question I cannot answer."

This was not a good beginning.

"Why not? Do you not know or are you not allowed?"

"Try again," Aryel replied enigmatically.

Not allowed, Kerri decided. Swallowing her momentary anger, she settled on a less direct attack. "Very well. Do you know of a body called the Alliance."

"Yes."

"Are you a member of this body?"

"I am."

"What is the Alliance?"

"You have seen what it is. An association of individuals."

"Very helpful! Does this association have any purpose other than self-importance?"

"It does. The self-importance...is a regrettable by-product which is not, fortunately, universal. Nor is it entirely avoidable. There will always be petty individuals in any such association."

If I were not paying attention, I would be sidetracked here, Kerri realized, *to personalities, pettiness, and self-importance. Arzelle and Val. But they are not central, I think. Deal with them later.*

"What is the purpose of the Alliance, then?" she asked.

"I cannot answer," said Aryel. "But I can assure you it is not evil."

"Evil," Kerri repeated, vaguely surprised. It was not a word that lived at the forefront of her vocabulary. People could be petty, nasty, small-minded, rude, and so on, but they were almost never evil, not in present day. In the Age of Dreams, yes, but not now. She felt faintly alarmed, as if the suggestion of the absence of evil was as much a suggestion of its presence. "Is it a good purpose, then?"

Surprisingly, Aryel seemed uncertain how to answer this. "I suppose it is good," she said after some hesitation. "It is necessary. That is, I believe it to be necessary. We all believe it to be necessary. It is what we are taught." She frowned and thought for a moment. "I would be unwilling to gamble that the necessity does not exist."

"Then it is an important purpose?" Kerri said, vaguely confused.

"Oh, yes, indeed. Vital."

"To whom? To the Alliance?"

"To everyone."

"But you cannot tell me what it is?"

"I cannot offer that information."

"In other words, I have not asked the right question." Kerri leaned back in her chair, thinking, making herself a second peanut butter sandwich. She had already wolfed the first. Aryel continued serenely quartering apples.

Kerri asked, "If the Alliance is vital—let us suppose that is true for argument's sake—then why is it kept such a secret?"

Aryel shrugged. "It is not really kept secret."

"Do not lie to me," Kerri interrupted scornfully. "If it is not a secret, what do you call it when no one ever speaks of it, when my own husband conceals his involvement from me, lets me experience the pain of suspecting his infidelity rather than be honest with me?"

"I grant you it is not spoken of in public," Aryel admitted, looking somewhat uncomfortable. "Nor in private to unaffiliated persons. It is...tradition, basically. The value of it is debatable, in my mind, but one does make promises. And keep them. There is no reason, really, for people outside the organization to know of its existence or purpose. It has no impact on their daily lives. But most people get an inkling sooner or later. In Academic life, it is almost unavoidable, certainly by your age. I have been expecting questions from you these years past, but you never asked."

"No, not me!" Kerri said bitterly. "I never had an inkling! No wonder I never got a Sponsor until now; I was so dense and oblivious." She paused. "That is not true. I did have an inkling. I shall not say more than that. But there are things one does not speak of or ask about. I thought this was one of those things. Therefore, I did not mention it either. In fact, I was led to believe...but never mind that. I shall just say I find it difficult to believe that the facts were there all along for the asking, or mentioning. Or you would be telling me now what I need to know. You would have told me long ago. You would not have allowed me to go on blundering through life wondering why I was somehow never able to measure up."

"You are quite right. The facts were not, and are not, simply for the asking. Although many young people do ask, in all innocence. That is one of the signs we look for. Usually, by that time, the individual has already been recruited and is well into the process of becoming one of us. It is a delicate process. Each person is given only the facts that are necessary at each stage."

"What do you mean, recruited?"

Aryel drew in a quick breath, realizing, as Kerri did, that she had let go of at least one item of unrequested information. "I mean, that those persons who show an aptitude, who are deemed appropriate candidates, are approached. Eventually."

"An aptitude for what? Appropriate, how? Who deems them appropriate? How are they approached?" She hesitated for a second, then added, "Why was I never approached?"

But Aryel made no reply, only gazed steadily, unsmiling, at her granddaughter.

The right questions, Kerri said to herself. *In the right order.*

"Who deems them appropriate?" she tried again, choosing an approach at random.

Aryel smiled faintly. "We have...certain colleagues who manifest an ability to discern whether or not the...essential element is present in a candidate. They are the ones who decide."

"This essential element...what is it?"

Again, Aryel waited, silent.

"You won't tell me what it is. No matter. I know what it is. And is it rare?"

"No, but the ability to detect it reliably is relatively rare. That is a talent we value."

"I see. And these talented people decided I do not possess enough of this... whatever it is. Here!" She broke off suddenly and got up from her chair, moving restlessly to the stove to fiddle with the fire. "Let us make things easier to talk about," she suggested hopefully. "Let us give this thing a name. We know what we are talking about. I simply want to know what to call it."

"By all means, give it a name," Aryel replied placidly. "Call it whatever you like."

"In other words, you will not tell me what it is called."

"Call it whatever you like," Aryel repeated. "It must be present in some small measure. The tiniest bit is sufficient."

Kerri closed the burner with a clang. "So. I did not even have the tiniest bit." She laughed and made a face at her grandmother. "Oops!"

"Yes," Aryel agreed. "They were wrong about you." She shook her head. "I knew they were. They had to be. And the thing is, when you were younger..." she broke off, frowning. "I have always thought I possessed some of that perception, myself. It is only an illusion, they say, but I was always certain you...were developing just as you ought. And in those days, others said so, too, those who are expert in such matters. It was only when you began to grow up that I began to hear reports that you seemed to be, well, lacking. Yet, not always. Some said you had it; others said there was no trace. It was very worrying—I can tell you that now. I was most concerned, but your father was confident things would eventually turn around to your advantage. They would see how eligible you were."

Of course, Kerri thought, *my father was one of Them. But Mother is not.*

Aryel continued, "I think he was beginning to worry also, when he died. It was not long after that when I finally insisted upon a definitive answer, and the answer was...no. The very best talent in the field declared that you were completely and unequivocally unfit for the Alliance. There were still others who disagreed with her, people who had known you as a child, people on the islands, but she...."

"Arzelle!" Kerri exclaimed. "It is Arzelle, isn't it? Arzelle Pendrake James. She's the one!"

Aryel nodded. "She is deemed one of the best. Her ability has contributed greatly to her consequence in the Alliance. She exercises a lot of influence on that account."

"Yes!" Kerri paced the floor, hugging both arms to her chest. "She always had that...that way about her. Peering in at me. Judging. But, Grandmother, she hates me! You know she does. She has hated me since she tried to get me in trouble for cheating on preliminary exams. She hated me before that. And she never stopped. Look what she did to me and Val? She hates me still. Didn't they take that into account?"

"I did try to point it out, but, to be fair to her, other experts corroborated her finding. If you had ever possessed...that which is necessary, it seemed to have flickered out of existence entirely by the time you were at University."

"They were wrong," Kerri paced, back and forth.

"They were *very* wrong," Aryel agreed. "Nobody understands how it could have happened."

But I understand, Kerri realized, stunned with the discovery. *I fooled them. I hid from them. The Veil. The Veil. It worked. It blinded Them. It stymied Them. It never occurred to Them I was doing it on purpose, turning off and on almost at will. They haven't got it. I'm the only one who has it—and maybe Loren and Greta, if I can teach them— but it is my secret. They don't know what to make of me. I am something entirely new.*

She fussed again with the fire, hoping that she did not look as gloating as she felt.

She had the sensation that great pieces of the puzzle were finally dropping into place. Finally, when she could trust her face, she turned and faced Aryel with a bland, innocent gaze. "Will there be any consequences to Arzelle?" she asked. "It would seem she is not the expert she professes to be. Or else a very great liar. Or both."

"She has a great deal to answer for," Aryel agreed. "Trust me, she will answer for it. There will be some manner of reprimand."

"Is that all? A reprimand?"

"She will sting far more from the damage to her reputation," Aryel said. "It will be some time before she can reclaim the kind of authority she has enjoyed in recent years. In any case, she can no longer harm you in any significant way. I should put her out of my mind if I were you."

I will never, Kerri promised herself, *turn my back again on that viper.*

Aryel added, "You had a right to know the extent of the enmity that woman holds for you, and what the consequences of that enmity have been. Oath or no oath, I was determined put you on your guard, but I have taken a very great risk in saying as much as I have said. I can tell you no more."

"Even if I ask the right questions?" Kerri protested. "There is so much more I want to ask you, whether you will answer me or not. Am I in danger? Is any one in danger because of me? Is this Alliance angry with me? Am I to be punished? Are they going to make Nick divorce me? I must know what I am dealing with here!"

Aryel shook her head. "I am sorry." She set down her cup with click of finality and got stiffly to her feet.

"I will ask someone else. I will ask and ask until I get answers. And if no one will answer me, I will find out for myself if it is the last thing I do!"

Aryel's face broke into a smile of triumph and relief. "That," she said with emphasis, "should be the *first* thing you do!" She placed the chair very precisely again the table and stood with her hands clasped on the back of it. "I must leave this house before I am tempted to cross the line again. And you need your rest."

"Are you not going to stay here tonight with me. You cannot think of going all the way back to Town this late. It is dark!"

Aryel chuckled. "I shall not return unattended. Everything is arranged. I am spending the night with Dean Salisbury-West and her husband. We are old friends, as you know. Tomorrow I must sail back to the Islands to let Sophia know you are well. If you have any letter you want me to carry for you, you can leave it with the Sea People up until sailing time."

"Will I not see you before you go?"

"I do not expect They will allow it," she said gently. "But give things a few days to settle. Should you wish to sail home for a visit next week, there would be no objection. You need to call on your Sponsor, after all, and we have a celebration to plan."

"They'll still let me have my Sponsorship? In spite of what has happened? And, if you go, will I be safe here alone? Are They sending anybody else tonight?"

Aryel, arrested in the middle of putting her arms into the sleeves of her coat, looked shocked. "Do you not understand?" she said. "Do you not realize? You speak as if you expect to be punished. Nothing could be farther from the truth. My dear, you have achieved something of great significance, something so rare it has happened only a scarce handful of times. Thrice that I know of. You have become a person of some importance, believe me. All three of you have become persons of importance. As for your privacy this evening, be assured that you will not be bothered again. You are quite safe, now that you are stable."

"Are they watching the house?" Kerri asked.

"I cannot say." Aryel tied her scarf firmly under her chin and took up her umbrella.

Kerri walked with her to the front door. "What happens next?" she asked.

"That," said Aryel, "is, to a great extent, up to you and your associates. There are many opportunities."

"Will no one help us?"

Aryel stopped in the doorway, as if considering her words. "No one will offer help." she replied. She turned and embraced her granddaughter. "But you will prevail," she said. "All will be well. Good night, my dear."

With a last fond pat, Aryel walked into the darkness. Looking past her, Kerri could see a light, low to the ground just beyond the front gate. Someone was waiting in the lane with a lantern. She heard the stamping and snorting of horses and the jingle of harness, heard a carriage door close. She listened and watched as the lantern light and carriage sounds moved away north up the lane toward the high road to Fernly.

And then she was all alone, with only the call of the wind through the trees, the patter of rain and the distant twinkle of lights in the windows of Greta's new country house. Greta and Loren were no doubt very comfortable and cozy there, but she would not join them, not tonight. There were certainly Watchers in the village. They would find out soon enough; no point in giving them satisfaction tonight. She went back inside and bolted the door.

Tomorrow, she decided. *Tomorrow I shall find the Private Library and read the hidden writing. Tomorrow I shall begin.*

The End

www.ingramcontent.com/pod-product-compliance
Lightning Source LLC
Chambersburg PA
CBHW071342020726
47502CB00001B/214